A BINDING OF BLOOD

A PRACTICAL GUIDE TO SORCERY

AZALEA ELLIS

Seladore Publishing

Cover art by James T. Egan of BookFly Design

To Jared.
… But I have promises to keep,
And miles to go before I sleep.

JOIN THE INNER CIRCLE**

Become part of the Inner Circle.
Instantly receive a free excerpt from Siobhan's illustrated grimoire.

https://www.azaleaellis.com/newsletter

I will send you new release updates, exclusive content like pre-release or deleted scenes, as well as news about giveaways or contests I'm doing (signed paperbacks, posters, etc.) and other cool stuff I think you might enjoy. Sometimes I tell weird stories about my life.

Support me on Patreon

https://www.patreon.com/azaleaellis

Read along chapter by chapter as I write the next book in the series, with early access chapters not available elsewhere, plus exclusive short stories/bonus chapters, and other goodies like various illustrated excerpts from Siobhan's grimoire and character portraits.

NOTE TO READERS

The world-building for this story is extensive and can be quite complicated. If you find yourself forgetting terminology or wanting a little more detail about a term, the end of this book holds a Glossary of Magical Terms.

Thank you for reading!

Azalea

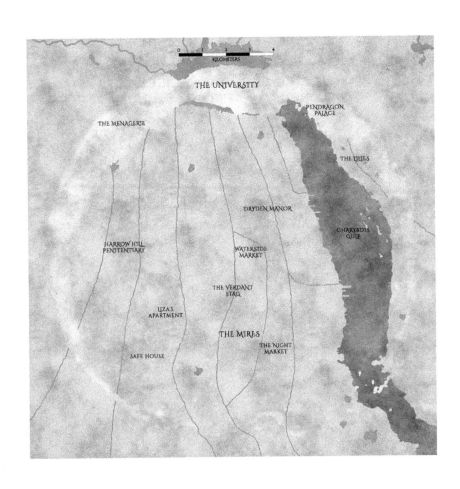

A PRACTICAL GUIDE TO SORCERY
RECAP

If you have not read the first book in the Practical Guide to Sorcery series, spoilers lie ahead.

Previously, in *A Conjuring of Ravens*:

Siobhan Naught unwittingly becomes a wanted criminal when her father steals a mysterious book during their visit to the Thaumaturgic University. Her hopes of becoming a student dashed, she runs from the coppers with the book. Later, in danger from being caught by their ambush, she meets Oliver Dryden, who tries to help her escape.

When the coppers corner them, she accidentally activates a transformation amulet that had been hidden in the stolen book, turning herself into a young man who looks nothing like her original form. With this new body, she deceives the coppers and escapes arrest. To have a chance at entering the University under a new identity, she takes a huge loan—one thousand gold—from Oliver and Katerin at the Verdant Stag, the criminal organization they run.

Oliver helps her create a new identity for herself as Sebastien Siverling, but she makes a bad first impression on Damien Westbay and his group of Crown Family friends upon their first meeting.

When Siobhan learns the coppers caught her father Ennis, she and Oliver enlist the help of local illegal thaumaturge Liza, who helps Siobhan contact Ennis with a spelled raven messenger. To Siobhan's disappointment, Ennis has tried to sell her—and the stolen book—to the Gervin Family in marriage, in exchange for benefits for himself.

Much disillusioned, Siobhan studies for the University entrance exam and works for the Verdant Stag, who actually seem to serve and help the people within their community. When young Theo, Katerin's nephew, injures himself, Siobhan unthinkingly uses some harmless blood magic learned from her grandfather to heal the boy, earning both Katerin and Oliver's ire for the reckless use of illegal magic that could get her executed, and them implicated by association.

As Sebastien Siverling, she takes the University entrance exam, but her results are poorer than she hoped, and the panel of professors who administer the verbal portion of the exam plan to deny her entrance. In a fit of rage, she refuses to be dismissed, casting a hastily prepared spell to prove that she has the only thing that matters to a potential sorcerer—a strong Will.

Professor Thaddeus Lacer, a famous free-caster and Siobhan's childhood hero, takes an interest in her and overrides the panel of other professors, forcibly admitting Sebastien Siverling under special circumstances.

Sebastien falls into her University classes with glee, learning with feverish enthusiasm. She keeps to herself except for a budding new friendship with Anastasia Gervin, a Crown Family heiress, and Damien Westbay, who remembers their first meeting and finds Sebastien abrasive, nurturing the pseudo-rivalry between them. One of their student liaisons, Newton Moore, also extends an olive branch of friendship, believing her to—secretly—be a poor student just like him.

When she is not studying, Sebastien brews alchemical concoctions for the Verdant Stag to pay back the debt she owes them.

Oliver makes moves to expand the power of the Verdant Stags, but things backfire when the Morrows, a rival gang, attack one of his warehouses with the help of a mysterious sorceress. Oliver sets off Sebastien's alarms, waking her in the middle of the night to give emergency aid to his people.

Returning to her female form, Siobhan uses the minor spell exercises she's been practicing for Professor Lacer to sling balls of shattered glass at the Morrows. When the fighting is over, she tries to help the Verdant Stag warehouse workers, some of whom have been severely injured. Unable to do much, she patches up what she can before the coppers arrive.

Trying to give the others a better chance to escape, Siobhan uses a harmless esoteric spell that controls her shadow, molding it into a frightening creature of tattered darkness with a huge raven's beak. The coppers are successfully frightened, but one of them shoots a grasping spell at Siobhan, tripping her and cutting her hand.

She and Oliver escape to a safe house owned by one of Oliver's subjects, but the coppers found some of her blood left behind at the scene and use it to cast scrying magic on her. Siobhan's warding medallion, given by her grandfather, holds off the scrying attempt—at the cost of Siobhan's Conduit—and they go to Liza for a more permanent solution.

Liza creates a divination-diverting ward, anchored in five disks that she inserts underneath Siobhan's skin. The ward uses her blood for power, and can activate at low efficiency on its own or be further empowered by Siobhan's conscious efforts.

Thaddeus is called to the scene of the crime to consult on the investigation at Titus Westbay's request. Given the available evidence and witness accounts, they come to some erroneous conclusions. Siobhan Naught—codename Raven Queen—is a free-caster with some unknown, nefarious purpose that involves curses and blood magic.

She fascinates Thaddeus.

Siobhan, now without a Conduit, contacts Ennis in jail again, hoping to retrieve her mother's Conduit from him, but learns that he gave it to the Gervin Family as a bond for his word in the marriage agreement he gave on her behalf. Enraged and desperate, she spends most of her remaining funds to buy a dinky, overpriced replacement Conduit, then breaks down in tears.

But she isn't the same person who came to Gilbratha with Ennis those months ago. She's no longer under his—or anyone else's—control. She takes ownership of her life and her choices, pulls herself back together, and returns to the University.

A Binding of Blood begins immediately after these events.

1

COMPETING FOR POINTS

SEBASTIEN
Month 11, Day 30, Monday 8:45 a.m.

WHEN THE SCRYING attack hit Sebastien, she immediately began empowering her new anti-divination ward. The five artifact disks that Liza had embedded under the skin of her back consumed her blood, making the skin around them prickle like it was being stabbed with needles. This provided magical energy, which Sebastien channeled through the small Conduit pressed between her ankle and the inside of her boot, right back into the spell.

Fortunately, there were only a few stragglers still lingering around the University dorm, and they were all hurrying to gather their things before class. No one paid any attention to Sebastien.

She cursed the coppers, dropped the luggage she had been repacking into the chest at the base of her bed, and hurried toward the bathrooms. Liza had warned her that, with the ward active, anyone paying enough attention might notice a strange difficulty focusing on her, which could have very unfortunate consequences.

If things had gone even a little differently when she and Oliver went to defend his warehouse and the people inside from the attack by the Morrows, she might be fully rested, clearheaded, and relatively safe. If that last attack by the coppers, when she was trying to distract them with her shadow-familiar, hadn't hit her, she wouldn't have fallen and cut herself, and they wouldn't have her blood. She could have returned to the University without fear.

And maybe, if she had gone long enough without giving them any more leads, living as Sebastien Siverling instead of Siobhan Naught, they would have given up searching for her.

Instead, she was trembling in a bathroom stall as she brought her strained Will to bear. The coppers had her blood, and if she failed, they would find her through it. If she was arrested, she would likely be executed, since they had branded her a blood magic user. Even if she somehow escaped that fate, she would forever lose her chance to study at the Thaumaturgic University of Lenore. And without the University, she might never gain the knowledge and power to become a an Archmage level sorcerer and a free-caster. The kind of power that meant she would never be vulnerable again.

The ward deflected searching tendrils of magic for the next few minutes despite the sheer power battering across the entire city through the coppers' scrying spell. It was a stronger spell than Liza had used to test the ward's strength, but the protective magic held.

Some part of Sebastien had hoped that the transformation into her male body might mitigate the coppers' ability to find her through the sympathetic connection to her blood, but it seemed that was not the case. Siobhan's blood was still her blood, even in Sebastien's body. Which would have been interesting to know in less dire circumstances.

Panting, Sebastien rubbed the back of her neck as the stinging sensation subsided. Her head was pounding again. Not as bad as when she had first strained her Will, but bad enough that she had trouble concentrating. She wished she could neglect her classes and spend the day in bed.

Instead, she steeled herself, made sure she looked calm and alert, and hurried toward the Citadel and Professor Burberry's classroom. She arrived a few minutes late to Introduction to Modern Magics.

Professor Burberry gave her a stern glance but said nothing as Sebastien slipped into the seat beside Anastasia.

"Are you alright?" the girl murmured to her, her eyes roving over Sebastien's face with concern.

Sebastien realized sweat was beaded at her temples and quickly wiped it away. "Fine. A little nauseated. Lost track of time in the bathroom."

Ana patted her hand sympathetically and pulled a potion out of her bag. "It's for stomach cramps, but it should help slightly with nausea, too. The cafeteria food is atrocious. Really, I don't understand why we cannot simply *purchase* a better meal. We have the gold for it, and you would think they'd be happy to take it. I'm going to start losing weight at this rate."

Sebastien took the vial and stared at it bemusedly. *'Great. There's no reasonable way for me to decline this. I hope it doesn't have side effects on someone who's perfectly healthy.'* Aloud, she said, "Can it be taken on an empty stomach?"

When Ana nodded cheerfully, Sebastien suppressed her misgivings and took a swallow.

Having satisfied the other girl, Sebastien settled into her ruse, hiding her fatigue as completely as she could. Though for once, her mind wasn't on her classes. *'It was well done to request Liza's help with the ward against divination. If not for that, my time at the University would definitely be up.'* She shuddered at the thought. Finding information on the coppers' scrying procedure and capability was a priority, as soon as she could slip away to do so.

'If I had known how all this would turn out, would I have stayed in bed when Oliver activated my bracelet's alarm? What would have happened to Jameson without me? He would probably still be dead.' Setting that thought forcefully aside, she consoled herself. *'It is possible that things could have gone* worse *if I wasn't there.'* If she was honest with herself—and she tried to be—she would still go with Oliver knowing what she knew now. She would just perform *better* the second time around.

During the lunch period, she ate quickly, then went back to the dorms and made herself a strong cup of wakefulness brew from some tea leaves she had stashed in her trunk, as the basic meal options didn't cover such "luxuries" as caffeine.

When she arrived at Practical Casting, she was finally more awake, though her heart was beating a little too fast and her chest held a sour tightness.

Sebastien did a double take after entering the classroom. Something was off. She frowned, looking around quickly, and then realized that the classroom seemed to have *shrunk*. She had noted on the first day that this was the biggest class, both in room size and number of students. Though that remained the case, with hundreds of students drawn by the allure of free-casting, over the first few weeks many people had stopped coming, leaving empty desks behind. Those desks were gone now, and the back wall seemed to have contracted toward the front.

Her muscles tensed with unease, and without quite realizing it, she had taken her Conduit from her pocket. Walking around the room and examining the doorway showed tracks, and she realized with awe that the dividing walls that broke up each floor of the Citadel into classrooms could be moved, shifted forward or back to change the size of the individual rooms. Constructing a building with such capabilities, at this scale, was a feat she doubted could have been accomplished without impressive magic.

She took her seat, close to the front of the room on the side farthest from the door, and waited.

A few more students arrived after her, but no one else seemed to notice the classroom's modification. At least, if they did, they weren't particularly surprised by it, instead chattering with their fellow students or hurrying to complete homework before the class started.

Professor Lacer strode in dramatically, his trench coat flapping helplessly behind him. He was a tall man with a hawkish gaze, and he kept his dark hair pulled into a knot at the nape of his neck. The hair of his short-trimmed beard was always a little wild, as if it was afraid of him and trying to escape his face. He stopped in the middle of the lecture stage, ran his eyes over the students, and nodded to himself. "Those of you remaining are those who will not be leaving my class because of unwillingness to put in the work. You may be lacking, but at least you have shown dedication, and you should have enough experience to avoid Will-strain with some more strenuous spell-casting. Now, it is time to make you stronger." There were some murmurs of excitement, and he waved them to silence. "How does a sorcerer become stronger?"

He paused as if waiting for an answer, but continued when no one spoke. "Through adversity. You are going to learn how to fight with your Will, and once you do, you will compete to see which of you is strongest. The winner will receive fifty University contribution points. Before you lament the unfairness of competing against those with more capacity, let me add that this competition will be broken up into brackets. There will be thirty points for the winners of each of the weaker brackets, for those of you who started out with less experience but have still managed to prove your determination."

He opened a cabinet behind his desk and pulled out a box of small tea candles, which he sat on his desk. "You have been practicing a spell to introduce movement to a small metal ball. In this augmented exercise, one of you will attempt to force the ball into motion while your opponent counters you, trying to keep it still."

He placed one candle on his desk and touched the edge with the tip of his finger. The wick sprang into flame. "In the real world, when you are casting *practically*, you may find that you do not have a convenient beast core or bonfire readily available to cast your spell, and yet, you must still cast. If your Will is a pipe, and your goal is to channel enough water through it to wash away a hill of dirt, many people assume the best way to achieve the goal is to increase the amount of water that can be channeled through it at once. They attempt to make the pipe larger. In other words, to increase their Will's capacity. To be truly powerful, however, the pipeline of your Will must be not only wide, but robust and efficient. A smaller pipe may spew water more quickly than a larger one, if its walls are durable enough to withstand the pressure. At risk of abusing the metaphor, pouring water through the large pipe may result in a deluge that slowly erodes the hill, but the same amount of water forced at speed through a small pipe can create an impact forceful enough to scour the entire hill away, or simply pierce right through it.

"*Efficiency* will allow you to use minimal resources to achieve greater effects, and without wasted power spilling everywhere—everywhere except where you actually needed it to go, that is." He examined their faces, his cynical expression stating quite clearly that he doubted they understood him.

Being close to the front, Sebastien heard him mutter, "Note: prepare visual aids next year," to himself before continuing at full volume. "Most sorcerers waste much of the energy they attempt to channel. If you can be efficient, a mere three candles will be more than enough power for most spells you will be able to cast before earning your Apprenticeship."

Some of the students looked skeptical.

The edges of his mouth drew down along with his eyebrows. "For those under one hundred thaums, one candle. Two candles under two hundred thaums. Everyone above that gets three candles. The restriction on power source should force you to focus on the quality of your Will, and not only the strength of it. Make it work. Two glyphs from now on, instead of three."

He ignored the groans of the students. "The next few classes will provide time for you to practice against each other. This tournament is your mid-term examination. We'll start a little early, since it will take more than a single class period, and winners will be decided on the day of this class's mid-term. For your mid-term score, I will be grading you on all the facets of your Will, not just its capacity. The contribution points you earn can be redeemed immediately, or saved and added to your reserves. If you haven't already, I suggest you take a stroll through the various rewards available in the Great Hall."

That reminder of the prize boosted the students' excitement, and with a slight loosening of his expression, Lacer waved them all down to his desk to retrieve their candles. "Partner up and start practicing."

As soon as Sebastien made it back to her desk, a girl whose name she didn't know pushed up beside her, holding a single tea candle in one hand and a chair in the other. "May I partner with you, Sebastien?"

Slightly taken aback by the informality, as well as the fact that she didn't know the girl's name, Sebastien nevertheless waved obligingly to her desk. The other girl only had one candle, so Sebastien set two of hers to the side to level the playing field. *'How fortuitous. One standard-sized candle flame is only about eighty thaums. Hardly enough to strain me.'*

With a wide grin, the pink-cheeked girl pushed the chair she had brought up to the other side of Siobhan's desk and sat down.

"Seb—" Ana called, cutting off when she saw the other girl sitting across from Sebastien already.

"Sebastien is already partnered with *me*," the unnamed girl said, her smile growing stiffer. She tossed a look over her shoulder to where a group of young women seemed to be paying a little too much attention to the three of them.

Ana frowned.

"I'll be your partner, Anastasia," a loud man said. Alec Gervin, with his lack of manners and self-important attitude, threw his arm around her shoulder.

Ana shook her head, "Oh, thank you, Alec, but I—"

"It's no trouble at all, cousin. Besides, you need someone who can serve as an actual challenge to you," he said loudly, throwing Sebastien a combative look that lacked any subtlety at all.

"I doubt that person is *you*," Sebastien muttered, but she waved her hand uncaringly when both girls looked as if they were about to argue with Alec. "Go ahead."

Once Alec had pulled Ana away, Sebastien muttered, "His ass must get jealous of all the shit that comes out of his mouth."

The girl across from her almost choked on a surprised laugh, then clapped her hand over her mouth to stifle her giggles. "Oh, you are so *bad*, Sebastien!"

Alec, not completely oblivious, shot them a suspicious look, but Sebastien was careful to keep her expression innocent.

'*At least the Westbay boy has some actual ability to back up his attitude. Gervin… well, I would be surprised if he got into the University without more than a little "help" from his Family.*'

"Do you want to attempt movement, and I'll attempt to stop you?" Sebastien asked. They would both be competing for control of the same main Circle carved into her desk.

The girl agreed and drew the glyph for "*movement*" inside the Circle on her side, then connected it to a smaller component Circle where she drew the glyph for "*fire*" and placed her candle. "Oh, I wish we could still use three glyphs. Only two is going to make this so much harder, don't you think, Sebastien? My name is Cynthia, by the way. I don't know if you…" Cynthia trailed off, flushing again.

"A pleasure to meet you, Cynthia," Sebastien said distractedly. "And I don't mind the restrictions. After all, the point of this class is to teach us to cast without any spell array at all." After a few seconds to think, she drew a somewhat obscure glyph she had learned recently, "*adversity*." She, too, used "*fire*" in her component Circle, before palming her Conduit, which she noted with a hint of jealousy was of much poorer quality than Cynthia's.

She would need to be careful. Spells that directly opposed the Will of another thaumaturge put strain on the Conduit that was greater than the simple measure of how many thaums were being channeled. Meaning the Conduit was more likely to shatter unexpectedly, even at lower levels of energy. She understood the need for the efficiency Professor Lacer had lauded.

Reaching the danger level on her Conduit might come sooner rather than later, for her, especially if she was pitting her Will against a series of opponents that grew increasingly stronger. Her new main Conduit, the one she'd just bought at an exorbitant price to replace the one that shattered, was rated at only two hundred and twelve thaums. She had another one, her backup Conduit—little more than a cloudy pebble—tucked into her boot, but the capacity of the two Conduits couldn't be added together. The backup was only meant to keep her alive long enough to redirect the magical energy and safely release a spell if her new Conduit shattered. It was a pity celerium couldn't be melded together like any other sort of rock and still work as a Conduit. But there was a reason it was special—and so expensive.

Sure, she could just throw the match to avoid the risk, once things got more difficult, but she didn't *want* to. Professor Lacer would be watching and judging them. *'I have to prove to him that I'm worthy to stay at the University.'*

So as she channeled Will and power into opposing Cynthia's desire to make the ball move around the edge of the Circle, Sebastien kept an eye on her candle out of the corner of her eye. She had considered keeping a hand cupped around it so she could gauge its heat output, and thus, how strongly she was drawing on its power. This would require putting a piece of herself within the spell Circle, though, which was *dangerous*. Professor Lacer would surely throw her out of his class for displaying such stupidity in front of him twice. *'I can learn from my mistakes. I can.'*

So, she gauged the stability of her candle flame visually, putting mental pressure on her Will like a fist squeezing water out of a wet cloth. Tighter, more compact, more directed. Like a housewife squeezing bread dough, she forced her Will into a tighter and tighter mass, till she was gently massaging it, whispering to it and cajoling it to receive her thoughts and desires and needs.

When the spell array glowed with overspill, it wasn't because of *Sebastien*. After Cynthia made a few dozen stymied attempts to get the ball to move, Sebastien suggested they switch. She would move the ball while Cynthia stilled it.

Again, Cynthia was no match for her.

Sebastien abruptly and rapidly varied both the amount of power she was putting into creating movement, as well as which direction she was attempting to move the ball, jerking it around despite the pressure of the Will trying to stop her.

This time, Cynthia had used the glyph for "*stillness*," but didn't seem to have a firm enough grasp on the mental aspect of opposing Sebastien, and was easily overcome whenever the force on the ball was anything other than steady pressure in one direction.

The spell array glowed brighter as the other girl grew tired and frustrated, and her candle flame began to flicker and flutter. "How are you so good at this?" Cynthia whined.

Sebastien drew back some of her attention from the spell, allowing the ball to stop jerking around spasmodically. "You're pushing harder, but not exercising enough control. Look at your candle flickering. The spell array's glow is from inefficiency, too. This is what Professor Lacer was talking about. Even if your Will had a greater maximum energy capacity than mine, I might still be able to beat you if my Will was more powerful than yours in other ways. You may conceptualize it however works best for you, but without a more compressed idea of what exactly you're attempting to accomplish, you're wasting too much effort on things that do not directly oppose *my* Will. Here, I'll put less energy into it," she offered, giving herself the chance to take a break. "Rather than continuing to blindly push as much power into the spell as you can manage, put more effort into a clear conceptualization of what you want."

"What I...want?" The girl's attention had completely fallen away from the spell, and she was biting her lower lip as if nervous, looking back at Sebastien with big, limpid eyes.

'Has no one ever explained how spellcasting works to this girl, or is she simply stupid? Either way, I refuse to spend the rest of class explaining the basic concepts. She should not be in this class with such a marked inability to focus,' Sebastien thought with some distaste. "Yes," she said aloud. "You want to keep the ball from moving. But specifically, you must want to keep the ball from moving *more than* I want to move it. You must want it more clearly and purely than I want it. You want me to *fail* at moving it, because there is no space within the conceptualization of your Will for me to succeed. Smarter, not just harder, as they say."

Cynthia was blushing brightly. "You're so smart, Sebastien. Thank you for helping me."

Sebastien noted the bright red of the other girl's face. *'I hope she doesn't believe such an attitude is attractive. Perhaps she has enough sense to be embarrassed to be so openly incompetent that she is seen to need advice from a classmate, especially a no-name like me. But flattery from someone so mediocre is unlikely to gain my favor. If she was going to be so shy and embarrassed, why ask to partner with me? Well, perhaps she was pressured into it by some kind of dare or bullying from her friend group.'* She settled back with a nod, and instead of the scathing, impatient remarks she wanted to make, said, "I'm sure you can do it, Cynthia. Just focus." Sebastien gave herself a mental pat on the back for her restraint and patience.

It took Cynthia a few more tries, but she did manage to improve. It still wasn't enough to best Sebastien.

Halfway through the class, Professor Lacer called for them to switch partners.

Ana looked to Sebastien and began to rise, but another girl from Cynthia's group of friends had lunged forward and slammed her palm on Sebastien's desk as if it was a race. The loud cracking sound echoed through the classroom, drawing attention. "Are you free?" the new girl asked with a sweet, almost shy voice that belied her earlier zeal.

"Sure…" she said warily, nodding her head in greeting. "My name is Sebastien Siverling."

"Helen Marvin," the girl replied, flipping shoulder-length hair back with a practiced head toss as she sat down. "Call me Helen."

Helen was better than Cynthia had been, and shot the other girl a smug look when Sebastien complimented her control.

'Is there some sort of feud going on between them?'

However, she was still no match for Sebastien. "I think you might win the whole tournament. Professor Lacer is probably expecting it, and is only putting on this show so that no one can accuse him of favoritism for awarding you points directly," Helen said.

Sebastien's mind blanked out for a second as she tried to figure out which part of the girl's statement was the most wrong and where to start with her rebuttal.

Helen didn't seem to notice, and continued speaking. "What will you buy, if you win?"

Still trying to figure out how to respond to Helen's previous statement, Sebastien answered this one. "Well, I haven't perused what is on offer in the Great Hall, and I'm not sure what fifty points can buy." Privately, she admitted that she would very much enjoy a more private room or some of the better meal options, which were only purchasable with contribution points.

"If you add Lacer's points to whatever you earn at the end of term exhibitions, you'd be able to afford the hairpin carved from live star-maple wood. That hairpin would be the perfect gift for…a girl you wished would take notice of you." Helen's smile wasn't over-wide, and she had looked away as she spoke, not with shyness, but as if to soften the impact of her words with nonchalance.

Still, Sebastien immediately understood her implication. She thought Sebastien was rich, and for some misguided reason also likely to gain the accolades that would get her contribution points before her fourth term. Helen wanted to attach herself to that success. Specifically, she wanted gifts like a magical hairpin from a wood known for its healing properties, likely meant to make her complexion dewy or her hair lush and shiny.

Sebastien shook her head decisively. "I'll do my best in this tournament, but Professor Lacer will give the prize to whoever deserves it most. People seem to have wildly overestimated his regard for me. Also, I don't plan to participate in the exhibitions." She paused, debating whether to make a cutting statement about her lack of romantic interest to deter the girl more directly.

"What? Why would you not enter the exhibitions? Don't you want future employers to notice you? What about the points? There are a ton of things here that you can't buy with gold." Helen's voice was loud, turning heads around them.

Sebastien straightened, tamping down her irritation. Her desire to avoid drawing unnecessary attention to herself wasn't something she could say aloud, or that the other girl would even *understand*, apparently.

Professor Lacer coughed pointedly, stopping beside their desk.

Sebastien jerked, straightening impossibly further. She hadn't noticed his approach. "Professor," she said, greeting him with a half-bow from her seat.

His glare seemed to cast a pall over their immediate surroundings. "Why have you stopped practicing in favor of inane chatter? Is it because you feel you have learned all my class has to offer, or have you simply admitted your own incompetence and decided to give up on self-improvement in favor of flirting?" His words were precise, clipped, and cutting.

"I apologize, Professor," Sebastien said. "I was negligent. We will return to practice immediately."

Helen nodded quickly, pale and seemingly unable to speak.

Lacer waited a few agonizing seconds before replying, "See that you do." He turned and walked away, his trench coat spinning out and slapping the side of Sebastien's chair as he passed.

Sebastien spent the remainder of the class in focused spellcasting. None of her fellow students even attempted to speak to her about topics other than the task at hand.

By the end of class, she felt the boost of artificial energy from the wakefulness brew and adrenaline wearing thin.

As the students filtered out, she thought she saw Professor Lacer throw her a dark look, but when she turned to meet his gaze head-on, he was facing away.

Damien Westbay swaggered up beside her as they walked down the hallway. He clicked his tongue like an old matron. "Tch, tch, Siverling. *Flirting?* I hope you bring more focus to the tournament, or I might end up crushing you without a fight, and that would be disappointing."

Sebastien threw him a glare, her mouth already opening to let some of the frustration and anxiety within her spill out on an appropriate target. The sight of his smug grin, less malicious than she had expected, gave her pause. *'Could he be...joking with me?'* She wasn't sure of that, but the thought dispersed some of her ire. "I'm sure Professor Lacer will give you the prize you deserve. In your case, that would be...a participation trophy." She gave him a smirk of her own and turned the corner into another hallway without giving him a chance to reply.

2

PAPER SPELLS

SEBASTIEN
Month 11, Day 30, Monday 4:00 p.m.

SEBASTIEN WORRIED that the Morrows would rally after their failed attack and attempt to retaliate against the Verdant Stags with more violence. In fact, if the Morrows did *not*, it might be seen as a sign of weakness. Consequently, the Verdant Stag needed to recover and prepare faster than the Morrows could.

Even having acknowledged that, she didn't have the mental energy to start brewing healing and battle potions for the Verdant Stag right away. Besides, Katerin could brew, and they had at least one other alchemist making concoctions for them. If they needed more, Oliver should have the funds to buy anything Sebastien could make from someone else. She was not the only supplier of the alchemical concoctions that the enforcer teams needed.

Trusting someone else to be competent enough to do what needed to be done was dangerous, but she believed Oliver would do his best to make preparations even if she wasn't there. He had proven he was willing to take the weight of responsibility that many people shirked.

Gritting her teeth past the renewed headache from casting in Professor Lacer's class, she went to the library. A private table hidden in a remote alcove sat thankfully empty. The natural light from the windows didn't quite reach it, but her throbbing brain found that a boon rather than a detriment.

Sebastien pulled out some paper and her fountain pen, using cryptic notes

—just in case someone were to somehow read them—to help organize her thoughts and rearrange her plans. Writing things down had often helped her settle her racing mind. *'I need to study emergency procedure and triage—to make up for the knowledge I was clearly missing during the attack. Hopefully I'll never need to use it, but...if I ever do, and I haven't tried to correct the mistakes I made with Jameson, I couldn't forgive myself.'*

The University had healers' courses, but only for those above Apprentice level. They started in the fourth term, once students had a stronger foundation. It was a complicated subject that required a lot of knowledge and power. She wouldn't be able to learn everything on her own, but basics about how to triage and stabilize traumatic wounds should be accessible.

'I need a variety of spells ready to go. Having a spell array memorized isn't enough. It would be best if I had them primed to cast without the need to stop and draw the array before adding the components. Such a delay could be fatal in the wrong situation.'

With her lack of skill with artificery and her lack of funds to buy artifacts or potions, alchemy was the best way to accomplish her goal. As soon as she had the time and mental fortitude, she would go to Dryden Manor and brew a variety of the most useful potions she could think of. Starting with the blood clotter. *'That's good, but I should have other contingencies in place, too.'*

The glass pane that had made her spell arrays portable was quite useful, if unwieldy and dangerous...and ultimately disastrous when she cut herself. She could see many scenarios where something like that could be invaluable. Actively cast spells weren't quite as conveniently ready-to-use as alchemical concoctions, but alchemy didn't have an equivalent recipe already developed for every spell. Pre-brewed items also couldn't have their effects changed on the fly, and the cost of component ingredients was often higher.

The glass pane would have been even better if she weren't forced to erase and redraw the Circle and Word every time she switched spells.

That's what the giant tomes of magic that some sorcerers carried around were for. Some laypeople mistook them for grimoires, whose pages held instructions and notes on the spells. Magic tomes instead held useable spell arrays. The pages and arrays were made of special materials and cost more than a normal artifact to make, but provided access to more castable spells than would fit in most artifacts, up to two or three dozen.

The military offered its soldiers a few portable arrays made of precious metals wrought into the desired shapes, but those would be even less accessible to someone like her, and certainly were not something she could lug around in an emergency.

Sebastien paused her cryptic scribbles, staring down at the cheap paper as the ink from her pen tip began to feather out and form a blot.

Even if she couldn't create a tome of magic from materials meant to handle spells, that didn't mean she couldn't set up the Circle and Word for a few useful spells ahead of time. Normal paper was a particularly poor surface for spell casting, but as long as it *worked*, some inefficiency could be excused. Even if the paper burnt up from the force of the magic flowing through it, it would just destroy the evidence. In fact, it would likely be a good idea to create a small spark-shooting spell array at the corner of each page, just in case she ever needed to quickly turn one or all of them to ash to keep them from being used against her.

The library, like the jail, had wards to notify them of sudden fluctuations of energy within a small area. Such fluctuations usually corresponded to magic being cast, which was prohibited due to possible damage to the books. Thus, she couldn't immediately test her theory, but that didn't stop her from bouncing up to feverishly grab research and reference texts.

She found a handful of low-powered but versatile spells that seemed like they would be useful to have on hand. Research on emergency healing measures was less successful.

Even with the help of the crystal ball search artifacts placed around the edge of the atrium, she found no information about blood transfusions except to mention that the Third Empire—also known as the Blood Empire—had performed them. Like all blood magic, they were illegal, and their use was considered high treason. Anything useful, like how to do them safely and properly, was restricted in one of the many underground archives.

Humphries' adapting solution remained the only viable alternative. The solution could be spelled directly into the veins in a blood-loss emergency. Its original purpose had been to keep creatures from the Plane of Water alive on the mundane plane, but it could also act as a filler and keep blood oxygenated. It was expensive and difficult to make, and didn't have a very long shelf-life, so it wasn't feasible for most people except dedicated healers to stock. She had heard of it, but never brewed it herself.

And...the recipe was only available on the second floor of the library. Which she did not have access to. She almost kicked the base of her crystal ball's marble stand in frustration. Despite this setback, she peered into the clear crystal and dutifully wrote down the locations of the books that contained a copy of the recipe. *'Just because I cannot go there myself doesn't mean I cannot get information from the upper floors. This is innocuous enough, not like the restricted archives. I just need to get an upper-term student to check the book out for me.'*

Her research continued through dinner, which she was much too focused to pause for, until ten, when the library closed and she was unceremoniously kicked out. Instead of going to the bed, she went to the dorm bathrooms. She would have preferred an empty classroom, but the Citadel closed at this hour, too. She checked to make sure all the stalls were empty, then sat down on the tile floor in one of the shower stalls and pulled out her notes and materials.

Using a piece of thread as a makeshift compass tool to ensure her Circle was as uniform as possible, and thus increase the spell's efficiency, Sebastien carefully inscribed a rudimentary barrier array onto the paper with her fountain pen. Grubb's barrier spell had been the weakest she found in the library, and at under two hundred thaums to manifest, the only one she could hope to cast, if feebly. It only protected against physical projectiles, but she had already proven that could be critical against a certain kind of opponent.

She took the components from her school satchel and placed them atop the correct spots on the paper, lit her tiny lantern for energy, and cast the spell.

The paper caught fire along the lines of ink she had drawn, and within a few seconds was nothing but ashes and wisps of smoke. The energy she had been channeling blew the white-blonde hair away from her face and scattered the ashes around the room, but thankfully didn't manage to do any damage to her mind or her surroundings as it escaped.

She sat back, rubbing at her forehead and letting out a disappointed puff of air. Still not completely deterred, she took out another sheet and redrew the spell. This time, she focused on being as efficient as possible, casting more slowly and bearing down harder with her Will. The paper began to smolder and smoke along the ink lines, and though the entire sheet didn't catch fire this time, the spell lashed against her Will, and she had to release it as pieces of the spell array disintegrated from the rest of the paper.

'That could be quite dangerous. What if an inner Circle containing important glyphs were to burn separately from the rest of the paper and blow away in the wind, leaving me with only part of a spell? Or if the entire paper caught fire midcast, and I got Will-strain from the backlash?'

She tried using a wax crayon instead of ink, but quickly found that the wax melted into the paper and only added fuel for any opportunistic spark.

'Behold. I have created a very tiny candle.' She shook her head ruefully. 'No, ink is obviously better than wax. Perhaps the inked parts are burning because the channel through which all the energy travels is so thin? Too much heat in a small space can set almost anything alight.'

Tiptoeing into the dorms, she retrieved a small ink brush from her chest of belongings. Using that, the third attempt was a bit sloppier, but the lines were definitely wider. It helped, but again, not enough. Pieces of the spell array smoldered and burned away, even with her only holding the small shield spell active for a few seconds. That wasn't completely useless, true, but it was close to useless.

She groaned and rubbed at her aching eyes. 'Perhaps it would be best to set this idea aside until I have access to materials better suited to channeling magic. If they aren't too expensive, that is...' Her eyes opened, and she stared down at the small glass inkwell beside her. She already had a material better suited to channeling magic. Her blood.

She hesitated only briefly, considering the illegality of using blood, even one's own, to channel magic, and then cast the hesitation aside. *'No one will find out, especially if I simply mix blood in with the ink. The blood will be unrecognizable. And if I find there is somehow danger of discovery, I can simply activate the self-destruct spark spell and burn away the evidence of "blood magic."'* Of course, this meant that the spell papers could never leave her person, but to fulfill their purpose of emergency preparedness, they shouldn't be out of immediate access, anyway.

The brief mental nod to legality out of the way, Sebastien quickly made a small cut in her forearm with her athame, letting her blood fill the inkwell to the top. A dab of skin-knitting salve left only a faint scar to mark the spot, which would fade soon enough. She mixed the ink and the blood thoroughly, then painted the barrier spell on yet another piece of paper.

This time, the small barrier burst to life like a bubble, shimmering faintly, and the paper endured.

Sebastien let out a small "whoop!" of excitement, then let the spell go. Touching the paper revealed the ink lines were quite warm, perhaps almost to the point of catching fire, but casting was still feasible. *'If I get my hands on some thicker paper, a little warmth won't be disastrous. Maybe a double-ply bound together with paste. It should last at least a minute or two per sheet.'* Parchment, even the relatively cheaper parchment from a goat or a cow, would be extremely fire resistant, but then it wouldn't be so simple for her to destroy any evidence that could lead to suspicion. Also, she still might not be able to afford it.

Having returned the spell components to her bag and carefully tucked away the paper and inkwell, she finally made her way to bed.

Only then did she remember the actual classwork that she needed to complete for Sympathetic Science the next morning. Normally, she would have completed it as early as possible, simply to get it out of the way, but now she was forced to resort to taking out her potion of moonlight sizzle and using its light to scribble her way through the assignment.

3

SLEEP RESEARCH

Sebastien
Month 11, Day 30, Monday 10:30 p.m.

Sebastien felt sick with fatigue by the time her head finally hit the pillow, and it wasn't much better by morning. For once, not even the promise of learning magic was enticing enough to motivate her out of bed. Only the thought of her absence being noted managed to haul her to her feet. The coppers made another attempt to scry her before she got very far, and after it had failed and the adrenaline left her system, she felt even weaker.

She dragged through her classes, having to rush to the bathroom quite suddenly when the coppers once again scried for her. At the end of the day, she went to the market to purchase better paper, as well as supplies for the most critical potions.

The owner of the small stationery shop she visited was exceedingly solicitous, and at first she felt uncomfortable with him hovering near her and asking questions, but he turned out to be quite helpful.

"If you are looking for a fire-resistant writing surface that isn't parchment, I recommend this one-quarter seaweed blend," the man said, herding her around to the other side of the shop. "Darker, rougher, and thicker than fine vellum, but strong and long-lasting for any project you would like to withstand the rigors of time."

"Is it totally flame resistant?"

He shook his head. "Unfortunately not, but it has good performance for the price. Don't be dissuaded by the appearance. Of course, if you are insistent upon a brighter, smoother sheet, we do have more flame-resistant paper made of special magical materials—the details are a trade secret—but that option is significantly pricier."

"No, no, this is fine."

"Wonderful!" The man was so excited that she wondered if he'd been struggling to offload the seaweed paper. "What size would you like? We can cut it for you here, free of charge."

Sebastien paused. The idea that she could get larger paper had never crossed her mind. She'd been stuck thinking that she would have something like a mini-tome of magic, filled with journal-sized spell arrays. But if that wasn't the case, it gave her even more options. "No need. I need a variety of sizes, so I'll be cutting it myself," she said, grinning almost as wide as the shopkeeper.

A couple of gold lighter, she made her way to Dryden Manor. Oliver himself wasn't there, but she set up the brewing station in his study anyway.

As she stirred the steaming cauldron over the small batch of grainy blood-clotting potion within, she had trouble focusing the full strength of her Will. Her eyelids would droop and her mind's grip on the magic would loosen without her even realizing it, only for her to jerk back to alertness.

The third time this happened, the magic almost slipped from her grip entirely. It frightened her enough that she stepped away from the cauldron and took a few minutes to cast some wakefulness magic on coffee pilfered from Oliver's kitchen. When she knocked back the mixture in a single swallow, coffee grounds and all, she got enough of a rush to make it through the remainder of the potion.

Oliver still hadn't returned by the time she'd brewed a small batch of blood-clotting potions. She took one for herself and left the rest for him with a scribbled note.

The servants persuaded her to stay for dinner in the kitchen, more than happy to add her to their table. As Sebastien stuffed herself to make up for all the energy she'd expended channeling magic, Sharon fussed over the circles under Sebastien's eyes and tutted about the University's poor food quality.

When Sebastien returned to the dorms that evening, she thought, '*I need to practice my new spells just like I practice the exercises for Professor Lacer's class if I want to be able to use them in a practical setting.*' The acknowledgment gave her no extra energy, however, so she went to sleep instead.

The nightmares came particularly strong, seeming to defy her attempts to suppress them with magic. After she woke with a pounding heart and a scream choked off in her throat, she gave up on sleep and used the time to study the theory behind the new utility spells she would be putting on paper.

She felt no better than the day before, and after lunch her body decided it was a perfect time to catch up on all her deferred sleep, so she went back to the dorms for a short nap.

Newton noticed her struggling to get out of bed in order to make it to Defensive Magic, and stubbornly hauled her off to the infirmary. "I understand the desire to perform to the best of your abilities, but you have to recognize when you are in need of rest, Sebastien," he said. "It won't go away just because you keep pushing. The pressure only grows worse. Trust me, I know from experience." He had shadows under his own eyes, and his clothes were a little more rumpled than usual.

"I've just been having trouble sleeping," she said. "I'm fine, really."

"You'll get sick if you keep pushing beyond your limits. If you're lucky, it'll only be physical, and not cause any damage to your Will."

"I'm missing class right now," she protested. "And Fekten just gives the lectures, not any reading or homework. If I'm not there, I'll miss the entire topic for today, along with the participation points toward my grade."

"The infirmary will give you a pass," Newton replied, undeterred. He waved, ushering her in ahead of him, as if to make sure she couldn't escape behind his back.

'They cannot know I had Will-strain. They might ask questions.' But she couldn't say that aloud, couldn't explain that she didn't want to seem any different than the other students to avoid drawing suspicion to herself.

To her surprise and relief, the woman who came over to deal with them seemed completely unsurprised when Newton volunteered the symptoms he'd noticed. "You're the third one today, and that's only of the students I've dealt with personally. Sometimes I think they push you all too hard. Are you experiencing any signs of Will-strain?"

Sebastien started to shake her head, but stopped when Newton raised his eyebrows skeptically. "Well, I have had some headaches," she admitted. "But I think it's just from the lack of sleep. The dorms, you know... I'm not used to sleeping with so many people all around me."

"He wakes up and practices casting in the middle of the night," Newton corrected.

The healer and student liaison shared a knowing look. "Well, I'm going to prescribe two days of rest from any practical exercises, as well as a mild anti-anxiety potion. The potion should last you for a couple of weeks, at single-sip doses. You can take it twice a day: once in the morning before breakfast, and once before bed. Please come back for more at the end of that period, if you feel you need it."

Newton gave her a thumbs-up. "I'll make sure he does."

Sebastien rolled her eyes, but neither of the other two seemed to find her exasperation worth noting.

They made her take the first anti-anxiety potion before leaving. While

Sebastien disliked the artificial sense of serenity, she had to admit that she had also lost any desire to attend Fekten's Defensive Magic class, as the idea of physical exercise sounded torturous when she could be resting in her little cubicle instead.

"I'll have one of your friends write down notes from Fekten's lecture," Newton said once he'd returned her to the dorms. "Rest easy, you won't miss anything important."

She hummed gratefully and found herself casting her dreamless sleep spell without even worrying that Newton was watching.

He drew the curtains around her bed, and she slipped into sleep while the sound of his footsteps was still fading into the distance.

She was still tired when she woke, but the nightmares wouldn't let her rest any longer. She briefly considered going back to the infirmary to see if they could do anything to make her sleep more restful, but discarded the idea. When she was a child and the dreams started, her father had taken her to more than a few healers out of desperation, but there had been nothing they could do. "Dreaming is natural," one had said, "and if the girl is having nightmares, perhaps you shouldn't tell her any scary stories before bed." Even when Ennis hinted at what she'd gone through before he came back for her, they had never been able to provide a solution. The dreamless sleep spell she had modified over the years was the only thing that seemed to actually help.

Besides, she didn't feel comfortable revealing such a weakness when she was surrounded by potential enemies. She would handle her problems herself, as she always had.

So she returned her attention to her research on sleep, going through the texts on the subject that she had borrowed from the library. 'If I'm never able to properly recover, any efforts to learn or practice other topics are useless. My Will is bound to grow brittle and snap even more quickly from desperate training without balance.' Most of the texts were useless to her, and were set aside after she skimmed through them thoroughly, but just as she was beginning to despair, she came upon a research journal written by Keeswood, a thaumaturge who had been attempting to learn what sleep actually did for the body.

Keeswood cautioned against attempts to avoid sleep altogether, citing an increased likelihood of becoming sick, decreased mental and magical functions, and, in extreme cases, hallucinations, paranoia, and even madness. Nothing she didn't already know. She was about to toss the book aside in frustration when Keeswood mentioned one particular experiment he had done on a pair of twins.

Using a spell that he explained only in the vaguest of terms, he had caused one twin to sleep *in place of* the other, allowing the wakeful twin to go for over ten days without sleep. Even this was not sustainable long term, because signs of fatigue still built up in the wakeful twin, while the twin who had been sleeping for the both of them fell into perpetual unconsciousness, not even waking for the eight hours per day that should have been possible.

In fear of damaging either of them, Keeswood had stopped the experiment. The wakeful twin had slept for a slightly extended period after the spell was released, but both recovered fully and returned to functioning normally after only a day.

Sebastien was captivated by the idea that someone or something else could do her sleeping for her. She quickly flipped through the rest of the research journal, but could find no more detail about the spell used to allow this. Standing, she pulled on her boots, preparing to go to the library and search for any other writings by the man, but realized with a bleary examination of her pocket watch that the library had already closed. She only then looked around and realized that most of the other students had returned to the dorms and settled down for sleep already.

With a deep sigh, she knelt over her pillow and cast the dreamless sleep spell as strongly as she could, setting her alarm for only a few hours later. 'Perhaps if I wake on my own, I can recast the spell before the nightmares have time to slip in. It might allow for more overall sleep, since I won't have to recover from them before being able to relax again.' She took another dose of the anti-anxiety potion, and was able to get almost a full night's rest by the morning.

She felt almost normal, but she didn't forget the research journal or the ideas it had sparked.

Despite Newton's good intentions, she did not give the casting pass from the infirmary to any of her teachers that day, feeling awake enough to at least complete the in-class exercises.

Professor Lacer seemed to be keeping a closer eye on her than normal, and that, too, kept her from being complacent enough to droop off. If she did, it would be the end of her, just like that boy who had supposedly been turned into a sheep and then expelled.

She stopped by the library once again after class and looked up every other text the author of the sleep-surrogate experiment had contributed to. Most of them were held in one of the restricted sections in the underground archives. She sought out one of the library student aides and enquired about accessing it. Without the contribution points to afford a pass to that section, and lacking the rapport with any of the professors that might get them to sign a special exception slip for her, in the end, Sebastien had been forced to *flirt* brazenly with the student aide to get a pass. She was desperate.

The young woman, who sported a tail marking her as one of the non-human students, could barely look Sebastien in the eye past her blush. She stammered that it would take at least a day to get a new pass created, and Sebastien promised to return when it was ready.

When Sebastien found her legs bouncing irritably as she tried to write a homework essay, she went to the simulation room in the big building out on the Flats, where students were permitted to practice spells and dueling for Defense class.

One of the utility spells she had researched for casting through paper was a fabric cutting spell that sent a single slicing line outward in an arc, the shape of which could be controlled to some degree by the caster's Will. Unlike many similar spells, it didn't require the target to be within the Circle, as it used compressed air as the cutting edge.

And of course, she could use it to do more than cut fabric.

It wasn't meant to work against humans, or any living thing. However, with extensive practice, and if she could channel enough power into it, it could still overcome the inherent barrier against invasive magics that most creatures maintained unconsciously, through molding the air rather than trying to attack directly with magical energy. It was meant as a close-range spell, and at longer distances the cutting edge would degrade severely, but it was one of the few potentially useful battle spells that someone of her level could cast.

She set to practicing it using one of the waist-high, slate-topped columns the simulation room had helpfully raised from the floor to use as a drawing surface, aiming at a dummy only a few feet away. Keeping the air compressed for long enough that the slicing edge could travel farther was still well beyond her. She experimented with varying the size of the slice, as well as how quickly she cast.

While she was practicing, she noticed Westbay enter the room and move past her to one of the more advanced stations. He proceeded to use a battle wand in a mock duel with a dummy, which moved back and forth and sent harmless bolts of light shooting at him. He was actually quite skilled, both in his footwork and ability to dodge, and his aim. If he had been one of the coppers chasing after her, she likely would have been hit with a stunning spell and captured.

She was still methodically sending arcs of slicing air toward her stationary dummy when he finished and walked her way again.

Westbay stopped beside her, mopping at sweaty hair with a fluffy towel while he watched her cast.

She did her best to ignore him, powering up another slice, this one with a wider arc.

"A slicing spell? Are you planning to murder someone? My Family's coppers will catch you, you know," he muttered.

Sebastien spun on him before even fully registering what he said, a hot rush of fear and anger rising up from her belly as if it had been waiting there to be triggered. She opened her mouth to let it out in the form of words, and only when the spell had already been released—the edge of the slicing arc heading directly for the left side of Westbay's chest—did she realize her mistake.

She tried to call it back, to direct the spell away, but it was too late. The edge, visible as a faintly glowing shimmer in the air, cut into him, slicing through his shirt and the skin below even as his eyes widened in belated surprise.

A red line of blood welled up, a crimson stain blooming on the crisp white fabric of Westbay's shirt.

Sebastien's face paled. *'What have I done? I'll be expelled.'*

4

FRIENDSHIPS FORGED BY ACCIDENT

DAMIEN
   Month 12, Day 2, Wednesday 5:30 p.m.

DAMIEN LOOKED DOWN to the quickly reddening slice in his shirt. Sebastien Siverling's spell had cut across the left half of his chest and his arm. For a moment, he wondered if he was going to die, carved right through but taking a moment to notice he was mortally wounded, like he'd read in one particularly violent detective story.

But, no, he judged with relief. The blood wasn't shooting out in huge arterial sprays. As the pain began to register, he felt his cheeks flush with shame. If Titus knew how careless he had been, needling a sorcerer while they practiced battle spells, Damien would be in for a tongue lashing at the very least. Even little children should know better. Honestly, he didn't even know why he'd done it.

He might not enjoy admitting it, but there was a reason Professor Lacer had taken Siverling as his apprentice. Siverling was obviously talented with magic, but also had a tongue sharp enough to match the professor's, and an air of sophistication that even Damien couldn't match, no matter how carefully he starched his collar or styled his hair. Siverling seemed not to even notice the rest of them unless interrupted from his constant study, and then the air of superiority—only partially covered by a facade of courtesy—was obvious to Damien at least, if not to all of their other classmates.

It was only when provoked that Siverling's true temperament slipped through, and Damien could admit that he found it somewhat enjoyable to bicker with the other young man. It had become a habit over the last few weeks, even as Damien began to understand Professor Lacer's choice. And, reluctantly, to admit that it had not been in error.

Siverling's face had gone pale enough to match his hair, those dark eyes standing out starkly against his skin. His angry expression slid away in favor of unadulterated horror.

Damien swallowed and raised his right arm, the uninjured one, to push his hair back from his face. Should he apologize? Probably, but it seemed strange to do so when he had been injured at Siverling's hand.

The other young man's jaw clenched, his teeth grinding the words like a pepper mill as he said, "Lie down on the ground and take off your shirt." Then Siverling was turning and running for the changing rooms.

Damien stared after his escaping form, blinking. "What?" Was Siverling seriously leaving him there to go get dressed? No, he'd already been wearing his normal clothes, so that couldn't be it. Damien looked to the dirty floor, the white dust of the Flats and whatever other filth people had stepped in tracked everywhere. "Lie down on that?" He would have to change his clothes afterward. His eyes were drawn to the crimson soaking his shirt, all the way down to the waist now. "I suppose it *is* already quite ruined," he muttered. Along with his sweat and the blood, a little dirt wouldn't make much difference.

He swayed on his feet.

Siverling, returned already without Damien noticing, grabbed him by the shoulders with a grim expression and pushed him down to the floor.

Damien realized Siverling's instruction had been meant to keep him from fainting due to shock or blood loss. "I should be fine if I get to the healers soon enough," he said. "There's an alarm ward trigger on the back wall, remember?" It would alert them to an emergency and summon someone skilled enough to keep students alive in even the most grievous states. Except, if the healers were called, they would notify his family.

"If my father finds out..." he muttered quietly. Realizing he had spoken aloud, he let the statement trail off. Even the thought was frightening.

Siverling must have caught the fear on Damien's face, because after a short hesitation, he said, "There's no need for a healer." He dug into the satchel he had grabbed from the changing rooms with practiced hands. "It's just a scratch, and we will have it healed in no time."

Damien stared incredulously at the other young man. "Just a scratch?" The pain was making itself known now, and the blood had finished with his shirt and was beginning to soak his trousers. He kept his eyes on Siverling's face so that he wouldn't focus on the blood. He had been injured a few times sparring with his brother or his dueling tutor, but the sight of blood still made him lightheaded. "Do you have a healing artifact in there?" he questioned. In a low murmur, more to reassure himself than anything, he added, "If there are no healers involved, my father need not know…"

The young man nodded tightly as he pulled out a couple of potion vials and the supplies to draw a spell array.

Damien frowned, shaking his head woozily. "That's not a healing artifact."

Siverling reached forward and tore Damien's shirt, widening the slices the spell had made to better expose the wounds.

"You are so forward." The words had slipped out before Damien realized what his stupid brain was thinking, and he would have been embarrassed, but he imagined almost anything he said could be excused by the circumstances.

"Lie back," the other boy ordered, accompanying the words with a firm push on Damien's good shoulder.

Damien complied.

"The wound isn't that deep. I'm not sure we need a blood clotter, but it's better to be safe. I don't want you bleeding out before I can handle this," Siverling muttered. He uncorked the potions, dribbling the first, and then the second across the cut from right to left.

The first was a wound cleanser, Damien thought. There was just enough in the bottles to generously cover the entire wound, and Damien winced at the burning as the wound cleanser killed any infectious agents. The blood clotter did its job immediately after. The bleeding stopped, but the slice was far from healed.

Siverling eyed it critically. "I don't think my skin-knitting salve is going to be able to deal with that."

Damien groaned, reaching up to touch it, but his hand was rudely slapped away by Siverling.

"Keep your filthy fingers at your sides," the young man snapped, picking up the spell supplies. "And stay still while I work." He leaned over Damien, drawing a large Circle on the ground around his entire torso, and then a mirrored pair over Damien's chest and arms. Siverling hesitated for a few moments when drawing the glyphs, glancing at the blood now forming a puddle on the floor.

Finally, he drew back and reached in one of his vest pockets for something he didn't find. He looked around and snatched up a small, contaminated Conduit that he had apparently dropped when he hit Damien with the cutting spell. He clenched it in his fists, glared down at Damien's wound, and took a deep breath.

Damien felt the weight in the air as Siverling gathered his Will. "Wait, wait!" he said.

Siverling met his wide-eyed gaze, raising his eyebrows impatiently. "What?"

Was he seriously about to attempt a healing spell? "You didn't even place any components in the Circle, and that Conduit wouldn't be fit for a goblin. It's going to backfire and injure both of us."

Siverling's scowl returned full force. "Shut up and stay still."

"If you could heal something like this with nothing from the Plane of Radiance and with that Conduit, I would acknowledge you as the second incarnation of Myrddin—"

Before Damien could protest any more, the other boy began to cast.

Damien didn't move, though he wasn't sure if it was for fear of distracting Siverling and causing the disaster he feared, or if it was because some small part of him was watching with anticipation and a growing sense of awe.

That second, smaller part of him was fully rewarded as the cut across his chest began to tighten and heal, as if time was being wound back, so slowly it was almost possible to miss it.

Siverling's brow beaded with sweat and his fist clenched so hard around the Conduit that his knuckles turned white. It took a lot longer than a certified healer would have managed, and there was a certain hair-raising discomfort that Damien had to steel himself against as his flesh moved. When Siverling finally finished, he released the spell with an almost tangible burst of freed power and sagged forward, breathing raggedly. He used some skin-knitter to seal the patch job.

Gingerly, Damien sat up and touched his chest. The slice was more than half-healed, red and aching, but not bleeding any more. After the skin-knitter finished, there would be a scar, so the spell hadn't been perfect, but it was still astounding. He turned to look at the spell array on the ground, his eyes marveling at the minimalist construction. There were no components except a little oil lamp to provide energy, and no instructions besides glyphs for mirroring, flesh, and healing. His heart was pounding when he turned back to Siverling.

He watched as the young man recovered from the overexertion. It had been snark when he said he would acknowledge Siverling as the second incarnation of Myrddin. But this...

Sebastien Siverling could end up the most powerful sorcerer of their generation.

At the realization, Damien let out a slow breath. How had he not heard of the Siverling family before? Were they simply that far from Lenore? Or perhaps fallen into such ruin that their name was no longer mentioned among the influential. It might explain why, despite Siverling's mannerisms and attire, he used such a cheap Conduit. Perhaps his family had spent all they could to ensure he would fit in amongst his peers at the University, and hoped that he could make it through the first few terms without bringing attention to the Conduit. Obviously, a better one would be needed soon if he didn't want to risk it shattering.

Siverling raised himself back up, his spine straight and his chin raised. "It's healed," he said. "There's no need to sound the alarm, or to contact your family. We may both continue on and forget this incident." He stared into Damien's face as if searching for something, then grimaced slightly. "Of course, I'm willing to provide a small favor as well, if you wish. I did ruin your clothing, after all."

It was only then that Damien realized Siverling had thought Damien was threatening him when he mentioned his father's wrath. He opened his mouth to explain and reassure the other boy, then closed it abruptly.

"A favor," Damien agreed. "And a ceasefire between us. I apologize for my previous actions, and I hope that we can be civil toward each other going forward." He hadn't been raised a simpleton, and even if he was still feeling a little lightheaded, he wasn't stupid. Alliances formed now would influence the future, as would enemies. Plus, he found himself undeniably curious about the other young man.

Siverling's eyes widened at the offer of reconciliation, then narrowed, but eventually he nodded. "Agreed."

"Lend me your jacket," Damien said. "Unless," he added, seeing Siverling's raised eyebrow, "you wish everyone to see the state of my attire and ask questions."

With a huff, Siverling gave him the jacket. After clearing the spell array and remains of blood from the ground, they left the simulation room together, heading back toward the dorms.

"Why aren't you participating in the exhibitions?" Damien asked.

Siverling shot him another inscrutable look before replying. "I have no need for points, and would rather spend my time learning something useful than preparing some spectacle purely to impress the judges and audience."

"You wouldn't need to do much extra preparation, I think. You could simply show them your skill at purely Will-based healing spells and gain full points. Healers command a sizable income, you know. Especially ones as talented as yourself. You might even be able to earn a little money while continuing on past the third term."

Siverling's face grew stony, and he stared straight ahead for long enough that Damien wondered if he had said something wrong. Perhaps he shouldn't have mentioned the bit about earning money. If Siverling's family wasn't impoverished, it would be gauche. If they were, maybe he was sensitive about it.

"I have no desire to ingratiate myself to those who would hold themselves above me while weighing my worth—as if I were a fat hog—nor do I feel the desire to peacock around for insignificant points and empty praise. I will not participate," Siverling said, his lip curled in a scornful sneer.

Yes, Damien had definitely offended him. "Well, to each their own. Personally, I would enjoy moving up from the dorms. Being stuffed in with the rabble makes it so difficult to properly relax, and I *know* someone stole my spare pair of boots." He scowled for a moment, thinking of what he would do to that person should he ever find them. "But there are other ways to gain points, such as the tournament in Practical Casting. If you would like to gain extra practice with competent opponents before then, you might join our study group again."

"Maybe."

Well, at least it wasn't outright refusal. With persistence and cunning, he could get Siverling's amity. Damien could be likable when he wanted to be. Even to people as insufferably rude as Sebastien Siverling. Perhaps a more direct overture of friendship was required. "You were practicing a battle spell, though I'm not sure I've seen that particular one before. If you have interest in dueling, both Rhett and I have some skill. His interest leans more toward competition, but I've received some of the same training our coppers get. I could pass along some useful tips, or help you hone your aim and footwork."

That seemed to catch Siverling's interest. "Right, your family is in charge of the coppers. Have there been any updates on that case you were talking about before?"

Damien suppressed a small smile. Perhaps it wasn't the dueling Siverling was interested in, but the detective work, like Damien. Well, that made sense, as the job was both worthwhile and fascinating.

"Yes, in fact. She made an appearance in a fight between two local gangs, though the circumstances behind the whole altercation are somewhat muddy. She injured several members of one group, but they were able to retreat when things became dire. Now, one would assume this meant she was allied with the second group in some way, but when the coppers arrived, they found her performing some sort of *sacrificial blood ritual* on one of them."

He grinned as Siverling's eyes widened, satisfied with the other young man's rapt attention. Perhaps he could share some of his old detective periodicals with Siverling. He would be bound to enjoy them. Then, at least, Damien would have one friend with whom he could talk about the latest fictional exploits of Aberford Thorndyke, consulting detective.

"Do they have any leads on her?"

He nodded. "Oh, yes. Well, she fought back against the coppers when they arrived, leaving her victim to his fate, but though we almost caught her, she managed to escape. However, one of the coppers managed to injure her, and she left a little of her own blood behind on the scenes. They have it and are scrying for her now. Of course, she's quite a powerful sorcerer, so she's managed to hold off the attempts so far. A couple of witnesses even say she was managing to cast spells using the *air* as the surface for her spell array, though I'm a bit skeptical about the veracity of those claims. We are quite confident she's still within the city, and they'll be bringing in some stronger scryers soon, I'm sure. I know my brother has access to a prognos or two, so I imagine it is only a matter of time before she's caught."

Siverling was still enraptured, so Damien went into detail, relating what he knew from the reports he'd managed to wheedle out of his brother, along with his own speculation. He continued until Siverling rubbed his forehead, wincing as if he had a headache.

Damien's eyes narrowed, and, as he paid closer attention, he noticed the trembling in Siverling's fingers. "You didn't strain your Will healing me, did you?"

"No," Siverling replied in a clipped tone.

Damien eyed him dubiously. He didn't need to be Aberford Thorndyke to make such an obvious deduction. "It's no use pretending you didn't, if you did. My brother always says, 'If you've strained your Will, it's a sign you chose the wrong strategy at least two moves ago. Do not just continue on bullheadedly, as that will lead to even more catastrophic failure.'" Damien felt even worse about the whole thing now.

"First, there was nothing to heal, because nothing happened, remember?" Siverling said pointedly.

Damien nodded slowly, pursing his lips.

"So there's no reason to go to the infirmary just for them to ask a lot of questions and prescribe a couple days of rest. Secondly, even if I had healed you, I wouldn't have hit Will-strain just from that."

Siverling glared at Damien until he nodded again, though he didn't believe Siverling's assurances at all. Obviously, he'd strained his Will from that ridiculous display of skill, but he didn't want anyone to know. "Well...you should take a break from casting spells for a completely *unrelated* reason, then." He gave Siverling a pointed look of his own.

When they got back to the dorms, Damien changed into a fresh outfit—one not covered in blood—but found Siverling gone when he emerged from the bathrooms. "Oh, well," he said, tossing his clothes into the fireplace, both to destroy the blood and to keep the events of that afternoon secret. All in all, it had been an exciting and fruitful day.

Almost an *adventure*, really.

5

THE MYSTERIES OF SLEEP

Sebastien
Month 12, Day 2, Wednesday 6:00 p.m.

Sebastien had, in fact, strained her Will again healing that idiotic boy. It wasn't so much the spell itself as it was trying to keep the Word almost entirely in her head while casting it. She wanted to leave no evidence of the Sacrifice for that particular spell. This way, even Westbay couldn't truthfully say that he'd seen her use blood magic.

She had panicked when she realized what she'd done. Harming another student with careless magic use was a big deal. *'Harming one of the Thirteen Crown Families, and a high-ranking member at that? One I'm known to dislike? Even if the University believed it was an accident, the slightest push from one of the Westbays would have a commoner like Sebastien Siverling expelled.'* It wouldn't even have to be Damien Westbay himself who complained. If any member of his Family wanted the University to take greater responsibility for his safety, she would be the perfect scapegoat. Even Professor Lacer might not be on her side.

So she'd acted as quickly as possible to cover up the evidence, removing any need for him to report the incident. She owed him a favor now, but that was a trifle. After all, she'd been willing to owe far worse favors to borrow tuition money.

Sebastien begged some headache salve from Ana, since she'd used all of hers as fuel for the fire a few nights before, when her warding medallion had been the only thing that kept the coppers from scrying her and Oliver.

THE MYSTERIES OF SLEEP | 31

the throbbing in her brain partially suppressed, she escaped to a

With the throbbing in her brain partially suppressed, she escaped to a dark, secluded corner of the library to do her homework. Very inefficiently.

Professor Lacer's exercises had fallen to the wayside for the last few days. *'I'm in no shape to do them now. I hope I don't fall too far behind before I'm recovered again.'*

That night, she took another dose of the anti-anxiety potion, but hesitated before trying to cast her dreamless sleep spell. She considered instead casting a very slow, careful, timed alarm spell on her pocket watch to wake her before she could slip too deeply into dreams, but reluctantly discarded the idea. Pushing too hard with Will-strain could make it worse, or even cause permanent damage. She had to rest as much as possible. *'All the more reason I need access to the remainder of Keeswood's research on the experiment that allowed one twin to bear the sleep of the other.'*

Two more doses of anti-anxiety potion when she woke in the middle of the night got her through to the morning. As she dragged herself off to the bathrooms for her morning ablutions, she lamented the life choices that had led her to this moment.

Without the esoteric pain-muffling spell to get her through the workout, Defensive Magic was even more grueling. When she accidentally tripped another student and caused a near-pileup while they drilled evasive maneuvers, Fekten snapped at her. "Are you a new-born puppy dog!? Out there in the real world, carelessness like that will get people killed. Keep your head in the game and your limbs to yourself!"

After classes, she scrambled to the library, where the blushing, stammering student aide gave her a pass to the restricted section where the majority of the sleep researcher's experiment journals were held.

'Information should be available to everyone in the first place,' Sebastien thought with irritation. Even once she had proven herself worthy of the University, she still had to fight for knowledge. They didn't want people who would only be there to reach Apprentice certifications learning anything truly useful or dangerous. Those who stayed longer would have the chance to earn the contribution points needed to get into whatever sections of the library they desired.

The door to the restricted archives was thick metal, spelled with what she thought was the same ward on the gate to the Menagerie. The new wooden token that allowed her into a specific archive shivered as she passed through the doorway. A short staircase led down to hallways carved from the natural white stone of the white cliffs that the University had been built into and atop. The hallways were narrow, the ceilings low, and the air smelled of ancient dust with a faint hint of paper and glue. *'The smell of undisturbed books.'*

The student aide was needed elsewhere, so she gave Sebastien quick instructions to the single archive she could access, warning her not to get lost.

"It's said you can still hear the screams and shuffling footsteps of those who wandered until they starved to death, if you listen," the girl murmured, her tail swishing with agitation. "It used to be a network of caves, and the only navigation aid is the archive code above each door. It's easy to get turned around down here."

"I'll be careful," Sebastien assured the student aide with a smile, repressing her impatience.

The girl blushed, said, "Good luck with your research project," and hurried away, pausing only to remind Sebastien not to mention the pass to anyone who might get her in trouble.

Sebastien found her way easily enough, ignoring the other metal doors along the tunnel despite her curiosity. She didn't want to set off any alarms by trying to get past a ward without the proper key. Finally, she pushed open the door to a dim room only a few meters on either side. It was quite different from the high ceilings and warm, bright light of the main library floors above. The air was still, the only movement in the room from her own entrance, but it smelled fresh, and there was no dust or spiderwebs on the rough ceiling or in the corners of the room.

She pulled every book with Keeswood's name on it off the shelves. Her fingertips burned with excitement as she scanned the pages. It was hard to concentrate on the words, but she was determined.

Two hours later, after flipping through the whole stack, she tossed the last journal onto the table and sat back with a scowl.

The series of handwritten journals had whole volumes missing, and sections of pages had been cut away in those that remained. 'Well, at least I know why they were restricted.' It had never been explicitly stated in the pieces of his journals that remained, but Sebastien gathered he'd been involved in some blood magic. She hadn't found a detailed explanation for the spell he'd used to join the sleep requirements of the two twins with no serious side effects, but he'd recorded other spells of a similar nature, and she was able to piece together an idea of how it had worked. Perhaps the details had been in one of the missing sections.

'If I want to use it, I will have to redevelop it myself.'

Leaving the library, she stopped by the infirmary again. She looked around cautiously to make sure the healer she'd talked with before wasn't on duty, then inquired about some headache-relieving salve. She didn't want to have to keep borrowing from Ana, and she wouldn't have time to make her own until the weekend. Plus, she was paying for the infirmary as part of her tuition anyway, so she might as well try and recoup some of her gold's worth.

When she finally got back to the dorms, she found a stack of book-bound periodicals on her desk. She eyed them suspiciously. 'Are they trapped?' They looked innocent, and nothing happened when she nudged the pile. They were fiction, touting the latest adventures of someone called "Aberford Thorndyke, consulting detective." *'Or did someone put them there so they can pretend I stole them and get me into trouble? But why would they put them in plain sight? At the very least, you'd think they'd slip them under the bed...'*

She looked up and saw Westbay looking at her from over his dividing wall. He sent her a wink and a thumbs-up.

Bemusedly, she realized he'd left them for her. *'Could it be, because of my questions about the case, he thinks I have an interest in detective stories?'* The friendly gesture was still surprising, and left her a little off-kilter, unsure if she should be suspicious of some deeper layer of motivation or simply amused at his obliviousness. Perhaps a little blood, a secret, and a favor owed him was all it took to befriend Westbay. *'Without a blood print vow to guarantee that favor I promised, I barely feel any pressure. Once enough time passes, even if he wants to get me in trouble for hurting him, the scar will have faded, and anyone he tries to tell will be suspicious about why he didn't report it when it happened. He's a little too naive.'*

After riffling through the pages of the detective stories to make sure nothing was hidden between them, she decided to humor Westbay by reading one, as each was short enough to be finished rather quickly. Her concentration was still a little too shot for schoolwork or further research, anyway.

To her surprise, she found she enjoyed the story. The plot was a little unbelievable, but it was fun to follow along as the fictional Thorndyke used his superior intelligence and observational skills to assist the coppers in solving baffling crimes, and she enjoyed the dynamic between him and his Everyman assistant, Milton.

Her pass to the restricted archive didn't allow her to check books out or even remove them from that room, so she had to return to the archive to continue her research. Over the next couple of days, she pieced together a better understanding of the author's work, taking pages of notes and checking out a few dense reference texts referred to in passing within the journals. The ones she had access to, anyway.

She wanted to pull her pale blonde hair out by the roots.

Apparently, she needed a deeper understanding of the workings of the brain and the immune system. Looking at the references meant for upper-term healing students, with tight-packed text and illustrations she barely understood, she drooped. *'No truly valuable accomplishment is easy, I know. But still...this had better turn out extremely useful,'* she grumbled mentally. Truthfully, though, she would be happy with almost any small measure of improvement.

In Practical Casting, Sebastien took the initiative to approach a young woman who she vaguely remembered was a commoner without much prior experience with magic, one term above her. "Would you like to partner with me today?" she asked.

The woman's eyes went wide, then darted around quickly, as if to make sure Sebastien was really talking to her. "Umm, I won't be very good practice for you. My Will's maximum capacity is only at a hundred thaums on the Henrik-Thompson scale?" she said, biting her lip.

"I don't mind," Sebastien assured her, sitting down on the other side of her desk without further preamble. "I'll work on improving my efficiency, and you can work on improving your capacity. Using just a single flame will be a good challenge for me." She placed a single tea candle in her Sacrifice Circle.

The woman looked around again, uncomfortably meeting the curious gaze of some of the other students, but silently nodded.

Sebastien's little plan worked well, as her opponent's enduring capacity was a respectable two-thirds of her maximum, meaning Sebastien only needed to channel about seventy thaums to keep up. Even this was enough to give her a migraine, though, and she slipped away to the bathroom to reapply headache salve. "I'm getting very tired of this," she muttered, staring at her bloodshot eyes in the mirror above the sink.

When she returned to the class, the students were rearranging themselves, and she realized with dismay that Lacer had instructed them to switch partners.

As she was looking around for a suitable partner, Anastasia Gervin caught sight of her and began to maneuver her way.

Sebastien pretended not to see her. She liked the other girl well enough, but Ana wasn't a suitable partner to slack off against.

Just as Ana was about to reach her side, and Sebastien had almost resolved to just grab the closest random student, Westbay hurried up from behind Ana, clapping Sebastien on the shoulder.

"Partners, Siverling?" he asked.

Ana stopped abruptly, looking at Westbay with wide eyes that narrowed suspiciously. "Really, Damien? Can't this rivalry wait until the actual tournament?"

Sebastien almost rolled her eyes, turning to Ana. "Westbay has convinced his friends of his illusion that the two of us are rivals, too?" she asked.

Westbay shooed away her words, smiling a little too casually to seem normal. "I don't know what you're talking about, Ana. I lent Siverling some Aberford Thorndyke stories. He likes detectives, too, did you know? He always runs off to the library right after class, so this is our best chance to discuss them." He didn't allow Ana to respond, his grip on Sebastien's arm steering them back to Westbay's desk. "So what did you think of the twist at the end, with the serial disappearances?" he asked loudly.

"It was a tad obvious," Sebastien said truthfully, wondering what Westbay was doing but deciding to play along.

"*Obvious?*" Westbay's head snapped around to Sebastien, and he scowled. "How could you possibly have seen—" He cut himself off, pressing his lips together with a sharp shake of his head. "Never mind. That's not relevant right now." He lowered his voice, leaning closer over the table. "Do you have a headache?"

Sebastien shrugged, drawing the numerological symbols into the carved Circle between them. A triangle, for the simple transmutation of heat to movement, and then a pentagram within that, because she thought it might help with actualizing the idea of opposition.

"I know you do. I noticed you go to the bathroom, and I can smell the mint of a headache salve."

Sebastien set the chalk down, staring expressionlessly at Westbay.

The young man continued, undeterred. "You chose to partner with Jones because she doesn't pose a challenge, and you still had to use headache salve. You shouldn't be here. You *definitely* shouldn't be here and casting magic. Did you think everything would be better after just a day? I know you're some prodigy who might not ever have experienced Will-strain before, but it takes two to three days of complete rest to safely recover. We covered this on the first day of classes. I know you were there."

"I'm fine," she insisted, lighting their candles and putting the iron ball on the edge of the Circle. "Hurry up and pay attention. Casting against each other using the same array is dangerous, and I would prefer not to be subjected to the effects of your inability to focus."

"Professor Lacer may be strict, but he isn't unreasonable. He's a bit snappish toward the students to keep us from messing around, but I know him outside the University a little, and I can assure you that he'd never force you to keep casting with Will-strain."

She pushed energy into the spell and sent the ball rolling uncontested. "You want to renege on our deal?"

"What? No." He lowered his voice further. "Is this about...my father?" He continued quickly, "I'm not suggesting we tell everyone what really happened. We can make something up."

"Professor Lacer will want to know what happened. You want to try and lie to *him* about it?" Thaddeus Lacer was one of the more common topics of student gossip. She'd overheard someone say that he had a powerful divination for untruths running all the time, and could know as soon as you said it whether you really did the homework. She didn't know if it was true, but if anyone had both the ability and the inclination to do such a thing, it was Thaddeus Lacer. He had little patience for fools and those who stood in his way. "I have absolutely no intention of taking such a risk."

"Well, okay, that's probably not a good idea. You could...tell the truth?" Westbay seemed to know it was a bad idea even as he said it, judging by the cringe on his face, but he bulled on regardless. "He might be angry, but—"

Sebastien cut him off. "Of course he would be angry. What I did—" She clenched her jaw. "If you heard the same story from someone else, what would your reaction be?" In the very best case scenario, Professor Lacer would simply be disappointed in her, and maybe he wouldn't let her stay for the next term. In the worst case scenario, he would be enraged by her second overt display of stupidity, injuring someone Lacer was presumably closer to than he was to her—she had heard him call Westbay by his first name, after all—and he would throw her out immediately. The University took it seriously when their students were endangered. Surely even more so, for the nobles.

She'd be that student people gossiped about with some ridiculous story, in which Professor Lacer turned her into a fish and hurled her over the east edge of the white cliffs—right into the Charybdis Gulf. She couldn't tell the truth, and she couldn't risk lying to him, either. Just the thought of approaching the topic with Professor Lacer had her heart pounding faster in her chest. She was *afraid*. Her headache grew worse at the increase in her blood pressure.

Westbay smoothed his hair back, making sure every strand of its waxed-perfect sloping style was in place. "Well. I know what my father would say. To be honest, I don't want him to hear about this any more than you want Professor Lacer to know. He'd be…disappointed."

"Yes, well, if Professor Lacer gets 'disappointed' in me, that's the end of my stay here at the University," she said, grinding her teeth.

"Right, because you're his app—"

She kept talking, uncaring of whatever weak argument he was trying to make. "So I will say nothing. *You* will pay attention and play along. Stop blabbering and start casting, Westbay."

Westbay glared, but, after a few tense seconds, he picked up his Conduit and turned his attention to the ball, opposing its slow rolling. He didn't put much effort into it, though from the disgruntled look on his face it seemed like he was struggling and failing. "At least you remember my name now," he muttered.

They kept the ball rolling slowly for a while, neither pushing very hard but outwardly keeping their focus for the benefit of anyone watching. Sebastien felt a tug of gratitude toward Westbay, and suppressed a grimace. *'If not for him, I wouldn't be in this position in the first place. Don't go soft just because he's being friendly now,'* she told herself. *'He is still an unbearable ass deep down. People don't actually change.'*

They continued on like that until Professor Lacer, who had been strolling along the rows of desks, occasionally stopping to give praise or a sharp rebuke, stopped beside their desk.

She couldn't help but tense up as he loomed over them, his presence bigger than his body could ever be. She kept her eye on the rolling ball.

Westbay seemed to feel the same, but he flicked a quick glance between the professor and Sebastien, and his candle flames flickered as his concentration wavered.

Sebastien tried to stay in sync with him, to keep the ball moving steadily, but she didn't quite manage it, and it sped up sharply for a moment.

She felt her back tensing straighter, and slowly pushed a little more power into the spell.

Westbay frowned slightly, as if he was struggling to keep the ball from moving.

"Stop," Lacer said, his voice cutting through the class despite its low volume.

Sebastien's heart clenched sickeningly. She released the magic, and the ball rolled to a stop, the sound of it louder than it should have been against the backdrop of the rest of the classroom. People were abandoning their own practice to look at the three of them.

Lacer waited, allowing the silence to become unbearable.

Westbay started to shift uncomfortably in his seat.

She stared at him, urging him mentally not to do anything stupid.

Finally, Professor Lacer spoke, his words carefully enunciated, precise, and somehow all the more menacing for it. "Were either of you, perhaps, under the impression that I am a blind half-wit?"

Westbay paled.

Sebastien swallowed. "No, Professor."

Westbay echoed her.

"In that case, do you think this kind of effort," he nodded his head to the table in between them, "is acceptable?"

Westbay looked at Professor Lacer, then back to Sebastien, wide-eyed. He tilted his head to the side, just slightly, a query.

Sebastien glared back at the boy, stony-faced. Poor performance on a single exercise in class was nothing compared to carelessly injuring a fellow student and then causing herself Will-strain while using blood magic to heal him.

That thought sent a cold centipede of horror crawling down her spine. If she *hadn't* healed Westbay, there might have been some chance to come clean. But if there was any chance at all that she would be accused of blood magic, it would be better for her to cut out her own tongue. Literally. Blood magic was high treason. She would be killed. "No, professor." Her throat was dry, and she swallowed convulsively.

"Try again," he ordered, his voice hard despite its low volume. He held his hand out to stop them when they turned their attention back to the spell. "This time, Westbay will attempt to move the ball clockwise and Siverling counterclockwise. Perhaps a more direct competition will stir your spirits."

Westbay quickly rubbed out and replaced his two glyphs, and they complied.

The ball moved counterclockwise in small starts as Sebastien poured on more and more power, her grip on the magic like a vise, and Westbay countered her.

They steadied out at a consistent rotation in her favor.

"Is that all you have? Push harder!" Lacer ordered.

Westbay looked at her uncertainly, but she was already complying, the ball spinning faster till it began to blur.

It slowed again as Westbay pushed against her Will. His candles flickered under the drain, and she realized suddenly how Professor Lacer had known they weren't truly trying. Their candles weren't showing any signs of true strain—no flickering, loss of heat, or dimming—when Westbay's Will was likely approaching two hundred thaums and she had already exceeded that amount. If she pushed to the normal limits of her ability, she could likely suck two candles completely cold.

She pushed harder, till her own two little flames looked like washed-out ghosts of themselves. The pain was like an ice pick through her brain, and her lashes fluttered as she realized she was losing sight in one of her eyes. Sunspots bloomed over her vision.

She swallowed down nausea, and slowly, carefully released the magic. The ball decelerated, and then reversed direction entirely. She sat even straighter, her chin high and her gaze focused vaguely straight ahead. She could have pushed through the pain, but it wasn't worth it. Severe Will-strain could cause permanent damage. 'My ability to cast magic is more important than even the University. I won't jeopardize that.' Additionally, her Conduit was only rated to two hundred thaums, and opposing another's magic put more stress on them. If she kept pushing, she risked her Conduit shattering. She had the weak backup inside the lip of her boot, so she might be able to avoid a total loss of control, but she had no gold to buy another replacement.

There was no way she could do what Lacer wanted. She accepted this, and kept her breathing even and her hands pressed to the table to keep her fingers from trembling as she waited for the punishment that would no doubt follow seemingly willful failure.

Professor Lacer didn't say anything at first, but she could feel his Will in the air, turning his gaze into a sucking hole.

The hair on her arms and the back of her neck lifted, and she was reminded of what it felt like to walk alone and defenseless through a dark room, with the absolute certainty that something cold and hungry was watching from the shadows.

But he said only, "See me after class, Siverling. In my office." He turned that horrible gaze on Westbay for a moment, who quailed under its force, then stalked back to the front of the room.

Westbay watched him walk away, then looked to her, and she could see the horror she felt reflected in his eyes. "Sebastien—" he whispered.

Slowly, minutely, she shook her head. "No," she mouthed back. "You promised," she said, slightly louder, but slowly. "Maintain your honor, and hold your tongue, Westbay."

She could only hope that Professor Lacer wasn't angry enough to expel her immediately. If she had till the end of term, at least, she was sure she could come up with a plan of some sort.

6

ALLIANCE WITH THE NIGHTMARE PACK

OLIVER
Month 12, Day 2, Wednesday 6:30 p.m.

TWO BODYGUARDS ACCOMPANIED Oliver as he rode through the dark streets atop his Erythrean horse. Even though his people successfully fought off the Morrows' blatant attack on the warehouse holding his new miniature farm, he was wary of their next move.

Oliver knew he was unlikely to be ambushed in Nightmare Pack territory, but the Morrows were known for their occasional recklessness, and it wouldn't be entirely unprecedented for his meeting with the Nightmare Pack leader to be a trap.

If anything happened, he and his two guards could fight back, and if the situation called for it, his horse could flee like the wind. Oliver wasn't so puffed up on his own pride that he couldn't admit that sometimes running away was the smart decision. One could always get revenge later.

Nightmare Pack territory was in the heart of the Mires, even poorer than his own territory, especially after the Verdant Stag's various programs to improve the quality of life for his people. Here, though, the number of non-humans was noticeable. Already, he'd seen signs of a hag, a vampire, and what was either a gremlin or a homunculus.

The gang provided three main things: a safe place for non-humans to live, less open discrimination, and a sense of community. But then, it also pressured the more powerful and useful non-humans to join the gang, supported certain kinds of crime, and made law enforcement even more reluctant to help those who needed them most.

Oliver and his bodyguards stopped at the gate in front of the Nightmare Pack headquarters, a once-proud manor with a small yard in the heart of the slums. They dismounted and handed their reins to a young man who hurriedly led the horses around to the back. If he was truly wary, Oliver would have insisted the horses stay out front, ready to go, but that would have been an insult, and an inauspicious start to the alliance he hoped to form tonight.

A man with the look of a wolf in his eyes and the shape of his jaw opened the manor's front door and bowed, motioning for them to step inside. "Welcome, Lord Stag. The pack leader awaits you."

The manor was old, the dark wood of the interior scuffed and scratched from many years of heavy, reckless traffic and sharp-clawed footsteps. The hallways were wide, the walls covered in lifelike paintings of nature and the hunt, and mounted with the occasional taxidermied trophy.

The man gestured silently to a set of open double doors, and Oliver stepped through alone.

The room beyond was expansive, with a burning fireplace at the far end, simple rugs and a mismatched scattering of comfortable chairs and couches filling most of the rest of the room. The windowsills spilled over with potted plants, and vines crawled up the glass. Stylistic sculptures of animals in different stages of transformation between man and beast were bolted onto stands or the walls, presumably to protect them from being accidentally knocked over and shattered.

Another man stood within, facing away from the doorway, his hands clasped behind his back. He was gazing up at a large oil painting of wolves falling upon a deer in the forest, but turned when Oliver entered.

His eyes were a light amber that seemed to shine in contrast to skin that was almost as dark as his hair, which hung in tiny braids to his shoulders. His cheekbones sat high and a thick, closely trimmed beard covered his chin. Despite the semi-casual suit vest he wore and the cultured way he held himself, the wildness behind his eyes was palpable. "Welcome, Lord Stag."

Oliver was suddenly hit with the irony of holding that pseudonym before a man like this. The leader of the Nightmare Pack was well-known to be a lycanthrope, which was the common name for those skin-walkers who could take on and off the skin of a wolf, transforming into the animal at will. Still, even in front of a wolf, a stag was not defenseless.

Oliver bowed in return, removing his mask as he straightened. They were alone, and as the one who had requested this meeting, it would have been quite rude to keep his face concealed. "Thank you, Lord Lynwood."

"No need for a title. I am no lord. I am the alpha, and I am not above my people. I lead them, I do not own them," the other man said.

Oliver couldn't tell if there was hostility in Lynwood's tone, or if he was simply sensing the watchful vigilance of a natural predator whose magic was not just something he wielded but a part of his body. So different from Oliver. "It is a beautiful painting," he said, diverting the topic of conversation.

Lynwood didn't give even the barest hint of a smile, though he turned to look up at the huge piece again. "Art, in its most pure form, is a melding of the unadulterated instinct and passion of a beast and the conscious control of a man. As I studied to gain control of the canvas, I found I also gained control of myself."

"You painted this?"

Lynwood's lips stretched into a small, satisfied smile. "To the outside world, many know me only as a somewhat eccentric artist. You might be surprised to learn that I fund a significant portion of our operations off sales of my work. Those with too much money in their coffers love to show off their deeper sense of artistic appreciation by paying exorbitant sums for grand paintings that hold a message they fear and yet pretend to understand." He gestured around to the other paintings and sculptures scattered about. "It is not all my own work. I encourage all those in my pack to find joy in creation as well as destruction."

"I admire your approach," Oliver said. "That's why I requested to meet with you today. I want to discuss a mutual endeavor that I believe could benefit both our people."

Lynwood turned, eyed Oliver assessingly, then motioned to a couple of chairs in front of the fire. "Please, let us sit, and you can elucidate."

Once they were both seated, Oliver said simply, "The Morrows."

Lynwood raised his eyebrows, a silent encouragement to continue.

"You've likely heard of the harassment the Verdant Stag has been facing from them. When I first opened the inn and created the Stags, the Morrows resisted, but I was determined and they backed down. Due to the small size of my operation, the lack of critical territory under my domain, and my willingness to spend extravagantly to hold the area, it would have cost them more to get rid of me than the Morrows could earn by holding the territory. Or such was my theory, anyway."

"I remember this time," Lynwood said, nodding.

"However, they continued to abuse the people in my territory, perhaps even more than before. In addition to their usual criminal behavior—the kidnappings for their whorehouses and fighting arena, selling the worst of their addictive alchemy products, threatening people for money and favors— they harassed anyone who wore my symbol or simply lived in the wrong place. So I created enforcers to protect my people."

Oliver gave a humorless grin, the show of teeth meant to speak to the wolf in the other man. Lynwood wasn't the first lycanthrope Oliver had met, and thank the stars above for that experience. "The Morrows respected my bound-aries once they had no other choice, at first, but recently they've begun their harassment again. This time, their attacks are pointed and brutal. It's obvious they hope to collapse my organization entirely by harrying us until we cannot keep up with the cost of the damage and those within the territory lose faith in us. They plan to then take back the entirety of what was once theirs."

"And how is this relevant to me?"

Oliver smiled again. "The Morrows overstep their boundaries. Just as they overestimate their infallibility."

"Oh?"

"I know they've made themselves a thorn in your side, too. They take your people for their brothels, and they have a particular interest in non-humans for their underground pit fights. I would assume they also feed addictive substances into your territory. They don't do all this overtly, perhaps. They don't want to drive you to retaliate in force. But they don't respect your authority, and they are harming your people."

Lynwood steepled his fingers together in his lap. "It's natural that we bicker and snap at each other. If one organization falls, another will rise to take its place, and who is to say the new order will be better than the old? Balance is important. Or, at least, the right kind of instability." Was Lynwood hinting that if the Nightmare Pack helped the Stags take out the Morrows, his gang might not actually benefit in the end? Perhaps there was some fear that the Stags would grow greedy and turn on them next, Oliver mused.

"That's where you're wrong. Balance is important, I agree, but instability is only preferable if you believe that order would not bring prosperity to you and yours. By all accounts, you are a reasonable man, Lynwood. I'm a reasonable man too, when not pushed to extremes. War is costly. I wouldn't choose it if I had other, more practical, options."

Oliver was telling the truth. The Morrows had attacked him and killed two of his people. It wasn't possible to back down now. They would crush him if he showed weakness. Even if by some miracle, they decided to stop harassing his people and let him keep operating, the Verdant Stag operation as a whole would still not be sustainable.

He was slowly being bled dry, and needed to increase the size and prof-itability of his operations to change the tide. If he could take out the Morrows and obtain even half their territory and operations—along with the more palatable streams of income—almost all of his problems would be solved in one fell swoop.

Oliver added, "In the interest of allowing as little instability as possible, I would suggest our two organizations agree to a nonaggression treaty, to be renegotiated in five years' time." This would give both of them time to consol-idate their hold on what they gained from defeating their common enemy, without worry that either side would grow greedy and attempt to take more than their fair share.

"You are suggesting that we would benefit from allying with you against the Morrows?"

"Yes. In addition to stopping their current persecution of your people, I have no doubt some of their operations would be better managed in your hands. The fighting arena, for example. I'm sure you could provide voluntary participants, and I hear the income from the betting is quite high. They have control of Avery Park, which would seem a welcome addition to your territory. Perhaps a portion of their shops in the Night Market could do with a different owner?"

Lynwood stared at the fire for a long moment, but when he turned back to Oliver, his expression was still firmly unimpressed. "Be that as it may, it would require this operation to be *successful*. We might be larger than the Morrows if you count only the size of our territory and the number of people it contains, but we do not share their monetary resources. I am loath to conscript my people to fight and throw away their lives for an ally that cannot even manage to protect themselves without our help."

"You'd be mistaken to think the Verdant Stag cannot protect itself. Surely you've heard of the consequences of the Morrows' last attack on us?"

Lynwood nodded, the intensity of his amber-eyed gaze revealing an increased interest in this particular topic. "Indeed."

"The Stags are merely more interested in supporting our own people and growing our interests than focusing unnecessary resources toward an extended skirmish. Additionally, even were we to take down the Morrows, we are still too small to hold the entire Morrow territory securely. It would be an invitation to others to try and take a piece of it, and the situation would spiral into endless conflict. That's useless to us. I hope instead that we could both benefit from the destruction of the Morrows."

Oliver paused, weighing his words. "Of course, our other option would be to take over only a portion of the Morrows' operation and leave the rest open to the power struggles of the other gangs, which would only serve to destabilize and inconvenience the rest of the city." The Nightmare Pack especially, since their territory was adjacent to the Morrows', but Oliver left that part unsaid, sure that Lynwood knew what he meant.

"I have my doubts that the Verdant Stag could take out the Morrows as easily as you insinuate, at least without outside help. If not us, then perhaps the one who came to your aid recently. I hear she is called the Raven Queen. If we were to agree to this alliance, would she be included in this nonaggression treaty?" Lynwood was obviously fishing, hoping to learn Oliver's connection to the mysterious rogue sorcerer.

"I do not control her, but we are acquainted, and she allows me some minor influence over her actions. The rumors about her are somewhat exaggerated. She is actually rather restrained, when not being harassed. She wouldn't attack the Nightmare Pack without reason, and doubly so if I asked her politely not to."

"The rumors may be exaggerated, but it is clear she is both bold and powerful," Lynwood said, seeming more interested in the Raven Queen than he had been throughout the entire previous conversation. "Would she be adding her efforts to our own against the Morrows?"

"Perhaps, though I doubt she would take a front-line position. Her support against the warehouse attack was impromptu. She is quite busy and doesn't take requests unless she finds them sufficiently valuable or…interesting." He was playing into Siobhan's reputation a bit, knowing that the less he said clearly, the more Lynwood would speculate, with his conclusions undoubtedly being more outlandish than the truth.

Oliver considered that Siobhan, a poor, self-educated young girl, was disguised as a young man with a completely different appearance and background, and secretly attending the University. He had to amend his previous thought. The truth was quite outlandish indeed. It was simply outlandish in a completely different direction than Lynwood would assume.

"How did you come to be associated with her?"

"A series of coincidences," Oliver said.

Lynwood eyed him with some dissatisfaction. "Would it be possible for me to meet her?" he asked finally.

Oliver suppressed his expression of surprise, though a man such as Lynwood might be able to glean it from the responses he couldn't control, like the change in his heartbeat or scent. "I could pass along your request, but I can make no guarantees."

She would want to be paid, no doubt, and they would have to ensure that meeting in person didn't disillusion Lynwood and endanger their alliance. All the rumors about her prowess were fabrications blown magnitudes out of proportion to reality, after all. It might be best to pretend to pass along the request and return with a denial. Or at least ensure the alliance was secure and the joint attack on the Morrows settled first, with the reward for meeting enough to make the risk worth it.

Oliver spoke before he had time to fully think through the idea, because he didn't want his hesitation to be too obvious. "She enjoys tributes. She might be more likely to give an audience to someone who…gently incentivizes her." He raised his eyebrows pointedly.

Lynwood pressed his fingertips together, settling back in satisfaction. "I understand." His eyes gleamed with even more interest. "I agree to your proposal, Lord Stag, pending the appropriate particulars."

"Wonderful." Oliver reached into his pocket and brought out a rolled-up map of the city. "Let us work out the generalities, at least. Details can be solidified over time." He laid the map over a short table. The area of their respective territories was painted with a translucent ink, with the parts of the city currently belonging to the Morrows divided between them.

Lynwood peered at it with interest, then pointed. "We'll want a bit more of this area, all the way out to the canal."

Oliver frowned. "That could be acceptable, if you're willing to give up a little more of this residential district."

They haggled over territory, and then went on to decide on the allocation of their respective combat forces, joint efforts to keep conflicts suppressed in the short term, and what businesses and enterprises each of them would swallow.

When they were both moderately satisfied, feeling that they hadn't gotten a very good deal but not an exceedingly bad one either—which probably meant it was quite fair to both parties—Lynwood asked, "So, I assume you have planned further than dividing up the territory. How exactly do you propose we bring about the Morrows' downfall?"

The edges of Oliver's mouth curled up a little too far in a way he knew made him look vulpine, but Lynwood didn't seem disturbed, his own lips pulling back to reveal sharp-edged teeth.

7

CHASTISEMENT

Sᴇʙᴀsᴛɪᴇɴ
Month 12, Day 4, Friday 3:45 p.m.

Wʜᴇɴ ᴄʟᴀss ᴇɴᴅᴇᴅ, Professor Lacer left immediately, not bothering to wait for the handful of students who wanted to linger and speak to him. "I have office hours," he announced as he strode past them. "Use them."

Damien and Sebastien shared a look of sick concern, and she took longer than necessary to gather up her belongings, trying to settle herself. Fearing that she would gather more ire by dawdling, she followed the gently curved hallway to Professor Lacer's office. She felt sick, not only because of straining her Will beyond its limits, but because she didn't know the extent of his anger toward her. '*I will plead with him if I need to. But only if I need to.*' She briefly considered trying to tell some sort of half-truth that would mollify him, but her mind was too scrambled to think through the options and their ramifications.

It had been such a stupid mistake, and she regretted compounding it with an attempt to hide it. It would be horrible to be expelled, but as long as she could keep her magic and her life, she would always find a way to claw her way back up again.

She paused outside the door for a few breaths, blinking in an attempt to clarify the vision in her right eye. She pressed her trembling fingers to her sides, straightened her back, and rapped softly on the open doorframe.

"Enter," Lacer said, his voice clipped. He'd sat at his desk and was scribbling a note. His scowl was harsh enough to toast bread. "Close the door behind you," he said without looking up.

She did so, stopping a few feet in front of his desk. She didn't dare to take a seat without his permission. She resisted the urge to fidget or wince with every ice-pick spike of the headache impaling her brain.

"Are you aware that without me, you would not be studying here?" he asked.

Her heart clenched. "Y—" Her voice broke, and she had to swallow before replying. "Yes."

"And you are aware that if you make *me* dissatisfied, I can have you expelled before the day is out?"

"Yes."

"Do you think there is anyone at this university whose opinion is more important than mine?"

"No," she said. '*Which is precisely why you can never know what I've been up to,*' she thought.

"Are you also aware that because of the special circumstances of your admittance, your performance reflects back upon me? If you perform poorly, or act inappropriately, my judgment will be in question. Honestly, I am currently questioning my own judgment."

Sebastien suppressed a wince. "Yes."

He stared at her until she wondered if she was supposed to say something else, the judgment in his gaze almost a physical weight on her body.

She couldn't tell the truth, but she was afraid to lie, and so silence was her only refuge.

Finally, he said, "Did Mr. Westbay ask you to lose to him?"

Sebastien blinked twice. "No," she said, her tone as neutral as she could make it.

"So you *chose* to pander to him. I am unsure if that makes it better or worse. I had thought you would have more pride than that."

She remained silent, sluggishly realizing that Professor Lacer thought she'd thrown the match with Damien because he was a Westbay, and that she was either afraid to openly best him, or was trying to get on his good side by making Damien look better than he was.

'*Professor Lacer hasn't noticed the signs of Will-strain? Perhaps he simply never considered that I could be that stupid.*' She was filled with relief. It was a plausible motive that had nothing to do with fleeing from the coppers, attacking another student, or using blood magic. She couldn't overtly agree with his assumption, though, in case he really did have some divination running to reveal lies. She bowed her head, the shame of the movement all too real. "It will not happen again," she promised, meaning every word.

"See that it does not. I will bestow my forgiveness this time. In future, if you are going to curry favor with others at the expense of your pride, do it *better*. I will not preach about honor and chivalry, but please, at least have the cunning not to embarrass me. You will comport yourself with my reputation in mind at all times. And in exchange for today, you will win at least fifty contribution points in the end of term exhibitions." He paused, as if waiting for her to protest.

"I understand," she said. Rather than worrying about drawing attention to the persona of Sebastien Siverling in the exhibitions, her immediate thought was to wonder how difficult it was to earn fifty points as a first term student. With what she knew of Professor Lacer's standards, it was likely a hellishly difficult demand.

"Good. Now get out."

She complied without hesitation. The relief was heady. A little scolding and a task to redeem herself. There had been no offensive spells, nothing to publicly shame her, and most importantly, no expulsion. It seemed that he hadn't even noticed her Will-strain. *'Could it be that the rumors surrounding Professor Lacer's temper are somewhat exaggerated?'* She wanted to laugh.

Damien Westbay was pacing in the hallway outside the door, fidgeting with his already perfect hair and unwrinkled clothes. He stilled when he saw her. "What did he say? I can talk to—"

The smile slipped from her face. She grabbed him by the arm and kept walking. "You will not talk to him."

"I'm sorry, Sebastien, it's not right that you're the one to get in trouble for this. I—"

"It's fine. He was angry, but only because I embarrassed him with my public weakness. I have to participate in the end of term exhibitions and earn at least fifty contribution points. That's it."

Westbay stumbled along beside her. "Oh. Well, that's...good?"

"Yes. Except I doubt I'll be coming back next term if I don't succeed."

"He's that angry? Sebastien...maybe we should just explain what happened?" he said reluctantly. "We could leave out the details of how I got hurt. There's no way I'd be expelled, I'm a Westbay, and we might even be able to convince him not to inform my father—"

"*I* could still be expelled," she snapped. "Can't you get that past your thick skull? I'm not worried about you, I'm worried about myself. The rest of us don't get to take the paved road through life, Westbay. There are *consequences* for our actions."

He was silent for a while, and kept walking beside her even when she released her grip on his arm. "Mood swings," he said finally, his tone placating. "You need to go to the infirmary, Sebastien. They can help with the Will-strain."

"No." The anger she was feeling was perfectly legitimate, but a vivid desire to strangle the bullheaded, oblivious boy had her seriously considering slamming him into an empty classroom.

The urge was strong enough that she had to concede, at least to herself, that her decision-making faculties were impaired.

"I'll drag you there myself if I have to. This isn't about your preferences or wanting to seem tough. It's not even about getting in trouble. This is about your safety, your well-being. I won't let you jeopardize everything just because you're feeling stubborn. Your judgment is impaired, so if I have to, I'll make this decision for you."

"Where did you grow the stones to act like this is any of your business?" she muttered, gritting her teeth. Before he could reply, she held up a hand toward him. "Alright, alright, stop. I don't need to go to the infirmary. I have a friend who can help me."

"Really?" He peered at her skeptically.

She scowled. "*Really*. I'm going there now. You may not have noticed, but I do have a working brain, even if it feels like it's being stomped on by a rabid cow right now. I know I need healing."

The worry and doubt smoothed away from his face. "Good," he said, nodding imperiously. "If you're not feeling better by Monday, do not come to class."

She rolled her eyes and walked faster, hoping to outpace him.

He jogged a little to catch up, but was thankfully silent all the way to the glass transportation tubes on the south side of the white cliffs. He waved as she used her student token to activate one. "Feel better soon! And don't come back until you do!"

She didn't wave back.

By the time she got to Oliver's house, the headache was making her nauseated.

Oliver took one look at her and said, "What happened?"

"Will-strain," she replied simply, her voice soft, because she felt like speaking loudly or opening her mouth too wide might send the contents of her stomach spilling out over his polished shoes. "My professor asked me to cast in class. I don't want to risk the healers at the University infirmary. Do you think I could see...whoever the Verdant Stag usually uses?"

"I'll hail a carriage," he said, though instead of doing it himself, he motioned to a servant, who hurried outside to the street. Oliver strode off into the kitchen and came back with a steaming mug of dark liquid. "I don't keep a lot of potions in the house. They don't work very well on me, so... The caffeine should help with your headache."

She took the mug gratefully, sipping slowly.

"The next time something like this happens, perhaps you should consider refusing to cast magic," he said.

"The *next* time?" she groaned.

Oliver gave her a wry smile, but it didn't disguise his worry.

The servant poked their head back through the front door and said, "I've got one, sir."

Sebastien took the mug of coffee with her into the carriage, which thankfully had shock absorbers to mitigate the bumps and jolts. After a few minutes of sitting and sipping, she felt well enough to talk, as long as she kept her eyes closed. "Has anything happened since I've been back at the University? Anything new with the Morrows?" She kept her voice low enough that no one would overhear them.

"Nothing big. There's been some harassment, especially on the edges of our territory, but we've been patrolling, and we've invested a lot into improving the equipment and number of our enforcers so we don't seem like such an easy target."

"That's good."

"We also made an alliance with the Nightmare Pack."

She opened one eye. "Who?"

"Another gang with no love for the Morrows. The leader would like to meet with you. Or, to be more specific, he would like to meet with the Raven Queen," Oliver said, lifting one side of his mouth in a half-smile that lacked real amusement.

He reached into his pocket and pulled out a folded piece of paper. It was another wanted poster displaying an evil version of her face glaring out underneath a hood. Only this time, the caption said, 'Alias: The Raven Queen. Dangerous practitioner of Forbidden Magics. Flee on sight. Report any information to law enforcement. Reward for information leading to arrest: Five hundred gold crowns.'

"Flee on sight?" she muttered. Five hundred gold crowns was more than many poor families made in a year. It seemed they were taking her more seriously after her recent appearance. Even the most copper-hating or loyal person might be swayed by such a large bounty.

Oliver folded the paper away and tucked it back into his pocket. "I'll let you consider the meeting when you are more lucid. There will be incentives."

"I'll have to do *something* to pay for the healer," she mumbled. "Pretending to be the Raven Queen shouldn't be much harder than pretending to be a boy."

There was a pause, and then he said, "It seems you've had it worse than us. Will everything be alright, once you return?"

"I hope so," she sighed. "The pressure keeps rising, but once I'm better, I'll be able to handle it. Is it okay for me to meet this healer as Sebastien?"

Oliver hesitated, then said, "Well, I'm taking you there as Oliver Dryden, not the leader of the Stags. Healer Nidson is discreet, and there's an easy explanation for how a University student got Will-strain, even if it is strange that you wouldn't stay to be treated there."

"We need to find a more thorough way to keep Sebastien and Siobhan separate. I can't be switching back and forth at will. Eventually, the wrong person will notice something."

"I have some ideas about that. We'll talk about it once you're better."

The healer retained by the Verdant Stag was brusque but competent, the type of person whose eyes wouldn't widen in surprise even if Oliver brought Myrddin himself, resurrected, into his home. Nidson gave Sebastien a quick succession of potions which calmed the pain and slowed her thoughts till they felt like cold molasses within her skull. Then he made her guzzle down a large mug filled with what tasted like a modified nourishing draught, till her stomach sloshed with every movement. He laid her down on a slate table with a Circle carved into it, then drew a spell array around her prone form.

She dozed off, opening her eyes some time later to see Nidson casting a healing spell with various exotic components as the Sacrifice, some of which she recognized, and some of which she could only speculate about.

She woke again in a carriage with poor suspension, every bump of the cobbled road jostling through her. She was slumped against Oliver, her head on his shoulder, wrapped in a blanket. He pressed a hand against her hair, keeping her from sitting up. "I need you to turn into Siobhan. Can you do that?"

She pressed the amulet against her chest and pushed at it with a small pulse of Will. The spike of pain this caused was dull and distant.

"Sleep," Oliver said. "You'll feel better when you wake up."

Siobhan did feel better when she woke up, except for the disorientation and the horrible pressure in her bladder. She was alone, but recognized the small, spartan room and the door made of iron bars.

She was at Liza's place, in the warded, secret section of her home. After relieving herself using Liza's enchanted chamber pot, Siobhan made her way upstairs.

Liza was sitting in the apartment above, among the magical reference books, animal cages, and growing plants, sipping dark liquid that gave off a whiff of nostril-burning alcohol mixed with the earthy bitterness of coffee. She was petting a neon-bright bird that sat trilling musically on her lap. Her eyes were bloodshot, with dark, puffy circles below, and she'd tied her curly hair back into a low bun to partially disguise its unwashed frizziness. "You're awake."

"I feel much better," Siobhan said. She had a faint headache still, but it was nothing compared to the horseshoe nails of pain that had been trying to chisel her skull apart, and she could see normally out of both eyes.

Liza grunted around a mouthful of alcohol-laced coffee. "You're lucky there's no permanent damage."

Siobhan acknowledged that with a wince. "What time is it?"

"About five in the morning. On Monday."

Siobhan's eyes widened. Whatever that healer had given her must have been an extra-strength tranquilizer. It might have even slowed some of her bodily functions. '*Or...Liza stayed up caring for me and casting spells to empty my bladder and bowels while I slept.*' The thought sent heat rushing to her cheeks. She coughed and looked away. "Oliver brought me here so I could sleep through the scrying attempts?"

"Yes. Of which there have been several. The coppers are more interested in you than I expected, child."

Siobhan rubbed her forehead. "Unfortunately. Thank you for taking care of me."

Liza waved a tired hand. "It is far from my first time caring for an invalid. At least you were still and silent. As long as this doesn't happen again, you may be forgiven. I am more concerned that the solution we came to is already proving insufficient. Did the divination attempts push you so far as to cause Will-strain?"

"Oh, no, that was something else."

Liza's mouth tightened judgmentally. "Something *else*," she repeated, supremely unimpressed. "Perhaps you should take a good look at your life choices." She tucked the bird under one arm and put it in one of the cages scattered around the room. "Come," she ordered, walking into the official part of her house through the attached closet door.

She made a second cup of coffee, eyed Siobhan, then added a moderate splash of liquor to it before handing it over. "Drink."

Siobhan accepted it awkwardly. She wasn't a fan of alcohol, but the caffeine was a lifesaver, and the minty burn of whatever Liza had added immediately provided a boost of vivacity, rather than the mellowing, depressive effect she remembered from her other attempts to drink.

Liza stared at her until Siobhan felt uncomfortable. She wondered if Oliver bringing her here was actually not okay. Or perhaps Liza was just trying to calculate how much coin she could extort from Siobhan in her weakened state. Finally, Liza spoke. "You need a more permanent solution to the scrying attempts if they are going to continue like this—and if your lifestyle continues to create moments when you cannot safely or consistently counteract them."

"A more permanent solution, like retrieving my blood from Harrow Hill?"

"Harrow Hill has some of the best wards in Gilbratha. Theoretically, I might be able to bypass them, but in practice, with only nine thousand thaums under my command, such a course of action would be like a dragon attacking a sky kraken—an act of hubris bordering on stupidity. Any mistake would only end up giving them more opportunity to track you down. If our last transaction was any indication, it also seems that you could not afford to hire me for such a project. However, there are more creative solutions you might employ. The blood need not be retrieved, as long as they cannot realistically use it to find you."

Siobhan's eyes widened, her attention caught on the mention of Liza's capacity. That was only a couple of thousand below the level when one could start thinking about getting certified as an Archmage, though a lot more went into being acknowledged as an Archmage than simple capacity. Siobhan's eyes narrowed. "How old are you?"

Liza rolled her eyes. "Well, you just put your foot in your mouth without hesitation, don't you?" she asked, but didn't seem to be actually offended. "I'm sixty." She was almost as old as Professor Lacer. Of course, neither of them looked like a commoner of the same age might, with all the magic they cast keeping them young. Liza looked closer to thirty. "Due to my *advanced age*, and my particular background, I have valuable experience and feel qualified to give advice on this. I participated in the Haze War, and I know first-hand that there is always a loophole that can be exploited in any ward or defensive system. If there's no loophole, one can be created. Often this weakness lies in human error and laziness and not the external defenses. Do some research. Necessity is the mother of innovation, as they say. Alternatively, you can hire *me* to find a more permanent solution, for the small sum of eight hundred gold crowns."

Siobhan sipped her minty coffee. "Do you have any particular ideas?"

Liza gave her a deadpan stare, apparently not tired enough to be tricked into giving up valuable information. "If you're feeling better, you can leave."

Siobhan hesitated, wondering if she should offer to pay Liza for the care and lodging while she'd been unconscious. Then she smacked herself mentally. If she could get away with something for free from the woman, she should run before Liza overcame her sleep-deprivation.

The sun was still a couple of hours from rising as Siobhan hurried out, and the streets were empty, a layer of unbroken snow covering everything. She pulled her cloak tighter around herself and felt the angry grumble of her empty stomach. Returning to Sebastien's form in an empty alley felt safest, even though she probably could have transformed in the middle of the street without being noticed. She was still wearing the same clothes she'd left the University in a few days before. Hopefully Liza hadn't thought that was strange. Women did wear trousers, after all, and even if they didn't fit her very well, no normal person would jump to the *correct* conclusion.

When Sebastien got back to the University, she grabbed a change of clothes and went straight to the showers, luxuriating in the warm water and solitude.

She was again asleep in her bed when the rest of her dorm finally woke. As the sounds of early morning preparation woke her, she realized she hadn't done any of her homework over the weekend. Rubbing her temples, she took a deep breath, then fumbled with the vial containing the anti-anxiety potion and swallowed a half-dose. *'I needed the rest. Missing one weekend's worth of homework won't lower my grade so far that I fail. Probably.'*

Westbay, who was just getting dressed as she left, gave her a questioning look.

She raised an eyebrow at him, and he nodded and smiled as if she'd instead given him a reassuring, "Good morning, friend!" With a snort, she left him to comb his hair three hundred times, knowing he would keep at it until he'd beaten every single strand into submission.

She pondered her situation as she ate the bland breakfast slop. Now that her mind was clear again, she realized she'd been acting irrationally. Maybe it was a byproduct of the original Will-strain, added to the ongoing stress that she hadn't been able to escape even before then.

She had been focused on peripherally important things, at the expense of neglecting the *biggest* problem in her life. This weekend could have been entirely disastrous if not for Oliver's quick thinking. *'What would have happened if I was unconscious and helpless outside of Liza's wards, and the coppers scried for me?'* She shuddered at the thought. *'What happens when they scry me while I'm in the middle of casting a difficult spell, and the distraction makes my concentration slip, and I lose control of the magic?'*

She forced herself to keep eating despite her sudden lack of appetite. She needed all her energy, and the basic meal options barely provided enough to sate a working thaumaturge's increased caloric needs.

'Letting the coppers keep my blood is unacceptable. I have to figure out how to stop their scrying attempts for good, before all the different pressures add up and something critical finally snaps. Either I'll get caught, or I'll lose control and succumb to Will-strain when they try and scry me at a bad time, or someone will notice when the seemingly unre-lated Sebastien Siverling is casting anti-divination spells at the same times the coppers are searching for Siobhan Naught. I want to help the Stags, and I need to repay my debt, and it would be wonderful not to worry about sleep any more, but I have to dig myself out of this hole before anything else. Getting rid of these scrying attempts will make my entire life easier. I need to completely reprioritize. I cannot believe I've been so complacent even as I thought I was trying my best to become prepared.'

Through her shirt, she rubbed the warding medallion her grandfather had given her, the fatigue and the shame mixing to form a prickle of tears behind her eyes. She blinked them back rapidly. *'I still have a long way to go,'* she admitted to herself.

Sebastien hurried to complete her homework before the breakfast period ended, taking it as easy as possible through her first two classes. As was becoming her habit when she had a problem, she headed to the library during her afternoon free period before Practical Casting. Such a comprehensive repository of information would surely have a solution hidden among the shelves.

She was in the glass tunnel between the main building and the library when the sirens went off, loud and piercing and screaming of danger with their unnatural tone.

Everyone dropped whatever they were doing, some panicking, wanting to move but not knowing where to go, others moving with purpose, and a couple looking around with anxious confusion.

"It's an Aberrant," Sebastien heard someone say.

She realized then that she'd frozen as soon as she heard the sound, and forced herself to keep walking. Her head swiveled back and forth, her eyes wide as they absorbed everything, searching for a hint of the danger.

One of the librarians opened the door to the library, waving for the students to enter. "Come take shelter! The building has wards, and if necessary, we can take refuge in the reinforced lower levels."

Sebastien moved as quickly as she could, her face feeling like a bloodless mask. The wails of the sirens rang in her ears till the sounds overlapped and drowned everything else out, like the surface of a lake in a rainstorm.

8

SIRENS

Sebastien
  Month 12, Day 7, Monday 12:45 p.m.

It wasn't the first time Sebastien had heard Aberrant sirens. However, the prior experience did nothing to calm her, as the sound only brought back memories she would rather have forgotten. She looked around for signs of chaos and destruction, but saw only panicking students and the faculty directing them all to safety.

Clutching her school satchel in one hand and her Conduit in the other, she joined the congregating students in the central atrium of the library. The whole ground floor of the building was filled.

"I heard someone say it was an Aberrant," a young woman said. "Do you know where it appeared?"

"It might not be an Aberrant," an older woman said comfortingly. "The sirens don't distinguish between different magical dangers. It could just be a rogue blood sorcerer casting some dangerous magic."

A nearby man said, "You know blood magic users are more likely to mutate into Aberrants, right? That's not exactly reassuring."

A boy fidgeted, looking around as if a monstrous mutant might pop out from behind one of the other students. "My older sister is a copper. She told me the last time the sirens went off, it was a loose elemental, an enraged sylphide from the Plane of Air. Someone attempted an over-ambitious conjuring without strong enough bindings, and it went wrong. The sylphide choked the air right out of a whole city block of people. Drowned without a drop of water."

He'd spoken loudly, and some of those around reached for their chests and throats as if to ensure they were still breathing properly.

Sebastien knew it was nothing compared to the destruction the right kind of Aberrant could wreak. *'At least you can reason with a sylphide.'* Fortunately, most people who lost control of their magic were simply killed or mentally disabled. It was rare for a spell to go so horribly wrong that the caster mutated.

"What if it's an attack on the city wards?" someone asked.

"That's ridiculous," someone else snorted. "Even the Titans would know better than to besiege Gilbratha. The wards are unbreakable."

"It could be the kraken."

"The kraken hasn't been seen for the last two hundred years. It's an Aberrant, I tell you."

"It doesn't matter what it is, nothing is going to get past the library wards. They were cast by Archmage Zard," the older woman said, one arm around her frightened friend.

That seemed to calm most of the students until one girl whispered, "But I have family in the city... What about them?"

"If they know what's good for them, they'll get to the shelters," a boy said.

Sebastien wanted to snap at them all to *shut up*, wanted to pace back and forth, wanted to cast some magic so she could feel like she was actually doing something useful. She pressed her way out of the crowd and brought her Will to bear. Creating a Circle with her hands flipped around so that her middle fingers touched her thumbs, with her pinky awkwardly curled around her Conduit, she brought out a hum from deep in her chest, casting the esoteric self-calming spell that Newton had taught her.

As she forced her body to calm, it became clear her agitation had been much stronger than she'd realized. Her heartbeat slowed, the stress-response chemicals burning in her blood cooled, and her muscles relaxed a little more with every deep hum.

When she finally opened her eyes, the panic of the other students seemed a little absurd. *'We're safe. And even if we weren't, sitting around and worrying about it won't make us safer. If we aren't already prepared, then it's already too late. Best to just get on with life.'* She didn't have the luxury of spare time to waste.

Sebastien nudged back through the crowd to use one of the search crystals, burning a card with keywords about divination in its brazier. She'd picked up an armful of books and was looking for an out-of-the-way table when she noticed Newton at a spot that would be perfect. With the library so packed, there weren't many other options.

"Can I sit here?" she asked. Her shoulders were beginning to tense again from the screaming of the sirens and the palpable tension of the crowd. The rationality she'd struggled to achieve was already being overridden by deep-seated wariness as her eyes flicked around mistrustfully.

Newton looked up a little slowly, as if he'd been focused on the hand-written sheaf of notes in front of him, but his eyes hadn't been moving across the page, just staring at the same spot. "Oh, hello, Sebastien. Sure, feel free to join me, as long as you don't expect entertaining company. I'm afraid I'm a little...preoccupied." His face was drawn, and though his posture was proper, something about his unfocused eyes spoke of deep fatigue.

She sat, her back a little too straight, even for her. "Even better. I'd prefer not to sit around speculating."

When the sirens suddenly stopped a couple of minutes later, Newton let out a deep breath, but his fingers kept worrying at his note paper until it was unusable. He somehow appeared both relieved and yet even more worried at the same time.

Sebastien tried to conceal her own relief. If the sirens were turned off, that meant the coppers believed they had dealt with the problem, or at least that it was contained and no longer a potential danger to the whole city. They would have to wait for confirmation before leaving the library, even so.

She eyed Newton. "That spell you taught me is useful. Especially for situations like this," she offered, trying not to make her concern obvious.

He met her gaze for a long few seconds.

"I also have some of that anti-anxiety potion from the infirmary left," she added.

He gave her a small smile. "Is this a role-reversal, Sebastien? You looking out for me?"

She shrugged. "Sometimes, when you're really tired, you don't realize how hard you're fighting it. Your body tightens up until you're like this taut little rock on the edge of a precipice. If you can rest, when you wake up everything seems a little more manageable, and you have the option to be flexible instead of shatter."

"Sound advice. Almost as if you know from experience," he said, his wry smile growing.

She rolled her eyes. "I'm used to fatigue. It's the people that bother me."

"Right," he said, sniggering behind his hand. But he took her hint and spent a couple of minutes humming, performing the same esoteric spell he'd taught her.

When he opened his eyes, she looked up from the irritatingly oblique divination reference she was trying to read.

"You were right, I'm tired," he said. "But I'm used to fatigue, too. It's the fact that my family is out there in the city, possibly in danger, that worries me."

"Oh." She had no idea what to say to that.

"They don't live in the best neighborhood," Newton continued. "And as you might not be surprised to learn, Gilbratha's emergency shelters are well over capacity in the poorer areas. Sometimes you need to bribe the guards to get in. And my family...well, my father's fallen ill. He's been out of work for the last few weeks, and without him—" Newton pressed his lips together and shook his head. "All of us Moores are stubborn. I'm just worried they chose to stay at home, block the doors, and hide under the beds rather than begging to be let into a shelter."

Newton had already been worried about money, spending his extra time tutoring and taking the student liaison job to ease the burden of tuition. If his family was poor enough without his father's income that they had to worry they couldn't spare the coin to get into the shelters, they almost certainly wouldn't be able to afford for Newton to continue his education. "Are there any other thaumaturges in your family? Someone you could trade messenger spells with?" Sebastien asked.

He shook his head. "My mom and sisters know some kitchen magic and a few esoteric things, but they're not sorcerers. They don't even have real Conduits. They're definitely not powerful enough to defend themselves, either. My grandmother might have been able to cobble something together, but she's going senile now, and I have her old Conduit."

"The sirens have stopped, so they'll probably let us out soon. You can go check on them personally. I doubt anyone will notice if you miss one class after all this pandemonium."

"You're right," he said, relaxing a little.

She hesitated, realizing it might be rude to ask, but couldn't stop herself from doing so anyway. "Was your father the main source of income for your family?"

He pressed his lips together. "Yes. And I know what you're getting at. I have no University sponsor. If he doesn't recover..." He took a deep breath. "Without my family's help, I cannot pay my own way. It's just too much. But if I leave now—" He paused, cleared his throat, and continued in a forcefully calm tone. "Apprentices don't earn enough to support a family and also save much, especially not at first. It might be ten years or more before I could return to continue my education. Maybe never, if healer's fees for my father become too much. I don't want to be stuck doing busy work for a Master for the rest of my life."

Sebastien wanted to suggest that Newton take his father to the Verdant Stag and see if they could help with something in the alchemy shop, or connect him to an affordable healer, but she didn't. Sebastien Siverling should have no way to know about the Verdant Stag's operations. *'I'll talk to Oliver about it. Maybe he can find some way to get the information to Newton's family more surreptitiously,'* she told herself.

The library doors stayed closed for over an hour longer, until the faculty in the administrative section of the building received word that it was definitely safe to release the students.

Newton and most of the other students left as soon as they were able, but Sebastien remained behind, reading about divination while she waited for her next class. She struggled to focus, her mind returning several times to what might have caused the rogue magic sirens.

Divination was the only branch of magic she wasn't particularly interested in. When she was younger, she'd had fantasies about getting tips from the spirits or seeing the future in a basin of water. It turned out that beyond basic things like dowsing for water or sympathetic scrying for a location, most humans weren't built for real divination. The very talented could get vague hints about possible futures or answers about specific questions, but Sebastien had discovered that she could rarely even tell which card was next in a shuffled deck, much less divine the future.

All that to say, she didn't have much knowledge or experience in divination, which meant trying to put a stop to the scrying attempts would require extensive research. She would wait to start practicing the actual spells, at least until tomorrow. She didn't want to push herself too hard when her recovery was still fragile.

She felt no more confident about her plan by the time she left the library for Lacer's Practical Casting class, but she was determined. There were no problems that a combination of magic, power, and knowledge-backed ingenuity couldn't fix.

'I'll need to prioritize, though,' she admitted. *'I can't handle practicing new utility spells, researching sleep spells, and trying to learn about emergency healing while also working on this. Everything but school work and getting my blood back from the coppers will have to wait.'*

All the students were still absorbed by the earlier sirens, and the class was filled with chatter while they waited for Professor Lacer to arrive. It was normal for him to stride in with his coat flapping behind him after all the students had been seated for a few minutes, but the minutes ticked by and Professor Lacer still hadn't arrived.

"He might not be coming," said Westbay, who had taken it upon himself to sit beside Sebastien.

"Because of whatever caused the sirens?" she asked.

"Sometimes he gets called away from the University to deal with special cases, if the Red Guard is going to be slow in arriving or the coppers need an expert consultant."

"There are rumors he was in the Red Guard at one point, too," she said slowly.

Westbay shrugged. "Who knows? There are a lot of rumors about him, and a good half of them are completely ridiculous."

"I thought... He's a friend of your Family, right? You don't know?"

Westbay gave her a flat stare. "I'm flattered you think so highly of me, but you know the ranks of the Red Guard are confidential, right? The Westbay Family does handle the internal security of the city, but I'm only the second son, not even finished with the University. They don't tell me anything actually important," he said with irritation.

The other students were starting to chatter about Lacer's absence, and when one person speculated that the Charybdis Gulf's kraken had taken him back to its sea lair because it wanted his seed for its progeny, Westbay raised his eyebrows as if to say, "See? I told you people make up the most ridiculous rumors."

She conceded the point.

Professor Lacer still hadn't arrived thirty minutes after his class was supposed to start, and whatever discipline the students might have retained had entirely evaporated away as they gossiped and worked on homework from other classes.

"I think it was probably an Aberrant," a man seated near to Sebastien said, immediately drawing the attention of the students close enough to hear him. "Gilbratha gets at least one 'creature of evil' per year, on average, so it wouldn't be a surprise."

The woman he'd been speaking to grimaced. "Someone experimenting with blood magic? Some evil spell?" She shuddered delicately. "I cannot imagine why anyone would dabble in such a thing, knowing the consequences."

Aberrants were actually quite rare, Sebastien knew, but it was true that most of the incidents came from thaumaturges dabbling in immoral things and corrupting their Will. If Gilbratha had one every year, it was only because of the high concentration of thaumaturges, both legal and criminal.

A younger girl, obviously a commoner by the low-quality fabric of her clothes, leaned toward the two. "Are all creatures of evil Aberrants? I thought some of them were...beasts, or evil Elementals, or something."

The man shrugged. "Well, they might be. Only people who don't really know what they're talking about use the more generic terms, like 'creatures of evil.' Commoners and non-thaumaturges. It's a catch-all for any living rogue magic element."

The woman said, "Well, Aberrant or whatever it was, the Red Guard has handled it now, and we will know soon enough, once they have finished their investigation. It did not take them very long to send the all-clear signal, so it must not have been particularly difficult to deal with."

Beside Sebastien, Ana nodded at that. "That is true. When I was a child, we were stuck in the basement shelter for almost two days. Mother was worried they were going to have to set up a sundered zone right in the middle of Gilbratha. A rather powerful sorcerer had corrupted his Will and broken while trying to revive a newly dead body. It took the Red Guard some time to figure out how to deal with the Aberrant that resulted."

Westbay looked dour. "I remember that. Titus was here at the University, and Father was dealing with the incident. It was just me and the servants the whole time, waiting for news. All Aberrants have a weakness, though, a counter to their ability. You just have to find it."

Sebastien frowned. "What about Aberrants like Metanite, or Red Sage? It seems like the Red Guard would have found their weakness by now, if they really had one. Metanite isn't even contained within a sundered zone." Sundered zones were the effect of the world's most powerful barrier spell, and could contain *almost* anything. They created perfectly, *unnaturally* white quarantine domes, and were used exclusively to keep the world safe from Aberrants that couldn't be otherwise killed or neutralized. Metanite had destroyed the one they put around it just as it destroyed literally everything else it touched with its void-black form.

Westbay shook his head. "Just because it can't be killed doesn't mean there is no counter. Metanite is slow and shows no signs of intelligence. With enough vigilance, space-warping magic is plenty to deal with it. And the Red Sage is contained within a sundered zone."

"But it's not *stopped*," Sebastien argued. "Whatever ability Red Sage has is either summoning people to hear its prophecies or manipulating reality to make them come true, even from within its sundered zone."

The spell that created sundered zones did not stop sapient creatures that could give their informed consent from *entering* the barrier, nor from exiting again as long as they had not been tainted by any tangible or magical effect within. Why this was, she didn't know, but the Red Guard usually kept people from entering—or tried to—with a secondary barrier, and often a wall, too. The Red Sage could see the future, supposedly, and whatever it prophesied would come true. Except it pronounced better fates to those it liked, and horrible ones to those it disliked, and all its prophecies came true in the most horrible way possible. Desperate people continued to find ways past the security measures in the hopes of bribing the Aberrant to receive a favorable prophecy, no matter the destruction the fulfillment of the prophecy would inevitably wreak on the world and lives of those around them.

"Sure, but the Red Guard *is* working to mitigate the effects of the prophecies, as well as limit who gets to speak to the Red Sage. There haven't been any major disasters in at least a hundred years. The Red Guard has almost entirely constrained it. Imagine what it could do, unchecked."

"But that's all they can do. Constrain it. Just the same as the Dawn Troupe. Dozens of people die every year to that one."

"Again, because people are stupid and visit the Dawn Troupe on purpose, in the hopes of winning a boon. That's not the Red Guard's fault. Anyone who *isn't* stupid or suicidally reckless is safe from the Dawn Troupe."

"If enough people don't visit, the agreement with the Aberrant is that it can go on a hunt," Sebastien said. "That's what it bargained. Don't you think that has something to do with why the newspapers report it whenever someone manages to get out alive with a boon? It entices the general idiot specimen to offer up their own life so it's not so *obvious* that the Red Guard actually has no way to stop the Dawn Troupe. And what about Lugubrious? Cinder Stag? That's to say nothing of those Aberrants that you and I have no idea about. Can you truly tell me you don't think they exist? Aberrants that they can't catch? Ones they don't even *know* about?" Sebastien's voice had grown harder, sharper, and she realized she was leaning toward him, glaring into his eyes.

People were staring at her.

"You know so much, Sebastien," a girl a few desks away said with a simpering smile that lacked any real thoughtfulness and made Sebastien want to smack the expression off her face.

Sebastien leaned back, looking away with a sharp exhale.

Ana eyed Sebastien. "You *do* know rather a lot about this."

"It seemed rather prudent to do at least basic research about creatures that are created without warning and can wipe out an entire city." Sebastien couldn't understand why more people weren't interested in learning every-thing they could about Aberrants.

At most, incidents would be reported in the paper, and there would be warnings about the danger of blood magic and unlicensed, improperly trained thaumaturges. She was sure someone was researching the beings extensively —how else would the Red Guard be equipped to deal with them?—but, as a normal person, a commoner, trying to get information about Aberrants or the mental break that created them was an exercise in frustration. Those in power probably didn't want to cause a panic, while the average person just wanted to go about their life peacefully, moronically pretending that it had nothing to do with them, wouldn't affect them. Even the University library kept most of that information on the third floor or in the underground restricted sections.

"It's a real threat. A danger to the entire world. Aberrants don't die of old age, and they keep being created," she added in a calmer tone. '*It only takes one to destroy everything you've ever known and cared for,*' she added silently.

"Maybe you should join the Red Guard," Westbay said. "They might not be perfect, but they do protect Lenore pretty well. They need people who are powerful and passionate about protecting the country."

Sebastien wasn't sure how to respond to that, caught between surprise, amusement, and denial.

Ana turned away from Sebastien, putting on a bright smile. "All that as it is, the Red Guard has no doubt performed valiantly in this instance," she announced. "Let us discuss something more pleasant? I've heard Professor Boldon was proposed to by one of his student aides."

The others were drawn in by this semi-scandalous declaration, and Sebastien took the welcome reprieve to chastise herself for allowing her interest in the topic to override her discretion. She was easily caught up in theoretical discussions, sometimes without properly taking into account her audience and what was appropriate to reveal about her opinions.

Not long after, a student aide walked in and told them that the class had been assigned to self-study in the absence of their professor. The student aide sat behind Lacer's desk at the front corner of the room and started scribbling on a paper while watching them, as if to record their adherence to the task.

Westbay quickly turned to Anastasia. "I'll partner against you to start, and Siverling can watch and give us some pointers."

Sebastien raised an eyebrow, but didn't protest.

Ana hesitated, looking at Sebastien. "You don't mind? We'll be competing against each other in a few weeks, after all."

Westbay shook his head condescendingly. "Siverling's not so selfish that he can't set aside practicing for a single period to help his friends. Right, Siverling?"

"...Right."

The two of them set up the spell array and competed against each other for a few minutes while Sebastien watched. Then, they stopped and turned to her expectantly. "Well?" Westbay asked.

She stared back at them for a few seconds. '*Where does this bright-eyed anticipation come from? Are a few tips from me so valuable? Well, I suppose I am better than either of them.*' She cleared her throat. "What do both of you visualize when you move the ball?"

Anastasia looked unsurely between Sebastien and Westbay. "Umm, I just imagine the ball...moving?"

"How? What causes it to move? It just moves on its own?" Sebastien asked.

"I imagine an invisible force behind it, pushing," Westbay said.

Sebastien tapped her forefinger thoughtfully on the table . "Westbay, your visualization seems to be a little stronger than Ana's. And you've both practiced this spell a lot, so there's not a ton of inefficiency. But...Will isn't just about how much energy you're channeling, or even how efficiently you do it.

At least that's how it seems to me. When you know exactly what you want, as clear as high quality celerium, and you want it really, really badly, it makes a difference. Knowing exactly what you want can be tricky, but an easy way to create effects like this is to think about how you might create them without magic. You could nudge the ball around with your finger, and that would work, but you'll never get real speed or efficiency out of that. Swinging it around like a rock in a shepherd's sling would be better. If you can handle it mentally, a geared crank that sends the ball shooting around two times, or a hundred times, for every revolution of the crank... My point is, the visualization matters."

Damien scribbled down a handful of notes on a spare piece of paper while she spoke. "I think I understand. Give me a moment to come up with a model."

Sebastien turned to Ana. "You don't care enough about the outcome. Don't ask, don't order, just...believe. There's a reason it's called the Will. You must become a god, a force of nature, and the ball moves because the laws of reality that you created say that it moves."

Ana stared into her eyes for a long moment. "Is that how you do it?"

Sebastien chuckled. "All good thaumaturges have to be a little narcissistic, I think."

"It sounds...appealing, that kind of control."

"Of course. Magic is...it's the fabric beneath reality. It's in everything. When you touch magic..." Sebastien shook her head, feeling visceral electricity running through her skin at the thought, raising the fine hairs all over her body and setting her blood alight. "There is nothing more worthwhile." Her hand had gripped her Conduit while she wasn't paying attention, and she released it, sitting back and rolling her shoulders. "Okay. Try again."

They did. The improvement wasn't huge, especially with them already having so much experience casting the same spell over and over, but it was noticeable. Maybe a five percent increase in power, and about the same improvement to their efficiency. It was enough to put a huge grin on Westbay's face and make Ana let out a rich laugh. They drew the attention of those sitting nearby.

"You really are a genius," Westbay said. "This is as good as if I just gained ten thaums in five minutes of work."

A girl whose name Sebastien had forgotten leaned in, tucking her hair behind her ear. "Are you handing out tips, Siverling? Teaching the class in place of Professor Lacer?"

"I don't have anything to say that you shouldn't already know," Sebastien said shortly.

Despite the fact that she'd just coached him, Westbay crossed his arms over his chest and gave their curious classmates a glare. "Focus on your own tables," he snapped at them.

And so, they spent the rest of the class period like that, with Ana and Westbay practicing while Sebastien watched and gave them little hints to improve their performance—and their classmates not-so-inconspicuously continued to eavesdrop.

9

THE INTERSECTION OF TRANSMUTATION AND TRANSMOGRIFICATION

SEBASTIEN
   Month 12, Day 9, Wednesday 2:15 p.m.

PROFESSOR LACER WAS BACK in the Practical Casting classroom on Wednesday. For once, he was there ahead of the students. He leaned against his desk, which displayed a scattering of components.

'A demonstration,' Sebastien thought with excitement. Professor Lacer's classes tended to be filled with a lot of practice, but he also often lectured on the kind of fascinating topics that were beyond the purview of their other classes. He introduced ideas and talked about spells that they couldn't explore at their low level of skill, but which were still fascinating. Sometimes he made them do thought exercises that seemed designed to force them to think creatively and come up with non-standard solutions to problems.

But everyone enjoyed the days when he demonstrated free-casting the most.

As soon as they'd all settled, Professor Lacer pushed away from the edge of his desk. "Just as our understanding of magic has changed as we created the modern practice of sorcery, our labels have evolved. Ancient humans had no concept of a delineation between transmutation and transmogrification. It was all magic. Now, we say that transmutation is based on natural conversion of form or energy, and transmogrification is a borrowing of concepts. Of ideas. Intangible properties. Today, we are going to explore the intersection of transmutation and transmogrification.

"Transmogrification intersects with transmutation in three main ways. One, when both are used for separate aspects of a spell to create a synergistic effect. Two, when transmutation is not enough, and so we boost the effects by adding transmogrification toward the *same* purpose, adding a punch of efficacy to efficiency, as it were. Three, when the caster is using transmogrification not toward an intangible idea, but to copy a process, or, as happens more often, to copy *part* of a process in addition to the *idea* of the process that the caster does not understand."

He crouched down and drew a Circle on the ground, about a meter across. "We will start with the simplest of intersections: spells that use both for a synergistic effect, transmutation for one facet and transmogrification for another."

He turned to his desk, moving a block of heavy clay, three small white balls floating in a jar of yellow pickling brine, and another jar of water containing a frond of seaweed and some sand to the floor. From his pockets, he pulled out his Conduit with one hand and a beast core with the other. The block of clay rippled and morphed into the shape of a turtle, surprisingly detailed and life-like. "A simple shape-change transmutation, using the provided clay and the energy from this beast core to mold it according to my Will. What comes next is, arguably, more interesting," he said.

Within the briny jar, the three white balls disintegrated.

Color and texture seeped over the turtle, turning it from clay to flesh and shell.

It came to life with a sudden jerk, like someone awoken from a nightmare to find themselves in unfamiliar surroundings.

"Pickled turtle eggs for the animation, the concept of the life that would have been, borrowed and molded into a lifelike simulation. Transmogrification. Let me point out that I have no idea if those eggs were fertilized or not, or if there were stillborn turtles within. And in case any of you have not been paying attention when we talk about theory, let me also point out that I have not created life. I have created a lifelike golem that will last as long as my concentration does."

A student raised her hand, and he nodded to her, indicating that she could speak.

In a slightly hushed tone that nevertheless was clearly audible in the classroom—the rest of the students held their breath, as if any disturbance would break the spell—she asked, "Is it possible to create life? I've heard there have been experiments, but the creatures always die as soon as they let the spell drop. Professor Boldon said creating true life was one of the inherent limitations of magic."

"Of course it is possible," Professor Lacer immediately dismissed. "If you believe anything is impossible, it is because you are too primitive to understand how it works, or too weak to make it happen. If a woman can create true life in her womb, a thaumaturge can create true life with magic. Eventually, someone will cross that seemingly impassable barrier, just like we have crossed so many before."

The girl sat back, frowning but silent.

Sebastien remembered Professor Gnorrish's class on the theory of spontaneous generation. *'Is it that we don't understand what makes something "alive," and so we cannot create life? Or perhaps there is something—a soul?—that requires too much energy, or that we are not giving the proper Sacrifices to recreate. But if that were the case, we would be able to measure the soul escaping from the body upon death, correct? I don't believe there is any evidence of that. Unless the "soul," or whatever it is that we're missing, doesn't actually reside within the body.'* It was a fascinating idea, with interesting implications. Who wouldn't want to escape death? If you could understand enough to create life through magic, surely that was a huge step toward staving off death. One might even be able to simply transfer themselves into a fresh body when they got too old. *'Of course,'* she thought wryly, *'Research into the topic would almost certainly be classified as blood magic, whether it deserved to be outlawed or not.'* Before she could lose herself to contemplation, Professor Lacer's spell drew her attention back.

Seawater burst out of the final jar, dispersing in an artful splash around the spherical confines of the Circle, and then seeming to expand impossibly while simultaneously disappearing.

The turtle rose up, swimming around the air as if it were in a dome-shaped aquarium. "And here," Professor Lacer continued, "I have taken that concept of buoyancy that a creature might experience surrounded by seawater and applied it to the area under my control. I have slowed down the steps of this spell so that you can see the delineation between transmutation and transmogrification, but in many other spells both effects are simultaneous. We go as far as we can with transmutation, and bridge the gap with transmogrification."

'It's true. Spells do that all the time. And it makes sense, if there isn't any actual difference between the two. The two T's are just labels we've used to explain what we've always been doing. A divider that's only in our minds.' It was an interesting way to look at things, as if she had tilted her head to the side and saw that the shape she'd thought was a square was actually a diamond, but it wasn't some world-shattering revelation. Things like this were why she loved this class, as tedious as the magical exercises could sometimes be.

Professor Lacer dropped the spell without further fanfare.

The turtle fell to the floor, lifeless and a little damp.

He picked it up and tossed it into a box beside his desk without care, then grabbed a glass bottle of amber liquid. "For the second most common intersection of the two, take this whiskey spelled to impart a sense of warmth and wellbeing by the shot. Alcohol does this naturally, and the fermentation and distillation are a form of transmutation, whether processed magically or not. The addition of transmogrification magic uses that *same* alcohol and a couple of other ingredients to boost the effects beyond simple inebriation."

"Do we get a practical demonstration of that, too?" a student called out. "I could do with a shot of warmth and wellbeing."

This caused scattered laughter, and even Professor Lacer allowed a small quirk to his lips. "Even if University rules allowed it, I would not be so reckless as to give students anything that would combine lowered inhibitions and a sense of wellbeing. You already mistake yourselves to be invincible."

He picked up a metal box, touching the controls to turn the walls of the artifact transparent. Within lay a shimmering, tapered slab of something that looked like dark oil.

'That's the same kind of evidence box the coppers use to keep things in stasis.'

"Finally, transmutation intersects with transmogrification without us realizing it. The spell cast using this fish is one interesting example." He opened the top, placed the box down, and then cast a levitation spell on the specimen using only his Conduit and the beast core for power. Even the Circle was maintained within his mind, and cast at a distance, just as he'd spoken of on their first day of class.

Sebastien grinned just to see it.

The fish floated between Professor Lacer and the students, turning slowly so they could see its flat, slablike form. "The dorienne fish survives and hunts using particularly impressive camouflage," he introduced. "It can see through its skin, and it processes the input from one side of its body and mimics it on the other with precise control of its pigmentation. The dorienne is only able to do this from one side at a time, and will turn to keep one broad side facing a predator or its prey, so that it remains effectively invisible."

He floated the dead, preserved fish into the Circle he'd drawn on the floor earlier, then placed a foot-wide mirror with a frame of ornate scrollwork across from it. "Although we are aware of how the dorienne fish works, those who first discovered it knew only that the fish could be invisible from one side at a time. They created a spell that seems to copy that process." He pointed, and the mirror became invisible, frame and all.

With a deep breath and a scowl of concentration, he moved slowly to face the students again. Now floating in front of him, the partially invisible mirror rotated to its visible side, and then around again. "The spell does not actually copy the process of the fish. Can anyone tell me how they are different?"

Sebastien leaned forward in her seat, her eyes devouring every movement as the mirror continued to spin at different angles around its axis. "It's actually invisible."

Professor Lacer turned to her. "Explain."

"With the way the fish works, light hits both sides. It's only changed what one of its sides looks like to *mimic* the effect of light passing straight through. The spell you're casting has made one side of the mirror invisible. When the invisible side is facing the light source, it casts no shadow. Light is passing right through it."

With a very slight smile, he floated the mirror over to the lamp on his desk to show the effect more clearly. "Mr. Siverling is correct. The dorienne invisibility spell is more power-intensive than it should be if the process were truly being copied. It killed its creator on his initial test casting. Transmogrification is unclearly defined. The trade for your Sacrifice is not always an intangible property. Sometimes, rather, it is a tangible process that you *could* create with transmutation, with enough study. Sometimes, transmogrification molds connotative associations, which are intangible and often beyond our powers of transmutation. But other times, transmogrification simply copies a state or process from the Sacrifice, whole-cloth. And occasionally it does one while the ignorant researcher who does not understand the limitations of their subject believes it to be doing another.

"This spell was created to copy the process of the dorienne, a much less power-intensive shortcut than the true invisibility spells of the time. And yet, in their lack of understanding, the creator of this spell did not copy, but drew on their *idea* of the dorienne's invisibility, never having noticed that the dorienne casts a shadow or understanding what this means."

He placed the fish back in the stasis artifact and then snapped his fingers.

Boxes appeared at the back of the classroom as if they'd been there all along—and they probably had been. "We will be moving on to another exercise today. You have had five weeks to practice moving a ball in a circle, and while you should continue to practice so that you do not grow rusty before the mid-term tournament, it is time to stretch your Will in other ways. Come up and grab a set of components. They are rated by thaum capacity."

Once all the students had filed down, retrieved the appropriate components, and returned to their desks, he continued. "You each have two bottles of dirt and a small dragon scale. Your dirt varies both in volume and the ratio of clay to sand. Those of you with a larger amount or sandier material will find this exercise more difficult. Your goal is to turn particulate earth into a solid sphere capable of withstanding pressure, and then back again. You will use both transmutation and transmogrification to achieve this. The dragon scale is to be used as a template of form as well as for the idea of its strength. In a month, you should be able to create a sturdy ball of earth from any combination of methods. From pure transmutation using pressure or heat or whatever natural process you can come up with, to accurately copying the internal structure of the dragon's scale, to imbuing your ball of earth with the defensive power of a dragon."

Professor Lacer had his own set of components on his desk, along with a steel mallet. He poured out a jar of pure sand. Under his hand, it glowed brightly with heat, flowing and melting into a sphere of opaque glass. "Transmutation," he said.

He slammed the mallet down onto it, shattering the glass sphere into powder and shards. "Fairly weak." The pieces drew back together before melting again into a ball. "Do not forget you must not only create the compressed sphere, but also return your component to its original state." The reformed ball crumbled into sand under his Will.

He picked up the dragon scale and laid it next to the pile of sand. The sand once again glowed and drew together into a sphere, but its surface was matte this time, and Sebastien thought she could make out the same patterning as the dragon scale sitting on the desk beside it.

"The simplest form of transmogrification," he said. "Copying. The internal structure of a dragon's scale is no more an intangible quality than its color is. Both are knowable, explainable by the natural sciences. And yet, spells like this have been labeled and cast as transmogrification by those who don't understand how these things come to be. I will move the sphere to the floor this time. I do not wish to damage my desk."

He brought down the iron mallet even harder than before. The sound of the impact was like the muffled crack of a frozen tree branch fracturing in the cold of winter under the weight of too much snow. The sphere was scuffed where the mallet had struck, but remained whole. He repeated this several more times to the same effect. Turning to one of the other students near the front, a strong-looking young man, Lacer called him up to take the mallet.

While the young man kept bashing away at the sphere, Lacer stood and continued lecturing, his words punctuated by the cracking sound of the mallet against the ball. "If I were to take the time to understand how the scale of the dragon is created, what the cells are made of and how their structure provides such defensive qualities, I could mold the sand without the need for a template to copy. The advantage of this method, as well as transmutation, is that as long as the transformation is complete by the time the casting stops, the changes will remain. I have created permanent change from a temporary application of magical power."

Finally, after a few dozen more whacks from the enthusiastic student, the sphere broke, falling to jagged shards like a piece of hard candy.

Professor Lacer had him stand by while he returned the pieces to sand once again, this time using the second jar as a component. "What you can copy in one direction you can copy in the other. Rather than disintegrating this through transmutation, I am copying the state of the sand."

The sphere's recreation took slightly longer the third time, and Sebastien imagined she felt the weight of Professor Lacer's Will brushing against the air.

When he finally held it up to them, it looked like the first time, shiny and semi-transparent. "This ball is a simple-structured glass imbued with the concept of a dragon's defense. True transmogrification, completely conceptual without any accompanying physical change. It is an actively cast spell, not an enchanted artifact, so the magic won't hold long, but while it does..."

He tossed the sphere to the man holding the mallet, who caught it clumsily, then placed it on the floor and whacked.

The sound was different, not such a clear crack, but deeper and hollower, as if the force of the blow had reverberated through something bigger than the sphere. The man repeated this dozens of times, but the sphere remained completely unharmed, pristine and unscuffed even after he began to pant and sweat.

Finally, Professor Lacer stopped him, once again turning the sphere back into sand, then levitating that sand back into its bottle. "Your turn," he said to the class. "Homework will be theoretical research: the glyphs and spell arrays you could use to make these effects happen. Three glyphs, maximum. Be creative, be exhaustive. Due next Wednesday."

Sebastien's jars weren't quite filled with pure sand, as the ones Professor Lacer used for his demonstration had been, but they were far from the clay dust she saw some of the other students working with, and there was enough to create a ball almost an inch in diameter. It would require both more power and more skill. With only middling success, she attempted to transmute the sandy dirt into a rock. By the end of the class period, she was frustrated with her dinky little Conduit. It kept her from crushing or heating the material with enough strength to create anything more than a lumpy ball with the consistency of sandstone.

10

USELESS CLUTTER

SEBASTIEN
Month 12, Day 9, Wednesday 3:45 p.m.

AS SEBASTIEN LEFT the Practical Casting classroom, Anastasia and Westbay fell into step on either side of her.

"That was amazing!" Westbay crowed, his grey eyes bright and glinting. "I can't believe Professor Lacer isn't an Archmage already. Did you see that turtle? He turned *clay* into *flesh*."

"Most impressive," Ana agreed. "Do you think he was making some sort of allusion to the task given to Myrddin by the dragon?"

"What?"

"Well, as you said, he's not an Archmage yet. That classroom holds several members related to the council of Grandmasters that he would need to confirm him. Perhaps he hopes to subtly influence the council's decision by pairing himself to Myrddin in the eyes of their beloved family members. At some point, they won't be able to deny him without being seen as petty and foolish to the masses."

"Well...I suppose that's possible," Westbay said doubtfully. "But do you think he even cares about the title?"

"Who knows? Titles can hold power. Freedom," Ana said, her fingers absently stroking the spine of the ornate pink journal she carried with her everywhere and wrote in every evening.

"What I want to know is whether that turtle was edible," Westbay said, turning to Sebastien. "If I were trapped in a dungeon cell, with only the stones in the wall around me and some turtle eggs, could I create an edible creature? Not a living one, but flesh that would provide calories and nutrition?"

Sebastien raised her eyebrows as they stepped into the Great Hall. "I doubt *you* could. Or any of us. Rather than flesh, stone to a simple sugar might be possible, and could keep you alive, if not healthy. Besides, if you're trapped in a dungeon cell and somehow have enough power to transmogrify stone into an edible, dead turtle, I think there are better uses for your efforts. Like escaping."

Westbay blinked a couple times before launching into a response, but Sebastien's attention was drawn to the far side of the Great Hall, where Newton was stepping down from the stage where the contribution point prizes were displayed. The older young man looked tired, but not much worse than he had a couple of days before. *'Is he looking for something to help his father? Or maybe something he could sell for gold?'*

The thought was a reminder of her own situation. Everything in this city cost too much, and she was running low on coins. After what she set aside to repay Oliver for Healer Nidson's fee, she was once again poor. Aside from the emergency gold hidden in the lining of her jacket and boots, she had a little less than eight gold crowns to her name. At one point, she would have considered that a fortune. Now, she knew how little it could actually get her.

She had a few contribution points by now, earned by performing well in her classes and on tests. *'Perhaps there will be something I could afford.'* "I'm going to look at the prizes," she announced, interrupting whatever Westbay was saying and striding away immediately.

Westbay grumbled, "Were you even listening?" as he hurried to catch up.

"No, not at all," Sebastien admitted. It was the truth, but just because she hadn't been actively listening didn't mean she didn't *hear*. "You said that in this hypothetical situation, maybe the dungeon cell had some sort of protective warding that didn't allow you to break out, and no one was coming to feed you because they were afraid you would attack them, so they were hoping to kill you through simple starvation, and wouldn't they be surprised when they came to check on you a month later and the cell was filled with turtle corpses, and you'd made turtle-shell armor and weapons and were ready and waiting?"

"Um."

She shook her head with exasperation. "Honestly, Westbay. You're like a child."

"I thought you said you weren't listening?"

"I wasn't."

Ana let out a long, low laugh. "Oh, Damien. You do have the most amusing outraged expression!"

Westbay had fallen behind in his confusion, and he ran a few steps to catch up with Sebastien as she climbed onto the stage. "You weren't listening, but you retained the information anyway? But what about when we first met? You forgot my name. In fact, you heard it *several times*, but *still* didn't remember it."

Most of the prizes were in display cases or otherwise warded against theft. Sebastien skimmed the summary cards beneath a row of wands as she spoke. "It's like my mind is a vast ocean. It can hold quite a lot, but all the useless information kind of settles to the bottom. Very hard to find anything down there in the dark, piled up with all the other clutter."

"*Useless information?*" Westbay's voice had grown decidedly shrill.

She rolled her eyes at him. "Don't be so dramatic. I remember your name now, don't I?"

He started muttering something about, "the most narcissistic, pig-headed, rude man...think you're the second coming of Myrddin...oh no, don't bother remembering useless information like my *name*," but she tuned him out again, browsing further.

She knew he wasn't actually upset, after all. His eyes were still light grey and he hadn't started fidgeting with his hair or clothes. '*If I irritate him enough, I wonder if I could get him to use that favor I owe him just to dull the razor of my tongue.*'

Unfortunately, *she* was the one who was irritated by the way he'd suddenly started hanging around her. She didn't trust his sudden turn toward amiability. But he was determined it seemed, and undeterred by her snark.

Ana, silently aware of Sebastien's frustration, gave her a crooked smile when Westbay wasn't looking.

Atop the stage were potion ingredients, spellcasting components of varying rarity, and even things like the powder of gemstones and precious metals that could be used as components or to draw a more conductive spell array. The professors, or perhaps higher-level student aides, had probably transmuted them from something much less expensive. Of course, none of the items on offer were legally restricted, but a few were probably hard to come by in the city market, regardless of coin on hand.

Then, magical items created by the professors. A multitude of artifacts, enchanted clothing, and strange alchemical concoctions. The artifacts ranged from the useful—a better lock for the storage chests in the dorms—to fanciful and strange—a pillow that sang lullabies out of its felt mouth.

There were even a couple of small Conduits displayed in one of the glass cases. Sebastien eyed them with interest, but they were far beyond what she could afford, even the smallest costing over twelve hundred contribution points.

Ana seemed particularly interested in the enchanted clothing, eyeing the glyphs embroidered into the cloth with a magnifying glass that she pulled out of a pocket. "That's a very elegant solution. I'll have to write father about it," she muttered.

Westbay focused on the divination supplies, staring at an artistic deck of cards and a rune-inscribed basin for far-viewing. "This is what Aberford Thorndyke used to catch the hen-thief terrorizing that rural village!" he exclaimed, grinning at her, his earlier ire forgotten. Westbay was taking seven classes this term, the last of which was Divination.

Sebastien grimaced at the reminder of her own struggles with that field of magic. If only she could foist the work off onto someone like him. She sighed at the thought. *'Even if I could find someone to do it, I couldn't afford to hire them.'*

A big book on a pedestal listed the other things she could buy, going into detail about what exactly she would be purchasing. In addition to purchasing better cafeteria food, there was also access to various upper sections of the library, private tutoring with University student aides of different levels and areas of expertise, and a list of the available—increasingly luxurious—dorm rooms. If she could afford it, she could live in a penthouse suite with a built-in kitchen and bathroom, all in pale marble and dark granite, and eat purple lobster three times a week.

If she had five hundred points, she could exchange them for tuition on a single University class. A quick calculation told Sebastien that if that exchange rate held steady, each point was worth about one silver crown, which was actually a significant amount.

Sebastien could afford some of the less interesting components and alchemy products, but nothing she particularly needed, and nothing she could resell for a good sum.

But the possibility had reminded her that she *did* have some things she didn't need.

Instead of accompanying Anastasia and Westbay to the library, she dropped off her new practice components from Practical Casting in her dorm cubicle and left for Oliver's house.

He wasn't home, but the servants greeted her happily, and Sharon forced her to sit down and have an afternoon snack that was really more like a full dinner, grinning and blushing behind her hands every time Sebastien showed appreciation for the non-University food.

When Sebastien was stuffed so full it was almost painful to walk, she went to the room Oliver was lending her and took the bags she'd brought with her that first night out of one of the closets.

Ennis's things. The bags she'd retrieved for him from that room at the inn, when she still thought he was a real father to her.

She took out one set of clothes. They were a little too short and wide for Sebastien, but she could make some adjustments so that they would fit her better. She was not very handy with a needle and thread, but that was alright.

It made sense to keep a simple set of male clothes with her, ones not as attention-drawing as the items in Sebastien Siverling's wardrobe. Perhaps someday she would need to present herself as a more mundane blonde man.

With Ennis's luggage slung across her shoulders, she started walking. She kept an eye out for anyone watching or following her, but saw no eyes that were anything more than curious. Sebastien dressed like Oliver—like she could feed a family of four for a month with the price of her perfectly tailored suit made of silky, thick wool and the stylish jacket over it. She looked like she was *actually warm*. '*And I'm hauling three bags stuffed with the worldly possessions of a nomadic conman,*' she thought. '*They're probably wondering where my manservant is.*'

Her shoulders hurt by the time she reached the Verdant Stag, but she didn't want to waste coin on anything unnecessary, like the luxury of a carriage.

She'd only been to the inn-slash-entertainment-hall a few times as Sebastien. There were a couple of musicians on stage, and people were filtering in as the sun set and they got off work, filling up the seats and ordering food and ale from the bar. People were betting with a bookie in front of the large chalkboard against the other wall. She recognized one of the Stag enforcers leaning up against the wall near a hallway.

Sebastien walked past all of them.

Theo was at the top of the curved staircase at the far side of the room, sitting with a book and what looked like a half-written essay. The boy leaned his copper-haired head back until it thunked against the wall behind him, his eyes closed and his mouth yawning open in a soulless gape of boredom.

A laugh barked out of Sebastien's throat without warning, and Theo jerked to awareness.

"Sorceress!" he yipped. His eyes widened and he looked around, covering his mouth with his hand, but there was too much other noise in the room below for anyone to have heard him. He took his hands away, examining her curiously. "You don't look homeless anymore."

She grinned at him. "Having trouble with your homework?"

"Ugh!" He rolled his head back dramatically again. "It's an assignment from Mr. Mawson, my tutor. I'm supposed to write an essay on the Black Wastes, but it's so *boring*. I don't even know what to talk about. They're black. The Brillig caused them thousands of years ago when we were at war with them, when they knew we were gonna win and they didn't want us to have anything good if they couldn't. And stuff dies there. How'm I supposed to say any more than that? I've never even *been* there. I've never been more than a day's walk away from Gilbratha."

Sebastien shook her head. "Whoa. Well, if you think the Black Wastes are boring, I must say it sounds like your tutor may be a teeny bit incompetent.

He left out all the interesting parts and wanted you to write an essay copied from a book?"

Theo's eyes widened, then narrowed. "What do you mean, interesting parts?"

"Well, like the stories of the adventurers who explored the Black Wastes to try and uncover the dragon corpses. The few who made it out alive told crazy —and I do mean *insane*—stories about the things they saw."

"*Dragon* corpses? What kind of things did they see?"

"Well, how long is your essay supposed to be?"

"Two pages."

She waved her hand carelessly. "That's nothing. Take notes. I will give you the information for the source material you can say you referenced if your tutor gives you problems, too." She settled next to him on the top step of the stairs, speaking slowly. "This comes out of Edward Leeson's third volume of 'History of the Indomitable Race,' which is actually kind of an ironic title, because..."

She told stories, repeating particularly interesting sections, answering questions, and helping him spell certain names while Theo scribbled as fast as he could to keep up with the information. Almost an hour later, he had three pages of notes and a cramping hand. "Okay. I think that's enough material," she said finally.

He sighed with relief as he stretched out his fingers, but still pouted reluctantly. "What about the other knight who went in with Briarson?"

She stood and began to walk down the hall to Katerin's office, and Theo gathered up his things and scrambled to walk with her. "Briarson said that his partner went to check the perimeter around their camp, but didn't come back until dawn, and when he did, he was glowing and shooting off sparks of green light, 'like a dandelion in the wind.'" She used her fingers to indicate the quotation, then knocked on the door to Katerin's office. "So Briarson shot him with an arrow. Well, six arrows. Briarson said his partner kept getting up again, so he had to keep shooting. No one knows if that really happened or if Briarson had gone insane by then."

When Katerin called for them to come in, Theo bounced into the room. "What happened then? Did Briarson get out?"

Sebastien shook her head. "No, he never did. We know all this because a later expedition found his journal. It had been enchanted to ward off the elements. That expedition confirmed Briarson's body was right there in camp, dead of unknown causes. And they found the arrows he'd shot on the other side of camp, broken and rotting. But they didn't find the body of his companion."

Theo's eyes were round. "Could he have...got up again? Like Briarson said?"

Katerin raised her eyebrows.

Sebastien shrugged, suppressing her smile. "No one knows. Maybe he was a hallucination. Or maybe he was real, but he wasn't Briarson's friend at all. Maybe Briarson's friend never came back from checking the perimeter."

Theo shuddered in delighted horror. "Titan's balls, I can't wait to rub this in Mr. Mawson's face. He never said anything about any of this stuff. Not the good stuff, I mean, just the death tolls and the loss of farmland and the boring recovery efforts."

"Language, Theo," Katerin reprimanded lazily, her accent throaty and biting. "And maybe he never said anything about that because he didn't think it was appropriate to regale a young boy with horror stories."

Sebastien winced.

"They're not horror stories! They're real! The sorcer—I mean, *he*"—Theo jerked his head to Sebastien as he bounced over to Katerin's side—"gave me all sorts of sources. This all comes out of real books that he read. It's for my essay on the Black Wastes, which are actually super cool and not boring at all." He waved the scribbled sheets of note paper at her.

Katerin sighed, but ruffled his hair with a smile. "Okay. *Real* horror stories, then. Make sure you thank *Sebastien* here. And that essay better be good enough that I can rub it in Mr. Mawson's face, too, when he comes complaining to me." She winked at him. "Now go to your room and finish your homework."

Grinning wide and gleefully as only a child could, he ran out. "Thanks, Mr. Sebastien!" he called over his shoulder.

"Err, I'm sorry if—" Sebastien started, but Katerin cut her off with a wave of her hand.

"No, no, it's fine. Great, actually." She stood, walking to the window and shutting the curtains against the night. "Oliver suggested a reward system to get Theo more focused on his learning, and it's been working to some degree, but Theo's only been dragging himself through it for the end prize. I overheard him giving himself a pep talk in the bathroom yesterday." The woman chuckled fondly. "It's nice to see him actually excited about learning for once."

Katerin's crimson hair and white teeth, especially after night had fallen, still made Sebastien think of a vampire. Or maybe it was something about the way the muscles around her eyes and mouth were tight with what was probably tension and fatigue, but looked a little like hunger, too. Her eyes roved over the leather and canvas luggage bags Sebastien had let drop to the floor. "What have you brought me?"

"The belongings of one Ennis Naught," Sebastien replied softly. "I was hoping to get your advice on the best way to sell them."

Katerin raised an eyebrow, but replied smoothly. "Nothing that would lead back to him, and through him to you, I hope?"

"Of course not. Good clothes, a warm, waterproof jacket, and fancy knick-knacks he collected to make himself seem cultured or richer than he actually was." Ennis had accumulated a lot for someone with such a nomadic lifestyle. Sebastien had taken only the bags that were light enough to carry, which meant she mostly had his clothes, and the rest had been left at the inn for the coppers. "It should be worth at least a few gold, even used."

"There's a shop about half a kilometer north of here. They'll pay for things like that, mostly from people who've died or commoners who are upper-class enough to wear only new clothes but aren't wasteful enough to throw away their worn purchases from last year. Tell them I sent you, and don't accept the first number they offer." Katerin scribbled their name and location on a scrap of paper and handed it to Sebastien.

"Thank you," Sebastien said. She turned to the door, then hesitated. "Are there any updates?"

Katerin eyed her thoughtfully, then took out a pipe from the drawer in her desk and began to fill it with a dark blue crumble that Sebastien recognized as dried etherwood leaves. The smoke was smooth and calming, and great for blowing smoke rings, but nonaddictive. Either it was laced with something else, or Katerin's smoking habit was purely recreational. "He's still in jail. They brought in a curse-breaker and a shaman to see him, with no luck. He's still telling the same story."

Sebastien frowned. "You mean...the truth?" *A shaman might help him to clarify his dreams or memories to give better testimony, but why a curse-breaker?*

Katerin placed the pipe onto a round glass coaster with a spell array molded into its surface. She paused to concentrate, frowning until a spark burst to life in the bowl of the pipe, orange smoldering in the depths of the dried leaves. "Well, yes. But I'm not sure they believe the truth, with the sudden notoriety of the Raven Queen. Our contact says most of them think he's just a pawn in the Raven Queen's scheme and doesn't know anything useful. But the coppers are unwilling to give up on Ennis just yet. They hope he might lead them to her involuntarily." She looked up, sucking on the mouth of the pipe and then tilting her head back to release a thick ring of light blue smoke. "She's contacted him twice already, after all."

"Ah." Sebastien ran her tongue across the back of her teeth. "But they're not torturing him, or threatening execution?"

"You sure you want to get rid of those bags?" Katerin's gaze was piercing, but her expression showed no actual curiosity.

"Yes." Sebastien gripped the straps of the packs tighter.

"It's just that someone who really does not care wouldn't be asking me these things, right?"

Sebastien shifted, her shoulders tightening. "Well, if I find myself slipping into feelings of worry or guilt, I need only to remember that, if Ennis Naught somehow gets out of jail, he only has himself to blame for giving my birthright heirloom ring—with a Master level Conduit—to the Gervin Family, which would have been worth more than enough to buy him new clothes and support him. Even after his *ungrateful* daughter sold all his things." Her voice petered out on a low snarl.

Katerin just stared back silently.

Sebastien straightened her shoulders, lifted her chin, and left for the address of the shop Katerin had given her.

She made five gold off the lot.

11

UNRESOLVED CURIOSITY

SEBASTIEN
Month 12, Day 14, Monday 9:00 a.m.

AFTER GETTING RID of Ennis's belongings, Sebastien spent the night studying, allowing her magic-casting faculties to rest, except for a single use of the divination ward against a scrying attempt. The coppers seemed to be trying at random times, hoping to catch her off guard, but with the way the ward worked, it would start to veil her even without her conscious aid, and the stabbing feel of it in the skin of her back when it activated was impossible to ignore or sleep through.

After a couple days of research, she determined that a map-based location divination was her best option. Her blood was almost certainly at the coppers' base, and Oliver was doubtful of their ability to access it. But that simply wasn't acceptable. There had to be a way to actually solve the problem, and pinpointing the location of her blood was the first step in doing so.

The spell she eventually settled on was meant to precisely determine the location of the separated piece of her blood on a map. With multiple castings, she could use more detailed, close-up maps to determine its location with increasing precision. Once she knew *exactly* where it was, she could destroy it.

'Maybe I could have a Lino-Wharton raven messenger fly in an explosive potion, or force my blood to escape from its confines with a telekinetic spell, or even get Liza's help with a switching spell or something. It is impossible for them to ward against everything.'

It also helped that the map-locating spell didn't require any overly expensive components, except for the tiny vial of mercury and an eagle's eye.

That weekend, Sebastien bought alchemy ingredients at Waterside Market again—which Oliver reimbursed her for—along with the ingredients for the scrying spell—which she had to cover herself. She then spent almost the entire weekend brewing for the Stags to try and pay off at least some of the interest on her debt. She focused on the more intensive potions that Oliver's enforcers would need, like the philtre of darkness and revivifying potion, as well as the blood-clotting potion, which she could produce a lot more of in a single batch. Every enforcer should be supplied with at least two.

Despite her inability to channel large amounts of energy through her new Conduit, she could still complete potions in smaller batches. These were worth more than many of the more common-use potions sold in the Verdant Stag's little alchemy shop, and she made a single extra dose in a couple of her batches for herself, so she still came out ahead.

It was likely that getting her blood from the coppers would take a combination of money and power, neither of which she had at the moment. Retrieving her blood, like figuring out a solution to her sleep problem, would likely be a long-term project.

A week after the rogue magic sirens had gone off, the coppers released a statement about their cause. It had indeed been an Aberrant.

Apparently, a prostitute had been attempting to cast an illegal, dangerous allure spell and had corrupted her Will. She'd broken under the strain and become a rabid creature of evil. The Red Guard had dealt with the Aberrant easily enough, and there were no lingering effects or danger.

Everyone was talking about it that Monday in Intro to Modern Magics. There was plenty of gossip and speculation, but no real details. Being as pleasant as possible, Sebastien even asked Damien Westbay, "Is that the full story? Have you heard any more details?"

He brightened perceptibly under her interested gaze. "My brother wrote to me that the spell she was trying to cast was new magic, something she cobbled together trying to do more than one thing at once. She was apparently disfigured, so she turned to magic out of desperation to attract customers," he said.

"What were the abilities of the Aberrant?" she asked. "Some kind of allure effect, I'm assuming." Usually, Aberrants had some relation to what the thaumaturge had been casting when they broke.

Westbay shook his head regretfully. "I don't know. He didn't go into detail. I could write him and ask, if you want?"

Sebastien hesitated, considering it, but shook her head. The last thing she wanted was for the leader of the coppers to know her name, or anything else about her. "No, that's alright. Thank you, though," she murmured, her thoughts turning inward.

Westbay beamed as if he'd won some sort of award.

Professor Lacer might know something, too, if the rumors about his past association with the Red Guard were true, but she was afraid to ask him for gossip.

Professor Burberry reeled back in the students' attention to introduce their project for the week, a color-changing spell. It was labeled a transmogrification spell, and they were all given half a dozen different items in bright colors to use as components, plus a little vial of yak urine, which was apparently known for its ability to help dyes stay color-fast. They would be casting the spell on a white mouse with the intent to overcome its natural resistance and change the color of its fur.

The rest of Westbay's group of Crown Family friends had been interacting with Sebastien more frequently, likely spurred on by his own sudden amicability toward her. They sat around her, Ana on one side and Rhett Moncrieffe on the other, with the rest of the group scattered close by. After a single silent nod to Sebastien, Moncrieffe turned to the pretty girl on his other side, who blushed under the weight of his attention. Sebastien was relieved he wasn't as pushy as Westbay.

As Burberry lectured on the details of the color-change spell, Waverly Ascott tried to read a book on summoning under the table while Brinn Setterlund gently covered for her and alerted her whenever she needed to pretend to be paying attention to the professor.

When the time came to cast the spell, Ascott succeeded without much trouble despite her lack of attention, then returned to her surreptitious reading, her straight black hair shifting forward to hide her face.

Ana caught the direction of Sebastien's gaze and leaned a little closer to murmur, "She dislikes Burberry because Burberry is prejudiced against witches."

Now that Ana mentioned it, Sebastien realized that there had been hints of that in Burberry's lectures. Sorcerers reigned supreme in their professor's mind. "But...Waverly is a sorcerer?" Sebastien murmured, turning her eyes back to the caged mouse in front of her whose hair they were supposed to be turning different colors.

"For now, yes. The Ascott Family doesn't approve of her interests, but she's preparing to make a contract with a powerful Elemental. She'll have succeeded by the time we finish with the University, if not sooner."

Sebastien was intrigued, and could admit she respected that kind of passion, even if she herself preferred the personal control of sorcery. Instead of a celerium Conduit, witches channeled magic through their bound familiars, which could be tamed magical beasts, creatures, or even sapient beings conjured from one of the Elemental Planes. There was less chance for a witch to lose control or go insane from Will-strain, as their familiar took on some of the burden of casting, and the witch would always find casting spells that were within the natural purview of her familiar's magic easier. However, spells that were antithetical to the familiar's natural abilities would be more difficult.

Witches gave up versatility for focused power and safety. And for some witches, maybe for companionship.

Sebastien returned her focus to her own spellcasting, but was distracted again as Alec Gervin snapped at the student aide leaning over his shoulder.

"I did exactly what you said! You're bungling the explanation. It's useless, I can't work with you. Send over the other guy," he said, jerking his head at the other student aide with a glower.

The student aide seemed taken aback, but Gervin was resolute and got his way.

To Sebastien's surprise, Westbay waved the reprimanded student aide over and made a murmured apology for his friend.

Sebastien grunted in disgust. "Surprising, that you and he share the same last name," she murmured to Ana.

Ana smiled demurely, her eyes remaining on her own mouse, which was cowering in the corner of its little cage. "Alec was never taught finesse. He's failing several classes, and he's afraid of what's going to happen when the Family finds out. His father, my uncle, is a horrid man. I've no particular love for Alec, but it's best to think of him like an abused dog. He lashes out at strangers because his master lashes out at him." Her smile grew crooked, a little wicked. "In fact, he's like a dog in many ways."

'That's no excuse,' Sebastien thought, but she was smirking too.

But as they were filtering out of the class, Sebastien brushed against Gervin, who was still glowering with those bushy black eyebrows. "Our student aide, Newton Moore, does paid tutoring," she murmured to Gervin. "He taught me a spell, and I found his explanation to be very clear. Perhaps you'd prefer working with him?" Alec Gervin could afford it, and from what she'd learned, Newton could use the coin.

Gervin scowled at her suspiciously, but she was already pushing past him.

On Tuesday, after Sympathetic Science, Sebastien stayed to talk to Professor Pecanty while the other students left.

"How can I help you, young man?" he asked in that lilting cadence that made everything he said sound like poetry.

"I've got a couple of questions about transmogrification." Pecanty nodded, so she jumped right in. "Does it actually matter the conditions when components are gathered? What's the difference between morning dew gathered before the sun rises or afterward? Or from morning dew and a bit of steam from a boiling cauldron?"

Pecanty's genial smile fell away, and he seemed to puff up a bit. "I think you're a little too young to be questioning the achievements in understanding of all those that have come before you. Surely you can see that the intrinsic properties of morning dew are very different than steam off your cauldron? This is *Sympathetic* Science, Mr. Siverling. If you still wish to question the expertise of myself and the people who have filled our library with books on the subject, please wait to do so until you are at least a Master of Sorcery."

Sebastien's shoulders tightened, and her chin rose involuntarily, even though she knew it wasn't a good idea to challenge a professor who was so obviously unimpressed with her. "Well, what about the different types of transmogrification? Professor Lacer mentioned it. Some of it's copying a template, and some of it uses ideas that are so vague as to be ungraspable. Are the delineations between different types of transmogrification officially recognized? I've never heard anyone talking about that."

"Transmogrification is all the same. If you do not understand, it is because your foundation is patchy and weak. Understanding builds upon previous learning and enough practice that the *feel* becomes instinctual. If you are too impatient to put in the long-term effort without succumbing to your need to force the world into your little boxes of classification and order, you will never progress past petty questions that have no answers. Go now, young man, and try to see the beauty in the book of poems I assigned, rather than analyzing every word for its technical definition. Believe me, this type of questioning will not serve you well in my class, or in this craft." He waved his hand at her and turned away dismissively.

Sebastien's heart was beating loud in her ears, and she felt her cheeks tingle with blood. Clenching her jaw hard to keep herself from speaking, she strode out of the classroom and up to the second floor, where she'd recently found an out-of-the-way classroom that had at one point been used as a supply room for the elective art classes. There was an old slate lap table with a carved Circle that had once been an artifact whose magic kept the rain and elements off the writing surface. Now, it was empty of energy and entirely mundane—which was probably why it had been abandoned. It was the perfect aid to help her practice her fabric-slicing spell on one of the walls. She left behind light gouges in the white stone until her anger had dimmed and cooled to embers rather than a fire devouring her rationality.

Panting, she put away the small folding table and set up a spell to practice sympathetic divination. *'Time to find my blood.'*

12

REVERSE SCRYING

SEBASTIEN
Month 12, Day 15, Tuesday 12:30 p.m.

SEBASTIEN DIDN'T WORRY about someone walking in on her. There had been enough dust in this room to tell her that it was rarely used and likely unmonitored, and she had locked the door just in case. She'd cleared out a little corner in the back of the room to practice in. She couldn't practice this divination in the dorms behind the paltry protection of her curtain, or in the public practice rooms, after all. It was illegal for anyone besides the coppers to sympathetically scry for a human.

As always, she started with the Circle. Divination was finicky. For power, the spell required special candles infused with scented oils and dyed certain colors, rather than a coal brazier or her much more convenient lantern. She set them evenly around the main Circle's edges, in the component Circles meant for them.

Then she placed the map, which covered the entirety of Gilbratha. It was fairly accurate everywhere except the Mires, which were haphazard and frequently changing, a sea of shanty houses built out of old wood and white stone stolen from the dwindling remains of the southern white cliffs.

The spell had a few prerequisites, and in some ways was more like alchemy than the actively cast sorcery she practiced in her classes. Actively cast spells would dissipate as soon as she released her Will, but with ritual magic, spells were not controlled by the Word of a spell array, but woven into and absorbed by the matter they were bound to through the practice of the ritual. The magic created a kind of multi-dimensional weave with its host, which was self-sustaining enough to be semi-permanent. This was what allowed potions to work months or sometimes even years after they had been brewed. As a trade-off, it took way longer and lost about a third of the energy immediately, with the remaining magical effect slowly degrading after that.

Sebastien used some small pieces of dirt, rock, and slivers of bark that she had collected from a relatively wide section of the city and carefully labeled. She placed them on the map as precisely as possible, corresponding with the places she'd obtained them, then added a handful of tent spikes, for their concept of anchoring.

She dipped her finger in the wax of the nearest candle, suppressing a wince at the heat of it. The wax quickly cooled as she drew her hand away, creating a film over her skin. She repeated the process with the other five candles until her fingertip had a thick coating of layered wax. Concentrating hard on her memory of each anchor spot in the city, she first touched a tent spike, then, as if pulling a thread from it to the map, she drew a hexagram around one of the pebbles. As she moved, slowly and deliberately, as if the spell was an animal that might attack if she startled it, she chanted in a low voice. "To the earth you are bound. Weight of stone, iron, and root. Foot to foot, head to head, heart to heart. As the roots of a tree are reflected in its branches, be as one." The candles flickered, and the wax at her fingertip grew a little softer.

'No mistakes. Your Will is absolute,' she told herself, redoubling her concentration. She could have done this from outside the Circle, using a long stick to write instead of her finger, but the book she'd learned the spell from had cautioned against sloppiness, and she knew from her work with alchemy that any feeling of detachment would work against the purpose of the spell, which was all about creating sameness and connectivity, to the point that in the eyes of magic, one became the other.

Panting once she finished, she cleared away the dirt, bark, and stone, putting them back into their labeled bags. She would need to use them again any time she wanted to recast the spell, because with such a short ritual, and the map being a precreated item that hadn't been inherently changed during casting, the spell's weave would unravel and degrade quickly.

A single pea sized drop of mercury—the most expensive part of the spell —came next. Her cauldron was much too big for it, so she used a small glass bowl the size of a finger cymbal, large enough to hold only a single swallow. She placed it in the center of the map instead of over any of the flames, dropping the mercury from its vial into the bowl. "To search and seek. To hark and peek," she began, slowly and deliberately adding the ear of a bat, an eagle's eye, and a tiny glass lens from a child's toy. She stirred, six times six, with a rod made of dehydrated sprite honey mixed with the powder of a lava-pepper. The rod shrank with each stir, until she was holding only a stub, and within the little bowl sat a trembling, mirrorlike ball of spelled mercury, still only the size of a pea despite the amalgamated components.

The final step was the actual divination spell, which did require a spell array. Moving the map and mercury to the side, she drew it carefully and consulted the book to make sure she'd not forgotten anything. She'd already studied the spell to ensure she fully understood the purpose of each glyph, numerological symbol, and word, but now she reviewed them all again. The map went back into the Circle, and a tiny dot of the mercury was placed in its center, with the rest set aside for future attempts. She caught the tip of a little bundle of dried herbs on fire in the nearest candle, snuffed the flame immediately, then waved the bundle about to let the herb smoke settle through the air.

Remembering how she'd seen Liza work at one point, Sebastien drew a hexagram with the smoke, then glyphs for *"key"* which could also be interpreted as *"answer,"* and *"discovery."*

Using one of her own hairs—which was much less likely to have people panicking and calling for the coppers than a drop of blood if she were to be discovered—she began to cast, focusing on how desperately she needed to know exactly where her missing blood was.

The most difficult part of the map-based divination spell was that she lacked the skill to work past the huge beacon that was the blood in her own body.

That was the downside to scrying for her own blood.

The upside was that if it was someone else's blood, with a weaker sympathetic connection, a sorcerer as unskilled and untalented at divination as she was might not have been able to successfully cast the spell at all.

The first couple of times she attempted it, the tiny dot of spelled mercury rolled across the map to the University, and more specifically, the western edge of the Citadel where the abandoned storage room was. She was scrying herself. "Yay," she said dully, sagging back as she released her draw on the special candles.

It would have been a small silver lining if her ward had activated, because she could have found a way to make that useful, but there had only been a gentle tingle in her back before it fell silent. Apparently, it was impossible to cast a divination spell on herself while simultaneously warding one off, as they were strictly opposing thought processes, and her mind couldn't split into two independent consciousnesses. This meant that she couldn't simply cast a scrying spell on herself whenever she wanted to sneak around without being noticed.

When the pin-head sized dot of spelled mercury lost its shininess—and its magic—she gave up. She only had so many attempts before she would need to buy more, and *"try harder"* did not seem to be the answer.

More research revealed a solution to the first problem. She found the answer, ironically, in a book that leaned more toward history than magical instruction. Liza had, perhaps, mentioned her participation in the Haze War for a reason.

It was the perfect example of how necessity—war—stimulated invention. The war had started over greed for Lenore's celerium mines and the foreign invention of an improved method for divination-based, long-range attacks. Silva Erde and several smaller countries had banded together against Lenore. This led to the counter-invention of an anti-divination fog. This "haze" was spread over the tactical areas and battlefields, blocking the targeting ability of enemy long-range attacks. The haze inspired the creation of a biological warfare philtre that spread on the air and thrived in the low-light of the haze. Of course, this led to an immediate improvement in wearable air-filtering and skin-protecting artifacts. Stronger divination spells began to filter through the haze. Reverse-scrying spells were vastly improved, making them much more dangerous for the distant attackers, who could be pinpointed through their own attacks and attacked in turn. Eventually, exploring the principles behind how the haze actually worked, Lenore discovered the existence of divination rays and revolutionized the anti-divination field.

While the concepts were mentioned, many of the spells themselves were still either confidential or beyond her access level, but the basics of reverse-scrying were available freely, since the concept far predated the recent military improvements.

As the book suggested, once a diviner sent out feelers, it was much harder to stop someone following those feelers back to the source. Sebastien could piggyback on the searching magic of the coppers' attempt to scry for her, thus overriding the pull of the blood in her own body to find the few drops they were using.

Of course, there were wards to stop that kind of thing, but apparently, they were expensive, prone to failing, and generally not useful for domestic law enforcement, because they had no need to disguise the fact that they were scrying for you. If you found and approached them, it only made their arrest of you easier.

Sebastien couldn't practice that variation successfully until they made an attempt to find her at a convenient time, but she still tried to increase her facility with divination spells. Holding off the scrying attempt at the same time as tracking it back would be very difficult, and if she wasn't prepared, either of the spells might fail. If the divination failed, she only risked Will-strain, but if the divination-diverting ward failed, she might actually be caught. The ward wasn't strong enough to hold off the coppers without her active participation.

The only reason she could—hypothetically—do both at once was because, first, the ward handled most of the actual work for her, only needing her to feed it more power rather than control the spell. Secondly, the ward against divination was shielding against *someone else*, which was the same target she was attempting to find. It was like two people hiding in a dark forest, both trying to find the other, which was conceptually possible, as opposed to attempting to move and be still at the same time, which...wasn't. Hopefully it worked. If it didn't, she was unlikely to kill anyone except herself, as long as she cast it in a suitably secluded area.

She set aside most of her free time all week to practice in the abandoned storage room, prepared to wake early and slip back out to eat breakfast before her first class started.

Her ire with Professor Pecanty flared back to life when she returned to Modern Magics on Wednesday, but she suppressed it.

Professor Burberry used a dab of hair-loss potion on the mice they had used to practice the color-changing transmogrification spell, then used another potion to help the fur regrow.

Some students' mice grew colored fur, somehow permanently, inherently changed by the spell. Most regrew the same solid white as before. At the place where the potions had been used, Sebastien's grew back a little splotch of white hair, which stood out starkly on its otherwise rainbow-colored pelt. She felt the uncomfortable prickling of shame as she stared at it. '*Maybe if Professor Pecanty would actually help me understand, I could do it better,*' she snarled to herself.

Professor Burberry handed out contribution points to those who'd managed to create truly permanent change.

Ana nudged Sebastien, giving her a small smile. "Don't be too harsh on yourself, Sebastien. I'm sure you can get it, if you try again. It's not as if your grade will be marked down just because you didn't manage to imbue the entire mouse with enhanced properties. You did change the color of the fur, and you did it perfectly."

Sebastien shook her head, and Ana looked like she might keep trying to comfort her, or encourage her, or whatever she was trying to do, but then Westbay came up holding his flower-patterned rodent and distracted her. "Do you think the colors would pass down to a child if I bred it with a white mouse? Or what if we bred a red mouse and a green mouse? Do we get brown mice babies?" He reached into his pocket and fed the creature a little piece of bread roll that he'd taken from breakfast.

"I don't know, but I wonder if brightly colored rabbits or other docile creatures might make a good gift product for children," Ana said. "My little sister would probably love a bright pink mouse."

Sebastien, with what she thought was incredible self-control, did not throw herself into practicing the color-change spell outside of class. Her focus remained on preparing for the reverse-scrying.

The only side project she allowed herself was making sure she had a dozen ink spells drawn on parchment and ready to go. With the fire-retardant seaweed paper, she actually didn't have to use her blood to keep the paper from burning up along the lines of the spell array. Sebastien had realized, after all the research into divination she'd been doing, how *incredibly stupid* her plan had been. By removing her blood from the barrier of her skin, she had made it theoretically possible for the coppers to find *it*, even if they couldn't find *her*.

'*How did the coppers not find me already? Do they know where I am and are just toying with me for some reason? Maybe they want me to lead them to my accomplices.*' But if that were the case, why would they have continued their attempts, over and over? She wasn't entirely oblivious, and she'd noticed nothing suspicious, no one watching her or going through her things.

Perhaps they hadn't found her yet, after all. If so, that might have something to do with how she kept her school supplies nearby constantly, and the divination-diverting ward had some minimal area-of-effect capabilities that affected perception around her. They had no way to find that blood without finding her, and she was *very thoroughly* warded. If she had left the inkwell or a paper spell with her blood far enough away that the coppers could conceivably find it *instead* of her...or if they had been using a spell with different divination outputs that would give them information *only* on the inkwell instead of broad information that included her...

Maybe they had been having the same trouble as her with scrying for anything small past the huge beacon of her body, but she didn't know enough about how the ward worked to count on that. With most wards, whatever was behind them would be completely blocked off, and that would only make it more likely for their magic to focus on the unwarded traces of her.

In shuddering horror, she had destroyed the whole inkwell along with the small paper spell array she'd created previously, then gone through all her things casting the shedding-disintegration spell over and over, ensuring not even a drop of blood-laced ink, or hair, or anything remained.

When her racing heart had calmed, she tried to think of any other critical mistakes she might have made. She held a trembling hand to her lips, holding in a tremulous laugh. With her track record, she probably had made more than one, and just didn't realize it.

'*The blood print vows I made, what about those? Could the coppers scry for those, even if they cannot find me?*' She had a copy of each, but so did Katerin and Liza. Liza's would definitely be behind wards, and she was pretty sure Katerin's would, too, but her own copies might not be safe. They were hidden with the stolen book at Dryden Manor. Of course, the spell did have restrictions against any *use* of the blood without one of the parties having broken their vow, but she wasn't sure if that also acted as a ward against divination. She resolved to make sure Dryden Manor was properly warded, and if not, learn to set up small anti-divination wards herself. Luckily, that was a small amount of blood, barely a drop, and would give off a much smaller beacon than the amount she'd added to the ink or the mass of her own body.

When she had calmed enough that her hand didn't shake, she laid down spell arrays, in ink only, on her seaweed paper. She made some of them large enough that she had to fold up the spell array to get it to fit inconspicuously within her bag, while others were small and ready to be used immediately, only requiring that she place their components for rapid casting. She'd decided on fourteen simple spells that she thought could help in a variety of emergency situations.

In the middle of the night, as if they were trying to catch her off guard, the coppers scried for her again. The prickling of cold needles in her back woke her as her ward went to work before she was even conscious.

'*The Citadel will probably be locked at this time of night, and besides, I don't have any time to waste.*' It wasn't as safe as her abandoned classroom, but instead she went to one of the more inconvenient bathrooms on the dorm's second floor, where there were fewer students. She checked the stalls rapidly, then shoved a wedge of wood underneath the door from the inside to keep it from opening. She'd taken the wedge from the door of a random classroom days before, for situations specifically like this.

She had all the components for the mapped divination spell, but casting the prerequisite magic on the map, which had worn off since her earlier practice, was torturously slow and difficult, with much of her attention split toward warding off the coppers' attention. The reverse-scry itself might have actually been easier than the setup, being more congruent in concept and intent.

She had barely finished anchoring the map and was only a couple of seconds into the reverse-scry when the five disks embedded in her back calmed, the pressure easing.

Rather than sigh in relief, Sebastien slumped forward, letting out a low groan of defeat. '*Did they sense what I was doing? Is that why they stopped? But it was so soon! The mercury had barely even started to tremble!*'

She paced for a while, her reverse-scrying spell waiting in the stall farthest from the door, some part of her hoping that the coppers would try again.

They did not.

Reluctantly accepting this, Sebastien quenched the candles, packed up the spell components, and tried her best to go back to sleep.

The coppers didn't try again over the next couple of days, and she worried that they really had sensed her attempt to find her blood and become more wary. It was...disheartening, but she continued to practice, just in case. She didn't have time to make real progress with the paper design, or practice any of the spells until they were second nature, so she focused on those she'd been long familiar with, or which she was practicing in Professor Burberry's Modern Magics and her other classes. Having them ready in her satchel made her feel a little more prepared, even if they weren't particularly powerful.

On Thursday morning, she got a little too engrossed with practice in the abandoned classroom on the second floor and forgot to stop for breakfast.

She hurried back to the dorms to put the divination components away in the chest at the foot of her bed before History of Magic. Professor Ilma always jumped into the lecture right away, and Sebastien would miss out if she was even a minute late.

In her hurry, she wasn't paying attention to where she was walking, and ran right into Tanya, their female student liaison and Newton's counterpart, outside the dorm as they both turned a corner.

Tanya was surprising solid, and rather than falling or stumbling, she spun around to snatch the spelled paper bird she had dropped out of the air before it could flutter feebly away. She didn't bother to stop, simply snapping, "Watch where you're walking, Siverling. You could put a lady's shoulder out."

"I'm sorry!" Sebastien called after her.

Tanya waved an uncaring hand in the air without looking back, her head bowed to read whatever message had been folded inside the spelled piece of paper.

As Sebastien grabbed the homework she'd left in her trunk and emptied her school bag of the bulky divination components, she heard the shuffle of hard leather on stone. She whipped her head around to see Westbay slouching against the entrance of her little stone cubicle, his chestnut hair perfect and his grey eyes staring out over the seemingly constant bags of fatigue under them. She wondered idly if the condition was genetic, because he slept almost nine hours every night.

She shoved the lid of her chest shut before turning to him. "What do you want, Westbay? Shouldn't you be getting to class?" The rest of the dorm was almost completely empty, except for a few students rushing off to their first class. Considering the sprawling expanse of the University grounds, they were already likely to be late unless they ran.

He shrugged. "It's just History of Magic. A different section than whatever class you're in. My professor won't even realize I'm gone. Say, have you read any more of those Aberford Thorndyke stories I lent you? I got the latest issue delivered. I can pass it on once I'm finished, if you're up to speed on the timeline."

Sebastien was torn between rolling or narrowing her eyes. '*He's not one to skip classes so nonchalantly. Is he truly that desperate for someone to talk about his little detective stories, or is he fishing? How long was he standing there?'* She reached for the curtain beside the opening to her dormitory cubicle. *'Best to be calculated in my response, let him feel comfortable enough to give himself away.'* "Sure, but I'm not finished with the stack you gave me before, so there's no—" Her tongue stumbled to a halt and her eyes widened for a moment before she controlled her expression.

Westbay looked at her with confusion.

"I just remembered something. Homework. Sorry, Westbay, no time to talk. You should go to class even if your professor isn't noting your attendance. History is important." With that rushed tumble of words, she pulled the curtain shut right in his face.

She was being scried.

As she pulled the components for the reverse-scrying spell back out again, she listened to Westbay's footsteps retreat. With hands quickened by worry, she pulled the components for the reverse-scrying spell back out again. It seemed she might not be getting to class after all.

After checking to make sure she was alone, Sebastien carefully laid everything out on the floor of her cubicle. In a way, the timing was lucky. Many of the most time-consuming parts of the divination were in the prerequisite spells cast on the components like the drop of mercury and the map. Without being an artifact itself, the magic on the map would wear off somewhat quickly, but it was still ready to go at the moment.

As quickly as she could, she drew the spell array, then placed the candles, the map, and the dot of mercury, along with a bronze mirror she'd polished herself and a few other components that would help her augment the target of the divination. She dabbed a bit of herb smoke around and began to scry. *Carefully.*

It was more difficult than she'd expected. Much more. It wasn't that she didn't have the power, though that was part of the problem. It was her concentration. The clarity and stability of her Will, for one of the first times in recent memory, proved unable to meet her demands. *'Maybe it's because I am so exceptionally untalented with divination,'* she thought bitterly.

Rather than stiffening, she relaxed and controlled her breathing, routing every last drop of energy and control to her Will.

A part of her attention went toward feeding the divination-diverting ward in her back, deflecting attention and slipping away from the prying tendrils of the rival sorcerer. That part was easier, and didn't require the same focus that reaching out through the city for a tiny missing piece of herself did. She couldn't get too focused on the spell, or her ward would grow weak enough that they might find her, but splitting energy and concentration like this was not something that came naturally to humans.

It was like trying to play two different songs on the piano at the same time.

The reverse-divination was difficult and complicated, while empowering the ward took only a couple of plinking notes, but it was still almost impossible to keep them going together. Trying to cast two actual spells at the same time would have taken the equivalent of four hands, and while she was reluctant to say that it was *impossible*, it would require both spells to be merged into a single, more complicated spell with multiple outputs, rather than two separate spell arrays.

The dot of spelled mercury moved over the map, and at first her insides tightened with frustration, because it was just finding *her* again, but then it rolled right over the spot where it usually stopped.

The mercury settled at a spot she judged to be slightly northwest of the student dorms.

She held the spell for a couple more seconds, staring at the map. Then she let the magic go, shoving everything haphazardly into her trunk, uncaring of the hot candle wax spilling onto her belongings. She didn't bother with a locking spell. It was too different from the magic of the planar ward, and she didn't want to risk failure.

'My blood is at the University.'

She shook her head. 'But the coppers have it, don't they? I expected to find it at their station, or maybe at the prison, or even a black site where they hold important evidence. So why is it at Eagle Tower?' She hurried from the room and out of the building, moving with purpose but without panic.

Eagle Tower was where the professors and high level students carried out their experiments, Sebastien knew.

'It could have been here all along, if my information was wrong from the beginning, but I don't think so. There's a reason the pressure is so much stronger this time. Did they give my blood to the University in hopes the diviners here could do a better job? The University does have a stake in my capture, after all. The book was theirs. But would the coppers give up such a big win? It seems unlikely. They're tenacious, as evidenced by the continued attempts to find me despite their ongoing failure.' She walked along the winding path into the cultivated woods between the Citadel and Eagle Tower. The scrying attempt was getting stronger as it went on, and had already been going for several minutes, longer and harder than most she'd fended off before.

'Maybe that's it. They've failed to find me and this is their next move. A better spell array than whatever they have access to at Harrow Hill, stronger thaumaturges, maybe more than one casting the spell at the same time. And they're close to me, even if they don't realize it. That'll make it easier. This is their sharper knife, their bigger hammer, the thing they pull out when they really need a win.'

As Eagle Tower appeared through the veil of trees, she looked up at the looming obelisk of pale stone. 'If they're powerful enough to find me, I have to stop them. Somehow.'

13

EAGLE TOWER

SEBASTIEN
Month 12, Day 17, Thursday 9:00 a.m.

SEBASTIEN HESITATED FOR A MOMENT, staring up at Eagle Tower. *'Should I just walk away? Avoid the risk and go to class along with everyone else, hide among the other students and hope no one notices me?'* Perhaps there was some future upside to walking away, but by the very nature of the future's inscrutability, she couldn't see what it might be. Besides, she knew she wasn't about to stop.

Moving ahead was risky, but it was also an opportunity. As long as she held off the scrying attempt—which was becoming increasingly difficult with every passing minute—the downsides seemed minor. At most, she'd be seen as a curious student hanging about where she shouldn't. Maybe she could learn something important.

So, after a pause to tuck her student token and restricted library pass into the pile of dirt and leaves at the base of the tree beside her, she kept walking. She didn't want the University to be able to look up the logs of everyone who had entered Eagle Tower and find her name on them. If necessary, she would wait outside for someone to leave and slip in behind them.

Luckily, it turned out the entranceway wasn't warded to require a student token like the Menagerie. She walked right in with no trouble.

The tower seemed even bigger on the inside, like a slightly smaller version of the Citadel. A hallway circled around between the single central room on each floor and the squat, wedge-shaped rooms on the outside. The walls of the inner room on each level were made of reinforced glass, so the researchers within were visible to those outside. Everything was brightly lit, giving off a feeling of clarity and cleanliness, and the researchers within would always be aware they were visible, which would help to keep their minds sharp and their experiments to the proper procedure.

It also let her see that she was on the wrong floor. As if designed to make navigating the tower more difficult, the entrance to the stairwell was all the way across the building from the main door, at the other end of the curving hallway. And when she got to it, the door was locked. *'This is where they require the student token,'* she realized. *'But it probably wouldn't even matter if I went back and got mine. I'm not authorized to be here in the first place.'*

Since the last time she'd been in a similar situation, two stories up on the outside of the crappy little inn her father had rented, she'd taken the time to study a few unlocking spells.

Unfortunately, the lock was visible to the rest of the floor, making it difficult to cast a spell without being seen, and she was a first term student at the University with a Conduit that could channel barely more than two hundred thaums. The mechanism was both physical and magical, and no doubt cast by someone much more experienced than her.

One of her paper utility arrays was an unlocking spell, and she could use the slate lap table she'd taken from the abandoned supply room to support the page and the necessary components at the level of the door handle, which would speed the process of casting. That was *if* she could manage to split her Will to cast that while still empowering the divination-diverting ward, which seemed both unlikely and foolish. Even if that weren't a problem, she'd still be doing it right in the middle of everyone, and she couldn't imagine that Eagle Tower didn't have protections against such rudimentary magic. There was a high chance she would fail and end up setting off an alarm.

She'd paused for a second too long, staring at the obstacle between her and where she needed to be, when a hand reached out from beside her and opened the door, holding it open for her.

She turned, looking a couple inches down into mercurial grey eyes. "Westbay," she said.

He waved her through.

She stepped into the stairwell, off-kilter. *'He followed me.'*

He waved a metal token at her. "You need one of these to get through the doors here. Maybe you didn't know, if you've never been in here before."

"And how do you have one?"

"I swiped it off some random person's desk."

On the other side of the doorway, within the silence of the stairwell, she stared at him. She didn't make fumbled excuses about why she was in Eagle

Tower. She didn't ask him what he was doing—before at the dorms or now—right here with her when they both should have been in class. Instead, she stared silently, as if she could read his micro expressions like letters strung together on a page, as if her eyes could pierce past his skull and see into his soul.

He stared back for a few seconds, but then his eyelids fluttered and he looked away. "I..." He swallowed. "I don't know what you're doing," he said, offering up answers to her unspoken questions under the pressure of her gaze. "I've just noticed some things lately. You've been...distracted. Or, focused, but just on something different. And I was curious. And...I thought maybe you could use some backup?" He grinned a little, slightly nervous but with a spark of real excitement. "Don't worry. No one saw me, and I dropped my student token under the same tree you did."

Sebastien had a sudden realization. *'He thinks we're in an Aberford Thorndyke story. This is just... He thinks we're about to have an* adventure.' She was simultaneously relieved that he wasn't a threat and irritated, almost offended, by his eager insouciance. *'Nothing matters to him, because there have never been any real stakes for him—nothing he stands to lose. Maybe he cannot even comprehend that it's not the same for everyone else.'*

"That's an interesting stealth spell you're casting," he said, squinting at her. "An artifact, or is it something esoteric? I can *feel* that you're here, but my eyes keep wanting to slip away, and I'm having trouble focusing mentally on you, like my thoughts want to slip around to the idea of you rather than the reality of you."

'If only that had kept you from following me, you thickheaded peacock.' She barely kept herself from snapping the words at him aloud. *'Or maybe he's more cunning than that, only trying to seem harmless so I will not realize the danger he poses to me.'*

"The spell is privileged information," she replied. "Family secret."

He seemed to recognize the hostility she couldn't keep from her voice. He raised his hands. "I won't pry. I was just curious. Everyone has their family secrets. But you *are* doing something?"

She was about to tell him to walk away and go read his detective magazines if he wanted a sense of excitement in his life when an upper-term student, a research assistant probably studying for Grandmastery, walked down the stairs.

He stopped and looked at the two of them. "Firsties? What are you doing here?"

Westbay stepped forward. "Bruner. I can't believe *you're* still here. What is it, your thirteenth term?"

Bruner narrowed his eyes. "Westbay? Oh. I—I didn't recognize you at first. Should have known by the eyes."

"No matter," Westbay said, waving his hand with regal nonchalance.

"We're on an errand for one of our professors. No time to chat at the moment, but maybe I'll see you at a Family gathering sometime."

Bruner's eyes widened, and then he bowed.

Westbay grabbed Sebastien by the arm and began to drag her up the stairs.

Bruner turned and bowed again as they climbed past him, stammering. "Oh, yes, definitely. I would be honored to attend a Westbay gathering. At your convenience. Thank you, Westbay, good to see you."

They left Bruner behind, and Sebastien swallowed the scathing words she had been about to say. "Useful," she admitted instead, grudgingly.

Westbay grinned. "Thank you. The Family name does come in handy from time to time. Now why are we here?"

Sebastien eyed him with consideration. *'He's irritating and spoiled, at best, but he hasn't told anyone about the accident in the defense building or my subsequent Will-strain. I still owe him a favor. Perhaps he doesn't want to get rid of an asset before it can bear fruit. And as he's just shown, he can be useful, through no merit of his own.'*

Aloud, she said, "No questions. In fact, don't talk at all." She looked around before motioning impatiently for Westbay to open the door for her.

"Where are we g—" He snapped his mouth shut halfway through the question, then lifted his hand to cover a smile that made him look like a child who'd just stolen a cookie from the jar and was reveling in the thrill of it. He tried to put on a serious face, but the excitement kept peeking through.

"You're an idiot," she muttered.

A spark of ire flared in his eyes, but slipped away just as quickly as it had come in favor of a rueful smirk. "And you're a porcupine," he muttered when her back was turned.

With saintlike self-control, Sebastien ignored him. She might even have found him harmlessly amusing if the situation wasn't so critical. She wasn't sure if it was her imagination, but as she climbed the stairs the pressure on her divination-diverting ward seemed to grow, until it felt like she was pressing up against some barrier to heaven with every step.

She discovered what she was looking for on the fourth floor of the tower.

It was busier than the floors below, filled with both coppers and a good handful of the faculty. The chair of the History department was there, along with some professors she was pretty sure were from the Divination department. Within the central, glass-walled room, a handful of coppers with sorcery experience were aiding a trio of prognos with the scrying spell. They stood around a huge Circle engraved into the marble tiles of the floor in precious metals and gems, with the type of components Sebastien had only ever read about in books powering the spell.

Her eyes flicked around, taking in the University staff and group of coppers watching this from the hallway. Both groups stood separately. Those from the University were tense, though some did a better job of hiding it than others, and although the coppers beside them weren't hostile, they were far from relaxed.

The University staff didn't want the coppers there.

'But why not? That doesn't make sense. One would think they'd be happy that the coppers have a better chance of finding me with the more powerful scrying array. Except there's some sort of conflict of interest here, but I have no idea what it could be about. What exactly is written in that book?'

Her observation and contemplation were finished in the mere two seconds that had passed since she'd opened the stairwell door.

She moved toward the closed door of a room on the outside of the hallway. Someone's office, currently empty, which she knew because no light came through under the door. She closed the door behind herself and Westbay and turned to the window that showed a view of the hallway and central room. Moving slowly, she peeked around the edge of the drawn curtain.

The pressure on her ward actually seemed to have ebbed slightly, but it hadn't gone away.

'I made a mistake,' she admitted to herself. *'There's nothing I can do here. But I'll watch and wait. Maybe…there will be an opportunity if I'm clever enough to notice it. If I can wait them out, maybe I could see where they keep the blood, if they take it back with them or perhaps even leave it here. Though it would be considerably easier if Westbay weren't looking over my shoulder.'*

"That's a divination spell," Westbay murmured. "Who are they looking for?"

She didn't respond.

He smoothed a nonexistent hair back from his face. "I have a spell that can enhance hearing. Maybe we could…listen in?"

That was enough to gain her attention, despite the increasing strain of empowering her ward against scrying.

His eyes slid off her. Without waiting for further response, he dug into the couple dozen pockets built into his suit vest and jacket for his Conduit and a writing implement.

Two minutes later, he'd used a thin black stick to draw a spell array on both palms. He didn't use any components, shaking his head at her offer of the small lantern she carried in her bag. "It barely uses any power. The warmth of my hand will be more than enough. This spell is all about… control." Somewhat comically, he placed his hands behind his ears, cupping and swiveling them like he was pretending to be a dog.

She caught the faint smell of honey. *'Are the components part of the array itself? Maybe honey for capturing sound and charcoal for filtering?'* She was curious, but it would be rude to inquire or study the spell array too closely. Some magic was a closely guarded secret passed down within families or from master to apprentice, and Westbay had just refrained from questioning her about the spell he thought she was casting to avoid notice.

"It enlarges the surface area that can capture incoming sounds, filters them, and lets me artificially focus my hearing," he murmured, wincing when he turned back to the hallway. "Loud." After a few seconds, his expression settled into fascination. "They're chanting. For the spellcasting. It's advanced. I haven't heard anything like it."

Sebastien straightened her shoulders and settled her mind. The Conduit in her off hand was flush with energy, the five Circles in the flesh of her back were cold and filled with the sensation of needles, and she imagined that within half an hour she would start feeling faint from blood loss. *'How long can this go on?'* It was becoming increasingly obvious that she was the metaphorical frog being slowly boiled alive, too stupid to realize the water was heating.

"Someone in the hallway just said something about the Raven Queen," Westbay said. He stared blankly for a moment, and then his head turned slowly toward Sebastien. "They're scrying for her...right now?"

She had a sudden vision of herself in jail, trying to convince the coppers as Sebastien Siverling that she had no idea why Siobhan Naught's blood kept leading back to her. *'Would they believe me, if I pretended to have met the Raven Queen and had my blood stolen by the "evil sorceress" to use as a red herring and lead the investigation in the wrong direction?'*

She shook her head. *'No, I'm sure they have wards against untruth, and obviously they have access to more than one prognos. They'd know right away if I tried to lie. And with enough reason to look into me, they'd tear my entire backstory apart.'*

She tried to estimate how many thaums of heat and blood she was channeling. *'Close to two hundred already. According to what Liza told me, they must be channeling many times that. There are so many of them, they can probably keep going well beyond what I can handle. Sticking around is no longer feasible, leaving me two viable options. I can ask Westbay to borrow his Conduit, which is surely rated much higher than mine, or I can run now and hope that I'm far enough away by the time their scrying spell breaks through my ward that they cannot catch me.'*

She felt flushed beneath her jacket and scarf, but resisted the urge to pace back and forth between walls that felt like they were closing in. *'If I borrow Westbay's Conduit, he'll wonder why I need it. He might connect the dots. If I run, at least I have the gold I sewed into the lining of my clothing and boots.'* There might still be time to get her things from the dorms. If she hired a carriage, she could be halfway out of Gilbratha before they found her. If it turned out she could, somehow, hold out longer than they could, she could simply return as if all was well. *'Or...should I attack Westbay and take his Conduit? If I could keep him from sounding the alarm until I'd escaped, I'd at least have a Conduit powerful enough to handle my Will. It would buy me a few more minutes, maybe half an hour.'* The thought made her feel a small prick of guilt. He was often irritating, but he hadn't done anything to truly deserve that. '*His family could afford to buy him twenty more Conduits without even cutting into the budget for their next high society ball. It wouldn't hurt him at all for me to take it, except for a blow to his pride,*' she reasoned.

She was considering it, thinking about how she might have him follow her back to the dorms, steal his Conduit, and then tie him up in one of the bathroom stalls before escaping, when someone she hadn't expected to see opened the door to the fourth floor.

14

SAVED BY THE ENEMY

SEBASTIEN
  Month 12, Day 17, Thursday 9:05 a.m.

TANYA CANELO, one of their student liaisons, looked around. She was breathing a little too hard, as if she'd run to Eagle Tower and up the stairs. She didn't notice Westbay or Sebastien in the small side office, her eyes landing instead on the spellcasters in the tower's central room. She stared at them for a few seconds with narrow eyes, then looked to the crystal wall clock on the other side of the hallway.

'Why is she here?'

Tanya touched her jacket pocket, then spun back around to the stairwell, hurrying to one of the upper floors, seemingly unnoticed by anyone else.

Sebastien's mind was grasping at mist, feeling that she was missing something, but too occupied by feeding the planar divination-diverting ward to bring her full mental capacity to bear.

She'd turned to tell Westbay they should leave, but was barely halfway through the sentence when the first screeching wail of a siren reached them. That distant siren was quickly followed by others, all sounding in concert, melding into one city-wide warning.

Westbay's head jerked back and he yanked his hands away from his ears, dropping the sound-enhancing spell. "Again? It hasn't even been two weeks since the last one."

A few seconds later, the pressure of the divination spell searching for

Sebastien disappeared. She felt a relief that not even the sound of the rogue magic sirens could ruin. Gilbratha's coppers were used to this, and prepared for it. They would handle the danger, and even if they failed, she was safe inside a heavily warded building, manned by people dozens of times more powerful than her. As long as the danger wasn't inside with them, she would most likely be safe.

Some of the people outside grumbled, some were obviously worried, but none hesitated to leave. Most headed downstairs, while a few of the staff went up instead, probably to man the watchtower and magical weapons set into the highest level of the tower.

A handful of coppers tried to join them in going up, but were rebuffed.

'There's conflict between the University and the coppers, beyond just wanting to catch me,' Sebastien realized. 'The University doesn't want to give the coppers access to their power at all. I didn't expect that. I thought the University was happily subject to the Thirteen Crowns, even if they had their own power structure.'

"This is terrible timing," Westbay said, scowling at the emptying central room. "They can't keep casting during a citywide emergency. I'm sure they would have caught her otherwise. There's a shelter in the first basement level. We'll have to join them." He brightened, moving toward the doorway. "Hey, maybe they'll talk about the investigation. We might learn something interesting."

Sebastien reached out and stopped Westbay from opening the door.

He turned to look at her curiously, able to focus on her normally now that the anti-divination ward was deactivated.

After thinking it over, she stepped back. "Never mind. Go ahead, then."

His eyes narrowed. "Are you not coming?"

"I have something to do first."

"I'm staying too, then," he said stubbornly.

"Whatever set those sirens off could be anywhere. It might not be safe," she tried, hoping to appeal to his logic. "I would wager the University has a higher incidence of Aberrants than the rest of the city. So many thaumaturges in a relatively small area. You should know the numbers. Your Family runs the coppers, right?"

He swallowed, hesitated for a few seconds, but still shook his head. "I'm not going to miss out on this. The curiosity would kill me. Unless you promise to tell me what you find?"

She should have known an appeal to logic was futile. "I promise."

His expression of hope collapsed. "You're lying. You'll just pretend you didn't find anything interesting if I don't come along and see it with my own two eyes. Otherwise, you would have brought me in on whatever this is from the beginning." He sniffed with irritation.

'He's not a complete idiot.' Aloud, she said, "We're not friends, Westbay, and

I've yet to see you do anything useful except throw your Family's name around. I had no reason to bring you in on this."

His look of irritation deepened into something harsher. "Oh, so you knew about the door-pass tokens? You had a handy spell to eavesdrop on what they were saying? I may not be a once-in-a generation prodigy, but you shouldn't underestimate me. I'm staying." He crossed his arms over his chest.

Sebastien scraped her tongue against the inside of her teeth to keep herself silent, turning to look out the window for any signs of stragglers or danger. She wanted to see if she could get into the divination room. If the thaumaturges were careless, maybe they had left her blood behind with the rest of the components when they evacuated. Maybe she could simply walk in and steal it back. *'All my problems could be solved through a moment of serendipity. But if Westbay comes along, he'll see me take it. Maybe, if it's there, I can steal it when he has a moment of inattention. If necessary, I'll force that moment of inattention.'* Her shadow-familiar spell might do the trick, if she could stretch it around to draw his attention from the opposite direction. She didn't know any spells to safely knock someone unconscious, unfortunately.

Once Sebastien was sure that the above-ground levels of the tower had emptied, they opened the door and moved into the hallway, the small sounds of their movement drowned out by the piercing sirens. Sebastien moved to the glass wall beside the door of the divination room, her eyes flicking over the components within. She didn't see her blood immediately, but she wasn't quite sure what she was looking for, either. *'It could be in any kind of container, or they could even have used it to create a prerequisite spell component and it could be unrecognizable.'* She moved her eyes to the spell array engraved in the floor, hoping to tell where it would be placed by reading the spell's Word.

The stairwell door flew open, slamming into the wall.

Both Sebastien and Westbay spun around toward it like startled rabbits, jumping about a foot in the air. Westbay even let out a small, high-pitched scream.

Tanya Canelo stood in the open door, obviously as surprised to see them as they were to see her. She was still breathing heavily, either from exertion or fear. She recovered from the surprise first, frowning at them. "What are you two doing here?"

Sebastien and Westbay shared a look.

Tanya's frown turned into a scowl. "Don't you hear the sirens? Why haven't you evacuated?"

Damien stepped forward, raising his chin like the young aristocrat he was, his previous anxiousness seemingly forgotten. "We heard the sirens. We were in the Menagerie when they went off, and we ran, but it still took us a while to get back. Eagle Tower is the first building we came to, but everyone was already gone when we got here. We're trying to find the shelter."

Tanya seemed suspicious, walking toward them slowly. "It's underground. Like all the shelters."

"Really? I thought it would be on the top floor. That's where they keep the weapons, right?"

"Are you qualified to fight against something powerful enough to warrant the sirens?" Tanya scoffed, rolling her eyes. "If not, you should be sheltering underground with everyone else. You may be a Westbay, but you're only a firstie. Getting greedy for glory will only get you killed." She looked up at the ceiling. "Come on, we need to go."

Damien scowled and muttered, "I'm not greedy for glory," but Tanya ignored him, looking at the ceiling again.

Sebastien was reluctantly impressed with Damien's deflection. Tanya might not totally buy his story, but she didn't seem to suspect the real reason for their presence.

Tanya grabbed Sebastien's arm and tugged. "Come on. If you're not both in the shelters within the next sixty seconds, I'm giving you both a demerit," she snapped.

Sebastien resisted the urge to growl in frustration. They would have to *run* to get five floors down within a minute. But that wasn't what was really bothering her. Something was strange about the way Tanya was acting. The skin of the other woman's neck was fluttering under the force of her pulse. *'Why is she so anxious?'*

A pressure moved through the air, like the instant before lightning struck, and Sebastien's inherent sense of danger screamed at her.

Tanya's expression twisted with sudden horror, and she yanked forcefully on Sebastien's arm, hard enough to pull her off balance.

Sebastien leaped into the force of Tanya's pull, reaching out for Damien with her free arm. They all stumbled a few feet away from the central room, and Tanya managed to fumble open a door to one of the outer offices.

They were halfway through the doorway, jammed together and plugging the opening like a cork, when the tension in the air broke.

The wave of pressure hit first, hurling them into the office, where they slammed to the floor.

The ceiling collapsed next, from the center outward.

White stones and waves of visible magic tore down from the floor above, destroying the central divination room. Glass burst outward as the reinforced windows buckled. Aftershocks of sound and color swirled around and lashed out as the suddenly released magic of whatever had been in the room above collided with and destroyed the divination components.

Sebastien lay in a pile with Tanya and Damien for a few seconds, covering her head with her arms. When things had settled, she raised her head slowly, carefully, not sure whether the ringing in her ears was from the explosion or the sirens.

The air was full of dust, some cloudy sections shimmering unnaturally with neon colors.

She coughed violently, then pulled up her scarf over her mouth and nose, wiping away the tears streaming from her eyes.

The outer edge of the ceiling above was still intact, and the frame of the doorway they'd all gotten jammed in together had protected them from some of the falling debris.

Sebastien looked around for the source of the damage, up through the destroyed ceiling into the room above. She squinted, but saw nothing moving. '*Were the sirens set off by some hazard within the tower itself? I'd assumed the danger was more distant. Somewhere else on the University grounds at worst. Stupid of me. Careless.*'

Tanya crawled to her hands and knees, coughing and retching, completely disheveled and coated in dust. Her sleeve had been torn back, uncovering her forearm and revealing a fractured spiderwebbing of thin scars, still pink and relatively fresh.

Sebastien stared at the skin for a few seconds, frozen, until Tanya pulled her sleeve down again. "Are you both alright?" Tanya rasped.

Westbay groaned.

The ringing in Sebastien's ears was settling.

Westbay weakly held up his hand and gave them a thumbs-up.

"No serious injuries. We need to move," Sebastien said, pulling him to his feet and then offering a hand to Tanya. "Whatever caused that could still be around." She looked up at the hole in the ceiling again, then over the fallen debris, searching for signs of danger.

Tanya let out another retching cough, but was stable as she regained her feet. She shook her head, holding her sleeve over her mouth to block the dust. "The floor above was being used for some alchemy experiments," she shouted over the noise of the sirens. "They must not have properly settled and stored whatever they were working on, and it exploded. The fumes could be hazardous, and the ceiling might not be sound any more. It could still fall on us."

"No breathing, no getting crushed by falling stones," Westbay croaked. "Got it."

Sebastien gave a last look toward the destroyed divination room, but gave up on the idea of searching it now.

Westbay waved to Tanya to lead the way. When the other woman's back was turned, he gave Sebastien a searching look.

Sebastien ignored it, staring at Tanya's back and moving down the stairwell as quickly as she could. A few pieces of rock had hit her legs, and she could feel the bruises already beginning to form.

When they arrived at the first basement level, which had a huge vault door made of iron on the far side of the room, Tanya knocked on the door and showed both her student token and the tower token that allowed her to open the doors. After a few seconds, someone on the other side unlocked the door and it swung open slowly, with a loud creak of untended hinges.

A professor scowled out at them, and Sebastien saw that there was a second door behind the first one, which led to a small room between them and the emergency shelter. 'Smart. It's not so easy to break through twice.'

The professor looked them over suspiciously, taking in their dreadful state. "Canelo. Were you attacked?"

Tanya shook her head. "There was an explosion. I don't think it's related to the sirens. Something on the fifth floor went wrong, collapsed the whole floor. I suspect someone was in too much of a hurry to evacuate to properly settle and clean up whatever they were working on."

"It's been almost ten minutes since the sirens went off."

Tanya rolled her eyes and jerked a thumb toward Sebastien and Westbay. "These two were out in the Menagerie. They got here late and didn't know where the shelter was. I had to retrieve them, and then...well." She gestured to herself and the signs of being caught in the alchemy explosion.

"No signs of Will-strain or other oddness in either of them?" the professor asked.

Tanya shook her head. "They're fine. A little too curious, maybe, and as stupid as most first-term students, but nothing abnormal. I'll make sure to *thoroughly* educate them on the proper procedures for evacuation when this is over," she said, giving the both of them a look promising punishment.

The professor nodded, and then an almost invisible wave pulsed from the door through them, a ripple in the air that prickled against Sebastien's skin. She thought it was the same revealing or maybe nullification spell that came standard in a copper's battle wand.

The professor turned and opened the inner door for them, apparently satisfied with the results of the spell.

The people within were tense, and immediately started to question the three new arrivals about the source of the sound and rumbling they'd all felt.

Tanya explained again, and those upper level research-aid students that had been on the fifth floor paled under the glares of everyone else, stammering to make excuses for themselves.

Sebastien took a seat in the corner of the large shelter, which, rather than being directly one floor down from the rest of Eagle Tower, was *attached* to the underground tower level like a component Circle might be attached to the main one in a spell array.

Damien joined her, a slight frown on his face. Thankfully, he remained silent.

Sebastien's mind worked swiftly as she watched the crowd, piecing together the things she hadn't even realized were clues until she saw the final pieces of the puzzle. *'Tanya got a note from someone, just before the coppers started scrying for me. She was in a hurry. When she got to the tower, she looked at the clock before heading to the fifth floor. She didn't evacuate with everyone else.'*

She fell into speculation, reminding herself not to stare at Tanya too suspiciously.

There was some worry among the others that another Aberrant had spawned, but a while later the professor who'd opened the door for them got a message through one of the spell arrays engraved into it. He threw back his head with a loud sigh and massaged his temples. "It was a false alarm," he announced loudly, the frustration clear in his voice. "*Someone* was careless enough to get Eagle Tower blown up for a *false alarm.*" He glared pointedly at the people from the fifth floor.

The whole room filled with grumbles of frustration and relief, and they filtered out.

Sebastien looked for Tanya in the crowd, tracking the other woman's dusty blonde hair as she headed toward the dorms. Not just anyone could set off the rogue magic sirens, and from the things she'd pieced together from reports and rumors of Aberrants, it wasn't a simple process that could be triggered by accident. *'That is simply too much of a coincidence.'*

As if noticing Sebastien's eyes on her, Tanya moved closer to them and said, "You should both probably go to the infirmary and get checked out."

"I'm fine," Sebastien said.

Tanya rolled her jaw with frustration. "Even if you're not hurting too badly now, that could just be the shock. Something in the air could have been poisonous. At best, you both likely will need a calming potion. You were just caught in an alchemy experiment that could have killed you." Having done her duty in warning them, Tanya strode off toward the dorms, where she had a room with an attached bathroom to herself.

'Tanya looked at the clock right before the sirens went off,' Sebastien repeated to herself. *'Did she know? Was it planned?'* She looked at her palm. The thin scars where she'd fallen on glass during the warehouse attack were almost invisible. She'd been extra careful to heal them completely before anyone had a chance to see them, just in case.

She'd recognized similar scarring on Tanya's arm. Except Tanya's scarring had obviously been deeper. The pattern matched what Sebastien imagined a wound from a glass ball exploding and embedding its pieces into the flesh might look like.

'Tanya was the sorcerer who attacked Oliver's warehouse. Which means Tanya is working with the Morrows. And she just blew up the divination room to keep me from being caught. Or, more accurately, to keep Siobhan Naught, the Raven Queen, from being caught.'

15

FAULTY DEDUCTIONS

DAMIEN
Month 12, Day 17, Thursday 9:00 a.m.

DAMIEN HAD NOTICED Sebastien growing distant over the last week or so, refusing to join him and his friends in their morning study group even when Damien invited him personally. Sebastien was often missing from the dorms, and hadn't been occupying his regular spot in a corner of the library.

In fact, Damien hardly saw Sebastien all week outside of class. It was like Sebastien was trying to distance himself from Damien, which left a pang of admittedly ridiculous hurt in Damien's chest. He knew Sebastien didn't particularly like him, which was understandable considering how they had met and their less-than-pleasant interactions since then, but he couldn't help but be frustrated by how easily the other young man dismissed him. It reminded him a little of his father. Perhaps that was why Damien took notice when he saw Sebastien hurrying down the Citadel's stairs before their first class period on Thursday morning.

None of the first term classes were held on the second floor. So why would Sebastien be up there? Was that where he had been hiding away?

Sebastien was walking quickly, heading back toward the dorms, seeming focused more on his own thoughts than the world around him, as he often was.

Damien looked to the door of his History of Magic class, then to Sebastien's quickly retreating back. He checked the time on his pocket watch. There were only a few minutes left before the first class of the day. He knew Sebastien had a different teacher for this period, one specifically requested by Professor Lacer instead of the rest of their student group's rather lackluster professor...but Sebastien wasn't heading toward a classroom.

Which meant he was doing something interesting enough to make him late for class.

Damien only hesitated for a few seconds. He settled his leather satchel on his shoulder and, without taking his eyes off Sebastien, told his friends, "I've got something to do. I'll see you later."

They questioned him, but he was already walking away, a rude maneuver that he'd seen Sebastien do more than once to anyone that didn't meet his standards for intelligent conversation. In his own way, Sebastien was just as arrogant as any member of the Crowns, despite the way he seemed to look down on all of them.

Sebastien was in such a hurry that he knocked into Canelo, their female student liaison, but luckily she was too busy reading a spelled letter to punish him.

As she passed Damien a few seconds later, he heard her whisper viciously, "By all the greater hells! How am I supposed—" She clenched her teeth, glaring at the paper as she continued to read.

Damien let her be. Her problems were none of his business. Which wouldn't normally have stopped him from prying in the name of chivalry, but he had something more interesting to focus on at the moment.

He walked lightly into the dorms, stopping in front of Sebastien's cubicle. He watched as Sebastien stuffed what Damien recognized as components that could be used in divination into his wooden chest. But Sebastien wasn't taking a divination class; Damien was taking one, and he'd never seen Sebastien there.

Sebastien's head suddenly whipped around.

Damien catalogued the micro-expressions on Sebastien's face: shock, fear, dismay, anger.

Sebastien controlled his response with impressive speed, but Damien had been trained for social warfare his whole life, and had been honing his detective skills on top of that. Being able to read what a suspect or witness *wasn't* saying aloud was critical to solving a case.

Sebastien slammed his wooden chest closed. "What do you want, Westbay? Shouldn't you be getting to class?" he asked irritably.

Damien considered admitting that he'd followed Sebastien out of curiosity, but that would make Sebastien even more wary of scrutiny. Damien's eyes caught on the stack of magazine periodicals he'd lent Sebastien sitting atop his bedside table, so he made up some nonsense about skipping class out of laziness to chat about the latest installment featuring Aberford Thorndyke, consulting detective.

He was almost disappointed when Sebastien didn't find that suspicious. Did he really believe Damien to be so vapid? Sure, he wasn't a genius power-house who could cast healing spells without any components, or impress the notorious Thaddeus Lacer enough to become the man's apprentice, but he was one of the best students in their class—and powerful and rich, moreover!

Sebastien was halfway through an equally inane response when something caught his attention. His words cut off and he stared into the air with what might have been surprise or alarm. It was as if he'd suddenly remembered something of critical importance. Coming back to reality, he rushed to get rid of Damien with some blather about forgotten homework, then literally pulled his curtain closed in Damien's face.

Rude. Damien glared at the curtain for a couple of seconds, then walked toward the dormitory doors, making sure to stride a little louder with anger. He heard the tell-tale sounds of Sebastien pacing, which definitely wasn't homework, and smirked to himself.

Damien would bet his entire monthly allowance that Sebastien was about to cast a divination spell. Likely the same spell he'd been casting in secret in some dusty upper floor classroom.

Damien stopped just around the corner toward the bathrooms and waited as class started without him. His patience and foresight were rewarded only a couple of minutes later as Sebastien hurried out of their dorm room and then out of the building. He didn't notice Damien, and Damien *almost* didn't notice him.

Sebastien was casting some kind of stealth spell. It didn't make him invisi-ble, simply unremarkable. Enough so that if Damien hadn't been on full alert, filled with excitement, he might have disregarded Sebastien's exit and kept waiting for him indefinitely.

Damien couldn't hold back a giddy grin. "This is just like the Case of the Unwatched Watchman!" he muttered. Leaving almost a hundred meters between them so Sebastien wouldn't notice the tail, he followed the other young man all the way to Eagle Tower, where Sebastien hesitated at the edge of the tree line for a few seconds before hiding his student token and striding through the front doors.

Damien dropped off his own token with rising excitement, then tried to seem as assured and confident in his right to be inside Eagle Tower as Sebastien had.

Sebastien had obviously never been in Eagle Tower before, because Damien found him stymied before the locked door of the stairwell. Damien hesitated, but decided it would be more entertaining—and less likely to make

Sebastien angry—if he stopped sneaking around and honestly inserted himself into whatever Sebastien was doing.

Damien had taken a tour of the place with Professor Lacer when he was younger, so he knew that they had special, metal tokens to access the stairwell and central tower rooms.

Serendipitously, he saw one such metal token lying abandoned on a desk in an empty side office. Human carelessness often made security measures useless. He looked back and forth to make sure he wasn't being watched, then slipped it into his pocket. Even if it was technically mischief, a Westbay was unlikely to get in serious trouble. His Family donated thousands of crowns to the University every year, after all.

Damien walked up behind Sebastien, who was still staring at the door, then reached past and opened it for him.

Sebastien stared down at him, nonplussed. "Westbay."

A little awkwardly, Damien explained the door-pass. He wasn't used to fumbling like this, not even with his father. Not anymore at least.

Sebastien stared at him until Damien felt like his skin was being metaphorically peeled away so the other young man could see his insides.

With continuing uncharacteristic gracelessness, Damien confessed to his curious snooping. "I thought maybe you could use some backup?" he finished hopefully, trying not to make it obvious how tight the rejection in Sebastien's gaze made his chest. Sebastien had kept whatever this was a secret so far, probably because he didn't really trust Damien, and didn't consider him a real friend. "Don't worry. No one saw me, and I dropped my student token under the same tree you did," Damien added.

If Damien was given a chance, he was sure he could prove that he could be useful when he was included. He *could* be a good ally to Sebastien. He knew how to keep his mouth shut and keep them both out of trouble. He could be fun.

Sebastien just kept staring at him, and even though Damien *knew* this tactic—making the other person uncomfortable with silence until they started talking to fill it, thereby giving up their conversational leverage—he still couldn't help speaking, as if he felt it would create a barrier between him and that black-eyed gaze.

But he only ended up making Sebastien more upset by prying into proprietary family magic knowledge.

Damien was worried Sebastien was about to either send him away or call the whole thing—whatever it was—off entirely, when an upper term student walked down the stairwell, and suddenly Damien had the chance to save the day by diffusing any suspicion and sending the man on his way grateful to have bumped into him, a *Westbay*.

Sebastien eyed him with reluctant appreciation. "Useful," he admitted.

Damien grinned, bursting with satisfaction, but tried to be humble about it. "Thank you. The name does come in handy from time to time. Now why are we here?"

"No questions. In fact, don't talk at all," Sebastien replied.

That only made Damien more curious, but at the same time felt somehow more satisfying. He was intelligent and observant enough to figure it out on his own.

Sebastien waved imperiously for Damien to open the door for him.

Without thinking, Damien started to ask where they were going, but cut himself off with a smile.

"You're an idiot," Sebastien said.

Damien's first reaction was immediate anger at the insult, but he quickly reminded himself who he was dealing with. Sebastien Siverling's tongue was almost as caustic as Professor Lacer's, and insults tripped from it seemingly without conscious thought or even intent to offend. Yet, Sebastien had accepted him as a partner on this little adventure, and Damien could see a spark of amusement in his eyes. Sebastien's real friends would have to understand not to take his words to heart and instead recognize the intention beneath them. Still, Damien didn't want to seem like a pandering pushover. "And you're a porcupine," he muttered.

Sebastien didn't respond, and Damien had a small epiphany. Were the minor insults, perhaps, not meant to be offensive? Was bickering Sebastien's version of friendly banter?

Damien nodded to himself when Sebastien wasn't looking. Yes, Sebastien may have been a genius with somewhat poor social skills, but the young man also had an interest in detective stories, a *grueling* work ethic, and a hidden kind interior that led him to heal Damien at risk to himself, offer advice to Alec—who he hated—and let students whose names Damien was sure Sebastien couldn't even remember listen in when Sebastien tutored him and Ana.

In fact, Sebastien was probably pretty lonely. Except for Ana and Damien, he ate alone, studied alone, and snuck around doing exciting things...alone. The only other person he'd seen Sebastien talking to of his own free will for longer than sixty seconds was their student liaison Newton Moore. It was sad, really.

Damien couldn't get angry at Sebastien for not being properly socialized. It must be hard to get along with other people as the only genius growing up in a small rural city like Vale. It must have been stifling, and probably part of what had caused Sebastien to grow such a prickly exterior. If he was poor, jealousy at the good fortunes of everyone around him might have played a part too, petty as that would be. Even geniuses could be petty.

Damien's contemplation ended as they entered the fourth floor of the tower. A team of coppers with *three* prognos were casting a divination spell on the University's spell array. That only happened when their own array wasn't powerful enough.

Sebastien was sneaking in to watch the coppers in an active investigation! It couldn't have been more perfect if Damien had come up with the idea himself.

Sebastien quickly led him into an empty side office, completely unnoticed.

Damien was jealous of that stealth spell, his heart pounding as he scurried to follow, hoping none of the coppers or professors would see him and give them both away. Inside, they peeked out of the window onto the spellcasters. Who, or what, was their target? Damien realized he'd murmured his thoughts aloud, but Sebastien remained silent. Damien smoothed his hair back, trying to regain his cool composure. "I have a spell that can enhance hearing. Maybe we could...listen in?"

Sebastien's interest in the question was enough answer for Damien, and he quickly set up the spell his brother had taught him as a reward for scoring so high on the University entrance exams. "They're chanting. For the spell-casting. It's advanced. I haven't heard anything like it."

When he heard the words, "Raven Queen," he understood why the normally rule-abiding boy would sneak out for this. "They're scrying for her... right now?" It was the case of the decade, if not the century, and they had a chance to watch her be found in person! If only they could be there for the arrest as well...

Sebastien was looking at him speculatively, and just as his lips twitched as if he were about to tell Damien something, movement at the door to the room drew his attention away.

With disappointment, Damien followed his gaze to their student liaison, Canelo. Her short, dirty blonde hair was windswept and her cheeks flushed.

She'd obviously arrived in a hurry, but after checking the time, she returned to the stairs and kept going up.

Damien pitied her. She didn't know what she was missing out on.

He focused on Sebastien, hoping he would continue with whatever he'd been about to say before her arrival, but instead sirens went off, so loud to Damien's enhanced hearing that it felt like a blow. It was the alarm for danger of a magical nature, and a warning for everyone to take shelter. It was the worst possible timing. The divination spell would have to be stopped and started again from scratch when it was safe, and they might not have a chance to watch at that time.

"Again? It hasn't even been two weeks since the last one. This is terrible timing. They can't keep casting during a citywide emergency. I'm sure they would have caught her otherwise. There's a shelter in the first basement level. We'll have to join them." It could have been worse, though. "Hey, maybe they'll talk about the investigation. We might learn something interesting."

When he moved to join the evacuation, Sebastien stopped him, but after a moment of hesitation, stepped back. "Never mind. Go ahead," Sebastien said.

Damien's eyes narrowed. "Are you not coming?"

"I have something to do first."

"I'm staying too, then."

"Whatever set those sirens off could be anywhere. It might not be safe. I would wager the University has a higher incidence of Aberrants than the rest of the city. So many thaumaturges in a relatively small area. You should know the numbers. Your Family runs the coppers, right?"

Sebastien was right, but the University buildings were all quite sturdy, and the professors were the best in their fields, skilled enough to quickly deal with the things that could have caused the alarm. "I'm not going to miss out on this. The curiosity would kill me. Unless you promise to tell me what you find?"

"I promise."

Damien wanted to hit him. "You're lying. You'll just pretend you didn't find anything interesting if I don't come along and see it with my own two eyes. Otherwise, you would have brought me in on whatever this is from the beginning." He sniffed, looking away.

Sebastien was too oblivious to apologize, and worse than that, acted like *Damien* was the one in the wrong. "We're not friends, Westbay, and I've yet to see you do anything useful except throw your Family's name around. I had no reason to bring you in on this."

The sudden pang of hurt caused by those words quickly morphed into anger. "Oh, so you knew about the door-pass tokens? You had a handy spell to eavesdrop on what they were saying? I may not be a once-in-a generation prodigy, but you shouldn't underestimate me. I'm staying." Damien crossed his arms over his chest, glaring at his companion.

They snuck out into the empty hallway, peeking in the windows of the divination room. Damien wondered how long it would take him to be proficient enough to cast such a powerful spell, if he ever could. As a human, he had no natural talent in divination, and his father didn't even approve of him taking the class, but he had the passion, at least. He hoped the University didn't crush him to the point he had to drop electives in upcoming terms.

He was so focused on the tantalizing divination room that, when the door to the stairwell slammed open, he jumped. He might have let out a small squeak, too.

"What are you two doing here?" Canelo demanded.

"Didn't you hear the sirens? Why haven't you evacuated?" she asked.

Sebastien was not the person for this job, Damien knew. Damien was the smooth-talker, the one with influence. He had to take the lead here. He stepped forward, trying to emulate his brother's easy authority. "We heard the sirens. We were in the Menagerie when they went off, and we ran, but it still took us a while to get back. Eagle Tower is the first building we came to, but everyone was already gone when we got here. We're trying to find the shelter."

Canelo walked toward them, moving slowly and silently, like a large cat. "It's underground. Like all the shelters." Her tone indicated that they were idiots.

Damien knew she wasn't stupid. The reason they were up here was obvious, and probably the same reason *she* was there. He gave her a deadpan look, letting the side of his mouth twitch up in a tiny, tiny smirk, just enough to show that he knew she was in on the joke. "Really? I thought it would be on the top floor. That's where they keep the weapons, right?"

She either didn't notice his subtlety, or decided to shove right through it, rolling her eyes. "Are you qualified to fight against something powerful enough to warrant the sirens? If not, you should be sheltering underground with everyone else. You may be a Westbay, but you're only a firstie. Getting greedy for glory will only get you killed." She looked up at the ceiling. "Come on, we need to go."

"I'm not greedy for glory," Damien muttered. He didn't know why people liked to accuse him of that, as if he were some sort of attention-hound. Compared to Alec and Rhett, he was positively unassuming. He enjoyed being liked, being noticed, but he didn't *need* it.

Canelo grabbed Sebastien's arm and tugged. "Come on. If you're not both in the shelters within the next sixty seconds, I'm giving you both a demerit," she said waspishly.

Then it started.

At first, Damien thought Sebastien was casting a spell.

He turned to the platinum-haired young man like a fish swimming through honey, the world slowed around him. Sebastien wasn't casting anything, not even his stealth spell, but there was a bladelike intent in his expression that Damien had never seen before.

Sebastien slammed into him, forcing him to stumble forward into a doorway.

Canelo tried to get through, too, and ended up blocking the way.

That's when something slammed them off their feet, and then the ceiling exploded.

Damien fell under Sebastien and didn't even try to move. Sebastien was still alive; Damien could feel his heartbeat and his breath over Damien's head.

He tried to listen for other movement, in case whatever had just destroyed the floor above them was creeping around looking for survivors.

Sebastien climbed off of him, a knee pressing painfully into Damien's kidney.

Beside him, Canelo crawled to her hands and knees, coughing and retching. She had a distinctive scar on her forearm, but covered it self-consciously when Sebastien looked at it.

Damien looked to Sebastien curiously.

The other young man seemed more interested in the scar than the explosion and possible danger, and suddenly, Damien realized how strange it was that Canelo had been on the floor above right before the explosion. In fact, it seemed like she'd gone there purposefully, just before the sirens went off. Almost as if she knew when they were going to sound, forcing an evacuation and leaving her alone.

"Are you both alright?" Canelo asked.

Damien lifted a thumb, his mind too occupied trying to digest the huge lump of suspicion to talk.

"No serious injuries. We need to move. Whatever caused that could still be around," Sebastien said.

Damien accepted Sebastien's hand and climbed to his feet. He covered his face with his scarf, suddenly less worried about whatever had caused the explosion and more worried about Canelo. He moved to stand beside Sebastien, keeping his eyes on the woman.

Canelo shook her head, shouting past her sleeve. "The floor above was being used for some alchemy experiments. They must not have properly settled and stored whatever they were working on, and it exploded. But the fumes could be hazardous, and the ceiling might not be sound any more. It could still fall on us."

"No breathing, no getting crushed by falling stones," Damien muttered sardonically, choking on dust. Canelo seemed a little too sure about the cause of the explosion, in his opinion, which only enforced his growing suspicion. "Got it." He waved for Canelo to lead the way down to the shelter. When her back was turned, he looked questioningly to Sebastien, but was ignored.

Down in the shelter below, Canelo deflected the suspicion they faced onto the people who'd been working on the fifth floor before the sirens.

Sebastien moved to the wall and sat against it, something dark and cold swimming behind those eyes, like a kraken in deep waters.

Damien slid down beside him, his own thoughts more than enough to occupy him. He ran through his memories, trying to piece together the clues that he must have missed at the time.

Tanya Canelo wasn't, in general, suspicious. She was capable, trusted enough by the faculty to be a student aide, and the kind of person whose competence was assuring rather than intimidating—like it could be in someone like Sebastien. She was rather handsome for a woman, but not attractive enough to gain favors. She was from a better family than some who managed to get in, enough so that her University contribution points didn't go into tuition or items that could be sold right back for gold crowns to keep their family from starving. Not a good enough family that she could be assured of a nice position after leaving the University, though. No, she still had to work for everything she got.

But Sebastien had known better.

Damien had thought Sebastien was sneaking into Eagle Tower for a bit of fun, but that hadn't been it at all. No, Sebastien was doing something much more serious, more dangerous, and more ridiculously...wonderful. And it made sense why he'd been so frustrated and adamant about getting Damien to leave. Not because he didn't trust Damien, or disliked him so much he couldn't stand to spend a few minutes sneaking around with him, but because Damien had no idea what was going on and might have caused *real* problems. The kind that just the word of a Westbay couldn't get them out of.

Damien knew this must be the kind of serious thing that he really shouldn't be excited about—and people might think something was dangerously wrong with him if he started grinning like a loon while sheltering from rogue magic—so he suppressed the urge to display his suddenly roiling emotions. He returned to his deductions with a serious face.

Sebastien had been doing some kind of advanced divination, and that had led him to Eagle Tower at the exact time the coppers were searching for the Raven Queen—when Canelo came in to sabotage the attempt.

The spelled letter Canelo had gotten? That had been a clue. One that Sebastien had noticed, even if Damien didn't. That was what Sebastien's sudden moment of realization in the dorms had been, when he rushed Damien to leave and went after Canelo.

Who had it been from? Someone who knew what the coppers were doing at the University? Someone who could set off false rogue magic alarms?

Damien pulled his knees up to his chest, suppressing a gasp of realization. Canelo had looked at the clock, just before going upstairs, and then she hid until the tower was clear. She'd *known*.

His heart was pounding in his chest, and he controlled his breathing, patting back his filthy, dust-coated hair with a slightly shaky hand.

Sebastien had noticed Canelo's scar. Why was that important? In detective stories, a distinctive scar like that was often the clue to finding an otherwise unidentifiable suspect or lead. Sebastien had recognized the scar...but he had been surprised to see it on Canelo. So, either Sebastien had previously come across her when she was disguised and remembered the distinctive mark, or he recognized the weapon that had inflicted the injury. Damien withheld from guessing the details without a better foundation.

Except, he did know that Sebastien had been missing from the dorms the same weekend the Raven Queen had made her latest appearance. Where had Canelo been that night? Had Sebastien been following her?

There were likely other clues that Damien had no way of knowing. Without Sebastien being forthright, he couldn't know the details, but some things were clear enough through the fog.

Canelo was either the Raven Queen—which seemed unlikely for multiple reasons, unless her entire identity was some sort of deep cover—or she was working with the Raven Queen in some capacity. She'd protected the Raven Queen from being caught, after all. It could have been as innocuous as Canelo being blackmailed or threatened into it.

And Sebastien? He was investigating the Raven Queen, searching for her on his own. That was why he'd been so interested in the case. Damien supposed Sebastien could want to catch her simply for his interest in detective work, and in some ways that fit Sebastien's personality—curiosity like a raging fire, never satisfied—but somehow it didn't feel right.

Damien remembered Sebastien's shitty Conduit. There was no way that thing could channel all of Sebastien's Will. Sebastien may be from a rural city like Vale, but he was far from a commoner. Except, when Damien had first met him, hadn't Damien insulted Sebastien for wearing a suit that was too big for him and in an outdated style, besides? He'd wondered about the Siverlings' monetary situation before, but unlike Sebastien, Damien knew enough about tact not to pry. Damien smoothed down his collar, *barely* even bothered by the dirt crusting itself into his skin, settling under his nails, and turning to tiny balls of mud in the corners of his eyes.

Either Sebastien's family was punishing him, someone was purposely suppressing him and his growth opportunities, or they simply didn't have the resources to provide better. Could it be, somehow, that Sebastien's family had fallen on hard times? Perhaps they'd put all of their wealth into their genius scion, cultivating him with the last of their resources in the hopes that he could restore them to their former glory? Or perhaps an uncle or a step-parent was afraid that Sebastien would grow up and usurp them. He would need to look up the Siverlings.

If it were true—and there wasn't some even more outrageous reason behind all this that Damien had missed, like Sebastien being an undercover agent for the Red Guard—then Sebastien was looking for the Raven Queen to get the reward. It was up to five hundred gold crowns by now. More than enough for a better Conduit.

The third option was that Sebastien was doing it for the glory, the recognition. To prove something, or get some sort of revenge. That, too, was something that fit Sebastien's character.

Damien looked at his classmate, who was still obliviously consumed by his own dark thoughts. Normally, he would have taken information like this directly to his older brother Titus. But if Sebastien found out he'd done that, it would destroy any chance of them ever becoming real allies. Sebastien was either going to die young or make something of himself, something great, like Titus or Professor Lacer.

Like Damien wished he had the talent for. He might not be like them, but he didn't need to be, exactly, if he could stand beside them and hold their respect. Power came in many forms.

The whole thing being terribly fascinating was merely an additional benefit.

Would Sebastien be terribly offended if Damien offered him a better Conduit? He could probably get one of the Family ones that Titus had outgrown. Of course, anyone who noticed the Westbay seal would think Sebastien was a vassal to the Westbays, which seemed like just the kind of thing Sebastien would hate, so perhaps that idea wouldn't work.

Damien wasn't sure whether concern or excitement were at the forefront in his pounding chest, but he knew one thing for certain. Sebastien would need help, and Damien was the perfect person to give it. He'd just have to convince Sebastien of that.

16

THROUGH A GLASS DARKLY

SEBASTIEN
   Month 12, Day 17, Thursday 11:30 a.m.

SEBASTIEN HEADED STRAIGHT for the washrooms. She ignored the stares of the other students, who were openly wondering what had happened to her and Westbay to become so dirty and disheveled during a rogue magic alarm. She took a thorough shower, retrieved her student token and secret library pass, then returned to the Citadel in time to catch the last bit of Sympathetic Science, which was useless since Professor Pecanty was as distracted as the students.

Westbay was uncharacteristically silent through the rest of the day, though he kept sending Sebastien searching looks.

As soon as Fekten's grueling Defense class was over, Sebastien wiped herself down with a damp towel, changed back into her high-class suit, jacket, and scarf, and left for the city below. She put a small smile on her face, not enough to be obvious, but enough to make her seem without a care. In her own mind, it was just a prelude to baring her teeth in a defensive snarl.

She didn't go straight to Oliver's house. She didn't even head in the same direction, and she kept going past the strictly upscale part of the city. She wasn't trained to recognize a tail, but she could follow common-sense tactics like taking a winding route, suddenly doubling back to surprise anyone trying to seem normal, and peeking in the reflections of glass shop windows to see if she could catch anyone watching her.

She stopped well before arriving at the Mires and made a loop back around to Dryden Manor, all without seeing anything particularly suspicious. People noticed her, as Sebastien, but no one did more than stare for a couple of seconds too long. Even so, her Conduit never left her hand. It rolled around inside her grip, which was sweaty despite the cold.

She walked straight in through Oliver's front door.

A male servant bowed lightly to her. "Welcome, Mr. Siverling. Mr. Dryden isn't in at the moment..."

"When will he be back?" she asked, unraveling her scarf from around her neck and stamping her boots on the welcome mat.

"I'm not sure..."

Sharon hustled out from the kitchen before the man could finish. "Sebastien! Welcome! Are you hungry?"

Sebastien smiled as genuinely as she could despite her anxiety. "No, thank you. I'm going up to my room to wait for Mr. Dryden. Please let him know I'm here when he arrives." Without waiting for a response, she hurried up the stairs.

Sharon called after her that she would be bringing tea and refreshments.

Once Sebastien was alone in "her" room, she pushed up her sleeve to reveal the series of thin wooden bracelets on her wrist.

After the fiasco the last time, when Oliver had set off the linked alarm on the bracelet and sent her fleeing from her dorms in the middle of the night, she'd taken a few spare moments to create more. Each was wrapped with a small section of colored thread. Different colors for different messages, still almost as simple as could be.

Grabbing one delicate bracelet near the weak metal bead that kept it together, she pulled, breaking it apart. Oliver's own linked bracelet would grow cold, indicating that he should return to his house immediately.

Each bracelet was single-use, but Sebastien figured that if she was having such frequent emergencies that she didn't have time to create replacements between them, she had bigger problems.

Sebastien didn't simply sit back and wait for Oliver, however. She fell to her hands and knees and crawled under the bed, retrieving the ancient book from its hiding spot. There were no signs that it had been disturbed since the last time she retrieved it.

'How much do Tanya and whoever she's working with know about me? Is there any information that could have leaked?' There were several possible ways someone could have learned to be suspicious of Sebastien. Anyone who knew Oliver's identity, and his connection to either Siobhan or Sebastien could have given away clues. 'Could his connection to me have been somehow related to the attack on the warehouse? Am I even sure that he's safe right now? He has his own bracelets, to alert me to an emergency, but if something happened to him, what could I even do?'

She opened the book and flipped through it quickly. It was the same as ever—frustrating and indecipherable.

'*Tanya is likely to be much more powerful than me. It's honestly amazing that a fourth-term student was able to almost collapse an entire warehouse by herself. Unless she was using an artifact.*' Sebastien tried to remember, but for once her memory failed her. There had been too much going on in the dark, with the storm and the screaming and the fighting, and she had been too full of adrenaline to pay close attention.

'*Don't panic. Be logical. What Tanya did today doesn't mean they actually know anything about me. So why would someone do that? Why might someone—the Morrows? —not want the Crowns to find me?*' She could think of too many possibilities, but all of them seemed ludicrous, like something out of one of Damien's stories. Anarchists that held a grudge against the established powers. Someone who knew what was in the book and didn't want the Crowns getting their hands on it. Someone who was using this event as a decoy to commit another crime while diverting suspicion to the Raven Queen.

Even Oliver could have sent Tanya, and Sebastien might have suspected him if she hadn't seen the scar on the other woman's forearm. Oliver would never have placed his employees in danger with that attack on the warehouse. The Morrows were Tanya's most likely allies.

She realized then that it might not be the Morrows at all, or not directly. '*There is someone with a motive, as well as the means. I don't know why, but judging by the aura of hostility, the University has some reason not to want the coppers to find me. What if that's why Tanya was there? But if she's working for someone at the University, how is she also connected to the Morrows?*'

Sebastien had to push the stolen book back under the bed when someone knocked on the door. She opened it to find Sharon on the other side with a tea tray, cookies and snacks, and a worried expression.

Sharon bustled in, setting up the tea tray on the table beside the bed. "Everyone has heard how difficult the University is," she said, her tone failing to be conversational, just a little too gentle and conciliatory.

"Yes, the workload is crushing," Sebastien agreed, resisting the urge to fidget in her desire for the woman to *leave*. "But it's nothing I can't handle."

Sharon stepped back from the table and pushed a cup of tea into Sebastien's hands, guiding her to sit on the edge of the bed. "Sometimes, when we feel overwhelmed by a problem, it's best to step back and look at it from a different angle. Find out what you can pare away, what's not absolutely critical, and then cut the rest down into manageable chunks. Be kind to yourself, Sebastien. If you aren't, who will be?" She patted Sebastien's hand like one might a dog's head, then left the room, closing the door gently behind herself.

Sebastien chugged the tea, ignoring the burning sensation as it scalded her mouth and throat and hit her stomach like a cauterizing knife, somehow staunching the steady bleed of her panic. She stared at the loose leaves in the bottom of the cup for a few seconds, then let out a long breath and retrieved the stolen book from under the bed again.

'Sharon may have no idea what's going on, but she's not wrong. Wild theories will not help me. I have very little real evidence with which to work, but at least I have a direction in which to investigate.'

She placed the book on the marble floor and stared at it. "What are you?" she whispered. She knew its secrets might hold the key to all her problems. If only she could unravel them. "Why are they searching for you so desperately? How does the amulet do this to me? Who created you?"

The book didn't respond, of course.

She knelt down, pulled her alchemy athame out of her bag, and began to peel back the leather wrapping of the outer cover, where she had first seen the edge of the space-bending array that contained the transformation amulet. She was gentle, but ruthless as she took the book apart like one might dissect a corpse, searching for any hint of its origins, purpose, or the magic that powered it. If she could find a spell array, even if she couldn't solve the key to its lock, she might still be able to break it with precisely applied force.

But it was just a book.

If not for its contents, it might even have seemed an ordinary book.

Suppressing her seething frustration, she put the book back together and performed a simple mending spell on it using some glue and a couple strips of leather as components. When she was finished, it looked good as new.

Bringing her hands to her chest, thumbs to her middle fingers, she brought her Will to bear on the idea of stretching out her muscles and relaxing her body like it was a coiled spring. A few minutes of deep humming later, she had broken the vicious cycle of her body causing anxiety to her thoughts and her thoughts filling her body with fight-or-flight chemicals. 'Newton's gift of knowledge is becoming increasingly useful,' she mused. 'I owe him.' It was only too bad that the effects were so temporary.

An anxiety-inducing thought popped into her mind. She couldn't be sure what had happened to her blood with the explosion.

Still, with her body and mind calmer, a piece of positivity rose to the surface. The reverse-scrying spell based off sympathetic divination had worked.

There were other potential applications for that. Her original idea had been to find a way to remove or destroy the coppers' sample of her blood once she pinpointed its location, but today had shown that even if she knew where it was, she couldn't necessarily do much with the information.

But her success with sympathetic divination reminded her that other kinds of sympathetic magic were also an option. 'Would it be possible to remotely destroy *any lost piece of myself that could be used to cast sympathetic spells affecting me?'* If she could do that, not only would she solve her biggest current problem, but she would never have to worry about missing a strand of hair or leaving her toothbrush out again.

Sympathetic magic worked through the impression that different items or ideas were, in fact, the *same*, and so should display the same characteristics and effects. With many spells, this was forced through Sacrifice.

For instance, a transmogrification spell that took the idea of "death" and "doused fire" from a pinch of ash and forcefully applied it to a man to curse him with impotence. Or, using duplicative transmogrification to copy a gold nugget from the matter of a clay brick, forcing the brick to become the gold in truth.

But when you had a piece of the original, it was even easier. The sympathetic connection was inherent. What was once a part of the whole always remained a part of the whole in some way, even after being separated. It was easiest to do sympathetic magic with things you had a strong personal connection to, like long-term belongings—or pieces of your own body. However, the longer a piece of the whole was separated from the rest, and the more the sample's state or that of the original changed, the less effective such magic became. This was especially true with living things.

For example, a branch taken from a tree could be used to find its parent when it was still fresh. Over time, the connection lessened. If the branch's bark was peeled and it was turned into a walking stick, the connection would weaken. If the tree itself were cut down and turned into furniture, it would be almost impossible to use the branch to find any of those pieces of furniture.

The coppers had been using a stasis artifact—the evidence box—to keep her blood fresh, but within ten years it would still become almost useless as both time and change weakened her connection to it.

Of course, she couldn't wait ten years. Turning into Sebastien didn't seem to help, despite how much of a change it was. Or, perhaps it *was* helping and in fact the only thing keeping her safe.

If she were to leave the city, the power and skill required to find her at longer distances would be untenable. She would be unreachable. But there was only one Thaumaturgic University of Lenore, and it was in Gilbratha.

"But the reverse-scry *worked*," she repeated aloud. "I found my blood."

She hadn't considered the full possibilities of this sympathetic connection before because of the same inherent limitation she'd faced when trying to locate her blood without the reverse-scry. How did you distinguish between which pieces of the whole you wanted to affect with the spell and which you didn't? By the very nature of sympathetic magic, they were all the same. If you wanted to curse someone using a piece of them, say to force them to spontaneously combust, you probably didn't care if the piece you were using burnt up, too.

But she very much cared if she caught fire while trying to destroy the blood held by the coppers.

'There has to be a way around that. With enough ingenuity and power, there is always a way.'

It might be possible if she could stay within wards that were *stronger* than whatever wards the coppers were using to protect her blood. Then someone outside both wards, maybe Liza, would try to break through, all unprotected pieces of Sebastien throughout the range of the spell would be destroyed, and the coppers' wards would fall before Sebastien's did. It would likely be more power-intensive than scrying over the same distance, but maybe Liza could handle it. Of course, as always with Liza, her fee would be crippling. An estimate of the work that would be involved in developing the spells for and setting up something like that made Sebastien wince.

Alternatively, they could somehow bound the area of the sympathetic destruction. If they could draw a really, really large Circle while ensuring that it wasn't broken or disrupted, they could enclose the entirety of a place like Harrow Hill Penitentiary within it. Then, a piece of Sebastien's blood or hair could be used to destroy only the matching pieces *within* the Circle, overpowering or bypassing any wards. Maybe. It was the same way the shedding-destroyer worked, only this would be targeted specifically to pieces of her rather than any human material. The problem with really large Circles was manyfold, though. They were conspicuous, easily disrupted by enemy forces or even coincidence, and the larger the area within the Circle, the harder it was to hold dominion over it with your Will. That plan would likely require joint-casting by multiple sorcerers who had thoroughly practiced the same spell together to avoid causing a disturbance in the flow of magic during spell-casting.

While theoretically possible, these ideas weren't practical. Which brought Sebastien back to the concept of reverse-scrying. Perhaps she could use the same reverse-scrying application she had just proved worked to pinpoint a target for her destruction—just as she'd pinpointed a target for her search. It was likely that her blood would be outside of whatever protective wards the coppers normally kept over it while they used it to scry. The idea filled her with energy, but she knew that it, too, was unfeasible for the moment. Destroying her blood would require more power than simply locating it, and that kind of spell would require an even more divergent split of her attention while being scried. She couldn't get it wrong, even once, so she would need to practice sympathetic curses on something else. In addition to her Conduit not being strong enough, her Will wasn't strong enough either.

Because of the sporadic timing of the coppers' attempts to find her, it wasn't as if she could just set up a time for Liza to catch their diviners in the act. Sebastien's frustration was returning, but she tried to comfort herself. *'Destroying it while they try to use it is a viable solution. I may not have all I need to implement that plan, but I will not always be so weak. I'm definitely going to need a better Conduit, though. This one is not acceptable.'* That was frustrating, because she truly could not afford better. If only she'd left Ennis to rot in jail instead of paying twice to contact him, maybe lack of funds wouldn't be a problem.

At the very least, she wasn't worried about the coppers using her blood to attempt to kill her. They desperately wanted the book, and if she died somewhere distant, out of their grasp, they risked never finding it. However, they could still curse her in other, more subtle ways. It was illegal, sure, but who knew if that would stop them should they grow desperate? She would be warned, at least, because one of the spells in the medallion her grandfather gave her warded against curses, but it could obviously be overpowered.

She frowned. If the coppers ever knew exactly where she was, they could kill her remotely to stop her from escaping, and then take their chances finding the book through divination cast on her corpse. That, too, would be a move of desperation and idiocy, but she wouldn't bet her life on them being calm and intelligent.

The sound of Oliver's arrival below shook her from her thoughts. It had been little more than three quarters of an hour since she activated his bracelet's alarm.

She hid the book, picked up the tea service tray, and walked to Oliver's office, prepared to confess both her foolishness and what she had discovered. This was a threat to both of them, and she hoped she could count on his help. After all, she owed him, through the Verdant Stag, about a thousand gold. If he tossed her aside because of how much trouble she was, he would lose any chance of recovering that.

She stopped mid-step, swallowing with a sudden resurgence of apprehension. *'That is not entirely true. The reward for aiding in my capture is five hundred gold now, and he could probably sell the book to the University for at least that much again. I suppose I just have to hope that he counts my future value higher than my immediate cost. He might seem softhearted, but he isn't foolish.'*

17

COMMISSION TO INVESTIGATE

SEBASTIEN
Month 12, Day 17, Thursday 5:30 p.m.

OLIVER STALKED into his office a couple of seconds behind Sebastien. His dark hair was windswept, his cheeks and nose red from the cold, and he was breathing hard. His eyes swept across the room and latched onto her, the question in them obvious.

Once the door was closed behind them and they were assured of privacy, she opened her mouth to speak but choked on the words. While he waited impatiently, she tried to formulate a coherent explanation.

"The coppers almost found me today," she said finally. "They moved to the University in order to use the divination room in Eagle Tower."

"*Shit.*"

"I wasn't expecting it, wasn't fully prepared," she admitted. "I—I did a divination spell to find my blood, piggybacking on their own scrying spell, and managed to find them. I wanted to gather some information, so I went to peek a little—as Sebastien."

Oliver stared at her, stupefied. "You went to peek. On the coppers *actively* scrying for you. You are aware that divination is more powerful at close range?" His tone was flat and incredulous.

"I thought the risk was worth it. The ward Liza made me has worked so well, I didn't assume they'd be able to break past it easily. And they didn't. They even had three prognos, and it took them a long while to ramp up to the level where it started getting dangerous for me. Still, I fully understand that it was a bad idea. I miscalculated. You don't need to say it."

He let out a puff of air, rocking back on his heels. "You said *almost* caught. What happened?"

She straightened her shoulders, forcing stillness to settle in her bones. "My miscalculation brought about an unexpected discovery. The female sorcerer who led the attack on your warehouse is a fourth-term student at the University."

His eyes narrowed, but Sebastien continued to the really shocking news. "She, or an accomplice of hers, more likely, set off the sirens earlier today while the coppers were in the middle of scrying for me. When everyone evacuated, she blew up the floor above the divination room. I assume to ensure they couldn't continue their divination spell after the false alarm was revealed."

"What."

"Her name is Tanya Canelo." The name sparked no recognition in him, so she continued. "She's one of my student liaisons. I'm not sure how long it will take them to fix Eagle Tower, but unless they can find or set up another ultra-powerful divination spell array, I'm safe for the near future. Which, crazy though it seems, appears to have been her goal. At least, I cannot figure out why else she would have acted as she did."

Oliver stared at Sebastien for a moment, then brushed past her to the liquor table at the corner of the room, pouring himself a glass. He offered Sebastien one.

Despite her abhorrence for sedatives in general, and liquor in particular, she accepted. It was disgusting, as she'd anticipated, but she welcomed the burn.

"Do you know what this means?" he asked.

"A University student is working for the Morrows, and has a rather significant information network. They have more access than we do," she replied immediately. "Alternatively, the University itself is working with the Morrows, and the information was easy to get because they're one of the involved parties. If that's the case, the Morrows might have *much* more access than we do. Also, someone doesn't want the coppers to find me. I suspect that someone may be part of the University itself. Some of the professors seemed reluctant for the coppers to be there. They were on edge and distrustful. However, I don't understand why they wouldn't want the coppers to succeed."

"Because they want to find you themselves," Oliver said simply. "The University and the Crowns have always struggled with each other. The Crowns are wary of the University growing so strong that it threatens their rule, and the University wants access to unlimited control and resources. It's in the nature of powerful thaumaturges to be ever hungry for more, and to chafe at the restrictions of 'lesser men.'" He swallowed the rest of his drink with a bitter grimace, then poured himself a little more. "Both want to find you first, and it seems they're not keen that the other should do so. The Morrows are aware of this. Even if they're not working with the University... If the Morrows could apprehend you and the book, they could trade you for money and favors to either of the two most powerful factions in Gilbratha—the two most powerful factions in the whole of Lenore."

It made sense. Today, it had worked in her favor, because either the Morrows or the University cared more about catching her *themselves* than that she was caught in general. But one thing *didn't* make sense. "What's so important about this book that they would go to such lengths to catch me?" She reached up to the amulet hidden under her shirt. "What is it? Have you heard any rumors?"

"I don't know what's in the book, other than that convenient little trinket you're wearing. Maybe there were other amulets, and they know you have one. I suppose they could be worried about spies or assassination, if they know what it can do, but you're right," he said, shaking his head. "If it was just that, it shouldn't matter so much *who* found you. There are surely politics at play that the two of us are not privy to. The coppers alone have already put several thousand gold into tracking you down. I estimate they burned one or two thousand on today's attempt alone."

"*Thousands?* On *what?*" Even the exorbitant reward for information leading to her capture was only five hundred gold crowns.

Oliver tilted his head to the side, bemused. "They have a whole investigation team focused on finding you. They've called in specialists. All those people have spent hundreds of hours gathering testimony and picking apart any crime scene they think might be remotely linked to you. They've been giving out bribes for information. But mostly, it's the scrying attempts. Their spell must immediately relay enough information to capture you, after all, not just a simple direction or a vague location. The base energy cost for a robust divination spell with a clear output is higher. The power required increases based on the area covered multiplied by that base power requirement."

"Would the spell really be that expensive? How much power could it take?" she asked. It was common knowledge that divination—all spells that reached outside the core Circle, really—got harder the farther you were away from your target. But she'd never seen a formula for how it worked with an area-effect spell like scrying for a target that matched set parameters. It wasn't like shooting a fireball in a straight line. Scrying sent out invisible feelers in all directions gathering information. Or something. The books she'd studied had been rather vague about the actual mechanics, and she hadn't spent extra time digging into the non-essentials.

Reading the lack of comprehension in her expression, Oliver eyed her speculatively for a long few seconds, seemingly hesitating about something.

Finally, he set down his drink and pushed some clutter to the side of his desk, revealing a large map of Gilbratha with different colored zones, arrows, and notes scribbled all over it.

"It's Caidan's Theorem, if I remember correctly? Are they not teaching that at the University anymore?"

It hadn't really been a question, but she murmured, "I'm not taking Divination," anyway.

"When you extend a divination over a greater distance, the power require-ment increases by a variable exponent that's...one-hundredth? One-hundredth of the spell's base cost." He nodded to himself. "It's not exact, and I'm pretty sure it doesn't take into account physical or magical barriers, but it's an easy way to make estimates. How much does a really basic divination spell cost, in thaums?"

"Umm, something like pointing a compass needle to a sympathetically linked object or dousing for water takes about twenty thaums to cast."

"That's even if you're casting right next your target?"

"Yes."

He pointed out Dryden Manor, then used a graphite pencil to draw a one-kilometer circle around it. "Okay, so let's do some simple math. You can use one-hundredth of a kilometer, or ten meters, as the base unit to measure distance. I remember that for sure. Assuming you are casting the simplest divination spell at a base cost of twenty thaums, and your target is one kilo-meter away"—he paused to scribble a simple exponential equation next to the penciled circle—"it will cost you slightly more than thirty thaums for the spell to reach it."

"Twenty thaums, times ten to the power of zero point-two," she muttered, trying to verify his math. Sebastien understood the concept of exponents, but she didn't have a lot of practice calculating them, especially ones that weren't whole numbers. Tentatively, she nodded. It felt strange, to be receiving a magic lesson from Oliver, of all people, instead of one of her professors.

Oliver continued. "Thirty thaums isn't that much. But say your base spell costs a moderate one hundred thaums to cast, which seems like a very conser-vative estimate for the coppers' attempt to locate and capture the Raven Queen. They'll want the output to give enough immediate data that they're sure to catch you. They could have cut down on the higher base cost for a more robust divination by shaping the spell's search volume into a downward-sloping cone, starting from Eagle Tower and reaching toward the south." He drew a smaller wedge within the circle he'd drawn to illustrate the smaller search area. "They have good reason to believe you're within the city, after all, and there's no need to waste power searching in a perfect sphere up into space. To reach a kilometer out they must spend..."

While the Circle and its bounds were spherical, Sebastien was vaguely aware of the more complex theory that could shape the output in various ways. "One hundred thaums, times ten to the power of *one*," Sebastien muttered to herself. This calculation was much simpler. "One thousand thaums per second. Is that right?" It seemed too much.

He gave her a slightly impressed quirk of the lips and a nod. "I'm no expert on divination, and what I did know I've mostly forgotten. Liza would probably be able to explain it better, and in more detail. But keep in mind, this is with an *unwarded* target. From what I understood from Liza, your ward could, with enough aid from you, make things multiple times more difficult for the coppers."

Sebastien reached back to touch the spot over the uppermost disk inserted under the skin of her back. "She really could have applied for a Grandmastery in artificery with it."

"Why did you think Liza was so expensive?"

"Because people who come to her are desperate, and have no other options?"

He huffed in exasperation. "There are plenty of thaumaturges selling illegal services in Gilbratha, Sebastien. *Liza* is trustworthy, competent, and her skills are well-rounded. That is a difficult combination to find. I won't give away what few of Liza's secrets I happen to know, but it seems like you are severely underestimating how lucky you were to receive her help. Liza is one of the few people I know of who could have created that ward, even in a city that hosts the University."

Sebastien nodded slowly to show that she was properly impressed. And she was. Maybe, if things had gone differently, she could have paid the University tuition fee to Liza and had an apprenticeship under her instead. Still, she preferred the more well-rounded education she was currently receiving, and nothing could replace access to the library.

"But back to the point at hand," Oliver said, "the coppers don't know where you are exactly or how strong your wards are, and yet are still pouring resources into finding you. They must at least be prepared for their spell to reach the whole of Gilbratha and its outskirts, as well as overwhelm your wards. Do you see? Having the high ground makes things significantly easier" —he pointed to the white cliffs—"though I don't remember the details of how that works, but all it means is that their base spell comes at a more reasonable cost."

Sebastien frowned. Something seemed wrong about this. Her study had been narrowly focused, as she had neither the resources nor the desire to become an expert diviner. However, it seemed that she might have missed some rather important elements of understanding. "If this is right, the volume of the search field is increasing *way* faster than the power requirements." She scribbled on an invisible paper with her fingers, trying to hold the rapidly increasing number in her mind. "Either the spell becomes more efficient over greater distances, or it becomes less effective."

He smiled approvingly at her. "The latter. Divination is an imprecise art. That's a large part of why it's not more widely used. With a very low-powered base spell, it might take weeks or even months of casting to receive accurate information if the edges of your search are very distant. When I was young, the diviner in my hometown took ten days to find my father's stolen prize horse because it had been transported multiple towns away. It had already been sold by the time my father arrived to take it back."

Sebastien was intrigued by the hint of Oliver's history, but he continued. "I've always imagined it like this: A divination spell sends out many little tendrils—strings, if you will—and those strings come into contact with relevant pieces of information and return them to the caster, filtered through whatever translation and analyses method the spell is set up with. The initial number of strings stays basically the same, even if they must reach farther, and so at greater distances they take either more time or more power to gather all the data, and are less likely to be one hundred percent accurate. Caidan's Theorem isn't based on volume, but on distance. I assume there are other equations that would deal with calculating the base cost of an area-effect spell of different shapes, or the accuracy of a divination at certain distances after certain investments of time." He flipped his pencil around awkwardly. "I hope I'm making sense?"

It was strange seeing Oliver unsure, especially while in the role of a teacher, as he was normally so confident and smooth. But even she wasn't so tactless as to point it out. Sebastien nodded absently. "Mostly, though it seems like this would be a rather imprecise method of estimation, what with all the possible variables and caveats." She wondered how accurate Caidan's Theorem really was. As Professor Lacer's class had shown, through training to be more efficient, different people could get entirely different results with the same amount of available power.

Sebastien eyeballed the map of Gilbratha, gauging its proportions. "The diviners needed to reach all the way from the University through the Mires. The white cliffs are a circle with a diameter of about twelve kilometers, and the Mires spill out to the south." That math was a little too much to do in her head, but she understood the point.

"At minimum, *if* that one hundred thaum base cost is realistic, they were prepared to power that spell with a twelve thousand thaum capacity. That's the lower limits for Archmage certification. I suppose it could be cast by a Master or Grandmaster with decades of experience, too. But they had six people joint-casting. They probably had doubts about their ability to over-power my wards. Or maybe the spell's base cost was a little higher. Even if it was only one hundred fifty thaums, suddenly the cost to find me would have been...over *a hundred thousand* thaums per second." The total energy value channeled into their search, which had lasted at least twenty minutes, was mind-boggling.

She let out a low breath as she wrapped her head around the idea, then shook her head in shock. "I was in the same building as them. If they were channeling thousands of thaums, even with my ward, how could they have failed to find me?"

Oliver frowned, rubbing his jaw. "As I said, they wouldn't have been searching in a perfect circle, to conserve energy. If most of their efforts were directed in a semi-conical shape, downward and toward the south, while standing in Eagle Tower you may have just been catching the edges."

"The pressure did seem to ease off a little when I reached the floor they were on," she remembered. "And they wouldn't have started off at full power for a joint-cast spell, because of the increased chance of spell backlash. They were ramping up slowly. If I had stayed on the grounds below, I would have taken the full brunt of the spell. So perhaps it was a good thing I went to spy on them after all."

"If so, only by coincidence, not intention." He still seemed a little peeved, giving her a pointed look.

Sebastien conceded the point with a one-shouldered shrug. "The cost of the components and beast cores alone..."

"Do not forget the hazard pay for joint-casting. Divination is one of the most dangerous crafts for a reason. And remember, they have attempted this *multiple times*, if not always with today's fervor."

Sebastien stared at the map, then met Oliver's dark blue eyes. "They should give up. It's foolish to keep wasting this level of resources, no matter how much they want to find me. They have to realize that divination isn't effective on such a large scope." It was also a further reinforcement of her conviction that divination as a whole was rather useless. If the coppers weren't forcing her to, she wouldn't have even studied it this much.

He shrugged. "Or perhaps this false alarm will instead encourage them. If they believe they forced a response from the Raven Queen, that she—you—feared being caught... And at such a close distance, you likely *were* in danger of them overwhelming your defenses. Divination has its uses, and they have no way to know what they're really up against. If today's attempt had worked, the coppers would have spent one to two thousand gold to capture you, retrieved the book, and at the same time *kept* the University from doing so. It could have been worth it."

Her shoulders slumped. "You're right. They have resources to burn, and at this point I've embarrassed them, too. It could even be a matter of principle to find me, no matter the tangible return on investment."

"Perhaps."

"Instead of burning gold like that, what if they used a less costly spell and just kept it going for hours, or days? At some point, my Will would fail due to sheer fatigue."

"That would be feasible if you weren't warded and had no way to tell they were searching, but it's too risky for them. It would be just as likely to drive you to escape the city as actually catch you. They want to surprise you with enough power to overwhelm your resistance, then rush to your location before you have a chance to escape."

"Dryden Manor has wards against divination, right? Just in case there's a piece of me left behind here..." She was thinking of the bloody thumbprint on her copies of the blood print vows made with Katerin and Liza. The blood print vows were inherently warded against outside tampering, so if the coppers did manage to find them, they would self-destruct immediately. This prevented those remnants of her from being used for anything nefarious, but who knew what information the coppers might get from them before that happened.

"The manor does have basic wards, more than enough to shield against whatever small signals that random pieces of hair or whatever else might give to a scrying spell. Not strong enough to shield against them finding you yourself."

She'd thought as much, but it was good to have reassurance.

Looking at the equation, she realized suddenly that her divination attempt might never have worked to find her blood if it were actually at Harrow Hill Penitentiary, because it was too far from the University. She'd read in one of the *negligently* vague divination books that having the high ground made scrying easier, but according to Oliver's equation she would have needed a capacity of almost a thousand thaums to overcome the distance, even though her divination spell was much less costly than the coppers'. If they were smart, perhaps they would try to break past her wards with a much simpler spell, and then immediately afterward cast something more robust to give them all the information they needed to actually catch her. "You're quite knowledgeable about divination. Is that your area of expertise, then?" she asked. She wouldn't have taken him for a diviner. Maybe a general sorcerer, like her, though she realized she'd never seen him actually cast magic. But he was too intelligent and charismatic to be anything but a thaumaturge.

He stared at her for a long few seconds.

She stared back, her eyebrows raised.

Oliver picked up his whiskey and moved to stand in front of his fireplace, gazing into it as if to avoid her. "No. My father was particularly interested in the craft. Not that it did him, or the rest of the family, any good. I spent some time between the ages of ten and thirteen rather obsessed with it, until I realized my folly."

He sounded bitter, and Sebastien decided not to press the issue despite her sudden curiosity about his past. She hated when people tried to pry into her own childhood, after all. There were some things a person just wanted to forget about. "Do you have any idea why someone at the University might be working with the Morrows? Could it have anything to do with why they attacked your warehouse?" she asked instead.

"I don't know, other than that if they're working together, there must be something illegal involved. Maybe smuggling? The Morrows have contacts in that area, and territory in the docks. It would make sense if the University is feeling suppressed by the Crowns' recent increase on restrictions for magical imports. Why the Morrows would attack my warehouse seems less to do with the Raven Queen, and more likely to be because they don't appreciate me encroaching on their business or territory. But I *don't know.*" He sounded almost as frustrated as her, and with a sudden, violent motion, he dashed his glass of whiskey into the fireplace.

The glass shattered and the flames roared higher for a moment.

Sebastien jumped, immediately tense, but as Oliver stared darkly into the greedy flames, she felt herself perversely calming at the signs of his anxiety. "I think we're safe," she said, sitting down in a chair closer to him. "Or at least not in immediate danger," she amended as he turned to her with an incredulous look. "All we can do now is prepare for the future with the information we've been given." She swallowed the remainder of the amber liquid in her own whisky glass. "Step one? We need more information."

He nodded. "Knowledge is power."

"As is magic."

"But we don't have enough of either at the moment."

As much as it rankled her, he was right. "Should I start watching Tanya Canelo, then? Secretly, of course."

"Yes, her and anyone associated with her. *Please* avoid recklessness. If she finds out you are spying on her, things could go very badly for the both of us. You might need help. Unfortunately, I'm not sure how to provide you with it. I don't have anyone else within the University. Not anyone we can trust, at least. Have you noticed anything suspicious surrounding your identity as Sebastien? Do you suspect she knows who you are?"

Sebastien admitted to herself that she was barely keeping up with her current tasks. She had no time to add any sort of meaningful surveillance on Tanya. She rubbed the edge of her empty glass, listening to the crystalline ring it gave off as she achieved just the right angle and amount of friction. "I haven't noticed anything. She did seem abnormally interested in me when we first met, but I thought it was just because of the way I got admitted. Since then, she's acted...normal. And as for help on the inside..."

She grimaced, knowing Oliver wouldn't react well to what came next.

"Damien Westbay was with me when Canelo pulled her trick. We weren't wearing our student tokens, but we were seen, and we sheltered with everyone else in Eagle Tower's underground attachment. If they're investigating, and there are records of everyone who was there, it might seem suspicious that we weren't logged by the building's wards. I don't think that'll be an issue—it's definitely not incriminating by itself—but Westbay... He may have connected some of the dots. About her, I mean, not about me. If he did, I'm not sure what he might do with the information. Might it be possible to use that, somehow? Perhaps we could further pit the coppers—and the Crowns—against the University, keeping them both distracted."

Oliver sat down opposite her. "One of the Crown Family scions was with you during this reckless stunt? That's the kind of relevant information I'd like to receive a little earlier in the conversation," he said, his voice hard.

She straightened her shoulders, tilting her chin up. "There was a lot of relevant information. The other stuff seemed more important. And then you distracted me with the divination equations."

He gave her an irritated look, but said, "I'm not sure you want to draw the coppers in right away. Not until we have a better understanding of the situation. There could be a better play."

"What if he wants to talk? To them, I mean?"

"You must find a way to dissuade him. Find out what he knows, and what he wants, not just in the short term but more intrinsically, and then guide his actions." Oliver leaned back, idly rolling his sleeves up past his forearms while he thought. "Damien Westbay doesn't have a particularly close relationship with his father, from what I've observed, but the opposite is true of his older brother, who is currently running the coppers. Use that to your advantage, if you can. Hint at things that might mislead him. Stall, if that's all you can do. I'll be working on gathering information on my end, too. I might be able to find out who set off the false alarm, and I'm going to be digging into any possible connection between the University and the Morrows. If it comes to it, perhaps he could be useful to set the coppers against *them* and relieve some of the pressure on us."

Social maneuvering was not Sebastien's strong suit, but surely she could figure it out if she put her mind to it. "Westbay has seemed rather interested in ingratiating himself to me. Do you think it would be too dangerous to make it known that I prefer this all to be kept a secret for the moment?"

"Oh? Is he only interested in gaining your alliance, or is he trying to engender a friendship?"

She palmed her Conduit, rolling it around absentmindedly as she ran through her memories of Westbay, trying to catalogue his attitude. She hesitated, but decided not to mention that she'd done blood magic in Westbay's presence, or rather, cast blood magic *on* him. Westbay hadn't even realized, and she didn't feel like admitting to any more stupidity. "He thinks I share his childish interest in detective stories because I've show interest when he talks about the investigation into the Raven Queen, and he saw me do a rather impressive piece of magic. That's when his attitude really changed. At first, I thought he just wanted to use me, but he's been inviting me to spend time with his friends, acting ingratiatingly, and overall pretending as if we're best mates. Even when I snap at him, he might snap back, but he just keeps trying to burrow closer, like a roundworm. Honestly, he seemed to think this morning was all some sort of adventure from an Aberford Thorndyke story. I couldn't get him to leave me be—he forced himself along. He doesn't seem to have a sense of real-world consequences."

Oliver stood, paced a little, and then stopped with his hands in his pockets, rocking forward and back on his heels while staring at the ground. Finally, he looked up and grinned at her. "That's *perfect*, actually. If you can play deeper into that part of his personality while also gaining his loyalty, you can make your friendship and all the feelings that come along with it indispensable to him. Over time, with careful handling, he might even become a valuable resource. He's a high-ranking member of a Crown Family after all, with both money and influence."

Sebastien narrowed her eyes at Oliver. "Are you sincerely hoping I can turn him to your cause? Overthrowing the Crowns' law and rule to create some kind of idealistic utopia for everyone else?"

Oliver's smile sobered, but didn't fall away entirely. "Unlikely, perhaps, but not impossible, with enough time and subtlety. He doesn't need to know what he's getting into right away. Perhaps by the time he realizes, it will long have been too late."

"Subtlety is not my strong suit, Oliver. Nor is manipulation. I'm too... sharp and grating. Too impatient." She paused, watching his face carefully. "I can control and take responsibility for myself. Tweaking someone's strings until they dance to my tune like a puppet? I don't have the dexterity for that."

"All the better. It won't be as suspicious coming from you. We'll keep things simple enough. Mysterious. He can fill in the blanks himself. You don't have to lie overmuch, just honestly and boldly keep secrets, and with the right original framework for the whole idea, he'll be drawn in to the mystique, to the *emotion*, like a moth to flame." Seeing her skeptical look, he said, "I'll help you. We'll walk through the whole thing together. It's easier than you think, I promise. You've already laid most of the groundwork without even realizing it, I'd bet. Sebastien Siverling, a mysterious, aloof prodigy who has been withholding his friendship and confidence, suddenly offering someone desperate for belonging and meaning the inclusion he didn't even realize he craved? It would work on a lot of people, but him in particular, I think."

She sighed with reluctant acceptance, feeling that Oliver was much too confident. "I will attempt it, at least. Then, with Tanya Canelo, would it be acceptable to recruit other students to aid in the surveillance? Her counterpart, the other student liaison, has expressed a willingness to work with me, and I know he's in need of gold."

Oliver paused, but finally said, "I'll leave that up to your judgment. Please be cautious. If we do this incorrectly, things could suddenly get a lot worse than they already are."

She nodded, subdued. "I will." It was a promise to herself as much as him. "I'll keep you informed. Please do the same for me." Oliver agreed, but Sebastien still didn't feel settled, lacking the internal, subconscious stillness that came with a fully realized plan. "We've got a way forward, at least, but no matter what we find out, it's not going to solve the original problem." She leaned forward, clasping her hands together, but almost immediately found that posture to be too weak. She straightened, pushing back her shoulders and raising her chin, letting her elbows rest over the sides of the chair with a confidence and surety she didn't feel. "Unless—and this would be wonderful for us, but seems a little too optimistic to hope for—unless the blood sample they were using was destroyed in the explosion, they still have my blood. And as soon as Eagle Tower is repaired, maybe sooner if there are any other powerful divination arrays available, they'll be searching for me again."

She flexed her shoulders, feeling the five disks under the skin of her back. "What we've done to mitigate the danger isn't enough. Is there really no way for us to get my blood back from them, or destroy it?" She explained the ideas she'd come up with while waiting for him to return.

He rubbed his face. "I understand what you mean, and you make some good points. Develop your ideas on the sympathetic magic. You should do that 'reverse-scry' again the next chance you have. I'll have my people put out feelers for more mundane opportunities. If it wasn't destroyed, they'll be taking it back to warded storage. Maybe if the blood was in transit, and we knew the route and the time, we could lay an ambush. That could be effective even without needing complex, powerful magic. Probably cheaper, too. As it is, I don't believe destroying the blood impossible, because no defense is impenetrable, but I don't have the ability to make it happen. Not without sending my people on a suicide mission. And I will not do that. Let us see how the next few weeks develop. However, if you want to take out another loan in order to hire someone like Liza to help you with development or casting a spell to destroy the blood remotely, I might be able to convince Katerin." He smiled encouragingly.

Sebastien carefully controlled her facial muscles to avoid scowling at him. Why should *she* borrow a huge sum to solve the problem that was as much his fault as hers, and which put him equally in danger? She resisted the urge to point that out, remembering her worries about being considered too steep a liability. Oliver might act like an altruist, but he had led her into an impossible position and was willing to take advantage of her vulnerability just like any other manipulative loan shark. He was a criminal. And sometimes criminals did drastic, immoral things to keep themselves safe. She needed to remember that. Even if he wasn't planning to betray her as a liability, he could have easily decided to *force* another debt on her in the name of resolving this problem.

She sighed, considering mentioning her other big problem—that she needed a better Conduit—but the thought of begging for help made her muscles clench and her throat close up. That problem only led full circle back to needing another loan. *'I'll find a way to handle the Conduit on my own. Once I do that, I'll eventually find a way to turn their divination attempts against them. There are options. I just need the resources to access those options.'*

Sebastien and Oliver talked for a while longer, discussing the details of their plans and the best reactions to possible permutations of events. He came up with ideas that she never would have, including one for Westbay involving a drink coaster, an astronomy potion, and the kind of pageantry that Sebastien found ridiculous, but which she was sure Westbay would love.

Sebastien was feeling a little more settled by the time the sun began to set. She stood. "I'd stay to do some brewing—I could certainly use the gold—but I've homework and spell practice left undone. Perhaps I could pilfer the kitchen for some bread and cheese to take back with me?"

He waved his hand carelessly. "I'll have them pack you a proper dinner, but wait a moment. There is one more thing I'd like to discuss with you."

She raised her chin, staring at him.

"Do you remember I mentioned that the leader of the Nightmare Pack, who the Stags are recently aligned with, wanted to meet you?"

"I remember something about him being a fan of the Raven Queen."

"Yes, well, your faculties were somewhat impaired at the time I mentioned it. Lord Lynwood asked to meet you quite insistently the last time we spoke. I made it clear to him that I don't control you, but I would pass along the request. I also made it clear that you expect a sort of…tribute, for doing favors like this. He says he's prepared something."

She raised an eyebrow. "A bribe, just to meet me?"

"More like payment. To make it worth your time, and in the hopes that you'll look favorably on him. Your reputation precedes you. I don't know what the payment is, or what exactly he wants from you, but if he gives you something of value, I'd be willing to split its worth with you. It could solve some of your gold problem, at least, and if he has a request you cannot fulfill, you could simply turn him down. It only requires that you act powerful and mysterious enough that he feels the meeting was worthwhile."

She crossed her arms. "Half of any tribute he gives me? Why should I agree to that?"

"I'm brokering the meeting."

Her chin rose. "Ninety-ten. That's an actually appropriate number."

"I also legitimize your claim to power and infamy. Sixty-forty."

"You had little to do with my supposed power and infamy. Simply refraining from telling him the truth serves you as much as it does me. I'm sure he took into account your powerful contacts when making this deal between your two gangs, and that legitimizes *you*. Seventy-thirty. And please remember, you're not the only one who could set up a meeting between the two of us. A meeting which I'm *only* willing to take because of the chance of payment. This is a risk for me. Things could go wrong. Things we cannot anticipate because we don't know why he wants to meet in the first place. It could be a trap."

"Lord Lynwood has honor. I doubt it would be a trap, but your point is taken. Seventy-thirty, agreed."

They shook hands.

As she was leaving, she stopped and looked back. "Oh. One more thing. Newton Moore is the student liaison I was mentioning. The one that might help with Tanya. His father is sick, and his family is in need of money. I don't know if they're within Verdant Stag territory, but..."

Oliver nodded. "It's good leverage."

She shrugged. "Well, that too, but he could use the help. He could be useful to you. Maybe even more so than I am," she admitted reluctantly. "Maybe someone could reach out to the Moores and see if there's a way to help his father, or if Newton's the kind of investment you'd like to sponsor through the University."

Oliver stared at her with consideration for a few moments, but then smiled. "Okay. I'll talk to Katerin about it."

Sebastien nodded and turned to leave, hiding her own small smile. Seeking help for Newton was a little thing, considering, but it had been a shitty day, and she really needed a win right now, even if it wasn't for herself.

18

A PACT OF STARS

On Oliver's instruction, Sebastien stopped by a small apothecary in the good part of town just before they closed and bought a single potion. He'd given her a purse of twenty gold for the new mission's expenses, but she still found the price of nineteen silver exorbitant and painful. In a small town, the same amount could have fed her for two to three weeks. *'Everything in Gilbratha is overpriced,'* she grumbled mentally.

Back at the University, a couple of hours after sundown, she stopped by Tanya's dorm door. Light shone through the crack at the bottom, and the movement of shadows showed someone was awake within. Sebastien listened for a while, but heard nothing.

Satisfied that she wouldn't gain anything from more snooping at the moment, she strode into the dorms and retrieved a few small items from the chest at the base of her bed.

Westbay's cubicle was only a couple away from her own. His curtains were still open, and he sat in bed scribbling on a piece of paper—likely working on one of the essays they'd been assigned. He looked up, meeting her gaze with some surprise.

"Come with me," she said. Without waiting for a response, she turned around and strode out of the room. She heard Westbay scrambling to put on his boots and coat behind her, but didn't slow, heading out of the dorm building and toward the Citadel.

She went to the classroom that Westbay and his friends used for their morning study group. The building was mostly empty by now, with classes over and those who wanted to study likely gone to the library to do so. She took a seat at the table.

When Westbay entered, she said, "Close the door." When he did so, she gestured to the seat across from her. It was an auspicious sign that he was obeying without complaint or hesitation.

He settled slowly into the chair, light grey eyes meeting her dark ones, full of questions.

She folded her hands on the table, staring at him until the silence became uncomfortable. Finally, she asked, "What did you see today?"

"What did I see?" he repeated, confused.

"I had the idea that you're not completely oblivious to what's going on around you. Was I wrong?"

Damien leaned forward, his shoulders loosening even as his chin rose and a small, satisfied smile stretched his lips. "You weren't wrong. I did see things. I saw that Tanya Canelo got a letter that made her anxious. I saw that you followed her, or whatever clue you picked up from that divination spell you were casting—I noticed that, too—to Eagle Tower. I saw that she seemed to know when the rogue magic sirens would go off, almost as if it was *planned*." He paused, searching for a reaction, but when she gave him none, he continued. "I saw that she hid while everyone was evacuating, and was in the perfect position to cause that alchemy explosion and stop the coppers from finding the Raven Queen. I saw she had a scar, and I saw that it meant something to you, but I don't know what. And I saw that you disappeared after classes, which probably has something to do with all this."

Her expression remained neutral. "Is that all?" It was more than she had hoped, definitely, but it could have been worse. Westbay wasn't a complete idiot, after all.

He seemed taken aback. "Well...perhaps I missed some things because I don't have all the connecting information to understand what's mundane and what's a clue. But I think I did fairly well for coming into your investigation cold. Don't you?"

'*My investigation? Well, that's about the best spin he could put on it. Except he has ties to real investigators, and none of them will have any clue who I am, or find it amusing that I've seemingly been withholding evidence on an ongoing operation.*' She remained silent for a few moments, trying to figure out the best approach. '*I wish Oliver was here. He may have coached me, but an hour is not enough to gain real skill.*' Aloud, she asked, "Have you mentioned any of this to anyone?"

Westbay shook his head. "No. I can keep a secret, Sebastien. I told you that. And I'm not an idiot. You don't go around talking about an open investigation where a possible enemy or criminal could hear you."

"Not even to the coppers?" she asked.

His eyes narrowed. "You haven't gone to them either," he said, as if defending himself.

She raised an eyebrow.

He frowned. "Unless...they know about you?"

She kept her eyebrow raised.

His frown flattened and his eyes went wide. "Or they have moles among the ranks," he breathed, "and you can't go to them."

He wasn't wrong. Oliver did have informants among the coppers, though that had nothing to do with this. Westbay was also making up his own answers to unanswered questions, just like Oliver had said he would.

"What's going on? With Canelo, and you...and the Raven Queen? Who set off those rogue magic alarms? Was it the Raven Queen? Tell me," Westbay commanded.

Sebastien snorted.

Westbay's eyes narrowed. "You owe me a favor, Siverling. Do I need to call it due?"

She bared her teeth at him. "That favor is the only reason you're in this room with me right now. But it's only a medium favor. Not nearly enough to get *that* kind of information. Besides, I'm not sure you're being totally truthful about your ability to maintain confidentiality, Westbay. Because you did indeed talk about an ongoing investigation with *me*, who you didn't know and had no idea that you could trust. All I had to do was show a little interest in the Raven Queen."

He gaped and stammered before recovering. "Well, that was... I didn't give out any critical information, and probably nothing you couldn't have found out by going to the right taverns after a shift of coppers were off work for the day. This is different."

"You've proven your mouth can be loose when *you* don't think it's important, or when you're around friends, or when you want to impress someone."

"This is different," he insisted, his nose flaring as he leaned forward. "I'd never talk about a case I'm involved in, whether the information was important or not."

"Not even to your closest family members? To your brother?"

"My brother? You...think Titus can't be trusted? Or someone around him?"

She waved her hand dismissively. "I think that if you'll tell a secret to your closest family member..." She leaned forward. "If you'll talk *at all*, that's it.

You'll talk. And even if it's only ever to that one person, even if it's only when it seems reasonable, even necessary, then that one person can be used against you. In your case, Westbay, there's one particular enemy that I'd like to avoid ever getting wind of what I—and possibly you—will be doing here." She waited a beat. "Your father."

He blinked, then shook his head. "My father? He's not—"

"I believe you know that's not true," she said firmly, cutting him off. She resisted the urge to swallow nervously or let her gaze slide away.

He stared back at her, small expressions she couldn't decipher flitting across his face. Finally, he said, "I'm not sure if you're insinuating something deeper, but you're right that he'd want to stop me, and you by extension. He doesn't respect me." His last sentence was simple, but even Sebastien could tell it held a wealth of emotion.

She leaned into it. "The man is a stain on the name of all nobility," she said, her voice low. Oliver had told her a strong, even offensive stance against Lord Westbay would be one of the best ways to keep his son's mouth shut.

Damien's eyelids fluttered at the words.

She pushed one step further. "He has no honor."

When Damien didn't immediately respond, she knew she hadn't misstepped. It was actually somewhat exhilarating.

"You're different from him," she continued. "And you don't *have* to be constrained by your name or your blood. So let me ask you, Damien Westbay. What do you want?"

He considered for a moment, then said, "I want to know what's going on. I'd like to help, as an ally."

Sebastien almost released a bark of incredulous laughter. *'Has he not even considered the danger, or that whatever I'm involved in might not be on the side of the "good guys" from those stories he likes to read?'*

"You might think I'm foolish, but there's a lot I can offer, Sebastien. I'm a Westbay—"

She cut him off. "Your name holds no meaning to me. It's your character I want to see." Oliver had said to make it personal, to make Damien feel *seen* and accepted. "What do you want?"

"You already asked that. I told you—"

"What do you want *out of life*? What mark do you hope to make on the tapestry of fate? What is your true goal, your real ambition? What will give you *worth*, Damien? It is not your last name. Answer carefully."

His nostrils flared as he took a deep breath. Despite the chill in the air that wasn't fully dispersed by the Citadel's climate spells, his temples were starting to bead with tiny dots of sweat.

It took him a while to answer, but she waited silently, her own heart rushing in her chest with the thrill of it. '*This is power, too,*' she admitted silently. '*I can see why Oliver likes it.*'

"I want to do something that people—" Damien broke off, and after another long pause he finally said, in a softer voice, "I want to feel like *I* matter."

It was sincere, and raw enough that Sebastien had to look away for a moment, feeling uncomfortable and a little guilty. "I can give you that chance," she said in an equally soft voice, returning her gaze to his. "If you would like to join my operation—and let me be clear that it is rarely as exciting as it was today, and is likely to be nothing more than a boring strain on your ability to complete your homework. If you'd like to join, I'd like to have you."

"Yes," he said, this time without an ounce of hesitation.

"You should have hesitated. So that I would know you really understood what you were promising. You'll be a probationary member of this team, and will be giving up the favor I owe you in exchange. I'm in charge. You'll be doing boring work, sometimes relegated to research. You won't get to know all the details. This will be nothing like an Aberford Thorndyke story, and you will never get to talk about it to anyone."

"I agree," he said, again without hesitation. "The reason I'm not hesitating now is because I already decided I wanted in on this. I'm fine with everything you just said."

"It could be dangerous. And you will have to prove your loyalty as well as your ability. You may occasionally have to do things that are unpleasant, that would embarrass you, or even go against the laws."

"I agree," he repeated for a third time, unable to keep the excitement from sparkling in his eyes.

She settled back, still somewhat unsatisfied. '*I wish I could get him to sign a blood print vow of secrecy, but even suggesting such a thing would send most people running to the coppers. I'll just have to risk it. If he hadn't inserted himself into things today and ended up getting too much information for comfort, I'd never bring him into it. But at least this way, I can keep him close and hopefully under control.*'

He frowned at her, a hint of irritation leaking through. "Are you still holding a grudge because of the way our acquaintance started? I've learned to look past your abrasive nature, Sebastien. You could do me the same courtesy."

She sighed. "Fine. Pending your initiation, you're a provisional part of the team, Westbay."

"Damien. You should call me Damien. I already call you Sebastien, after all. Unless!" He paused dramatically, perking up. "Should we have code-names? I could be Nighthawk. Or Shadowbane. You could be..."

Sebastien raised a hand to forestall him. "*Damien* is as far as I'm willing to go. Take what you can get." She had more than enough identities to keep track of already, she didn't need another.

He seemed a bit disappointed, but perked up quickly. "What's this initiation, then? Who are the other members of your team? Are you part of an organization? Or on a secret mission from the coppers?" When she didn't answer, he inhaled sharply, his eyes going wide. "A secret mission from the *Red Guard?*"

"You are letting your imagination run away with you," she said, standing. "Come with me." She led him into the Menagerie, walking till she found a spot far enough away from the light-bordered cobblestone paths that their night vision wouldn't be affected, where there was a wide, clear view of the sky.

Damien matched her silence as she picked up a stick and scratched a Circle into the leaf-strewn, dying ground, big enough for the both of them to stand inside.

It was windy, which it often was this high up, and the flurries carried dead leaves and the premonition of snow. The moon's glow filtered sideways through the trees, but the sky was clear and cloudless. The stars were clearly visible. Sebastien looked up at them with satisfaction.

Damien cleared his throat. "What are we doing here?" he asked in a hushed voice.

She lowered her head to look at him. "Perhaps you didn't really understand what you were getting into. Do you want to go back? We can forget everything that's happened tonight. It's not too late." Of course, she didn't really want him to be frightened off. She wanted to bind him with shackles formed entirely in his own mind. That was the purpose of most initiation rituals, after all. Oliver thought it would be more effective with a group of people to lend to the sense of ceremony, but she didn't have that luxury.

"What does that mean?" he asked.

"You can be just Damien Westbay, University student who goes to classes and has fun with his friends. You won't be a part of this, but nothing will be expected of you. Maybe you will find a way to matter on your own."

He stared at her for a few seconds in the darkness. She couldn't tell what he was thinking, but just when she was growing worried, he stepped forward, joining her within the Circle.

She smiled. "Stay here." Turning around, she pulled the shallow bowl she'd retrieved from the dorms out of her pockets. There was a small stream nearby, and she dipped the bowl into it, filling it with a couple ounces of water. She returned, handing the bowl to Damien. "Hold this."

He cupped it carefully, holding it in front of his chest with both hands.

She stepped back into the Circle with him, bringing her Will to bear. Like when she was brewing a potion, she used her Will to reinforce every movement. It lent a feeling of meaning, of ritual importance to the process, even for the parts that magic wasn't technically required for, and during which she wasn't channeling any actual thaums of energy.

Here, she simply fed her Will into the Circle, consuming slight amounts of heat from the dome around them and adding a tension to the air as she claimed authority over everything within. It took barely any effort, but Damien would be able to feel it in his hind-brain, and it would lend gravitas to the impromptu ceremony.

She reached into her pockets and pulled out three small vials. "State your name."

He swallowed. "I am Damien Corolianus Westbay."

She resisted the urge to make a comment about his ridiculous middle name. "Damien Corolianus Westbay, I exhort your silence." She took a drop of the first vial's herbal oil extract on her finger and touched it to his forehead, staring down into his eyes, which seemed almost as dark as hers with nothing but the light of the stars to illuminate them. "Will you keep our secrets, knowing when to speak and when to remain silent?"

"I will," he whispered.

She increased the pressure of her Will, though still she was casting no magic.

She anointed him with the second vial's drop of oil. "I exhort your loyalty. Will you support us and our efforts faithfully and fully, with true heart and steady hand?"

"I will."

She increased the pressure once more, then touched him with the third oil, the sharp smell of peppermint only increasing that feel of unreleased tension. "I exhort your resolve. Will you persevere through hardships and the wear of time, exerting yourself to fulfill our cause?"

"I will," Damien said for the third time.

Sebastien pushed harder with her Will, till she approached the limit of her ability to coil potential force without anything to apply it to. She pulled the astronomy potion out of her pocket and poured it into the shallow bowl of water, then supported his cupped hands with her own. "Our purpose," she said, leaning forward slightly and trying to sound serious, "is freedom...and enlightenment. Drink, and look up. See beyond the edge of the sky."

He hesitated, but she gave him a shallow nod of encouragement, and he lifted the shallow bowl and drank down its contents in a couple of quick gulps.

As soon as he lowered the bowl, she released her Will at once with a mental outward thrust, just to be safe. It barely did anything, causing a small flurry of leaves and sending a couple of animals that had been hiding nearby scurrying away in alarm. But the sudden lack of tension was palpable.

Damien gasped as he looked up at the night sky.

This particular potion had been Oliver's suggestion. It wasn't mind-altering, addictive, or harmful in any way, except if the user took it and then looked into a bright light. It improved long-distance night vision, making the stars seem brighter, clearer, and more colorful. It also supposedly emphasized the dark emptiness of the rest of space. In essence, the potion created a poor version of the effects of a telescope while allowing a much wider field of view.

Many of those who had taken this particular potion for the first time reported an overwhelming wave of emotions bordering on awe, with the awareness of how small and insignificant they were—and the Earth was—compared to the vast, terrible beauty of space. Intense emotions would make Damien feel more bound to the promises he'd made and to their shared secret.

Damien's eyes filled with tears, and he blinked to send them spilling down his cheeks, breathing hard as he gazed up in wonder. "It's—I don't—"

"Shh. I know. Just see. Just let yourself be conscious." She waited a few minutes, until the tears had stopped flowing and his breath was beginning to slow, then said, "Repeat after me. I am small, as are we all."

He did as she said, still staring up at the sky.

"But I am not without purpose. We are not without meaning." She pulled the novelty drink coaster she'd gotten from Oliver out of her pocket. It was black marble embedded with a light crystal.

Using the stone disintegration and reformation exercise Professor Lacer had assigned them, she'd managed to mold the original circular light crystal into a thirteen-pointed star, working to pull out its edges in tiny sections. She didn't want to give Damien something he'd recognize from some high-class artifact shop, after all.

"There are stars in this world, too," she finished. When he'd echoed her, she said, "Look at me."

Slowly, he drew his gaze back down to the earth.

She twisted the black marble disk, slotting the inner section into the outer, and the light crystal activated, a star among darkness. She handed it to him in her cupped hands. "You may be one of them, if you prove yourself worthy."

He squinted against the mild glow of the light crystal, but took it reverently.

"This is the sign of our people," she said. "If ever anyone comes to you with one, you will know you can trust them, and should help them if they need it."

Letting out a shaky breath that fogged in the air and refracted the light of the crystal, he nodded. "Does it...this group, or order, does it have a name?"

She rolled her eyes. "What's with you and wanting a dramatic name for everything?"

He looked up from the light, the mystique of the moment lessened. His lips quirked up in amusement, and he scrubbed the tear tracks from his cheeks, sniffing hard.

"No," she said, deciding not to make something up on the spot. "We have no name. Things that have names get talked about. Besides, we need no label to constrain us."

"Freedom and enlightenment?" he echoed from her earlier words. "How exactly does that work? What do we actually do?"

"We do what is needed to fulfill our purpose, especially where others do not. Think on these principles. On what it means to be a light in the dark. I cannot give you the answer. It must be understood on your own." It was vague nonsense, but the best she could do with no real answer prepared.

He frowned over this for a moment, then asked, "How many of us are there?"

"You're only a provisional member, remember? You don't get to know everything." She picked up the bowl, which had dropped on the ground at some point, and jerked her head in the direction of the University. "Come on, let's get back."

"What do I need to do to become a full member?" he asked, following her back onto the lit path.

She shrugged. "There's no specific assignment. You'll prove yourself or you won't. There's no penalty if you don't, but your involvement—including the ability to ask questions—is limited as a provisional member."

He mulled this over for a few moments before carefully tucking the drink coaster into a pocket on the inside of his jacket. "What's my first assignment, then?"

"We'll be gathering information on Tanya Canelo and her associates. I want to bring on an informant to help us keep track of her," she said. "Not another member, just a contractor. You won't have enough time to do it by yourself."

He nodded slowly. "Okay. Who?"

"Newton Moore," she said simply.

A smirk grew on Damien's face. "Oh, that is perfect. He has a flawless excuse to spend time with her. They're both student liaisons, and they have at least half their classes together. But can he be trusted?"

"You'll help me judge that. He won't know anything about what's really going on, but we still need him to be both thorough and discreet. From what I know of him, he has both qualities."

"We should conduct the interview right away. I don't want Canelo getting out of our sight for a moment," he said gravely.

"I agree. And we will be doing more than personal observation, if we can manage it. But for the moment," she said, checking the time on her pocket watch with the approaching lights of the University buildings, "I'm pretty sure Newton is tutoring someone in the library. What do you say we catch him as soon as he's alone?"

Damien smoothed back his hair, straightened his clothes, and took the lead, striding straight toward the circular building.

19

FORMING A TEAM

SEBASTIEN
Month 12, Day 17, Thursday 9:15 p.m.

DAMIEN HAD to stop outside the library and adjust to the brightness of the lights illuminating the path and the doorway. He still winced when he entered, shielding his potion-dilated eyes even though the building's shimmering walls and the ceiling were dimmed, not shining with daylight-brightness.

"Do you think he'll agree?" Damien asked her as they made their way toward the private room Newton usually booked for tutoring.

"I'm not sure," Sebastien admitted. "It might depend on his sense of honor, or his regard for the two of us compared to *her*."

They slipped inside the private room as Newton was packing up, with less than an hour left until the library closed. His clothes were wrinkled, his eyes tired, and his fingers smudged with ink and chalk.

Damien closed the small room's door, then locked it.

Newton's eyes trailed this movement, and then went to Sebastien. "What's going on?" His tone was too weary to seem alarmed, even if he had been inclined to anxiety.

"Do you remember the offer you made, concerning employment?" Sebastien asked.

Newton nodded slowly.

"I'm here to take you up on it, a bit sooner than perhaps either of us expected."

"You want to hire me?" Newton asked her, looking to Damien questioningly.

"Why don't you sit?" Damien said, gesturing to one of the newly vacated chairs around the table. "The job is contingent upon your performance in this impromptu interview."

Still obviously confused, Newton obliged.

The two of them sat across from him. To Sebastien's relief, Damien didn't immediately try to take over the flow of conversation, deferring to her to start.

"What I require is of a delicate nature," she said. "The kind of thing that might call for you to lie to a classmate or friend, but nothing that forces you to harm the innocent or do anything truly distasteful. Is that the kind of thing you can handle?"

Newton hesitated, but nodded. "Hypothetically, yes. But... Sebastien, what is this about?"

"Your silence is the prerequisite for saying any more, whether or not you decide to take the job. Can you agree to that as well?" she asked.

He hesitated, then leaned forward, lowering his voice. "Are you asking me to help you cheat on the mid-term exams? Because, to be honest, I really don't have a way to make that happen, and I'm also not sure that either of you would benefit very much. Westbay already scored among the top three hundred incoming students, and you cannot be that worried about your own results, Sebastien. Besides, it's the end of term exams you should really be worried—"

Sebastien stopped him with a hand gesture, unable to hide her smile. "No, Newton. It's not that at all." She looked to Damien, then back to Newton. "Can we trust that you'll keep this conversation private? I want your oath, or we walk out this door right now."

Newton straightened, looking more alarmed. "I swear on my name and honor, unless I judge that what you tell me will bring serious harm to yourselves or others, I will not divulge the contents of this conversation. Now please explain."

"We want you to spy on Tanya Canelo!" Damien burst out before Sebastien could say anything, vibrating with poorly suppressed excitement.

Sebastien could have strangled him. Damien could be smooth and cunning just long enough for her to let down her guard, and then slip into this childish obliviousness and ruin it.

Newton's face sped through a series of expressions, too quick for Sebastien to decipher them, and finally settled on wary interest. "I don't understand." He paused, losing focus for a moment as his gaze turned thoughtfully inward.

"Or rather, I understand the actual words you're saying, but...why? What would I be looking for?"

'At least he didn't immediately refuse. He's considering it.'

"Everything," Sebastien said simply. "Even the things that don't seem particularly memorable. We want to know every time she leaves your sight, anyone she speaks with, even the things she researches for homework projects."

"Can I ask why?"

"No, you can't," Damien said.

"We have good reasons," Sebastien said. "And no intention to place ourselves or other students in harm's way."

Newton rubbed one of the ink splotches on his fingers, staring at her. "Did Tanya *do* something? Offend you?"

She smiled. "She did something. It didn't offend me personally. And before you ask, it's the kind of delicate matter that we cannot take to the authorities. We could do this without you, but..." Sebastien reached into her pocket and pulled out the small purse Oliver had given her. It held the operating expenses he'd supplied for this mission; Tanya being associated with the Morrows and the Morrows possibly having a connection to the University—and its power— was relevant to him as well as her. After purchasing the astronomy potion, of which she now had several useless doses remaining, the purse contained eighteen gold and one silver. If she needed more funds, she would have to ask for them. She pulled out one gold crown and set it on the table, then pushed it with her finger toward Newton. "Two gold a week," she said, leaving the coin in front of him. "That's a signing bonus. Either you trust me or you don't."

Damien eyed the purse with some surprise, as if trying to gauge how much was hidden within.

Newton looked down at the coin, then up at her, his bloodshot eyes inscrutable. "I trust you," he said, palming the coin. "So tell me again, and in detail. What do you need me to track?"

Sebastien didn't try to restrain her smile. "I'm happy to be working with you," she said. She didn't know if he actually trusted her, or if he was simply desperate for the chance to make extra coin, but it didn't matter as long as he did what was asked of him.

She proceeded to detail exactly what that was. "We'll want detailed written reports and a verbal review twice a week," she finished. "Be discreet. Take the opportunity to get into her confidence, if possible. If you find something particularly important you can earn a bonus, but we don't expect you to place yourself in any dangerous situations."

When they were done with the instructions, Newton left to get started. As his solo dorm room was directly adjacent to Tanya's, he would be able to keep tabs on her in the evening and early morning.

As Newton was leaving, he turned back to face Sebastien. "Thank you for thinking of me for this," he said, adjusting the strap of his school bag nervously. "And, umm, for pointing Alec Gervin my way." He gave her a mischievous grin. "I'm charging him three gold a week for one-on-one lessons, and it's going to be even more for the exam prep sessions."

She grinned back. "I heard from someone knowledgeable that it works best to treat him like a dog."

Damien flopped his head back and groaned, not without amusement.

Newton grinned wider. "Treats, praise, and plenty of exercise. Got it."

When Newton had gone, Sebastien locked the door again. She took a seat and crossed one leg over the other. "Your first assignment is researching and developing other ways we'll be able to keep track of her. I'd like to put a ward on her door, so we know when she goes in and out, especially at odd times. A tracker would be even better. Use the library as a resource. It will have all the knowledge you need, as long as you're skilled enough to compile it. If you get stuck, come to me. If you need assistance casting, I can also help with that. In fact, I would prefer to. Be circumspect about letting anyone else understand what you're doing."

Damien nodded without hesitation. "I already have some ideas. I'll bring you a solution by tomorrow night. Perhaps it won't be as elegant as some of the things my brother's people come up with, but speed is of the essence, right?"

"We'll have time to improve the system, if nothing happens. If something does happen, we need to be aware, even if it's not exactly elegant," she agreed. "As long as it's subtle enough that she won't become suspicious."

Damien bounced on his feet, swinging his arms like a child who'd eaten too much sugar. "I can't wait to get started. I'm going to start looking up references." He hurried off into the stacks without waiting for a response, muttering, "I wish the library were open later. Only half an hour to check out everything I need..."

Sebastien watched him go with a bemused expression. She checked out a few books of her own and took them back to the dorms to finish her homework, then practiced Professor Lacer's extra exercises. In some ways, it seemed a little foolish to be doing that with everything that had happened in the last day, but it wouldn't do to be so afraid of what the future might bring that she ran around like a chicken with her head cut off and failed to *prepare* for said future. Improving her Will was something she could never neglect.

She had moved on to the third auxiliary exercise, which seemed to complement the new main exercise. It was very simple, only requiring her to create a ball of compressed air, and had similar principles to the air-cushion spell she'd learned years before to make bumpy wagon rides more comfortable.

With her small, contaminated Conduit, she could only compress a small volume. This exercise required a simpler thought process than the three-dimensional maze or the skewed sympathetic movement spell, but unlike the original ball-spinning exercise, at no point did inertia make the process easier. It seemed to actively fight against her with every second, pressing back against her Will with equal and opposite force, always vying to escape and disperse through any point of weakness.

Being forced to cast with a sub-par Conduit was starting to noticeably improve her efficiency, which was about the only upside. Out of the initial five bonus exercises, there were two left that she had yet to attempt. Though she had wanted to gain a basic measure of competency in all of them by the mid-terms, she knew that was probably impossible by now. All the extra things she had to worry about had hampered her progress.

There were no more attempts to scry her, which wasn't necessarily a surprise but *was* a relief. She felt like someone teetering at the edge of weight-lessness on a rope swing, not sure yet if she would fly off or drop back down. The coppers could just be biding their time, or maybe Tanya had really disrupted their ability to try again, at least for now. She tried not to be too anxious waiting for the moment when they would surprise her again.

The next morning, she got a letter from Oliver, brought by a runner and then delivered by the Administration office. She broke the wax seal and tore through the redundant paste seal below that. He'd been conscious of security, even though the only thing inside was a meeting time and a note to arrive a few hours early.

The Raven Queen would be meeting with the Nightmare Pack leader that Sunday, an hour after dark, approximately thirteen minutes after six, when the moon would be highest in the sky. It was an oddly specific time, but some people were prone to dramatics.

20

NOTICING CONFUSION

THADDEUS
Month 12, Day 17, Thursday 11:55 p.m.

AFTER RETURNING from the site of the false rogue magic alarm, which was still cordoned off while the investigators scoured the area for evidence, Thaddeus had learned of the failed scrying attempt on the Raven Queen. Suddenly the timing and effort that had gone into disrupting the whole city's lives for a couple of hours that morning had made sense.

Now, much later, he sat in one of the many rooms in the network of restricted archives beneath the library, looking through an ancient text written in a long-forgotten language. Despite the importance of his research, he found himself distracted.

Setting off the city's rogue magic alarms was not simple. No ordinary citizen could do it. The effort that had gone into faking the scene was impressive, considering the limited time the culprit must have had between setting off the alarms and the arrival of the Red Guard. It had seemed senseless, at first, before he realized that it was quite the perfect distraction.

When the sirens had gone off, Thaddeus had requested all the details, as he always did, and had hurried to leave the University when he was told it was an Aberrant, Master-level, and an Eldritch type. He'd hoped to arrive in time to see it in action, and to study it before the Red Guard took it—or its remains —away to one of their black sites. The Aberrant earlier that month had been a particularly interesting specimen, an anomaly, and he'd been hoping for a repeat, though he knew the chances were exceedingly low.

The Red Guard had arrived before him and had already cordoned off an area around where the beacon had been sent from. They were sweeping the area thoroughly, but the citizens had evacuated to the nearest shelter already, leaving the street eerily still, silent except for the piercing sirens.

The signs of what seemed to be a violent Aberrant attack were obvious.

The doors lining each side of the street in about a two-block area were smashed in, some torn entirely off their hinges. Blood, guts, and organs were splashed haphazardly in and around each doorway. The blood was already half-curdled, sitting in stinking, oozing, jellylike lumps rather than spreading and pooling. The bodies were in pieces and entirely unrecognizable, missing head, limbs, and any other identifying features.

As he wasn't an active member of a Red Guard emergency direct response squad, Thaddeus had to stay on the edge of the cordon with one of the communication and containment team members. But that didn't stop him from casting diagnostic and warding spells.

He caught no signs of the Aberrant. As time passed and the communication team member beside him reporting a similar lack of success from the direct response team, Thaddeus grew increasingly alarmed.

"Could it be a Nightmare?" one of the containment team members muttered to his partner.

Even the words sent a cold centipede crawling up Thaddeus's back. He crouched down to draw out the most comprehensive and obscure ward against mental interference that he knew.

No Aberrant was exactly the same as another, but they came in broad types.

A Nightmare, especially one at Master level, was the kind of thing that could warrant an entire village and all the people within being quarantined and then firebombed indiscriminately in a desperate attempt to deal with it. Nightmare-types were named such because they could control, in some way, the subjective experience of the people trying to take them down. They used stealth, subversion, or mind-control.

Thaddeus had seen Nightmares that could walk right past a prognos without them realizing they were in danger. Others could insert themselves into your memories as an innocuous friend that you believed was harmless and amicable, despite any and all evidence to the contrary. Others were barely mutated by the change, passing as the humans they had once been, while inside they were twisted and corrupted.

This ward wouldn't help if the Aberrant was invisible, or could transform into an animal, or travel through the reflection of the shop windows, but all those were things he could handle. The sanctity of his mind was paramount.

It wasn't until the direct response squad found the huge buckets filled with traces of blood and offal that they began to suspect the truth. The buckets were from a nearby butcher's shop, and had been stashed in a back room of one of the smashed-up houses.

When they found the pair of coppers who had set off the rogue magic sirens, that suspicion became a near-certainty. The coppers were lying on the ground in another house, drunk to the point of unconsciousness and relieved of the artifact that allowed all law enforcement teams to trigger the alarms.

The direct response squad levitated them back, tossed them into a quarantine ward, and forcefully sobered them up with a couple of potions. The inebriated coppers could have been the product of an Aberrant with particularly strange abilities, but Thaddeus already suspected they had all been duped.

Fighting severe hangovers, both coppers denied triggering the alarms. They didn't remember anything past stopping for lunch in one of the now-emptied pubs.

Whoever had done this was competent. The alarm-triggering artifact law enforcement teams carried was complicated, and required various inputs to send off the call for help and activate the alarms. Either the perpetrator had known the password string and the various codes to communicate danger levels to the Red Guard, or they had extracted that information from the coppers. They'd taken the artifact with them, too, and must have started falsifying the scene immediately after the area was evacuated, then escaped shortly before the arrival of the Red Guard.

Of course, all this evidence wasn't enough to make them let down their guard. They had to verify that the blood and offal were all from animals, cast divinations to confirm that the broken-down doorways were damaged by a standard concussive blast spell, and search for signs of curses, erased memories, and replacement or subversion of the two coppers. No two Aberrants were exactly alike, after all.

Hours of tedium later, and with only a little bit of work as an expert consultant on Thaddeus's part, they had determined with surety that there had never been an Aberrant at all.

The Raven Queen, possibly one Siobhan Naught, had foiled the attempt to find her flawlessly.

He wondered if she had some further use for the alarm-triggering artifact she, or her agent, had taken from the coppers. Unlike the last time she'd had an altercation with law enforcement, she hadn't shown herself directly. Even the report of the Master level Eldritch-type hadn't matched her description or that of her shadow-raven companion.

The Raven Queen seemed the type to make a show of it. She would poke fun at their inability to stop or catch her, or leave behind some gift that would perplex and frighten them. This had been skillful, but it lacked her bold, playful signature. He doubted she'd been directly involved in the operation.

Thaddeus stared sightlessly at the arcane glyphs on the ancient parchment laid carefully on the desk in front of him, simultaneously fatigued and filled with restless energy now that he was back at the University.

He wondered again what had been in the book she stole. Those higher up in the University and the Crowns surely knew, and thought it was important. Important enough that they were treating it like a national secret. Casual questions had lent no information, even to him, and he wasn't sure he wanted to be seen being *too* interested.

If she were looking at the text before him—records of those who had lost themselves to magic thousands of years ago—would she be able to read them? Would she understand the significance of his research?

He dismissed the thought along with the desire behind it. She was too volatile, too inclined to risky undertakings to be a viable partner. And his work was too important to gamble.

Perhaps, though, that would make her the perfect test subject.

Again, he dismissed the idea. It was too reckless to even consider.

As much as he hated to admit it, sometimes he got lonely, being the only one with big ideas, the only one who really seemed to see and *understand*.

Maybe that was part of the reason he had finally decided to take an apprentice, provisional or not. He had seen potential in the Siverling boy, both in the perspective that leaked through in his test answers, and in his Will.

There was an intangible quality of the Will that had nothing to do with practice or even intelligence. It was that hidden part that was vaguely categorized as "force."

Thaddeus had always likened it to an all-consuming hunger. A bloodlust. A lack of self-imposed limitations. That was what it really was. And he could see that quality in the boy's dark eyes.

Maybe Thaddeus had taken an apprentice in the hopes that he could, through imparting his own knowledge and ideas to someone with a similar lack of self-imposed limitations, create a companion for himself.

He had found himself recently disappointed in that choice, with Siverling deliberately underperfoming in class for Damien Westbay's benefit. Thinking about it again, Thaddeus grew irritated. The memory of the boy refusing to keep casting past Damien's limit and then staring Thaddeus down in his office afterward niggled like an itch in the back of his brain.

Thaddeus lifted his head, latching on to that itch. It wasn't just irritation. It was confusion—something didn't make sense. Why would someone like Sebastien Siverling, proud and angry, bend his neck to a Westbay? Were he the type to do that, he never would have gotten into an argument or rivalry with the other boy. He wouldn't have had the gall to look Thaddeus in the eye.

Thaddeus grabbed onto his confusion, tearing it open. He delved into his memory of that day.

Siverling had been prone to wincing, some better hidden than others. He had been sure to face away from the light. He had kept his hands under the table, pressed against it, or in his pockets. He'd spoken as little as possible, *moved* as little as possible, maintaining impeccable posture. And despite Thaddeus's watchful gaze, he had *refused* to keep casting over approximately two hundred thaums.

Damien had been worried for him.

"Will-strain," Thaddeus whispered.

He straightened, leaning away from the table. How had he not seen it? He was more than familiar with the signs. He knew Siverling was the type to push his limits like he didn't quite believe they *existed*. The boy was a reckless fool, and eager to prove himself.

Thaddeus stood, moving as quickly as he could while still taking care to put the ancient parchment back into its spot gently. Siverling had already proved himself too stubborn to come clean. Otherwise, he would have done it immediately and saved himself Thaddeus's ire.

No. Damien was the weak link here.

Thaddeus strode through the winding archives up into the library proper, which was closed to students and dark at this hour. He created a floating light above his head with a thought. It followed him all the way to the student dorms, which were also dark, and as silent as a building that housed thousands of young adults could be at midnight.

It took him a couple of tries to find the ground floor room with his apprentice's student group.

When he did, he snuffed the light, then cast a spell that would muffle sound in a large bubble around himself. He was just tall enough to see over the edges of the cubicles, so there was no need to pull back the curtains on every random student. He walked through the aisle separating the young women and men, noting the occasional sloppy wards placed by the barely competent "firsties."

Damien's bed was only two removed from the end, where Siverling had pressed his small bed and himself into the corner of the walls, like a cornered animal.

Thaddeus flicked back the thin curtain in front of Damien's stone cubicle, strode inside, and clasped his hand over the boy's sleeping face.

Damien woke with a gasp, scrabbling frantically at Thaddeus's hand.

Thaddeus stayed still until the boy realized it was him and stopped fighting. Then he took his hands away, wiping the saliva off his palm with a grimace of distaste.

"Professor Lacer," Damien croaked. "What are you doing here?" He looked around, wild-eyed and panting.

"That day in my class, when Siverling couldn't beat you—he had Will-strain. For some reason, he was keeping this a secret." He raised one eyebrow in a menacing, silent query.

Damien pushed himself into a sitting position, shaking his head. "It's not what you think."

"Oh? Then what is it?" he asked darkly.

Damien looked toward Sebastien's cubicle, though he wouldn't be able to see anything with the cubicle between them. Still, the thought of the other boy, so close, seemed to calm him. His breathing slowed, and he sat up more fully. "Well, obviously you think it's something that warrants waking me up in the middle of the night like some assassin. I don't know exactly what conclusions you've drawn, but I assure you, Sebastien is...he's a good person. He deserves to be here. He's smart, and driven, and maybe someday he'll beat your record for the youngest Master of free-casting."

Thaddeus raised an eyebrow at that.

Damien swallowed, but continued. "Coming here, to me, in the middle of the night was an act of...alarm."

"Or insatiable curiosity and a disregard for social norms," Thaddeus said.

Damien blinked at him. "Umm. Well. I'm not going to sate your curiosity." He drew himself up a little straighter, lifting his chin defiantly. "But I can tell you that if you were alarmed, you don't need to be. Sebastien is responsible."

"Or *you* are gullible." Thaddeus considered him for a moment. "Do you think being a Westbay will protect you from the consequences of defying me?" He stared into the boy's eyes, imagining himself boring into those wide pupils like a maggot searching for answers.

Damien shuddered. His eyes seemed to darken, and for a minute he reminded Thaddeus of the older Westbay brother, Titus, uncowed and defiant. "I'm more than a Family name, Professor Lacer. I respect you, but I will not be cowed by you."

Thaddeus smiled and stepped back. "I see he has a loyal friend in you. That's good, I suppose. He's foolish enough to need someone around to help him get out of trouble. As long as you don't help him get *into* it, too."

"It wasn't his fault," Damien admitted, his cheeks reddening. "I'm not going to say anything more about it. I promised my silence."

Thaddeus was slightly irritated, but he couldn't deny some equal measure of satisfaction. Whatever he had done, Siverling had created a loyal and powerful ally. Those were useful.

Damien poked a finger upward, as if remembering something. He spoke slowly, as if sounding out the idea even as he spoke it. "However, I will say that you should provide better for your apprentice—provisional or not. How can he prove himself to you without the proper tools? If he's going to win contribution points at the end of term exhibitions, he's going to need a better Conduit."

Thaddeus stared at him a moment, then spun around, leaving Damien and stalking to the end of the room. He pulled back Sebastien's curtains more gently than he had Damien's.

The boy woke as soon as Thaddeus took the first step into the little cubicle.

Siverling tensed, but he wasn't disoriented, his black eyes immediately locking on to Thaddeus while his hand slipped under his pillow. Likely palming his Conduit. His *sub-par Conduit*.

Siverling watched him approach, saying nothing.

Thaddeus leaned over him, speaking softly. "Do not speak. Listen, and *hear me*. I know that earlier this month in my class, when you refused to perform to the best of your abilities, you were hiding Will-strain." He watched the boy for a response, but there was none, not even a hitch in his breath or a flutter of an eyelash. "I don't care about whatever foolishness caused you to reach that point. Mr. Westbay has assured me of his silence on the matter, even in the face of threats. However, my tolerance requires that you understand one salient point."

Thaddeus let his voice grow softer, as with a certain type of person that was more intimidating than growling or shouting. "You will not place yourself or other students in such grave danger ever again. I do not care if you have stretched your Will to the end of its limits by torturing small animals or performing depraved sexual acts with some of the more questionable members of the student body. As long as you do not bring shame to my name. I *do* care that you *do not* afterward disregard the safety of yourself and everyone around you by continuing to cast. You could have killed yourself and half the students in that classroom with your stubbornness. Never again." He whispered the last part, then stared into Siverling's eyes in silence.

Siverling nodded jerkily.

"The correct thing to do would have been to refuse to cast *at all*. Ideally, with a pass from the infirmary."

Siverling nodded again.

"Good. You will regret it if we are forced to have this conversation again."

Another nod from the boy, who was still following Thaddeus's original order not to speak.

"Now, onto the second matter. Show me your Conduit."

Slowly, suspiciously, Siverling pulled his fist from beneath his pillow, unclenching it to show the pitiful chunk of raw, uncut celerium within.

Thaddeus plucked it up, weighing it in his hand and then creating a light behind it to see its clarity. He sneered with disgust, tossing the disgraceful shard back at his apprentice. "That thing could barely be expected to support the Will of a child of thirteen."

Siverling just stared back up at him, blinking against the brightness of Thaddeus's light.

His silence, rather than being gratifying, was beginning to irritate. "Speak, boy. Did your family not provide you anything better?"

Siverling's eyes narrowed at that. "I'm on my own. I know it's not very good, but I've been being careful with it. It's a good lesson in *efficiency*," he said challengingly.

Thaddeus snorted. "It is a lesson in *impoverishment*, and leaves you no room to grow. Come with me. No dawdling."

Siverling's jaw lifted. "Am I being expelled?"

"No, you imbecile. I am rectifying this problem, which you should have come to me with as soon as you knew."

As soon as Siverling had thrown on his jacket and boots, Thaddeus straightened his own jacket and strode out of the room. They were joined by Damien, who said stubbornly, "I'm coming too," when both Thaddeus and Siverling gave him surprisingly similar expressions of refusal. Thaddeus didn't have the inclination to argue at the moment.

When they stepped out into the night air, both boys flinched at the chill. Thaddeus took a deep breath, somewhat enjoying the bite against his lungs, and let his muffling bubble fall away. "Did the University's loaner program not have anything better than that? Or did you shatter theirs and are trying to put off having to pay?"

Both of them looked at him blankly. He exhaled heavily, his breath fogging in the air. "The University offers low-level Conduits to first-term students who need them. All students should have been made aware of this when they signed up for their classes."

"Never heard of it," Damien said.

"Perhaps they thought I didn't look poor enough," his apprentice muttered darkly.

"Indeed," Thaddeus said. "In any case, you are beyond needing a low-level Conduit, so the point is moot."

When he led them toward the east instead of one of the other University buildings, Damien asked, "Where are we going?"

"To my lodgings. As a professor, I have been afforded a small cottage on the grounds. I keep my old Conduits there."

The two boys shared a look of surprised excitement.

He had them stay in the entryway while he retrieved the Conduit from his warded safe in the back room. He tossed it to his apprentice, who caught it, wide-eyed. "I won that one off a particularly foolish noble in a rural tavern. He tried to have me killed for the offense, but I disabused him of that notion.

This Conduit was better than my own at the time, and I used it until I outgrew it. Do not make me solve this problem for you again, Siverling."

The boy looked up at him, his expressions vacillating rapidly between several different emotions. "I will not. Thank you, Professor Lacer."

Beside him, Damien was smiling rather smugly. No doubt the boy felt pleased to have orchestrated this.

"You will return that to me when you have outgrown it. Now go! Back to the dorms with you," Thaddeus ordered, scowling. "It is well after curfew, and you've rudely kept me awake too long already."

With his fist clenched around the Conduit, Siverling gave him a stiff bow, then turned and left without another word, copied quickly by young Damien.

As Thaddeus had noted before, a disregard for even the *idea* of limits was necessary for all truly great thaumaturges. Siverling's disregard was a little too broad, though. Will-strain was a sign that you had *already* lost control, and continuing past it was the kind of madness that turned promising young men into corpses, or worse.

As Thaddeus prepared for sleep, one of his few true indulgences in life, he found the edge of his lip curling up in a slight smirk. By rights, he should be furious, but instead he found himself ruefully amused. "Children," he muttered aloud.

At least Siverling wasn't *boring*.

21

THE CONSTITUTION OF COCKROACHES

SᴇʙᴀsᴛIᴇɴ
Month 12, Day 18, Friday 12:30 a.m.

DᴇsᴘIᴛᴇ ʜᴇʀ ᴇxʜᴀusᴛIᴏɴ, Sebastien had trouble getting back to sleep after Professor Lacer's impromptu nighttime visit. She had left Professor Lacer's house with Damien, who looked just as shocked as she felt, practically marching on her heels.

Sebastien grilled him on everything Professor Lacer had said, but there really wasn't much to go over. However Lacer had figured out the Will-strain, Damien hadn't helped him, and she couldn't really fault Damien for mentioning her Conduit when it had gotten her a new one—one so much better it almost made her want to cry with relief.

Now that her Conduit problem had been solved, she realized it had been rather obvious. She had instinctively wanted to keep her new, sub-par Conduit a secret, and not only because she didn't want anyone wondering what she'd been doing to break her old one on the same weekend the Raven Queen almost got caught. She'd unconsciously believed that if the University found out, they would expect her to immediately rectify the situation or be kicked out. Celerium was ridiculously expensive, exponentially so at higher capacities, and students without a proper Conduit were endangering not only themselves but others.

But it was more than that. She hadn't believed she could rely on or trust anyone but herself. It had been a long time since she learned that she was the only one in this world she could count on. *'Maybe…maybe I can at least consider the option that someone else might actually be willing and able to help me when I need it,'* she thought, feeling uncomfortable with the idea. It didn't feel safe to think like that. But the proof was in her hand. Professor Lacer hadn't even asked for anything in return.

The Conduit he had loaned her was still raw and unfaceted, but had been set in a metal ring with an attachment for her to hang it as the counterweight for her pocket watch. It was a little cloudier than the one set in her mother's ring, now in the Gervin Family's hands, but still large enough that she estimated it would support six or seven hundred thaums. She would need to have it tested.

Damien was rather smug about the whole thing, but she was actually too tired to snap at him. She felt like she'd lived weeks over the course of that single day, with enough stress and mental exertion to fill it all.

Sebastien used her new Conduit to cast her dreamless sleep spell. It channeled magic like silk, and she poured as much into the spell as she wanted without worry.

On Friday, she woke still exhausted, and was thankful to only have the two classes: Modern Magics in the morning and Practical Casting in the late afternoon.

She spent the middle of her day in the library, on the ground floor in a spot where she could watch the staircase nearest Tanya Canelo, who was on the second floor where Sebastien couldn't go.

She was reminded by the reduced number of bracelets hidden under her clothes on her forearm that she'd wanted to figure out how to cast that paper bird spell that was so common on the University grounds. It would be much more convenient to be able to send a secure message to Oliver, Katerin, or now even Damien, without needing to create a new pair of artifacts from scratch every time. Plus, just the ability to send a complete, nuanced message would make it worthwhile.

To her disappointment, while the spell's details were easy enough to find, it wasn't a viable option for her. Creating the paper alone was a long, complicated, and expensive process. It needed to be, for the paper to handle the magic and maintain the integrity of the animation and homing spells over even moderate distances.

Apparently, the folded birds were a type of enchanted artifact. The University Administration center staff saved time on the folding by casting a continue-motion spell, which she actually knew. It was a complex spell array, and finicky, but you could essentially give yourself an extra set of arms or a dumb assistant as long as you could concentrate on keeping the magic active.

All you had to do was demonstrate the action as one of the inputs of the spell, and an invisible force would continue the action, *exactly*, for as long as you could power it. It was good for things like stirring a pot continuously if you wanted to leave your hands free for something else. The woman she'd learned it from had used it for spinning thread and then weaving cloth.

There was another, more advanced version that Sebastien didn't know. The mimeo-motion spell would allow duplication of the continued motion in multiple places. People used it most commonly for producing multiple copies of books. A scribe could write one page while the magic copied their actions across a couple dozen other sheets of paper. The spell would then continue making dozens more copies without the scribe.

It was one of the great innovations of the Third Empire, under the Blood Emperor's reign, and the biggest reason that books had become widespread and even marginally affordable. Unfortunately, it was largely useless for any magical application. It couldn't be used to create a dozen potions at the same time, for example.

Returning her thoughts to the paper bird messenger spell, Sebastien considered trying to get her hands on some of the sheets that someone else had made.

More discouragement hit when she learned the homing spell did not work on some magical extra sense. The paper bird simply moved to preprogrammed points or followed the homing beacon of the staff and student University tokens that everyone carried. The homing spell also grew more difficult to cast over distances more than a kilometer or two.

She gave up the idea of having her own paper birds sending messages at that point. *'The University must be spending more on that little trick than people pay to send the messages. It's just another way for them to show off.'* There were other magical methods to send messages to people, but all those she knew of were beyond her reach, either in resources, magical power, or knowledge, and most of the time in all three areas.

'It looks like I'm going to have to make a few more bracelets.' Damien would need a set of his own, after all. She might as well make some for Newton, too, while she was at it, and have them be part of a network, like her other bracelets were part of a network with Oliver and Katerin.

After that disappointment, Sebastien tried to study, but kept getting distracted trying to wrap her head around her piling mountain of problems.

Before she knew it, the morning had passed, and Tanya walked down the stairs, accompanied by Newton, who shot Sebastien a surreptitious thumbs-up behind Tanya's back.

Sebastien didn't follow. She didn't want to make her interest in the other woman obvious.

The library emptied as most students went to lunch, but Sebastien's stomach felt too sour and knotted to eat. "My life is falling apart," she muttered. With a dramatic groan, she let herself slump forward until her forehead bumped the table.

"As bad as all that?" an amused voice asked from behind her.

Sebastien jerked up, turning to the woman who'd spoken. "Professor Ilma!" She tried to keep from focusing on the embarrassment so that she didn't make it worse by blushing.

The blue-tinted woman sat down across the table from Sebastien. "Siverling, correct?"

Sebastien nodded.

Professor Ilma's eyes drooped with boredom, her expression of disinterest belying her words. "It must take a lot for the life of a bright, motivated young man such as yourself to fall apart."

Sebastien didn't respond, staring at her History professor as she tried to figure out how to respond without seeming suspicious.

Professor Ilma stared back, content to wait.

"My problems all seem to compound upon each other," Sebastien said finally. "That's all."

Ilma nodded, as if she'd expected that. "Real life problems are like that. Sometimes, one catalyst problem can create an avalanche as time passes, as it impacts a delicate balance of unstable components. We see this repeated over and over again in history. And yet, here we are, none of these—at the time catastrophic—events have stopped humankind in the long run."

'Is she trying to encourage me?'

"This is not coincidence. We can take personal lessons from the greater lessons of people and times past." Ilma raised her eyebrows, as if expecting Sebastien to agree, but when Sebastien only nodded bemusedly, she sighed and straightened.

Her voice took on the tone she used while lecturing in the classroom. "We've discussed how precarious it has been for the human species many times throughout history. Yet now, we are the dominant species of the most fertile lands of this continent. I don't believe it's some individual inherent superiority that has allowed this. There is a tendency to focus our attention on great men who did great deeds, as if they were important. And sometimes, they were, but generally they were only able to accomplish these great deeds because of an overall shift in the surrounding culture or established powers."

Ilma pushed back from the desk, standing to pace like she did in her classroom. "Great men do great deeds with the force of a society behind them. Now, some would say that this ability to form groups of many individuals that help each other and work for mutual benefit is proof that the human species has a moralistic advantage, duty, and *right* to power and prosperity. But communities are not the purview of humans alone. And I would question whether this ability to form them is truly altruistic and a sign of morality, or whether it's simply a matter of humans being so *weak* that this large super-organism of a city, or a country, is the only way for the individual to survive. Cooperation is utilitarian."

The woman's volume rose with passion, seemingly lost in her own thoughts. "If we are truly governed by morality, how can you explain the aggression, the persecution, the *genocide* against not only other species but *ourselves*? It is almost as if we cannot stop our inherent proclivity for aggression even when it's not good for us. So, I posit that the real reason we have managed to survive is twofold. One, despite being so weak magically, we are extremely versatile. Like cockroaches. And like cockroaches, we breed quickly."

Ilma stopped, seemingly realizing her audience, and turned back to Sebastien. Clearing her throat awkwardly, she retook her seat. "My point is, humans are versatile and incredibly resilient, not only as a species but as individuals. If you are searching for an answer to a complex problem..."

She shook her head. "Decisions, *solutions*, aren't always as binary as we like to think of them. It's not always a good deed or an evil one, greed or altruism, left or right. And it's *also* not always some combination of the two. The middle path can be even worse than one extreme or the other. However, sometimes people realize this and jump to say that *no* right path exists. Or that all paths are equally valid. Both of these are usually just as incorrect as a simple binary answer. Though they might seem wiser, they are, in truth, useless. Humans don't need useless answers. We need *utility*." She stared at Sebastien as if expecting her to understand now.

Sebastien frowned, fascinated by the impromptu lecture despite her initial bemusement. "I understand what you're saying, but..."

Ilma sighed again, speaking before Sebastien could continue. "Humans are versatile and hardy. Like cockroaches," she repeated. "Whatever complex, intertwined problems you have, they are not insurmountable. It's not that there are no answers to complex problems. There are usually *many*. It's just that they're hard to find, and even harder to implement. If you cannot find a solution, look at your problems from a different angle, pull in new resources, and don't be afraid to be ruthlessly utilitarian. Sometimes the solution is to kill whatever problem is too resource-intensive to deal with."

Sebastien thought all of that seemed reasonable, but she still wasn't sure how to apply it to her specific situation. "Thank you," she said, nonetheless.

Professor Ilma's bored expression was back again. "Go to lunch," she said. "Food is one of those resources humans need to solve problems."

As Sebastien gathered up her things and left, Professor Ilma called after her. "Don't forget your essay due on Tuesday!"

Ilma's advice swirled around Sebastien's mind, and she found herself thinking of it suddenly at random moments for a while afterward.

"Kill whatever problem you can't deal with," she muttered to herself. Her Conduit problem had already been solved, and to be fair, it was the most critical bottleneck in solving the remainder of her problems.

She had two surplus Conduits now, the one she'd bought recently, and the even smaller one she'd had since she was a child. Professor Lacer had intimated that she could keep the one he'd lent her as long as she needed it—at least as long as she stayed at the University. Perhaps she could recover some of the gold she'd spent.

She bundled up in her expensive wool jacket and a thick scarf and headed into the city for Orbs and Amulets, the Conduit "boutique."

"I'd like to return a Conduit I bought here a few weeks ago," Sebastien informed the attendant.

The woman's face lost its welcoming smile. "All sales are final. However, we will purchase *undamaged* celerium for a marked-down price."

Sebastien held up the small piece of crystal. "How much?"

The woman took it and used a spectacle device and a bright light to examine it, then said, "Forty-five gold."

Sebastien's jaw almost dropped. "I bought this Conduit, *from this shop*, less than three weeks ago for seventy-eight gold crowns." Her voice grew hard. "Are you telling me celerium prices have dropped that much since then, or are you just trying to swindle me?"

The woman's expression tightened, but she didn't back down. "Prices haven't fallen, *sir*. As you should know, there is a thirty percent tax on magical products, and that includes celerium. In addition to that, we have overhead."

That was ridiculous. Sebastien said as much. "Especially because so little time has passed that I doubt you've reported or paid tax for the original sale yet. And there is no need to pay taxes on *returned* items, which by definition have not actually earned a *profit*. I still have my proof of purchase, this isn't some random Conduit off the street."

The woman sniffed. "All sales are final," she repeated. "I'm happy to purchase this Conduit, but according to our policies there are no returns, receipt or no. Forty-seven gold is as high as I can go."

Sebastien's finger's twitched with the urge to strangle her. She grabbed up her sub-par Conduit, spun, and strode out of the shop without another word. After she'd muttered angrily to herself for a few minutes, she tried her luck at a few other shops. While some offered slightly higher prices than Orbs and Amulets, none came close to the original seventy-eight gold she'd spent on it.

Frustrated, she began to trudge back to the University. *'Maybe I could sell the Conduit through the Verdant Stag. At least that would allow me to avoid the magic tax.'*

She was glaring down at her boots when a small flutter of brightness caught her eye. She stopped.

At the corner of a building, in the bottom mouth of a downspout gutter, a sprite with glittering dragonfly wings was struggling to haul a thick piece of what might have been scrap leather, or might have just been a piece of decayed animal found on the streets, into the gutter.

Sebastien grinned and stepped closer, squatting down to watch it.

The sprite bared its tiny, sharp little teeth at her, glaring with its lidless insect eyes, but when she didn't move to attack, it continued struggling with the piece of scrap it had selected for its nest.

She caught a glimpse of the two half-larvae children within, who looked much less humanoid and had not yet sprouted wings. "This is a bad place to make a nest," she said to them. "The rain is going to come and wash you all away."

The adult sprite buzzed a little at her, but of course it didn't understand.

Sebastien took off her scarf, wrapping it around her hand and reaching out for the sprite to see if it would let her pick it up.

It attacked viciously, but didn't fly away as it might have done if not for its children. Its teeth cut through the yarn of her scarf rather easily, but didn't injure her hand beneath.

Still, Sebastien drew away. She didn't want to ruin her scarf—it had been expensive—and the sprite was too distressed to handle relocation. It might hurt itself out of panic.

It chittered and buzzed at her, and even flew at her face a few times to try and drive her away.

"Stop that! I'm trying to help you," she said, ducking back. *'Maybe a box, or a pot, something I could put them in to hold them safely and securely.'* She had nothing like that on her person, but she might be able to borrow one from a nearby shop or home. *'Or maybe I could cast a docility spell on them.'* She'd watched Liza cast one on her ravens a couple of times, and was confident she could replicate it.

She stared at the angry, frightened creature for a while longer. The children within were wiggling, expressions of distress on their tiny, alien faces. They looked cold.

Tilting her head to the side in consideration, Sebastien slowly brought her Will to bear, not casting any magic, but letting it emanate from her like she did when preparing potion ingredients, before they went into the cauldron. There were other types of magic than those cast in modern sorcery. The animists of old had used no Circles, no spells, and no structured magic to create and control their domains. Yet, within them, they spoke to and seemingly controlled everything from the animals to the trees, having connected the life of the land to their own.

Animals were said to be sensitive to both magic and intent, though tests had been rather inconclusive. With her Will activated, Sebastien took a while to examine her own feelings of benevolence toward the sprites, and her surety that they were in danger. She tried to push all of that feeling into her Will, to let it carry her desire to communicate. "I don't want to hurt you," she whispered. "You are not safe. I want to take you to a new nest. It will be warm and dry there. You can trust me."

The adult sprite glared and buzzed even harder at first, but Sebastien kept pushing her thoughts into her Will, simplifying them into pure emotion.

When she reached out a second time, the sprite struggled a bit in her scarf-covered hand, but not as viciously as before. Sebastien fumbled out her little vial of honey from her vest pocket, clumsily opened it with her free hand, and offered it to the sprite.

The creature was immediately entranced. It shoved both its arms into the vial as far as it could push them, coating its forearms and pulling back with both hands cupped full of the sticky amber liquid. It ate in big, messy gulps, oblivious to the world.

Sebastien picked up the children and the bedding, too, holding the nest within the shield of her scarf. Sprites could get confused if they were relocated without the pheromones soaked into their nest.

The sprite ate the entire way back to the University, demanding more honey for itself and its children several times, enough to use up half her vial and have its belly bulging full.

She dug out a space for them at the base of a tree that had some protective bushes around it, adding a little trench so that any water could flow away rather than fill their new nest and drown them. She gave them their bedding, including the piece of ratty leather, and added some cotton from her own magic supplies, which she fluffed up, along with one of the lava peppers she'd taken from Modern Magics when they were practicing the spark-shooting spell. It wouldn't provide much heat, but even a little could help get them through the winter.

The sprites seemed completely uninterested in her, and in no way grateful.

Still, she smiled down at them. She felt better. Her frustration and fear from earlier in the day had melted away. "I can handle this," she whispered to them, then left to go do her homework assignments.

22

A SIMPLE SOLUTION

SEBASTIEN
Month 12, Day 18, Friday 8:00 p.m.

DAMIEN WAS true to his word. That evening, he brought her his plans to keep Tanya Canelo under surveillance, complete with spell array notes and designs. He had found a small ward they could carve onto the underside of Tanya's door that would alert them when it was opened, and a couple of different designs for a tracker that they would somehow need to get onto her person.

The proposed tracker designs weren't active, and so wouldn't require constant spellcasting, nor were they artifacts that would keep working even without input from either Sebastien or Damien. Rather, they created sympathetic beacons that would point the way to Tanya like a compass when the linked item was used as a divination component.

"It will work," Sebastien said, looking over Damien's notes.

He smiled, but smoothed back his hair nervously. "Ana would be better at this. She's taking Artificery. She'd probably have some design we could carve into the sole of Tanya's shoe or some other ingenious idea."

Sebastien looked up. "That's a great idea, actually."

Damien hesitated. "Err, well, yes, but none of the books I found had anything like that, and I don't have any experience with spell design..." There was a reason why spell theorists and designers were paid so well. It was almost as dangerous as free-casting, if not quite so glamorous.

Sebastien pointed to one design, a disk that was carved and spelled on both sides. After it was split in two, one half could be used to find the other until repeated castings caused the material to disintegrate. "Let's put it into the sole of her shoe. Her boots have a one-inch heel. We can cut it open, insert it inside, and then seal the boot heel back together seamlessly. I know a leather-mending spell."

"How will we get hold of her boots?"

Sebastien smirked. "She doesn't wear them into the shower."

Damien's face split with a grin of excitement.

They planned Operation Sentinel—as Damien insisted on calling it—that night, and found a cow leg bone to use as the material among the kitchen scraps from dinner. One of the cafeteria workers was happy to give it to Damien.

The two of them cast the linking spell together to give it as much power as possible. Technically, that part wasn't a requirement, just as no linking spells had been done on Sebastien's blood to allow the coppers to use it to search for her, but the extra step made sympathetic spells a lot easier. Sebastien cut the bone disk in two with repeated, careful castings of the same slicing spell that had gotten her involved with Damien in the first place.

They implemented Operation Sentinel early the next morning, before most of the other students were awake, while Tanya completed her daily ablutions.

It succeeded without any problems, which Sebastien found faintly unsettling. 'I'm a little too used to things always going wrong. I've come to expect it,' she mused. 'Well, things still have time to go wrong,' she assured herself wryly. The hardest part of the operation had actually been carving the tiny ward array on the underside of Tanya's door without removing it from its hinges or being seen by the occasional person walking through the hallways, even at that early hour.

Based on a combination of anxiety and a lingering lack of confidence in Damien, Sebastien wanted to stay at the University over the weekend to keep an eye on Tanya, but the crushing weight of her ever-increasing debt and her empty purse drove her back to Oliver's house to spend Saturday and most of Sunday brewing, taking a few minutes here and there to make a few more batches of linked bracelets.

While there, she mentioned that she had an extra Conduit she could sell to Oliver, but he wasn't particularly optimistic about quickly finding a buyer who could afford the celerium at current market price. "Our thaumaturges already have their own Conduits, and most of our clientele is either too poor to afford one, too uneducated to need one, or both." She was willing to sell it for less than a licensed shop, but she hoped to make as much off it as possible.

She gave a simple set of ward bracelets to Damien and Newton so either could immediately alert her if Tanya left the University grounds. She instructed Damien to follow and monitor Tanya from morning till night. "Be *discreet,*" she emphasized.

Damien scowled. "I *know,* you've told me several times already. I promise I'm not going to sit there staring at her and be following two steps behind when she goes to the bathroom! I grew up in the Westbay Family, Sebastien. I think I can handle it."

"Don't get snippy, it's a valid concern. You tend to draw attention to yourself. I'm not sure you have much practice being discreet."

"I could say the same of you," he said, crossing his arms and giving her a challenging stare.

She opened her mouth to refute this, but he raised his eyebrows, and she hesitated. Despite not wanting to admit he had a point, she could see the evidence was stacked in his favor. '*People of greatness rarely go unnoticed,*' she consoled herself. '*Perhaps they need to exert extra effort and time in practice, learning to keep the weight of their sheer consequence from drawing curiosity and regard.*' She struggled for a minute between a perverse pleasure at that idea and the more basic truth that it simply meant she had failed in her true goal. "Alright," she said finally. "Good luck."

Damien watched her leave with some curiosity, but he hadn't tried to pry her own plans out of her, which she reluctantly appreciated.

'*Hopefully someday soon I won't have so many crises to solve and will be able to simply spend my days like any other student, giving no one any hint of secrets to pry into.*'

So, after another trip to the market, Sebastien spent another weekend at Dryden Manor brewing for the Stag enforcers. Her new Conduit made it a little easier, and she thought that, with a bit more time to improve her Will, she might be able to make more of the simpler potions in a single batch and thus increase her profits.

In two days, she earned about five gold more than the interest accrued for the whole week. It was a lot, but still not nearly enough, and thinking of the debt hanging over her head made her irritable. '*If I hadn't paid Liza to talk to my father, I'd have at least a hundred gold left right now,*' she grumbled mentally.

She stopped casting as the sun began to set, hours before her meeting with the Nightmare Pack gang leader, partially to reserve her strength in case it was needed, and partially to listen to Oliver's lecture—which he called "advice"— on how to act and what to be mindful of around Lord Lynwood and his people.

"It would be best if you attend the meeting alone, for appearance's sake. The Raven Queen needs no escort, neither for fear of enemies nor to listen to her negotiations," he said.

"I expected that," Sebastien agreed. "I was also thinking, maybe you could cast a weak divination spell targeting me? To activate the ward Liza made me, I mean. The effects on my physical body—difficulty focusing on or thinking about me—could be useful in maintaining the Raven Queen's aura of mystique, and might keep them from looking too closely and noticing something wrong, too."

Oliver stared bemusedly at her for a moment, then said, "I'll send a message asking Katerin about it. She's not a diviner, but she can probably handle something low-level, if that's all you need. I doubt she'll mind."

Sebastien shrugged. "That works too."

Oliver hesitated, then stood up and went to his desk, where he pulled out a small package and handed it to her. "I got you something for tonight. Open it."

She did, and found two ornaments of black and crimson feathers attached to thin, splayed wires. She looked up at him. "They're pretty, but what are they for?"

"They're raven feathers. The red ones have been bleached and dyed. They go in your hair, behind your ears. It's a kind of headdress. They're common among the People..." He coughed a little awkwardly.

She nodded to show she wasn't offended that he'd guessed her heritage, at least the part that showed through. Her grandfather had always been pleased that she looked nothing like her wastrel of a father. 'The blood of the People runs strong,' he had said.

"I thought they were fitting for the queen of ravens, a kind of crown for someone who has no need for gold or jewels," he added. "Do you want me to help you put them in?"

Sebastien hesitated, but wasn't sure why, so she handed them back. "Yes, please."

His fingers were gentle, brushing the rim of her ear as he pushed the wires into her hair.

Her skin burned where he touched, and the wires were cool as they slid against her scalp, weaving into her hair as if alive. She startled.

Oliver chuckled. "It's an artifact. The wires hold the feathers steady and then conceal themselves, so it looks like the feathers are growing out from your skin." He stepped away, assessing her, then nodded. "Perfect."

Her gaze slid away from his. "I'm going to look in the mirror." She hurried down the hall to the bathroom, where she took a few deep breaths to suppress the frustrating blush in her cheeks. "Don't be a brainless ninny," she muttered to herself, scowling at her reflection. She rubbed her ears harshly to rid them of the lingering sensation, then judged the effect of the feathered ornaments.

They did indeed give her a faint air of otherworldliness, even as Sebastien. She could imagine the effect would only be enhanced against the ochre skin and high cheekbones of her face as Siobhan. If only her eyes glowed gold or she had facial tattoos or something similar, the effect would be complete.

After a couple more minutes to make sure she was entirely calm—and there was no way she'd get surprised into blushing again—she returned to Oliver's study. "Thank you," she said. "Now tell me more about this place that's going to act as a safe house for my transformation."

"It was the simplest solution, really. No one will think it strange if Sebastien Siverling occasionally visits a brothel, and Siobhan Naught would fit right in among a group of beautiful, exotic women. It's the perfect place to hide in plain sight, using people's unconscious biases and associations against them." He slipped her a leather-bound booklet. "Identity papers for one Silvia Nakai, declaring you a citizen of Gilbratha. Silvia is legally employed at the Silk Door, and if she gets into any trouble with the law, she can call upon her wealthiest and most influential patron to help her. One Lord Oliver Dryden." He coughed a little awkwardly.

"Lord?" Sebastien echoed, flicking through the proof of one more false identity.

He shrugged, leaning against his desk and crossing his legs at the ankle. "Technically. It's foreign and basically a defunct title, with the destruction of my family as a boy, but it still affords me a measure of influence."

"I hope it will never be useful, but thank you." She wondered how much the false identity had cost him, but didn't ask.

"My investigation into who set off the false rogue magic alarm has borne no fruit," Oliver offered, changing the subject. "The coppers have no idea."

"Perhaps Tanya will slip up, and we'll be able to follow the trail to her accomplices. Everyone makes a mistake eventually." 'Myself included,' she admitted silently.

"You're right. We have people watching the Morrows as well. Eventually someone is going to slip up."

With sunset approaching and little time to waste, Oliver hired a carriage to take her to her midpoint destination.

The carriage driver gave Sebastien a knowing look as she stepped down into the street. "Have fun, milord."

She ignored the man, staring up at the large building made of creamy white bricks. The sign above had words rather than a picture like it might have in the slums, where stores couldn't trust that their patrons could read. In unadorned lettering, it read, "The Silk Door."

Sebastien entered through a side door. Within, soft music played. The lighting was mellow, the furniture dark smooth wood and soft plush cushions. A couple of girls lounged about in tasteful but impractically light dresses, kept comfortable by the fire raging at all hours and the warming stones laid under the floor.

It was a high-end brothel, discreet and comfortable.

Without pausing to speak to anyone, Sebastien followed Oliver's directions, walking up the stairs and down two hallways to a private, locked room.

The workers weren't stupid, and would probably notice her strange comings and goings given enough time, even if she didn't interact with them and the little room she used was well away from the trafficked areas of the building. But they also wouldn't talk to the coppers. Their clientele was strictly confidential, and they had all taken vows.

She pulled out a key and entered. The room held little more than a well-appointed bed, but it was clean, and connected to another hallway and staircase, these ones private. She moved to the closet, where a nondescript but still stylish dress and accessories were waiting for her.

She stripped out of Sebastien's clothing, pressed the dark matte stone artifact against her chest, and changed back into Siobhan.

She shrank a bit, her hair grew dark and long, and her skin gained an ochre tint. Looking into the small mirror inside the closet door, she confirmed that her eyes were the same as always, dark and fathomless.

Siobhan stared into them for a while, taking comfort from the sudden vertigo of the change. She wiggled and flexed until her brain remembered how long her limbs were in proportion to each other and the floor. Then she put on the dress, smoothed her hair, and spread bright scarlet cream over her lips, very carefully making sure not to smear it.

It took a quarter hour to prepare and cast the color-changing spell to fix the section of hair that Katerin had bleached. Lynwood would be expecting the Raven Queen, not Siobhan the Verdant Stag contractor, or even Silvia the courtesan.

Since she'd previously had trouble with this spell in Professor Burberry's class, she squeezed every last drop of clarity and intent into her Will that she could manage. The spell worked well, perhaps even a little too well, leaving her hair a black that was so dark it almost shimmered blue.

Finally, she put the feathered ornaments back on, watching as they settled, lending a regal mystique to her presentation.

She transferred her spell components, the paper spell arrays, and Silvia's identification to her new clothing and more stylish leather satchel, which was not nearly as convenient or spacious as her school satchel. "Women's fashion," she muttered disapprovingly.

When she looked nothing like the young man who attended the University, she exited the brothel through a different door than she'd entered through.

23

REQUEST A BOON

OLIVER HAD BEEN RIGHT. The Silk Door was safe in its sordidness, as long as Siobhan didn't make a scene. It was a place where neither of her identities would seem strange, but which she could reasonably still want to avoid talking about or being trailed to or from, without seeming suspicious.

Shortly before the assigned meeting time with the Nightmare Pack leader, Siobhan walked up to the gate in front of the manor address Oliver had given her.

Katerin was already casting a weak divination spell with Siobhan as the focus. She enjoyed the way no one seemed to notice her as she moved through the darkening streets, even at the expense of the prickling coldness radiating from the disks under the skin of her back.

Siobhan had learned her lesson with the blood-mixed ink, and instead of giving Katerin something that someone else might also be able to scry for, like a piece of her hair, Katerin was attempting to locate Siobhan's bracelet that was a match to her own. It was close enough to scrying for Siobhan directly that the ward still worked to block it, though not as efficiently.

There was a guard in front of the Nightmare Pack manor. He jumped suddenly when she stopped in front of him. White-faced, the Nightmare—as the Nightmare Pack members called themselves—took a single look under her hood and bowed deeply. "M-my apologies, Mistress. You startled me."

Assured that the anti-divination ward was working as intended, she simply nodded silently.

The guard hurried to open the gate for her and usher her to the front door of the manor, where a few hissed words sent another servant scurrying to fetch Lord Lynwood at top speed.

Lynwood, a dark-skinned man with many small braids and bright amber eyes, appeared shortly afterward. He also took one look at her and bowed deeply.

'It's a sign of respect, that he's come to fetch me himself.'

"I am Lord Lynwood, the leader of this group. We call ourselves the Nightmare Pack. I place myself at your service."

"Well met," she murmured.

Lynwood straightened, and with a boyish, awkward hesitation she wouldn't have expected from the wolf-in-tailored-suit Oliver had described, he held out an elbow for her to take. "You are the one they call the Raven Queen?"

"A name I did not choose for myself. But yes, that is what they call me."

"Does the name displease you?" he asked.

She hummed noncommittally again, and said, "You may call me that, if you wish." She pushed the hood of her cloak back, waved off the servant who stumbled forward with an offer to take it from her, and accepted Lynwood's arm. She was as tall as him, and his eyes slid off her own when they met.

"I apologize for our lack of courtesy," he said. "We had thought..." He cleared his throat. "Well, we thought you might appear out of the shadows or come through the window."

She carefully kept her mouth from dropping in shock, and then suppressed an amused guffaw. *'What does he think this is, some sort of fairy tale? The rumors circulating about the Raven Queen must be absolutely outrageous.'*

Oliver had warned her to speak as little as possible, especially about topics she didn't understand, and to adhere to formality when she did speak. *'It is better to remain silent and be thought a fool, than to open your mouth and remove all doubt,'* she quoted mentally. So she simply said, "That would have been rude," with the barest hint of a smile.

"Right." Lynwood nodded, then finally began to lead her down the hallway.

They had been walking for a few seconds when he said, "You smell of sweet dreams."

She was prepared for his strangeness this time, and didn't falter. *'Is he being literal? Perhaps his heightened senses are picking up the herbal tinctures I use in my dreamless sleep spell?'* She simply hummed in response.

The house was big and beautiful, filled with art, greenery, and signs of life, and she felt some part of herself start to relax.

He led her into the drawing room, where about a half dozen people were waiting for them. The light crystals were very dim, with most of the illumination coming from a roaring fireplace. A couple of those within were servants, and the others were likely high-ranking members of Lynwood's organization.

Two chairs were aligned against the wall near the fireplace, larger and more ornate than the rest of the furniture in the room, like thrones in comparison. A woman prognos stood closest to the chairs, while the others stayed a couple meters away. The single large eye above the bridge of her nose was in the path of a long-healed, jagged cut that ran from high on her forehead down to one cheek. The injury had ruined the eye and left her obviously blind.

'Is it right to call her a "woman," when she's not human? But "female" just sounds like I'm talking about an animal, and she is a person. Do prognos, or other species, have their own terms for man and woman?' Siobhan wondered.

Lynwood led Siobhan to the chairs, but as soon as they drew close, the eyeless prognos gasped and recoiled.

Siobhan felt the increased pressure on her anti-divination ward and fed more power into it through the Conduit she had hidden inside the lip of her boot. 'She must be using a divination spell to sense the world around her in lieu of her lost vision. I can only hope she doesn't notice anything strange about me.'

Lynwood stared at the woman, who ducked her head and murmured an apology. He looked to Siobhan with a touch of renewed wariness, then took one seat, offering Siobhan the other. "This is my sister-by-choice, Gera. Would you like refreshments, Queen of Ravens?" he asked.

One of the servants immediately stepped forward, offering a plate laden with wine, cheese, and fruits.

Siobhan waved the servant away. She was too nervous to eat, and she thought it might damage her mystique. "My thanks, but no."

Lynwood shared a meaningful look with one of the others standing to the side.

Siobhan hoped she hadn't offended him.

"We would like to thank you for agreeing to meet with us." Lynwood motioned to the other servant, who hurried forward and kneeled before the two of them, holding a tray with three wooden boxes on it. "We were not sure what tribute you might find preferable, so we prepared a selection. Please choose whichever pleases you best, Queen of Ravens."

The servant opened all three boxes with the slow fanfare that signified treasure. His fingers were trembling faintly, and he didn't dare to meet her eyes.

Siobhan had to hold back a gasp as she saw what the Nightmare Pack was offering her simply for her presence. It might be rude, but she *could* take one of these items and walk away without fulfilling whatever request they had.

"Phoenix ashes," the servant said, introducing the vial in the first box.

Phoenix ashes were an incredibly rare spell component, used in powerful healing, fire, and supposedly even spells that could affect one's destiny. Most famously, they were said to have been used by Myrddin to resurrect his recently deceased lover. There were only a few grams within the vial, but if the ashes were what they said, she could sell each gram for at least a hundred gold —maybe more—to the right buyer.

"The wolf-pelt of a skinwalker," he said while opening the second box. This was less valuable, monetarily, but just as rare, and usually not something you could buy on the open market, or even the black market. The animal-form pelts of skinwalkers were usually burned with their users when the person died. Prepared properly, they could give someone a lesser version of the animal-transformation skill of the skinwalkers themselves. Used as a component in other spells, they could tame some of the rarer and more vicious beasts, or be used in binding the most powerful of familiars to a witch's service.

The last box was a black stone polished into the shape of a flattened oval, about one-third the size of Siobhan's palm. When the firelight hit it, a six-rayed star of light shone out of the depths of what she suddenly realized was a gem.

"A black star sapphire," the servant said, darting a glance at her.

She'd never seem a gem of any kind that big, but she'd heard of star sapphires. They could be used as components in space-bending spells of various kinds. She'd heard the story of a king's messenger who used a black star sapphire to step between the shadows, traveling faster than any mortal man could otherwise, bearing a message to an allied kingdom in the space of a single night, and then back again the next.

She couldn't properly judge how much it would be worth, especially in Gilbratha, but estimated it would normally be less expensive than the phoenix ashes but more valuable than the skinwalker's wolf-pelt. But what drew her to it wasn't its properties when used in spells.

Sapphires were one of the gems that could be used as a passable replacement for celerium as a Conduit. And with the current price of celerium, it was likely that other gems were also rising in worth. If it was natural, and not thaumaturge-created, it might even be the most expensive of the three. Most thaumaturges had trouble duplicating the same level of quality that was found in nature. Like all other substitutions for celerium, a sapphire was less efficient, and would heat after extended, heavy spellcasting, *and* be more likely to shatter under the strain. Still, this one was large enough that it had to be better than her old Conduit. '*Several times better, in fact, if I estimate correctly,*' she thought.

Siobhan hesitated between the phoenix ashes and the black star sapphire, trying to weigh which was worth more in the current marketplace conditions.

If Conduits weren't so expensive, it would have definitely been the phoenix ashes, but the lack of supply changed things. And more pressingly, she wanted a Conduit.

Professor Lacer had lent her one, but it wasn't *hers*. If he ever took it back, or something else happened to divest her of it, she would be reduced to relying on her useless, dinky backup again. If she took the star sapphire, she would have security. It was even something that most people wouldn't immediately associate with the word "Conduit," since it wasn't celerium.

She had been through enough in her life to know you couldn't rely on anyone else or the things they gave you. One could only rely on themselves and what they had the strength to *take*.

'If I take the ashes, seventy percent of the selling price should still be enough to get me a better backup Conduit than the one I have now, especially if I can sell my current one for anything close to what I paid for it. However, word of phoenix ashes being sold would definitely spread, and I'm not sure how the Nightmare Pack might feel about me immediately exchanging their gift for money.' She looked to Lynwood and the others, but didn't have the skill to read their expressions.

'If I take the sapphire, what about Oliver's cut? I could probably convince him to let me pay it off slowly, but if not, seventy percent of the sale price would still get me a backup Conduit, if not one quite as powerful as the sapphire itself. I also have to consider how distinctive the sapphire is. It cannot be used in both my identities.'

In the end, personal desire won out over considerations of greatest utility. The star sapphire called to her. It was as simple as that. She reached for the polished gem, feeling its cool, smooth weight on her palm. "This tribute pleases me," she said.

Lynwood and Gera glanced at each other, despite her lack of working eye.

'I hope they're not upset that I chose what might be the most valuable among the three,' Siobhan thought. There had been a lot of subtle looks between her hosts, and it was a little worrying that she couldn't decipher the silent conversations they seemed to be having around her, *about* her.

'Was it a test? I suppose we'll see shortly if I failed. In any case, I'm not giving my new Conduit back.'

Lynwood turned back to her. "There are rumors about you and your formidable abilities. I wonder if you could help me judge the accuracy of these rumors."

'So now we finally get down to it. Best not to brag too much, so I don't have to live up to unreasonable expectations. Still, the Raven Queen has to be worth the tribute they just paid to have this meeting.' Rather than volunteering information, she nodded, as close to regally as she could manage. "Ask."

"I have heard you take another form, one composed of the wings of night herself."

Siobhan was conscious of Gera standing right beside them. While the blinding of the eye would have made it more difficult for the woman to use her divination abilities, it was obvious by the continued pressure on Siobhan's divination-diverting ward that the woman was not crippled by this. She might know if Siobhan lied.

So, Siobhan said, "I do take another form, one in which people see me as they wish, or as they fear." She continued silently. *'The rumors must be exaggerated by distorted retellings and the imagination of fanciful minds.'*

"Men say that those who earn your wrath have tortured dreams, and that those dreams only grow stronger with time until they start to seep into reality."

'That sounds like a dreamless sleep curse and the hallucinations that come with extreme fatigue.' She shook her head. "If a weak-willed man crosses me and begins to have nightmares, is it a measure of my threat to him or of his own poor mental constitution?" She paused, considering her answer, but was wary of being *too* vague. The key was to be truthful, but in a way that did not undercut the mystery of the Raven Queen. "I have laid no curses. Well, not within Gilbratha," she amended. Shortly after Ennis retook guardianship of her in her youth, she had placed a weak curse on the threshold of a particularly dislikable young man's house.

"But your magic has no need of the glyphs and symbols that the humans use to ground their spells?" Lynwood asked insistently.

'Is he trying to confirm that I can cast esoteric spells?' She tilted her head to the side, confused. "I can channel magic through the modern spell arrays, but in truth no magic of any species requires glyphs and symbols. They are an aid, a powerful one, but they are oftentimes also a crutch. While I may not yet be able to freely cast whatever magic might come to mind without Circle and Word, I do have a few...*tricks* that need no such mundane tools."

"You are young, still?"

She was growing even more confused. *'That should be obvious. He's looking right at my face. Maybe he's wondering if I've used glamours or rejuvenating spells? He thinks maybe the Raven Queen is an older woman pretending to be young? It would explain the ridiculous rumors about me being so capable.'* She gave a single nod of agreement. "Young enough," she said, trying for some sort of cryptic middle ground.

"These questions are not the reason you requested my presence," she said, keeping the uncertainty out of her voice and making it a statement instead.

Lynwood looked to Gera again, then back to Siobhan. "You are correct. I apologize for my circuitous interrogation. We have need of someone with power over the domain of sleep. When we heard about you, we thought perhaps you could help where many of our more traditional methods have failed."

"I do have some knowledge in that area," she admitted, "but not all things are within my power. Please be more specific." If they wanted her to go dream-walking or some such, she would be of little use, but ironically, she did probably know more about sleep-related spells than most professionals, due to her personal interest over the past many years.

Lynwood motioned to the door, which had been closed behind them, and one of his people standing off to the side opened it, ushering in an old maid holding the hand of a young boy, who looked to be between eight and ten years old.

"My son cannot sleep," Gera said softly.

Siobhan looked between the boy and Gera, but failed to see a resemblance. The boy looked almost like a normal human, having two eyes on either side of his nose instead of one in the middle of his forehead. Except for the abnormal paleness of his skin and the dark circles under his bloodshot eyes, he would have been unexceptional.

'He must not be a full-blooded prognos,' Siobhan assessed. "He is your biological son?" she asked.

"Yes." Gera nodded, motioning to the maid to step back.

Siobhan's eyes widened as the boy's skin glimmered ever-so-faintly from the light of the fireplace shining directly on him. 'Not only part prognos, then.'

The boy blinked sleepily up at her, expressionless.

"The boy is dying," Lynwood said. "All mortal beings need to rest. With every passing year, his dreams grow stronger, and without the ability to block them, he grows wearier and weaker."

The boy didn't seem to find this news surprising, still staring at her while blinking slowly.

"You want me to stop the boy's nightmares?" Siobhan asked. The sides of her mouth twitched, and she clamped down on the bubble of amusement trying to rise up through her chest at the absurdity of the situation. She knew plenty of spells for that, sure, but she hadn't even managed to stop her *own* nightmares.

24

TO SLUMBER BUT NOT REST

SIOBHAN

Month 12, Day 20, Sunday 6:25 p.m.

"NOT NIGHTMARES," Gera, the prognos woman, said. "Visions. My son is part prognos, part sylphide, and, as you might have noticed, he carries a drop of fey, as well."

The fey ancestry was the source of the shimmer in the boy's skin. '*A member of the fey hasn't been seen for centuries. Some of the books even say they're extinct. Add that to being a prognos-mix cambion from the Plane of Air, and he might be the only one of his kind in the world.*'

Siobhan could guess part of his problem just from common knowledge. The sylphides were powerful, humanoid elementals from the Plane of Air, given to song, laughter, and knowledge carried on the wind. Combined with the predisposition for divination that the prognos had, and the strangeness common in all the stories passed down about the fey, it was unsurprising that the cambion child had powers beyond his control. "Tell me more about the visions," Siobhan requested.

"He has had them since he could first speak," Gera answered. "Maybe before then, too. They come to him on the wind, incomprehensible pieces of the present and past. They are incoherent, but intense. When he is awake, he can mostly block them out. Only a few of the strongest slip through. His abilities are not like my own, and not like those of the sylphides we have invited to see him, either. They are a curse." Her voice broke, and she pressed a hand against her face, taking deep breaths.

The boy looked to his mother, then slowly back to Siobhan, a tiny hint of a frown between his brows.

Lynwood took over while Gera worked to regain her composure. "Some of the supposed experts we have contacted have suggested that the visions may become more coherent when he has reached maturity in a few decades. He grows slowly—slower even than the prognos—and as time passes the strength of his visions is outpacing him. They plague him even when he is awake, and rouse his mind from sleep like a beast harrying his limbs."

Gera raised her head. "The healers say that he will die if he cannot sleep, but they have no long-term solution to the problem."

The healers were right, according to everything Siobhan had read on the subject. She peered at the boy assessingly, watching every slow blink and muffled flicker of emotion as he listened to his mother and uncle pronounce his fate. "What has been attempted to cure him?"

Gera took a deep preparatory breath. "He has seen half the healers in the city, it seems, and some experts in non-human physiology and divination as well. Most have been completely useless. They've cast spells and given potions to calm him, to put him into a deep sleep, to keep his mind active and in control while he sleeps, to suppress divination abilities, to ward off nightmares, and even prescribed such treatments as bloodletting at his energy points to release 'bad humors.' He's had healing potions and revivifying potions. There were a few who said he was cursed or haunted and tried to release him from this." Gera scowled, the expression twisted by her scar. "One suggested we place him in a large, completely sealed room to cut him off from the flow of the wind."

"That did not go well. Did any of these treatments show promise?"

His mother smiled wryly. "You are correct. The sealed room caused severe panic attacks, and by the time we realized what was happening, he was hysterical with fear. It took him months to recover from that incident."

"The man was punished for his incompetence," Lynwood murmured, and Gera nodded.

"Some of what once worked has lost its efficacy as he grows older," she continued. "When he was a toddler, the calming magic was enough. When that grew insufficient, the sleep magic took over. Keeping his mind active while sleeping was a particular disaster. Suppressing his divination abilities was...unpredictable. Sometimes it seemed to work, and sometimes it provoked crazed raving and had him flailing about enough to injure himself."

"We were worried it might have other ill effects," Lynwood said.

"The bloodletting left him weak, but did not do the same to his visions.

The healing potions helped for a time, if not helping him to sleep then reducing the effects of his fatigue, but eventually his body developed a tolerance for them. When attempts to dispel a malicious influence had no effect, most concluded that he was not cursed or haunted, but a couple of those who came to help told us that the evil influence on him was simply too strong to dispel."

"Nonsense, if you ask me," Lynwood interjected.

"What of the attempts to block nightmares?" Siobhan asked.

"Only mildly effective when he was younger, and without benefit for years now. We were told that my son would die within the year if we could not find an effective treatment. There have been some more...radical suggestions, but I would not maim my son or curse him for life if there is any other option. Currently, we give him a powerful narcotic potion meant to cause the sleep of the living dead. We commissioned a master alchemist to modify it so that its effects are strong, but fast-fading. It does allow him to rest, but..." Gera gestured meaningfully to her son, who was swaying on his feet, his eyes trailing through the empty air as if watching something invisible to the rest of them.

'Hallucinations? If he's to that point, he does indeed need urgent help.'

"But too deeply," Lynwood finished. "He is insensate for twelve or more hours at a time, and often soils himself while he sleeps. And when he wakes, he is groggy and clumsy the rest of the day, almost as if he has not truly rested at all." He nodded meaningfully to the boy, and Siobhan realized that perhaps some of his daze was not from lack of sleep, but a side effect of the potion.

Lynwood added, "His mind and emotions are muffled, except for sudden, wild flares. He fractured a rib in a sudden laughing attack last month, and his nursemaid swears she saw him about to stab a knife into his own abdomen the week before last. This sleep of the dead is a stopgap measure at best." He reached out for Gera's hand, squeezing it tightly while he turned to face Siobhan more fully. "This is my sister by choice, rather than by blood. The boy is my nephew. The Nightmare Pack would be grateful if you would grant us this boon and help him."

Siobhan took a long while to think, staring at the boy. While she hadn't the deep pockets or connections of the Nightmare Pack, she too had consulted healers and shamans and anyone Ennis had access to that they thought might be able to stop her nightmares. All had failed, and over time, through endless trial and error and sheer desperation, she had developed her own spell to deal with the problem. It was only partially effective, but better than anything others had offered, and cheap enough to cast that she could actually afford to do so. However, it sounded as if the boy's condition was worse than her own, and she wasn't even sure that her dreamless sleep spell would stop visions.

Nevertheless, her research had taught her a lot about sleep, and one of the things the prognos woman had said sparked an idea in Siobhan's mind. Sleep was mysterious at best, even to the most learned of healers and researchers, but it seemed clear that the body used it both to heal and to process, cataloguing the experiences and thoughts of the day. It allowed long-term memories to settle, and without it, dreams would start to slip into the waking world in the form of hallucinations.

Siobhan had been restricting her own dreams for years now, and hadn't had any problems with decreased brain function. Her mind was a steel trap. Of course, her dreams did manage to slip through after only a few hours of rest, so she was not suppressing them completely. That healing and revivifying potions had mitigated the boy's problem, even for a time, showed that the most critical function of sleep was whatever it did to heal and effectively reset the brain, like recharging a battle wand.

She'd never been able to afford healing components for her own efforts. The closest she had come was coffee beans loaded with wakefulness magic, and that hardly counted. Siobhan's fingers caressed her new black Conduit, fascination causing her thoughts to focus just on the edge of true Will engagement.

"Your son has no need of a sedative," she said. "It is not that he cannot fall asleep, but that he cannot rest. He has fallen asleep over a dozen times since he came into the room," she said.

She was sure he was falling into what the University's library books had called "micro-sleeps" with almost every slow blink. "He's already exhausted to the point of death. First, he needs something to calm the fear and desperation that are likely making his visions worse."

"Will you help, then?" his mother asked.

Siobhan hesitated. "I cannot cure him," she stated. "Because he is not sick."

Gera's knees buckled, but she caught herself on the edge of Lynwood's chair with a whimper and straightened.

Siobhan lifted a hand in a calming gesture. "He must learn to master his own nature, either through age and experience, or through practice and discipline. But I have several ideas for another short-term solution, one that could give him a semblance of normalcy and the time to learn that discipline before the visions once again outgrow him."

"Yes," Lynwood and his sister both said, almost simultaneously.

"I will design something that your people should be able to handle without me," she said, giving herself an excuse for why she wouldn't just be freecasting some spell that would have the boy dreaming of frolicking in a meadow. "After all, I cannot attend to the boy every night. I assume you have access to resources like components from the Elemental Planes?"

They both nodded readily.

She wasn't surprised. After all, Liza could access components like that, and if they were willing to go to such lengths as described for the boy, the cost of extra-planar components wouldn't bother them. "Good. We will attempt the simplest of my ideas first, to judge if my theories are sound. Take down a list of items and bring them to me here. Gather a handful of thaumaturges, too. At least three, at most...however many you can call upon, as long as they are competent and can be trusted."

Lynwood waved to one of his people who had been standing silently by the side, and the woman hurried to grab a scroll and a fountain pen.

Siobhan listed her requirements. "Crystal—preferably clear, uncut quartz. Also amethyst and polished moonstone. Eagle or gryphon feathers, from a creature too young to have mated." She herself used eagle, but gryphon feathers would likely be more powerful, and they could afford them. "Strong, clear liquor. Some herbs—these should be fresh: Valerian root, preferably grown in a place where human footsteps do not often pass, night vanilla, chamomile picked at sunset, lavender grown in a place that has a frequent northern wind, and poppy flowers, as pale in color as you can find."

The specific guidelines on the growing and harvesting conditions of the components might or might not make much difference—she couldn't get a clear answer on that from Pecanty—but she needed all the help she could get, and hopefully the extra effort of gathering components that matched her specifications would make her seem more legitimate. People valued what cost them, after all.

Seeing that the woman was scribbling frantically, she continued. "You will want to create a permanent Circle and spell array, but for tonight bring me wax from the Plane of Earth and the powder of all the gems I mentioned, plus either gold or diamond dust. Finally, something from the Plane of Radiance, still-living. A small star-maple sapling would do. If you cannot find that, then any slow-growing plant from the Plane of Radiance might do as a substitute. A beast core or three will power it all."

The woman scribbled a little longer, and then finally looked up.

"That is all," Siobhan said.

With a nod from Lynwood, everyone but himself, his sister, and the boy rushed from the room.

Siobhan stood, moving forward and reaching out a hand to the boy's shoulder, steadying him. "What is your name?"

"Millennium," he said in a small voice. "But everyone just calls me Miles."

"Miles. Go find a chair and rest. In a few hours, you will sleep without dreams," she said.

He stared back at her as if to assess the truth of her words, and though his eyes had trouble focusing on her face, they didn't slide away from her under the compulsion of her anti-divination ward. "I hope so," he said, full of vibrant emotion for the first time.

She hoped she could keep her promise. She knew objectively that she might not be able to, but the energy and focus she felt at the prospect of a problem to solve, given all the resources Lord Lynwood could provide—including other thaumaturges to supplement her immature Will and a Conduit that would no longer hold her back—made her believe she could do it. She was hungry for the challenge.

"Get me paper and pen," she ordered, walking over to one of the tables.

Lord Lynwood's sister complied, and with only a bit of focus remaining on keeping her ward up, Siobhan turned the rest of her mind toward creation. '*A modification of my own dreamless sleep spell. Better components, more power, and with a healing factor. It needs to be actively cast for the whole duration of sleep, rather than placed and released like I do with my own castings. If I can improve his rate of regeneration while he sleeps, simply boosting his own natural processes, perhaps he won't need as many hours, and there will be less chance of him growing a tolerance to repeated healing spells or potions. Alas, if only I could get someone to cast this spell on me...*'

She looked up some time later, a finished spell array fresh under her pen, to find herself surrounded by scribble-covered papers, her hands smeared with ink, and her fingers cramped from writing.

Lynwood's people had returned, and brought with them almost a dozen other people—likely the thaumaturges she had requested. One of the other tables was covered with spell components, and among them sat a small star-maple sapling in a pot. The sheer efficiency was astounding. She couldn't have been working for more than a couple of hours.

Siobhan pried open her fingers to release the pen and stood.

The other members of the room quieted their low murmurs and turned to face her quickly, some squinting at her and some not even attempting to meet her gaze.

"We have gathered everything you ordered," Lynwood said.

"We will be casting what I suspect is a newly created spell today," she said to the newcomers. "If any of you are not comfortable with your ability to do so without endangering yourself or your fellows, leave now."

A few feet shuffled, betraying their nervousness at her words, but no one walked out.

"These are the best thaumaturges among my people," Lynwood said. "They will learn and obey, at your discretion, Queen of Ravens."

Siobhan tried not to smirk at that. '*Too bad I don't have a group of sorcerers to boss around on a daily basis.*' She realized immediately after thinking it the folly of that wish. '*No, wait, that might actually be horrible. Most people are imbeciles. I don't want to be stuck leading a group of imbeciles who cannot do anything without constant instruction.*'

"Follow along, then," she said. "Nothing we do tonight should be beyond your comprehension or abilities, and I do not enjoy repeating myself."

First, she made the crayon stick to draw the spell array with, mixing the wax with the crystal and gem powder. They'd provided both diamond *and* gold dust, so with mixed feelings of heartache at her own inability to afford such things and pleasure at the chance to use such fine components, she added both to the wax crayon. The Circle and Word array drawn with it would handle more power than something simpler or cheaper, though not as much as a permanently engraved array made of solid precious metals. As she mixed the wax with the multi-colored dust, she channeled her Will in the same way she would when making a potion, every component touched with magic and intent.

Then, waving a hand for the others to clear a large spot on the floor and bring in a mattress, she drew the array, every glyph and angled line touched with her Will. There was no energy to channel into this, no active spell, but her grandfather had taught her that there was more to magic than the parts that were easiest to quantify.

Next were the herbal tinctures, drawing out the oils through crushing the plant matter and soaking it in bottles of alcohol.

"Process matters. Magic may be a science, but beyond our understanding it becomes an art," she explained to those watching her work, not bothering to turn and see whether they understood what she meant, or if it was obvious that every competent sorcerer started applying their Will long before they actively cast the most powerful spells.

They placed the mattress in the center of the large spell array, and the components in the outer Circles. Siobhan walked along the whole thing, inspecting the lines and glyphs for damage or mistakes, and explained, in as much detail as she could, the purpose of all the interconnected pieces.

She stopped at the head of the mattress, motioning for Miles to climb onto it. "Most important in all of this is not the components or the power. It is your Will, tuned perfectly. Think on the spell till you feel it in your belly and the dark places of your mind. We will begin casting in a few minutes. I will join you, but merely as a guide. You will provide the impetus on your own. Discuss amongst yourselves," she said with a wave of her hand.

She rolled her shoulders, the thrill of magic a delight that made her bones itch and her thoughts bloom. She turned to Millennium, climbed onto the mattress, and sat next to him.

She spoke in a low voice, soft enough not to be heard over the talking of the others. "Can you cast any magic, Miles?"

The boy, more awake than he'd been before, despite the late hour, shook his head. "Not yet. I'm only ten, and my mom says it's not safe if the visions make me lose concentration. I could hurt myself or someone else."

Siobhan herself had cast her first spell at the age of eleven, a simple levitation spell on an acorn, under the watchful eye of her grandfather. It had been a bit early, but he was insistent that only stupid, immature children needed to wait till the traditional age of thirteen to begin an apprenticeship. It was lucky, because if she had waited, she might never have had the chance to learn from him at all. "You're not afraid of magic, though, right?"

Miles shook his head, but paused with his mouth open, suddenly hesitant. The silence drew on.

"You're a little afraid?" she guessed. "Because of your visions and everything they've done to try and fix them?" She gestured to Lynwood and the boy's mother, who were both watching them intently from across the room. "Which hasn't been so pleasant, and sometimes, has been quite torturous." She herself had taken a couple years off practicing magic after the...*incident* that led her father to taking over his duties as a parent again.

Miles nodded. "They've been talking about you...whether to call you here or not. They're afraid of you. But they're afraid of what I might do if they don't fix me, too. And I'm dying," he said matter-of-factly.

"Tonight will not hurt," she said. "And it will not be frightening, either. At the very worst, nothing will change and you will wake up as soon as your visions slip through. But if things go well, you will wake up in the morning feeling better than you have in a long time. To make sure you can fall asleep, I want to try something."

"Okay," he said in a small voice.

She knew that sometimes when she was exhausted beyond all reason, it actually became harder to fall asleep. "I'll need you to sit in my lap, with your back against my chest."

Slowly, awkwardly, he moved to climb into the scoop of her crossed legs. His small body was cold and faintly trembling, either from the chill or sheer exhaustion.

She reached her arms around him, touching her middle fingers to her thumbs, with the large black Conduit gripped to her palm by her pinky and ring finger, a little awkwardly. She pressed her hands against his sternum.

Miles copied her.

She took a deep breath and let it out with a low hum, like Newton had showed her.

As soon as Miles caught on to her rhythm, she began to cast the esoteric calming spell on the both of them. The spell wasn't meant to work on someone else, but with him being so small and close, and going along with all the prerequisites except for actually casting himself, it wasn't that hard to bend the magic in this way.

A few minutes later, Miles was slouching against her limply, his eyes closed and on the brink of sleep, the only indication that he was still awake being the purring sounds coming out of his throat along with her own deep hum.

She released the magic, settling him back on the bed and drawing a thick blanket over him to hold in some warmth. She sent a servant to fetch a wrapped, hot brick, and then tucked it next to the boy's feet so it could warm him up slowly.

Without further preamble, she announced, "It is time," with what she hoped was sufficient gravitas.

The other thaumaturges quickly moved to stand at equal distances around the outer Circle.

She moved to the head of the bed and, with a finger dipped in herb-infused alcohol, drew a small Circle around the boy's head, straight on the pillow. Aloud, she walked the others through the process as she cast her normal dreamless sleep spell, which would facilitate Miles falling asleep but probably wouldn't keep him that way.

Then she stepped back to the head of the larger Circle drawn on the floor. They would be actively casting through the night for Miles, keeping him asleep, dreamless, and facilitating his body's natural healing process.

She pulled her hood up to cover her face. Her ward remained active, but she reduced the attention and power she was channeling into it. Her mind couldn't handle the split concentration when casting something new like this, even with all the others to provide power and stabilize the spell.

Siobhan was the first to start casting, drawing upon the trio of beast cores sitting within one of the component Circles for power. She channeled it with ease through her new Conduit, as smoothly as the one Lacer had lent her.

The other thaumaturges joined in, one by one.

Siobhan thought she could feel it when Miles fell asleep. Slowly, she increased the amount of energy flowing through her Conduit and the lines of the spell array, drawing on the star-maple for healing and the other components for dreamless sleep. Her companions did the same, till the air thrummed faintly against the hair on her arms and the array began to glow.

At this rate, the boy would have slept for the equivalent of two or three days by the time the sun rose, and without the accompanying problems with pent-up bodily processes that would have normally interrupted such a long rest.

After about half an hour, when she was sure the others had the hang of it and was starting to feel the crush of true fatigue herself, she released her grip on the spell and stepped back. The spell array flared for a moment with inefficiency, and she frowned. '*I was channeling under three hundred thaums, at best. The spell shouldn't have been so strained by my departure.*' She looked suspiciously at the others who were still casting.

Lord Lynwood and Gera were standing a few feet away, staring avidly at the sleeping boy. They both turned their attention to Siobhan as she moved toward them.

Gera's scarred, blind eye was weeping, and she bowed deeply before Siobhan could say anything. "I thank you," she choked out.

Siobhan was too tired to go through the long-winded standard niceties. She'd been brewing all day, and after this, she just wanted to collapse into her own bed. "You were lucky that this is my specialty."

"Is it working, then?"

"It seems so. The spell does not force him to remain unconscious, so if his rest were being disturbed by visions, he would wake. You will need to have someone cast this on him every night for the time being. It need not be this large a group after this first time. Millennium will wake rested and will only need maintenance going forward. One or two moderately powerful thaumaturges should be enough. However, none of them are particularly *good* at this spell, and I doubt a lack of practice is the problem. I have a number of suggestions."

"Speak them," Lynwood said.

"The boy should be trained. Give him physical and mental exercise each day. Exercises that focus on clarity—some call it meditation—could be helpful, if he can master them deeply enough, and he need not actively channel magic to learn that. As for your casters..."

She sneered. "Keep them awake, like the boy has been kept awake. When they are truly desperate for sleep, only then will they understand how the spell is properly cast. When he has rested, they will be able to as well."

Lynwood frowned at them. "I will do as you say, Queen of Ravens." He hesitated, obviously wanting to speak.

She waved an impatient hand at him.

"Might depriving them of rest make them more likely to lose control of the magic? This spell you have designed...is it meant to be cast by someone without your particular advantages?"

She sighed. "If your people are so incompetent that a little fatigue has them miscasting, you should replace them. I hear first term students at your Thaumaturgic University deal with such conditions on a regular basis. This spell is not special. It is not even particularly difficult. It works as it does for me because I know what it is to be *desperate* for oblivion."

Lynwood and Gera bowed again, said some more words of thanks and praise, and, in a moment when no one was looking at her, Siobhan strengthened the force of her anti-divination ward. Its effects seeped into the physical world so well that she was ignored, even by the prognos, as she left the building.

Outside, she smirked up at the University atop the towering white cliffs to the north of the city, visible by their light crystals twinkling in the dark night like so many stars. She broke one of her bracelets to let Katerin know she could finally stop scrying for her.

'That should fortify the Raven Queen's reputation. What a fruitful evening.'

25

COLD SWEAT

GERA
Month 12, Day 20, Sunday 11:30 p.m.

GERA WAS the first to realize that the Raven Queen had gone. They had all been distracted for a moment, watching Miles sleep with relief, and sometime while they had all forgotten to think about the unsettling creature, she had disappeared. It was almost like the stories, the ones told in the small, remote villages, among creatures with long memories and uninterrupted oral tradition, and among those skinwalkers who hadn't forgotten that their other form was as much a part of them as the human one.

Gera, at least, was more convinced than ever that they had called upon a creature of night.

The stories were ancient, and the names given to the mischievous, sometimes benevolent and sometimes horrifically vengeful, shapeshifting creatures of dream and shadow were inconsistent. The stories of their abilities and physical characteristics were also inconsistent, and to be truthful, Gera had long thought them only fanciful children's tales, meant to amuse, thrill, and frighten.

It was Lynwood who had been hopeful when he heard the rumors, but Gera now saw that though the tales may have been twisted over time with the retelling, they had some basis in truth.

When she pointed out their missing guest to her brother-of-choice, they sent their people—those who were not busy with the casting—to search the mansion and grounds for signs of her, but all came back with nothing.

Gera found the Raven Queen's disappearance almost as relieving as it was frightening. She had to tamp down the little fear at the back of her head that said the creature might simply have disappeared from their perception and be watching them even now, hidden in some shadow.

She sidled closer to the ring of spellcasters standing around her son, examining his face for signs of distress. She'd been frightened when the Raven Queen had enfolded Millennium within her darkness and began to produce that deep, harmonized hum. Even the thought of it raised the hair on her arms, and she rubbed them briskly to force away the feeling.

Her brother placed a cloak around her shoulders. "Miles is unharmed. Perhaps you have gone so long without seeing him peacefully asleep that you have forgotten what it looks like," he said softly.

Gera pulled the cloak tighter around herself, the movement reminiscent of a child huddling under the covers for fear of the dark. "Requesting an audience with her was dangerous. It was more of a risk than we realized."

"It was worth it," he said, gesturing meaningfully to his nephew. "But, yes. I found her...unsettling. Her gaze was black. Empty, almost. I had to force myself to meet it, but for more reason than simple fear. All my instincts told me to look away, to ignore, to forget. That the Raven Queen was utterly inconsequential, which was even more frightening as I knew it to be untrue. You were startled when you sensed her, too. What did you see?"

Gera's eye had been brutally wounded when she was younger. Though she no longer had her physical sight, that did not take away the talent of a prognos, and she had learned to make up for her disfigurement with a specialized divination spell. In some ways, the spell was more powerful than sight, as it did not rely on light or angles to gather information. Everything within her sphere of influence was known to her, from every angle, with an emphasis on even the smallest movement. Her new sight lacked only color.

She shuddered at the memory of the Raven Queen walking up to her that first time. "To my senses, she was an empty hole in the world."

Her brother's eyebrows rose.

"She could be felt by where she wasn't and seen through her effect on the things around her. Not directly."

"She was very much present to my senses. She smelled of the same herbs used in the spell for Millennium, but underneath that...it's very hard to differentiate and explain." He breathed deeply, as if her scent still lingered. "It was like darkness, and old blood, and the smell of the air just before a spring thunderstorm. It was my first reassurance that she was more than a powerful witch or sorcerer. Then there were the feathers growing out of her scalp, woven into her hair, which was no natural color. It shimmered blue, like the oil-spill iridescence of a raven's feather. And the eyes—too dark, like she hadn't realized humans have *both* iris and pupil."

"Considering how she slipped away, I suspect she can choose whether to make herself manifest at all, and if so, in what form," Gera murmured.

"She came to the front door. Most of the stories say they enter houses by the night wind blowing through a window or through the shadows stretching under the doorframe. She said it would be *rude* to do that."

Gera snorted. "Well, she said that she was young. Whatever 'young' means for one of her kind. Perhaps she has a better understanding of our modern sensibilities."

"Or she was being mischievous. She has displayed a penchant for the dramatic." Lynwood smiled, sharp-toothed.

Gera's frown deepened at his attempt at humor, still on edge. "She was pleased with the stone? I would not want that 'mischievous' nature pointed toward Millennium."

"Yes, the stories are correct on that point, it seems. I was slightly worried when she refused our food."

"It is good we took the time to contact a lore-master before requesting an audience," she said.

"Indeed." The smile slipped from Lynwood's face. "I shudder to think what she might have done if she was displeased. I've heard rumors on the street about what she's capable of. I wonder how Lord Stag managed to make her acquaintance."

They were silent for a few moments, and then Gera said, "We should deepen that alliance with the Verdant Stag."

Her brother looked at her searchingly for a few seconds, then nodded. "Yes. We should."

26

THEORETICAL EXERCISES

SEBASTIEN
Month 12, Day 23, Wednesday 10:45 a.m.

THE FIRST HALF of Sebastien's school week passed rather uneventfully. There had been no more scrying attempts, and she couldn't help but hope that the coppers might be waiting for Eagle Tower to be repaired. If she were exceedingly lucky, and she barely dared to wish for it in case of disappointment, her blood could have been lost or destroyed in the explosions, leaving them completely without recourse—and her safe.

'In any case, I cannot do a reverse scry to retrieve or destroy it unless they resume attempts. So other than Oliver's tendrils looking into how one might steal or destroy warded evidence, I'd be best-served focusing my attention on something I can actually control.'

Without any progress to be made regarding the scrying attacks, she'd returned to her previous mission: solving the problem that was her lack of time and energy.

In Natural Science on Monday, Professor Gnorrish had no experiment waiting for them. Instead, the blackboards at the front of the room were covered with chalk diagrams and charts.

"Some of you may question why we spend so much time and effort on the Natural Sciences, trying to increase our understanding of the world, when there is nothing transmutation can do that transmogrification cannot. Others have wondered the same, and I believe the results of their experiments speak for themselves. To those of you who mutter among yourselves that this class is useless, who wonder why you should learn these things when they have no real utility, who have no desire to discover all the irrelevant details about how things truly work..." He turned to the blackboards. "The Natural Sciences have value beyond themselves."

Sebastien was already beginning to decipher the significance of the data behind him, extrapolating meaning from the labels.

"We will go through the studies that prove this today," Professor Gnorrish said. "In our first example, researchers took a baseline sample of subjects casting the color change spell. As I understand, you all have recently practiced this same spell in your Introduction to Modern Magics class, so you should be familiar with it. Researchers quantified the efficiency of casting, the area affected, and the resistance of the new color to change." He pointed to one set of data on the graph behind him.

"Then, they had the subjects cast an analogous color-changing spell using dye and their understanding of light. Transmutation instead of transmogrification. They measured the same metrics as before." He pointed to a second set of data. The performance was noticeably poorer than the previous attempt.

"When they had a proper baseline for both transmutation and transmogrification, the researchers put the test subjects through an intensive course on color and light theory. They then had the subjects cast the transmutation spell again. As you might guess, they improved dramatically."

Sebastien's heartbeat was like slow thunder rolling through her body. Her sense of time slowed as she realized what was coming next and started to extrapolate what it meant for her.

"Then, they cast the spell a fourth time, this time using the principles of transmogrification. This was not an increase in sheer power. It was an increase in skill. As you can see, learning to *understand* what they were trying to achieve, even when casting a transmogrification spell, created a marked increase in every single metric." He pointed to the final set of data on the board. "This ranged from a five percent overall improvement to, in the most strikingly affected subject, *twenty-three percent.*"

Professor Gnorrish was uncharacteristically somber, staring out at them. "If there are things which our greatest arts and all our power cannot achieve, we must study the underlying principles until we have revealed that which was once a black box of unknowable phenomena. Only then will we surpass the previous limits of our species."

'This is what I need," Sebastien thought. 'It's what I've been missing.'

Professor Gnorrish spent most of the class going over similar studies, and as excited as Sebastien was by the topic, she had trouble focusing on the lecture past her own racing thoughts. *'I need to learn more about the human brain, and what exactly happens to it when we sleep.'*

As soon as the bell rang to announce the lunch period, she went straight to the library and pulled all the books she could find on the subject. A quick skim showed which ones would be useful and which were completely beyond her current standard of comprehension. She checked out a full dozen, and had to take most of them back to the dorms because it was too much to carry through the rest of her day.

Practical Casting ended the school day with another fascinating lecture from Professor Lacer about mental exercises they could perform before casting that would improve the clarity of their Will. She had already been doing much of it, but Lacer seemed to have a deeper and richer understanding of, well, *everything* than she did.

Afterward, Damien and Sebastien met Newton near the eastern edge of the Menagerie, surrounded by trees and plants that would shield them from curious eyes.

It was time to pay Newton for a week of work, something Sebastien was all too conscious of. It wasn't that she begrudged him the payment. No, he had obviously taken the task seriously. He gave them an extensive written log of Tanya's actions accompanied by a quick verbal report of the highlights, every other day. He deserved to be rewarded for his diligence. It was just that she wished the payment didn't have to come from her own pocket, even if the funds had been provided by Oliver. Once the coins were in her hands, she felt pained parting with them.

"She went to her dueling club yesterday," Newton reported, "and I couldn't follow her there. I've listed some of the other students that are also in the club who she seems friendly with. And I learned that she's looking to change her student aide department next term. Rather than working with incoming students, she's interested in a move to the History department. Which is reasonable, because it's less work, but it's unusual to change departments between the winter and summer terms."

"Good work," Sebastien said, slipping Newton his payment.

Newton tucked the coins away with a satisfied smile. "I'm off to catch her at the library. I've got a student to tutor, but she'll be around too."

As Sebastien and Damien headed for the Citadel, Damien said, "You remember my friend, Rhett Moncrieffe? He's a member of the dueling club. He's practically obsessed. Perhaps I can sit in on one of the sessions, and if that bears any fruit, either we bring in another informant or one of us joins the club?"

Although Sebastien was frustrated by the idea of adding one more thing to her plate, she agreed. "Let's keep an eye out for anything interesting in the History department too. What's the specific post she's angling for? Would she gain access to any otherwise restricted magic or sections of the University? Is there anyone helping her to get the job?"

"This would be easier if either of us was a little less conspicuous," Damien said. "It's too likely that otherwise unremarkable snooping or questioning will become the topic of gossip with one of us involved."

'He's not wrong,' Sebastien admitted.

Setting aside the frustration threatening to dampen her mood, she stopped by the dorms to pick up some of the reference books she'd dropped off earlier and made her way back to the library.

She waited till no one seemed to be looking, then used her illicit pass to the low-security restricted section to slip through the locked door. Her pass was only good for one of the many rooms in the underground levels below, and she had to be careful not to get lost finding it.

After Damien had noticed her coming out of the Citadel's second floor, she'd wanted a more private place to do anything truly questionable. She couldn't take any restricted texts out of the library, anyway, which made the restricted archive the perfect place to lurk out of sight.

The aroma of old paper, parchment, and leather counterbalanced the scent of dust, with the faintest hint of dampness kept carefully controlled for the sake of the books. She breathed it in deep, then exhaled into the solitude, smiling a little to herself.

Her shoulders, which she hadn't even realized were tight with strain, slumped with relief even as she did the same into an old wooden chair at the corner of the room. After a few moments of stillness, she got up and retrieved a half-dozen more books from the shelves without even needing to read the titles.

The light crystal near the door wasn't bright enough, so she took out her bottle of moonlight sizzle from her satchel, gave it a good shake, and set it on the table.

Her new sapphire Conduit was pressed into the lip of her boot, which was slightly uncomfortable due to its size, but the best place she currently had for it. 'Perhaps some sort of leather holster that I could hide under my clothes,' she considered. 'That would keep it against the abdomen, or maybe the small of my back.' All that was needed to use a Conduit was skin contact, but holding it in the hand always made channeling easier, so she didn't want to make it entirely inaccessible.

Having a sufficiently potent Conduit and a suitable backup meant one less problem, but left her with a baker's dozen remaining.

She was as exhausted as ever, and as much as she didn't want to admit it, felt herself straining and fraying at the edges under the stress, the school workload, Professor Lacer's extra exercises, and her lack of sleep.

Her identity as Siobhan Naught was still wanted by the coppers for theft and blood magic.

She was destitute when compared to the heightened expenses of living in Gilbratha, and on top of that, including the exorbitant interest, owed over a thousand gold crowns to a criminal organization—a criminal organization that required her to perform undetermined favors to pay them back. The same criminal organization that technically owned thirty percent of her beloved black star sapphire.

She had a priceless, stolen, encrypted book that she hadn't made the first bit of progress decrypting.

Her father was in jail and, at some point, would likely be sent to work in the prison mines.

She still had nothing concrete on Tanya.

And Professor Lacer, probably the smartest, most sheerly *capable* thaumaturge in Gilbratha, seemed to think she was a reckless imbecile. And she couldn't refute him, even in her own mind. Which was almost the worst of it.

'*If I could get rid of the need to sleep, or even reduce it to a few hours a night, I'd regain all those lost hours. The creature that takes over my need to sleep will need to take over the healing and processing for me too.*' She needed to learn as much as possible about how the brain worked and sleep's effect on both it and the body. If she could amass a huge wealth of knowledge, even if it wouldn't directly fix her problem, it might be enough to let her cast a spell to fix the problem with transmogrification. '*I suspect I'll still need some downtime every night, whether that's true sleep or simply a forced rest to allow my mind to recover, and every few days I'll need to let the spell drop entirely. It'll have to be in artifact form, since having to hold an active spell twenty-four hours a day somewhat defeats the purpose...*'

She was engrossed in her thoughts, scribbling away under the slowly fading light of the potion bottle, when the door on the far side of the room— the other door into the room, the one that never opened—opened.

She didn't jump or jerk. She froze.

She parsed the shape of Professor Lacer's knee-length, dark jacket out of the corner of her eye. When she turned slowly to look at him, he was already staring at her.

She didn't try to cover up what she was working on, hoping that a lack of guilt would keep him from feeling suspicious. She could have gotten a pass to a minor restricted section from any of the Professors. She might have every right to be there.

Lacer seemed to dismiss her, walking through the bookshelves until he found whatever it was that had brought him to the room. But instead of leaving with it, he stopped in front of the table she was sitting at. His presence was like an unstable tower blocking out the sun, impossible to ignore, giving the person below the faint sense that it might come crashing down atop them at any moment.

"Don't be rude, Siverling," he said, motioning to the tabletop, which was mostly covered in open reference texts and pieces of paper. "Clear some room."

She raised her gaze to meet his, not sure whether to be terrified or relieved by the sardonic quirk of his eyebrow. She scrambled to clean up the area in front of him.

He sat, placing a book on the table. He picked up her blue potion bottle, shook it to make the light brighter again, and began to read.

Sebastien stared at him for a bit, but he ignored her, turning the pages of his book just barely too fast, enough to make her wonder if he was actually reading.

Feeling awkward, she returned her gaze to her own work, and after a couple minutes of discomfort that only she seemed to feel, she decided she was being ridiculous. *'If he's about to get me in trouble, sitting here like a scared rabbit won't stop him.'* She picked up her pen and took a note about the different chemicals the brain replenished during sleep, copied from the book in front of her.

Almost half an hour had passed in silence like this, and while she still thought the whole thing was strange, she'd lost her anxiety and was engrossed in study.

That was when he finally chose to speak. "How are you enjoying your classes?"

She looked up at him, but he was still staring at his book, which he was already halfway through. "I love them," she said.

"Really? All of them?" His tone was inscrutable, but if she had to guess, she would say he was skeptical.

"Well, Pecanty is a bit..."

Professor Lacer looked up to meet her gaze.

"Stodgy. Set in his ways. Damien called him 'uncurious,'" she said.

"Uncurious," he repeated. "Do you agree?"

"He discourages unorthodox questions and associative thinking," she said, her lip curling up into a sneer. "He's a pompous academic more concerned with looking like an intellectual than exploring the depths of the field in which he is—supposedly—an expert."

"Are you sure?"

She didn't look away. "Yes. I've tried to ask questions and start discussions several times, only to be condescended to as if I am some daydreaming child too immature to realize that original thought is so *naive*."

Lacer nodded. "Pecanty is an idiot. He was hit by an experimental curse when he was younger. It turned his brains into taffy. He was saved, but he's always been a bit off since then. It seems that having new thoughts is difficult for him."

Sebastien couldn't tell if Professor Lacer was joking.

His eyes were wryly amused, but his voice was serious. "But *you* are not incurious, it seems?" he asked, looking pointedly to the books and notes in front of her. "I hardly think this could be work for any first-term class. Independent project?"

She ran her tongue across the back of her teeth. "Theoretical exercise. I'm very curious." She tried to give her tone the same ambiguity that his had, deadpan and yet not seeming as if she expected him to take her words at face value. Her heart was beating a little harder as she waited for him to react.

"I'll take a look," he said, holding out an expectant hand. "I am very good at theoretical exercises. Maybe I can help."

Slowly, she gathered up the loose papers she'd accumulated over the last few days of study and handed the stack to him.

He read through it almost as quickly as he'd read the book, his eyes flicking over her notes, questions and sloppy spell diagrams. "It is a binding spell at heart," he murmured. "Not a vow, but an ongoing exchange?" He read for a while longer, then set down the stack. "Getting rid of the need to sleep? A little clumsy, but an intriguing idea. At least it is not some continuous stimulant spell. That would have killed you. Hypothetically."

"And this?"

"It will have an inherent loss of efficiency over time, but as long as you only run it sporadically, the idea has merit. I would tell the average first-term student off for being an insufferable dimwit if they told me they were preparing to cast this. You need more than power for this. It will require finesse. I see the spell is broken into multiple steps, and you've noted extended casting times for a stronger buildup of power, which is smart. I should almost think you have experience casting similar spells."

She kept her face impassive. She'd modeled parts of this spell, including elements of the structure and the *"connection"* glyph, from what she could remember of the Lino-Wharton messenger spell.

Perhaps it wasn't a subtle dig, because he continued with barely a pause. "Still, I would warn any student at your level against attempting this spell. The thaum requirement would be rather high." He stared at her pointedly, a reminder that he thought her a reckless dimwit. "Especially if they had no practice casting spells of a similar nature, either by the whole, or by similar component factors. The magic would be wild with its newness, its lack of history. The study you are doing there"—he nodded to the biology book in her hand—"would be useful, but insufficient without power."

'I'll need to practice binding and healing spells, then. And get my Will capacity tested again.' "I understand," she said aloud.

He seemed skeptical, but returned his attention to the papers, continuing his dissection. "However, it's obvious you don't have any true foundation in spell theory. Your base symbol is the pentagram, which might be the most common for more powerful transmogrification spells, but for applications like this it is not the perfect channel by itself. I would suggest incorporating a hexagram for its connection to wisdom, intelligence, and the transfer of aid."

She leaned forward, grabbing her pen to make a note. "That makes sense. But why not an octagram? This is an exchange spell. Wouldn't the octagram's association with balance be more useful?"

"In truth, several of the symbols are associated with balance. The octagon and octagram, specifically, are more suited toward stable systems. The balance between creation and exchange. While the octagon might be useful in creating something like a miniature ecosystem spell with little loss, the octagram is associated with true balance between creation and destruction. Justice. What people from the East might call karma. *This* is not a true equivalent exchange."

He gave her a pointed look, and she nodded in concession.

"And because you *agree* with that statement, something might go wrong if an inexperienced spellcaster like yourself tried to cast with an octagram. Doubly so if you felt any guilt about what you were doing to the other party."

She felt the urge to shift in her seat, suddenly uncomfortable, but there was no accusation in his tone.

"However, the clumsiest part of this is your use of glyphs. The Word is crude, obviously cobbled-together by someone with a limited pool of experience. There are better choices to describe this spell, by far." He pulled over one of her papers and motioned impatiently for the pen, then scribbled a quick series of glyphs and their connotative translations.

Sebastien stared greedily at the alternative piece of the Word he'd just provided. "*Forceful-given-transfer-gift, sleep and dreams. Forceful-taken-transfer-gift of harmony, rest and healing.*" A couple of the glyphs were foreign to her, and he'd arranged them in a different order. It was the core of the spell, really. She would write the entire process and instructions out longhand as well, for stability, but the glyphs channeled and molded magic in a way that letters and words didn't. With a simple scribble, Professor Lacer had just greatly decreased her chances of losing control of the spell. "Thank you," she said simply.

"Come to me again when you have made further progress with the spell design. I will check it over for you. And...I hope I do not need to make this statement aloud, but your common sense has not impressed me nearly as much as your Will. A spell like this, even if cast between two perfectly consenting parties for the purpose of research, could be classified as blood magic." His eyes were lit from beneath by the bottle of moonlight sizzle, giving his gaze an eerie quality. "The world is not kind toward...curiosity in this direction."

She stared back at him silently for the space of a few breaths. She realized that the electrical charge in the air was a silent compact between her and Thaddeus Lacer, youngest free-caster in a century, one of the most powerful casters in the country, and likely also the most interesting. The man about whom she'd searched out any stories or news articles she could find since she was a child...approved of her efforts. He was helping her, and warning her to keep it between the two of them—to keep it from those who might not understand.

She felt impossibly, entirely *awake* as she silently acknowledged his warning.

He stood abruptly. "Wait here." He walked away, exiting through the door she'd come in. He returned a few minutes later with one of the thickest books she'd ever seen. He placed it with a thud on the table before her.

A Comprehensive Compendium of Components, the cover read in gold-embossed leather. She opened the book to a random spot, flipping carefully through a few pages. The illustrations were painstaking, with the occasional gleam of precious metals or powdered gem, the letters looping and ornate. Each page had concise but detailed information on a component: different stages of growth, best conditions to harvest them for varied effects, and the various spells they were commonly—and uncommonly—used in. Many of the components were familiar, but even more were not.

She stopped on a particularly gruesome page. Harpy intestines were definitely not on the list of approved spell components. Particularly not when used in a ritual while the harpy was still alive. While not considered human by the Crown-approved definition, they were close enough that many components from their body parts were illegal. *'That's why this book is restricted. It truly is* comprehensive.'

"You should be able to find the proper components and Sacrifice within," Lacer said.

"My pass doesn't allow me to check any restricted books out, and there's no way for me to put this back wherever you took it from," she admitted.

He picked up the book, and, unsmiling, turned to the nearest bookshelf. He leaned down and inserted it between two other books on the lowest rung. "The library has no wards or alarms against misshelved books. A dreadful oversight. Sometimes books even get...lost."

"Yes," she said, tilting her head to the side consideringly. "Quite dreadful. Dangerous, even, for the impressionable minds of young students."

For the first time she'd seen, Professor Lacer actually smiled, a smirk stretching across his face. It disappeared almost as quickly as it had come. "Remember to submit your efforts to me for oversight when you are ready," he said. Without waiting for a response, he took the book he'd originally come to the room for and walked out through the same door he'd entered through, disappearing somewhere into the network of underground rooms.

Sebastien sat staring at the closed door, with all the resources she needed to design the spell that would do away with her need to sleep now at her disposal. That was fantastic.

But she was almost more thrilled to have somehow gained Professor Lacer's approval.

27

SNOWFALL & SPILLED SECRETS

Sebastien
   Month 12, Day 24, Thursday 11:55 p.m.

Sebastien retrieved the *Comprehensive Compendium of Components* from the shelf after Professor Lacer left.

There was an index at the back of the book that gave page numbers by keyword, which was immensely helpful as it meant she didn't have to flip through a few *thousand* pages one-by-one. She spent the rest of the evening reading through the pages containing relevant keywords. Only when the library closed at ten o'clock did she reluctantly leave. She didn't want to find out what would happen if she was still inside a restricted section after that.

At *best*, she would simply be trapped in the room all night and have to find a way to deal with an extremely full bladder without the proper facilities. At worst, it would set off an alarm and she would be found.

Thursday dawned gloomy, cold, and still. Great masses of cumulus clouds hung low and heavy in the sky. The air held the tension of a bent twig just about to snap, without the wind that was normally a constant at the University's altitude.

Shortly after the third class of the day, which was most people's last, the clouds broke and began to dump feather-like snowflakes. There had been several sprinkles of snow already that year, but none so perfectly suited to playing, and students of all ages spilled out onto the grounds, getting into snowball fights and creating things out of the malleable material.

Sebastien watched from a bench under a tree, working on homework for one of her less rigorous classes under the cover of the evergreen canopy. At other times, such ruckus and noise would have distracted and irritated her, but at the moment she only smiled slightly to herself. Things were going well for her.

Two witches competed along with their familiars to create the best-looking sculpture of a dragon, packing the snow even higher than their own heads while their familiars did the more detailed carving with tooth, claw, and magic.

A sorcerer furrowed a complicated design into a swath of clear snow, taking great care where he placed his feet and snappishly shooing away any students who threatened to get close. After about a half hour of work, he took out a little house made of sticks and what Sebastien thought must be a beast core, because there was no other obvious source of power, and placed them as components. Then, with a dramatic lifting of his arms and rumble in the air, the snow within the Circle rose and compacted into the shape of a small, simple house, complete with chimney and square openings for windows.

This drew cheers and applause from those who had been watching, and the sorcerer invited one of the girls from the crowd inside, which deepened the blush of her cheeks, already rosy with the cold. She accepted, even though the "house" was small enough that they both had to duck to get through the opening for the front door.

'That looks useful,' Sebastien thought longingly. 'I wonder if it could be cast on dirt, too. I wouldn't have to sleep in the open the next time Father and I are traveling between cities and there is nowhere to beg shelter, or no coin to pay for it.'

With a belated twinge, she remembered that she wouldn't be traveling with Ennis ever again. 'Still, that doesn't mean I'll never be somewhere without a proper roof over my head,' she reasoned. The spell was likely energy-hungry, but if she was able to draw out the casting to match her Will's capability and power it with, say, a campfire instead of a beast core, she could still cast it. It would just take much longer and be less dramatic. But with ingenuity, even an Apprentice-level sorcerer could cast interesting magic.

The snow house demonstration led to a general interest in fort-building, which led to people forming factions and attempting to bypass or destroy opponents' forts while protecting their own, with some sort of freeze-tag and flag capturing mechanics mixed in.

When she finished her homework, Sebastien had a quick dinner and again made her way into the library, which was uncharacteristically empty, except for those huddling in the atrium to warm themselves after frolicking in the snow.

The books in the small restricted room below kept Sebastien company for the next handful of hours, and she finished a preliminary version of the sleep-proxy spell that incorporated Professor Lacer's suggestions in an updated casting structure and spell array.

Of course, she would have him look it over again before she actually tried to use it. On top of all the studying into the Natural Sciences of the topic she still had to do, she also needed to practice binding and healing magic. Many more hours of practice would help grow her Will strong enough to channel a more powerful spell like this. She hoped she wouldn't have too much trouble getting her hands on a few of the rarer components and a couple of ravens.

She would have preferred to avoid ravens because of the whole "Raven Queen" thing, but they were well-suited to the spell, relatively easy to feed and care for, and could be found cheaply in almost any magical market. It would be much harder to find—and then care for, say—a couple of raccoons, which were another viable option.

Her most immediate problem was that she doubted she could afford everything the spell required, even though she'd purposefully chosen weaker, cheaper options where possible. *'I will have time to make a bit more gold before I'm able to cast it. I can gather the components slowly while I'm practicing and improving my Will. And I bet there are some useful potions I could make for the Verdant Stag that require healing and binding magic.'*

That evening, Sebastien was woken up after only a couple of hours of sleep, about halfway through her first rest of the night. She checked the time and found it was only a few minutes before midnight, which was also the official curfew. She was confused until she realized that the ward they'd set on Tanya's door had just alerted. It usually went off several times throughout the day, but at set times.

Tanya had a small toilet in the corner of her room, so there was no reason for her to need to leave when all the University buildings were closed and all the students were in bed.

Sebastien sat up and tossed aside her covers, threw back the curtain enclosing her half-walled section of the dorm, and rushed to Damien's bed. She clapped a hand over his sleeping mouth.

He woke up with an arching, futile gasp, scrabbling at her forearms with wide eyes.

"Shh!" she hissed. "Myrddin's balls, you're so dramatic, Damien. Get up. *Discreetly.*" She took her hand away slowly, watching to make sure he didn't start screaming or flailing.

"Dramatic? I'm dramatic?" he ground out past clenched teeth, one hand pressed over his heart. "You realize the actual *discreet* way to wake me would have been a shake or whispering my name? Why do people keep doing this to me?"

Sebastien ignored him. "She's leaving," she whispered, already hurrying back to her own cubicle. She'd only deigned to wake him because she had no spells that could enhance her hearing well enough to spy on Tanya from afar. Otherwise, she would have preferred not to involve him.

Damien immediately understood who she was referring to. Behind her, he scrambled out of bed and began to dress with more haste and less silence than she would have preferred.

She retrieved the bone disk that would let her sympathetically track Tanya's shoe and set up the tracking spell on the portable slate table with folding legs that she'd taken from the abandoned classroom. Her little lantern was plenty of power for this simple spell, with Tanya not having had enough time to move very far from the dorms.

The tracking function itself consisted of nothing more than a stick in the center of the spell array, with one burnt end that would point toward the disk they'd put in Tanya's shoe, like a compass. The stick spun to point northwest, vaguely in the direction of Eagle Tower.

Damien crouched down beside her, looking at the stick. "She's returning to the scene of the crime," he said in an ominous tone.

"Take over," she said, moving to get dressed herself. By the time she finished, the stick was still pointing the same way. "We're following."

She led the way while Damien held the slate table, balancing it carefully so the spell components didn't shift or fall out of the Circle. They paused in the dormitory building's doorway, looking out.

Outside, it was still snowing, though more gently than earlier in the day. The clouds had thinned enough to let in the light of the moon, but were still thick and low-hanging enough to reflect the lights from the ground back down. The University kept light-crystal lamps glowing around the outside of their buildings and along their cobbled pathways, lighting up the snow, refracting off the white flakes in the air, and then bouncing back down from the sky.

The world was aglow.

It was the kind of fairy-tale scene one could only experience within the cradle of a big city. In the wilderness, a cloudy night was the darkest black you would ever see.

Sebastien peered at the snow with some worry. If too much snow got on the spell practice table, it could disrupt the chalk array symbol and glyphs. And, while they may not need the spell to find Tanya at all, because her footsteps were very apparent in the snow, their own footsteps would be equally noticeable if she came back the same way.

She turned around. "We can't go out this door. We have to circle the building. Hurry!" She motioned for Damien to drop the spell, then grabbed the bone disk, slightly burnt stick, and the lantern off the folding table, tucking them away.

A couple of minutes of tromping through knee-deep snow later, they made it back around to the north side of the dorms, but stayed away from the lights of the building so that their trail wouldn't be so obvious to the naked eye.

They made it to Eagle Tower following Tanya's trail from fifty meters to the side, but, contrary to their expectation, the trail didn't lead to the front door.

In fact, it bypassed Eagle Tower entirely, continuing on past it.

Sebastien stopped Damien behind a tree, then quickly touched up the chalk spell array on the table and recast the sympathetic locating spell. "Just to make sure she isn't cleverer than we thought," she murmured. The twig pointed further to the northwest, the same direction in which Tanya's footsteps continued. "The Menagerie," she murmured.

"What could she be doing there?" Damien asked.

"I don't know, but it's a problem. There's only one gate accessible through the student tokens." The gates were warded, and would block anyone without a University token from passing.

He pursed his lips. "It'll set off alarms if we try to jump the fence, and one of the groundskeepers will come to investigate. There are too many valuable things inside the Menagerie for them to be lax about thieves. But if we go through the gate, they'll have a record of us entering right after her. If she does something like last time, we could be under suspicion."

"That too. But the more immediate problem is that I have to cover our tracks or she'll see she was being trailed when she comes back through the gate and there are suddenly two more fresh pairs of footsteps in the snow. We'll just have to hope she doesn't give anyone a reason to look at the records. If she does, we can give a different excuse for our presence. You said students come here to harvest moonbeams and fairy wings, right?"

"Hallucinogens? My father would—" He grimaced and shook his head, shuddering.

She took the slate and chalk from him, and when they had made their way closer, turned around and set up a gust spell, which was a simple thing that did nothing more than shove air through the Circle as fast as she could power it. She'd used the same spell in her escape from the University on the day that had started everything, but the spell was common enough that she wasn't worried about being recognized just for knowing it.

With sufficient force, she was able to blow up enough snow to cover their tracks, though the effort left her panting and sucked the little lantern flame completely cold with each burst. Luckily, the array on the bottom of the lantern allowed her to relight the wick with little effort. She was conscious of its light drawing attention to their position, and wished it had a way to darken or cover the glass. Damien was using his cloak to block the light, but it wasn't perfect.

Once they reached the gateway and Tanya's trail, they stepped exactly where she had, avoiding disturbing the snow until they found a good place to split away from her trail again. Sebastien thought the whole thing rather irritating. *'Would it have been too much to ask for Tanya to conduct her nefarious business at a more convenient time and location?'* she seethed.

Any appreciation she had earlier felt for the outdoors was spoiled by the need to sneak through it. Her jacket was too thin, the knee-high snow fell into her boots and melted into her socks, and every accidental noise cut easily through the night air. With idle vindictiveness, Sebastien contemplated casting the only real curse she knew—a minor thing meant to make the victim attractive to flies and other biting bugs—on the threshold of Tanya's door.

Finally, they found Tanya standing on a small arched bridge over a half iced-over stream. She stood with a man whose back was turned to them, but who still seemed strangely familiar.

Damien and Sebastien crouched behind a group of dingleberry bushes to watch, ignoring their offensive smell.

Sebastien ran through her memories like a bloodhound, tracking down the one that had caused her sense of deja-vu.

'Munchworth.' He had been the professor to meet her and her father when they first came to Gilbratha. He had laughed at even the idea of sponsoring Siobhan through the University, which had likely been the catalyst for her father stealing the encrypted book out of spite. Munchworth had again almost stopped her from entering the University during the verbal examination, and would have, if not for Professor Lacer.

The realization was almost enough to make her breathe his name out loud. She recognized the way he was constantly moving some part of his body like a nervous jitter. *'I saw him here before. Weeks ago. And Tanya was here, too. I didn't see them together at the time, but is it possible they were meeting? Is this a weekly thing? Did they meet here last Thursday, too, after she blew up Eagle Tower, and I just missed it because I wasn't prepared?'*

It didn't take Damien long to get his hearing spell ready, his hands cupped behind his ears and carefully angled toward their targets till he caught the sound.

"She's saying something about discretion," he murmured. "I think she didn't want to meet tonight." His eyes widened. "And *he* just said that if the worst should happen, he'll just tell people she's his mistress. Unless she gets caught, in which case she's his mistress who's blackmailing him."

Tanya's body language grew visibly agitated, the line of her mouth harsh as she responded.

Damien turned to Sebastien. "She didn't like that."

Sebastien nudged him. "Stay focused."

It took a few seconds for Damien to regain the right angles for his "ears" to catch their conversation. "...paranoia and trying to find an excuse to overstep their boundaries on sovereign land," he said, his voice taking on a caricature of Munchworth's tone. "We're sticking to the idea that the Crowns just don't *like* that the University is independent and want to 'investigate' the accident so they can get their men in where they don't belong. Again. No admission that any malfeasance occurred. We've got them blocked, and we'll keep them that way. Enough of the staff are on our side, and if it ever came to it, I think you'd find more than a few influential people want to limit the Crowns' power."

Damien switched to the stereotypical, sweetly high-pitched tone that men seemed to use whenever they were imitating women. "What about Westbay?" Damien's eyes widened, but he didn't lose focus this time. "If he mentions something to his Family about me being there..."

Munchworth waved his hands impatiently. "Proximity does not equal criminality. Especially because, as far as our faction is concerned, there *was* no criminality. As long as you avoid being caught in a situation with *no* deniability, we can deny and deflect. You should be focusing on finding her. There's a meeting soon, right?"

Tanya nodded silently.

"Here," Munchworth said, shoving something into Tanya's hands. "Go to the meeting. You might need coin to grease people's tongues if they're not interested in the goods."

She tucked what looked to be a full coin pouch away. "Our 'friends' might be reticent to just give away some of the stock."

Munchworth snorted. "Then remind them who they're dealing with. I want that book, Canelo. Spend what you need."

"We need to be discreet, too. I've heard...rumors. She already gave me a warning," Tanya said, absently touching her covered forearm. "I don't want to give her a reason to come after me in the middle of the night."

"Surely you don't believe that drivel? The lower city is made up of uneducated peasants with Wills so weak they'll be frightened of their own shadow. They make up stories to relieve the boredom and hopelessness of their existences. Perhaps your pedigree is showing through," he said with a sneer.

Tanya didn't respond to the scathing insult, even though Sebastien felt insulted by proxy.

"Find out what her connection is to those upstarts. It is your job to bring me solutions, Canelo. If you cannot do that, I may start to regret our arrangement."

"Don't underestimate me," she said.

He chuckled. "You'll have your assignment change next term if you can provide results. And a recommendation from me to any Master who's willing to hire you, when the time comes."

Tanya snorted. "When the time comes, I'll be the one hiring people." Without waiting for him to respond, she trudged away.

Munchworth waited a couple of minutes and then left in a different direction, muttering ungraciously to himself.

Damien and Sebastien stayed hidden until they were sure they wouldn't be discovered, then began to retrace their own steps. Just in case, Sebastien used the gust spell to erase large sections of their trail.

"That man was a professor, right? Who were they talking about? I mean, obviously the Raven Queen, but the rest?" Damien whispered as they walked between the trees, the dorms visible in the distance. "Their 'friends,' and the 'upstarts?' What meeting?"

'*Probably the Morrows and the Stags. I've no idea about the meeting, but hopefully we can find out by following her again.*' Sebastien shook her head and said, "I don't know. But that wasn't just any professor. That was Munchworth. He teaches Titanic History and Lore, and…"

"He was involved in the theft," Damien finished for her. "The Raven Queen and her accomplice were here for a meeting with *him* when they stole the book." He was silent again for a while, then said, "I've been thinking. There seems to be a conflict between the University and the Crowns. Both of them are trying to find the book, right?" He looked to Sebastien.

Sebastien nodded.

"And neither of them wants the other to have it. And Munchworth mentioned that their 'faction' is keeping the coppers from investigating University matters. So maybe there's internal strife, too. Is it possible that the University, or some part of it at least, 'lost' the book on purpose to keep it out of someone else's hands?"

Sebastien kept trudging, her breath escaping past her scarf and hanging heavy in the cold air. She'd never considered that, but it did seem awfully coincidental that her father had managed to steal it in the first place. "It's possible," she said softly, blinking away the snowflakes melting on her eyelashes. "Would that be a simpler explanation than the alternative?"

Damien frowned. "That a powerful, free-casting user of blood magic stole it?"

'*That a man with no magic at all managed to grab it in a moment of pique due to simple negligence on their part. That a young woman with only a few years of formal training managed to escape with it.*' "Yes," she said aloud.

"I don't know."

'*I don't know either,*' she agreed silently. '*I don't even know what's inside the book, except for the amulet hanging around my neck right now. Could someone have sent Ennis to steal the book without him realizing it? Maybe they never planned on him giving the book to me and us splitting up.*' She huffed into her scarf, her breath billowing out around the edges. '*Maybe I'm reading too much into it. This isn't the first time he's stolen something, after all, and with all their questioning and curse-breaking, the coppers don't seem to have found evidence of any nefarious influence on him.*'

Damien was silent for a while. "We don't have all the variables to solve the problem yet," he finally said. "That's what Aberford Thorndyke would say. Though he'd probably have noticed about fifteen different clues by now, and would just need to put them all together in the big revelation."

"Well, this is the real world," she said wryly. "Aberford Thorndyke has the advantage of a writer slipping in little hints, arranging 'coincidences' in his favor, and making sure he has all the opportunities he needs to tie everything up nicely. His whole life is full of contrived plot devices. In addition, there's some hindsight bias at work. Once we know the answer, it *seems* like something a genius could have deduced, but in some of those stories, if you put down the book just before Thorndyke does his big revelation, and go back through from the beginning trying to figure it out yourself, you'll find that there is either missing information or *other options* that the evidence hasn't narrowed down yet. But once you know the correct answer, it's impossible to be truly objective about what the evidence points to. In some of the stories, Thorndyke's conclusion seems to be geared more toward shocking and awing the reader with his intelligence than pointing toward a *realistic* culprit. I think I could argue convincingly against him on several of the cases I've read."

Damien stopped to stare at her. "Really?"

"Of course." She started to go into greater detail, but he held up a hand to stop her.

"No. I mean, you...you've, in your head, come up with arguments about who's the real culprit. Which you would argue with Aberford Thorndyke about."

Sebastien stared back at him, one eyebrow raised. "Well, if he's wrong, he could be ruining someone's life while letting the real guilty party go free."

Damien stared at her for another few seconds, then clamped his hands over his mouth to stifle hysterical laughter.

Sebastien had to half-drag him back into the dorms to keep him from collapsing in the snow. *'Obviously the stress is getting to him.'*

28

A CONVENIENT CONCOCTION

SEBASTIEN
   Month 12, Day 26, Saturday 7:00 a.m.

TANYA DID nothing suspicious on Friday, even in the dueling club meeting that Damien sat in on.

The weekend seemed the most likely time for the meeting Munchworth had mentioned, and while the three of them couldn't keep watch on Tanya for literally all the hours of the day, they could try.

Sebastien, however, wasn't willing to sacrifice her normal weekend activities just to spy on Tanya. She needed the gold that brewing for the Verdant Stag gave her, and she planned to search for the components she would need to cast the sleep-transferring spell. Even one week lost was a week that Eagle Tower was closer to being rebuilt, a week more of wasting time and energy scrabbling to keep up while struggling to get enough rest, a week closer to the kind of strain that would mean more than a few days recovery time. And a week more interest owed to the Verdant Stag.

Sebastien refused to let Tanya make things *worse*, not when she was so close to a solution.

Both Newton and Damien would remain behind, but she would take the linked bone disk with her when she left.

Damien argued against that, and while she agreed that it would have been better if they could *both* locate Tanya magically, he had the advantage of actually being able to follow Tanya physically. He also had Newton to help, and as big as the University grounds were, there were only so many places she could go. Out in the city, she could disappear easily.

Plus, Damien was in Divination class. If any of them could find her without the tracking disk, it should be him.

Sebastien didn't necessarily expect Tanya to leave, but since Sebastien had to, this was the most logical way to handle it. She needed the disk more.

And she was honest with herself—if not with Damien—that she also felt uncomfortable giving up the control the linked disk provided. It was illogical, but she couldn't shake the fear that he might learn something very bad in her absence if she wasn't there to supervise.

'If Tanya comes into the city, I'll be able to track her to the Morrows' hideout,' she consoled herself, ignoring Damien's frustration. *'Damien doesn't actually need to be there.'* She would search for Tanya every hour the other woman was out of her sight, and move to track her down immediately if the stick pointed in an unexpected direction. If something went wrong, Damien or Newton could alert her by breaking one of the bracelets she'd given them.

On Saturday, Sebastien went to the library to find healing and binding spells that she could practice, ideally ones that were alchemy-based so she could also get *paid* for them. The revivifying potions were close to healing magic, but they did not have the same purpose as the spell she was developing, and she wasn't comfortable relying on them as her only form of practice. What she needed was closer to the skin-knitting salve, but stronger.

While the library was absolutely filled with scrolls, books, and other information-recording media, much of the most useful information was not available on the first floor. Of what *was* available, many of the spells required more energy than she could channel or components she couldn't easily access.

'Call it paranoia, but there must be a conspiracy to keep knowledge out of the hands of those the University doesn't trust. If, even after graduating with an Apprentice certification, a thaumaturge has had no access to more powerful or dangerous magic, not only does it reduce their threat level if they ever turn against the powers that be, but it also keeps them from channeling the kind of difficult, powerful magic that would keep their Wills growing to the level of a Grandmaster or Archmage. Without challenge they will stagnate, remaining easy to control.' Simply increasing the intensity of a spell's output had diminishing returns, just as muscle growth would plateau if someone only did the same exercises over and over. To grow, the Will needed to be stressed in *new*, interesting ways, but many thaumaturges spent their lives casting the same few spells, or variations thereof.

Generalized healing potions were both difficult to make and very expensive, and in most cases, unnecessary. If Sebastien were stabbed somewhere that wasn't immediately life-threatening, why use a forty-gold healing potion when she could use a six-gold blood clotter along with a five-gold revivifying potion and a six-gold muscle regenerator, then top it off with stitches and a bit of skin-knitting salve for less than another three gold? By using a solution specific to the problem, she could save about twenty gold, and even more at the Verdant Stag's prices.

General healing potions were good for things that were difficult to diagnose, when you didn't know what kind of ailment or injury you might encounter and wanted to be prepared for everything, or in the rare case that other treatments couldn't cure your specific condition.

Or, if you were rich and just wanted to feel better *right away.*

A general healing potion could have saved Jameson, maybe even past the point that a blood clotter and flesh-fusing potion would have made no difference.

Sebastien found a minor healing potion that worked by boosting the body's natural response, lending some of its own power to the healing and taking the rest from the stored nutrients and energy of the injured person. The reference text said the potion would struggle to fix anything larger than a moderate wound, which it defined as a small dagger perforation in a non-critical place, a non-separated fracture in a single bone, or about six square inches of severe burn. Rather than a standard healing potion, it was better classified as a regeneration-boosting potion.

The potion took time to work, and it was apparently uncomfortable, but it could keep someone alive in an unexpected emergency, and she knew Oliver would be willing to stock the Verdant Stag and his enforcers with them. Fortunately, it was also rated at a low enough thaum requirement that she could actually brew it.

It was much harder to find a binding spell that she could practice. Binding magic, at its core, was simply an ongoing restriction or exchange that used a living creature.

The blood print vow was binding magic. It didn't force, but compelled, both parties to keep the agreement they'd made, in exchange for the same compliance from the other party. If either party broke the agreement, they would be punished with the release of their blood print to the other, for whatever use the wronged person desired. It was about as mutual as these types of spells could get, and even so, still blood magic.

Which should have been a hint to Sebastien how difficult it would be to find low-level binding concoctions for alchemy.

The Lino-Wharton messenger spell was binding magic. She gained control of the raven's movement and senses, for a nominal exchange of the vitality and intelligence of the Sacrificed raven. The exchange was unequal at heart, and the ravens were necessarily alive during the casting and could not choose to refuse, which was yet another reason why this type of magic was so likely to be restricted.

A witch's contract with their familiar was binding magic too. While the

University didn't focus on teaching witchcraft, it did have quite a lot of information about the training a witch undertook before binding a familiar. A book titled *Basic Contracts and Companions: Preparatory Exercises* held a lot of short-term contract spells that could be used on summons, conjurations, and even mundane animals that Sebastien would have been strong enough to cast.

But she hesitated to take that route, because all of the resources for the training would have to come out of her own pocket, and she wasn't planning to delve further into the craft of the witch after she was proficient enough for the sleep-proxy spell. It seemed a waste, as much as any knowledge of magic *could* be a waste. By which she meant that *really*, she avoided that alternative mostly because she couldn't afford it.

There was a potion, the draught of borrowed gills, which allowed someone to breathe underwater by dropping a small, living fish into a mucusy concoction and then gulping the whole thing down whole. The fish was kept alive inside a bubble of potion within the stomach for a few minutes, during which time the fish's ability to filter oxygen from water was transferred to the drinker's lungs. The fish died quickly, both because of the incredible strain of its inherent property being sucked dry by a much larger being, and because the protective mucus around it eventually gave way to the stomach acid and dissolved the fish alive. To avoid drowning when this happened, the drinker needed to exhale as much water as possible and immediately return to breathing air.

She was surprised to find this openly available, because according to the supposed rules of what constituted blood magic, this should have been illegal. Blood magic included, among a host of other rules, spells that used a still-living being as a Sacrifice that would be harmed, or any magic that was unnecessarily cruel in execution or caused undue pain. Apparently, people didn't care enough about the well-being of a common fish to ban the spell. Of course, that didn't mean that she couldn't still be accused of blood magic for casting it if someone powerful decided they wanted a reason to convict her.

It would probably have worked as a training spell, but she doubted she could get Oliver or Katerin to agree to buy it in large quantities. Still, she wrote it down in her grimoire. Gilbratha's east side was sliced through by the Charybdis Gulf, after all. Perhaps there were uses for an inconvenient, dangerous water-breathing potion that someone would be willing to pay for.

Eventually, after spending half the day searching, she finally found a concoction she thought would work in *Arcane Alchemy, Vol. III*.

The group proprioception potion let everyone who drank from the same batch instinctively know where the others were for a period of time. It was a vague extra sense that worked even without being able to see the others of the group, like a person could tell where their elbow was, even in the dark. It was not blood magic, because it did this by dint of the main component—

a magical sea lichen that connected and disconnected any singular part of itself at will, still somehow communicating with the greater whole to capture prey and then confine it until it starved to death. The lichen fed off the nutrients of its prey's decaying body, filtering them out of the water. In this case, the exchange given to the lichen for its properties was a simple sugar solution.

No one would complain if a lichen were used as a still-living component.

The potion would be useful for any stealth operations, but also in chaotic emergencies where one person getting separated and lost could be dangerous. Additionally, an instinctive knowledge of where everyone else in a combat team was would allow a small group to work much more effectively together. After all the trouble with the Morrows, she was sure Oliver would be interested in anything that could give his lesser numbers an advantage.

She checked to make sure Tanya was still studying with Newton on the library's second floor before she left, and then made her way down to Waterside Market.

She didn't have enough gold to buy all the components she would need for the sleep-deferring spell, but Katerin would reimburse her for any alchemy components used for the Verdant Stag, and Sebastien could at least compile a price list for the rest. While she was shopping, each clink of coins paid from her shrinking purse causing another pang of regret, she wondered about the wards around the Menagerie.

'If I could find a way to fundamentally change the nature of a harvested component, or disguise them within some sort of concealing ward, could I essentially have a free magical market at my fingertips? Surely I'm not the first to have come up with that idea, though. The University has likely already patched the kind of obvious security holes that an amateur like me can think of.'

She bought the more common ingredients first, most from the relatively cheaper market stalls that didn't ensure the same kind of preservation and freshness as the more expensive permanent storefronts. She went to one of the cheaper shops for the remaining components she needed for the new potions she planned to brew that weekend. They also had a couple of the less expensive items needed for the sleep-deferring spell.

The person working the counter directed her to a more elite alchemy shop a few blocks north of the market for the rarer components.

When Sebastien found it, she knew immediately that everything inside would be expensive. The interior was all marble floors and dark wooden shelving, polished to gleam in the light of the many spelled light crystals illuminating the shop. Components sat in the shelves, some behind protective glass or under preservative spells.

Sebastien found a small jar of water imbued with energy from the Plane of Radiance, a vial of moonseeds, and a tiny little jar holding the soporific pollen of an elcan iris. Each cost a handful of gold, but the shelves still lacked the most important components.

Sebastien went to the counter and waited for the tall, thin woman behind it to finish with her current customer.

"Welcome to my humble establishment. How can I help you, sir?" the woman asked in carefully cultured tones.

"Thank you. I'm looking for a sempervivum apricus, and if you have it, a mandrake root. Both still living, if possible. I didn't see them on the shelves. Do you stock those components?"

The woman nodded. "Yes, I believe we have both in the back. I'll need to see your thaumaturge certification, Journeyman or higher."

Sebastien stared at her. No one else, not even the shop she'd just come from, had done more than glance perfunctorily at her student token.

"If you're still an Apprentice, proof that you work for a certified Master is also acceptable," the woman said.

"This is the first time I've actually been asked for that," Sebastien said, giving her a sheepish smile. "I didn't bring any proof with me."

The woman's mouth tightened, but she nodded, and said with some pride, "This shop abides by the Crowns' law."

Sebastien didn't hide her frown. "Well, I suppose I cannot purchase them at the moment, then, but can I at least inspect them? I need to report back to my Master. If he wants them, he'll probably come back and buy them himself."

The woman hesitated, but Sebastien stared at her expectantly until she gave in.

The sempervivum apricus was a low-growing succulent plant from the Plane of Radiance. The shop owner brought out a small specimen growing in a pot. Its juicy leaves grew in complex rosettes, and tiny motes of light traveled beneath the semi-transparent skin along with the water and nutrients, barely bright enough to shine through the membrane.

It was one of the "low-light" lifeforms from the Plane of Radiance, which meant that, with the proper conditions, it could survive on the mundane plane, though it still preferred the bright sunlight and long days found farther south.

The mandrake root was similarly small, but its pot was much bigger, dwarfing the dark green, wrinkled leaves sprouting from the middle. The main part of the plant, the root, was covered safely by well-packed soil. A faint, unpleasant sound filtered through the dirt and pot, making both Sebastien and the shop owner wince.

"How much?" Sebastien asked.

"Eighteen gold for the sempervivum, forty-three for the mandrake."

Sebastien didn't have to fake the surprised rise of her eyebrows. "Really?

My master said he got a sempervivum with two offshoots for fifteen gold last month. And he expected *thirty* for the mandrake. How old is it?"

"The mandrake is at least three years old. I assure you, my prices are fair. Supply for many components has fallen slightly, while demand, if anything, has risen. If your master isn't interested, I'm sure I'll find another buyer."

Sebastien shrugged. "Well, I'll tell him. Thank you."

With a slightly sour smile, the woman sent her off, returning the components to the back room.

Outside, Sebastien let out a slow breath, trying to force her shoulders to relax. *'That was close. If she'd known a mere student, uncertified, was trying to buy those components, would she have reported me?'* She shuddered. *'Well, I didn't give her my name. But if that's how strict people are with the rarer, more powerful components, how am I going to get my hands on them, even if I do manage to save up the funds?'*

On the way to Oliver's house, she considered where else she might acquire what she needed. *'Maybe I could ask Liza where she gets hers. Or, if that still doesn't work, maybe I could pay her a small fee to purchase them on my behalf.'* The thought of how much the spell might end up costing her was depressing.

She was still scowling when she reached Oliver's house, and she slipped up the stairs to his study before the servants could notice and delay her.

She knocked, shuffling the packages in her arms. "It's me."

"Come in," Oliver called. He was sitting behind his desk with the ever-present pile of paperwork, sipping a large, steaming mug of coffee. He looked tired, but less *exhausted* than he had been in the aftermath of the Morrows' attack on his warehouse. He eyed her silently as she set up at the alchemy station against the wall. "What did you do with Lynwood?" he asked.

She paused in laying out the components of the minor healing potion. "Very fortuitously, Lynwood was interested in one of the only areas in which I have real expertise. His adopted nephew was having trouble sleeping. I acted mysterious, designed a spell to help the kid, and helped cast it for the first time to make sure it worked. Why, is he upset about something?"

"Very much the opposite," Oliver said slowly. "So much so, in fact, that he sent you a gift to show his appreciation for your work."

"Oh." Suddenly remembering the other gift, she pulled the ovaloid black star sapphire from her pocket. "Er, this is the tribute. I was hoping that maybe I could keep it, and be in your debt for the thirty percent cut? I'm in need of a Conduit, and this will help me to brew more doses at a time for the Verdant Stag. And avoid scrambling my brains into puree by accident," she added dryly. "When my other Conduits sell, they should make up for a good part of your cut."

"I think I can do you one better than that," Oliver said with a small smile. "The impact of your meeting on Lynwood was better than I expected. In fact, he's been increasingly accommodating in general. He was very insistent that I pass along his message of gratitude and friendship toward you along with the gift." He pulled a small box out of one of the lower drawers on his desk.

Sebastien approached the desk, both curious and bemused. "I tried to be mysterious, like I said, and I kept the anti-divination ward up to keep them from looking at or thinking too hard about me—I didn't want them to be too observant and see through the facade—but I didn't actually do anything very impressive."

Oliver opened the box, revealing the two tiny mottled eggs sitting on velvet within. "Pixie eggs," he said.

Sebastien's eyes widened.

He nodded, a wide, predatory smile slowly stretching across his face. "Unfertilized, but still fresh. Few in this city but Lynwood could get their hands on such a thing. Your 'unimpressive' act earned an unasked-for bonus of approximately four hundred gold. It should cover my thirty percent cut of both this and the worth of your new gem and still leave, minimum, a few dozen gold for you."

She took a deep breath. Her heart was pounding, sending a flush to her cheeks.

"We'll need to appraise the gem, of course, but if I can find the right buyer for these, it could even be seventy or eighty gold coming your way. I'm thinking of approaching Liza first. She's a valuable contact that I want to cultivate, but mostly it would feel good to pry some of my gold back out of her greedy fingers."

Sebastien grinned back. "That would be a boon from the fates themselves. Perhaps I could get some of the payment directly, rather than toward my debt? I'm working on a...special project, and some of the components are quite expensive."

"Does that project have anything to do with the new components on the alchemy table? I recognize a couple that are generally used in regeneration spells."

"Well, yes. I need practice with healing magic, and I thought you could use a cheap, general-purpose wound healing potion. Your enforcers could carry it, and maybe some of the wealthier people in your territory could afford to buy it, too. I've also got the recipe and components for another potion I thought you might find useful."

Oliver was curious, and after she explained the potions to him, they haggled a bit over how much the Verdant Stag would pay her to brew them.

As she returned to the alchemy station to get started, suppressing her smile of triumph, she asked, "I need a couple components that I can't get without a University certification. Do you think Liza might know a place that doesn't ask too many questions?"

Oliver gave her a wry look. "Most certainly. From my limited experience, you can buy almost anything in the Night Market. You might pay a premium for the lack of questions, but as long as you have the gold and you aren't silly enough to get yourself stabbed and stripped of your valuables in a dark alley, that will be the place to go. Many of the shops require passwords or recommendations from a trusted customer, though. Ask Liza about it, but don't pay her for the information."

Satisfied that her problems were being shot down one by one, she searched for Tanya's direction—the magical compass pointed north to the University—and then fell into the process of brewing. The healing potion came first, because it was the most difficult, and she wanted to be fresh while casting to avoid mistakes. It was a bastard cousin to the types of healing potions that could regrow a chopped-off finger or refresh burnt and blistered skin, but it still took more power than her old Conduit could have channeled, and she felt her Will stretching to its limits.

An hour and a half later, she carefully portioned the regeneration-boosting potion into two small vials, feeling that foggy fatigue that came from concentrating hard for long periods of time. Two doses were so little that she had to be careful not to let the brazier beneath her cauldron burn too high in case she evaporated all the water and burnt the potion to the bottom of the cauldron, but it was almost more than she could handle.

It also made her more money in the same amount of time than any of the other concoctions she'd made.

Next, after repeating her search for Tanya, she moved on to the group proprioception potion. Sebastien took her time reviewing the steps and the proper thoughts that would focus her Will for this type of magic, since it was well outside of her prior experience. After taking some time to rest, she started brewing, again a smaller batch than normal, only three doses, but this time because she was uncertain how efficient her Will would be at channeling the magic.

'I don't really understand proprioception, and it's hard to imagine gaining an entirely new sense. Maybe if I could test out a batch for myself, I'd understand well enough to make it better the next time.'

This potion had a short shelf-life, so she couldn't make it in bulk and just let the Stags stock up on it. But that was okay, because she didn't have the time or Will capacity to make it in bulk anyway.

She was starting to tire by the time she finished with that, so she made a batch of skin-knitting salve to be sold in the Verdant Stag's alchemy shop. By then, the sun had gone down and the chill from outside was overwhelming even the roaring fireplace and the warmth from the brewing.

She ate dinner with Oliver, where he made her laugh so hard she almost choked on her food telling her a story about a childhood mission carried out with his older sister. They had banded together to get rid of a new governess whose ideas about the "proper behavior" for a young lady didn't agree with their own. He smiled fondly when he spoke of his sister, but didn't say where she was now, and never told stories about her as an adult.

Sebastien knew better than to ask.

After that, she went to the Silk Door, going through the transformation process from Sebastien to Siobhan in a way that still felt anything but routine and left her disoriented within her body for a few long minutes.

Siobhan's clothes still smelled faintly like the herbs and wax from the spell she'd cast on Millennium the week before, which she found soothing. *'No matter what body I wear, my mind and my magic are my own. My Will doesn't change.'*

Siobhan hailed a cheap hackney and rode it to a corner a few blocks from Liza's house. She exited reluctantly into the cold, dirty streets to walk the rest of the way. *'Being cautious is more important than being comfortable,'* she told herself, but it didn't make the trek any more pleasant.

She climbed the rickety metal staircase and used the lion-shaped door knocker, but no one answered.

Somewhat gingerly, eyeing the animated metal lion with distrust, she knocked again, but still no one answered. She was turning to leave, realizing with disappointment that Liza was either sleeping, ignoring her, or had gone out, when one of the bracelets on her wrist grew suddenly, uncomfortably cold.

She ripped it off hurriedly, worried that it would cold-burn her skin, then stared at the colored string wrapped around it.

This particular bracelet was linked to Damien.

Siobhan realized she hadn't divined Tanya's direction in the last couple of hours.

Fumbling with the need for haste, she crouched down at Liza's doorway and set up the spell, which was already drawn in thick brush lines on a piece of seaweed paper. The spell pulled harder on her Will than it ever had before, probably because of her distance from the target.

For the first time that day, the burnt stick pointed in a different direction than north toward the University.

Siobhan stared at it for a few seconds before letting out a huge, disappointed sigh. Once the spell components had been safely stowed in her satchel, she headed out on a path to intercept her prey. *'Curling up in my warm bed with a book is not in my cards tonight, apparently. This had better be good, Tanya.'*

29

AN INTERVIEW

SIOBHAN
Month 12, Day 26, Saturday 7:15 p.m.

SIOBHAN ONLY KNEW Tanya's direction relative to her, not the other woman's actual location.

After walking a few blocks away from Liza's house, she hailed a shoddy, two-wheeled carriage—one where the driver didn't sit underneath the fabric roof with her—and gave him directions.

She shoved her star sapphire Conduit into the lip of her boot, against her skin, to free up both her hands, ensuring the movement of the rickety carriage didn't fatally disrupt her casting. The Conduit borrowed from Professor Lacer was at the bottom of her bag, since even though it technically could be connected to Sebastien, she didn't feel comfortable leaving it in her little closet at the Silk Door.

When the stick spun around sharply, reversing direction just as they passed an intersecting street, she knew she was close. Siobhan got out, paying the driver with a silver crown from the purse Oliver had given her for investigating Tanya, and looked around.

The only people still outside were the homeless, huddled around bins of fire or bundled up in ramshackle shelters built of trash and scraps. Some of the houses leaked a bit of flickering candlelight through their poorly insulated cracks. Whatever streetlamps the city might have placed in this area had long been vandalized for the spelled light crystals within, which could be used personally, or more likely, sold for a few coins. Luckily, the moon was bright enough and high enough in the sky that she could still make her way, and her little lantern was ready if she needed it.

The scattered people still outside were mostly too miserable to bother paying attention, but those who did notice her eyed her with an assessing hunger that made it obvious she wasn't safe.

Her alchemy athame was in her pocket, but, while the stamina to run away had been beaten into her by Professor Fekten's Defense class, she had no skill with a blade, and the little athame would be unlikely to defend her if she was backed into a corner.

The problem with sorcery was that it didn't lend itself to instantaneous casting, for those without the skill to free-cast. Still, she had a dozen-plus useful spells already drawn out on seaweed paper in her bag, a handful of emergency potions, and, if things got truly desperate, the low light was the perfect setting to cast her shadow-familiar spell for the most dramatic effect.

After quickly checking Tanya's direction in the darkest corner she could find, Siobhan began to move. She kept her shoulders back and walked without hurry, turning her cloaked, shadowed face toward anyone who looked at her a little too long. Her confident, aggressive body language seemed to deter any inappropriate interest, but she wished she had some divination magic to push against so she could activate the ward in her back and go unnoticed. 'Hells, I would even appreciate Damien's company right now.'

This part of the Mires stunk worse than anywhere in Oliver's territory, and in the dark, she even stepped into a few patches of what she thought might be frozen human feces. 'The stench would be unbearable in the summer. And the threat of disease... No wonder the Verdant Stag needs so many healing concoctions.'

After a few minutes of searching, she came upon a bright jewel of a street amidst the squalor.

It wasn't rich—or even clean—like the northern parts of the city, or the Lilies where all the Crown Families lived. It wasn't even particularly bright. Its light came from open fires, lanterns, and a few spelled crystals mounted above the doors of the shops. But it was still awake and alive, even this far into the Mires after dark.

Siobhan looked around greedily, noting the riot of things for sale among the small, wheeled stalls and in the grubby windows of the shops: everything from questionable "meat" pies and alcohol to dried chameleon skins to a tiny, still-living squid in a glass jar. 'Spell components. This is the Night Market,' she thought with awe.

She gave her head a quick shake, reminding herself that she wasn't here to sightsee or shop. She was following Tanya Canelo. 'What reason could she have for coming here? Is she buying restricted components? Or perhaps it acts as a discreet meeting place with the Morrows? Munchworth did mention a meeting.'

Siobhan quickened her pace a little, scanning the hectic street for the other sorcerer.

Not long after, she caught the quick flash of Tanya's short blonde hair as the woman turned a corner ahead of her.

Siobhan followed with the best combination of stealth and speed she could manage, keeping her hooded face just a little turned away, only watching Tanya out of the corner of her eye just in case her target looked back to see if anyone was watching her.

Tanya led Siobhan to the edge of the Night Market, where the lights and people grew sparser. When her pace began to slow, Siobhan ducked into the shadow of a doorway just before Tanya looked around apprehensively.

The woman pulled up her cloak, covering her head and short blonde hair, then withdrew something large and dark from her pocket and held it up to her face. After a few adjusting movements under her hood, Tanya stepped forward and knocked a pattern against a nondescript door.

Siobhan memorized the knocking pattern immediately.

After a few seconds, a little slot in the door that Siobhan hadn't noticed slid open at eye-height. Someone inside said something, Tanya replied, and the slot closed.

The door opened, allowing Tanya to slip inside.

Siobhan cursed internally. She'd been too far away to hear what they said, which could have been a simple greeting, but more likely was some sort of password.

After a few seconds of searching for any watchful eyes, she slipped closer, hiding in a nearby alcove that had been formed from a poorly planned addition to an existing building. It provided just enough space for her to tuck away in the darkness, not quite perfectly, but hopefully *enough*, if she was careful not to move.

Over the next twenty minutes, ten more people came to the door, answered one of three phrases from the doorman with one of three responses, and were let inside. Each of them were wearing hoods, making their features impossible to see. Siobhan strained to memorize their voices, but, with a sample only the length of a sentence, she was skeptical how well she could reproduce any of them.

When a few minutes had passed with no more arrivals, Siobhan considered her next move. *'Tanya is inside. I need to see what she's doing. But even if I can get through the door, is it safe for me to do so? What if someone within notices that they don't recognize me? What if they attack? Should I call Oliver as backup? But even if I alert him through the ward bracelet, how would he know where to find me?'* Without more information about what was going on inside, what dangers she might face, she couldn't make a plan. *'But I can't just wait out here when I know something is happening inside.'*

She circled the building, searching for any other possible entry points, but the windows had all been bricked over, and the back door was locked with a heavy iron contraption, with bars inserted onto the wall on either side to withstand attempts at forceful entry. They had been careful.

She briefly stepped back far enough to see the roof, searching for a chimney. She had the wild idea that maybe she could climb onto the roof and listen in through the chimney if the fire below wasn't lit. But the brick stack was smoking, and there were no good places to haul herself up onto the roof, which, on second inspection, was too steep to try and climb considering the snow and ice melted into the wooden shingles. She imagined herself slipping and falling to the street, cracking her skull open against the cobblestones, shuddered, and vetoed that plan.

Siobhan resisted the urge to pace, her fingers flexing and reaching for her Conduit unconsciously, only to remember she wasn't keeping either of them in her pocket.

Finally, she stopped, pulled the feathered hair ornaments Oliver had bought her for her meeting with Lord Lynwood out of one of her pockets, and slipped them on under her hood. '*Best to differentiate my criminal persona as much as possible,*' she thought.

Then she walked around to the front of the building, and with her heart pounding and her head held high, she knocked on the front door.

The slot resolved from the wood—some kind of magic—and then slid open, revealing a man's eyes and bushy eyebrows on the other side. He squinted at her, shifting a little to let some of the light behind him spill onto her face, which she tried to keep as concealed as possible within the shadow of her hood.

"What kind of demon feasts on the corpse of a thought?" he asked.

"Speak not of such things lest they speak of you," she replied.

His eyes narrowed at her and he stared for a few long seconds. Too long. "This is a private club," he said finally, then shut the slot. Its edges melted back into the rest of the door, adding a certain finality to his statement.

Siobhan stared at the closed door for a few moments, the muscles in her shoulders and back straining with disbelief, dismay, and frustration. '*I'm sure I got the password right. Does he know everyone who enters? Are people scheduled to come at very specific times, and I'm off? Or... What was it that Tanya slid underneath her hood? What if it was a signal of some sort? A...mask?*'

She turned to find someone walking toward her only a couple of meters away and almost jumped in fright.

She managed to avoid such an obvious tell, but her muscles clenched so hard it sent a spike of pain shooting up her back and into her skull.

The other person was hooded like the rest, but held a lantern in their hand that gave off enough light for Siobhan to see the mask beneath.

Siobhan stepped away from the door warily.

The masked person stared at her for a moment.

Siobhan tugged her hood further down and was already spinning away when Liza's familiar voice said, "Wait."

Siobhan wasn't so stupid as to blurt out Liza's name, but she did stare at her for far too long, mentally resolving the image of the cloaked, masked person in front of her with the sharp-tongued, gold-greedy sorcerer with a hidden core of kindness whose house she'd just come from.

Liza walked to the door, knocked, and when it opened, exchanged a different password phrase with the man on the other side. "I have invited a prospective new member for consideration," she added.

The man's eyes looked sideways toward Siobhan, and he nodded. "Wait here." He closed the slot again.

Liza pulled Siobhan to the side and walked to the edge of the block. She looked around suspiciously and then lowered her mask. "How did you learn about this meeting?"

"I overheard someone talking about it and followed them," Siobhan said honestly, though leaving out the most critical details.

Liza rolled her eyes with tangible irritation. "Do not mention that to anyone within," she said quickly.

"I thought this was a meeting for people aligned with the Morrows. I didn't expect to see you here..." Siobhan stared at the older woman suspiciously. *'Liza has no allegiance to Oliver. He was clear that her loyalty couldn't be bought when he first told me about her. But I hadn't thought she might be working with both sides.'*

Liza snorted at her, the sound more angry than derisive. "I will work with whoever I choose, girl, and I will take no censure for it. But I have no particular truck with the Morrows. This is a meeting of thaumaturges that the official, legal factions might not approve of."

"Oh." Since Liza was exactly the kind of thaumaturge legal factions wouldn't approve of, her presence was ironically appropriate. For that matter, Siobhan herself also fit the conditions.

"My recommendation can get you in the door, but if you want to become a member, you will need to pass the inspection. A prognos examines new members for duplicity, and there is a blood print vow not to reveal the important details of the meeting except to those you invite as prospective new members, and also not to talk about it in general with those you think might be a danger to it. Do not embarrass me. No acting awed, prying too much at the other members, or asking too many questions. In fact, if you can manage it, keep your mouth shut entirely." Liza looked to either side of Siobhan's face, at the red and black raven feathers growing out from behind her ears and around her temples. "Nice touch."

Siobhan grazed them with her fingertips self-consciously. "Thank you."

"I expect a fee for acting as the intermediary here," Liza added, slipping her mask back on and turning to walk toward the door.

Siobhan's eyes narrowed. She thought quickly, then caught up with Liza and said, "While I appreciate your help, it's little effort on your part. Perhaps a favor, instead of the standard compensation?"

"You may have an *interesting* title, girl, but I don't see how anything you can do would be valuable to me." It was a hint that Liza knew Siobhan was the Raven Queen, but apparently didn't find that impressive, which made sense seeing as she'd cast magic with Siobhan and knew better than most what she was actually capable of.

"I have a specific favor in mind, actually, and it has little to do with my hair ornaments," Siobhan replied with a tiny smirk. "Oliver has recently come into some pixie eggs. Fresh."

Liza's eyes didn't widen behind the holes in her mask, but something about her gaze grew more piercing. "Fertilized?" she blurted.

"Unfertilized." Liza didn't seem too disappointed, so Siobhan continued. "Two eggs. He's planning to sell them to someone willing to pay a premium, but I can convince him to offer you the chance to make a deal, first."

"You have that kind of influence?"

Siobhan shrugged with careful nonchalance. "It's just a meeting. If the both of you can't come to an agreement, that's not my fault. I think he can do that much for me. I'm the reason he has the eggs in the first place, after all."

Liza's head turned toward Siobhan fully at that, but they were back in front of the guarded building, and the door opened slightly behind them, spilling light into the street. They both turned and moved quickly inside, the chance for further conversation gone.

The door guard was standing with two other people, one of them a prognos, as Liza had warned. All three wore masks—though the guard's covered only the lower half of his face—and of course the mask of the prognos had a single large eye hole in the middle of their forehead.

The prognos's round eye was rimmed with kohl, and judging by the shape of their body, Siobhan thought her a woman.

The third person was a nondescript man around Siobhan's height. "Please, come with us," he said with an understated sweep of his arm. The hallway was narrow, so Siobhan and the man walked in front, with the prognos following behind.

Liza turned the other direction, leaving Siobhan to her fate.

As they walked, Siobhan felt the barest niggle of prying eyes and searching tendrils against her planar divination-diverting ward. Her thoughts turned to the soothing, chill smoothness of the black Conduit against her leg, but she didn't feed any extra power to the ward. *'It must be the prognos. It's subtle enough.*

Much less than the pressure of getting close to Gera. I wonder if what I feel could simply be this woman's natural talent for divination? Prognos notice and correlate details in a way entirely beyond most humans, but it doesn't mean she's casting a spell. In any case, no need to overreact. The ward can deal with this much all on its own, and I don't want to be seen as aggressive in the midst of a building full of suspicious, likely powerful thaumaturges. I just hope their questions aren't too invasive and their oath not too restrictive.'

The man opened a door into a small room, and Siobhan entered ahead of them both at another wave of his hand, her eyes flicking about for danger, taking in every nondescript detail about the room and her escorts' body language. There was a table in the center, a wooden chest in the corner, and a chalk spell array already drawn on the floor, covering most of the room.

Siobhan was pretty sure it was a ward against lies. Many of the stronger wards against untruth were illegal, because taking away the free will of a human was one of the definitions of blood magic. *'But that's not likely to deter these people.'*

Her heart was beating too fast, and, despite the chill that had seeped into the building, she felt the prickle of sweat on her back. *'Why do I keep getting myself into situations like this? I must have brain damage. If this goes horribly wrong, will Liza hear me if I scream? Would she help?'*

The man motioned for Siobhan to sit at the table, which had a chair on either end, then moved to the chest, where he drew out a couple of components and placed them in the spell array on the floor.

The prognos woman sat across from Siobhan while the man began to cast the ward against untruth.

Siobhan felt the strange tension in the air trying to seep under her skin, into her ears, and past her eyes. Into her brain. She shuddered violently.

"It can be unsettling," the man said quickly. "Just try to relax. It's easier if you don't try to fight it, and it'll be over after a few questions."

That was not reassuring in the least.

The prognos pulled out two pouches. She poured a Circle of pale, dull sand onto the table with one hand, skillfully adding a few simple glyphs that Siobhan vaguely recognized as directional focusers for spells that acted in some way outside of the bounds of the Circle.

In this case, based on the fact that obviously the woman was about to do a divination, it was focusing a direction for the suffused input of all the little details of sound, air pressure, and light that would be the clues it used to make deductions. Non-sympathetic divination—divination for extrapolating information based on data input rather than something like dowsing for a sympathetically connected item—was difficult, dangerous, and could give subtly or even blatantly incorrect results.

The woman unlaced the mouth of the second pouch and began to shake it with a certain slow rhythm, staring at Siobhan. Whatever was inside clacked around like dull stones.

Siobhan felt the draw on the magic of the disks in her back increase from a trickle into a growing stream. Together with the discomfort of the ward against untruth, she was profoundly on edge.

Her back had grown sweaty and was prickling, though her fingers were chilled and stiff. She curled them tight around the wooden arms of the chair, then very consciously released them and let her hands rest naturally. She stared back into the single, large eye of the prognos unblinkingly, letting her mind fall into that familiar focused state that prefaced casting magic.

"Try to answer with a simple yes or no. Are you a member of law enforcement, public or private, or employed by any member of law enforcement?" the woman asked.

"No," Siobhan said.

The woman shook the pouch one last time and then upended it over the middle of the sand Circle on the table. Bones spilled out. The pull on Siobhan's ward spiked sharply.

The bones could almost have been chicken leg bones, but they weren't shaped quite right for that.

'Finger bones,' Siobhan realized. 'Humanoid. Probably human. All a little different, and more than ten of them.' On closer inspection, she saw that runes were carved into every inch of their surfaces.

The woman looked down at them, her eyes flicking over the patterns they'd made. The skin above her eye contracted in what was probably a frown underneath her mask. She looked up to Siobhan, and then quickly back down. "Let's try that again. Maybe a little more simply this time."

She gathered up all the bones, put them back in the bag, and began the slow rhythmic shaking again. She stared at Siobhan even more intently this time.

Siobhan stared back, feeling the ward kick in again. She instinctively renewed the supply of blood and as much of her Will as it needed to boost its function. The prying, peeping, invasive sensation made her want to lunge across the table and rake her fingers across that eye. She wouldn't mind sending a slicing spell or two at the man powering the room-sized ward, either. 'Reacting like that would be a mistake,' she warned herself.

This time, the woman asked, "Are you a copper employed by Gilbratha?"

"No," Siobhan responded again.

The woman threw the bones again.

Siobhan gritted her teeth at the pull on her ward as the bones fell, clattered together, and settled. She thought one of her eyes might have twitched involuntarily.

The woman stared at the bones once more. She looked to the man, then to Siobhan, then back to the bones.

"Something wrong?" he asked, a slight edge to his voice. "Do I need to call Peters?"

The woman shook her head quickly. "No. I'm just...not getting anything. It's contradictory, or maybe like the bones are answering an entirely different question than the one I thought I asked." She stared at them a while longer, looked up to Siobhan again, and then quickly gathered up the bones. "Let's try something else. Something less reliant on interpretation."

She took out another pouch, this one small, and shook three many-sided dice into one hand. She closed her fist around them and asked, "Are you a copper?"

"No," Siobhan said. She was beginning to wonder if maybe she should let the divination attempts through, but the ward worked without her conscious input, and pouring more power into it was instant and instinctive, like how she might jerk away from a hot poker before even realizing she was being burned. Even if she wanted to let the divination through and allow herself to be bare, *seen* by the eye and *touched* in places that should have been dark and secret, the prognos would have to overpower the ward, still.

The woman blew on the dice, and, with an arching twist of her hand, let them tumble onto the table.

She paled.

"What is it?" the man asked, his voice strained with agitation.

The woman swallowed, staring at the dice, all three of which had fallen on the same symbol. "I am prying into secrets beyond my ken. The dice give a warning to look away."

Siobhan sincerely doubted the woman was correctly interpreting that. It seemed most likely to her that the spell was trying to explain that it had been diverted by her ward, turned away impotently.

"Whether or not she's a copper is secret knowledge?" the man asked.

Siobhan could see his hand sneaking into his pocket, and feel the compulsion against untruth waver as his focus faltered. "Be careful," she snapped, turning to him with a frown.

He drew out a wand, pointing it toward her, and the compulsion wavered even more violently.

"You're about to lose control of your spell," Siobhan said slowly and clearly. "Either focus, or let it drop. I will *not* be in the range of backlash if something goes wrong due to your *gross incompetence*."

The man paled, but his focus on the spell solidified rather than releasing the magic. "What are you doing? Why isn't the divination working?"

Siobhan turned back to the woman across the table from her, raising her empty hands a little to show that she wasn't a threat. She couldn't lie, but that didn't mean she had to answer his questions exactly as they were asked, either. "It's not the question that's the problem. It's me. I doubt you have access to any type of divination that will work against me. Is that going to be a problem?"

"Won't work? She's a *prognos*," the man said incredulously, but neither of them responded to him with even a glance.

As if in answer, Siobhan slowly raised her hands even further, to the sides of her hood, and drew it back, revealing the feathers sprouting from her scalp. She could only hope that some rumor of the Raven Queen had reached these rogue thaumaturges, and that they were as inclined to believe them as Lynwood had been.

The woman stared at her, her eye focused on Siobhan's darker ones, only flicking to the feathers. "Do you..." She swallowed. "Do they call you the Raven Queen, my lady?"

The man sucked in a breath.

Siobhan stared back for a few seconds too long, and the prognos looked away.

The man half-lowered the battle wand, then raised it again, as if he wasn't sure where to point it. The ward spell was wavering again.

"Some may call me that," Siobhan admitted. She turned to look at the man. "Please don't be alarmed. I mean you no harm. That will not stop me if you attack first, though."

The prognos turned back to meet Siobhan's gaze. She swallowed. "Put the wand *down*, Gerry," she said, her voice hard. "I apologize," she said to Siobhan. "We did not know."

'*My reputation must really be getting out of hand if this is how they react. I wonder if Lynwood or one of his people has been spreading tales about me.*' Siobhan realized only then that she'd stood at some point and was looming over the woman. She sat down again slowly. "I did not tell you," she said, trying to sound agreeable. "So there is no way you could have known. Now, we are at an impasse. I cannot pass your test if you cannot ask these questions, and yet, I would like to join the meeting before it ends." It was true. '*Who knows what Tanya is doing or talking about with everyone else while I'm stuck here?*'

"I—" The woman's voice broke, and she swallowed hard. "I ask only for your promise of truthfulness, Queen of Ravens. That will be more than enough proof for us."

"You have it," Siobhan said after a moment of thought. '*It's not a lie, because I do plan to be truthful as long as they don't ask anything too prying, and I can't be sure yet that they will.*'

To her surprise, at a sharp look from the prognos, the man released the spell to stop her from lying.

'*Are you serious right now?*' Siobhan thought incredulously. '*They're just going to take my word for it? Maybe they're worried that the ward will insult me, since I've already given my word. If so, my reputation is far more honorable than I am.'*

"Do you hold any animosity toward this group or its members?"

Siobhan gave her a small, ironic smile. "Not toward the group. I have somewhat...undecided affiliations toward the individual members. But I have no plans to cause trouble that would spill over to affect the whole."

"Has one of us offended you?" the woman asked, her voice a half-whisper.

"One of you has caused me some trouble, but also saved me some trouble, and I'm positively disposed toward at least one other member. As I said, I am not here to bring trouble. I'm here for the meeting."

The woman ran through a series of other, similar questions, and Siobhan answered vaguely but truthfully.

Less than two minutes later, the interview was finished, they'd given her a nondescript mask to conceal her identity, and the man was motioning for her to precede him back down the hallway toward the main meeting room.

Siobhan stopped in the doorway of the interview room. "I hope this doesn't need to be said aloud, but I will do so anyway. I expect that neither of you will reveal my identity to anyone else. That includes gossip about my appearance or abilities, or even that I was here tonight. I value my privacy just as much as anyone else wearing a mask here."

They both agreed readily, assuring her they wouldn't leak any information about her.

'Hopefully they keep their word. I don't want Tanya getting spooked because the Raven Queen goes to her secret meetings. By all the greater hells, what a mess.'

SECRET THAUMATURGE MEETING

Siobhan
  Month 12, Day 26, Saturday 7:55 p.m.

As she walked down the hall with Gerry, Siobhan reached up to adjust her new, nondescript mask. "So how do these meetings work? Give me an overview of the relevant information."

He cleared his throat nervously. "Identities are private, obviously. Though some do more to protect theirs than others, we don't allow unmasking or the use of any moniker besides a codename, which you can choose to provide to the other members or not. There is an arbiter who helps to control the flow of the meeting. He's the one you'll see sitting at the big table. We offer item appraisal, for a fee, and all exchanges of both material goods and information must be completed here. We mediate most exchanges to ensure that members are not cheated, stolen from, or attacked within these walls. There is…a small premium on all exchanges." He looked to Siobhan as if worried that she would object to this.

'And that appraisal fee and "small premium" is what makes it worth it for them to set this up in the first place.' She didn't respond aloud.

They both stopped walking as the hallway opened up onto a large room filled with a semicircle of chairs arranged in a vaguely horseshoe-shaped arc. The open end was occupied by the arbiter, sitting behind a large table.

"Umm, the first part of the meeting is for those who have something to sell," her escort continued in a low voice. "After that, we open the floor to requests. Then there's an opportunity for open exchange of information. That's the end of the official meeting, and any parties who have a transaction to complete will stay afterward to do so under our surveillance. We send members out at staggered times, in different directions. And, umm, I'm sure you won't have a problem with being followed, but generally we expect all members to take a different route to the meeting place every time."

His voice had been low, but a few of the members had noticed the two of them, and their turned heads were drawing more attention. There were a few dozen people.

'*How many unlicensed thaumaturges are there in Gilbratha? Of course, some of these people could very well have licenses, or have gone to the University for a term or two to learn the basics.*' In many ways, it seemed foolish for the University and Crowns to make it so hard for people to learn magic the official way. Their exclusivity could be *creating* rogue elements. Kicking early-term students out for under-performance was the same—counterproductive, and maybe even dangerous.

If someone like Oliver was in charge, he would take all prospective students who proved themselves worthy, and for those who couldn't afford it, there would be loans that kept them in debt for a good portion of the remainder of their lives—and working in jobs he needed—ensuring the return on his investment into their education. People who flunked out would be put into jobs that suited their limited abilities, keeping them useful and integrated into the system, too.

'*Do the coppers know about organizations like this? They must.*' It wouldn't surprise Siobhan if someone in a position of power was benefiting from allowing it, either directly by secretly running the whole thing, or indirectly through the bribes they received to ignore it.

Siobhan drew her cloak down farther over her masked face. She walked toward the group with no further hesitation and took an empty seat at the end farthest from the arbiter.

People turned to look as she passed by and sat down. The meeting had already started. She was late.

There were a handful of other people standing at the corners of the room, and several doors opened up off the sides, leading into small adjoining rooms. '*Guards, probably both to protect the members and protect against them. And I'd bet those small rooms are to handle the exchanges in a slightly more private way after the meeting is over.*'

Liza was there, slouched nonchalantly on her chair, giving off a sense of irritated superiority even with her features covered. Siobhan recognized her mostly from the fact that she was the only one other than the arbiter seated at an individual table. It was the unfolding cube artifact that Liza had termed a "portable office."

Some of the other members were obviously non-human, and for the more distinctive of them, the masks they wore might not have actually done much to protect their identities.

Siobhan found Tanya easily enough.

Tanya didn't do anything in particular to give herself away, but Siobhan was intimately familiar with the other girl's boots—the same ones she had sliced open to put the tracker in the heel. *'Shoes are one of those things people don't think about disguising. Luckily I don't have that problem, because Sebastien's shoes are too big for Siobhan's feet.'*

The man who'd helped interview her hurried over and whispered something into the arbiter's ear, who then said, "A new member. Welcome. Let us continue, then."

One of the members had been in the middle of his offering, and leaned forward immediately. "This design can keep minor and common spirits confined. It will resist attempts at dissipation, and my experiments showed that only the weakest spirits were able to escape in that manner. It's particularly useful against spirits with more ordered natures, but none of the four wild spirits I tested escaped, despite one being unusually clever."

A man so short his feet dangled from his chair asked, "How much?"

"Forty-five gold," the first man responded, an obvious smile in his voice, "Or two hundred grams of shade dust."

"How about fifty grams of shade dust and a natural adder stone?" a woman offered.

The short man slumped back in discontent, not deigning to counter-offer.

The seller looked around to see if anyone else was going to speak up, but no one did. He seemed more than pleased when he said, "Deal."

The arbiter nodded and said, with a tone of boredom, "Noted."

The next member presented various rare components that Siobhan probably wouldn't have been able to buy at Waterside Market. They had restricted components that the Crowns allowed, but tracked from seller to buyer, entirely illegal components, and components that were simply rare and valuable. Human fingernails, overgrown to the point of curling. Various parts of a mermaid, which included the human-mimicking tentacles and organs from the main body, which she doubted the being could have lived without. The fangs of a rare flying snake that lived much closer to the equator, and other, equally strange offerings.

After that, someone offered to teach how to cast the mind-muddling jinx, which caused the victim trouble reading and comprehending. They suggested this could be used on people signing contracts, receipts, or other binding documents that would benefit from lack of attention. Several people took them up on the offer, despite the requested price of fifty gold.

'I'll be careful to take note if I ever have trouble concentrating on something someone wants me to sign,' Siobhan thought uneasily.

Next was something more innocuous. Lightweight cold box artifacts, meant to preserve food, potions, or ingredients, with a signature, secret upgrade that not only kept them cold, but also suppressed putrefaction and dehydration, like a counterfeit combination of a normal ice box and the evidence boxes the coppers used.

The prognos woman had come into the room and taken a seat against the far wall. The arbiter called her up to appraise the artifact. When she confirmed its quality, a handful of people put in orders for one of their own, including the arbiter himself, on behalf of the organization.

'This is profitable,' Siobhan thought. 'The lack of the thirty percent magic tax alone is a huge draw. It's the kind of thing the Verdant Stag might want to explore, once they're big enough to ensure the whole thing wouldn't spiral out of control and blow up in their faces like a poorly controlled fireball spell.'

People continued to offer and bid on things for sale for the next few minutes, but Tanya remained silent. Siobhan worried that whatever the other woman had come here for had already passed while she was stuck in the onboarding interview.

Finally, there was a longer pause than normal. The arbiter looked around. "Are there any more offers?"

When no one spoke up, the arbiter cleared his throat. "Then let us move on to the requests."

Tanya immediately became tense, her foot tapping nervously for a couple of seconds before falling still.

This time, people asked for what they needed, whether that be components, magical creations, or information. Someone even requested a bodyguard. They offered a price, and sometimes people who could fulfill the need haggled or bid against each other. Sometimes no one accepted the request.

Tanya was one of the first to speak up. "I'm offering one hundred gold, as well as three green beast cores with a combined energy value of ten million thaums, for useful information about the Raven Queen. I can split up the reward between multiple people, if more than one person has relevant knowledge."

Sebastien always found it hard to estimate the price of things in Gilbratha, but thought the beast cores, which were respectable in both color and energy value, were probably worth about half as much as the gold. Maybe less, because that energy value was split between three of them. Like celerium, prices dramatically increased with higher quality. These ones would allow someone with a twenty five hundred thaum capacity to cast for about an hour before the last beast core ran out of power and crumbled like an overworked Conduit.

She herself, with her much lower capacity, could use them for ten hours or so. The convenience made trying to purchase one from someone besides Tanya seem tempting, but even if she only wanted one with a total energy value of a million thaums, which would last her about an hour, she could do a lot of other things with the five gold that would cost. She could buy three non-magical reference books, a good dress with gloves and a hat, or food for two weeks with that same amount. And besides, her lantern, with its adjustable flame, still met her casting needs for the moment.

'Perhaps once I pay off my debt I can indulge in such luxuries.' Hiding a beast core in her boot, next to her sapphire Conduit, would mean she was never completely helpless.

In the silence after Tanya's request, some of the other members looked around, while a couple shifted uncomfortably. Finally, a man said, "If you want concrete information, not just rumors, that's going to be hard to come by. What little I know, at least, is common knowledge. She stole something from the University, she's powerful, a free-caster, and practices blood magic. If we get into *rumors*...she's a shape changer, and can travel through and command the shadows, which is why they're having such trouble catching her."

Siobhan nearly choked on her own saliva. *'What.'*

Someone else said, "I have an investigator-adjutant contact. I can ask them for more information, for the right price. They're not directly on that case, though, so while I might get more details, they probably won't have access to any truly classified material."

Liza said nothing, her bored posture never changing. She didn't even look toward Siobhan.

Tanya leaned forward. "Does anyone have information about her connection to the Verdant Stag?"

There was silence again, and then someone shrugged. "I heard she might come if you make a pleasing enough offering. Maybe Lord Stag knows what she likes, or has some sort of agreement with her."

Someone else snorted. "Or maybe the Morrows just pissed her off somehow."

The man who'd offered the design of a spirit-trapping spell array said, "I could do a summoning ritual to connect the two of you. It would slightly skew both of your fates to make a meeting more likely."

A woman shook her head quickly. "I warn against that. Very iffy results. Even if that kind of compulsion would work on her, what kind of meeting? I certainly wouldn't want to run into the Raven Queen in a dark alley."

A man with horns curling out from under his mask said, "I agree. I have access to someone with relevant information about how to set up a meeting with her. Lord Lynwood did it. You'll need to prepare an offering for her in addition to my payment, though. I can give you an answer at our next meeting."

Siobhan resolved to ask Lynwood and his people not to go around spreading rumors about her.

Tanya hesitated, but steeled herself and nodded to the horned man. "Okay. I'll pay seventy gold and twenty beast cores to anyone who can confirm a meeting with her, along with details about this offering she requires."

"She'll choose the time and place of the meeting," the man said. "Is that okay?"

Tanya seemed supremely uncomfortable, but again she nodded.

The meeting moved on, and someone else asked for a recipe for a strong dissolving tincture. They offered either twenty gold in payment, or the exchange of a recipe for an all-purpose antidote, or a potion of night vision.

'A dissolving tincture? I have access to a recipe for a strong acid,' Siobhan realized. 'I could probably make money offering access to knowledge from the University library.' She didn't immediately jump to say she could fulfill the man's request, though. 'I have no idea who these people are. Someone might recognize the type of information I could sell and make connections. I need to wait until I have a better idea of what I've gotten into. As of right now, I still haven't done anything illegal. Technically.'

Those thoughts almost made her hesitate to speak her own request, but she pushed through. "I am looking for sempervivum apricus and mandrake root. Both still living."

A chubby man immediately raised his hand. "I have both. I'll sell them to you for forty-five gold, or an appropriate item in trade."

Some quick mental math told her that his prices were actually slightly higher than the component shop that had turned her away, if she took off the thirty percent tax the Crowns placed on all magical sales. "Do you have any need for regeneration potions?"

"Not healing?" he asked, hesitating. "Well, I suppose. I'll want them appraised, of course, but if they serve, I'll take six in exchange for the plants."

"Agreed," she said, smiling underneath her nondescript mask. Each potion took slightly over three gold to make, and she could make two in a couple of hours. She'd just saved herself twenty-six gold in exchange for a weekend of work.

As for her seller, a licensed shop would have sold each potion for about twenty gold. Even the Verdant Stag was going to sell them for over seven gold. So, unless he had an alchemist that was willing to sell to him at sub-market prices, he'd just agreed to a deal that left him anywhere from breaking even to making an extra seventy-five gold.

At the end of the meeting, the arbiter said, "We are also willing to purchase certain items. For the time being we are interested in communication or protective artifacts, elemental components, and celerium."

A few people offered to sell things to the arbiter, and when their haggling was done, the man spoke again, sounding as if he was lazily reciting a memorized spiel. "This may be a reminder for our old members, but be sure to watch for the signs about our next meeting. You can find the locations on the list pinned to the wall, there." He pointed to a piece of paper. "Memorize it, as well as the translations of meaning. This meeting is adjourned. Those who wish may exchange information freely amongst yourselves. If you have agreed to an exchange, please wait for one of us to mediate it."

'If people selling or buying information have an arbitrated trade, that means the meeting organizers get all that knowledge for free. Of course, people might decide not to allow the mediator, but without them they have no insurance that the information given is worth what was promised. That makes this whole arrangement doubly profitable for the people behind it.'

Keeping a surreptitious eye on Tanya and an ear open for any interesting conversations, Siobhan moved to the wall to read the paper pinned there. Apparently, the meeting's organizers paid various households and shops to put sympathetically linked origami decorations in their windows. The organizers would change details of the decorations remotely, and all the members needed to do was pass by one to see when the next meeting was or get a warning that it had been cancelled and to be wary.

The organizers sent Siobhan and Tanya out in different directions and at different times, but it wasn't hard for Siobhan to find Tanya again.

She followed her from a distance all the way back to the University. She watched the other girl walk back to the dorms, then waited a few minutes while holding the compass spell, but Tanya seemingly hadn't moved from her room.

Siobhan was exhausted and wanted nothing more than to find a dark alley somewhere, change back into Sebastien, and flop into her own bed. Instead, she turned around and walked briskly back into the city. *'I can't get sloppy.'*

She changed into Sebastien at the Silk Door, then walked to Oliver's house. Despite her warm clothes, her fingers and feet were frozen through by the time she arrived. The servants were gone for the evening, so Oliver opened the door himself.

He was surprised to see her, but waved her in and up to his office, motioning for her to stand, shivering, in front of the fire while he stoked it higher. While she warmed, he went down to the kitchen and made coffee for both of them.

When he returned, Sebastien cast a bit of perfunctory wakefulness intent into the dark liquid. She offered to do the same for him, but he shook his head, already sipping from his cup. "There's no need. Now tell me what happened. Did Liza help you?"

"She did. Just not in the way I was expecting. I followed Tanya Canelo—the girl who blew up Eagle Tower to keep me from being caught—to a secret meeting of thaumaturges. I'm now their newest member."

He sipped his coffee, not seeming particularly shocked. "That *is* momentous," he said calmly. "Tell me more."

31

ATTACK STRATEGY

SEBASTIEN
Month 12, Day 26, Saturday 11:30 p.m.

SEBASTIEN QUICKLY REPORTED what little she and Damien had found throughout the week and the events of that evening. "I missed Tanya's meeting with the Morrows. Unless they have some other stealthy way to communicate with her, she must have met with one of them on the way. If you get me a map, I might be able to estimate the path she took based on her angle from my location, but I'm not even sure how long she was gone from the University before Damien warned me. In the worst case, it could have been almost an hour."

"This is good," Oliver said, moving to pull a rolled-up map from one of his cabinets. "Actually, very good."

She stared at him.

"Not that you lost track of the girl. I'm talking about the secret meeting. I've wanted to get an eye into a place like that since I came to this city. You can vouch for a Verdant Stag member to join!"

She shook her head. "The rules state you must have been a member for at least six months and have brought a certain amount of value to the group before you can recommend new members."

He was visibly disappointed, but said, "Well, next time, make note of what people offer and need, and let me know. There might be some good business opportunities for the Verdant Stag. I'll give you a couple gold for each meeting."

"Five gold," she offered immediately.

"Ridiculous. Three gold."

"For something that could get me caught and sent to jail in my female form? Your false identity papers aren't enough to keep me safe from that. Four gold. You'll be saving a lot more than that by avoiding the magic tax, even after the arbiter's fees."

"Fine. Four gold, but only for any meetings that provide valuable supplies or information."

She glared at him, but conceded. It wasn't a lot at the kind of scale she was now working with, but every little bit helped.

He laid out the map and turned to her expectantly.

Based on her memory of her own location and Tanya's changing angle relative to her, Sebastien estimated a large swath of the city that the other girl could have accessed.

"You've just pointed out the majority of Morrow territory," Oliver said. "Not exactly revelatory."

Sebastien clenched her jaw until her teeth creaked, holding back her frustration. "I'll do better next time."

Oliver hesitated, staring at the map, then said, "There might not be a next time."

"What do you mean?"

"I'm planning a joint attack on the Morrows with the Nightmare Pack. We're going to oust them and take over their territory."

Sebastien took a sharp breath.

"The student liaison is a good source of information, but any of the Morrows' leaders should be, too. If I can question them, spying on her outside the University might not be as critical. Once the Morrows are defeated, it's even possible her whole operation will fall apart."

"Eliminating the Morrows altogether... Hah!" Sebastien let out a single, breathy laugh. "It's definitely the most direct way to deal with your problems, but I hadn't thought it was an actual possibility. I'm assuming you've got a plan? And enough manpower? Are you just going to be going after the leadership, or the lower-ranking members as well?"

"Not only will we be neutralizing their leadership, but we also plan to take out lieutenants and capture the most critical resource points and trade stations. That way, even if someone slips through our grasp and wants to mount a counterattack, they won't have the resources to do so." he said, growing more excited the longer he spoke. He stood and returned to his desk, motioning for her to follow him. "The Nightmare Pack are dedicating a lot of their resources to this venture, which is how we're able to do this. Not just manpower and weapons, but their authority and reputation also. Without them, even if we did manage to take out the Morrow leadership, it would be difficult to hold their territory against rebellion and other gangs. Our current plan is to initiate joint strikes on several different points of interest at once."

"Look," he said, pushing piles of paper and other clutter to the side to reveal a large map covered in different-colored notations and scribbled comments. "This is going to be the largest offensive the Morrows have ever dealt with. We're hitting eleven different major assets at the same time, and six minor ones. No plan survives contact with the enemy, of course, but we've tried to make the strategy as shatter-proof as possible."

Even the amount of surveillance work that must have gone into developing this plan was impressive. "You're pouring a lot of resources into this."

"I have to, or they'll keep bleeding me dry. It's either expand or die. You know that as well as anyone. I'm putting everything I can into this, because it has to work."

"Are you sure you can trust the Nightmare Pack not to turn on you once the Morrows are finished? They're much bigger than the Stags, aren't they?"

"Lord Lynwood and I made a vow of nonaggression for the next five years, so I trust them as much as that's worth, as long as he remains their leader. Beyond that, though, they became especially accommodating after their visit with you. I don't think they have any intention of suddenly turning on us."

They cared for the boy Millennium quite a lot, apparently. They might need her help again if the current spell stopped working as he grew older.

"Besides, we're both getting a good deal out of this," Oliver added.

She noted small symbols marked in green. "Healing stations?"

"I'd like to minimize the death toll as much as possible. All the attacking teams will be supplied with basic emergency aid supplies, but it won't be enough. Anyone who is seriously injured can retreat or be brought to one of the healing stations to receive more extensive care. Life is precious. Not just ours, but theirs too."

She held back a small smile. She might not agree with all of his ideas, but there was something endearing about the kind of person who would think like that. Sebastien tilted her head to the side. "Did I understand that correctly? You want to minimize deaths on the Morrows' side, too?"

"Their lives are valuable. And I don't mean just because they're sentient beings, though there's that too. This isn't an altruistic decision. We're not going to be able to get every last member of the Morrows, or their families. Leaving them alive—hostages, in a way—both discourages hasty retaliation and long-term revenge. Some of them have to die either way, but others can be ransomed back to their families or any other Morrow who escaped our grasp, and for exorbitant prices. That will further drain them of resources they might otherwise use against us. Even if they realize this, if any high-ranking member of the Morrows wants to retain their legitimacy, they'll have no choice but to ransom their men for honor's sake—even if it hurts them financially."

Sebastien frowned, thinking this idea over. "Like taking knights and lords as prisoners of war. They're worth more alive than dead. But what if they don't get ransomed? Trying to keep them secure and healthy would be a further drain on *your* resources, and, with the new territory, you're going to be stretched pretty thin. What do you do with someone who has no one to ransom him?"

The edges of Oliver's mouth turned down grimly. "The Morrows are well-known for their disregard of the citizens within their territory. They act like little lords, placing themselves above the law. And that territory will be my territory. Their people my people. And I've made a name for myself as being fair and just. I do not allow heinous crimes within my territory. There will be some ransoms, but also trials—and executions—to help legitimize Verdant Stag authority. If any are innocent, or mostly so, perhaps they'll be offered a job in exchange for their freedom. We're building the holding cells now. This plan relies on the prisoners not escaping or being broken out by their colleagues. A few more weeks and we'll be ready to implement the plan. I will use all their lives to the greatest benefit."

Sebastien didn't know what to think about that. It made her uncomfortable, but she couldn't point out any flaws in his logic. Oliver could appear benevolent at times, but he was no fool, and not as soft as he seemed, either. "The coppers won't be a problem? You have no authority to hold trial, and an execution is no different than murder."

He shrugged. "They don't care so much about murder in places like this. Murders happen every day. Unless it becomes egregious, many of the coppers spare only nominal effort to bring the perpetrators to justice—unless someone important or wealthy is affected. We'll bribe a few people to look the other way, and keep it from becoming a spectacle. We will use both magical and mundane means to ensure we do not execute the innocent, don't worry."

That hadn't been what she was worried about. "You really do want to take over Gilbratha," she murmured.

He looked up, meeting her eyes unflinchingly. "Of course."

She stared into the bright fervor in their blue depths, a foreboding of danger shuddering through her.

"It will take some time—years—but I've always known the eventual purpose of all this. If we can take Gilbratha, with its people, resources, and defenses, we will hold the strongest position in Lenore. From there, with time and care, we can grasp even more. But first, the fledgling Verdant Stag must start by overthrowing the Morrows. Our first real enemy," he said, turning back to the map.

Sebastien swallowed, her throat dry. People were going to die along the way for Oliver's ideas. She resolved that she wouldn't be one of them. "And the Morrows don't know this is coming? It seems too big an operation to keep secret. If you're spying on them, they could be spying on you."

"Oh, they know *something's* coming. It's impossible to keep our preparations entirely unnoticed. But only a few on our side know the details, and we're going to keep it like that for as long as possible. In addition, we'll be doing our best to sow panic and confusion amongst the Morrows during the attack. A complete surprise might be impossible, but that doesn't mean they'll mount an effective response."

She nodded slowly, still frowning down at the map. There was at least one healing station within ten minutes of each major target. "If there had been something like this in place when the Morrows attacked the warehouse, Jameson might still be alive," she murmured.

Oliver was silent for a few seconds, then said, "Yes. I'm trying to learn my lessons, Siobhan."

Sebastien turned to look at him. Normally, he was better about using the name of her current body.

He didn't seem to realize his slip. "We still don't have enough competent healers to fill all the stations, though. They'll be set back from the worst of the fighting, and not even the Morrows should have an incentive to attack them, but I'm having trouble getting healers to agree, especially when I can't tell them the details ahead of time. It's not just the fighters I'm worried about. We're in the middle of the city. It's unlikely all civilians will escape unscathed."

Sebastien clenched her jaw. She knew the world wasn't fair, but it grated at her bones when innocents were dragged into danger.

"That's why I was hoping you would assist at one of the healing stations."

She jerked her head up to look at him. "I'm not a healer."

"I know. But you're familiar with the basic use of alchemy to mitigate injury. I've seen you use blood magic to heal someone more than once, and you're not the type to fall apart at the sight of a little gore. You'll be placed with an actual healer, not on your own. They can instruct you if there are things you don't know how to handle, and you can assist them."

The muscles of Sebastien's shoulders and back tightened with dread until she felt little electric tingles of protest running through her spine. She instinctively wanted to deny his request, but she remembered the blood print vow she'd done with Katerin. She couldn't refuse any favors that acted as repayment of her debt, unless she found them morally reprehensible.

And how could acting as a healer to save not only the Stags, but civilians and even the enemy, be immoral? "I'll have time to prepare?" she asked past a tight throat.

"Approximately three weeks," he said.

'*I can do a lot of brewing in three weeks, and a lot of study on trauma care.*' She rubbed her neck, already anticipating the long hours of fatigue. '*It feels like I'm a hamster in a wheel that never gets anywhere.*' She raised her head, her eyes narrowing as she reeled in a sudden idea. "Rather than in gold toward my debt, can I be paid for my help with a stake in one of the businesses the Verdant Stags control? Say...three percent of the ongoing net profits from the alchemy shop?"

Oliver's eyebrows rose, and then he laughed. "You *are* a clever one. But I don't think so." He shook his head. "You have to pay off your debt first before you can negotiate things like that. You'll be paid the same rate as any other healer's assistant at Apprentice level on this mission. Forty gold. A month's pay for a single night of heavy work."

She couldn't deny that was fair. The amount he'd given her last time was to partially make up for everything that went wrong after he called her out of bed to help in the middle of the night. "I agree. But of course, any brewing I do between now and then will be paid separately."

They worked out a code for extreme emergencies using the linked bracelets they both wore on their forearms. If necessary, she would break one of the bracelets, and Oliver would use one of the other bracelets as a divination target.

Because of the way the divination-diverting ward worked, she would have to place the target bracelet somewhere away from her body, and if she was forced to move, it would be no use. But if that happened, she had multiple bracelets, and could leave a trail of metaphorical bread crumbs.

Oliver paid for her carriage back to the University. It was a nice one that even had a shielded brazier of coals within to keep the riders warm.

The dorms were dark and mostly silent. It was well past curfew, but Damien was still awake, sitting up on his bed and waiting for her to return. He hopped up as soon as he saw her and motioned for her to follow him from the room.

With a sigh, she trudged after him into the bathrooms, where he checked every stall before turning around to say, "I don't know how she slipped away. We looked for her as soon as we realized, and I broke the bracelet as soon as I knew we weren't going to find her immediately."

Sebastien nodded tiredly. "You did fine. She's slippery, but I found her."

"What happened? She's been back for a couple hours already. Was she meeting with whoever Professor Munchworth was talking about? What were you doing?"

Sebastien considered simply telling him he didn't have the right to know before he'd proved himself, but was certain this would require more effort than making up a simple lie, as Damien was sure to argue. "She met with someone. I'm not sure who. I couldn't see their face. She traded some of the gold for beast cores. If she did anything else, it was before I caught up to her."

"Beast cores? Why would she want those?"

Sebastien shrugged. "To trade or to use. You can make guesses as easily as I can."

Damien had more questions, but she brushed them off. "I don't know, Damien, and even if I did, that doesn't mean I would tell you. You've got a long way to go before your curiosity entitles you to information." *'And if I have my way, it never will,'* she added silently.

She slept well, for once, and in the morning went to the library, trailing behind Tanya and Newton.

Tanya headed up the stairs for the second floor, but Sebastien called Newton's name as the young man moved to follow her.

Newton walked with her, putting a few meters between them and the stairs. "Is everything okay?" he asked, his voice lowered. "Is this about me losing track of T—"

She shook her head, cutting him off. "It's fine. This isn't about her. I was wondering if I could ask you a favor."

Newton nodded, raising his eyebrows as he waited for her to continue.

"I need the recipe for Humphries' adapting solution. But it's on the second floor. I was wondering if you could bring me this book so I could copy it?" she asked, handing him a slip with the potion reference's location.

"Umm, sure, I can do that. Why do you need it, if I can ask?"

She'd already thought what to say, just in case he asked. "I met a young girl whose mother is an Apprentice under a sorcerer. The girl has a blood disorder that requires constant visits to a healer, and...well, her mother is struggling to pay for treatment. I happened to hear her pleading with the healer while the girl waited outside."

"Oh," Newton murmured.

Sebastien nodded. "This won't fix the problem, but it's a lot cheaper than healing spells, and her mother should be strong enough to brew it. Maybe it'll help them get back on their feet."

Newton's grip on the piece of paper tightened, and he hurried off to the second floor with a sharp nod.

When he returned, Sebastien copied the recipe onto a couple loose sheets of paper. The potion was difficult and power-intensive, and some of the components were relatively expensive, but she could brew it—if only in very small batches. Flipping a few pages, she also found the modified piercing spell that would let someone funnel the solution directly into a patient's veins, overcoming the natural defensive barrier of their skin.

'That would work for blood transfusions, too.' It was just another example of

how the delineations between acceptable and unacceptable magic were so arbitrary.

"Thank you," she said, handing the book back to Newton.

"No need for thanks. I wish there were more people like you out there," he said with a soft, knowing smile.

She shuffled awkwardly. "Err, how's your father?"

"His lungs rattle with every breath," Newton said, his smile turning strained. "But we found a healer who's willing to take payments, and there are a couple of people who might be willing to lend us some gold."

Sebastien wondered if this healer and lender were both from the Verdant Stag, but couldn't just ask. "Let me know if I can help," she said. "I know a couple people with enough coin that they probably wouldn't mind lending some to you."

"Thank you, Sebastien, but really, you've already done more than enough to help me."

She shook her head. "Not really. I've pointed some opportunity your way, and that's it. You're the one who's helping yourself."

He rolled his eyes at her, but his smile had lost its strain as he left, returning to the second floor to keep a subtle watch over Tanya.

Sebastien folded up the recipe for Humphries' adapting solution and put it in her pocket. She held her fingers over the pocket, a feverish rush of determination warming them. *'I will not let anyone else die the same way as Jameson, at the least.'*

32

DRILLS

Sebastien

Month 12, Day 31, Thursday 2:30 p.m.

Over the next few days, no one reached out to Oliver or any of his people to request a meeting with the Raven Queen. Sebastien found this puzzling, but since she was unsure how to respond if they did request one, she was fine postponing the problem as long as possible.

If she met with Tanya as the Raven Queen, they'd have to set a system in place to make sure they avoided any traps by the University faction behind Tanya. It was dangerous, much more so than meeting with Lynwood had been. However, she might be able to get information from Tanya in return, maybe even figure out what was going on behind the scenes with the University, the Crowns, and the ancient book.

Oliver could even use the meeting to gain an upper hand against his enemies, like using Tanya to feed the Morrows false information.

Still, the danger and uncertainty left Sebastien's muscles so tight that she had to use Newton's esoteric humming spell to forcefully calm herself several times.

On the bright side, her gold problem was slightly alleviated, taking a portion of that pressure off her shoulders. Oliver had indeed sold the pixie eggs to Liza, and after appraising the star sapphire, Siobhan was owed a little over ninety gold. She took eighteen to pay for the ingredients for the regeneration potions she was soon to owe the man from the secret meeting, and let the rest of it go toward paying off some of the interest she owed the Verdant Stag.

After that, she had paid off all the interest accrued up to that point, and managed to shave down the principal to, oh, only about *nine hundred fifty gold!*

She wanted to pull her hair out. *'Fifty percent interest is a nightmare. At least it isn't compounding. Yet.'* If she couldn't pay the balance off within a year, whatever interest she owed would be added to the principal balance, and she'd start paying fifty percent interest on that, too. It was decidedly ironic that the Verdant Stag did so much to help people, like selling life-saving potions well below the market value, and yet practiced lending with terms so predatory most people would owe them for life. *'I wonder how much of Oliver's apparent philanthropy is actually a cloak for his desire for power?'*

She, Damien, and Newton continued to keep watch over Tanya, but other than a couple of paper bird messages that they had no way to intercept, she did nothing suspicious. Perhaps Tanya was waiting, too.

Sebastien spent her free time studying emergency first aid—the best way to keep people with traumatic wounds alive a little longer so someone with actual skill could save them—and still managed to slip in some time reading about the purpose of sleep.

On Thursday in Fekten's Defensive Magic class, Sebastien was shown once again the distance between her and her goals.

As always, they started the class with a workout, while Fekten lectured in a voice that had no trouble traveling clearly to all the students.

"The biggest problem using magic in a dangerous situation is the difficulty of casting while moving. There are ways to get past this. Artifacts and battle alchemy, tomes full of spell pages, or even the wrought-metal, portable Circles the army provides. Each have their downsides, but these downsides are never more apparent than when attempting to *shield*," Fekten yelled.

He walked among them, occasionally stopping to goad someone into more effort, or to do the exercises right alongside them, only better, while never stopping his monologue. "A shield must be large enough to cover the body, and most are power-intensive. Except those cast by complex artifacts, most shields will require a large Circle drawn on the ground around the caster and whatever they are trying to protect. This goes against everything I have taught you about how to survive in a dangerous situation! What are the rules of survival?"

Without pausing whatever exercise they were doing, the students shouted back, "To stay alive, use stealth to escape! Hide under stationary cover only when you cannot run! Dodge only when you cannot hide! Shield in place only when you cannot dodge!"

Sebastien's voice was weak past her panting, but she repeated the words with as much force as she could. They were Fekten's mantra, and he added more to them every couple of weeks. If Fekten suspected that one of the students hadn't been listening, or wasn't filled with enthusiasm, he assigned additional exercise to the entire group.

She assumed Fekten would begin to teach them something about fighting back when he thought they were competent enough to live through such an attempt. *'Which means it might be years.'* She gave a mental whimper.

Satisfied, Fekten nodded and continued. "I have seen dozens of stupid thaumaturges die inside their shield Circle! No shield protects against everything, and even if you manage to stand against one enemy's attacks, are you more powerful than two people, or ten, working together? Can you shield their fireball spell at the same time you block the rock they've thrown at you just behind it? Can you block a broadsword swung with enough force to split you in two at the waist, or an explosive potion launched from a hundred meters away? Half of you cannot even *cast* a shield!"

He breathed hard for a moment, from passion rather than exhaustion, stopping beside Sebastien's group to do pushups with them, which he did with only one arm.

"The correct way to keep your heads attached to your bodies is to avoid the conflict."

Sebastien almost rolled her eyes. *'Wasn't that the same argument I made in the entrance exam, when he asked me about my hypothetical response to the Blood Emperor? What kind of double standard is this, that the only one it's not acceptable to run away from is the one most likely to kill me with the wave of a hand? Does he not realize the hypocrisy?'* It would have surprised her more, except she was seeing more and more how blood magic was so arbitrarily defined, hated on instinct and faith rather than rational consideration of the specific situation. Among those who had internalized these beliefs, it was a huge social faux-pas to even suggest that *some* blood magic could be used for good—on the same level as admitting that you thought sea kraken were sexually attractive, or that people should be able to marry their children.

Fekten continued. "The greatest weapon in the battle to live a long life is knowledge. Understanding yourself comes first. An incorrect assessment of your own abilities will leave you broken and dead like so many before you, as you make plans and take actions you cannot follow through on. Understanding your enemy comes second. For magical beasts, this means understanding their dispositions, abilities, and habitats. With superior knowledge of the dangers they are likely to face, someone weaker can prepare against a specific opponent—targeting their weaknesses—rather than hoping to crush them on a level playing field.

"For humans and other sapient beings, of course this also includes understanding their capabilities, the personal and external resources they have access to. But it also means understanding their flaws. You cannot deal with someone who is full of hubris and quick to anger the same way you would deal with a reasonable person. It is understanding their desires, not only their greed, which dictates what they are likely to do to take control of what is not theirs, but what they *value*, which often dictates what lengths they will go to when protecting the things that hold value to them. A mother protecting her children can be more vicious—and recklessly aggressive—than a soldier fighting for glory and coin."

Fekten signaled a station change, which let each group of students move on to a new exercise, and kept lecturing. "Once you understand your enemy, you can avoid being seen as a viable target, either by passing beneath their notice, or seeming too much of a threat to risk attacking. You can turn their urges and desires against them, so they're distracted, exerting their energy on fighting against a different opponent, or even ripping themselves apart with internal conflict."

Fekten passed Sebastien, stopping to correct her form with a couple of nudges. This close, his presence was even more intimidating—not just from his large, muscled form and loud voice, but the intangible press of his Will, which was like a choking fog. "The second-best way to keep your heads attached to your bodies is to be *prepared*," he continued. "Your body must be in the proper condition to react to danger and successfully carry you through it. Your mind must have the knowledge, and also the proper conditioning, to guide you through even when you're so afraid you piss yourselves. It is not so easy to reason when under stress. It is best to do your reasoning beforehand, and then practice your response until it becomes ingrained in your flesh. And, if possible, you should be externally prepared, as well. Artifacts for when your Will reaches its limits. Potions for when your body gives out. Allies for when your strength alone is not enough."

He signaled for another station change.

Sebastien's group was on the jump-rope station next. She'd always thought the game childish, but now, as she threw herself into the complex footwork and rabbit-quick hops that Fekten was trying to drill into them, she knew that jump-rope had probably been introduced to children by some sadistic devil chuckling to itself at their naivete and eventual, inevitable, horrible disillusionment. She choked down the food she'd eaten at lunch, which seemed determined to escape her stomach.

Fekten shook his head sadly before finally calling a halt to the conditioning part of the class.

"No punishment exercises!" Damien gasped, his hands on his knees and sweat pouring down his face. "Yay."

Another student, lying on the ground like a suffocating fish, aimed an ineffectual kick in Damien's direction. "Don't jinx it!"

Fekten had them clean up the equipment, then move from the open white flats to the building with the simulation room.

Inside, humanoid mannequins with "battle" wands were arrayed in several circular groups, facing inward.

Fekten led the students in a quick review of the basic footwork he'd been teaching them, then chose a handful of students to face off against the mannequins.

Rhett Moncrieffe, Damien's Crown Family friend, was in the first group and performed stunningly. As the mannequins surrounding him shot colored balls of light that would burst open and dye whatever they hit in bright colors, Moncrieffe spun and twisted and dodged.

The mannequins shot faster as time passed, their rhythm more unpredictable.

Moncrieffe kept going beyond the point that seemed possible, until Sebastien had to wonder how he was even perceiving all the spells coming his way.

Finally, he was hit in the back of his hip by one bright blue shot, while avoiding three other simultaneous shots from the other mannequins. He fell to the ground, winded, and the students watching and idly practicing their own footwork in anticipation let out a cheer.

Apparently Moncrieffe was the star of the first-term dueling team, and had been training for this since he was three. He was expected to win trophies, and already had a growing fanbase among the other students.

Damien sidled over to Sebastien. "Do you want to bet on how long you can last?"

Sebastien shot him a dirty look, not even bothering to respond. Damien had made no secret that he found it hilarious the first time she fell on her face during dodging drills. He seemed to take particular pleasure in crowing about the few things she was bad at.

Fekten handed out contribution points based on their rankings in these practical exercises. Moncrieffe had earned dozens already that term, Damien had earned over twenty, and Sebastien was approaching *one whole point* from all the small fractions of points she'd gathered.

As Fekten pointed at her for the next round, Damien slapped her shoulder and yelled. "Go! Double 's'! Slither like a snake!"

Some of the surrounding students laughed and repeated this mocking cheer.

Sebastien scowled as she took her place in the center of a ring of mannequins. *'I'm not even that bad,'* she grumbled mentally. *'Barely in the bottom half of the class.'*

Under Fekten's torture, she was strong enough and fast enough to throw herself around before the blasts of light could reach her. But she was just bad at dodging, especially while trying to remember to use the footwork Fekten was teaching them. Her mind moved quickly, and she could react quickly—if not as instantly as Rhett—but it was all conscious calculation. She had to think about every move her body made, and she couldn't even get into a rhythm of movement like she could for something like jump-rope. It was never instinctive, and as the attacks became quicker and required her to move in more complex ways, she couldn't keep up the mental calculations with enough time left to send instructions to her body.

Sebastien started out perfectly, but began to show the signs of strain after only a couple of minutes. Her movements grew jerky, clumsy, and a little too forceful as she scrambled to keep up with the increasing speed. She threw herself to the ground to avoid three shots that would otherwise have hit her in the legs, chest, and head, and then rolled quickly to the side as she saw a mannequin lower its arm to shoot her on the ground.

She tossed herself upright, the movement weaker than she would have liked after all the pushups, then had to backpedal to avoid a shot that almost brushed her nose. She retreated right into another two shots, one in the kidney, one in the back of the head.

She tried not to slump too obviously with defeat. The attacks were mostly light and a sprinkle of dye, with barely enough force to injure. Still, Fekten was quick to point at her. "Siverling! You just got your brains splashed over the ground, and if that didn't kill you, the mutilated kidney would have you bleeding out in under two minutes. Out."

She turned to rejoin the group of waiting students, but Fekten waved her over.

"You think too much," he said, his voice still loud but not a projected yell meant for the entire room. "You need to learn to act on instinct. Practice until the movements are engraved into your body, so that you no longer need to think to respond, only do what you have done thousands of times before. You might never be great, but you could be passable, at least."

Sebastien said, "Yes, Fekten," as the man had told them all to address him, but didn't feel particularly optimistic as she rejoined the group, where Damien was still trying to stifle his laughter. *'When will I ever have time to practice all this thousands of times?'*

It wasn't that she scorned the man's advice. She'd already tried practicing on her own, tuning the mannequins to an easier setting so she could have more time before getting overwhelmed. That was how she'd gotten to her current level of mediocrity. And she *had* gotten better, but not because her muscles somehow retained the memory of what to do. No, she had simply begun to memorize the best movement to make to avoid more complex attacks, and could immediately implement it rather than have to calculate it first.

Trying to do that until she reached even Damien's level would have cost her almost as much practice every week as Professor Lacer's class did. And if she had to choose between Defense and Practical Casting, it was no contest.

'There's another option to solve the dilemma between escaping and casting. Just become a free-caster. I'm sure Professor Lacer could shield while running away. If he ever needed to run away.'

OLD WIVES' TALES

SIOBHAN
   Month 1, Day 7, Thursday 6:30 p.m.

As WAS the nature of time, it passed—all the way into the new year. Sebastien had to cast a deafening hex on herself to get to sleep on New Year's Eve, and double-check her intrusion alarm wards so she could feel secure going to sleep in a room full of other people, many of whom were somehow intoxicated. '*I hate wealthy, well-educated young adults,*' she lamented, pulling her blankets overhead. '*I wish I were as frightening as Professor Lacer. He could just open the door and look around for three seconds and be guaranteed peace for the rest of the night.*'

She confirmed that there would be no secret meeting that weekend, then spent most of it at Oliver's house doing alchemy to prepare for the upcoming attack on the Morrows. Her Will had grown enough that she was able to prepare a few more doses of the less intensive items per batch, and accordingly, her payment for a weekend of work increased. She'd made almost twenty gold in only two days of work.

To be fair, it was exhausting work, and it pushed her to her limits by the end of the day, but it meant that she could make more in a week than the interest on her debt over that same time.

Early the next week, the secret organization's paper ornaments, placed in windows throughout the city, changed. There would be another meeting that Thursday.

Oliver gave Sebastien a pouch of gold and a list of things he wanted her to see if she could buy.

She left before Tanya, changing her appearance at the Silk Door and then returning to the base of the white cliffs to lie in wait.

She had instructed Damien to stay behind when Tanya left that evening, and was relieved to see that he followed her instructions without grumbling.

Siobhan was Tanya's only tail, as far as she could tell.

She followed the other woman from a distance, but Tanya didn't stop to talk to anyone or enter any buildings. After Tanya had arrived at the secret meeting spot, Siobhan waited a few minutes before entering herself.

She wore her own mask this time, not trusting the one the organizers had provided. If it were her, she would have secretly cast tracking spells on all of them to give herself the upper hand over the members. Knowledge was power, after all.

This group of masked, dangerous thaumaturges still made her feel awkward and on edge, but she tried to keep this nervousness from her body language. *'They don't know who I am or what I'm here for. No one here has any reason to wish me ill. Tanya is completely oblivious.'* She was sure there were more guards in the room than there had been the last time, and she kept imagining she felt the eyes of the meeting facilitators on her, though they weren't staring whenever she turned to look.

During the first part of the meeting, where people made offers of what they had to sell or trade, the chubby man she vaguely recognized from the last meeting raised his hand and said, "I brought the sempervivum apricus and mandrake for the person who wanted them last time."

"And I have the regeneration potions," Siobhan said with a slight raise of her hand.

The arbiter made a note on the paper before him. "We will handle the appraisal and exchange after the meeting."

Siobhan paid close attention to what people offered, and managed to buy a few of the things on Oliver's list. Liquid stone potions, for fortifications and stabilizing people with broken bones. A batch of philtres that, when breathed in, created a sealed bubble inside a punctured lung, keeping someone from drowning in their own blood. A couple of minor healing potions, which could be used when something like her regeneration potion wasn't enough. And an artifact that stored large masses of water inside a folded space and then released it again in a powerful spray. It did not contain any weight-affecting spells, so would be almost impossible to carry when fully loaded with liquid, but with the help of a couple horses, it could be used to put out fires, or even to attack crowds. Additionally, with the right kind of damage to the artifact, it could probably cause a deadly explosion of water.

Tanya sent a few distrustful looks Siobhan's way, probably because it was obvious she was gearing up for some sort of altercation. The other girl didn't seem to suspect Siobhan of being the Raven Queen, however.

Tentatively, Siobhan pulled out a pouch from her pocket. She cleared her throat. "I have some celerium for sale. One small conduit, rated at one hundred thaums, for twenty gold. One conduit at two hundred twelve thaums with a spot of contamination, for sixty-two gold. And a shattered conduit that was originally rated at two hundred fifty thaums, for twenty-five gold." She had calculated the sale price based off the current market price, deducting a little for the absence of magic tax, and a lot due to the shattered nature of the larger conduit. Celerium pieces couldn't be merged back together, and only the weakest child would be able to channel through the remaining shards. Celerium grew exponentially more expensive with increasing size and clarity, so most of the worth of her old Conduit was gone. Still, celerium was used in a few powerful spells, and was a fantastic material for drawing robust, high-capacity spell arrays, so it could be used for something.

The arbiter looked around to meet the eye of the prognos woman, who was sitting in the corner.

"I'll give you seventy-five gold for the two unbroken Conduits, contingent on appraisal," a woman said.

Siobhan frowned.

The fat man she'd done her other trade with said, "Eighty gold for the whole lot, and I will throw in a pound of etherwood leaves, too. Easy to resell, or they can be smoked yourself if you enjoy them."

Her stated price would have been one hundred seven gold for everything, but she had acknowledged ahead of time that she would go down to one hundred gold if someone wanted it all. Eighty gold was too little, and the only person she knew who smoked etherwood was Katerin.

"These prices are ridiculous," a woman muttered sourly. "Wait a few months till the shortage is over and you'll be able to get that celerium for half the price."

The fat man hesitated, but said, "My offer stands. I like to build up relationships with useful people."

'*Why would he assume I'm useful? Does he need a source of regeneration potions, perhaps? I hope none of the facilitators let any hints about me slip.*'

"One hundred fifteen gold for all the celerium," the arbiter said suddenly.

Siobhan straightened, staring at him from behind her mask. Many of the other members were surprised as well. That was *more* than the combined individual price for all three Conduits.

A few people, including Tanya, looked between the arbiter and Siobhan with suspicion.

She tried not to show her surprise, in case the man changed his mind, and was grateful for the mask that had covered her facial expressions. "Any other offers?" she asked.

No one spoke up.

"Alright. One hundred fifteen gold," she agreed.

Finally, the offerings portion of the meeting was over, and they moved on to requests.

Tanya spoke up immediately. "I previously requested help setting up a meeting with the Raven Queen. Was there any success?"

The man with the horns, who had offered to help her last time, gave a nervous cough. "I tried, but my contact refused to help. They were afraid to talk about the Raven Queen at all. Wouldn't even say her name. Apparently, Lord Lynwood is cracking down. I suggest you go to the Verdant Stag and ask there. The red-haired proprietress has connections to Lord Stag, and he should be able to get you an audience."

It seemed as if perhaps Lord Lynwood had heeded Siobhan's relayed request for him to limit his people's gossiping with a little more vehemence than she'd anticipated.

Tanya's scowl was obvious in her voice. "I'm not paying for that kind of 'help,'" she snapped. "If I wanted to go to the Verdant Stag, I could have done that already."

The man shrugged.

"This transaction was unsuccessful," the arbiter said, sounding a little tense, in contrast to his normal tone of boredom. "There will be no retaliation from either party. Please be aware that violence is prohibited. As the request was not met, no payment is due."

Tanya sighed deeply and adjusted her mask. "The previous offer still stands. Anyone who can give me relevant information about the Raven Queen or set up a meeting between us will be rewarded. Gold. Beast cores. I also have access to various unusual or restricted components, if you have a very specific need. But I'm not interested in trading for anything except the Raven Queen."

Siobhan again considered setting up the meeting between Tanya and her alternate persona herself, but decided against it. *'I need to talk to Oliver before I make such a risky move. It might not be worth it.'*

One member raised his hand tentatively. "I've overheard a couple o' the coppers talkin' over drinks at my pub. Might be just as filled with rumors as the rest o' the stuff on the street, but I'm happy to tell you, and you can judge for yourself."

Tanya agreed, and the arbiter noted down their meeting, sending a very subtle glance Siobhan's way.

'Oh. Of course he's tense. He knows I'm the Raven Queen. The interviewers must have mentioned something. Everybody gossips,' she thought with a sigh. She wasn't sure

if it was a good thing or a bad thing. The people in charge probably wouldn't want to sell her out to the coppers to get the reward, not with their reputations on the line, and the pseudo-misunderstanding might even have been the reason he offered such a high price for her celerium.

During the general information exchange at the end of the meeting, a woman with an old-sounding voice said, "There are rumblings of blood and violence in Gilbratha's future. It is like a violin string pulled too tight, on the verge of snapping and slicing through flesh. Take heed. Be wary."

"That's pretty obvious to anyone with eyes and ears," someone else said.

A woman nodded. "I say stock up on the necessities and a good lock for your door. It's always best to be prepared."

"As a reminder, I have single-use stunning artifacts," someone else interjected opportunistically. "It's enough to escape in an emergency or incapacitate a burglar who's broken into your house in the night."

No one said anything more specific about this upcoming danger. *'I wonder if it has anything to do with the attack on the Morrows,'* Siobhan thought, but was quickly distracted as one of the organizers waved her and the component-seller over to a side room, where the prognos woman from Siobhan's admittance interview bowed deeply to her.

Tanya was walking to her own secure room with the man who'd overheard gossip about the Raven Queen in a pub, but Siobhan didn't worry about missing anything, because she couldn't have listened in without being caught anyway.

The prognos gave only a perfunctory nod to the chubby man, who looked at Siobhan with more interest after experiencing the disparity in their treatment. Siobhan's regeneration potions were pronounced acceptable, as were the two plants the man had brought, their pots concealed within a plain wooden box, and they traded.

The man left, and the woman called in the others that Siobhan had traded with on Oliver's behalf. When it was all finished, and they had gone, she said, "I will take the celerium, if that is acceptable to you."

"Sure." Siobhan handed the small pouch over. She felt some regret at parting from her oldest Conduit. Her grandfather had given it to her as a child, and it had been with her until now. Second-hand Conduits sometimes held a weak sympathetic connection to their original owners, from being kept so close and used so intimately, but unlike a piece of her body, the connection would be weak, and fade quickly. Nothing powerful enough to harm her could be cast with it.

The woman handed over a full purse of gold before even looking into the pouch.

Siobhan was surprised. "Are you not interested in verifying my claims of quality? I could have just handed you a pouch full of pebbles."

The woman swallowed heavily, her eye having trouble meeting Siobhan's. "I trust in your honor," she said weakly.

Siobhan tilted her head to the side. *"Really?"* That just seemed foolish. She had verified all the other transactions. It was part of her job, whether she trusted the members or not.

The woman's hands were white-knuckled around the celerium pouch. "If you had given me a pouch of pebbles, would you have submitted to my protest about the matter? If you lied to me, what could I do about it?"

"That is ridiculous," Siobhan said before she could think better of it.

The woman rocked back on her feet, her knuckles whitening further. "I will appraise them immediately. I apologize, I meant no insult." She fumbled with the mouth of the pouch, peering inside.

Siobhan sighed, amazed at how gullible people could be. The woman hadn't seemed this frightened of her the last time. "Not all rumors about me have any basis in truth," she said, making her voice as soothing as possible in an attempt to calm the woman. "I am not dishonest, and if somehow I had given you pebbles instead of celerium, I would expect you to complain, and either refuse to pay me, or ask for equivalent recompense. I do not commit random acts of violence. I know you told the arbiter who I am, but I'm not so angry as to retaliate. However, I *would* appreciate it if you refrained from adding even more nonsense to the rumors."

It was rather disheartening to feel like an axe murderer threatening a defenseless woman who was trapped in a small room with her. The Raven Queen's reputation might have some benefits, but it could have downsides too, if people felt they were trapped or in danger and decided to resort to excessive force to "protect" themselves from her. A cornered rat would bite, and the real Siobhan Naught couldn't match up to her shadowed reputation.

The woman barely seemed comforted, but she nodded and whispered, "I understand. Thank you." She gave Siobhan a couple of tentative glances then said, "I suppose I am being a little ridiculous?"

It was more of a question than it should have been, but Siobhan nodded. "You are."

The woman let out a breath, then laughed. "I'm sorry," she said again. "It is policy to let the arbiter know when one of the members might be particularly dangerous, but I *promise* I haven't been gossiping about you. I may have been listening to too many distorted rumors, though." She hesitated. "Could I ask a question?"

"You may, but I do not promise to answer." Siobhan's divination-diverting ward was active at a low level, of course, but she didn't want to risk trying to lie to a prognos.

"Why can't I focus on you? I can think about you when you're not in the room with me, but standing so close to you, I just have the urge to look away or think about something else."

Siobhan considered that this might be a dangerous question to answer, but decided that she couldn't be the only person in the city warded against divination. *'Hopefully the effect isn't distinguishably strange enough for it to be something a passing prognos might find suspicious about Sebastien Siverling.'*

Aloud, she said, "For the same reason you could not divine if my answers were truthful. By your nature you cannot help but see deeper, and I am immune to divination." That was an exaggeration, but of the kind Siobhan didn't mind spreading. Maybe if people thought it was impossible, they wouldn't even try. On a whim, Siobhan decided to push it one step further. "Those who try too hard may find that though they do not see me, *I see them.*"

"Oh," the woman said softly.

"Goodnight," Siobhan said. By the time she left, Tanya had a significant head start, but Siobhan was able to catch up with the other girl and follow her back to the University. Tanya walked hurriedly and turned a few corners rather abruptly, and Siobhan almost lost her a couple of times, but thankfully could rely on the compass divination spell to keep from needing to follow suspiciously closely.

She watched Tanya ride up to the University grounds in the clear tubes that wove over the cliffside, then turned back toward the Silk Door. Her breath fogged up in the cool air under the light of a streetlamp. *'I made almost one hundred and twenty gold tonight! I wonder what I can sell next time?'* She held back a squeal of excitement.

3 4

THE PENULTIMATE PIECE

SEBASTIEN
Month 1, Day 9, Saturday 9:00 a.m.

AFTER CHANGING BACK INTO SEBASTIEN, she went to Oliver's house to drop off the purchased packages for the Verdant Stag in his office. Over a hundred gold went to pay down her debt, though she kept fifteen gold for herself. '*I'm making progress.*'

She put her two new potted plants in her room, turning on the light crystal lamp and placing it right beside the sempervivum apricus. They needed a lot of light to survive, and, with it being winter this far north, the illumination from the gloomy sky through the window wouldn't be enough.

On Friday, she decided to go back to Professor Lacer, but the thought of seeing him reminded her of the auxiliary exercises, which she had been somewhat slacking off on. During the free period where her second class of the day would have been, she slipped into the classroom used by Damien and his little study group, which was empty. She secretly stole some of Damien's coffee, then spent the whole period practicing a simple spell that compressed air into a ball. It seemed to augment the rock-creation and disintegration spell that Professor Lacer had introduced in class, but she found the extra control she gained from it was particularly useful for improving the range and size of her fabric-slicing spell, which used an edge of compressed air.

That evening, she took time to review and clean up the sleep-proxy spell she'd been working on for the last few weeks. It was the most complex spell array for anything she'd ever considered casting, largely because she had tried to make the Word as comprehensive as humanly possible, including the equivalent of pages of detailed instructions in tiny script which spiraled around a long section of the edge.

On Saturday morning, she rolled up the extra-large sheet of paper she'd written the spell array on and put it into her satchel, anxiety turning her stomach sour.

Professor Lacer had told her to bring it to him when she'd finished improving it. Showing what could easily be construed as evidence of intent to cast blood magic to a professor sounded like an absolutely idiotic idea. But since he *already* knew she was working on it, hadn't expelled her, and instead actually helped her with it, it's not like this second review would place her in any *additional* danger.

From what she'd seen of Professor Lacer so far, it seemed more likely he would expel her for trying to cast it without a final review by an expert than for the spell itself.

His only office hours that didn't immediately follow one of his teaching periods were early in the morning on Saturday. Sebastien suspected this was meant to deter those without a true reason to see him, since most students would be sleeping in, and those who weren't might prefer breakfast to his oppressive demeanor and scathing tongue.

She knocked on his door.

It opened, seemingly on its own. Professor Lacer was sitting behind the desk with a mug of steaming black coffee. He motioned her in, closing the door behind her with a nonchalant wave of his hand, within which he held a small beast core for energy.

Without preamble, she took the rolled-up paper out of her bag and handed it to him.

He took it with a slightly raised eyebrow and laid it flat across his desk. "This is quick work," he murmured, his eyes flicking over the spell array as he sipped his coffee.

'*It's easy to work on it when I can't sleep,*' she thought.

He waved absently for her to sit down.

About ten silent minutes later, he looked up. "Passable, for a first term student. At least you've done your research. It should not immediately blow up, with the right Will."

Sebastien let out a soft breath, deflating slightly. She swallowed. "On an unrelated note, I'd like to use one of the school's Henrik-Thompson artifacts to test my capacity. Would you be willing to facilitate that?"

His eyebrow raised again, and he stared at her for a moment.

She stared back, sitting stiffly.

He stood abruptly, and she almost startled. Downing the rest of his coffee, he rolled up her spell notes and handed them back to her. "Come," he said, motioning with his wrist. "Do you know how to calculate thaumic requirements?"

She hurried to follow him. "I understand the theory. We've done a little practice in Burberry's Intro to Magic and in Natural Science, but the calculations are beyond me for this spell."

"Hmm," he said inscrutably. He led her down a couple of curved hallways to a door near Burberry's classroom. It was a storage closet. He pulled a Henrik-Thompson testing artifact off one of the shelves, placing it on the floor in the middle of the room. He looked around and then pulled a small brazier off another shelf, lighting it with a snap of his fingers. "Well, go ahead. I will take the measurement reading," he said.

Her star sapphire Conduit was still tucked uncomfortably inside the lip of her boot, pressing against her calf, but the one he'd given her was in an easily accessible pocket, secured from loss by the chain threaded through her vest and attached to her pocket watch.

He eyed it with satisfaction, nodding slightly.

She sat down on the floor cross-legged, focusing her Will to prepare for a hard push.

With a wave of his hand, Professor Lacer created a sucking motion in the air behind her, pulling the door closed on the two of them.

For a moment, she felt trapped in this small, dark room with a powerful, dangerous man standing over her. Then she reminded herself how ridiculous she was being and began to pull energy from the brazier, pushing it into the spell array attached to the crystal ball of the artifact.

She bore down with her Will, tightening her grip on the magic, commanding the power to flow, more and more, until the storage closet filled with light.

She felt the strain as she reached the edge of her capacity. She breathed into the stretch, holding tighter and pushing farther, just a little farther.

Finally, she reached the point where she could go no further without snapping. She held the magic for a second, then two, and then released it slowly, making sure it didn't burn her like a rope slipping too fast through her fingers.

She rolled her shoulders and her jaw. Something inside her mind felt stretched, but not strained. Loose and relaxed.

"Three hundred fifteen thaums," Professor Lacer announced, giving her a sidelong glance.

It was more than she'd hoped. It meant maybe she could try to cast the spell soon, rather than waiting weeks or months to become strong enough.

"How many hours a week do you spend casting?"

Sebastien stood, dusting off her backside. "I don't keep track. I just practice till I'm too tired to go on."

He stared at her for a moment, then quenched the flames in the brazier and returned the items to the shelves they'd come from. "Your Will is not as abysmal as I feared, but it will not be nearly enough to cast that spell. Even with the variable casting times you have built into the process, you would need at least five hundred thaums of enduring capacity to finish the casting in less than four or five hours. Perhaps six or even seven hundred. The final step would take you perhaps three hours, at that strength. I did not calculate it precisely."

Sebastien's stomach dropped somewhere down around her feet. Or at least it felt like it. Enduring capacity wasn't the same as maximum capacity. She could hold about two-thirds of her maximum for long periods, and even then, casting at the edge of her limit for three hours in a single stretch would be quite a feat. She needed to gain another two or three *hundred* thaums before being able to cast the spell. If she had been practicing magic for a few thousand more hours, gaining a few hundred thaums would be much quicker. But for someone at her strength, it would take her another thousand hours of practice or so, at the very least.

She slumped.

Professor Lacer eyed her for a while longer, then spoke as if he didn't notice her discouragement. "New spells must be tested before being cast on anything, or anyone, of importance. I am sure you have heard the somewhat famous example of Master Susva, who perished while testing new healing spells on himself."

"Yes," she said. "He damaged his body's ability to create more blood and died several weeks later. He didn't understand the theory behind what he was doing well enough, which is a common danger for spell-creators. Running a diagnostic spell on a test subject like a mouse might have saved his life."

"Come with me," he said. He led her back to his office, where he scribbled something on a paper card.

She moved to the fire in the corner, took out the rolled-up paper with the evidence of her sleep-proxy spell, and fed it into the low flames, making sure no little bits escaped. She told herself it wasn't out of spite, but caution. She'd already done the same to the rest of the notes she'd taken. The only parts that remained outside her mind were in her grimoire, and that was warded against intrusion.

Professor Lacer noted her actions with an inscrutable look as he handed her the card. "This book should be in the library. It explains how to run a proper experiment and interpret the data. Professor Gnorrish is competent enough, but he will not be running his first term students through this type of rigorous analyses." He paused, then said, "Your improvement might be quicker than you think. If you look in the more advanced research texts on the subject, you will find that not everyone advances at exactly the same rate. You have talent, Mr. Siverling. That will only become more and more apparent over time, and with dedication."

'*Is he trying to cheer me up?*' she wondered. Normally, hearing Thaddeus Lacer admit that she had talent would have made her ecstatic. Even now, it was... pretty awesome. "Thank you," she said. "Is there any way to increase channeling capacity more quickly? Special exercises, or a spell...?"

"Many thaumaturges throughout history have asked that same question. If I were to give advice, I would tell you to continue doing whatever you have been doing."

Somewhat disappointed, she moved to tuck the card into her pocket, but caught a glimpse of writing on the back and flipped it over. It was a ticket for one contribution point. She looked up to him with wide eyes.

His lips twitched in a flicker-fast hint of amusement. "One point, for curiosity, and the good sense not to let it turn into foolishness. Learning how to thread the needle between greatness and recklessness is of the utmost importance. Complacency will lead you only to mediocrity, but recklessness in search of greatness can provoke horrors you have never imagined."

She tucked the card away in her vest pocket, trying not to grin. "I will not be reckless," she promised. "I understand the danger."

"Do you?" He seemed skeptical, but waved a hand at her before she could answer. "Off you go now. I expect this little extracurricular project will not affect your performance in next week's mid-terms."

"Of course not," she said, remembering her shameful performance on the entrance exam. "I won't let people question your decision to have such a mediocre student admitted."

His eyebrow quirked up again, and this time his smile was a bit slower. "See that you don't," he said without looking at her, focused on a half-read sheaf of papers on his desk.

Sebastien shut the door to his office behind her, her emotions a mix of buoyant light and sinking dark. '*An extra two hundred thaums, minimum. That could take me until I've finished my third term and gotten my official Apprentice certification. It's great that the spell is tenable, and it's even better that Professor Lacer seems to have acknowledged me, but it doesn't solve my problem. Is there any way to reduce the spell's power requirement without lowering its efficacy?*' Thinking of spending the next year or more in her current situation made her eyes burn with stymied rage.

'*I have to find a way. Not recklessly. It may not be worth my life, but it's worth a lot. How can I cast a spell that I can't cast?*'

35

FIRST FALLEN

SEBASTIEN
Month 1, Day 11, Monday 2:15 p.m.

IT WAS impossible for Sebastien to have the sleep-proxy spell ready before the mid-terms, which had been her goal.

Instead, she spent most of her weekend the same as the one before: brewing, resting, and then brewing some more, till her brain was foggy and her stomach screamed for calories. She wanted to try brewing some of the other potions that the Verdant Stag enforcers might find useful in a fight, like the liquid stone potion or the bark skin potion, but there was no time. With her limited resources, she needed to prioritize what she knew would be the most useful.

Monday dawned with a tangible air of panic. It was the week of mid-terms, which would be held Wednesday through Friday in lieu of the normal class schedule, and a good portion of the students seemed surprised to realize they only had two days left to prepare.

Sebastien reviewed the notes she'd taken since the beginning of the term and spent some time looking up the things she felt vague on, but didn't bother to panic. She'd been diligent throughout the term so far, and at this point there was little to be gained by a couple more days of frantic cramming.

Professor Lacer started the mini-tournament in his class that day. As he had promised, they were getting a head start on the tournament, since with over two hundred students remaining, completing it would take longer than the extended period they had been assigned for the mid-term on Friday.

The students arrived to find that the classroom had been rearranged. Six desks had been moved to the lecture stage at the front of the room, with a large area cleared around them. A chair sat on either side of each desk, and an empty glass wheel with an iron sphere inside sat atop it.

The tournament brackets were written on the blackboard at the front of the room. There were three sections, grouping people who had started the class under one hundred thaums, between one hundred and two hundred thaums, and then everything above that.

The students crowded closer to the blackboard to see who they would be paired up against for the initial match, chattering excitedly amongst themselves.

Professor Lacer had been sitting at his desk when they came in, reading through a bound sheaf of papers. When the bell rang, he stood up. That simple movement was enough to quiet the entire classroom. "Our class's miniature tournament starts today. We will use this time to go through elimination rounds, narrowing down the number of matches we need to get through on Friday. A single loss will see you disqualified. If any match lasts longer than twenty minutes, both sides will be disqualified. I have requisitioned a couple of student aides to keep track of wins and losses and keep things going smoothly, but I will personally be giving each of you your mid-term score." He gestured to the two student aides, who waved to the room.

"What are we being graded on?" a student asked.

"Your Will," Lacer said simply. "To be clear, your performance today is a chance to either confirm the assessment I've made of each of you throughout the term so far...or surprise me. I have made a reasonable estimation of both your dedication and your skill. Your grade will depend on the effort you have put into improving during the term so far, as well as your ability to demonstrate your grasp of the various aspects of a powerful Will. I will be noting your capacity, your efficiency, your force, and your soundness. If you do surprise me... Well, hope for your own sake that it is positive—a show of extra capability under pressure—rather than disappointment."

He moved to the front of the room and walked slowly past them, watching each student critically in a way that reminded Sebastien of Fekten. "In case any of you have forgotten, this class is called *Practical* Will-based Casting. There will be no theoretical or written portion to this exam. What matters is your ability to perform in a real-life situation with real stakes. Remember, the winners in each bracket will get contribution points in addition to a grade.

"Let us begin. Six matches at a time, from the top." He waved his hand impatiently and the first twelve students scrambled to find their partners and arrange themselves under his impatient stare.

"The desks have been marked with a direction, clockwise or counter-clockwise. If the sphere moves in your direction for more than three consecutive seconds, you have won."

When the first twelve contestants were seated, the spell arrays were written, and the student aides had their pocket watches, clipboards, and pens ready, Professor Lacer nodded sharply. "Begin." He watched intently as the students obeyed.

Damien, Ana, and Sebastien stood to the side, watching. Sebastien was in the third bracket. She leaned closer to Damien, murmuring, "Do you know who S. Vanderville is?"

"Simon Vanderville," Damien murmured back, not taking his eyes off the contestants. Less than a minute in and half of the matches had already been decided, with one side being unable to keep their opponent from moving the sphere against them for three consecutive seconds.

She glanced around at the stronger students in the class. "Okay. But who is that?" she asked. "Can you point him out?"

Damien's eyebrows rose, but when he looked at her sincere expression, he sighed and rolled his eyes in amusement. "I forgot. You erase 'unimportant things,' like peoples' names, from your memory." He jerked his chin toward a familiar looking man standing across the room. "That's Simon. You've actually partnered with him several times, Sebastien."

Vanderville noticed her looking and gave her a solemn nod.

"He doesn't stand a chance against you," Ana said, giving Vanderville a sweet smile that contrasted her words.

Vanderville blushed and looked away.

Damien snorted. "Of course he doesn't. Sebastien couldn't even remember his name. He's going to crush Vanderville like an ant."

From her vague memories of practicing against him, Sebastien thought that was probably true. "Well, I'll try not to be too ruthless about it. I want to make sure Professor Lacer has enough time to judge both of us thoroughly. If I just win in the first three seconds, that wouldn't be fair to Vanderville."

Damien stared at her for a second, his eyes narrowing. "Do you think you could? Win in the first three seconds, that is?"

Sebastien ran her tongue across the back of her teeth as she contemplated the question for a few seconds. "I think so. If for no other reason than that it would probably take him off guard."

Damien nodded, rubbing his fingers together thoughtfully. He turned to Ana. "What would you say the odds on that are?"

"At least three to one," Ana replied immediately.

Damien turned back to Sebastien. "Do it. Don't go easy on him." With his fingers digging through his pockets, Damien turned away and began to weave through the crowd, murmuring something to the people he passed, occasionally pointing out Sebastien and his upcoming opponent to them.

Sebastien frowned after him, then turned to Ana expectantly. "Is he taking bets?"

Ana smiled serenely. "As children, we used to do it frequently to get extra coin for spending, until all our friends refused to wager with us anymore. He's always enjoyed that look of surprise and dismay on people's faces when he's proven right."

"Smug little shit," Sebastien muttered.

Ana elbowed her in the side, not hard enough to really hurt.

Sebastien laughed. When Damien looked her way, Sebastien mouthed "Fifty-fifty," to him.

With an expression of reluctance, he nodded and continued working the crowd.

"Wait. Should I be looking worried right now?" she said. "If I look too confident, they might not want to bet against me." Ennis had loved to gamble, often to their detriment, but he'd also been a schemer who did whatever possible to tip the odds in his favor. Sometimes that worked out, and more often it got them into even more trouble.

Ana sighed deeply and walked away to chat with another group of students. At first, Sebastien thought she'd irritated the other girl, until she heard her say, "I know Sebastien probably doesn't have a chance against Vanderville, but he's my friend, so I'm still going to bet on him. What do you think? I heard Vanderville's a third term student, on track to be a student liaison next term. Sebastien's been practicing, but...he was up studying all night. He must be exhausted. Am I going to lose my coin?"

Some of the group members immediately agreed, with some variation of amusement and excitement, that she was going to lose her bet, and briefly consoled her before going to place their own wager with Damien.

Sebastien concealed her smile, doing her best to look both exhausted and secretly apprehensive.

The first set of matches took less than five minutes, with each desk being vacated and filled again under the direction of the student liaisons as soon as a winner was declared.

Professor Lacer, leaning against his own desk and observing, never moved from his spot or dropped his concentration, though his lips moved frequently as he muttered under his breath, and his pen scribbled notes as if controlled by an invisible hand.

After a few rounds of matches in the first bracket, Sebastien realized she wasn't gaining much from watching, thereby wasting precious time, so she took out a book and moved to the edge of the room to read.

She became engrossed in her reading, and was surprised when one of the student aides approached her with irritation. "Siverling? It's your turn."

Sebastien hurriedly tucked the book back in her satchel and walked through the crowd to take a seat across from Vanderville at the desk. She drew her own preferred glyphs onto the Circle and began bringing her Will to bear.

She didn't start channeling any of the power from the three small tea candles prepared for her. She was just preparing, coiling up like a snake about to strike.

As soon as the student aide said, "Start," Sebastien unleashed all the tension she'd been gathering. She sucked at the candles, riding the edge between extinguishing them and drawing as much power from their heat as possible. Her Will bore down like a clenching fist, squeezing as much utility out of the power as she could.

The sphere spun around the wheel so quickly it turned into a blur.

Three seconds later, the student aide said, "Winner, Siverling!"

Vanderville stared at the ball as it slowly lost momentum. He looked up to Sebastien, then down to the ball.

He looked like a puppy that had just been struck by lightning and didn't understand what had happened.

Sebastien felt a little bad for him. "Better luck next time." She stood and met Professor Lacer's gaze, but his expression didn't give anything away.

Damien was jumping up and down with excitement, shaking Ana's arm. "Did you see that!?" he exclaimed.

There were quite a few looks of shock and dismay among the other students, likely those who had bet against Sebastien.

Sebastien gave Damien a small smirk as she passed, the crowd parting for her as she returned to the edge of the room and took out her book again.

Damien spent the remainder of the class period extracting coin from the people who owed him. He won his own match against a studious-looking girl, though it took him almost thirty seconds to Sebastien's three. He didn't seem particularly surprised by this outcome, but shook hands with his defeated opponent genially.

Ana took her opponent off guard by chattering, and then yanking the ball out of their magical grasp when they were distracted.

"She's devious," Damien said, grinning.

When the bell rang to signify the end of the period, the class had finished all the initial elimination rounds and a handful of the second-level matches too.

As they made their way back to the dorms, Damien counted the money and handed Sebastien her cut.

She grinned, infected by his enthusiasm. She'd just made nine silver from a little bit of showing off, which was probably pocket change to someone like Damien, but throughout her childhood would have meant several days of food, or a couple nights in an actual bed rather than sleeping in a barn or a tent set up in a field. Now, it could buy her the components for two blood-clotting potions, or a new pair of insulated leather gloves. University students were much too rich. "That little trick won't keep working over and over," she warned.

"Oh, don't be such a downer, Sebastien," Damien said. "What do you say we go down into the city tonight and get a real meal with our winnings? I cannot stand another night of cafeteria slop while watching upper term students eat lobster and pheasant. It'll be fun! And we need the energy for the upcoming tests. Come on! We can get the whole gang together."

Sebastien frowned reluctantly. Any restaurant Damien picked was sure to be expensive, and as much as she wanted a good, filling meal, she also had the weight of her debt to the Verdant Stag hanging over her, and her need to prepare for not only the mid-terms, but her upcoming job as an assistant healer.

"Come on," Damien wheedled. "You can make fun of Alec as much as you want. Doesn't that sound refreshing?"

Ana let out a snort of amusement. "Damien's right. You need to take breaks to perform at your maximum potential, Sebastien. I know a nice restaurant with great musicians, not too ostentatious. The Glasshopper has the most delightful desserts, and I really do mean *delightful*. There is even pudding that they set on fire when they serve it to you!" She reached out and tugged on Sebastien's sleeve, batting her lashes over those big blue eyes.

"I suppose," Sebastien agreed reluctantly. *'If I pretend winnings are not fungible, I can pay for it with the unexpected windfall I just made and not feel too pained.'*

There was a crowd in the dormitory hallway, blocking them from getting into their dorm room.

"Something's wrong, " Sebastien said, taking in the expressions of the students milling about.

Damien reached out to grab another student's elbow. "What happened?"

"Someone died," they said.

The words knocked the exuberance out of Damien's eyes. "Who? Was it in our dorm?"

The student responded, but Sebastien wasn't listening. Two infirmary employees were carrying a stretcher with a cloth-covered body through the doors, and the crowd pressed back and parted to give them space.

They passed right by Sebastien. Her senses took in every detail as the sounds around her seemed to blur and soften, like she was hearing them from underwater.

White cloth, contouring around the body and features just enough to make what lay below obvious.

The smell of hastily cleaned vomit and feces. Bodies released when the life left them. It was common.

No crimson, no smell of blood.

The person's hand slipped from the side of the stretcher and flopped down as the small procession passed through the crowd. It was almost voyeuristic, that peek at what lay beneath, and it felt like a perverse glimpse into something that should have been shrouded.

Without thinking, Sebastien reached out, grasping the dead boy's pale wrist between her fingers and slipping it back under the protective covering of the white cloth.

His skin was still warm.

It was only once the stretcher was out of sight that the sound of the world rushed back in.

Near the doors of their dormitory room, a girl wailed, collapsing to her knees as two of her friends held her. Tears streamed down all three of their faces.

That, too, seemed like something private that Sebastien wasn't meant to see. She turned her head away as a lingering pair of healers from the infirmary tipped a potion against the girl's lips, urging her to swallow.

Her wails of anguish cut off as the potion sedated her, and they carried her off too, leaving her two crying, but less hysterical, friends behind.

A warm hand slipped over the top of Sebastien's, and she looked down to see that at some point, she'd grabbed Damien's wrist and was squeezing it in a bruising grip. She let him go immediately, looking away from his expression of sympathy.

She turned back, not quite sure where she was planning to go, just wanting to get away from the dorms, the too-close crowd and the feeling of suffocation.

Tanya was standing right beside her, arms crossed over her chest, an inscrutable expression on her face.

Sebastien met her eyes for a second.

Tanya sighed. "Will-strain," she said. "He won't be the last."

The words reverberated in Sebastien's mind with a rumble of premonition.

36

MID-TERMS & TOURNAMENT

SEBASTIEN
Month 1, Day 11, Monday 4:00 p.m.

THE HEALERS PASSED around calming potions to all the students, leaving a bottle inside the cubicle of everyone who wasn't there to take them directly.

Sebastien wasn't stubborn about it. She took a dose—a single swallow—right away, then left the building for a long walk through the Menagerie, trying not to think past the magical haze of well-being the potion imparted.

She returned a few hours later, after the sun had set and the cold was bitter enough that she noticed it through the waning power of the potion.

Back in the dorms, she learned from gossip she couldn't help but overhear, that the dead boy had been practicing magic with his friends, who were all cramming in what study they could before the tests. They had returned to the dorms together, and he'd complained of dizziness and lay down to take a nap.

His friend, the girl who'd been sedated and taken to the infirmary, had tried to wake him about half an hour later, when the smell of vomit and shit suddenly became noticeable.

It was too late. He was already dead.

The healers declared it an aneurism caused by Will-strain.

That evening, before lights-out but after all the students had returned to the dorm, Tanya and Newton stood at the front of the room and gave another lecture about safety and ensuring the health of their minds and magic. "Go to sleep early tonight," Tanya said, "and take a calming potion if you need one.

Please be careful not to cast any strenuous magic under the effects of a calming potion though, as it can impair your control. My advice is not to worry about the mid-terms or any other schoolwork. Your sanity and your life are more important than your homework, and this was a blow to all of us."

"It will take time to recover," Newton said in a rough voice. "We're here for you if you need help, as are any of the healers, and your professors, too."

Sebastien cast her dreamless sleep spell with as much power as she could pour into it, then used the esoteric humming spell that Newton had taught her to relax her body, and took another swallow of calming potion before sticking waxed cotton in her ears to block out the sounds of the other students. Finally, as prepared as she could be, she went to sleep.

Tuesday was subdued, and they only had morning classes.

Damien seemed shocked by the death and kept wanting to talk about it, going in circles about how horrible and sad it was without really saying anything new.

Sebastien went through that conversation with him a couple of times, then foisted him off on Ana and his other friends. It wasn't the first time she'd seen death, of course, but she kept remembering the feel of the dead boy's skin under her fingers, still warm. 'One in fifteen of us will die or go insane before we become Masters,' she reminded herself. 'Tanya was right. He won't be the last. But I won't be one of them.'

She forced herself to focus during her classes, and after on the basic books about emergency healing she'd borrowed from the library.

The latter at least gave her some comfort.

On Wednesday, normal classes were cancelled in favor of two extra-long exam periods, one before lunch, and one after lunch.

They started the day with Professor Gnorrish's mid-term examination for Natural Science. The exam was a more elaborate version of his normal tests, with a lot of extra questions and some interactive content with pictures, like Sebastien remembered from the entrance exam. She could answer questions about everything they had covered in class, but when it came to higher-level extrapolations based on a deeper understanding of those same concepts, she found herself stymied at least half the time.

At least this test wasn't never-ending like the written entrance examination. She was able to get through the whole thing with enough time to go back to some of the questions she'd been unsure about and think on them a little harder.

After that came Professor Ilma's exam for History of Magic. That one only had twenty questions, but they all needed to be answered in short-essay format. Sebastien knew Professor Ilma well enough by now not to bother regurgitating anything from a book. Instead, she made her own arguments and even openly admitted on a couple of questions that she had no idea about the answer, yet still gave all the evidence that might support *some kind* of conclusion.

She was still scribbling frantically when the bell rang to signal the end of the test period, groaning in dismay as she tried to finish her current thought in still-legible handwriting before someone stopped her.

After almost five hours of test-taking, she was exhausted, but that evening she asked around in the dorms and managed to find some second term students who also had Professor Pecanty in order to ask them about his tests. She and he thought nothing alike, and she was worried that his tests would be as subjective as the literary analyses they did in class.

"Oh, yeah," one second term student said. "Pecanty's the worst. Each test is going to have a randomly assigned essay question at the end. He told me my analysis was 'shallow and simplistic.'"

Another student snorted from the corner. "That's because you're writing to the topic, not the teacher. I have a system. Gets me a perfect score every time."

"You're such a suck-up," the first student said.

His friend shrugged. "Well, we have this room because of the contribution points he gave me. Don't complain too much while you're benefitting from my largesse."

Sebastien turned to the man with eagle-eyed interest. "What's your system?"

"Easy," he said, not even looking up from the magazine she recognized as the latest Aberford Thorndyke story. "I make as many connections as possible, always. If there's a short answer or essay question, I try to make at least two allusions to another story or poem we've talked about in class. Bonus points if it's a play or opera I saw outside of the University, or a story one of my many fake aunts, uncles, or grandparents told me when I was little, accompanied by some poignant memory. In addition to that, I try to use at least five vivid, poetic 'feeling' or 'sensory' words. He really loves it when I mention a smell or a taste. For example, a strong, salty sausage might remind me of my mother's bloody hands in the winter, pale with cold, and the iron and shit I smelled as the pig she'd slaughtered bled out into a steel bucket, its squeal of terror still ringing in my ears." His tone had taken on an imitation of Pecanty's rhythm as he spoke the last bit. He waved his hand leadingly. "Like that."

Sebastien nodded with wonder. "Can you give me some more examples? Just so I can get the feel of it?"

The boy laughed. "Dream on, firstie. I'm busy reading, so go bother someone else. Unless you're willing to trade contribution points for it? I've been wanting to upgrade my meal plan..." He looked up, eyebrows raised expectantly.

She pressed her lips together and shook her head. "Thank you for your help."

He looked back down, losing interest in her immediately.

Sebastien asked for advice from a couple other students who had experience with Pecanty, but got nothing as good as that first offering.

The Sympathetic Science exam was first on Thursday, and she was careful to make even more connections than reasonable, backing them up with sensory allusions that otherwise had no connection, when necessary. She even tried to make her handwriting as beautiful as possible, because that seemed like the kind of thing that Pecanty might subconsciously favor. When she finished the test, she went back over every written answer, making sure that, where possible, she'd made at least two allusions and used at least five evocative emotional or sensory words.

'If this doesn't work, there's really nothing I can do. Except something like...blackmail?' Sebastien shook her head at that fanciful thought and hurried quickly to lunch. She wanted to eat as soon as possible so that her stomach would be settled before the Defensive Magic exam.

Despite her efforts, she arrived on the white flats slightly queasy, though she thought that was more due to misgivings about the grueling physical torture she was about to experience than the food sitting uncomfortably in her stomach.

Using whatever magic allowed him to rearrange the stone of the white flats, Fekten had set up an almost comically difficult obstacle course. The students were to complete it as quickly as possible, with their grade depending on their speed for each section, and then take the written exam.

Looking at one section of the course where they were meant to leap across a scattered path of columns raised a meter above the ground, Sebastien swallowed heavily. Another section required them to climb up a rope to cross a tall wall, then slide down the other side into a tunnel that was somehow filled with water. 'I'll be surprised if no one gets seriously injured.'

As if that thought were some sort of prophecy, Fekten introduced the gathered students to the healers he'd called in to supervise his mid-term.

Sebastien took a deep breath and massaged her neck, trying to let go of her anxiety. She would have cast Newton's humming spell, but there wasn't enough time for it to really settle into her body before the test started. Instead, she cast the pain-muffling spell she often used for Fekten's class. All it really did was help her to *ignore* the discomfort, not lessen it, but that was enough to let her push through.

The obstacle course began with a one mile run, and concluded with a sprint through a corridor lined with light-shooting mannequins, just like those they'd been practicing their footwork against.

Sebastien finished the course with a time slightly better than the middle of the pack, but wasn't provided the opportunity to recuperate. She followed the students who had finished before her as they ran to the desks set up in the biggest room of the sim building. Throwing herself into a desk with a blank tests already waiting for her, she pulled out her pen and released the pain-muffling spell.

Her handwriting was even worse than normal, with the occasional ink-smudge from sweat, but she felt confident in her answers on all the various dangers and tactics that Fekten had been lecturing about every class period. It was actually even *easier* to remember it all with her lungs aching for air and her muscles burning with fatigue. Probably because that was the state in which she'd learned it to begin with.

She stumbled away from the white flats to the dorm showers, and then took a nap in an attempt to recover from her listlessness. *'I cannot wait until something else can do some of my sleeping for me.'*

She was still sore on Friday morning, but didn't have much trouble with Burberry's test in Modern Magics. The professor had brought in a few people to help get through all the students in the time they had, some of them student aides, and some that seemed to have been hired specifically for the task.

Each student was required to display competence with three randomly chosen variations on the spells they had been practicing that term, along with a written test, which, like Gnorrish's, had interactive content.

Sebastien didn't push too hard on any of the spells. Her control was developed enough that she didn't need to show off her power, too. She wanted her Will to stay fresh for the tournament.

Sebastien arrived at the Practical Casting classroom about ten minutes early, but there were already students gathered, and a couple of them were competing against each other in their tournament brackets while Professor Lacer supervised.

A girl approached Sebastien and said, "I'm your next opponent. Do you want to get a head start on the matches? Professor Lacer said we could."

"Sure." Starting ten minutes earlier could mean ten more minutes of recovery between it and the subsequent match.

They set up, waited for Professor Lacer's assistant proctor to note their names, and then began to cast.

Sebastien's opponent was familiar with her trick from the first match and was able to withstand the initial powerful push. "Did you really think the same trick would work twice in a row?" the girl asked.

Sebastien shrugged. "It's not like I lose anything in the attempt. Besides, if I did not push hard, what if *you* took *me* by surprise instead?"

They settled into the struggle. The girl was strong, but after a few minutes it became apparent that she lacked practice. Her Will was neither as clear, sound, nor as forceful as Sebastien's.

As time went on, the girl's candles began to flicker and flutter.

Sebastien sensed weakness and pushed even harder.

Her opponent squeezed her fists and glared at the ball that kept inching against her in little bursts, never quite for three seconds at a time, but growing ever-closer. Her face began to turn red from the effort, but she eventually pulled too hard and one of her candles was quenched. The cold wick emitted a small trail of smoke.

That was it. With three candles against two, Sebastien won immediately.

Damien and Ana arrived just as Sebastien was getting up from the table.

"No!" Damien cried dramatically. "I missed it? Sebastien, you should have stalled! I didn't even get a chance to make any bets."

Ana elbowed him in the side. "Damien. No one was going to bet against Sebastien again after what happened last time."

Damien held his chin in his hand, frowning thoughtfully as he looked Sebastien up and down. "Not necessarily. He just needs to be up against an opponent no one thinks he can beat..."

"And then what if he loses? Why don't you just enjoy the winnings you already have and be content?"

"Sebastien definitely won't lose," Damien said.

"How can you know that? He's in the most difficult bracket, against students from upper terms..."

They continued to dispute the issue, but Sebastien tuned them out.

The other matches finished, too, and when the bell rang, Professor Lacer announced, "We finish the tournament today! Since this is the last test period of the week, the matches can continue on even after the period technically ends. With the number of students still remaining, this seems likely. Anything after the test period ends is entirely optional, and will be for contribution points, not your grade."

Despite how fatigued most of the students probably were at the end of the mid-terms, most seemed enthused to see this contest through to the end. Of course, at least half of them had nothing to do except spectate today, having already lost their own matches on Monday, which probably contributed to their high spirits.

This time, Sebastien actually watched the matches with Damien and Ana. They murmured observations to each other, and she took note of those in her bracket who she might have trouble with.

Sebastien's second match was also against a woman. Her opponent was good. Neither of them had a marked advantage with only three candles to draw on, and they struggled back and forth, slamming at each other with bursts of unsustainable power that they had to release lest they quench their flames.

Sebastien bore down with her Will, tuning out everything else but the flames, the movement of the sphere, and her pure denial that the other woman could best her. Five minutes passed, then ten, then fifteen.

If neither of them won soon, they would both be disqualified at the twenty-minute mark.

Eventually, though, Sebastien began to gain the edge. The longer and harder she pushed, the more eagerly the magic responded to her. The air of the Sacrifice Circle around her candles grew chilled, but their flames never sputtered. Each pulse of extra power she funneled into the spell flowed only more smoothly.

In contrast, Sebastien's opponent couldn't maintain the same level of focus and control she'd started the match with. She didn't degrade drastically, by any means, but there was no space for mistakes.

Sebastien moved the ball, not quickly, but inexorably, and her opponent couldn't stop it in time.

"Winner, S. Siverling," the student aide muttered, going to write her name on the blackboard next to her upcoming opponent.

Sebastien rolled her neck, which was a little stiff from staring down at the table for so long. She had Damien point out her next opponent, a man who was sitting away from the rest of the crowd with his eyes closed, a slight grimace on his face.

Sebastien felt a little apprehensive about competing with someone so calm, but reassured herself that she could win. *'I'll freeze the table if I have to. Everything within the Circle belongs to me, and it might be enough for one surprise shove of power that doesn't rely on the candles.'*

However, when the two of them were called up to compete, the man pushed reluctantly through the crowd, met her gaze, and shook his head. "I don't think I can. I've got a headache, and I think I might be approaching Will-strain."

Professor Lacer waved the man away with a flick of the wrist. "Understood. Be sure to go to the infirmary if you need to," he said, the pen on his desk still scribbling away by itself. He looked at Sebastien, then back to the man, adding, "I commend your good sense."

"Forfeit, win goes to Mr. Siverling," an aide said.

A couple of students groaned.

Sebastien looked around for the perpetrators, but the boys she suspected refused to meet her gaze. *'Are they rooting against me?'*

As if to make up for this, a group of young women standing to the side gave her excited smiles and gestures of encouragement. "You can do it, Sebastien!"

The next matches took more time, as the more powerful people were pitted against each other. Damien lost his third match, but put up a strong resistance, and Professor Lacer even gave him a small nod of acknowledgement when it was over.

Sebastien suppressed a spike of jealousy.

With a dogged determination that Sebastien found surprising, Ana also won her match, but then excused herself from the tournament to avoid Will-strain.

By Sebastien's fourth match of the day, there were only a handful of contestants left in her bracket. She sat across from a young man who was growing a thick winter beard, which was impressive for a student their age.

"Nunchkin," he introduced himself, giving her a small bow.

"Siverling," she said, crossing her arms.

In his Sacrifice Circle, Nunchkin wrote the glyph for *"wax"* instead of *"fire,"* or even the less-common *"heat."*

Sebastien had a premonition of doom as soon as she saw that, but it was too late to respond to it even if she could think of some way to do so, because the student aide was already counting them down. The match began to a chorus of cheers from their classmates.

Sebastien slammed on the sphere immediately, and it moved under her Will, but not for long.

The sphere sat still for a long while, trembling minutely under the opposing forces. Then, slowly, it began to shift in Nunchkin's direction, against her.

Sebastien stopped it, but she could do no more than that. It sat trembling again, and then slowly rolled against her.

'No.'

The sphere stopped again, but Nunchkin just kept on pouring more and more power into the spell.

Her eyes flicked up to see that the wax of one of Nunchkin's candles was visibly disappearing, as if a few large, invisible ants were nibbling at it.

Turning matter directly into movement was an incredibly advanced conversion. Using matter as a power source rather than a transmutable component was possible, but generally inefficient and gruelingly difficult. It was why most sorcerers used flames, beast cores, or even something like the power of the flowing water in a river to provide the energy for their spells.

Running out of the specified form of energy and having the spell resort to using matter instead was one of the most common ways to lose control of your magic and get Will-strain. Put plainly, it was beyond her.

The little spots of missing wax grew.

Sebastien's eyes narrowed. As the spots grew larger, she could see their shiny, liquid edges, and faint shimmers in the air.

'But maybe he's not using the wax directly. Could he be using his Will to create a wick-like construct, and burning up the wax? If he's using the light as well as the heat, that might be why I can't see any visible flames.'

Her epiphany had cost her. In just this moment of distraction, Nunchkin had pushed the ball against her for almost a full revolution of the glass wheel and was about to win.

In a sudden effort, Sebastien used the idea she'd come up with earlier and sucked all the heat from the table beneath her Sacrifice Circle. The frosted-over section of the slate table groaned from the sudden temperature change. It was enough to match Nunchkin and even push back for a moment, but not to keep her going for the full three seconds as he increased his own spell's power to oppose her.

Still, it had bought her a little time to think.

Wax did not need a wick to burn, technically. The wick was useful because it drew melted wax up into the heat of the flame and burnt it there. Most of what the flame was devouring was actually the wax, not the wick at all. The problem with trying to burn wax without the wick was that the substance would disperse the heat throughout its volume, making it difficult to maintain the combustion point. The wick kept a small amount of liquid wax at the right spot, without enough volume to disperse the heat before it caught fire and was converted into more heat, light, and various gasses.

With the incredibly rudimentary spell array that Professor Lacer insisted on, what she did with the magic could be any number of things that used *"heat"* for the purpose of creating *"movement."*

A candle flame created around eighty thaums, give or take. Three candles left her stymied at a little under two hundred fifty thaums, total. But there was much more energy than that within the entire candle.

Sebastien drew on the heat in the melted wax of one of her own candles, experimentally, pulling at the part around the base of the flame, drawing it up into the wick.

It worked.

The flame flared higher, the inefficiency of the burn clear in the dark tendril of smoke that began to curl up from the flame's orange tip. Suddenly, she had more energy to work with, maybe an extra dozen thaums.

'I have all the power I need. It is only a matter of Will. Always, always, only a matter of Will.'

Nunchkin actually revealed a small smile, though he didn't look at her, his eyes trained on the sphere with unwavering focus.

Splitting her concentration on creating movement in the wax—as little as it was—with controlling the iron sphere made things more difficult. But it was more than worth it for the extra power.

She repeated her trick with the other two candles, sending their flames flaring angrily higher.

She had the upper hand again, for a moment.

But it was only a moment.

With the inexorability of the setting sun, Nunchkin kept pouring on more and more power.

Sebastien would never have been able to keep fighting back if she hadn't spent so many hours practicing the sphere-spinning spell.

Nunchkin's spell array was glowing with inefficiency despite his prowess.

Hers didn't, not even the barest flicker.

The candle flames flared higher and higher until they were like small torches, ready to burn out before their time. She *knew* there was enough heat in the candle wax...

But her Will could only channel so much.

The sphere began to move against her, once more.

She slammed her Will against it like she might throw her body against a barred door, but Nunchkin was unfazed, and she felt the taut fist of her Will start to tremble with strain. '*I have to let go,*' she realized. '*I've lost.*'

She did so with careful control, watching the sphere spin the wrong direction, faster and faster until it became a blur.

She almost didn't hear it when the match was called in Nunchkin's favor.

As she stood up from the desk, Damien slammed into her, grabbing her arm and screaming in her ear to be heard past the cheers filling the room. "Planes-damned, I'll kick an earth-aspected weta if that wasn't one of the most impressive things I've ever seen!"

Damien pulled her through the crowd, high-fiving people as they passed, crowing unintelligibly amid the noise as if he himself had just won the entire tournament.

Luckily, Nunchkin drew most of the attention away from them as they got to the edge of the crowd.

Rubbing her forehead, Sebastien moved to an empty desk a distance away from the front of the classroom and slumped down into the chair.

Even Ana was grinning widely. "Good job, Sebastien. That was indeed very impressive. I'm sure Professor Lacer was pleased."

Damien nodded, still vibrating with excitement. "What you did with the candles? Oh, I think I gasped out loud when I saw it! I never even thought of doing something like that, but the rules definitely don't say you can't, and Professor Lacer must not have a problem with it, or he would have said something."

Sebastien sighed, letting her shoulders slump. "I don't know what you think was so impressive about that display. I *lost.*"

Damien's excitement dimmed, and he shared a look with Ana.

"You put up a remarkable fight," Ana said. "You proved that your Will isn't only powerful, but sound, forceful, and clear."

"You're only a first term student, Sebastien," Damien said. His voice was gentle, as if explaining something worryingly simple to her, and he doubted her ability to grasp it. "Nunchkin is a fourth-term. And I heard someone saying he's taken this class *twice* before."

Sebastien's eyes widened.

"So you see, no matter how much of a prodigy you are, you can't expect to beat that kind of experience, and—" Damien cut off as Sebastien let her forehead thunk onto the table.

"Sebastien?" he asked.

She raised her head, unable to keep the disappointment from her face. "You're telling me I lost to someone who *failed* this class the first two times?"

Ana raised her eyebrows and lifted a hand to her mouth to disguise sudden amusement. "I think you may be focusing on the wrong part of that statement, Sebastien."

Damien blinked a few times, then shook his head as if to clear his thoughts. "Umm. Yes. What Ana said. Let me explain this—"

Sebastien waved away their counterproductive attempts to console her. "It's okay. I've got time. I'll catch up to him. I definitely won't fail this class and have to retake it!" she announced, clenching her fists.

"Yes, well...good," Damien said, seeming a little confused.

They returned to watch the last couple of matches between semifinalists, and Sebastien kept an eye out for other tricks she could appropriate.

Nunchkin and a girl with a fierce glare were the two finalists.

Nunchkin's opponent used the same technique as Sebastien to increase the amount of power she had to draw on, and came closer than Sebastien had to taking Nunchkin out in the beginning of the match, but still failed to beat the pressure of his slow, relentless ramp-up.

Nunchkin was declared the winner of the largest bracket, as well as the overall tournament, and awarded the biggest contribution point prize. He smiled humbly and gave a bow to Professor Lacer.

Sebastien wanted to scowl, but realized that would be childish, and so tried to keep her expression bland, if not exactly pleasant.

"Well done!" Professor Lacer said in a loud voice that cut through the chatter. "Well, to *most* of you. It is time for the prizes. As promised, the winner of each lesser bracket will receive thirty contribution points. However, those of you who put up a good fight or displayed some piece of exceptional control or ingenuity will also be rewarded for your efforts."

The students cheered, laughing and yelling and generally making a ruckus as Professor Lacer called students out from the crowd and handed them a ticket noting their points, murmuring a few words of praise to each.

To her surprise, though she hadn't even gotten to the top three of her bracket, Professor Lacer called her name.

She pushed through the muttering crowd—someone said something about her being at Apprentice-level capacity already, but she wasn't sure who—and took the ticket.

Five contribution points.

Lacer didn't smile, but it was almost as good when he said, "Impressive problem-solving and control under pressure."

Struggling to hold her own expression to merely professional satisfaction rather than profound relief—and even a little bit of glee—she gave him a shallow bow. "Thank you."

He nodded and called the next name.

Sebastien tucked the ticket into her pocket, patting it in satisfaction as she returned to Damien and Ana. "Well. I suppose I didn't do *too* badly."

Damien rolled his eyes hard enough they might have gotten stuck. "Right."

"So. Restaurant? Live music? Teasing Alec?" Ana asked, flashing Sebastien a winning grin.

Sebastien was in too good a mood to refuse.

Besides, her brain and Will both needed a break.

She needed to be fully rested for the attack on the Morrows, after all.

37

THE GLASSHOPPER

Sebastien
Month 1, Day 15, Friday 6:00 p.m.

Ana's choice of restaurant was indeed amazing.

Everything about the Glasshopper was subtly expensive, from the fine uniforms of the waiters, to the spells woven into the floor around the tables to keep conversations from being overheard. Nothing gaudy like gold filigree or eye-catching enchantments, just dark woods and marble.

There was a small string and brass band on the stage, accompanying a woman with rounded, bright-colored feathers sprouting from the sides of her face and scalp where her ears and hair would have been, on a human. She swayed on stage, crooning in a soft, chocolatey voice that somehow managed to reach the whole building equally. Her feather-lashed eyes were closed, and her voice shivered over Sebastien's skin like a sensual, ephemeral touch.

"Is that a siren?" Sebastien whispered in awe. "They're so rare, I've only ever heard of them, never seen one."

Ana sighed in appreciation. "They always have the best music. This is the best restaurant outside of the Lilies."

Alec Gervin's mouth had dropped open, and there might have been a little bit of drool at the corner of his lips. The waiter had to prompt him several times before he jerked back to awareness and followed them to their table.

Sebastien was in a good enough mood that she didn't even take the opportunity to cut Gervin down to size.

Waverly Ascott was without a book for the first time Sebastien had seen her. "Bring the dessert sampler," she told the waiter as soon as they'd been seated. "Enough for everyone." She pulled her dark hair back from her face, tying it in a high ponytail as if preparing for battle.

Brinn Setterlund sat next to her, examining the miniature, living tree in the center of their table with interest. He reached forward to stroke a branch, and Sebastien wasn't sure if it was her imagination, but it seemed to shift, caressing his hand in return.

"No appetizers or entrees?" the waiter asked, entering Ascott's order on a small journal-sized artifact that would send the information directly to the kitchen.

"If we're not full after the dessert platter," Ascott said.

"Good idea," Ana agreed.

"Bring some champagne too," Rhett Moncrieffe said, lounging half sideways on his own chair, the smile on his face belying the boredom in his tone. "We just finished our University mid-terms. We're celebrating."

"Congratulations, young masters," the waiter said.

When the desserts arrived, they drew a gasp from Sebastien.

Ana grinned at her. "I know. Exquisite."

Each confection was a tiny sculpture. There were miniature pixies made of toffee and flakes of phyllo dough so thin they were translucent, a dragon made of a dozen different types of chocolate, and sprites with shimmering wings of all different colors that melted at the first touch of a tongue.

The pièce de résistance were the grasshoppers in the center. They were made of crystallized nectar that glittered like crystal, bright and transparent, and they moved as if they were alive.

Ascott snatched one out of the air as it tried to jump off the table and twisted off its head. She popped it into her mouth and closed her eyes in bliss as the spell-animated confection twitched and stilled in her hand.

"Glasshoppers," Sebastien murmured, suddenly understanding where the restaurant got its name.

Alec Gervin's mouth had fallen open in dismay. "Did that... Can it feel pain? I don't want to eat something that's still alive. Where are all its organs?"

Damien rolled his eyes. "It's animated, not alive, Alec. No different than a dueling board piece. An edible toy."

Sebastien looked at the other confections, which didn't seem to be animated. "Are there other magical dishes on the menu?"

"A few other animated desserts," Ana said, ripping open the chocolate dragon's stomach to reveal miniature sweetmeat entrails. "There are also some dishes with magical ingredients, like the golden-apple pie or ice lion carpaccio. But you have to try the creme brûlée. They set it on fire!"

That was a little disappointing. "They could do so much more!" Sebastien said, ideas immediately popping to her mind. "It wouldn't be so impossible, with a combination of alchemy and artificery. The dishes could impart flashy little effects, like letting the customers blow bubbles out of their mouths, or create temporary glamours to give them rabbit ears, or jinxing them to talk backward for the next few minutes."

Ana lifted one shoulder in a half-shrug. "Not a bad idea. The costs would be rather outrageous, but that only makes it more exclusive and desirable. Perhaps someone in the Rouse Family would be interested, even to sub-contract. It might fall under their 'entertainment' domain."

Sebastien couldn't help but think of what Oliver might say about the way the current system stifled industry and potential growth, but was distracted soon enough by the arrival of their champagne. She'd tried the drink before, when Ennis was schmoozing someone wealthy, but never anything like the offering from the Glasshopper. The bubbles burst in her nose and *tickled* until she, and all the others at her table, were laughing from the sensation. She was careful not to drink too much, though, ever-conscious that she was never truly safe.

They ate and drank and chatted about nothing in particular, and Sebastien found herself thinking that, while they were rich, entitled, and sometimes snobbish, Damien's friends weren't entirely horrible. Brinn Setterlund, with his quiet stillness and slow smile, was probably her favorite.

When the siren on stage ended her set and a new musical group arrived to take her place, Moncrieffe went over to flirt with her.

Sebastien did a double-take as the woman handed him a cloth napkin, and Moncrieffe swaggered back to their table a little unsteadily.

"That was a *siren*. Did she just give you her contact information?" Sebastien asked incredulously.

Moncrieffe smirked at her, patting the pocket with the napkin proudly. "Her address. I'm invited for a 'private show.'" He wiggled his eyebrows dramatically.

The others groaned good-naturedly. "Please, spare us the details," Ascott said acerbically, tossing a cream-covered berry at him.

Moncrieffe caught it with his mouth. Even *he* looked surprised by this act of dexterity, considering his current state of inebriation, which sent them all into a round of laughter.

After a while, with their bellies full and the champagne no longer bubbling, the mood grew somber.

"I heard another student in our term ended up in the infirmary for severe Will-strain," Brinn said in a soft voice, playing with Ascott's small fingers. "She was in one of the other groups. Her mind is gone, and the healers are not optimistic about her chances of recovery."

"I heard about that," Gervin said, his tongue a little clumsy from the alcohol. "She can still feed herself and use the chamber pot when prompted, though. She's stuck in her hallucinations and doesn't respond to human stimulus."

"How do you know this?" Damien wondered aloud.

"I asked," Gervin said simply.

"There have been a dozen or so already this term, if you combine deaths and the permanent, debilitating injuries," Moncrieffe said, his head in Damien's lap as he tried to coax Damien into scratching his scalp for him. "You don't hear about all of them. Not the kind of thing the University wants to advertise, you know. I imagine you would become rather numb to it all after a while, anyway. *I* know this because there are some lovely young ladies working in the infirmary."

Brinn hummed. "Do you think they push us too hard?"

"Yes," Alec said immediately.

"It seems like if they were truly worried about our safety," Brinn continued, "they would not increase the pressure on new students with the ten percent mandatory failure rate. It's dangerous to everyone, not just those at the bottom of the list."

Ana was using a knife and some sticky dessert leftovers to turn her napkin into a tiny dress for the only remaining sculpted pixie. "Magic is dangerous, but there are wards *everywhere*. Both small and large. They do a lot to mitigate the danger that students might cause themselves and others."

'Why didn't those wards stop the explosion in Eagle Tower?' Sebastien wondered. 'Did Tanya deliberately damage them first? And if so, would the evidence of that have been destroyed by the alchemical explosion? How likely is it that Tanya would be found out?' Sebastien was entirely unsure, partially because she didn't know enough about the power of the people who might be willing to cover up for Tanya. No one had questioned either Sebastien or Damien about that day.

Rhett, still resting on Damien's lap with his eyes closed, said, "There's no reason to be so desperate over it. Students who fail can just retake that term. It would be even more unsafe if the University let them continue when they're not fit to do so."

Sebastien almost scoffed. 'Not everyone can afford to retake a term. Many of the students who are most likely to be at the bottom ten percent are commoners who must get their Apprentice certification and a good job right away, or their families will be ruined. Even only taking the minimum four classes for all three terms, the absolute minimum it could cost is nine hundred gold, and that doesn't take into account a Conduit, or the books and tutoring it takes to pass the test in the first place, or anything else.'

Damien, to her surprise, shook his head. "If that policy was really to keep the incompetent students from having a chance to do too much damage, then why are there *more* deaths in the upper terms?"

"People get cocky," Moncrieffe replied immediately. "They think they're experts and they get a little too confident. It would be worse if the upper terms were also filled with people without a strong foundation in sorcery."

Brinn sighed. "Maybe. It is sad, though."

Ascott squeezed his fingers, and he smiled at her.

"Well, what's the alternative?" Moncrieffe asked with a complacent shrug. "*Not* learn magic?"

"That's excessive, of course," Ana said.

"Not accept those who are statistically more likely to hurt themselves with it, then?" he asked.

"Poor, less-educated people, you mean," Sebastien said.

"Exactly. Everyone knows the risks, and they accept them. The University is doing what they can to mitigate the danger."

Sebastien wasn't sure that was true, but she wasn't going to argue with Moncrieffe, who was even more stubborn and self-assured than the rest of Damien's friends.

"It is true that accidents as well as deaths have gone down significantly in modern times," Damien conceded. "Some people, like my father, actually want to go back to the old, harsher ways. He thinks this 'softness' is stunting the potential growth of our nation."

"Having more of our future thaumaturges *dying* would stunt the growth of Lenore," Ana snapped back, glaring at the doll-sized dress she was wrapping around the dessert pixie.

"Of course it would," Damien said with a helpless shrug. "But good luck using logic to win an argument with my father, or people like him."

"The man is a sadist," Ana snapped, a little too loudly. She looked around, realizing her error, then to Damien, who didn't respond. She pressed her lips together as if to keep any more poorly considered words from slipping past them.

"Enough of this depressing talk," Moncrieffe said, sitting up from Damien's lap. "What we need are more drinks." He raised an arm to wave down the ever-attentive waiter.

Damien looked to Sebastien searchingly, but she kept from showing either sympathy or any particular interest in Damien's home life. She knew *she* hated it when people pried, as if her life were a piece of juicy gossip meant to entertain them. She wanted pity even less. "You were in the top three hundred of the entrance examinations, right?" She didn't really need to ask. She knew, because she'd heard him bragging about it enough times. "Do you think you managed to maintain that rank this time around?"

Gervin groaned and turned to the approaching waiter. "Whiskey!" he ordered. "And no talking about grades. I don't wish to think about that. If my scores weren't good enough... Well. Lord Westbay and my father are friends for a reason." He turned, a little awkwardly, toward Sebastien. "That tutor you recommended, Newton Moore, he *is* rather good."

She waited for Gervin to continue, but apparently that was all he meant to say. "He is," she agreed.

When the waiter brought the alcohol, Sebastien even let herself be coerced into having a single shot of Whiskerton's Whiskey of Well-being, which—as advertised—made her feel like she was being held on her grandfather's lap, in front of the fire, about to fall asleep with the deep knowledge that he would never let anything bad happen to her.

Of course, something bad did happen to her. Had happened to her.

Now it was up to her to protect herself.

She refused to have any more of the whiskey, even as the others did, slipping away instead to check on Tanya's location, which was just where it should have been.

Alec insisted loudly on paying the bill for all of them, and Sebastien didn't protest too hard when she saw the prices. Her portion alone would have been about three gold. She could have eaten simple meals for weeks on that price in a smaller village.

When they left, most of the others were drunk. "Do not drink and cast," she reminded them. "Alcohol and magic do not mix."

Brinn's face was flushed, his eyes glassy, and he tried to climb a tree on the side of the street as they were walking back to the University, forcing them to drag him down and away.

Ascott muttered something in a language Sebastien didn't understand, then took out a sobering potion and forced a partial dose down Brinn's throat. "It will make you have to pee," she warned.

"I'll drain my dragon," Brinn slurred reassuringly. "Don't worry, I know how to do it. Do it all the time. 'S easy." Which all the others thought was the most hilarious thing they'd ever heard, for some reason.

Feeling like a mother with small children, or the shepherd of a flock of cats, Sebastien herded them back to the University.

They took the transport tubes that crawled up the white cliffs, and the others spilled out at the top, laughing and loopy.

Alec had thrown up inside one. "Oops. Umm. Call one of the servants, I seem to have made a mess." He stumbled out, barely avoiding falling in the pool of his own vomit.

Sebastien glared at him hard enough that if she were a free-caster, she might have set him on fire. "Give him some of that sobering potion, Ascott," she ordered. She stared at the disgusting puddle, wondering if she knew a spell to handle the situation, because she definitely wasn't going to touch that with her hands. She knew a spell to draw water down towards a Circle marked on the ground, but it was meant to quickly dry oneself off after getting wet, not to mop a chunky liquid sideways along the floor.

In the end, she took out a piece of paper from her satchel and wrote a note apologizing and asking the workers who would find it—and the vomit— "Please bill Alec Gervin for cleaning services and any inconvenience."

Grumbling the whole while, Sebastien managed to get everyone back to the dorms and, relatively quietly, into bed. She didn't bother trying to get them to drink water or any more potions. *'Let their hangovers punish them on my behalf,'* she thought vindictively.

Luckily, at least half of her other dorm-mates were still awake, exuberant with their freedom from the mid-terms, so her group didn't cause too much trouble.

On Saturday morning, Moncrieffe was the only one besides Sebastien who wasn't sick and exhausted, which was astounding considering that he'd imbibed the most out of all of them.

Leaving the others with a smug smile, Sebastien got an update on Tanya from Newton, made sure she had the bone disk to track the other girl if she slipped away again, and ordered a hangover-relief draught from the infirmary for Damien, so he could properly do his job keeping watch while Sebastien was gone.

She spent the whole day brewing Humphries' adapting solution. It was a slow process, requiring her to distill her water to purify it, before using that distilled water to brew. The instructions assumed the brewer would be making at least seven liters at a time, but not only was Siobhan too weak for that, her cauldron wasn't big enough, and she would have had to borrow a stock pot from the kitchen to brew in, which wasn't ideal.

Instead, she brewed in two-liter batches. About one liter was a single dose when using it as a blood replacement for an adult human. Severe blood loss might require more. This alchemical solution was even more magically intensive than the regeneration-boosting potions, though, to be fair, the dose size was also much bigger.

She'd waited until close to the attack to make it, both because she needed her Will as strong as possible, and because its shelf life was short. This way it might still find use even if they didn't need it immediately.

She finished off the day with a single batch of the regeneration-boosting potions and returned to the University. Thankfully, Tanya had done nothing suspicious while Sebastien was gone.

On Sunday, she did no brewing. She spent most of the day in the library reviewing her study on emergency healing. That evening, knowing she wouldn't be able to slip away to follow if Tanya escaped the others, Sebastien considered giving the bone disk to Damien.

Instead, she sat down with him in a quiet section of the library and said,

"I've heard rumblings of violence in the city tonight. Some skirmish between criminals. If Tanya leaves, just let me handle it. It might not be safe for you."

Damien wasn't satisfied by this at all. "What? No, I can handle myself, Sebastien. I've had plenty dueling training. I do better than *you* in Fekten's class."

"When you can cast your own broad-spectrum ward spell, or dodge well enough to beat Rhett in a duel, you can place yourself in mortal danger."

"*You're* going out!"

"I'm not going to be in that part of the city. If Tanya leaves, *she* might be. You're no match for her, Damien. Trust me. A little extra information isn't worth the danger. Still, let me know if she leaves. I'll keep track of her from afar."

Damien scowled mutinously.

'This is a problem,' she thought to herself. '*I'm going to have to come up with better arguments and excuses if I want to keep working with him while still keeping him in the dark. He's too curious—too nosy—to just be a good little soldier and follow instructions.*' She at least had the comfort of knowing that if he tried to follow *her* in any way except mundane tailing—if he tried to scry for her—she would know and be able to counteract it. Still, she needed to be careful with him and prepare in case his gullibility wore off. '*I should deal with this as soon as possible, before it becomes even more hasslesome.*'

"Damien," she said, trying to seem compassionate rather than irritated. "Do you remember your vow?"

The scowl slipped away and he straightened. "Of course. I vowed my silence, to keep our secret, knowing when to speak and when to remain quiet. I vowed my loyalty, to support us and our efforts faithfully and fully, with true heart and steady hand. I vowed my resolve, to persevere through hardships and the wear of time, exerting myself to fulfill the cause. Freedom, and enlightenment. I—" He swallowed. "I saw beyond the edge of the sky."

He said the words seriously, almost reverently, but all Sebastien could think, hearing them recited with surprisingly perfect recall, was, '*I can't believe I came up with something so cheesy. It's like something out of a cheap adventure novel.*'

"How long has it been since you stood before the stars and made that vow, and you're already forgetting?"

"I—I'm not forgetting! I just—I want to help!"

"You're not ready," she said softly. "And you're not needed, either. There are other people who are more prepared and able to deal with dangerous situations outside the University. You don't need to know about those people. In fact, it's best that you don't. This world can be darker than you imagine, Damien." She looked away, her fingers pressing a little too hard against the wooden arms of her chair.

"It takes time, and a lot of it, to prove your strength, your dedication, and

308 | A BINDING OF BLOOD

your competence," she continued. "I hope you don't prove me wrong about you. I told you this would be boring. It's not a story. There is no glory to be had. You and your job are important, but *you are not entitled to more.* If we feel that you are undermining the integrity of our mission because of greed, petulance, or impatience, you will be removed."

He was staring at her with too-wide eyes.

She sighed. "That was not a threat. Trust me, Damien. If you are needed, you will be called upon. Until then, please be content to play your part. It may not be glamorous, but perhaps that's because you don't understand its importance."

The agitation had gone from Damien's shoulders and his cheeks were slightly pink. "I'm sorry," he murmured. "I won't jeopardize the mission. I've come to my senses." He fiddled with his collar self-consciously. "I guess I was acting somewhat like a Petunia, right?"

Sebastien stared at him blankly for a couple of seconds, then realized he was talking about the character of Aberford Thorndyke's niece. In several stories, the headstrong girl jumped into dangerous situations beyond her ability to handle and only caused more trouble for the other characters who then had to rescue her—at danger to themselves or the greater goal. "Well, at least you're not Investigator Amherst."

Damien rolled his eyes so hard his head lolled back. "Give me a stunner to the skull if I ever act like *him.*"

Having gotten her way, and thus in a more accommodating mood than usual, Sebastien slouched to the side. She took an invisible pipe out of her mouth, affected an extra-deep voice, and said, "Amherst, you do an absolutely fantastic impression of a gorilla whose mother dropped it from the tree as an infant one too many times."

Damien's mouth dropped open. "Radiant Maiden, was that a Thorndyke impression? Did you just make that line up on the spot? It was perfect! Do another. Another!" He leaned forward, so eager Sebastien thought he might grab and try to literally shake the words out of her.

She slipped her watch out of her vest pocket, making a fake expression of surprise. "Oh, is that the time? I really must be leaving. Sorry, ta ta, goodbye." She got up and hurried from the room with a stride that was only just below a jog.

38

THESE VIOLENT DELIGHTS

OLIVER

Month 1, Day 17, Sunday 9:15 p.m.

A TRIO EXITED THE MORROWS' main warehouse near the docks, illuminated only by the crystals of the streetlamps.

Oliver waited to assure himself of their identities, then moved to intercept them with a couple men of his own. He recognized the slightly wide gaits of those who were more used to the pitch and roll of a ship's deck than the steadiness of dry land. Even if the Morrows did know that they were surrounded and being watched, and were trying to trick him and his people into letting someone important escape, he doubted they would be good enough actors to fool him.

The short man at the front of the trio drew a battle wand as soon as Oliver stepped from the shadows, sinking into a fighting stance. His companions did the same.

Oliver's wand was in his hand, but he didn't lift it. "Captain Eliezer," he greeted. "I mean you no harm."

The man and his companions had just left a meeting to inspect the latest shipment of delivered goods with Lord Morrow. Captain Eliezer had, some time before, agreed to smuggle certain items for Oliver, but apparently didn't recognize him by voice alone. "What is the meaning of this?" Eliezer demanded.

With a *pop* of suction, Oliver removed his mask.

Eliezer recognized him then, but did not seem comforted. "Lord Stag," he said, his wand still pointed at Oliver. "This seems a rather inauspicious meeting."

"Does it? I had hoped that wouldn't be the case. You and I have mutual interests, after all."

Eliezer's eyes narrowed, his wand dropping slightly as he peered around into other dark shadows and past curtained windows, where more of the Verdant Stag and Nightmare Pack forces were gathered. He seemed to realize he stood little chance in an altercation, even with his backup. "I don't suppose you're also here to warn me off? No more work with the Morrows, if I know what's good for me? Things seem to have taken a much more antagonistic turn since the last time I berthed in Gilbratha."

Oliver smiled at that freely offered piece of information about Eliezer's meeting with Lord Morrow, knowing it was deliberate. "No. That is not my purpose here tonight. You may deal with who you wish. However, you may have trouble completing future business with the association of people formerly known as the Morrows."

"Formerly?"

"Soon to be formerly," Oliver amended.

Eliezer squinted sun-wrinkled eyes at him. "You are quite confident."

"I am extremely confident."

Eliezer paused, assessing the shadows once more. "The majority of my business is with this 'soon to be former' group..."

Oliver shrugged loosely. "I'm aware, but don't worry too much, my good man. There may be some transition pains, as I'm not sure my organization will need the same things as theirs did. You may need to take a few oaths of secrecy for the sake of our security measures, but rest assured that you will have continued business, no matter the name of those in charge. You have a reputation as the best smuggler in the city for a reason, after all."

"Why the ambush in the middle of the night, then?"

Oliver smiled, not bothering to moderate the expression.

Eliezer tensed, unsettled.

"If I am correct, you haven't taken any oaths of secrecy *yet*. I'm interested to know about the shipment they just received."

Eliezer hesitated, but Oliver just kept smiling at him, and the older man gave in soon enough. "You'll keep me out of this? I'm in the business of shipping, and that's all. I'll have no truck with your power struggles."

"Of course."

Ten minutes later, Captain Eliezer left with his men, and Oliver knew more details about the internal layout of the building, the number of men within, and the weapons delivered in the shipment than his people had been able to gather with weeks of preparation.

"What a stroke of luck," Oliver murmured, putting his mask back on.

He sent a couple of his men to tail the captain, just in case the man didn't want to stay out of the power struggle as fully as he'd proclaimed.

Just a couple of minutes later, spark-shooting wands sent up thick showers of bright green and yellow sparks from high points all around the city. They were clearly visible against the dark night sky, and the Stags and the Night-mares launched their simultaneous, joint attack on a dozen-plus locations and high-value targets at once.

As Oliver and his men closed in on the Morrows' building, everyone pulled out the battle potions that had been prepared. They only had a few protective bark-skin potions, so the enforcers who would be in the vanguard, and thus mostly likely to take spell-fire, had been assigned those. Everyone had a potion of diviner's sight in their utility belts, specifically created by another alchemist to counteract the philtres of darkness that Siobhan had brewed for them over the last few months. They also had one-use mask artifacts that would protect against Siobhan's philtres of stench, which had already proven their effectiveness.

A trio of overpowered concussive blast spells broke open the reinforced doorway, and the men beside it tossed in the philtres of darkness. Clouds of black, light-devouring particles exploded within as soon as the delicate vials shattered, accompanied by surprised, confused cries of alarm from those within.

Distant sounds of impact and screams from the left side of the warehouse told him the same was being done there.

The philtres of darkness were followed by philtres of stench, and the cries from within changed tone to include horror and disgust.

Satisfied that the enemy was mostly neutralized, Oliver gave the signal to enter, but before the vanguard could do so, a shimmering barrier popped to life over the doorway and shuttered windows.

Someone within had activated a building-wide ward.

Oliver raised his wand and tried a concussive blast. The ward rippled from the force, but held. He switched quickly through all the spells in his battle wand, but none penetrated. It made sense, as most wards were created to block at least the most common assault spells. Remembering Siobhan's work-around for that, he tried to toss another vial of darkness in. It shattered against the ward, spilling a huge cloud of darkness out around the door and covering their group.

He could still see through the magical darkness, though things were greyscale and a little distorted under the effects of the diviner's sight potion. It might have actually been a good thing, as it concealed them further from any enemies.

He picked up a rock off the street and tried that next. No luck.

He stepped closer and touched his pinky finger to the barrier, which was rippling and shimmering under similar attacks by the rest of the Verdant Stag soldiers. The ward didn't repulse him, or dissolve his flesh, or anything truly nasty, but it didn't let the finger through, either.

That was alright. They hadn't come unprepared. Stronger, comprehensive-purpose wards could either be broken by an exact counter-spell or overpowered through brute force.

His people knew this, and had already started to barrage the ward with battle spells, hoping to bring it down through overwhelming power. That was wasteful—he'd paid for every charge of spells put into their battle wands—and who knew how long it would take?

"Stop!" he called. "Bring out the augers! One on each wall!"

One of the support team Stags rushed forward with the device. The auger was a drill artifact that he'd had imported from his home country, Osham. The drill itself was physical, a spiraling, razor-sharp piece of hardened metal, but its movement was powered with magical energy. This allowed more power and greater efficiency than a purely magical drilling spell. Osham used the drilling artifacts for mining and other difficult excavation, but he was sure they could be utilized in non-traditional ways as well.

The enforcers used a liquid stone potion to anchor the augers to the ground, then activated them. Silently, they began drilling into the ward that surrounded the building like a skin.

The ward rippled violently around the tip of the drill, which kept pressing inexorably deeper.

The clouds of darkness within began to dissipate one minute after they had been released, leaving the Morrows able to better see and navigate. People appeared on the edges of the roof above, shooting spells , arrows, and battle potions down at the anti-Morrow alliance without hesitation.

Oliver's people quickly poured out large, half-dome barriers of liquid stone, which hardened enough to protect small groups from the weaker offensive spells. They shot back from behind the hastily created shields. Bright flashes with the colors of magic lit up the night, throwing ever-moving shadows about.

Oliver took out a fleetfoot potion, a wit-sharpening potion, and a bark skin potion, using all three in quick succession. Being well-supplied was one of the perks of being the leader. He flitted around, shooting spells at those above with much greater accuracy and avoiding their return attacks. He blasted one Morrow back, sliced deep into the chest of another, and tripped yet another as he was trying to escape.

That man fell off the edge of the roof, slamming into the ground below with a meaty *crunch*.

The Morrows had known something was coming, and this warehouse, where they brought most of the newly smuggled stock before redistributing it, had been well-protected.

But there were still more of the alliance members than there were Morrows, especially after the philtres of stench had done their job on those unlucky enough to be in the main warehouse area.

A few of his men made it to nearby rooftops, setting up liquid stone battlements to shoot from behind and negating the height advantage of those on top of the Morrow warehouse.

All the while, the augers drilled away, unperturbed.

Under such strain from multiple points, the ward dropped in only a couple of minutes, which seemed much longer than it really was. That was a fifth of the time even the most competent ward-breakers would have needed to bring down such a powerful barrier, and had required maybe a twentieth of the magical power that overwhelming the ward with spells would have taken.

Osham had its own problems, to be sure, but they didn't stymie nonmagical advancements for fear of disrupting the established industries. In Lenore, the results of so much industry being controlled by only thirteen powerful families became obvious. Many of them were impeding the advancements that could come from a freer market due to either complacency or fear of diluting their own power, and it wasn't just hurting the lower classes, it was weakening the nation.

As soon as the ward dropped, their vanguard threw in new philtres of darkness, but some quick-thinking Morrows within managed to cover and stifle them before the light-absorbing clouds could fully expand, leaving only a dark grey haze over a good portion of the warehouse.

Oliver gritted his teeth and cursed, but there was nothing to be done about it. Delaying further would only put them in a worse position. The vanguard had been prepped for this, and the head of his enforcers didn't even need Oliver's command to enter.

Mr. Huntley had a shielding artifact of his own, which he, as the point man, held up in front of the door to shield others entering behind him, but it could only absorb a couple of spells before failing.

Oliver slipped in, moving quickly to circle around the edge of the room with the others. It smelled fishy inside, as if new seafood had been layered over old, crusty, and sometimes putrid remains, and there were still halfprocessed fish and sea creatures strewn about the tables and floor within.

The enforcers attacking from the left side of the building were entering too, but they had the cover of darkness.

Huntley absorbed a fireball, a stunning spell, and then a maliciously shaped spell that might have been a hemorrhaging curse. The foggy concussive blast spell that finally overpowered the artifact slammed Huntley into the side of the doorframe behind him. He bounced off and fell to the ground, clutching at his ribs.

One of the others dragged Huntley out, shoved a lung-sealing philtre down his throat just in case the broken ribs had punctured them, then sealed him in a quick layer of liquid stone to prevent him shifting around and causing further damage as they retreated with him toward the nearest medic station.

Oliver narrowly dodged a glowing piercing spell that gouged a deep wedge out of the stone wall behind him, then hopped over a puke-green spell that he didn't recognize. He almost slipped on a slimy octopus tendril—which he was pretty sure someone had physically *thrown* at him—and would have fallen painfully if not for the fleetfoot potion. His eyes flitted about the large room, searching for dangers and the most important targets.

Toward the end of the room nearest him, farthest from both entrances, was the door to the other half of the warehouse. A tall, hefty man was crawling toward it, eyes and nose streaming with tears and snot, and vomit splattered down the front of his flashy red suit. Another large man in much less ostentatious clothing was trying to support him with one arm while waving around a battle wand in the other.

Oliver smirked. "Well, hello, Lord Morrow," he murmured, his voice too low to be heard over the sounds of battle. He shot a stunning spell toward the duo.

The man with the wand, probably one of Lord Morrow's personal guards or a high-ranking member of the gang, adroitly switched his wand's output to a half-dome shield that sprung from the tip of the wand just in time to block Oliver's sizzling red attack.

He shot back a concussive blast spell, but his aim was high.

Oliver lunged forward, throwing himself onto his hands and knees as the spell passed overhead, then springing back up to sprint toward them. The spell *whumped* into the wall behind him, shattering stone and blasting out shards that hit Oliver in the back, but not hard enough to injure him.

He was too close to completely avoid the next blast, which caught him in the arm with enough force to crack some of the bark armor and spin his entire body around. He didn't resist, switching the output on his wand as he went through a full spin. He pointed the wand at Lord Morrow and his bodyguard as steadily as he could, time seeming to slow under the combined effects of the wit-sharpening potion and adrenaline. He stumbled to right himself, hunching down to brace as the third concussive blast exited the bodyguard's wand.

He couldn't dodge the next expanding, foggy blast, but he kept his wand up, activating the personal shield at the last possible moment.

The concussive blast threw him off his feet and wrenched his shoulder, but rather than the spell simply being absorbed by his shield spell, it bounced back at the enemy duo.

They weren't prepared for that, and it caught them straight-on, slightly weakened but still more than enough to knock both of them off their feet, too.

He switched back to the stunning spell setting on his wand before they could get up or defend themselves, then shot both of them. Twice. Not to be vindictive, just to be sure.

Oliver climbed back to his feet and quickly took the bodyguard's battle wand. As he was searching Lord Morrow for hidden artifacts or weapons that could be a problem when he woke, the hefty man jerked forward.

Oliver snapped back, barely fast enough to escape the crushing headbutt that Lord Morrow had tried to give his face.

Eyes wide beneath the mask, he punched Lord Morrow in the face before even taking the time to analyze the situation.

One of Oliver's rings released a bright red pulse upon impact, and Lord Morrow fell back again, his eyebrows sizzling.

Oliver looked appreciatively at the ring artifact that held a pressure-triggered stunning spell. He was so distracted that he almost didn't dodge the slicing spell that came from the side. He took out the Morrow that had sent it with an idle returned stunning spell, then looked back to the gang leader in front of him warily. Oliver was not a small man, but Lord Morrow was built like a bear, broad and with a layer of winter fat covering his muscles.

Oliver nudged the man with his foot.

No response.

He stomped down on the man's knee.

That caused a frown, but Lord Morrow didn't seem to wake or try to get away from the pain. The stunning spell didn't put its victim into a coma or keep them from feeling, so a little response was normal under extreme stimulus, just like one might have when experiencing a nightmare.

Keeping his wand pointed toward the man's neck just in case, Oliver crouched over him again, his freehand rifling through Lord Morrow's clothes. He found the cause of the bearish man's resilience soon enough.

Lord Morrow's leather-lined jacket was a warding artifact. It must have absorbed the first two stunning spells that hit his body. He had only pretended to be unconscious to take Oliver by surprise.

Moving as quickly as he could while still being wary of the men before him, and the fighting around him, which was quickly dying down as the alliance gained control of the room, Oliver stripped Lord Morrow all the way down to his underpants, inspecting even them to make sure no more nasty surprises were lurking.

Then, he did the same with the bodyguard, who was actually unconscious. By the time he was finished, the other Morrows were also subdued, and his people were searching them, tying them up, and inspecting the rest of the warehouse. The wounded were being treated or taken to the nearest healer.

They had won.

This was one of the most important targets, but hopefully, the distant sounds of fighting throughout the city told a similar tale for the others.

In a single night, the Verdant Stags would go from a small, insignificant organization to controlling one of the largest sections of territory within Gilbratha.

Oliver laughed out loud at the triumph of it, what this meant for the Verdant Stag and all the people they would encompass. He was different from Lord Morrow, and things under his rule would *be* different. He wasn't averse to the trappings of power and wealth, and the life that afforded, but it wasn't his main goal. He felt *happy* just imagining all the good he could do. That particular feeling of satisfaction was hard to get anywhere else, and it made everything he had to do to achieve it worthwhile.

39

HEALING

As was becoming routine to her, Sebastien went first to the Silk Door, where she took up the name Siobhan along with her real body. This time, she rebleached the front section of her hair, again using the color-change spell rather than an alchemical concoction, and tied it in a severe bun. Noticing that the rest of her hair wasn't just dark, but actually an iridescent blue-black, she fixed that, too. *'Another difference between Siobhan Naught and the Raven Queen. Or rather, between Silvia Nakai and the Raven Queen.'* She again wore the fake horn-rimmed glasses Katerin had gotten for her when she was doing the street-corner flag wards throughout the Verdant Stag's territory. She didn't wear the red lip cream. Being Sebastien was out of the question for this, but hopefully, she could just be Silvia, a nondescript healer's assistant, not the Raven Queen.

Once upon a time, her name had felt like something intrinsic, a thing that held meaning when describing her basic identity. If someone had asked her who she was, she would have answered, "Siobhan Naught," without hesitation, and meant it. It was a label that encompassed all that she was. Now, if someone asked her that same question, she would have had to check what skin she was wearing and what role she was playing before answering. The only thing left of her was her insides—her mind and her magic—and of course no human remained unchanged over time. All living, growing beings were in a constant state of slow metamorphosis. *'There will come a time when I am different. But, I hope, never a time that I no longer recognize myself.'*

She took a roundabout path to the address Oliver had given her. She slipped through the back door, which had been left unlocked, into the back room of a shop where the normal supplies had all been moved to one side of the room. The shelves were stocked instead with potions, bandages, and a few basic medical artifacts. Two large, square operating tables sat within, and one wall was lined with cots.

The room was empty. Something about being alone in a strange place, in the dark, made her feel like she was being watched from the shadows.

"Hello?" she called, her voice weak enough that it wouldn't travel very far.

No one responded.

'The healer must not be here yet.' She closed the door behind her, found a light crystal, and began to set up, organizing her own potions and familiarizing herself with the prepared supplies. The operating tables both had a large Circle engraved on their smooth surfaces. One had a pentagram and pentagon within the middle, and the other a hexagram and hexagon. With those four options, the tables should be enough to cover almost all of the basic healing spells.

The minutes stretched on, and Siobhan found herself pacing back and forth in an attempt to release some of the nervous energy building up inside her.

When the distant sounds of fighting reached her, the healer still hadn't arrived.

A few minutes into it, when she was wound so tight she felt like a string that might snap, frantic pounding on the door made her jump.

There were no back windows, so she had to open the door to see who it was.

As soon as she did so, two men pushed past her, one supporting the other.

The injured man was badly burned. The skin across his head, neck, and one arm was already bubbling up, and he smelled uncomfortably like burnt hair mixed with roasted pork.

"You're the healer, right?" the uninjured man asked, puffing from the strain of supporting his almost insensate teammate.

Siobhan shook her head. "No. I—"

Behind them, a woman followed, her battle wand out and her eyes scanning the street for danger. "Is this the wrong place?" she asked demandingly. "We were promised there would be a healer here."

"It's the right place," Siobhan said. "But the healer hasn't arrived. I—"

The burned man sobbed pitifully. His face was badly blistered, one eyelid melted into the surrounding skin, and his ear on that side mostly burned away.

Siobhan swallowed past the nauseating smell and pushed her shoulders back. "Get him onto the table," she ordered, pointing to the one with the pentagon and pentagram. She couldn't cast any of the real healing spells that required a hexagram, anyway. She strode over to the shelf of potions. "I'm not the healer, I'm an assistant. I can't do everything, but I can help."

The man and woman worked together to heave the burned man onto one of the tables, which only drew out more pained sounds from him. "Fritz," he mumbled.

The man grabbed his hand and squeezed it. "I'm here, buddy. I've got you."

Siobhan tied on a full-body apron and returned with a potion and a jar of salve.

She uncorked the potion and fed it slowly into the good side of the burned man's mouth. "This will help with the pain," she told him. "You're going to be okay, I promise."

He swallowed obediently, shivering slightly from what was likely shock.

She followed that up with one of her newly brewed regeneration-boosting potions, letting him drink it rather than trying to pour it evenly over the huge swath of damaged flesh. This way, he could heal from the inside out.

"Turn him to lie on his good side. Someone hand me a pair of scissors and a pair of tweezers." She fished the chalk out of her pocket and walked around the table writing glyphs. Her secret Conduit was pressed between her calf and the upper shaft of her tall boots, creating a painful indentation in her calf, but she couldn't reveal it, so she pulled out the one loaned to her by Professor Lacer. It wasn't likely to be recognized, and there was no way to track its use. She cast a simple, improvised spell to slowly draw some of the heat from the man's burns, which would keep him from continuing to slowly cook.

The high strength pain-relieving potion kicked in as she worked, and the man let out a long breath of relief, tension easing from his body. His breathing deepened as he slipped into unconsciousness.

Fritz returned with the tools she'd requested, which Siobhan used to cut and pluck away her patient's clothes from his burned skin. "What caused his injuries?" she asked.

"Fireball spell," the woman replied succinctly.

Siobhan hummed thoughtfully. "Any coughing or liquid in his lungs?"

"No."

'Probably no internal burns, then.' "Did the fireball blow him away? Did he smash into anything?"

"No. It wasn't concussion-modified," the woman said. "Just heat."

"That's good. He'll have scarring if he cannot afford to pay for the strongest healing spells, but he'll live as long as I can keep his skin on his body."

Fritz swallowed audibly. "How likely is it that you can't? Keep his...skin on his body, that is."

Siobhan scowled down at the sweeping burns. She couldn't get all of the cloth and ash out of the wounds, but figured that was a job for someone more skilled, anyway. As long as he didn't die right away, she'd done her job. "I don't know. If the healer ever arrives, I'd say it's quite likely he'll come out of this with some scarring. If not, I'll at least be able to keep him alive through the night. For the rest..." She shrugged, perusing the wound-cleansing potions on the shelf for a brew mild enough not to tear away the burned skin.

She found a bottle and poured it liberally over the unconscious man.

"Do you have any idea where the healer might be?" Fritz asked. "It's just... It looks like you're all alone here. Our orders were to drop off any wounded and get back to the battle, but maybe we should stay. You might need protection."

Peering at the pieces of dirt, ash, and cloth that were flushed out by the gentle bubbling of the potion, she said, "You can stay for now. I might need an extra pair of hands or two when we get more injured. One of you should guard the door in the meantime."

Siobhan had cleaned her hands while waiting for the healer to arrive, but still rinsed them again in a basin of strong alcohol she'd poured in the corner. All the healing books she'd read had been rabidly paranoid about the possibility of infection, which often could not be treated without true healing potions or spells, and were a leading cause of delayed deaths. Infection had long been thought to be caused by bad humors, but according to Professor Gnorrish and the latest medical books, it was actually caused by tiny animal-like creatures too small to see with the naked eye, which would breed within a person like maggots in a piece of meat. Bacteria. Alcohol killed them.

Assured that she wouldn't be infecting the man with her touch, she dipped her finger into the fresh jar of burn salve and began to gently daub the gooey substance over his burned skin. She'd only covered a couple of inches when shouting from down the street drew her attention.

The woman's battle wand was in her hand as she peered out the door, but whatever she saw made her relax slightly. "Allies, carrying injured!"

Siobhan took a quick glance outside, turned around, and said, "Help me move him. I'm going to need the operating table, and he isn't in critical condition." Being as careful as they could not to jostle his burns, they moved him to one of the cots just as the new group hurried in the door.

They brought more burns, a broken leg, and what she thought was a punctured lung from a broken rib.

Siobhan slipped into a fugue of focus, rattling off orders, questions, and prioritizing the injuries as well as she knew how.

The punctured lung was the worst, but other than her blood magic flesh-mirroring spell, she didn't actually have any way to fix it. She gave the injured fighter a whiff of a strong anti-coughing philtre, then cast a modified version of a simple sinus-clearing spell on him. "Do. Not. Cough," she warned.

The spell drew up globs of blood and phlegm, which spilled out of his mouth in a horrific, lumpy mess into the bowl she had waiting. The man tensed, holding his breath in an attempt not to hack at the disturbance to his lungs.

She held up the anti-coughing philtre again, letting him get another soothing breath. "Breathe shallowly." She gave him a blood-replenishing potion next. "Does anyone have a lung-sealing philtre?" she called. She had bought some for the Verdant Stag at the secret thaumaturge meeting, but there were none stocked on the shelves.

"I do!" a man belatedly volunteered, fumbling it from the half-stocked utility belt around his waist. He dropped it, but with quick reflexes, Siobhan managed to catch it before it hit the floor and she delivered it safely to the patient.

The man took as deep a breath as he could, and the philtre did its job, coating the inside of his lungs with a seal that would add pressure to the wound and help to keep him from drowning to death in his own blood.

Siobhan sent him to one of the cots in the corner. "You're still bleeding. We're waiting on the healer. If you feel your lung start to fill up again, ring the bell and I'll come clear it out for you. No talking, no coughing, slow breaths," she ordered, shoving a cheap brass bell she'd pulled from one of the shelves into his hand.

'At least we're well-stocked,' she consoled herself.

Everyone with burns piled their affected parts or their whole bodies onto the table and she drew the heat out of the burned flesh, then removed any large pieces of debris or cloth from the wounds, repeating the same process as the first time. Those who were the worst off got enough pain-relieving potion to knock them unconscious.

She made Fritz rub down with alcohol, then put him on burn salve duty. "It's too simple to screw up. Dab, don't rub. Be generous with the salve, we have plenty. Clean your hands thoroughly between each patient."

She turned her attention to the man with a broken leg. The leg wasn't exactly mangled, but a jagged edge of bone was jutting out of his shin, and the limb was bent unnaturally at the break. Judging by the pallor of his foot and the rotten grape-purple bruising all around the wound, she doubted blood was flowing properly past it. 'He's going to lose that foot if I don't do something. Maybe I could knock him unconscious with a pain-reliever, take him into the main room of the shop and send the others away, and see if I can at least get the bone in place and the blood vessels reconnected with the flesh-mirroring spell? These people might be suspicious of the secrecy, but they're not healers. I could make up a plausible excuse...'

She was contemplating the wound while the pale-faced patient stared at her.

"Can you fix it?" he asked.

"Of course I can!" a man barked from behind her.

She turned to see Healer Nidson, the same man Oliver had taken her to when she got Will-strain.

Nidson was guarded by three men with wands. His white shirt was splattered with blood, his hands, knees, and shoes covered in what looked like a mixture of mud and blood.

Siobhan almost collapsed with relief. "Thank the stars above," she muttered.

Nidson looked around with a critical eye, then turned his gimlet stare on Siobhan. "You'll brief me while assisting. Go get the wound cleanser! Strength five. And I need a sink and some alcohol. Find me a clean apron. And be quick about it!"

Siobhan pointed him to the wash basin in the corner, gave him a fresh bottle of alcohol, then scurried around to retrieve the rest of what he'd requested, explaining the injuries she'd assessed and what she'd done to treat them as she went.

He was ready and up to date a few minutes later, just as another wave of injured people arrived.

There were people from the Stags and the Nightmare Pack, but also unconscious men wearing the red of the Morrows, and even a few civilians. The wounds were worse.

"Morrows were prepared," one of the men gasped. "Half of them had overpowered blast wands. Took down the side of a building on us. Civilians got caught up in it. We grabbed who we could. There are more there, some dead. There'll be—" He stopped to cough violently, then croaked, "There's more wounded on the way, as soon as they can get here on their own or we can fetch them."

Nidson initiated a quick diagnosis of that man using an artifact that sent out a pulse of light and sound, and then read its dials and scales for the result. "No obvious internal bleeding. You're good to go."

The latest batch of people were wounded in ways that were beyond Siobhan's ability to help directly. She could deal with cleaning wounds of the pieces of wood and stone that had been embedded in flesh by the concussive blasts, and she knew enough to give the proper basic potions. But she could do nothing about caved-in abdomens, shattered skulls and pelvises, broken spines, disrupted internal organs, or internal bleeding...not even simple concussions. For those, she gave pain potions, blood-replenishers, and revivifying potions, just trying to keep them all alive long enough for the healer to see to them.

It was honestly amazing to watch Nidson in action. He had been brusque before, but seemed unpretentiously competent. Now he was like a snappish, efficient whirlwind. He used telekinetic spells to move bones and flesh into the proper position, tossed around minor healing potions like they were water, and even broke out some components from the Plane of Radiance to cast specialized healing spells on the particularly grievous wounds.

He bossed her—and anyone else who stood nearby for a little too long—around with rapid-fire instructions, sending uninjured men back out into the fight. Their cots quickly filled up, and anyone who was conscious or stable enough to move was relocated to the main part of the shop and laid out on the ground.

In this way, they worked through the wounded even as more poured in.

Some died, or were already dead when they arrived, carried by people who were exhausted and often injured themselves.

Siobhan realized that she had been wrong to think that normal healing potions were inefficiently expensive. Being general purpose and simplistic was their greatest strength. She could dose people on the edge of death with one general healing potion instead of a series of different specific potions and spells, providing what they needed much faster. She could use a healing potion without taking the time to diagnose the injury as thoroughly, leaving specific problems until later. Some of those being brought in had already taken one of the mild healing potions the enforcers had been supplied with, and in some cases it had saved their lives. Even civilians with no medical training and no skill in magic, their eyes blurry with blood and their hands shaking, could use one.

Siobhan had also never considered that someone could be so severely injured that they might literally not have enough room in their stomachs for all the specific-purpose potions they would have otherwise needed.

There was a fire spreading from one of the battle sites, caused by careless use of a fireball spell. They were getting more civilians with burns or smoke inhalation, so many that Siobhan worried the previously excessive stock of burn salve would actually run out.

It was worse than Siobhan had expected. Not worse than she could have imagined, but it still rattled something deep within her. The darkest moment came when a grandmother with a mangled stump for a hand begged her to save her grandson, whose legs had both been blown off. The woman had tied the stumps with strips of her own clothing, using just her good hand and her teeth, then ran the whole way to them with the boy on her back, following directions from the Nightmares—Nightmare Pack enforcers—who had been fighting in the street around her.

Siobhan thought the boy was dead, to look at him, but Nidson pronounced his heart to be still beating. "He's lost too much blood, though. I don't have any of the more powerful healing potions left, and anything else will take too long."

"Humphries' adapting solution!" Siobhan cried, lunging over to the shelf where she'd placed the large bottles earlier that evening. She shoved two into his hands.

"Are these still fresh?" he asked.

"I brewed them myself just yesterday," she assured him.

Nidson wasted no time placing the boy on the operating table. Using a fountain pen with a thick ink, he drew out the modified piercing spell, centering it precisely over his pale arm. He used a tiny needle to barely prick the skin at the center of the array, then pressed the wax-covered mouth of the bottle over it and began to cast, forcing the liquid directly into the boy's bloodstream.

Five minutes later, three liters of liquid had been transfused into the boy's body with minimal waste, and he was breathing normally. His color hadn't recovered from the deathly pallor, but that was because the adapting solution wasn't red like blood.

Nidson moved on to the boy's leg stumps, but Siobhan took an extra moment to look at the unconscious child's face. *'He's alive because of me. I did better, this time.'*

Nidson was almost finished sealing the boy's stumps when the guard at the doorway screamed in alarm, shooting a spell from her wand before leaping out of the way.

Half a second later, the doorway exploded.

The open door was blown off its hinges, and the blast edges caught those closest, tossing them off their feet and peppering them with shattered pieces of brick and shards of wood.

Siobhan reacted in time to cover her face with her arms, flinching back from the blast and shrapnel. She was far enough away that it only rocked her back on her heels and left her with a handful of bruises where she'd been hit.

Nidson had reacted even faster than her, pulling the boy off the table onto the floor and shielding him with his own body.

A mixed group of Nightmare Pack and Verdant Stag fighters had been by the door. Some of them had moved in time. Those who hadn't were lying on the floor, injured or unconscious. The concussive blast spell had been a little off-center, impacting more against the side of the building than directly through the doorway, which had probably saved their lives.

Siobhan's ears were ringing from the pressure of the shockwave, and people were screaming in fear and pain, but she still heard the female guard who'd gotten off a return shot shout, "Morrows!"

'They must have followed some of our own people,' Siobhan thought. "Get away from the doorway!" she screamed. "If anyone has a shield, raise it now!"

People were crawling or being dragged away. The female guard stepped past them, falling to one knee in the doorway with her fists, wrapped by knuckle guards, held in front of her.

Another concussive blast hit, this one more on target, but a circular shield flared out from the woman's fists, wider than the doorway and almost as tall, blocking the blast and allowing the injured to make it farther into the safety of the room. The woman let out a grunt past gritted teeth from the strain of the impact as she absorbed a second attack, this one a fireball that spilled around the edge of the shield, licking at the ceiling and the walls and singeing the woman's skin.

"Give back our men!" screamed one of the Morrows from the street. "I want Andrews and Jacob or I'm going to collapse that building on top of you!"

Siobhan grabbed one of the stone operating tables by its leg and heaved it toward the doorway. "Step back!" she screamed at the guard.

The woman shuffled out of the way, her fists still raised with the faintly glowing shield.

From the corner of her eye, Siobhan saw one of their attackers release another spell. With a heave, she tipped the table over in front of the doorway and fell to the ground behind it, knees to her chest and her arms around her head.

The table cracked with the impact of the attacking spell—another concussive blast—but didn't shatter completely.

The woman was kneeling over Siobhan, her fists still raised. She'd reinforced the table with her shield artifact, keeping it from breaking, but the table also protected her from the brunt of the blow.

Siobhan crawled to her feet. 'We're trapped in here, like rats in a box.' She popped her head up above the edge of the table for less than a second, taking in the attackers scattered around both sides of the street, some peeking out behind doorways or the corners of alleys. She scrambled for her bag.

Some of the civilian patients were running to the front of the shop, hoping to escape out the main door, but many more were unconscious or not stable enough to move.

Some of the enforcers still well enough to fight headed that way, too, and Siobhan hoped they were going to circle around and attack the Morrows from the side or behind, not simply escape. She hoped, but she couldn't depend on them. She'd run scenarios like this through her mind several times since Oliver asked her to help with this operation.

'Do I have any effective long-range attacks except for the makeshift slingshot spell I used against the Morrows last time?' The problem was, the Morrows were scattered, not grouped together under a single shield spell, and if she moved to the doorway to attack them, they were much more likely to hit her than she was to hit them. The barrier of the operation table would only hold for so long. It would be suicide.

She could slip out the front of the shop, circle around, and try to surprise them, but it still left the problem of being one against many, with them scattered about and difficult to hit.

No, she needed an attack that could cover a wide area all at once.

And she had prepared just the thing.

She carried her bag back to the doorway, fishing out a philtre of stench. There wasn't enough wind to push the debilitating cloud toward their attackers, but she had a solution for that problem too.

She selected one of her paper utility spells.

The table, reinforced by the woman's knuckle-guard shield, which was beginning to falter, took another hit. An arrow from a forearm-mounted crossbow shot through the doorway, but the shooter had terrible aim and it embedded itself harmlessly in the back wall.

Three other fighters were now helping the female enforcer, ducking down to shelter from attacks and then popping up to send out return fire. It seemed to be helping, reducing the rate at which the Morrows could sling spells at them.

The building around the doorway had taken several more blows as the Morrows' aim deteriorated under the pressure. None of the Morrows seemed eager to come closer and make themselves a more obvious target.

Siobhan threw the alchemical bottle into the street, where it shattered. The stench expanded outward in a vaguely visible, sick-looking cloud.

As quickly as possible, she ducked back down and placed the paper spell array for her gust spell against the inner side of the table, using a bit of moderate-strength glue to paste it on. The Circle bound a spherical area under her command, which in this case meant that she also controlled a section of air on the *other side* of the table's surface. The side facing the street.

She realized belatedly that she needed a power source, and as she turned to look for one, the healer said, "Here!" and tossed her the beast core he'd been using to perform healing spells.

Siobhan wasted no time extracting energy from it. She was exhilarated by the deep well of potential she could feel within the small vessel. It was like holding a miniature sun, or a bolt of lightning, or all the crushing power of the world's largest waterfall.

She only needed a fraction of that power, and she used it to create wind. The Circle for this spell was small enough that she was able to create some real force from the gust.

The philtre of stench blew down the street, and though some of the Morrows had been smart enough to pull up their scarves or cover their face with an elbow, it wasn't enough to save them. The particles were small, easily filtering through cloth, and no one had thought to cover their *eyes*.

The philtre was more than just stench. It was also an irritant to any of the more delicate mucous membranes and a minor emetic.

Siobhan adjusted the angle of the breeze several times on the fly, using only her Will to change the spell's output in this simple way. She kept her head below the edge of the table for the most part, only popping up occasionally to readjust her aim.

The Morrows were dropping. Some vomited violently in the street. Some were blinded by their streaming eyes and hacking out mucus. Some decided that attacking the emergency healing center wasn't worth it after all and ran away.

The shielding artifact the female enforcer had been using gave out, and a spell chipped the table, sending some fragments of broken stone flying at Siobhan's face. Thankfully, her fake glasses protected her eyes.

Some of the enforcers who had escaped out the front of the shop did indeed circle around, taking shots at the escaping Morrows.

Siobhan tried to be careful not to send the magical stench at her allies, but it was hard to control, and they couldn't get too close without being affected.

The philtre ran out after a few minutes, letting off only a trickle of fumes rather than a billowing cloud, and Siobhan released her gust spell.

"Guard the doorway," she said to the fighters still inside. She went to the wash basin in the corner, wetted some bandages, and then tied them around her face, covering her mouth and nose like some kind of partial mummy.

One of the unconscious patients on the cots had a battle wand lying next to him. Siobhan took it.

The overturned operating table was mostly broken by that point, so it was easy to drag one side of it out of the way.

Siobhan stood in the doorway for a minute, clearly visible and ready to dodge aside, channeling every bit of reflex that Professor Fekten had managed to drill into her body.

No one attacked her.

Still ready to drop to the ground or lunge out of the way at a moment's notice, Siobhan stepped into the street. The lingering stench was horrible, forcing her to choke down a gag. She'd never been particularly squeamish, but there was a reason part of the process of brewing this potion required a protective barrier around the mouth of the cauldron.

Quickly and methodically, she stunned every Morrow she could see until the wand ran out of charges. A few more tried to escape, but the enforcers from the Nightmare Pack and the Verdant Stag that had circled around stopped them.

She grabbed hold of the closest unconscious Morrow and dragged him toward the makeshift infirmary. Her allies picked up on the idea quickly, and helped her haul the others in. Oliver wanted hostages, after all.

Inside, Healer Nidson was already on his feet and working again, using the second table.

Waving for the enforcers to follow her, she dragged her prisoner into the main part of the shop, dropped him, and used a spell to remove any extra liquid from his mouth, throat, and lungs. *'I don't want any of them to die from choking on their own vomit.'* She repeated the process on their other new prisoners, then quickly checked to make sure none of them had potentially fatal wounds.

Her fingers were trembling around her Conduit, and the room swayed a bit when she stood. One of the Nightmare Pack enforcers, a man with two curling goat horns springing out of a mop of tangled hair, caught her elbow.

Siobhan nodded her thanks to him, clumsily pulling the damp bandages away from her face and wiping her streaming eyes. "Check them for weapons, then tie them up securely. Re-stun them if you have to. We cannot afford to waste pain-relieving potions keeping them unconscious."

She returned to the back room, blinking away tears and suppressing the urge to cough. She felt like she'd rubbed her eyeballs and throat with a slice of onion. Staring around at the wounded lying on cots, and on the floor, those still waiting for treatment, and those already dead, she felt a buzzing sense of detachment for a moment. *'This cannot be what Oliver had planned, can it? Something must have gone wrong. Is it even safe for us to stay in Morrow territory? What if they win the fight and come to kill us all?'* She pressed her hand to her chest, where her heart was beating too hard. She hadn't thought she was afraid, but the burning in her veins and the lifting of the hair on the back of her neck was undeniable.

She looked around wildly, sure that something dangerous was in the room with her.

"Girl, are you listening?" Nidson barked.

Siobhan jerked back to awareness, turning to him belatedly as the irrational fear receded.

He fished in the pocket of his jacket under his now-filthy apron and tossed her a small bottle. "Take that and get back to work. I need three lung-sealing philtres and some liquid stone." He turned to point at a group of patients. "When you've done that, dose those three with a regeneration-booster, and him with a mild healing potion. I'm worried about cot number three, he didn't move when the first blast went off. Check his heartbeat and his eyes for dilation. And I need my beast core back."

The healer continued to rattle off instructions, and one part of Siobhan's brain catalogued them while the other focused on the vial he'd prescribed her. The scribbled label on the side named it a wit-sharpening potion.

Wit-sharpening potion did not in fact make you any smarter, but it could make you temporarily more aware and improve performance in situations that required multitasking, as long as you didn't take too high a dose and become overwhelmed by sensory input. It was also addictive.

She took the single swallow remaining in the vial and tossed the empty bottle in the box where all the other empty jars, bottles, and vials were piling up. Almost immediately, she felt her focus tighten, her brain organizing the steps she needed to take to complete all her tasks as efficiently as possible.

'There is no time to waste, and I will not leave these people to die.' She felt for the battle wand she'd secretly slipped from one of the captured Morrows' insensate fingers while taking them captive, now tucked in one of her inner pockets. The glyph next to its activation lever told her it was filled with only stunning spells, nothing more powerful, but she was pretty sure there were a few charges left. *'If more enemies come, we'll fight them off, too.'*

HAVE VIOLENT ENDS

OLIVER
Month 1, Day 17, Sunday 9:30 p.m.

THE DOOR to the back room of the warehouse was locked and thoroughly reinforced, enough that a few concussive blast spells did barely any damage.

While one of the others handled the bodyguard, Oliver dragged Lord Morrow onto a chair, tied both his arms and legs to it, then used a rope passed underneath the chair to tie his arms and legs together as well.

The Morrows that had been on the roof were brought down. All those who were severely injured were restrained, stunned unconscious, and given basic first aid before a team took them off to the closest medic station. Meanwhile, the rest remained, unconscious, tied up, and waiting to be taken to the holding cells. Cells that Oliver had paid an exorbitant amount to have set up on short notice.

The alliance's contracted wardbreaker came in when they were sure the front half of the warehouse was clear, going to work on the door to the back room. They could have used the augers again, but were worried about setting off traps. Also, since this warehouse would soon belong to Oliver, he didn't want to damage his future property any more than necessary.

The wardbreaker took a few minutes to examine the door while the others looked through the boxes of goods stacked around the warehouse. At first glance, this location appeared to be legitimately used to process seafood caught in the Charybdis Gulf. But some of that seafood was used as a cover for other, less conventional deliveries. They found packets of illegal components tucked into the stomachs of several creatures, and piles of restricted components covered with thick layers of unpleasant things like stinking sea slugs or thorny sea urchins. The Morrow workers had been in the middle of processing the incoming shipment when the attack began, but it seemed like the most valuable things were missing.

There were no artifacts, no celerium, no components from the Elemental Planes.

The wardbreaker called out to get Oliver's attention. "This is exceptionally well-done. It might take me an hour or two. If you're in a hurry, you can try to overwhelm the ward instead, but that will come out a lot more expensive for you in the end."

"So that's where you were keeping all the interesting things," Oliver murmured, looking down at Lord Morrow's pale, unconscious body. "Keep working on cracking it," he said more loudly. "We'll see what I can get from him." From his utility belt, he took out a small paper packet of magically enhanced smelling salts that had been "repurposed" by one of the coppers on the Verdant Stag payroll.

They were torturously strong—literally—and woke Lord Morrow up immediately. The man flinched back, wide eyes rolling around like a stuck pig as he took in his current situation. "You'll never get away with this!" he bellowed hoarsely. "We will erase you and your people from the face of the earth for this insult! And don't think you Nightmare Pack degenerates will be able to squirm your way out of it, either," he yelled, catching sight of a man with curling horns and a tail.

The Nightmare just smiled at him mockingly.

Red-faced, Lord Morrow—who was not a real lord by birth, only by affectation as the leader of an organization large enough to afford him the title—turned back to Oliver. "*You.*"

"Me," Oliver agreed, staring down at the man through the eye holes in his mask. With the artificial darkness behind those eye holes, Lord Morrow would know nothing of Oliver's expression, but his satisfaction was clear in his voice. It only made Lord Morrow's face flush redder.

Oliver hadn't woken him to waste time monologuing. "I have some questions for you. Whether you answer or not, you are going to die either way. But if your answers prove useful, the innocent members of your family may be spared. I am not a cruel man."

Lord Morrow spat at Oliver, but the fleetfoot potion hadn't quite worn off yet, and Oliver dodged easily. "You don't have my family," he snarled, "and the only words I have for you are maledictions."

Oliver had never believed in the power of maledictions—a curse spoken with a wronged person's dying breath—and even if he had, Lord Morrow hadn't lived the kind of life for this ending to be an injustice. "This world is not fair," he said. "If you get what you deserve, it is by coincidence or expended effort. But in this case, Lord Morrow, it seems you really will be reaping the fruit of what you have sown."

He leaned foreward. "I do have your family. We attacked your home first. They put up the wards, and your guards tried to fight back. When your wife realized it was hopeless, she abandoned the guards to buy time, set the traps, and escaped with your children. They went to the safe house. The one you prepared for a day like this. The one you thought no one knew about. My men were waiting for them, but they haven't been harmed. Much."

Lord Morrow roared and jerked against his restraints, trying to spit at Oliver again. "I'll kill all of you! All of you!"

A Nightmare lunged forward and kicked at Lord Morrow's side, knocking the air out of his lungs.

"You won't." Oliver almost felt guilty about how pleasant it was to solicit such reactions from a man he so despised. "You could have avoided all this, you know. I was content to grow slowly, but you made that impossible when you started attacking my people, in my territory."

"You think I'm stupid? You were sneaking around like a weasel behind our backs, trying to take over our source of product. Did you think we wouldn't notice? Did you think we would let that go?"

Oliver experienced an instant of confusion before making the connection. "Really? Because I used the same smuggler you did? That's why you attacked?" The warehouse incident had been shortly after his first meeting with Captain Eliezer, but he'd never connected the two. It made even more sense that Lord Morrow would have warned Eliezer off working with him again tonight. "But that can't be it. You were harassing us before that."

Lord Morrow laughed. "Those were warnings against getting too uppity. Which you failed to heed. You don't know who you're messing with, whelp. The Morrows have backers stronger than you could ever imagine. That bitch, the so-called Raven Queen? I'll have her fed to the dogs!"

Oliver had no doubt the man meant the threat literally. He'd heard the stories. Though he felt a powerful urge to slap Lord Morrow across the face, he suppressed it. "The University, right?" he asked. "They are your backers. Well, not all of them. Just one faction."

"If you think my contacts will just take up working with you once you've gotten rid of me, think again!" Lord Morrow said, uncertainty seeping into his voice for the first time. "You'll never be able to hold my territory or my business."

"Enough of this," Oliver said, suddenly impatient. He didn't need Lord Morrow for details about their operation and contacts. He had many captured lieutenants for that, and his enforcers were already working on waking and questioning them. He only needed Lord Morrow to save him some time getting into the warded back room. "I need the password to the back room. If you don't give it to me within the next ten seconds, I will give the order for my men to kill your oldest son. If you still refuse, it will be your wife next. Then your younger children, descending by age."

In truth, Oliver had no intention of killing the younger children. Lord Morrow's oldest son had committed enough crimes that he was going to be executed anyway, and his wife was complicit in many of his crimes. The younger members of the family would be tried for their own actions and punished accordingly, but Oliver doubted very much they deserved death.

Lord Morrow sneered. "Just because you were able to guess they escaped to a safe house means nothing. You cannot threaten me with something you do not control."

Oliver hadn't been sure he would need Siobhan's group proprioception potion, but he'd kept a set of vials for himself anyway, just in case. He realized now might be the perfect time to use them. "I thought you might say that," he said. "Proof is being delivered as we speak." He turned around and walked out of the warehouse without another word.

Outside, their people were guarding the building to make sure no Morrow backup attacked them by surprise.

Oliver handed two of the three group proprioception potions to a Nightmare with big yellow eyes, chosen because she was an owl skinwalker and also happened to own a watch. "Go deeper into the Morrows' territory. North of Lord Morrow's mansion, somewhere you won't be seen. In exactly five minutes, break one of these potions and hit the remains with a fireball spell. Make sure it's completely destroyed. Wait another three minutes, then do the same to the other."

The woman looked at him strangely, but accepted the task, moving into a dark corner to transform in private.

Oliver waited four minutes, then returned to Lord Morrow. He forced the last of the three potions down the man's throat.

Lord Morrow, probably thinking it was some kind of interrogation potion —which would actually have been quite useful to have on hand—tried to gag it up. But before he could succeed, the effects took hold, and his eyes widened. "What is this?"

"Do you feel that? It's a simple potion that connects you to two other people. Your son, and your wife."

"Lies."

"You can feel them. You know it's no lie," Oliver bluffed. "Don't you sense the kinship? They share your blood. And if you do not give me the password, you will share in the sensation of their death. You will feel it as they slip from this world."

Some of the enforcers around him shared uneasy looks, probably imagining experiencing such a thing themselves, but no one tried to intervene.

Lord Morrow glared at Oliver's serene, black-eyed mask and said nothing.

After a nonchalant look at his watch, Oliver lifted his wrist to his mouth and said, "The son. Do it."

Nothing happened for a couple of seconds, and Lord Morrow was just beginning to smirk. His expression was aborted immediately as his whole body convulsed, his wide eyes rolling back in his head.

The woman must have destroyed the first linked potion. Oliver had not expected such a strong reaction.

Lord Morrow shook, red-faced and breathless for a moment, then let out a wailing keen.

The sound hurt Oliver's ears, and made something inside him flinch.

The tied up man sagged forward finally, panting. "My son! What have you done? *My son!* I'll kill you for this. Slowly, in the street for everyone to see."

Oliver kept his tone neutral. "Your wife is next. The password?"

Lord Morrow glared at him, gritting his teeth for a good thirty seconds, but as soon as Oliver moved to lift his wrist to his mouth again, the fight seemed to finally go out of the big man. "It's a two-part verbal password, and I only have one part. But it doesn't matter!" he added quickly, seeing Oliver lift his arm again. "The ward is also keyed to my body. I can pass through with impunity. If you just take me to the door, it will open under my hand, no password required. But you must promise me the rest of my family is safe."

"As long as you cooperate, they will be safe until they are tried for their crimes. The results of that are up to them."

Lord Morrow agreed quickly.

Oliver's eyes narrowed, but he still ordered two of his men to untie Lord Morrow's arms from the chair, keeping his ankles bound to each other so he couldn't try to run. Oliver kept a good grip on Lord Morrow's left arm, his eyes trained on Lord Morrow's face as the man reached for the handle.

The handle turned.

Lord Morrow threw himself forward, uncaring as he hit the door and fell forward into the room beyond, dragging Oliver with him through the ward.

The ward stayed firmly in place behind the two of them, keeping the rest of Oliver's men from entering or coming to his aid.

Lord Morrow stared at him in surprise, looking back at the intact ward. "B-but that's impossible!" Obviously, he had assumed that the ward, keyed physically to him, would keep Oliver out. If it were someone else, perhaps it would have.

Oliver had fallen on the arm holding his battle wand, and before he could free it and attack, Lord Morrow rolled over onto him.

Oliver hooked his own leg around Lord Morrow's still-tied legs and continued the roll until he was on top of the much broader man. "There are exceptions to every rule."

Lord Morrow grabbed the wrist holding Oliver's wand, squeezing until Oliver physically couldn't help but drop it.

He punched Lord Morrow in the face, with the hand wearing the ring artifact, but apparently it only had had one charge remaining, and nothing happened.

Lord Morrow's free hand scrabbled for Oliver's face, his fingers sinking into the shadowed eyeholes of Oliver's mask.

Oliver jerked back, and the mask ripped away from his skin, ripping the remains of his fading bark-skin armor with it.

With both of Lord Morrow's hands temporarily occupied, Oliver reached for his utility belt, scrabbling frantically for something, anything.

Lord Morrow tossed aside Oliver's mask, smiling ferally up at him, then reached for Oliver's neck, just one of his hands big enough to close around it. He squeezed and lunged up to try and pin Oliver beneath him again. "There is only one sin, and it is *weakness!*" he snarled.

Oliver's fingers closed over a potion vial, and without even stopping to check its contents, he brought it up and smashed it into Lord Morrow's face.

Liquid stone spilled out, quickly overwhelming the blood spilling from both Oliver's hand and Lord Morrow's face where the shattered glass cut into them both.

It expanded rapidly, building up and pouring over Lord Morrow's face. Liquid stone potion was not intended as a weapon, and contact with living flesh purposefully inhibited the conversion process so that workers using it didn't accidentally entomb themselves in stone if a vial broke. Still, straight to the face, it would expand more than enough to kill a man.

The man sputtered, drawing his hands back to wipe off the quickly hardening goop.

Oliver tried to restrain the large man's arms, but his strength was no match for Lord Morrow.

Still, with the other man distracted, there was nothing to keep Oliver from going for his wand, which he did, breaking off large chunks of hardening stone from his fingers so that he could grasp it.

With it in his hand again, he stood tall, looking down at the panicking man in front of him, who had barely avoided suffocation by liquid stone. Lord Morrow was no fool, and even with both eyes caked over and coughing gritty mud out of mouth, he knew he'd lost the advantage.

"Wait, wait!" he yelled, even as he contorted himself, trying to reach the rope still tying his legs together. It was no use. His head and torso were encased in the hardened goop and stuck to the floor.

Oliver shot him. The wand, despite their struggle, was still set to a stunning spell.

Lord Morrow collapsed.

Coolly, Oliver adjusted his battle wand's settings, stepping a little closer so that he could aim properly with his trembling hand. "If there is no strength to be gained from hope, I will pull resolution from despair," he whispered, paraphrasing a half-remembered quote from a bedside story his sister had told him as a child.

The next spell sliced right through Lord Morrow's neck, separating his head from his body and leaving a gouge in the hardened liquid stone encasing him.

Blood gushed out, rapidly at first in a pulsing flood, and then quickly slowing.

It pooled over to Oliver's shoes, coating their sides and bottoms.

Oliver stepped back, letting his huge, foxlike smile recede in favor of a grimace of distaste. "You taint everything you touch," he murmured. "What a waste."

Finally, he was able to look around. The ward was still in place over the open doorway, and the men who had been firing spells at it, trying to break their way through to help him, had fallen still. One of them had placed an augur in the doorway, probably figuring the risk of triggering traps was worth it with his life in immediate danger, and it was spinning into the empty air, digging into the ward. Oliver sighed and waved for them to stand down.

While he waited for the ward to be broken the safer way, Oliver turned to the rest of the room, stepping over Lord Morrow's body and the pool of blood, which was steaming in the cold air. Absently, he cracked off the caked stone from his clothes and skin.

Shelves filled with boxes sat against the walls, with a few tables in the middle of the room. There were three hinged iron doors set into the ground beneath the tables, hidden but not invisible. Oliver inspected them first. He might not survive any more surprises in a single night.

The hatches were locked, and when he used his battle wand to break the locks and pull them open, he discovered that the ward around the room blocked them, too. But it didn't block his sight into the tunnels that extended down beneath. Having a basement in Gilbratha was rare, because the water table was high, and magic was required to keep a subterranean room dry.

These tunnels would have been expensive, but all the more valuable because they were so unexpected. He would be sure to let his people know to search any other of the Morrows' prior properties for similar additions.

After closing the hatches, he moved to place some of the boxes on the shelves over them. It would slow down anyone trying to come through into the room from below. He never actually got that far, because he almost dropped the first box he picked up in surprise.

It was full of beast cores. *Hundreds* of beast cores, ranging in size and color. Enough to power all of a thaumaturge's spells for the rest of their very long life.

He put that box down and moved to the next. It was the same.

A few minutes of frantic investigation showed that about a fourth of all the goods in the room were beast cores. Even without the recent price hikes caused by the Crown's import restrictions, the room held the equivalent of two hundred thousand gold, just based on a quick estimate. Perhaps more, if there were any of particularly fine quality. If sold, these beast cores could fund the Verdant Stag for a year or more, even with their expanded territory. It was more than his own inheritance and personal investments made in five years. And most of the boxes were labeled with the same incomprehensible shipping address, a string of letters and numbers. Oliver couldn't decipher it, but he didn't need to. He already knew who the Morrows were working with.

The University was secretly stocking up on an exorbitant amount of beast cores, in addition to other restricted, powerful components that would have otherwise been taxed as well as tracked.

But why?

He looked around again, then picked up one of the beast cores. He'd heard that thaumaturges could somehow sense the power of a beast core roiling beneath the surface, but it just seemed like a pretty rock to him. He moved it around, peering into its colored, crystalline depths. "The beast cores, and the book. They're preparing," he breathed.

41

A SACRIFICE OF LIGHT

SEBASTIEN
Month 1, Day 18, Monday 5:00 a.m.

SEBASTIEN GOT BACK to the University before the sun rose. Most of the students were asleep, but a good number were still up, likely because of the widespread fighting in the city below. She slipped past any students she crossed paths with, avoiding notice with a combination of patience and the occasional distraction. She wished again that she had some way to activate her divination-diverting ward on command.

She'd washed the worst of the grime off herself at the Silk Door, taking a couple of extra minutes to turn her hair back to the blue-black of the Raven Queen before she transformed, but leaving behind Siobhan's body didn't get rid of the fatigue. She felt tired in *all* the ways—mentally, physically, emotionally.

A quick check showed that Tanya was still inside her room when Sebastien returned.

Mumbling at Damien when he questioned her, she took a shower and managed to get a couple of hours of rest before the school day started. The wit-sharpening potion had worn off, and she felt slightly detached from the world, as if an ephemeral blanket were wrapped around her, muffling her senses and delaying her reactions.

She hadn't had a chance to talk to Oliver or Katerin. If not for the fact that the fighting had eventually stopped, with a group of Stag enforcers arriving to take away what had become dozens of Morrow prisoners, she wouldn't have known the outcome. She was still ignorant of the details, but she presumed if the Morrows had won, her night would have ended very differently.

Damien proved his worth by supplying her with delightful, sublime, life-saving coffee, brewed strong enough to melt a spoon and already imbued with wakefulness magic.

She almost cried out of gratitude.

There was a lot of distracted discussion about the night before, with rumors of varying credibility already circulating. Most agreed that several of the most influential gangs in the Mires had gotten into a battle, with chaos and collateral damage ensuing.

The fighting was over and the fires had been put out before morning, but now the coppers were dealing with looting. There had been a call for volunteer healers from the University. Some of the students in that career track would be able to get practice working on the poor, who couldn't complain if their healer's skills were sub-par because they weren't paying anyway.

At breakfast, Tanya was visibly alarmed to hear all the gossip, but other than asking the other students for details, she didn't do anything suspicious. She didn't talk to Munchworth or any of the other professors. There were no other signs that anyone had contacted her or that she was reaching out, either.

Sebastien assumed Tanya was biding her time, and was a little impressed with the girl's dedication to maintaining her cover. It could be hard to maintain procedure even when you thought you were safe and unwatched, especially when something like this happened.

Still, Tanya would have to do something soon. And when she did, they would be watching.

Newton, however, pulled Sebastien and Damien aside at breakfast to let them know that he was leaving to check on his family, who lived near one of the areas where there had been fighting the night before. "Tanya said she wanted to come with me, but I convinced her that at least one of the student liaisons for our group needed to stay behind. Other students might need our support, after all."

Damien and Sebastien shared a quick glance. *This is horrible timing. But there's no way I can refuse to let him leave. And even if I tried, I couldn't force him to stay.*

"Go. We'll keep an eye on things here. Let me know if you need anything. I might be able to help."

After Newton left, Damien said, "We'll have to take turns watching Tanya throughout the day. There's no way we can monitor her during classes, but we might be able to keep an eye on her between them in case she tries to talk to anyone suspicious or slip away."

They set up a schedule to do that while seeming as normal and unsuspicious as possible. One of them would slip away at least once during every class to use the compass divination spell on the bone disk and make sure Tanya didn't cut out in the middle of a class. It was the best they could do with the resources at hand.

Sebastien stopped by the Administration center in the library before classes, and among the crowd of students doing the same, inquired if there were any letters for her. As she'd hoped, there was a note from Oliver, dropped off early that morning by a runner. The name on the outside of the letter indicated it was from Fortner's, the high-class bespoke clothing shop he frequented, but she knew it was really from him.

Sebastien went into a bathroom stall to open the letter. The outer page was an actual advertisement from Fortner's, but inside that was a small square of paper. In a hurried scrawl, it read, "My niece's violin recital went fairly well. She managed to win first place, though it was a close battle between her and the next girl. She made a fumble in the first movement, and her rival was unexpectedly well-prepared with a powerful piece of their own. Still, she prevailed. She has blisters that might take some time to heal, and I expect some snide words from those who aren't so happy at her success, but she's on track for the all-city competition, and I expect her to move forward from this even stronger."

Sebastien read it twice to make sure she hadn't missed anything within the cryptic message, then turned it over and drew a spark-shooting spell array on the back. She burned the entire thing to ashes in a couple of seconds, crumbled the ashes between her fingers, and dropped them into the magical chamber pot, which filtered into its holding tank. Finally, she washed her hands, trying to make the pale blonde man in the mirror look less anxious.

In her first class of the day, Introduction to Modern Magics, Professor Burberry looked less pink-cheeked and bright-eyed than Sebastien had ever seen the older woman. "As most of you know by now, yesterday night the city was rocked by war between a handful of the criminal organizations that make their claim on the less affluent areas."

This drew the scattered attention of the students like dangling a piece of bacon in front of a dog.

She continued, "The Crowns have mobilized the coppers to control any violence, looting, and property damage. The Order of the Radiant Maiden and the Stewards of Intention are both temporarily taking in those who have been injured or lost their homes to fire or spellwork. We've sent some of our own higher-level students with healing expertise to help as they can. If any of you have family affected by this, you can get a pass to leave for the rest of the day in the Administration office. Above all, however, I would like to stress that the Crowns have this incident firmly in hand, and we at the University stand behind them. There will be increased patrols to ensure the safety of the citizens in these tumultuous times and relief efforts to help those who are affected get through the aftermath, and those responsible will be arrested. The worst is over. Please don't worry about it. Remember, as students, you are here to *learn*."

Several of the students left, presumably to get passes from the Administration office, and Burberry gave her lecture without further allowance for distraction.

'*I wonder if Oliver realized it would get this big. The Crowns will have to make at least a token response. They have to be seen doing something. And maybe they'll even make a real attempt, if the spectacle of this embarrassed them enough. The coppers didn't particularly care about the Verdant Stag, at least not before the Raven Queen came along. But now...*'

She didn't know enough to truly speculate, but she was apprehensive. '*This cannot have been the optimal outcome.*'

Sebastien fumbled through her classes for the first half of the day, for once unable to care that she was missing a chance to learn. She revived only long enough to keep tabs on Tanya. Luckily, a lot of the other students were similarly bleary in the aftermath of their mid-term celebrations followed by the pandemonium of the night before, so she didn't stand out.

A nap during the lunch period, while Damien kept an eye on Tanya, and yet another cup of coffee helped refresh Sebastien for Practical Casting.

Which was fortuitous, because Professor Lacer conducted an impromptu assessment of their progress in the last exercise he'd assigned—using three different methods to turn sand into a rock.

He had them come up in groups. With a beast core in his hand, he crossed his arms, leaned against his desk, and watched them perform the sand-to-stone transformation using transmutation, duplicative transmogrification, and true transmogrification. The pen on the desk behind him scribbled notes. Rarely, he commented, giving a student with particularly poor performance scathing admonitions, or someone with an impressive showing a few words of praise and tips to further improve.

Sebastien didn't perform as well as she would have liked. Her transmutation was passable. She used heat and pressure to form a very small pebble at first, which she added to bit by bit.

"Your understanding of the process is still not complete enough, and that is creating inefficiency," Professor Lacer said, frowning. "You could do this at least twice as quickly with more thorough study and some practice."

Sebastien wanted to melt into the floor, but she straightened her shoulders and nodded. Her duplicative transmogrification was faster, the sand taking on the characteristics of the dragon scale they'd been given.

Professor Lacer plucked the ball of textured rock off the table in front of her. With a slight narrowing of his eyes and a faint ripple of magic in the air, it crumbled in his hand. He dumped the dirt back in front of her. "Barely passable," he said. "Too brittle, more like glass than dragon scale. You lost at least thirty percent of the durability during the process of duplication. Next time, take your time before casting and get a better grasp on the dragon scale, both in your feeling of ownership and your attention to its details. Weigh it in your hand. Taste it if necessary."

Sebastien noted his advice, but lamented her own lack of preparation. Obviously, Professor Lacer was hinting that she was not on the right track, and might not satisfactorily grasp the auxiliary exercises he'd assigned her and Damien by the end of term. She took her time with the final variation, true transmogrification, trying to make her Will as clear and forceful as possible.

Once again, Professor Lacer shattered the resulting rock with a spell. This time, he frowned but said nothing.

Sebastien suddenly realized that this was actually worse than being offered correction and advice. *'It shouldn't have shattered so easily, right? A real dragon scale wouldn't have.'* She went back to her seat, trying to figure out where exactly the spell had gone wrong. While others went up to the front to be assessed by Professor Lacer, she practiced the transmogrification, over and over, forming the ball of idea-infused rock and then returning it to sand.

When the assessments were finished, Professor Lacer introduced the third main exercise of the term.

He was even more crisp than usual, seeming irritated enough that none of the students dared to let out a peep or hint at any distraction that might draw his attention and ire.

"The mid-terms are over. Congratulations to some of you. Grades and rankings will be posted by the end of the week in the Great Hall. We will not wait for them to move on. There is little enough time to beat some basic competence into your heads as it is. This time, we will be using something new as the Sacrifice."

'I'm falling behind,' Sebastien acknowledged with a sinking feeling. *'I have already fallen behind.'*

Professor Lacer had given her five exercises to work on privately. As they progressed through the in-class exercises, it was clear that the bonus ones were meant to augment these. She was still working on the air compression exercise, and had planned to start the next one—changing the color and shape of a candle flame—in a week or two. If she hadn't been distracted with everything else, like keeping track of Tanya, developing the sleep-proxy spell, and all the time she spent working for the Verdant Stag, maybe she would have had time to keep up.

Professor Lacer walked to one of the empty student desks in the front row, his Conduit in hand. "Many thaumaturges become set in their ways of thinking. They are stuck within the patterns of thought they have worn in their own minds, like a carriage wheel becoming stuck in a rut. This presents itself in various ways, but there are many such barriers between the average sorcerer and a free-caster. Magic does not have limits. *Humans* have limits that we impose upon magic. One such obstacle that we create for ourselves is the type of energy source we use. It is accepted that most any type of matter can be used in basic transmutation spells—living, nonliving, from solids to gasses, in any particular cellular structure. Thaumaturges accept that they can turn mud into a brick, or even into a diamond, with enough power. But when asked about where that power comes from, you get the same handful of answers every time. Too many thaumaturges never cast with any energy source besides fire or a beast core. You need to practice thinking in other ways while your minds are still malleable."

On the desk in front of Lacer, the spherical area marked by one of the component Circles carved into the surface disappeared.

Sebastien looked closer, her interest piqued. *'No, not disappeared. It's not invisible—that is a bubble of shadow. He is intercepting all the light passing through the Circle's boundaries.'*

"There is nothing in magic that restricts the source of energy. For some reason, humans find using heat more instinctive than, say, a lightning bolt. Some theories suggest that is because it is easy to associate the fire, which consumes its carbon-based fuel in exchange for heat and light, with our consumption of the fire in exchange for a magical effect. Yet, it is considered an advanced application to use the energy inherent in a slice of bread to power a spell, despite the fact that human bodies use that same type of energy to power our own continued existence. Most would find it much easier to access that power by setting the piece of bread on fire."

He looked down to the little dome of darkness atop the table. "We will be practicing with light as an energy source. A simple transmutation spell, with light energy as the input as well as the output. Some of you may find this easier than others." He met Sebastien's eyes for a brief moment. "The least limited among you may have already cast spells like this."

Sebastien thought of the amulet that gave her this form, pressed even now to her chest underneath her clothes. *'Maybe it uses some kind of esoteric power?'* She had wondered before, many times, how it worked. The transformation magic had not degraded, nor gotten any slower, nor left her with any pain or weariness when it activated.

She caught herself lifting her hand to rub the amulet through her shirt and consciously refrained. No artifact could contain unlimited power. When they were created, they were charged with a certain number of spells, which would either contain their own power source—this was more common—or pull from some external power source, which she knew was possible but had never seen in action. She had only learned the vague theory of it from her grandfather.

Distracted for once from Professor Lacer's lecture by her thoughts, Sebastien's eyes narrowed. The artifact was also special in that it could trigger with even a minor application of her Will. *'How does it even recognize Will? To do so, the effects of Will have to be somehow quantifiable in the first place, which is something we haven't managed to do even up until now—but the amulet does it, and would hypothetically be very old. Perhaps it uses transmogrification for this instead of transmutation. After all, some animals seem to be sensitive to magic being cast around them, and even humans feel a kind of hindbrain "awareness" around powerful thaumaturges in the middle of casting. That could be more than the senses subconsciously picking up on subtle energy spillover from spell inefficiency.'*

In any case, this was not an issue that she could afford to be complacent about. Things went wrong when she got complacent. And she had been using the amulet rather a lot lately. If it ran out of charges, she would have absolutely no way to fill it again. *'Maybe the book it came in contains instructions on how to cast the spell. That would make sense.'*

Professor Lacer pulled out a small carving from his pocket, placing it in the second component Circle on the desk and recapturing her attention. "There are varying difficulty levels for this exercise."

A spot within the central Circle of the desk brightened, then resolved into a replica of the carving. It expanded to be easily viewed by the whole class: a crude carving of a little boy with his dog at his feet. At this size, with only the Sacrificed light from the much smaller component Circle, the image was vaguely thin, like someone could poke a hole in it with their finger. "The easiest method is to replicate the image of a spell component..." The image turned, but it was flat, and the back was nothing more than an exact mirror image of the front. "Two-dimensionally. The next level of difficulty is maintaining a three-dimensional visual illusion."

This time, when the image flipped around, it wasn't flat, but instead showed the side and back of the boy and his dog.

He picked up the carving and tucked it back in his pocket. "After that, you may attempt to remove the source material entirely. You may start again with the two-dimensional..." The image of light resolved into silhouettes of darkness upon a light background, again the boy and his dog, but in a slightly different pose, one Professor Lacer had created himself.

"But those who wish to achieve true mastery should introduce a real challenge." The silhouettes began to move, the dog wagging its tail and the boy reaching down to scratch behind its ears.

Sebastien grinned. *'It's not so different from the kinds of shadow-plays I've seen in the market.'*

Except, under Professor Lacer's sudden frown of concentration, the moving silhouettes gained realistic, rich color and shape. A background appeared around them, a field of green grass with a single tree in the distance, with a wide blue sky above. It seemed to gain substance, losing that semblance of thin illusion. The spell Circle was like a window into another place.

Sebastien was close enough to see individual blades of grass, and when the wind blew within the dome atop the desk, she thought for a second that she felt it on her skin.

The boy and his dog were real, not a crude wooden carving, and when a shadow passed over them from above, they reacted with surprise and fear.

They ran. The boy kept looking up and back over his shoulder, until he missed a gopher hole in the ground and went into a tumbling fall. When a dragon slammed down in front of them, the illusory ground trembled.

The dog took up a defensive position in front of the fallen boy, its hackles raised and its teeth bared as it barked viciously and soundlessly at the much larger dragon.

The boy scrambled to his feet and began to back away.

With a deep breath, the dragon gathered its magic, releasing it in a stream of fire that washed over the dog, vaporizing its fur and incinerating it where it stood.

The boy broke and ran.

The dragon hopped forward and happily snapped up the dog-shaped meat snack, then swayed after the boy until it moved out of the viewing window Professor Lacer had created.

The students stared at the scorched ground for a few seconds before Professor Lacer released the light-transmuting spell. When he did, it was like he'd broken some sort of bewitchment hex over them, and a few people suddenly started breathing again or let out nervous laughs.

"Anyone who manages a passable version of a three-dimensional image from imagination will get contribution points. Movement is not necessary, and will be beyond most, if not *all* of you. Do not let that discourage you from trying, however."

As he walked back to his desk, he said, "Homework is, as always, at least three fully fleshed spell arrays that you could use to create these effects if you were not in Practical Casting and forced to use a minimalist array. As you practice casting, three glyphs are allowed, two is recommended, and anyone still casting with three by the time we move on to the next exercise should be aware that their laziness is unacceptable and will be the main obstacle between them and true progress. Start your attempts now, with a focus on consuming all the light available so that you may repurpose it."

He settled back into his desk chair and began to look through a stack of papers, ostensibly intent to ignore them for what remained of the class period.

Sebastien had indeed cast with light before. She had done so during her disastrous entrance examination. But then, she'd also used heat to augment the spell, and when all was said and done, she'd probably come close to giving herself Will-strain. But much more often, she had done so through her shadow-familiar spell, which she had been casting since she was a child. The Sacrifice of light was why her shadow grew so unnaturally, opaquely dark, and it provided the extra power that her warm breath through the Circle of her hands lacked.

She took a moment to write out the symbol and two glyphs, trying to settle the perspective of pulling on light for power in her mind. '*Plants do it. Why not me?*'

She started out with the simplest of exercises, trying to replicate the image of a single copper coin.

She looked up and toward the back of the class, where Nunchkin was working on a three-dimensional light construct. She couldn't see the spell array on his desk, but would have bet that he had already advanced to using only two glyphs. Sebastien straightened and turned her focus back to the small Sacrifice Circle where she'd drawn the glyph for "light". '*I'll start with a two-dimensional static image. I can focus on restructuring the light once I've mastered drawing upon it. This shouldn't be so hard. It's light to light, not like I'm trying to use the light to power a movement spell. I've cast the shadow-familiar spell enough times that this should be easy.*'

It was not easy. Using only two glyphs and without the thrice-repeated chant of the esoteric shadow-familiar spell, the magic seemed to be deliberately trying to slip out of her grasp, as if the light were water trickling through her cupped hands.

By the end of class, she at least had the Sacrifice consuming enough light that she couldn't see anything inside it, a little dome of black being repurposed into an undefined blob of light hanging in the middle of the larger inner Circle.

She could have made it easier by adding the third glyph, but refused to give in to the temptation. '*I want to be a free-caster. If this is hard enough to make me give up, I should save my money for something with a better return on investment than University tuition, because I will never achieve true greatness.*'

Nunchkin's Sacrifice Circle was just as dark as hers, but he had already begun to form a blurry three-dimensional image of what seemed to be a silver crown, rather than a vague blob.

Sebastien's Will was already fatigued as she exited the Citadel for the day, surrounded by milling students, and made her way to the library.

Tanya was still in class for another hour, and if she maintained her regular schedule, should be joining Newton at the library directly afterward.

Damien waited outside to keep an eye on her in case she broke her routine, but if she came to the library as expected, he wouldn't follow her inside. Despite volunteering for this duty, he complained bitterly about sitting by himself on a cold bench, to Sebastien's complete lack of sympathy.

Remembering her earlier inspiration about the transformation amulet, she searched the shelves for information on historical feats of artificery. *'There has to be a clue, somewhere. Maybe I have simply been searching in the wrong place.'*

42

CONNECTIONS

Sebastien found a book by an author who loved alliteration a little too much. If she wasn't specifically searching for that topic, she might have passed over *Ancient Achievements, Accomplishments, and Attainments in Artificery* due to the ridiculousness of the title alone.

Reading through its contents, however, she was glad she hadn't.

Normally, artifacts were charged with a finite number of spells, each spell fully formed and contained within the spell array until a set trigger released it into the world. Myrddin had been the first to develop artifacts that could gather their own power for a spell. *Supposedly*. Myrddin had a lot of fantastical feats incorrectly attributed to his name that had either been done by others, or had no actual historical corroboration. There were more stories about Myrddin than there were about all the other famous thaumaturges combined.

According to the book, he had developed several versions of these self-powered artifacts—some of which were now lost arts—and which she was pretty sure from the lack of citations or evidence that the author had at least partially come up with himself, based entirely on his own speculation about how such magic would work.

The spell arrays of the simplest self-charging artifacts contained the parameters to gather and transform energy as part of their activation and release process, and creating one was a Grandmaster-level feat. Her grandfather had owned an ever-cold ice box that kept itself charged through the very heat it removed from the space inside. *'That's how my medallion works,'* she suddenly registered. It could pull heat from its surroundings to power any one of several different protective spells. She lifted it out from under her clothes to look at the gold surface, where the glyph indicating the anti-scrying spell was warped and melted. When it protected her against the coppers' first attempt, it had overloaded. She hadn't considered what its heat-drawing nature meant, because she'd rarely had occasion for the medallion to be used enough that a normal artifact would run dry.

As long as the spell array held, it would continue to work. The problem was that the shielding spell wasn't efficient enough, and would either reach a point so cold it could no longer draw in heat, or the spell array would degrade further and become non-functional. Self-powered artifacts couldn't cast truly endless spells, as eventually the spell array would break down—and more quickly with heavy use—but they were still widely coveted. If that happened, she wasn't sure what the danger might be. *'Would the shielding spell simply stop working? Would it be like the Circle being disrupted while casting? Explosions, backlash, and peculiar magical disasters?'*

Sebastien hadn't spent much time mulling over this idea before, but she was now realizing that it sounded rather dangerous. Even if the spell array was undamaged, if the artificer didn't know what they were doing, the user might end up freezing themselves to death as their battle wand gathered up energy to shoot a fireball. This method of self-charging would require the artificer to be able to *quantify* the energy and its transformation process well enough to code that into the spell, from the beginning of the process to the end, while including safety precautions and limits. Sebastien wasn't an artificer, but it seemed rather difficult.

The second method listed in the book, which Sebastien had never seen in practice, allowed an artifact to access a distant energy source, like a heat-gathering spell array, through a sympathetic connection. *'How far away does that work? What happens to everything in between when the energy starts flowing from the source to the artifact? Wouldn't houses, trees, and random people be fried to a crisp, or electrocuted, or... Actually, it sounds like a really great way to cause mass destruction.'* The book didn't give details about how, exactly, this process worked, but perhaps there was a reason she'd never seen it implemented.

The third method, which had been lost to time if it ever existed at all, had the artifact accessing external power through a receptacle. For instance, a beast core that would slot into a Sacrifice Circle in one of the artifact's sub-arrays—an ammunition cartridge, basically. *'At least that method seems like it would be reasonably safe.'* Remembering her own experience with using beast cores, whose power seemed almost eager to be used, she wondered what exactly the limitation with using them for self-charging artifacts was. *'Perhaps* there's some limitation with quantifying the energy of a beast core, or maybe it's more a problem of containing power surges, so it doesn't all rush out at once and blow up the artifact or something?' Frowning, she continued reading.

The final postulated method was for the artifact to open up one or more tiny planar portals and siphon pure elemental energy in both the quantity and quality necessary for the spell.

Out of all the methods, this one seemed the most impracticable to Sebastien. She couldn't even imagine how one would go about doing that. Since they couldn't be created by anyone weaker than a Grandmaster of artificery, they were rare and expensive. Creating stable planar portals was on a similar level of difficulty, and notoriously dangerous.

While those were interesting thought experiments, it was a footnote at the bottom of the page that made her freeze, leaving her wide-eyed and momentarily breathless. 'Myrddin was rumored to have developed artifacts that could be triggered with Will alone.' The claim wasn't substantiated, and the author considered it to be one of many false rumors, since no one had ever found such an artifact, and the original source of the rumors was unclear. 'But that's how the amulet works. I have physical proof that it's possible.' A fumbling search through the book's index for keywords didn't come up with any other historical artificers who were likely to have done such a thing. A search through a more modern list of advancements still did not turn up that particular ability.

'Did Myrddin make my amulet? Write that book?' It was a ridiculous question, improbable to the point of being impossible. But someone had made it, and if it was true, it suddenly made sense why the University would be so desperate to recover the book. If her speculations held any weight, the book could be worth more than its enormous value to collectors and historians.

Sebastien thought back to Professor Gnorrish's class some weeks before. If a sorcerer could truly understand a process, down to its very molecules, well enough to reproduce it given only a piece of chalk, they could cast spells that replicated the process. Triggering an artifact with Will alone might signify an understanding of Will greater than anyone alive in the world today. It was the kind of knowledge that many would be willing to kill for.

But not all the pieces of this puzzle fit seamlessly together. 'If the book and the amulet really are relics that could be reasonably connected to Myrddin, why hasn't the University shouted their success from the heavens? Surely their expedition recovered more than the one book. Even if they had no intention to sell any of the relics, the prestige benefits alone would seem irresistible.' Perhaps they were waiting until they had retrieved her stolen book, or had some other reason to refrain from crowing about it like a rooster at dawn.

'Maybe it doesn't have anything to do with Myrddin after all. Maybe they have no idea what's written within, any more than I do. But if they really believe the Raven Queen stole one of Myrddin's journals...'

She stared at the yellowed pages of the reference book, unseeing. *'They'll never stop.'* She smacked her cheeks until they stung, bringing her mind out of its spiraling thoughts. She didn't have proof, just speculation. Acting as if she knew what was going on when she really didn't could lead her to making catastrophically bad decisions. And even if it were true, it didn't actually change her current situation.

Ancient Achievements, Accomplishments, and Attainments in Artificery didn't have much more of value, but it did lead her to a discovery of the existence of an artifact meant to evaluate the energy stored in other artifacts—without having to take the other artifact apart. It didn't detect magic directly, but worked by cooling down the artifact and then measuring any extraneous sources of heat. Most artifacts slowly leaked some of the energy from their captured spells, and in an extremely cold, controlled environment, this was measurable.

Such an artifact would be able to tell her how many of the small spell Circles within her commandeered battle wand were still charged—without the need to take it to an artificer and answer unwanted questions. It might even tell her something about the amulet.

Lost in thought, Sebastien jerked upright when someone pulled out the chair next to her. Her eyes were stinging, and she realized she'd somehow forgotten to keep blinking. *'I'm tired.'*

Newton sat down beside her. His hair was windblown, his clothes wrinkled and smudged with ash on his arms and legs, and the dark circles under his eyes stood out against his pale face. A smattering of blonde stubble grew from his chin. "I'm glad you're here. I didn't get a chance to give you my report yesterday. And something happened."

Sebastien straightened. "With Tanya?" She pulled out her pocket watch to check the time. To her horror, her research fugue had extended through Tanya's fourth class of the day and twenty minutes more besides.

Newton glanced toward the Administration offices, where Tanya was waiting impatiently at the end of a long line of students.

Sebastien let out a slow breath of relief.

"Yes. I just got back, and she pulled me aside to talk. She wanted to check on me and ask about my family, but she was also asking for more information on what happened. She seemed agitated when I told her the Morrows had been ousted from their former territory. She specifically asked about"—he lowered his voice—"the Raven Queen. She seemed surprised when I told her I hadn't heard any credible rumors about the Raven Queen being involved, but she still wanted the details."

"What did you tell her?"

"I really don't *know* much. I was focused on my family, and the fighting was so widespread. But I heard the Raven Queen flew above the battle in a black mist that was invisible against the night sky."

Sebastien rolled her eyes. "If the mist was invisible, how could anyone have seen it to tell stories about it?"

Newton nodded sheepishly. "Yeah, pretty ridiculous, but, umm, Tanya seemed interested, almost like she thought it could be true. I also told her I heard the Raven Queen attacked a whole squad of the Morrows and took their bodies with her when she disappeared. And I heard someone prayed to her for protection and was able to escape through the darkness without notice, a veil of invisibility safeguarding them until they reached safety."

Sebastien refrained from rubbing her throbbing temples. *'This is getting ridiculous.'* "Most people don't actually *believe* those stories, though, right? It's just ridiculous rumors?"

"Of course they don't. But no one knows exactly what she can do, so it's hard for anyone who tells crazy stories to be judged absolutely as a liar. Anyway, that's not exactly what I wanted to talk about. My family's home was caught in one of the fires."

"Are they okay?"

"Shaken. Frightened for their future. A couple light burns on my mother. She ran back into the house to save some of our things. A magician with this water-spring artifact pulled by a carriage put out the fire before our whole house could burn down, but...it's not livable, and it will be a big job to repair, especially at this time of year. The fire, the smoke, plus the force of the water, and then sitting there drenched... A lot of our things are damaged."

'That's the artifact I bought at the secret meeting. Or one just like it.'

"The worst of it is that the smoke and being out in the cold all night trying to get to safety took a toll on my father's lungs. But everyone is alive, and none of them were seriously injured. Except...well, it means there's no chance I'll be able to stay on at the University next term. And I mentioned that to Tanya. She..."

Newton glanced up again to peek at Tanya in the line, ensuring she still was paying no attention to them, and lowered his voice again. "She swore me to secrecy and said she knew something that might help me. A way to make money. She hinted that it was illegal, or at best, very questionably legal. That I would have to take a magically binding vow of secrecy. And that it might involve some danger to me. So, Sebastien, I really need you to answer some questions for me."

"I'll answer what I can," she said.

"Working for you, I've been getting closer to her. She's driven, smart, and capable. I know she considers me her friend. Reporting on her every move while knowing that she trusts me...it makes me wonder about myself sometimes. Where do I draw the line for what I'll do to further my own goals? I used to pride myself on my integrity. But I also have to wonder if it's all a facade on her part, too. So just tell me. Is she harming people? *Why* am I watching her? What exactly is she trying to get me involved in? Is she danger-ous?" Newton stared at Sebastien intently.

"Relax," she said. "Your body language is conspicuous." She slid the book she'd been trying to read closer to him. "Pretend you're explaining something to me."

Newton did a passable job.

It could be dangerous to give Newton answers, but she worried that he might decide to quit helping if she didn't.

Putting a slightly confused frown on her face, Sebastien said, "I don't know all the details, and of what I do know, I can't tell you everything. However," she said quickly, forestalling the protest that was obviously on the tip of his tongue, "Tanya is involved with people who perform criminal acts that include violence against innocents. She has participated in these acts personally. There is corruption inside the University itself that goes beyond her. And there's a reason she's particularly interested in what happened last night."

Newton swallowed several times, shifting in his seat like he wanted to get up and pace but was forcefully suppressing the urge. "But she was *here* last night? She didn't have anything to do with the attacks...right?"

"She didn't directly participate in them, no. But that's likely only because she didn't know they were going to happen. She's been directly involved in at least two civilian deaths. That I know of. You're keeping watch on her for a good reason, Newton."

This didn't seem to reassure him. "This is way too much. I'm just trying to get my Journeyman certification. I don't want to be involved in...whatever this is!" He waved his hand vaguely.

Sebastien hesitated, but said, "You don't have to be. You can stop if you want. But as long as you don't get caught, you should be perfectly safe."

Newton stared at the book for a moment, then forced a slow, calm breath that reminded Sebastien of the spell he'd taught her. "About this...meeting, or whatever it is she wants me to accompany her to. Do you think she suspects? Is she trying to lure me off campus so she can get rid of me?"

Sebastien suspected she already knew what Tanya had been hinting at. "Can you tell me more about what she wants you to do?"

Newton swallowed painfully, looking down at the book in front of him and pointing to a specific line to keep up the ruse of helping her. "She said she had an answer to my money problems, if I was willing to take a risk. She said there would probably be no direct danger, but that I would have to take a vow of secrecy. She said she'd pay me to carry a battle wand and watch her back, but that if I wanted to put some of my tutoring expertise to bear, I could make a lot more coin from the kind of information that only a University student has access to."

That confirmed it. "There are plenty of thaumaturges in Gilbratha that aren't officially licensed to practice, or who are interested in magics that aren't officially sanctioned. If I'm guessing correctly, she wants you to accompany her to one of their meetings. They'll pay for things like spell arrays, restricted components, or other magical equipment. Some of the people are probably just there to avoid the Crown's magic tax, but others could be dangerous. However, I've heard there's a well-enforced restriction on violence at the meetings, so unless Tanya expects to start a fight, I'm not sure why she'd want backup. It could just be that she's worried about navigating through the city alone after all the violence. The streets might not be totally safe. Or it could be that she plans to make some extra stops along the way."

"Should I agree to go with her? I don't want to get involved in anything... well, *criminal*. I don't want to hurt people."

Sebastien turned through a few pages of the book while considering how to respond. "You'll have to decide that on your own. You're definitely not obligated to agree. It is a risk, but the possibility of profit is real, and we might be able to use whatever information you gather."

"But I'll be sworn to secrecy. I won't be able to tell you anything, really."

She hesitated, then said, "I have a contact that attends the meeting. You can discuss events with other members, and they can tell me." Really, it would just be a meeting set up with her in her female body. They would have to be *very careful*.

"If you already have someone there, why would you need me?"

"Because Tanya might talk to you about the details. My contact is a stranger to her. Still, if something goes wrong...they might be able to act as backup for you. Just something to consider. Also, we would pay you extra for the risk. But you'll still have your assignment with me even if you decide not to do this." She hesitated again, but decided it was only fair to be candid. "Also, there might be other options to get the money you need. I do have some contacts, and we might be able to work something out. This isn't your only chance in the world."

She wished she'd had someone to say the same thing to her when everything was going wrong. It was only by luck that Oliver and Katerin weren't worse, and that her deal with them was something she could stomach. She might have made much worse bargains out of desperation, were she in Newton's spot. "Though, to be clear, what I could connect you with probably wouldn't be as lucrative as the danger of accompanying her."

Newton's shoulders visibly loosened. He laughed. "Wow. If you would have told me I'd be having this conversation at the beginning of the term..." He shook his head ruefully. "I'm just a bookish commoner who's too stubborn to admit I don't belong here. I wasn't meant for these things."

Tanya paid the Administration worker for the paper bird messenger spell and moved to the stacks of special paper that she would write her letter on.

She glanced over at them, and Sebastien gave her what she hoped was an unsuspicious smile.

Newton didn't even notice.

"We sometimes find ourselves in extraordinary situations," Sebastien said. "And then we discover that there are extraordinary depths of resourcefulness within us."

"How did you get involved in all this? Contacts in secret meetings, digging up corruption in the University, rubbing shoulders with the children of Crown families?"

Sebastien let out a breathy laugh. "I, too, never expected to find myself having this conversation. Truly. But life has a way of surprising you. Especially when you demand more out of it. The world twists in strange ways to keep up with you."

"I'm interested in these other opportunities to make some coin, but I think I'll do it. Go with her, I mean. As long as there's going to be backup there."

"In that case, let me be clear that I intend no one at that meeting any harm. You are not associated with Gilbrathan coppers or official law enforcement of any kind. You have no plans to discuss relevant information about the meeting to any non-members. You are there for your own mercenary benefit only."

He blinked at her.

"They will ask you," she said. "This way, you can answer honestly."

He gave her a slow, confused nod, but there wasn't time for more questions, because Tanya had finished sending her letter and was heading their way.

'*She was most likely contacting Munchworth, or someone else here at the University. Even if the paper birds have a delivery beacon with one of the Morrows, I doubt she'd be so reckless as to contact them directly right now.*'

Tanya dropped into the seat across from Sebastien with an irritated huff.

"Thanks, Newton," Sebastien said, pulling the textbook back over to herself. "That makes sense."

"No problem." He looked up to Tanya, and Sebastien was impressed with his composure, despite what he had just learned about the other girl. "Is everything okay?"

Tanya waved a dismissive hand. "Well, you know."

Sebastien wasn't sure they *did* know.

That must have shown on her face, because Tanya brought up a knee, tilting her chair away from the table to rock back and forth on its hind legs, and said, "I needed to ask one of the professors for instruction, but with everything going on I can't get hold of them. Had to send a bird."

"Is it worth it?" Sebastien asked. "The contribution points for being a student liaison?"

Tanya snorted. "Of course not. They make me do all kinds of *shit* that I don't want to do." She was grinding her teeth. She stopped talking to rub her jaw, then said, "There's a reason why you don't see a lot of high-class students working as student liaisons. We don't do this for the contribution points. I mean, the points don't *hurt*, but the whole point of getting a position like this is to put it on your resume once you're looking for employment. I don't want to be poor and insignificant my entire life. I have ambitions, Siverling."

"I can understand that," Sebastien said.

Tanya peered at her assessingly for a few moments, rocking back and forth. "Maybe you can," she said finally. "How did you manage to do it?"

"Do what?"

"Build all those connections. Even if you make a mistake, or make enemies, you have a safety net. You won't be expelled before reaching Master, and you'll easily be able to get a position as a research assistant to attempt Grandmastery. You're pretty much assured a job after graduation, etcetera. A lot of people will see who you surround yourself with and hesitate to make an enemy of you."

'*What?*'

Sebastien tilted her head to the side and said aloud, "What?"

Tanya scoffed. "Come on, Siverling. Damien Westbay, Anastasia Gervin, and Professor Lacer? I mean, I've heard you insult Alec Gervin to his face... and you're still here."

Sebastien blinked. "Well...I suppose I could get a low-level position in the coppers through nepotism, and Damien Westbay probably has enough influence to keep me out of minor trouble, but he's definitely not going to pay my way through the University, and he can't keep me from being expelled. To be candid, Professor Lacer vouched for me to get me through the entrance exam. I offended some of the other professors and almost didn't make it. But that means my future here depends on him, and he's already threatened me with expulsion multiple times."

Tanya seemed to find this both surprising and amusing. When she was finished laughing, she wiped the wetness away from her eyes. "But he's not actually going to do it, right? If he was, he wouldn't have taken you as his apprentice."

Sebastien again found herself saying, "What?" She felt as if the world was tilted just a few degrees off-center—this whole conversation wasn't quite making sense.

"I mean, that was a pretty big decision on his part. You know how he is. He's got a personality like a barbed razor blade. But he's not going to actually expel you unless you do something *really* outrageous or start failing all your classes or something."

Beside Sebastien, Newton nodded. "That's probably true."

Sebastien shook her head rapidly. "Oh, no. Okay, I think you have a misconception. I'm not Professor Lacer's apprentice. He just used his veto power over the entrance council to get me admitted."

Both Tanya and Newton stared at her silently, their expressions a mix of confusion and incredulity.

Sebastien looked back and forth between them. "Really. And I became friends with Damien...by accident."

Tanya started laughing again and almost fell over backward when her chair overbalanced.

One of the librarians sent a death glare toward the three of them, pointing to the clearly visible sign requesting a quiet, peaceful atmosphere.

Tanya gripped the table and slumped over it, her face pressed into her elbow to muffle the disruptive volume of her mirth.

Sebastien looked to Newton for support.

He shook his head. "You definitely are Professor Lacer's apprentice. It was on the announcement board for special accomplishments."

She remained silent.

"When the entrance exams ranking results came out? It's displayed to everyone."

Sebastien hadn't returned to the University to see her ranking after taking the entrance exam. She'd known it would be poor. She'd barely been admitted, after all. 'Green five-fifteen' echoed in her mind. She found herself mirroring Newton's shaking head. "That's impossible."

"What's impossible?" Damien asked. He'd waited some time to follow after Tanya into the library, and was now staring down at her shaking shoulders with suspicion. "Is she crying?"

With a few shuddering gasps, Tanya regained control of herself. "Oh, I needed that," she muttered.

"We're discussing apprenticeships. Do you remember who Professor Lacer's apprentice is?" Newton asked Damien, his own lips twitching in suppressed amusement.

Damien moved to pull out the chair next to Tanya. "What? It's Sebastien. Is this some kind of joke?"

Sebastien's eyes lost focus. She stared into the middle distance. It all made a horrible, embarrassing amount of sense. "But you and Ana are doing the extra exercises, too?" she asked feebly.

"Well, I wasn't willing to fall behind some rude commoner," Damien said with a rueful smile and a shrug. "And Ana's a good sport. I badgered Professor Lacer into allowing it, since it's all individual work and doesn't require any extra time on his part."

"If you want proof, you can go look at the special accomplishments display for this term," Tanya said, waving to a series of framed papers on the wall near the Administration center.

Sebastien got up and walked over to them in a daze. She found her name next to Thaddeus Lacer's easily enough. "Oh," was all she could say.

'I'm apprenticed to Thaddeus Lacer. I am the apprentice of the youngest Master of free-casting in a century. And somehow I had no idea.'

43

NERVES WRACKED

SEBASTIEN
Month 1, Day 18, Monday 6:00 p.m.

DAMIEN FOUND Sebastien's ignorance hilarious. He kept falling into random giggling fits whenever he thought of it, despite her increasingly ferocious scowl.

Tanya was similarly amused, leaving Newton the only one with a bit of sympathy for Sebastien.

Sebastien almost wanted to stop by Professor Lacer's office and ask him about it, but the thought of his reaction was even more mortifying.

Besides, Damien admitted that when they spoke, Professor Lacer had called her his *provisional* apprentice. That barely meant anything, really. He may have made her his apprentice to get her past the entrance exams, but it seemed likely that he would negate that once it was no longer necessary, or if she disappointed him.

She did her best to put it out of her mind. Nothing had changed, only her understanding of the situation. There was nothing she needed to do with this information.

With both Newton and Damien around to watch Tanya, Sebastien didn't really need to be there.

Most of Sebastien's professors—those who had some measure of compassion for their students, unlike Professor Lacer—had temporarily reduced their students' workload. She decided to take advantage of the extra free time to work on some of the things she'd been neglecting.

She went to the supply closet that held the Henrik-Thompson testing artifact, hoping that it would have other useful items, like the artifact-scanning device she'd just learned about, but was disappointed.

She hesitated to ask one of the Artificery professors, but when she firmed up her resolve and found the man from her entrance examination to make the request, he was happy enough to give access to the one in his classroom.

Looking around at all the complicated gadgets and tools for creating the miniature spell arrays, Sebastien regretted that Professor Lacer had restricted her to only taking six classes per term. 'No, what are you thinking?' she asked herself, looking at a spool of gold wire. 'You cannot afford either the time or the funds to be a competent artificer. There will be time to learn more about this craft later, once you have made something of yourself.'

The professor sat at his desk across the room, wearing a set of complicated, multi-lensed goggles and leaning over something delicate and shiny.

Sebastien arranged herself so her back was blocking his view, just in case. She was pretty sure owning a battle wand required a license. She examined the artifact before putting it into the larger metal dome, which was already wafting out cold air from its open mouth. The wand was bigger than the name implied. Only the most expensive wands with the most exquisite construction were the size of twigs. Most were more like batons, tapered cylinders that easily reached an inch thick at their base, and in an emergency might even be used to beat someone about the head.

This one wasn't fancy, and gave off no hint of precious metal or multiple different types of spells within. You pointed and pulled the embedded node on the side, and it fired a stunning spell. Of which the scanning artifact told her it had three remaining, based on the three rings of miniature Circles within that were radiating minute amounts of heat.

Glancing surreptitiously over her shoulder to ensure the professor was still paying her no attention, she slipped off the amulet and scanned it, next.

According to the scan, it had no charges remaining. 'Either I happen to have just run out, or whatever charges it holds are too efficient to be tracked.' Not sure whether to be disappointed or relieved at the continued mystery, she hid the amulet away again, thanked the professor, and forced herself to return to the dorms for a nap. Then, she practiced Professor Lacer's exercises, focusing on all the different aspects of her Will while creating a ball of compressed air, until she felt herself start to grow more at ease with the spell.

The next couple of days were uneventful. Other than the suspicious letter Tanya had sent via spelled paper bird, she was keeping to her normal routine as a student aide. But Sebastien knew the woman would slip up eventually. Probably soon, considering what had just happened.

Oliver sent Sebastien another coded note requesting she come by over the weekend to brew healing concoctions, as apparently the Stags were having trouble supplying their increased territory. She had already been planning on it, of course, but noted that she should buy any useful healing supplies at the next secret meeting, which she hoped would be soon. The Verdant Stag would need more than she could supply on her own, and Oliver would reimburse her, with her fee on top of that.

After classes on Wednesday, while Ana, Damien, and Sebastien were studying in the library, Ana sat scribbling furiously in the pink notebook she often wrote in, a harsh frown on her face.

Sebastien would have thought nothing of it, but Ana was the type to smile with almost creepy pleasantness even while enraged. She'd done so only that morning when one of the male students "accidentally" rubbed against her derriere. Right before shoving his food tray into him, splashing hot oatmeal over his chest and face with a sweet, "Oops!"

Meaning something that could cause Ana to frown so unpleasantly had to be serious.

"What's wrong?" Damien asked.

"I need to go check on my little sister," Ana replied, already preparing to leave.

"I'll come with you," Damien said immediately, already standing. He hesitated, looking to Sebastien as if realizing that he might have misspoken.

With Damien off campus, it would leave only Sebastien and Newton to watch over Tanya, but Sebastien nodded quickly anyway. Some things were more important. Damien had been Ana's friend far longer than he'd been Sebastien's ally.

She even offered, "Do you need any help?" but the pair was already hurrying away too quickly to hear her.

Checking to make sure Newton was still with Tanya, Sebastien moved to the supervised practice rooms, where she spent a couple of hours trying to catch up on Professor Lacer's exercises.

Ana and Damien were still gone when she returned to the dorms, and Sebastien guessed they might be staying the night at the Gervin estate. '*I hope everything is alright.*' Damien did have the bracelet she'd given him, so if anything went truly wrong, he could at least let her know, even if there was nothing she could do about it.

Sebastien cast her dreamless sleep spell and lay down. She was hoping to get a few hours of sleep, and then wake to work on some homework in the middle of the night while a little more refreshed. Just as she was falling asleep, however, the alarm ward they'd placed on Tanya's door went off.

Sebastien pulled the rattling, cold stone from under her pillow and stared at it in frustrated disbelief. It was as if Tanya had somehow divined the worst possible moment to get up to something suspicious. *'I'm tired. I don't want to follow Tanya out into the freezing elements and hide in the dark listening to her from afar...'*

Sebastien considered letting Tanya go unsupervised in favor of sleep, trying to convince herself that the other woman wasn't necessarily up to anything nefarious. Instead, Sebastien leapt to her feet in sudden anxiety.

Without Damien, she *couldn't* actually listen to Tanya from afar. Sebastien had spent a little time researching sound-enhancing spells, but what she'd found worked by amplifying received sound through the casting surface. These spells all created a slight but obvious echo that could easily give her away to Tanya and Munchworth if they were paying attention, even if she managed to hide or suppress any light given off by the casting or Sacrifice flame.

Her mind raced as she tried to come up with a solution. She could attempt to recreate Damien's spell by hashing something together, but there was very little chance she would get it just right, and new magic was wild. Dangerous. She was trying to learn from her mistakes, not recklessly undertake more of them. That would be a last resort.

'Why didn't I place more importance on finding a way to cast a divination spell focused on myself, at will? If I had the ward going at full strength, I might even be able to sneak up on them in the dark.' Even if she could have cast a divination on herself while simultaneously avoiding its grasp, though, the spillover light from her lantern and the probable glow of the spell array would give her away. The divination-diverting ward didn't make her invisible or impossible to notice, after all. If she could cast with light as a power source, she could have minimized her chance of being noticed, but she was nowhere near ready to do that. Now she wished she'd bought herself a beast core, despite the uneconomical prices.

'You're rambling. Focus. I need real solutions,' she snapped at herself mentally, wrenching on her boots and jacket.

She checked her pocket watch. Less than half a minute had passed since Tanya left her room. *'I can't listen in from a distance, and I can't sneak up on her. But I'm pretty sure I know who she's meeting, and where. I don't need to sneak up on them if I'm already there. Lying in wait. Hidden.'*

It was a gamble. Maybe Tanya wasn't going to meet Munchworth at the Menagerie. She could be doing anything, going anywhere...

Moving as fast as she ever had in her life, Sebastien used her little slate table and the bone disk to track Tanya's direction. She was headed north, which meant she probably wasn't leaving University grounds. She would swing west soon, if the Menagerie was her goal.

Already moving to the dormitory doors, Sebastien snuffed her lamp, stuffed it into her pocket with the bone disk, and wrapped her dark scarf around her head to cover her pale face and hair. She didn't want to stand out in the night like a beacon.

As soon as she was in the hallway, she ran. She burst through the opposite doors Tanya had exited through, sprinting around the Citadel to the east and onward to the Menagerie gates. She had to get there far enough ahead of Tanya that the other girl wouldn't see her. Sebastien could only hope that Munchworth wasn't already there and waiting.

At least this time there was no fresh snow to leave suspicious tracks in. It was trampled and dirty and the paths were covered in patches of invisible ice —which immediately sent Sebastien sprawling painfully.

Cursing silently, breathing too hard to spare any air for spouting obsceni-ties, she climbed off her bruised knees and elbows and kept running.

The little bridge where Tanya and Munchworth met last time was empty. Sebastien slowed and glared around suspiciously, looking for any other forms hiding in the dark. Her breaths were seeping out through the gaps in her hastily wrapped scarf, clouding puffy and white in the moonlight. Her lungs protested the shock of suddenly filtering such a great quantity of frigid air, and she coughed as stealthily as she could while searching around for a hiding spot.

Eventually, she decided the best hiding spot was actually under the bridge itself. There were a couple of large boulders near the bank that would help to conceal her form if she huddled into them.

It was a precarious descent. The rocks were slippery, and the edge of the little stream was iced over and concealed with piled snow. Sebastien cracked through the ice with a splash, but managed not to face-plant into the freezing water. "Titan's balls!" she hissed. She crouched down in the darkness under-neath the stone bridge against the lumpy side of the boulder and remained still, muffling her breaths with her scarf.

She wanted to cast the compass divination on Tanya again, or at least take out her pocket watch to estimate how long she would need to wait for the girl to arrive, but she resisted the urge. She was too likely to be noticed.

To her relief, though, she had been correct.

Tanya arrived first, clearly audible from the little bridge above as she stamped her feet and muttered vague threats toward "that pompous idiot."

It took long enough for Munchworth to get there that even Sebastien was beginning to wonder if he'd stood Tanya up. Then when he did arrive, Sebastien worried suddenly that one of them would use a revealing spell of some sort to ensure their privacy, but he started speaking without hesitation. "What was so urgent that you could not send it in a message? I was under the impression that you do not have much time to dawdle about tonight. Do you have something for me?"

Tanya seemed to hesitate, but then blurted, "This is a bad idea. I...I don't feel comfortable doing this. I can go to the meeting, but—"

Munchworth cut her off. "You called me away from my bed just to whine? What exactly do you think your job is? Do you think you are in a position to make demands, or even *suggestions*?" His voice grew louder as he berated her. "You do not decide. We decide. You either perform satisfactorily, or you *fail* and you are *useless*."

"I'm not incompetent," Tanya said in a tightly controlled tone, "but I object to being treated like a disposable pawn in a reckless strategy that's just as likely to backfire as bring about positive results. Aligning ourselves against the Verdant Stag and the Nightmare Pack, both of which have dealings with the Raven Queen, is a bad idea. I have already been warned once. I doubt she will spare my life a second time. I have reason to believe that a member of the Stags or the Nightmare Pack is *also a member* of the meetings. That's what I've been trying to tell you. It became obvious after the attack. Don't you see the implications?"

"It is no surprise that there are criminals at these meetings. That is largely the *point* of them."

"They know who I am!" she cried, barely keeping her voice low enough that it wouldn't travel through the night. "They've heard my request for a meeting with the Raven Queen, and they probably passed it on to her, but she *refused*. They've been selling Conduits, I think from people they attacked or killed. They're dangerous."

'She's talking about me, but why would she assume I got the celerium through nefarious means?'

Tanya continued, "When I start asking the questions you sent me, they're going to make connections. The Raven Queen has already shown she can move directly against the University without repercussion. She's warned me in person. Do *you* want to be assassinated? Wasn't that book she stole on its way to *your* office at the time? She knows where you work. She probably knows where you sleep. You are making an enemy who is out of your league, and you're tossing me into their jaws like some kind of disposable, unshielded pawn."

Munchworth scoffed angrily. "I am a professor of the Thaumaturgic University of Lenore. We are the most powerful magical institution on the entire continent. Even the Thirteen Crowns fear us. This upstart who calls herself the Raven Queen is nothing more than a petty thief and a dramatist, feeding the fear and ignorance of the population to bolster her reputation. She makes threats and pulls stunts because she is *not* powerful enough to face us directly. *We* will anger *her*? *She has angered us!* We will stand for this no longer, and if she knows what is good for her, she will hide away in the shadows, for the fist of our wrath will spare none!" He breathed hard for a few seconds.

"The cowardice of your common blood is showing true, Canelo. Rid your mind of petty superstitions and represent the University with the mettle of a *real* sorcerer."

Tanya's heavy breaths were audible, and Sebastien could imagine her anger, but the woman didn't reply aloud.

"You're increasingly becoming a hassle, Canelo. Remember, we wield both the carrot *and* the stick." There was a pause, and Tanya must have responded nonverbally, because her harsh breaths remained while Munchworth's heavier stride walked off the bridge and retreated toward the entrance.

Sebastien stayed still beneath the bridge, trying not to shiver or let her teeth chatter.

Tanya stood atop the bridge for a few minutes, then suddenly burst into cursing. She took a few deep breaths, muttering, "By all the greater hells," in a desperately strained tone that sounded as if she might be about to burst into tears. After a few more minutes of hunkering in the cold, Sebastien heard her say, "Okay, okay," in a calmer tone. "I do what I must. At least I won't be entirely helpless, or alone."

Tanya finally left, and after waiting a long while to be sure she wouldn't be observed, Sebastien surreptitiously followed her.

44

THE SIVERLING LINE

DAMIEN
Month 1, Day 20, Wednesday 6:30 p.m.

WHEN ANA REPORTED trouble with her little sister Natalia, Damien immediately volunteered to go with her. He had some idea what the Gervin Family was like and what the young girl was facing without Ana around to shield her, just as Titus had shielded him. Already preparing to leave, Damien hesitated belatedly, looking to Sebastien. Without Damien, Sebastien would only have Newton as a backup to keep watch on Tanya.

Sebastien nodded easily, shooing him off with a flap of his hand.

As they strode determinedly away, Damien asked Ana, "What happened? Is Nat okay?"

Ana's expression was carefully neutral, but a muscle pulsed in her jaw. "Natalia is unharmed. Physically, at least. She was frightened by the fighting last night. Cousin Robbie teased her that I had died, and then he locked her in a supply closet. She was stuck for several hours until one of the servants found her and let her out. Mother scolded her for having cried so hard she made herself ugly and dirty, and of course Robbie denied any wrongdoing. So, Nat got in trouble for lying."

"I'll give him a good thrashing," Damien said, grinding his fist into his palm.

"She tried to," Ana said, her voice growing rough. "Father saw. He was with

Uncle Randolph, so I'm assuming he was embarrassed, and she was punished. Nat was a little too hysterical to explain everything coherently by this point in her message. I could barely read her scribbles past the ink blots and tear stains."

"Robbie's a grown man now. It's shameful to be picking on a small girl like that."

"I'm sure his father encourages him. Anything that could undermine the female heirs' ability to lead this Family in Father's eyes." Ana's hand fisted in the delicate fabric of her suit vest above her heart as if to squeeze the beating organ, leaving enraged creases in the material.

They took the tubes down and hailed the best-looking carriage waiting by the side of the street. Even with the carriage bouncing along with enough urgency to stress its cushioning spells, it took a tense half an hour to arrive at the Lilies. The Gervin Family's estate was cut out of the far east side of the white cliffs. The mansion sat close enough to the base, near the waters of the Charybdis Gulf, that when it stormed, a spray of sea foam would hit the cliff's edge.

They both remained silent, but Damien's mind was active. Smoke from the smoldering remains of the fires had drifted over the water from the city, making his eyes sting as he looked out of the carriage's small window slot. Usually, the smoke would have been blown away already, but the air was unusually—ominously—still.

Late Sunday night, Damien had watched from the edge of the white cliffs as the fires that preluded that smoke broke out. Even though he had under-stood he couldn't help, he hadn't been able to let the worry go, so instead of pretending to sleep while Sebastien was out who-knows-where, he'd bundled himself up and snuck away, looking down on the city as the violence Sebastien had predicted broke out.

It had been more than a "little skirmish." Even from so far away, Damien had seen the flashes of magic, and the wind carried him faint sounds of explo-sions. He even imagined he heard the occasional scream.

Not long after, some of the University staff had come out to look. The beginnings of a fire lit up a portion of the Mires in orange, light diffusing through the smoke and setting everything glowing. He hadn't bothered to try hiding from the staff, and they'd barely spared him a perfunctory admonish-ment to return inside, which he ignored.

"It won't reach us here," one of them said.

"Still, best to be prepared for the unexpected."

Finally, a female guard insisted he return to bed. When Damien tried to protest, she said, "You'd best hurry up before I remember that it's past curfew and give you a demerit."

Damien had been almost ready to tell her he was the youngest Westbay and dare her to punish him, but instead he'd slumped in defeat. He was self-aware enough to know when his anxiety was making him foolish.

Sebastien would give him a horrible tongue-lashing if he heard Damien was drawing that kind of negative attention to them. After all, someone might wonder why Sebastien was missing from the dorms after curfew, too.

The only upside was that Tanya seemed to be oblivious. Her door hadn't opened the entire night. Damien had wished desperately that he was advanced enough in the craft to do a general, exploratory divination on both Tanya and Sebastien. He wanted to check to see if Tanya was likely to do anything dangerous or suspicious, and make sure Sebastien was still okay. Unfortunately, his Divination class had barely progressed past basic deductive divinations like telling the suit of the next card in a deck.

Damien had dozed fitfully and woken when Sebastien finally arrived around five in the morning, before the sun had risen. He'd been agitated, ready to snap at Sebastien for any slight he could find, but he stopped when he got a good look at his recalcitrant friend.

Sebastien had seemed unharmed, but Damien noticed the clues he failed to hide. Sebastien's eyes were bloodshot and his face even paler than normal. There was grime in the creases of his neck and what looked like traces of dried blood around his fingernails.

"What happened?" Damien asked, keeping his voice low to avoid waking any of their dorm-mates. "Are you injured?"

Sebastien dug into the trunk at the base of his bed for a change of clothes. "I'm not."

"Then someone else was injured? Something happened. I can tell."

Sebastien sighed. "Some civilians were caught up in the fighting. A young boy got his legs blown off."

Damien had paled.

"I had to help him. He'll live, but, for him, the worst is probably yet to come. I doubt his family can afford healing powerful enough to regrow his legs. I...don't want to talk about it anymore, Damien."

Damien kept his mouth shut as Sebastien went to the bathrooms and took a long shower. He'd wanted to ask what Sebastien had gone out to do in the first place, and what the fighting had been about. But he couldn't. Damien felt useless. All he had done was keep an eye on Tanya.

Sebastien was beginning to warm to Damien, but still didn't seem to like him very much. First impressions were valuable, and he had botched theirs. Professor Lacer had been right to reprimand him. It was foolish to make enemies so blindly, even when they seemed inconsequential. Now all he could do was slowly try to change Sebastien's mind.

Sebastien had drawn his curtains closed and plopped onto his narrow bed with a sigh of exhaustion.

The other students began to stir soon after, and Damien had been quick to throw his most dangerous glare around when anyone made too much noise and threatened to prematurely disturb Sebastien's rest.

Sebastien had slept for only a couple of hours.

Damien tried to convince him to go to the infirmary and get a pass to skip his classes, but Sebastien refused. In the end, all he would accept was an extra strong cup of coffee, which Damien imbued with a little magic to boost its effects. It was a trick his mother had taught Titus, and which Titus had passed down to him, despite the stigma of "kitchen magic."

Damien was jarred from his thoughts as the carriage slowed to a stop at the manor gates. He paid the driver as Ana strode ahead. He knew he was walking into a similar situation now. He would be moral support at best, unable to actually do much, but he knew from experience that sometimes it helped to have someone just...*be there*. Ana had done the same for him more than a few times over the years.

At the front doors, Ana blew past the servant that tried to take her coat and scarf.

Damien smiled apologetically to the servant and agreed to the offer of tea and refreshments. "Send them up to the library in twenty minutes or so."

Ana's house was quite different from his own, filled with bright colors and fresh flowers even in the middle of winter. It was just the right temperature, and the air inside held not even a hint of smoke. Her mother took pride in things like that, redecorating frequently and inviting people over for parties and balls whenever she wanted to be particularly extravagant.

Damien didn't want to thrust himself awkwardly between the two sisters, so he went to the library to wait for a few minutes. He browsed the books idly, his thoughts returning to the blood he'd seen caked around Sebastien's finger-nails. He couldn't imagine exactly what it might be like to find a child missing their legs and on the edge of death, but he knew it must be horrible, and he knew that, were it him in that situation, the child would have died.

But Sebastien was special. It was obvious, in his sheer skill with magic, but there was more to him than met the eye. Even beyond the secrets that Damien knew.

His fingers trailed over the spine of a book, his eyes idly reading without comprehending. He paused, reading the title again. *A Genealogy of Notable Figures of the Thirty-Second Century, B.C.E.* The book itself was completely useless to him, but it sparked an idea and renewed the flames of curiosity that had never quite died down.

He looked around, noting the recurring theme among the other books. The Gervin library was full of records. A lot of genealogies, history, and plenty of not-so-subtle gossip about other people's ancestors.

When the tea tray was brought up, he took it from the servant and made his way to Nat's room. He knocked on the door, then opened it with a smile, keeping any anger or concern from his face. Nat needed to be cheered up, not reminded of what she already knew well enough. "I come bearing gifts for the lady Natalia, in the hopes that she might gift me a few minutes of her lovely company."

Nat's face was swollen and blotchy from tears, but she nodded happily enough.

Nat and Ana were both sitting on the canopied bed, so Damien sat the tea tray at the foot, kicked off his boots, and climbed in with them. There was plenty of space. He served the girls tea and scones with butter and jelly and made light conversation, telling stories from the University that had Natalia giggling until she fell over. She particularly loved stories about Sebastien, and Damien found he had more of them than he realized.

As she ate and drank, he foisted more snacks on her and embellished anecdotes of Sebastien's obliviousness, grumpiness, and his secret soft-hearted core.

"What Family is he from?" Nat asked.

"He's not one of the Crowns," Ana said, running her fingers idly through her little sister's hair.

"Really?" Nat looked down, frowning with disappointment.

"It's not like that matters," Damien said. "We might have the advantage of bloodlines and opportunity, but there's plenty of skill among the lower classes. And plenty of garbage among our own," he added darkly.

Nat shrunk into herself a little, like a turtle tucking its head, and Damien quickly changed the subject.

After the ordeal of her day, and now finally being filled with food and liquid, she started drooping into sleep soon afterward.

When she was down, Damien and Ana slipped out of the bed and walked to the balcony, carefully closing the door behind them.

"Is she okay?" he asked.

"It was an ordeal for her, but she'll be fine. For now." Ana clenched the balcony railing, staring out at the city. "This is why I didn't want to leave her. She's all by herself without me. She's only *eleven*."

"You managed when you were her age. She's going to be okay. And she's not alone. You're not gone, you're half an hour away, and you talk to her every day."

Ana's grip only tightened, and she rocked back and forth a bit.

Damien nudged her shoulder with his own. "Nat's stronger than you think. Don't underestimate her."

Ana's fingers tightened, but then she let out an almost inaudible sigh and released her grip. "You're right. I just worry about something like this happening again. She was trapped in that closet for *hours* with no way to call for help. I think Cousin Robbie paid off some of the servants to purposely 'not notice' her screams. Our manor isn't *that* big."

Damien ran his fingers over the simple wooden bracelet Sebastien had given him, which was hidden beneath his shirt. "You should get her an emergency alarm artifact. Something that will let you know when she's in danger, even if she can't write to you."

Ana brightened immediately. "Yes, that's a great idea! I don't know why I never considered it before. I suppose...you don't normally assume a child needs an emergency alarm within the safety of their own home."

Damien only hoped Nat never needed to use it for anything worse than being trapped in a closet.

"You can go back," Ana said. "She'll probably sleep for a couple of hours. I want to be here when she wakes so she isn't frightened."

"Actually...I was wondering if I might use the Family library?"

"Oh? Whatever for? We don't have many relevant study texts at a University level, and there aren't any of your cheap detective periodicals."

Damien refrained from commenting on her slight. "I was hoping to look up a list of notable families. I'm curious about the Siverlings."

Ana raised a knowing eyebrow. "Interested in Sebastien's history?"

Damien rubbed the back of his head sheepishly, then realized he was mussing his hair and smoothed it again. He looked away. "I'm just curious. Gossip and genealogy and all that is your Family's wheelhouse. I don't want to pull up confidential information or anything, and that's the only type of special information my Family would have access to. Sebastien never talks about his family, you notice?"

"I already looked into them."

Damien's head jerked around to look at her.

"Don't be so surprised, Damien. Of course I would. I sleep next to Thaddeus Lacer's mysterious new apprentice every night, and no one's ever heard of him before."

"What did you find?"

"It was difficult to find anything. At first I thought he was..." She paused, playing with the collar of her jacket. "Well, I thought he was a commoner from a family just wealthy enough to afford his tutors and admission. No one particularly special."

Damien knew that even if Sebastien was a commoner, he would still be exceptional. "At first? You changed your mind," he stated.

"Recent records about anyone with the name Siverling are impossible to find. At least without hiring an investigator, and I didn't think that was warranted. But I found a more distant mention of the name. The Siverlings were a maternal offshoot line of the ruling Family of Lenore from before the

Third Empire. Supposedly everyone in the line was executed by the Blood Emperor."

Damien's eyes widened. "Do you think it's the *same* Siverlings?"

She shrugged. "Who knows? But it's definitely a curious coincidence. Especially since he seems to have popped out of nowhere."

Inheritance via a maternal line was often contested, and allowed only if there were no more direct descendants through a paternal line, but if it wasn't a coincidence, and Sebastien really was descended from the king of Lenore before the Blood Empire... "What would that mean?"

"Probably not much. Maybe it would make him a more desirable match for some Crown Family daughter. With the right backers, he could make a claim to power...and probably face either open execution or a deniable assassination, depending on how much support he had."

Damien could imagine it, a family living in secrecy for generations for fear that the Blood Emperor or the Crowns would take offense to their very existence and finish them off. "How likely is it to be true?"

"The king's third daughter married into the Siverling family. Her husband was the king's Court Sorcerer. She was pregnant when she died, and all the records say the child died with her. I did a little digging... She would have been at least eight months pregnant. With the right spells and a good nursemaid, eight months is old enough to survive outside the womb, if the child was delivered early or cut out of his mother's stomach immediately after her death. But it's extremely unlikely, although I'll admit that it makes for a dramatic and intriguing story."

"Unlikely maybe, but it *is* possible. And if we think so...maybe someone else does, too. Could someone have found him living in Vale, in obscurity, and convinced him to take up his true family name again? Perhaps funded his way through the University, connected him to Professor Lacer?"

"*Possible*, yes. It's *probably* unconnected, though. He's been staying with a man named Oliver Dryden, an exiled noble from Osham. The man seems to have very little personal ambition. He's a philanthropist with a bleeding heart, according to my father, and wouldn't have any reason to take advantage of Sebastien. I honestly wouldn't consider the connection to those other Siverlings at all except..." Ana's lips quirked up at the corners. "Well. Sebastien has something of a way about him. Blood runs true, you know."

Damien remembered the first time he'd realized Sebastien was truly special. He'd made a joke about him being the second coming of Myrddin.

Damien wasn't crazy. He didn't think Sebastien was the literal incarnation of history's most powerful thaumaturge. But if Sebastien held the bloodline of both the king and a man who would have been one of the most powerful sorcerers in the country, it made some sense how he could be naturally talented enough to draw Thaddeus Lacer's eye.

"There *is* a simple solution to our curiosity," Ana said.

"There is?"

"We could just *ask* Sebastien."

Damien considered it for a second, but shook his head. "I don't think we should. He can tell us if he wants to. That kind of thing...there are probably a lot of good reasons to keep it secret. He never talks about his family or his childhood, and I feel like maybe that's deliberate."

Ana hesitated, but nodded. "I agree."

Damien's eyes narrowed. "There's something else. Do you know something?"

She rolled her eyes in exasperation. "Sebastien is our friend. I don't want to gossip about him."

"You love gossiping, you liar," he said, daring her to refute it with a pointed look. "Besides, it's just me. I'm not going to tell anyone else, and you know he's my friend, too. If there's something relevant, isn't it best that both of us know so we can have his back?"

"It's nothing you shouldn't have noticed yourself. And I don't want to speculate about what it means. Just..." She cleared her throat. "Okay. Sebastien is incredibly self-assured. To the point of arrogance. But that arrogance is universal. He doesn't treat even the most obvious sponsored commoner any different than he treats you or me. And the way he studies, it's *obsessive*. I thought at first he was just trying to live up to expectations or something, but sometimes it seems like he's worried all this is going to be taken away from him, and he's trying to cram as much knowledge as possible into his mind before the spell ends. And you're right, he never tells stories about himself. It's not just that he avoids talking about his family or his childhood. He's never mentioned a pet, or his favorite food, or even what he wants to do after graduating. And mostly...he has nightmares, Damien."

Damien nodded slowly, realizing everything she said was true. In fact, the only thing he knew about Sebastien's family was from an offhand comment about how free-casting ran in his family, too. He, of course, knew that Sebastien's dreams had something to do with the secrets he kept. Sebastien would have taken the same oath as Damien, while looking at the stars. He, too, wanted freedom and enlightenment, whatever that meant *exactly*. Sebastien had spoken about that boy with the missing legs a little too matter-of-factly.

But Damien had never given much thought to the fact that Sebastien had trouble sleeping. He knew Sebastien had nightmares, and probably insomnia too. It was just one of those things about Sebastien, like him being grumpy in the mornings, and how much he loved good coffee but never bought any of his own, and how he ignored the increasingly frequent flirtatious looks from the female students like he didn't even notice them.

"Yes, he does..." Damien said encouragingly, waiting for Ana to continue.

"He has nightmares *every night*. That's why he's always practicing in the wee hours and seems exhausted in the morning. I think something bad happened to him. Something he doesn't want to talk about. So even if he is one of *those* Siverlings, it doesn't mean his life before this is anything he wants to remember. And maybe that's why he studies like he does. Being here is a way out for him. And if it is...I don't want to take that away from him by making him talk about it."

The thought that something or *someone* had actually *caused* Sebastien's nightmares had Damien's heart beating a little too hard, his cheeks flushing even brighter against the cold. When Sebastien had said, "The world can be darker than you imagine," there had been a shadow in his eyes, hidden thoughts swimming behind their placid surface. It seemed wrong that someone like Sebastien, who was strong and smart and who *cared* so much, could, in other circumstances, be the victim of something that scarred him internally so much that he couldn't escape the memories even in sleep.

"Sebastien isn't a victim."

Damien only realized he'd said the last part aloud when Ana nodded. "Exactly," she said. "It's not how he thinks of himself, and not how he would want anyone else to think of him. So let's not make him tell stories he would rather leave behind just for the pleasure of being in on a secret. Whether his last name has any significance...well, it doesn't really change who Sebastien is, right?"

She was right, of course. Damien told her so.

She laughed. "Damien, haven't you learned by now? I'm always right."

He smirked. "Except when you disagree with Sebastien."

They laughed, and didn't talk of it again.

45

THINGS GO WRONG

NEWTON
Month 1, Day 20, Wednesday 9:00 p.m.

NEWTON HAD CONSIDERED TURNING Tanya down when she asked him to accompany her to a secret meeting of criminal thaumaturges. He had no desire to be involved in the dangerous game Sebastien and his Crown Family friend were playing with the University, and he dreaded anyone finding out his part in it. Accompanying Tanya with a battle wand seemed like the stupidest decision a normal person—someone who just wanted to get their Journeyman certification and move on—could make, a trap door that would dump him into this morass with no way to escape.

In the end, though, when Tanya knocked on his door shortly after curfew, the promise of a solution to his other problems was too tempting to pass up. He needed the coin. His family was depending on him.

Their entire household: his parents, his Grams, and even his sisters, had been saving since he was young to put him through the University. When they talked about their hopes and dreams, it always revolved around his future, and the knowledge that once he was established, he would help them as they once helped him. When he'd gone to check on them after the fighting and the fire, his Ma had broken down crying.

Not about the half-burnt house, or Pa's failing lungs, or the loss of all the worldly belongings she hadn't been able to carry in her arms, but because Newton would no longer be able to become a Journeyman. Two hundred gold a term—the minimum to take four classes—would be beyond their family's means now. If he had to take more than one term off, he would have to pay the three hundred gold admission fee again, too.

Newton's father had been fairly well-paid for a commoner, making about three hundred gold a year. That was much better than their neighbor Mr. Carlton, who worked unskilled labor wherever he could find it. With that, Mr. Carlton made about one hundred thirty gold a year, which was not enough to support a family on alone. This was why it was common for everyone from grandparents to children to live together, each contributing what they could to the family's livelihood. Even doing that, some families still barely squeaked by when it came time to pay taxes.

An Apprentice-certified sorcerer could make four hundred eighty gold a year, if they found a good Master willing to let them work for their business. Legally, Apprentices weren't able to sell magical items or services to others under their own banner.

Newton had the basic certification, but he hadn't received any good work offers the term before. He hadn't particularly been looking, because he had assumed he would be able to get his Journeyman certification at least, and maybe even the extra two terms for a specialized Journeyman. A good Apprentice-level position would be enough to support his family on, and maybe, in ten years or so, he could save enough to return to the University for further certifications. The best jobs in Gilbratha were almost always given to those who put on an impressive show in the end of term exhibitions. If he could just make it until then...

He sighed, shaking his head at his own foolishness. It wouldn't do to be too greedy. Even if he needed to drop out right away, mid-term, he should still be able to find something that paid well enough to keep his family fed and housed. Sometimes a person needed to make sacrifices.

Newton had wanted to cry, too, when he saw the tears streaking his Ma's soot-stained skin and the wrapped burns on her arms. He'd controlled himself because he knew that would only make her feel worse.

His family's dreams for him weren't rooted only in what they hoped to get back from him once he had power and riches. It might be easier if that were the case. No, they all wanted a better life for him than what they could hope for themselves. And they were willing to sacrifice for it.

The pressure to succeed became crushing at times.

So now he was walking through the dark streets with Tanya. The air had been clear up atop the white cliffs, but down in Gilbratha proper, thick fog had rolled in, giving the city an eerie, muffled quality.

Tanya had given him a battle wand charged with stunning spells—which was the most expensive item beside his Conduit that he'd ever held, and which was illegal for him to have. His hand stayed wrapped around it within his jacket pocket. His eyes felt gritty and sore with lack of sleep, and the muscles in his neck hurt because he kept clenching his jaw without realizing it. He'd been having to use the calming spell his Grams taught him to get even a semblance of rest over the last few days, but it wasn't enough.

Tanya was wearing a mask, and they both wore hoods deep enough to keep their faces in shadow even when they passed the occasional streetlight, but he could tell from the way her head moved constantly that she was watching for danger, or perhaps pursuers.

When they reached their destination, a nondescript building with a slit in the door that slid open when she gave a special knock, he felt relieved for about half a second. She gave a strange, disturbing passphrase, and everything seemed to be going fine.

Then Tanya told the man behind the door that she'd brought a new prospective member.

He looked at Newton, then waved them in. He pointed them down the hallway, and they were met quickly by another masked man who looked at Tanya and said, "We prefer to be notified of new applicants at the prior meeting," with censure in his tone.

Newton's hand was sweaty around the battle wand. He carefully released his grip and removed his hand from his jacket pocket, wiping his palm on the side of his pant leg surreptitiously. Tanya had assured him that the meeting itself was regulated by the administrators, and thus safe enough, and Newton didn't want to come off as a threat, especially if he wasn't technically supposed to be here.

Tanya didn't reply.

The man turned to Newton instead. "You will be interviewed by one of our prognos. If your answers are acceptable, you will be allowed to join the meeting."

Newton nodded jerkily.

"At least you got here early," the man muttered, opening a door to reveal a person sitting at a desk. A large spell array was drawn over the floor beneath them.

The person behind the desk turned their head toward Newton, and he almost jumped when he met the gaze of their single, bright eye. He shuddered, hoping the response wasn't obvious.

The man tried to send Tanya off to the meeting room, but she refused to leave. "I'll stay with him," she insisted.

"You cannot," the person at the desk said, her voice marking her as a woman. "The interview must be conducted without outside influence."

Tanya hesitated like she wanted to argue, but finally stepped back and let the man close the door, shutting Newton in with the two masked strangers.

The man activated the spell, a ward against untruth, and Newton felt it take hold. It didn't muffle his thoughts, exactly, but he still felt the urge to shake his head, like water was stuck in his ears.

The prognos woman jangled a pouch of bones while asking him a series of questions. She poured them onto the table after each question to read whatever truth she'd divined.

He answered truthfully, and was glad that Sebastien had the forethought to assure him that he wouldn't be giving information to non-members, and that he wasn't affiliated with anyone who wished the group harm. Newton was a little suspicious of Sebastien's claim that he and Westbay, and thus Newton himself, weren't affiliated with the coppers or law enforcement, but apparently not so suspicious that the prognos thought he was lying.

He exited the room about fifteen minutes later, now masked like everyone else, to find Tanya waiting in the hallway.

"Okay?" she asked.

"Okay," he said, nodding.

She turned and walked back the way they'd come, and Newton followed, listening as she explained the meeting etiquette in a low voice. "Keep an ear open for any rumors about the Raven Queen," she murmured to him as they entered the room where a large group was already waiting, many of the masked members talking amongst themselves.

Wearing a mask himself made Newton feel slightly better, but he remained on edge. How could he not, surrounded by potentially hostile strangers, in a group that would all get sent to Harrow Hill if the coppers found out about them?

Most of them were talking about the gang fighting that had swept through the city earlier that week.

"The shop my nephew works at had all the windows blown out," one man said. "And then the looters made off with quite a bit of the inventory before the coppers got around to clearing the area."

"Lost inventory and broken windows," another replied with a sarcastic scoff. "Oh, the horror. The Stewards of Intention sanctuary near my house is full of the injured and newly homeless. Some of us thaumaturges might ride out this instability none the worse, but many who were struggling are going to slide into poverty with no way to recover. Crime is up because desperation is up, and that will not go away any time soon."

A woman looked between the two men. "I heard the Stags offer jobs to people in their territory, and loans to get healing, and their enforcers handle crimes the coppers don't care about. Perhaps recovery will be quicker than you think."

The first man crossed his arms over his chest. "Who do you think started all this? It was the *Stags* that attacked the Morrows! They're not interested in helping, they just want territory and power, just like all the other thugs!"

Another man stepped up behind the woman. "Well, *I* heard the Stags and Nightmare Pack attacked with non-lethal measures. They weren't even trying to kill any of the Morrows, just capture them. It was the Morrows who caused the real damage. They didn't care about killing bystanders or starting fires, which shouldn't be a surprise to anyone who actually lived in their territory. I've lost count of the number of young women who come to my clinic to deal with the *consequences* when a Morrow boy thinks he can take what he wants because of a red M on his shirt." His sneer of disgust was audible in his voice.

A squat woman who'd been standing a few feet away spun to face the arguing group. "And who told you this story about these *saints* taking over Morrow territory? Live capture? That's the most ridiculous thing I've ever heard. Sounds to me more like someone is savvy to the benefit of a positive public opinion. A lot easier to hold a territory where everyone's so naive they're actually *happy* to have you initiate war in the streets so you can take over running the brothels and the drugs and the fighting rings. 'Meet the new boss! Nothing like the old boss. No, really, *we promise!*'"

Yet another person joined in. "I've actually lived in Verdant Stag territory. Whatever you want to say about them attacking and causing all this, I can tell you first hand that they do what they say. I'm not claiming the leader is some bleeding-heart altruist, but they really do have enforcers to protect the people. There's an alarm system set up on the edge of every street corner. If there's a crime, or a fire, or you've been trampled by a horse, you can pull the Verdant Stag flag and a team will come to help you. And they have a little apothecary set up in the back of their headquarters with the cheapest prices I've ever seen. They can't be making a profit off that."

A woman shrugged languidly. "Some gang is always going to be in charge. New boss, old boss, who cares? Someone smart will make good use of the opportunities offered by this volatile situation and get themselves into an advantageous position with the Verdant Stag or the Nightmare Pack. And if the Verdant Stags are soft-hearted enough to make that easy? Even better."

That sparked a new round of argument, but the arbiter banged his wooden gavel until the room quieted, then instructed everyone to sit down and get to business.

If not for the violence the Verdant Stag caused, Newton might have actually been favorably disposed toward them. His father had been to see one of their healers when they couldn't afford one in Morrow territory, and he had no love for the Morrows. His family had only avoided paying "protection" to them due to his Grams and her not-so-secret skills as a hedge witch. That, and her stubborn recklessness in standing up to the gang.

One of them had tried to beat and mug his mother on her way home from the market once, and would have succeeded if not for a sharp-eyed, kind copper who ended up escorting her all the way home.

His father had taken one look at her black eye and flipped over the kitchen table in rage.

The Morrows went after anyone affluent enough to afford their predation, and plenty of those who couldn't, too. Sometimes, they demanded worse than a bit of coin.

Newton had to dismiss these thoughts as the meeting began. Masked thaumaturges were offering items and information in exchange for coin or trade in other items and information. Newton pushed back his nervousness and spoke up, offering casting information on the handful of spells he had prepared.

Tanya didn't do the same, perhaps because she wasn't allowed by her secret employers.

Newton only took the four basic classes, so he had no specialized spell-casting formulas to provide, and only a couple of the members were interested in what he was offering. Newton had to look to Tanya for a small nod to be sure he was haggling for a fair price, and in the end got an agreement for twelve gold crowns in exchange for a specialized mending spell and an extremely simple heat-containing artifact.

He settled back into his chair with relief as others offered their own goods and services, mentally calculating his earnings. Adding what Sebastien and Tanya would both pay him for being here, he could make fifteen gold in a single night. His job as a student liaison for the University made him a little over forty gold every term, and the accompanying contribution points were worth another five or six. If he could do this just a few more times, along with the money he made from tutoring, he would be able to pay for his own tuition. If he brought spells the other members would be more interested in, it could be even sooner. He had earned enough money in a single night to keep his family fed for an entire month.

It was suddenly viscerally easy to understand why people fell into a life of crime.

Newton jerked himself from his dazed state, returning his attention to the meeting. The fatigue and frequent rushes of anxiety were getting to him. He pushed himself to be more attentive so that he could gauge what magic information would be most valuable. Eventually, the meeting transitioned from offers to requests.

When a hooded woman spoke, requesting healing components, artifacts, or concoctions, Tanya stiffened beside him, her head swiveling to stare at the speaker.

Newton followed her gaze, wondering what was so interesting about the other woman. She was tall, and she sat with supremely confident posture, but her request seemed fairly innocuous. When she turned her head, Newton caught a glimpse of what might have been a red feather woven into her hair, which seemed a rather over-the-top fashion accessory, but she was masked like all the others. Perhaps Tanya had recognized her voice, or there was some important clue in the supplies she was requesting that Newton hadn't picked up on.

Tanya settled back into her seat, shaking her head silently when Newton sent her a questioning look, but she seemed even more on edge than she had been, and he found his hand creeping back to the pocket with the borrowed battle wand tucked inside. Not that he wanted to *use* it. The thought made him shudder. No, it just felt reassuring to know there was an incapacitating spell within his grasp.

Tanya only grew tenser, until, with an exhalation that sounded as if she'd been holding it in since the meeting had started, she loudly requested any information on where the Morrows were being held and what was being done to them.

Newton's gaze slid toward her with an inexorable sinking feeling. It shouldn't have surprised him, really. Obviously, he'd known she was involved in illegal doings, and Sebastien had warned him that those doings included the deaths of innocents. But he hadn't known she was working with the Morrows. And she must be, for what other reason would she be asking about this? Did that mean someone higher up at the University was also working with the Morrows? But for what?

"I assume they have been executed," one member offered.

"No," a man said, shaking his head. "They're imprisoned. I know a little about the conditions the Stags are offering for their release. Three gold for a private conversation about it," he offered.

A woman scoffed. "*Please.* That is not proprietary information. The Stags have been more than open about it with anyone who asks. The Morrows are being held somewhere secret, and they say Lord Stag is going to hold court and put them on trial for their crimes against the citizens. And I heard a rumor that they'll be either ransomed or executed, depending on the severity of their crimes and their status within the gang."

The man crossed his arms and sent the woman a glare that was obvious even through his mask.

Tanya looked around, her fists clenched at her sides, mostly hidden under the folds of her cloak. "Does anyone have information on where they are being held? Or what"—she cleared her throat—"what the security measures are?"

A few members shared glances.

Newton's palms were sweaty again. What reason could anyone have for asking that unless they were interested in breaking the Morrows free? That just seemed like it would cause even more mayhem, destruction, and bloodshed.

After a few seconds of hesitation, a man raised his hand. "I've an idea where they are. No proof, but I'm not sure what else they could be doing in that location. I've noted a few interesting comings and goings, and someone was hired to ward the place beforehand. The information'll cost you."

"Gold? Beast cores?" Tanya offered.

The man rubbed his hands together in his lap with as much awkwardness as avarice. "Umm, gold. Two hundred crowns. It's fine if you supplement with beast cores if you don't have enough."

Tanya's scowl was audible in her voice, but, to Newton's surprise, she didn't haggle. "Fine."

It was no wonder that she'd wanted backup, carrying that much wealth on her person. Bank cheques could be used for large transactions if you were wealthy enough to afford an account. His family had opened one to save the funds for his tuition in a place that couldn't be stolen by one of their neighbors, but obviously you wouldn't want to pay for anything illegal with a cheque, in case the paper trail led the coppers right to you.

The meeting moved on, but the hooded woman who'd asked for healing supplies earlier stared at Tanya a little longer than the others.

When the meeting ended, Tanya mingled with the crowd, her back never turning to the woman, while Newton went into a small side room to exchange spell information for gold under the watchful eye of an administrator. When he was finished, Tanya completed her own transaction with the man, and then whispered in the ear of an administrator, who nodded at her.

She and Newton were sent off soon afterward. Tanya walked quickly, turning corners at random for a few minutes before she calmed. "Keep an eye out for tails," she murmured to him.

"Tails? You mean, someone following us?" He at least had the foresight not to look around wildly. Even if he had, the fog was becoming so thick that he doubted he'd be able to see anyone more than a hundred meters away. He was a little nearsighted, and glasses were expensive.

She nodded. "I know what they're doing, and they know I know. That woman at the meeting, the one that asked for the healing supplies? She works for the Verdant Stag, I think. Her purchases are a little too coincidental."

"And you work for the Morrows," Newton muttered.

"Not exactly." Tanya hesitated, but shook her head. "Affiliated, at best. But the Verdant Stag isn't going to care about technicalities. The Raven Queen definitely won't."

"The Raven Queen?" Newton asked through numb lips. "Is that why you wanted me to listen for people talking about her?"

"I don't know what her agenda is, but I think maybe the Morrows offended her. I mean, why else would the Nightmare Pack suddenly team up with the Stags to go after the Morrows? I've heard rumors about her kind. Relentlessly vengeful."

Something about the way Tanya was walking, the lines of stress around her eyes, and how her fingers clenched around her own wand suddenly gave Newton a sense of foreboding. Tanya was frightened, maybe even terrified, and it was quickly rubbing off on him. "Her kind? Do you mean a blood sorcerer, or is the Raven Queen some other species?" He couldn't help but look around for something hiding in the shadows.

"Both, maybe. Who knows which of the rumors are true. If the Morrows were smart, they would have found a way to mollify..." She trailed off, and just when Newton was about to ask, "What?" she grabbed his hand and yanked him down a narrow side street.

She slipped into a bouncing half-run, and he followed, looking behind them. "A tail?" he asked.

"Maybe. Someone in a hood, might have been from the meeting. Following a couple blocks back."

They slowed to a walk again once they reached the next street, but doubled back the way they'd come rather than continuing toward the University. Tanya was still on edge by the time they'd made a loop, but as far as Newton could tell, no one was following them.

Tanya stopped them in the shadow of a spacious four-way intersection where one of the streetlamps had gone out, either having run out of power or had its light crystal stolen. They waited for a few minutes, suspiciously watching every hint of movement within the thick blanket of fog choking the streets.

Newton hoped Tanya was being excessively paranoid, but the thought that maybe she wasn't left him a little light-headed. He slid a hand under his mask to rub his dry, tired eyes. If they were being tailed, wouldn't it be better to keep moving? He removed his hand and adjusted his mask so he could see out of the eye holes again, and almost screamed when Tanya darted a hand out and grabbed his arm in a bruising grip.

With one finger held up over her mask where her lips would be, she leaned out from the corner and pointed to a hooded figure one block to the west of them. Tanya pulled back, shielding them behind the corner of the building they stood next to. "They realized we noticed them," she said, her voice almost inaudible. "They're following along beside us, one street over."

"Are you sure it's the same person?"

"Only one way to find out. Get your wand ready."

"What?"

"We'll close in like a pincer. You from the north, me from the south. I can question them, find out what they know, what they want from me. I'm not going to let myself end up like the others."

"No, Tanya," Newton said, his horror a distant thing that made his lips slow. "Shouldn't we run?"

"That will never work. We have to flip the tables. Don't worry, it's two against one." She raised her hand to forestall further argument. "And I'll call for reinforcements. Not all the Morrows were captured, and at least some of them will still be active and responsive to a flare beacon. This is what I hired you for, Newton. You're already here, and you can't back out now. We'll take that person by surprise."

And so, pulling the battle wand out of his pocket for the first time since she'd given it to him, Newton made sure the handle was twisted into the active position and would send out a stunning spell with a simple tug of his forefinger on the embedded lever.

Trying to keep himself from hyperventilating, he jogged north and prepared to cut around and block their possible pursuer. He wondered where exactly his life had gone wrong to lead him to this.

46

THINGS GET WORSE

SIOBHAN
Month 1, Day 20, Wednesday 11:00 p.m.

SIOBHAN HELD BACK a growl of aggravation when she realized she'd lost track of Tanya and Newton for the third time that night. *'Curse you for being so paranoid, Tanya.'*

The meeting had started late, and now it was almost midnight. It was cold, the streets were slippery with ice and so foggy she had a hard time keeping sight of them from a block away. She just wanted to drop off the supplies she'd purchased and return to her bed, but she was stuck doing her due diligence in case Tanya and Newton stopped somewhere or talked to someone interesting. Even if she hadn't cared about what she might learn, she'd promised Newton that he would have backup. They had left the meeting before her, and she'd had to use the compass divination spell to find them.

Then, they'd suddenly escaped her sight again, despite how innocuously far back from them she'd been walking, almost invisible with all the fog. Assuming that Tanya was jumpy because of what had happened to the Morrows, Siobhan decided it would be less conspicuous if she were to follow them back to the University from an adjacent street, rather than trailing directly behind them.

But apparently they'd veered off again.

Stopping at the darkest point between two streetlamps, she set down the small box of healing potions she'd bought, crouching to cast the compass

386 | A BINDING OF BLOOD

tracking spell on the disk connected to the one in Tanya's boot, using one of her paper utility spell arrays. In the alley next to her, the red M of the Morrows had been painted over by the glowing yellow eyes on black background of the Nightmare Pack, Oliver's new allies. *'I need an artifact that will scry me on demand and activate the spillover properties of my divination-diverting ward.'* She had an agreement with Katerin to scry one of her linked bracelets if she ever encountered an emergency, but while hasslesome, this situation didn't quite count. An artifact would allow her to turn the effect on and off at will, even several times in a single hour. She resolved to look for a more convenient solution as soon as she had the opportunity.

The burnt stick swung around, pointing toward Siobhan, and for a second, she was confused. She realized what it meant too late as Tanya's voice came from behind her.

"Raise your hands and stand up slowly. I have a wand pointed at your back, so don't try anything funny."

Her mind racing furiously, jarred out of the fatigue and frustration that had apparently been clouding her judgment, Siobhan activated the spark-shooting array drawn in the corner of the page where she'd added a daub of wax to help accelerate the fire. The seaweed paper was fire resistant, not immune, and it immediately caught on fire, destroying the evidence of her spellcasting.

By the time Tanya realized what she was doing and yelled, "Stop!" it was too late.

Siobhan then lifted her hands and stood as Tanya had instructed.

In front of Siobhan, a hooded man walked up with a wand in his outstretched hand. It had to be Newton. They had closed in on her from both front and back. *'Does he realize I'm his promised backup?'* There was no way to let him know, if he didn't.

She turned her head enough to see the wand pointed at her from behind.

"Step away from the wall, into the street," Tanya ordered.

Siobhan obeyed, her hood still up and her mask covering her face. *'What will I do if they find out who I am? Would they turn me in to the coppers?'*

"Don't move." Tanya jerked her head toward the supplies on the ground. "Check what they were doing there."

Newton moved to the sidewalk, looking quickly through the box, then picking up the bone disk and saving the stick from burning up along with the paper. "Um, those are the things she bought, and this is...bone."

Tanya urged Siobhan to move closer to the nearest streetlamp.

Newton followed, using its light to examine the disk. "I think it was a divination spell."

"Were you *tracking* us?" Tanya demanded.

'Neither Newton nor Tanya have any idea who I really am. I can still find a way out of this.' Siobhan remained silent.

"Guard her," Tanya said.

Siobhan stood still, watching the slightly trembling tip of Newton's wand as Tanya tinkered with something behind her.

'I hope that's not shackles.'

A flare went off with a sharp pop and a shriek. Siobhan flinched as the red light shot into the sky, illuminating the blanket of fog with a diffused penumbra as it burst above them.

'A flare beacon. There's no way that was anything other than a call for backup. But who was she signaling?' It was unlikely to be the coppers, based on the previous lack of cooperation between the University and the Crowns, not to mention the fact that they'd just come from making illegal trades with questionable thaumaturges. The University might have someone available and on call to respond to emergencies, or it could be someone from the Morrows or another criminal organization that had escaped Oliver's roundup. She wasn't sure which would be worse.

"You have no chance of getting away," Tanya announced, a hint of nervousness leaking through what she probably meant to be an imperious tone. "Your best bet is to talk. Who are you? Why were you following us? Are you working for the Verdant Stag, or the Nightmare Pack?"

'I could refuse to speak, but that will just encourage her to use violence, and only postpones the inevitable when whoever she called arrives. I need some way to shift the paradigm here. Bribes? Threats?' Siobhan considered breaking the bracelet that was connected to Oliver's. She could break it to let him know that something had gone wrong, but it would take some time to find her and then come help her, and Tanya or Newton might hit her with whatever spell was in those wands if she made such a suspicious movement. No one knew where she was, or what she was doing. If she disappeared tonight, it might be for good.

She had her paper spell arrays, a few useful potions, and her stunning-spell battle wand, but all of those were in her bag, and would take time to retrieve and use. She would need a distraction or a barrier between herself and them to make those options feasible.

She could turn back into Sebastien and reveal herself, but that might not necessarily mollify Tanya, and it would completely wreck the delineation between her two identities.

It was too late to pretend to be Silvia, or any other random civilian. She was wearing her original body, which Tanya had definitely seen the wanted posters for, so as soon as they took off her mask and hood she would be revealed. The only real option was to rely on the exaggerated reputation of the Raven Queen and hope that she could threaten or coerce them into letting her go.

The silence had stretched out, and Tanya barked, "Talk!" The tip of her wand pressed between Siobhan's shoulder blades threateningly.

"It is not you I want, Tanya Canelo," Siobhan said, her attempt at a dry, calm tone ruined by the rough crack of tension that broke her voice. She swallowed, trying to wet her dry throat.

Tanya drew in a sharp breath. "How do you know my name?"

Siobhan ignored the question. "You have chosen your alliances poorly."

Newton's wand dipped briefly, his free hand clenching and unclenching at his side.

Siobhan hadn't meant to implicate him, and hoped that wasn't the way Tanya would interpret the words. "They use you for their own ends. They ignore your fear and your attempts to reason with them. When you are alone and in need, will they return your loyalty? Or will you be tossed aside and silenced, an inconvenient liability?"

"What do you know of my alliances?" Tanya demanded, angry but with shallow confidence.

Siobhan turned slowly to face Tanya, her hands still up in the air. "I have seen your shadow pace at night as sleep evades you, Tanya Canelo." It was even true, though she declined to mention that the shadow was visible under the crack at the bottom of Tanya's dorm room door. "You still have a chance to walk away tonight, to return to your bed and your troubled dreams without true harm."

Tanya's knuckles were white around the base of the battle wand. "You're bluffing. New—" She cut off before completing Newton's name. "Check her bag and her pockets."

Newton shuffled closer, shrinking back for a moment when Siobhan turned her head to look at him. "Sorry," he muttered as he took the strap of her bag and slipped it off her shoulders.

Siobhan was grateful that she'd had the foresight to leave anything that might connect her to Sebastien back in the room at the Silk Door. Newton *might* be sharp enough to have recognized her school satchel. This bag, smaller and less conveniently filled with partitions, held components, paper spell arrays, and the wand in a secret pocket along the bottom, which she had added with some clever application of a mending spell. That was all. Still, best not to let him look in it at all. "Newton Moore. Your family would miss you. Your Grams taught you better than this. Make a wiser choice."

He released the strap, dropping the bag like it was a hot coal, stumbling back from her. "How did—how did you—"

"*Who are you?*" Tanya demanded again.

"You already know the answer to that question, Tanya," Siobhan murmured. "Or at least, you know the name they call me."

"What does she mean? *What does she mean*, Tanya?" Newton demanded tightly.

She didn't answer him. "Take the bag out of her reach at least, Newton."

Gingerly, looking at Siobhan as if waiting for her to snap and attack, he did so, sliding the strap over his arm but leaning away from the bag as if he was afraid it would blow up.

The best way to make a sorcerer harmless was to remove access to their Conduit. They hadn't managed that, as her black sapphire was tucked inside her boot, but the second best way was to remove access to their supplies.

"You're bluffing," Tanya said to Siobhan, lifting her chin challengingly.

'Of course I am, you idiot woman,' Siobhan thought. 'Just let me go before it's too late.' She lowered her hands slowly.

"Hands up!" Newton yelled.

"It is okay, child," she said to him, turning her head far enough toward him that she might be able to dodge if he tried to shoot her out of nervousness. "I mean you no harm. You have not made the same poor choices as this one." When she was assured that he wasn't about to panic, Siobhan returned her shadow-concealed gaze to Tanya. "You've been asking questions about me on behalf of your masters. Reckless."

"Take off your mask and hood," Tanya said. "If you're the Raven Queen, prove it."

"The Raven Queen?" Newton whispered.

Siobhan tilted her head to the side. "There really is no need for masks, I suppose." Everyone already knew what Siobhan looked like, after all. Her likeness had been plastered on wanted posters across the city. "I will remove mine if you do the same. I know what you look like already, so there is no need to hide." It would place her at a disadvantage to be the only one with readable facial expressions. Time was running out before whatever backup Tanya had called arrived, and making her and Newton feel a little more vulnerable might help facilitate her escape.

Her two captors shared a look, and Siobhan was careful to remain still so as not to startle them. Finally, Tanya nodded.

They each removed their concealment, moving slowly. Standing within the circle of light from the streetlamp, which quickly gave way to the darkness of the fog, it seemed like they were the only three in the world.

Tanya and Newton's eyes were drawn to the feathers extending from Siobhan's hair first, and then roved over her face.

She felt exposed, almost naked in her vulnerability. Some part of her expected the coppers to jump out from behind a corner and arrest her on the spot.

She stayed very still, her head cocked a little to the side. 'I've used the stick. Now, to try the carrot.' She met Tanya's gaze, which was a little watery from either fear or the cold. "It is not too late to make a different choice."

"What do you want from me?" Tanya whispered.

"Tonight? Simply that we go our separate ways, and neither of you are harmed."

"You were the one following us!"

"Coincidence. If I wanted to *harm* you, I could have done so long before tonight. But time is running out. They will be here soon." She could hear the faint echoes of words and the running footsteps of a group approaching through the fog. "There are other options, a different path to what you need. For both of you," she added, sparing a glance for Newton, who looked like he might be sick, his lips pale and trembling and his eyes bloodshot. "You may request a boon from me and mine in exchange for your services. I can be quite generous with those who please me."

Tanya licked her lips. "And the Morrows?"

Siobhan waved her hand in a falsely nonchalant motion. "It is the end for them." The muffled echoes of footsteps were drawing closer.

"What did they do to offend you? I never—I was—"

Whatever Tanya was going to say, it was too late, and she cut off as a motley group of a half-dozen men rounded the corner. Their leader pointed at the three of them. They wore strips of red cloth tied around their upper arms, a sign of the Morrows.

Siobhan slipped her hood back up quickly to conceal her features. She was somewhat surprised that they were either stupid or bold enough to openly wear the symbols of a deposed gang. 'Some of them must have slipped through the cracks. They are lower-level members, most likely. Perhaps there is still room for me to escape. Perhaps a bribe?'

The man in the lead glared at all three of them. "Who called?"

"I did," Tanya said with a grimace, still staring at Siobhan.

Newton lowered his wand and hunched his shoulders, shrinking back to the side of the nearest building, near where he'd set Siobhan's bag at the edge of the light.

The man looked Tanya up and down, too slowly to be polite. "You a Morrow? I don't see the M."

Tanya huffed. "I'm affiliated. How else do you think I got the flare beacon artifact?"

"Could a' stolen it. Could be a trap," one of the others offered.

This led to a general muttering and shifting, and a couple members lifted battle wands of their own toward the trio.

"I recognize her," a smaller man piped up from the back of the group. "Saw her visitin' the boss a couple times at the Bitter Phoenix."

The leader puffed up his chest, glaring down at Tanya. "Well, the boss ain't around no more. Why you callin' for help? This one givin' you trouble?" He peered suspiciously at Siobhan. "She one of the Nightmare Pack?"

Tanya's eyes flicked from the man to Siobhan and back, unsure.

He seemed to pick up on this, because after a second of silence, he reached out and grabbed Tanya's arm. "Take their wands," he ordered.

Tanya tried to jerk back from him, but his grip was strong. Though she raised her wand, she hesitated, looking between the trigger-happy Morrows and Siobhan. Her hesitation cost her.

Her wand was wrenched from her grip by one of the Morrows.

Newton gave his up willingly enough, but still received a rough shove as thanks.

"We're supposed to be allies!" Tanya growled.

The leader, who Siobhan mentally dubbed Chief, grinned humorlessly at Tanya, raising the wand he'd taken from her to point at Siobhan, who was nominally unarmed. "That agreement was with the old boss. You and I will need to make a new deal." He jerked his head. "Let's move. I don't want to stick around for anyone else that flare beacon might have attracted. The coppers are patrolling all night lately, and those Nightmare Pack bastards go rabid at the sight of us."

Wands trained on their three captives, the Morrows picked up the box of potions with pleasant surprise, then took them a few blocks away. Seemingly by random, Chief picked out a brick, three-story building with boarded-up shop windows across the ground level and dark apartment windows above on the third. The door was locked, but they broke it open with some difficulty and brute force, ripping the inner lock free from its moorings.

The inside of the shop, which took up and area the height of the first two floors, was filled with high-end wooden furniture, some completed and some halfway through assembly. It was a woodworking shop. As the Morrows searched for a light-crystal lamp and turned it on, Siobhan's eyes flicked around.

There were two other doors besides the one they'd just broken through: one to the side that looked like it might lead to a storage closet, and another at the back, at the top of a short series of steps. Her eyes flicked to the high ceiling, listening for movement that would signify people waking up in the rooms above. It would be simplest if the building was empty. The variable of civilians could throw a wrench in even the best escape plans.

The Morrow guarding her motioned for Siobhan to back up toward the side of the room. She did so until her legs bumped against a heavy table. "Keep your hands up," he warned.

"So what can you offer me, girl?" Chief asked Tanya. "Any reason I shouldn't just hold you and these other two for ransom?"

Newton let out a small, distressed sound.

The Morrow holding him gave a disgusted grunt and dropped his arm. "Don't try anything stupid," he warned, turning away to light another of the lamps on display, which he took to the counter and used to start rifling around, probably hoping to find any poorly secured coin. He grabbed random small items that caught his interest and shoved them in his pockets.

Siobhan dubbed him Sticky Fingers.

Newton backed up to the front wall, bracing against it and dropping Siobhan's bag beside him. She hadn't even noticed him pick it up. He placed his hands together, thumbs to forefingers, and began the hum for his calming spell, ignoring the disgruntled surprise of a couple of their captors.

"What is he doing?" a fat man with unfortunately saggy jowls demanded, pointing his wand at Newton. Siobhan named him Bulldog.

Tanya motioned for them to calm down with her raised hands. "It helps him keep from panicking. He's not accustomed to situations like this." She lifted her chin, glaring at the leader. "So, you're going to hold us for ransom? Ransom by *who*? Your bosses are all locked up, and if you're hoping for someone to pay you, they'll need to be free first."

Chief coughed—a gruff, blustering sound. "Perhaps I just have to kill you three, strip you naked, and throw you in the nearest canal, then. If you can't offer me anything..." He trailed off threateningly.

Newton's hums grew a little louder, as if he were trying to drown out their voices.

A muscle in Tanya's jaw jumped as she ground her teeth. "I'm working to free Lord Morrow. I'm sure he'll be in a generous mood if he knows you were helpful in doing so."

"Ehh...that's not exactly what I'm wanting to hear, girl. Word on the street is, Lord Morrow is dead. As for the rest of them...I kinda prefer my sudden rise in station now that they're gone. Well, if you know where Lord Morrow stashed the Morrow operation funds, I might be interested in that."

Despite the turn toward threats of violence, Siobhan was encouraged by this development. She didn't want the University involved, and apparently not every member of the Morrows knew about their connection. Additionally, this proved that Chief was both stupid and open to a bribe. Perhaps she could offer for them to take her to the Verdant Stag for the ransom they wanted? She could use one of the wooden and pewter bracelets around her wrist to alert Katerin of an emergency, and when they arrived the Stag enforcers could take out this entire group of idiots.

"I can offer you a beast core. Three million thaums of power. One for each of us," Tanya said.

Every Morrow head in the room turned to look at her.

"Oh?" Chief's grin returned. "Search them," he ordered.

'*A competent leader would have thought of that long before, especially since Tanya and Newton were openly carrying battle wands when they arrived.*'

Tanya's eyes flicked to Siobhan, almost as if she expected Siobhan to get them out of this mess somehow.

'You should have let me go earlier, and then none of us would be in this situation!' Siobhan wanted to scream.

Sticky Fingers, who had been rifling around the shop counter, reached for Siobhan's bag, which was sitting at the still-humming Newton's feet.

Newton also looked to Siobhan, a spike of anxiety returning to his expression, which had been momentarily loosening under the effects of his spell.

Siobhan pushed back a flare of embarrassment, because when nothing happened to the man searching her bag, Newton would know she had been bluffing.

"I'd like to propose a counter offer," Siobhan said, thinking quickly and speaking slowly. "You can ransom both us and our belongings from someone who can afford it. You have the authority to treat with other gang leaders, as the new head of the Morrows, I assume?" As long as the Stags came out victorious, and Siobhan didn't get injured or killed in the crossfire, she would walk away no poorer, with all her belongings.

The attention turned toward her.

One of the Morrows held up a lamp to better see her, while the one who'd been guarding her pushed her hood back so that her face was clear.

"And who are you?" asked Chief, grimacing with disgust at the feathers sprouting from her hair.

Introducing herself as the Raven Queen might not be the smartest decision this time. What if their avarice didn't outweigh their fear and aggression?

Near the front of the room, Sticky Fingers shifted around. As soon as his eyes landed on Siobhan's uncovered face, they widened. He looked back toward the shop counter, then again to Siobhan. His expression twisted with shock and horror. The hand holding a wand shot up, pointing at Siobhan. "It's a trap! It's her! Run, run away, *it's her!*"

Before anyone could respond to what he'd said, his finger clenched, tugging on the trigger of the wand, and Siobhan had a fraction of a second for stunned, horrified realization as an orange spell coalesced at the tip and shot toward her.

Her latest wanted poster was tacked to the cork board beside the shop counter.

It was too late to dodge—they were only a few meters apart. She instinctively threw up her hands, closing her eyes and ducking her head.

There was a moment of stunned silence in which she had time to recognize that she hadn't been hit by what she was pretty sure was a fireball spell, though she could feel the heat licking at her face and hands.

She opened her eyes tentatively.

The fireball hung in the air in front of her outstretched hands, roiling and expanding as it lost the cohesion and power of its condensed form.

She was as stunned as everyone else until she felt the burning cold of her warding medallion against her chest. She stepped quickly to the side, letting the fireball slide past her. It whooshed across the room and impacted against the brick wall on the other side, its energy dissipated enough that it left nothing more than scorch marks.

"Idiot!" Chief screamed at Sticky Fingers. "You'll burn the place down around us!"

The skin of Siobhan's chest was rapidly beginning to hurt, and she resisted the urge to curl up protectively around herself. *'The spell must have been coming at me perfectly dead center for the deflection spell to stop it rather than shunt it to the side.'* It was meant to be an energy-saving measure to deflect rather than to simply shield, which was probably how her grandfather had stuffed so many protections into a single artifact, but with the perfect angle, that apparently backfired. *'Once again, Grandfather saved my life.'*

But the danger wasn't over. After one more stunned second, which Sticky Fingers used to fumble with this wand, he pulled the trigger again. Thankfully, this time the spell wasn't orange.

Siobhan was prepared, sidestepping the rapidly expanding, almost invisible spell and taking only a bruising blow across her arm. Behind her, furniture was overturned and chunks of brick were blasted from the far wall.

But the other Morrows were spreading out, their own wands raised toward her, and she knew the situation was quickly degrading. *'I have to run.'* But she had very few options without her bag of components and pre-drawn paper arrays, and there were Morrows between her and the door.

With a distraction, something else for them to shoot at instead of her, maybe she could dive for her bag, break a philtre of darkness, and escape with Newton in tow. Tanya might escape if she was quick-thinking and nimble on her feet, but she would have to fend for herself. Siobhan couldn't save both of them.

Siobhan raised her hands to her mouth, cupping them into a Circle, and rushed through the chant for her shadow-familiar at a low mumble. "Life's breath, shadow mine. In darkness we were born. In darkness do we feast. Devour, and arise." Then she added a huge exhale to power the spell with the heat of her breath. The truncated ritual was a greater strain on her Will, but she pushed the magic into her shadow with only a single repetition of the chant instead of three. She had no time for three.

She used the same shadow form she'd used last time when the coppers were attacking, a tattered form of darkness with a fluttering cloak and a huge beak extending from the hood that covered its head.

Tanya dodged a spell with a smooth sliding movement, then leapt for Sticky Fingers, pushing his wand arm away and smashing her forehead into his face.

Siobhan sent her risen shadow moving away from her to the side, trying to draw their spells harmlessly into the back of the room. She hoped the construct was dark and substantial enough to be a proper distraction despite her rushed execution of the spell.

She spun toward Newton, crouching low.

His mouth hung open with horror, his glassy, bloodshot eyes locked on the unnaturally tall shadow-form behind her. His hands were still cupped in front of his chest, but it was obvious that the self-calming spell had been forgotten. Her bag sat at his feet.

Tanya cursed as she grappled with Sticky Fingers.

The others were screaming. One spell shot past over Siobhan's crouched head, and a couple more of different colors passed harmlessly through her shadow familiar, which she let ripple but not disperse.

All the hair on Siobhan's body rose at once with a tingling urgency. An instinct that lived somewhere in the back of her mind screamed at her to run, to *escape*.

A pressure moved through the air, a shiver that hurt her eyes and scraped along her teeth and spine.

She released her shadow-familiar spell almost too fast for safety and let her crouch continue downward, pulling herself into a fetal position, her arms shielding her head.

With a crack that was more hindbrain sensation than sound, the world twisted.

Siobhan's eyes rolled back into her head as reality ceased to conform to its normal pattern.

She felt all the things at once, tasted emotions, heard the ripples of space, and felt time shudder through her skin.

It was over in an instant, almost too fast for her brain to grasp what was happening, which she could only be grateful for. She suspected that extreme briefness was the only thing that allowed her to maintain her sanity.

She lay on the smooth, polished wood of the floor, letting out a few sobbing breaths as warm tears spilled down her temple. The scream of fear in the back of her mind was still going, and as her brain regained control of her body, she climbed clumsily to her hands and knees. She was already bruised from slipping on the ice, and this had only made it worse, but that concern was far from the forefront of her mind.

In the spot where Newton had been, stretching out a couple of meters, was a hollow sphere of randomly connected, faintly vibrating strings, like a shell made out of thread-thin vines. Crouched within, in a vaguely fetal position, was a dark form, indistinct under a mat of more strings, which grew over the form like old mold.

BLIGHT

SIOBHAN
Month 1, Day 20, Wednesday 11:20 p.m.

SIOBHAN STOOD, staring at the sphere of web-like strings. She realized, with a distant horror, that the strings were red and pink and white. The colors of the inside of a body. It seemed, for a moment that stretched on forever, that the world had stilled.

All was silent.

Then the strings began to vibrate. The movement was gentle and soft, but produced a faint noise, like a thousand distant cellos playing the same deep note. A few strings were spread out against the wall and floor, like vines.

With a sudden breath that set the world into motion again, Siobhan stepped backward, bumping against the table and making its legs shudder over the wooden floor. Her bladder tried to release under the effects of mindless terror, and she realized barely in time to keep from pissing herself. Her leg muscles were trembling uncontrollably. Siobhan braced herself on the table to keep from collapsing again.

'*What was that? The world broke, just for a moment. Or my mind did.*' Whatever it was had affected Tanya, too, but not the Morrows.

Tanya was on the floor next to the man she'd attacked, struggling to crawl to her feet.

The Morrow closest to what had once been Newton screamed.

It was a thoughtless sound, not an intimidating yell or a frightened cry, but the mindless, hoarse shriek of terror of an animal in the night.

He raised the wand in his hand and shot a concussive blast spell at the Aberrant. From as close as the Morrow was standing, the blast spell would have broken a human's ribs, tossed their body back hard enough to knock them unconscious against the brick wall, and probably ruptured a couple of organs.

The foggy spell washed over the Aberrant, rippling out against the vibrating strings that contained its form like a bucket of water splashed into a pond, going through and past and impacting with a loud, dull sound against the front wall behind it. The humming strings were agitated at its passing, but seemed unharmed. The tips of the strings, spread out like vines, writhed curiously.

The Morrow man kept screaming and shooting one overpowered concussive blast after another, till the bricks of the front wall began to shatter and crumble and the boarded-up windows were blown clear again.

Siobhan covered her mouth. She held in the convulsive sob that wracked through her body so hard she felt she might choke on it.

The other Morrows joined the first in attacking, one almost hitting Tanya with a fireball as she crawled across the room toward Siobhan.

The fireballs were moderately effective, singeing and withering the Aberrant's flesh-colored strings, but weren't enough to actually catch the thing on fire.

The slicing spells cut through the strings, and could get through the protective sphere, but not all the way through the lumpy mass within. They didn't seem to be doing much real damage. The strings sprouted offshoots from their severed edges and wove themselves back together again with nothing more than a vague scar to show for it.

"Kill it!" Chief screamed. The barrage of spells was enough to collapse a large section of the front wall Newton had been leaning against when he lost control and send a couple of pieces of burning furniture tumbling into the street.

The Morrows quickly ran out of the offensive spells they'd chosen. One or two at a time, they paused to switch the settings on their wands or replace them with another offensive artifact that still had a charge remaining. Each spell within a multi-option artifact like the more expensive battle wands had its own pool of magical energy to draw from, so when they were out of one, they had no option but to switch to something else, and when they ran out of everything useful, they would be helpless.

The man who'd attacked the Aberrant first was still screaming, his wand outstretched but empty of concussive blasts, and him too insensate to switch to a new spell.

The strings nearest him were growing through the air, extending in a liquid pour and hardening in place as they went. It looked like a snake's slither, and gave Siobhan the same sense of foreboding as they approached him.

He didn't move, just kept screaming and trying to fire an empty wand.

For a moment, when the first string touched his neck, nothing happened. Then, the skin bulged out in a boil, like the growing bud of a flower.

The bud sprouted.

The man's neck unraveled, strands of his flesh and blood rising up and disentangling themselves from the rest of him, as if he had been made of millions of tightly packed strings all along. The inside of his throat was visible for a moment, and then his screams choked off as the strands continued to spread, his body slowly coming apart like an unfurling flower of human thread.

The remaining Morrows spread out and retreated toward the back of the room, knocking carelessly into the displayed wooden furniture, their horror tangible. One of them had started to sob, his arm shaking so badly his slicing spells were shooting harmlessly past the Aberrant and disappearing into the fog outside the front wall.

Siobhan took another step back, her eyes opened as wide as they could go, her hand clamped over her mouth.

Still crawling, Tanya grabbed the edge of Siobhan's cloak.

Siobhan looked down into Tanya's desperate face.

"Help me. Save me. Please," Tanya croaked.

The words were ridiculous, a sign of desperation making the other woman reach for whatever feeble hope she could find, but they still acted like a shocking splash of cold water to wake Siobhan from her horrified stupor. She reached down, grabbing Tanya's arm and helping her to her feet. Above Tanya's head, her eyes flicked around, cataloguing the situation and their options.

Newton had been near the shop's front door when he lost control, and a whole section of the wall was now missing entirely, but there was no way they could escape past his still-spreading tendrils. There were a couple of boarded-up windows at the far end of the front wall, but strings were already growing toward them, and by the time she and Tanya managed to break the boards free they would likely have reached the windows.

The Morrows were between them and the stairway leading up to the higher floor.

Behind them was the door to the other room.

"Come on," Siobhan ordered, her voice barely loud enough to be heard past all the screaming and the battle spells. Still holding Tanya's arm, she hauled the other woman around the table, weaving through the furniture toward the far door. *'Maybe there will be a window that we can crawl out of.'*

Siobhan yanked on the handle. It was locked. She held back a whining moan of frustration, the hair on the back of her neck prickling as she imagined the strings weaving through the air, searching for her. *'Can I break down the door with a few kicks? If only I had my bag, my supplies, I could open it easily.'* Siobhan still had a few different writing implements, and even though she didn't have her lantern, she could use the heat in the air to power the spell...but the lack of proper components would make it more difficult.

She peered at Tanya, who was trembling, her bloodless lips pressed together. The other woman should still have all her supplies, including a handy beast core and whatever else she'd been carrying. "Open the door," Siobhan ordered her, turning to face the room again. Tanya was a fourth term University student. She would be faster than Siobhan, anyway.

"O-okay," Tanya stammered behind her.

The Morrow who'd been subsumed by the Aberrant was completely string already, the double-thump of a heartbeat spreading through its vibrating, hollow mass, and its own searching tendrils already spreading toward the other Morrows.

It reminded Siobhan of a fungus, spreading, seeding, and sprouting more of itself. This was the kind of Aberrant that the Red Guard labeled a Blight-type. If allowed to get out of control, they could cause true devastation.

Chief had calmed, and was shouting orders. He and two of the others were moving the furniture into a barricade piled up in the middle of the room, trying to block off the strings of Newton and their subsumed comrade.

Sticky Fingers, the one that had shot at Siobhan, was still on the floor, unconscious and untouched on the wrong side of the barricade, but apparently they had given up hope for him. Blood was pooling around his head from whatever Tanya had done to him.

The remaining Morrows had moved to stunning spells, conserving their charges, only shooting a single spell at a time.

It was the first thing that actually seemed to have an effect on the Aberrant. Wherever the crackling red spells hit, the strings stilled in a couple of meter radius, silencing their humming and slowing their inexorable growth. The Morrows were using the time this bought them to strengthen the barricade.

But the strings weren't just growing through the air. They were also spreading along the darkness of the far wall and even up toward the high ceiling. The Morrows' barricade wouldn't save them.

One of the Morrows had climbed the steps to the door at the back of the room and was kicking at it, no doubt hoping to break open an escape route, just like Siobhan and Tanya. Every kick was preceded by a loud scream, as if the man thought that would give him more strength, and the strings growing along the wall seemed to surge faster in response to the desperate sound.

He noticed them, screamed again, and threw himself back toward the middle of the room.

The strings detached from the far wall, growing back the way they'd come, following him. He kept screaming, pointing wordlessly at the strings that were now coming at them from the side of the room as well as the front.

Behind Siobhan, Tanya let out a sob of relief as the lock clicked open and the door swung inward.

A quick glance was all it took for Siobhan to realize there would be no escape from this room. It was a storage closet—full of tools, wood, and supplies in crates and on shelves. There was no window, only brick walls.

When they were both inside, Tanya moved to close the door behind them, but Siobhan shook her head. A closed door wouldn't stop the strings. They could slip through the cracks. Better to be able to see, to know what was happening.

The man who had been trying to kick open the shop's back door calmed enough to aim his wand and shoot two stunning spells, which stilled the strings reaching for him entirely. He quieted, his eyes wide, panting heavily, and then suddenly jumped as if he'd been stung by a hornet.

He looked down in horror at something Siobhan couldn't see.

She could guess what had happened, though. One of the strings had slipped through the barricade and touched his leg or foot.

He tried to run, but stumbled. Soon after—quicker this time than with the first victim—he began to unravel, one leg unfurling into an amorphous cloud of flesh-colored strings.

Siobhan pushed back her sleeve, picked out the correct bracelet by the colored string tied around each, and snapped it decisively, shoving the now-unlinked remains into a pocket. It wouldn't tell Oliver where she was, but he would know that something had gone wrong and she was in immediate danger. She chose the next bracelet by the pattern and color of the string she'd tied around it. She slipped it off without breaking it and, aiming very carefully, threw it out the window and into the foggy street as hard as she could.

She'd never assumed she would be in a situation like this, but she and Oliver had agreed on what to do in a dire emergency. He would have a divination cast using the pair to the bracelet she'd just thrown away, and as long as the target was far enough from her that her divination ward didn't act to protect her by blocking it, he would find her. She hoped.

The Morrows had grasped the situation. A couple of stunning spells knocked the latest victim unconscious, slowing the strings sprouting from his body. Unfortunately, their path to the back door was soon to be blocked off.

Bulldog, the fat man with unfortunate jowls, noticed her standing in the storage closet's doorway. He pointed toward her and Chief hesitated, looking around wildly for any other option, but, seeing none, nodded.

The three remaining Morrows began to head toward Siobhan and Tanya, navigating through the overturned furniture.

The younger one who had started crying—Siobhan dubbed him Sniffles—was holding a lamp to keep an eye out for sneaking strings waiting in the shadows to touch them.

The strings from the original core of the Aberrant had reached Sticky Fingers now. They crawled over him in several areas, but he was still human. Siobhan wondered for a moment if he'd died, and the strings only took root in living flesh, but his chest still rose and fell slightly.

Siobhan let out a loud, shaky breath as the realization hit her. '*The Aberrant is ignoring him.*'

The other three Morrows were getting closer to her, and as they pushed a fallen cabinet out of their way with a loud scratch across the floor, the strings nearest them began to grow in their direction.

"Lady Raven Queen, we're begging your pardon!" Chief yelled at her as they approached. "Please give us your protection, we'll give you anything you want—"

Siobhan's hand shot out toward him in a stopping motion, and he froze mid-step, the two behind him jostling a bit at the unexpected halt. She lifted her index finger slowly and pointedly to her lips. With her other hand, she pointed at what had once been Newton, then pointed to her ear. "It can hear you," she mouthed silently.

48

PULLULATION

Sɪᴏʙʜᴀɴ
Month 1, Day 20, Wednesday 11:25 p.m.

Cʜɪᴇꜰ's ᴇʏᴇs ᴡɪᴅᴇɴᴇᴅ, but he nodded dramatically to show that he'd understood Siobhan's message and began to tiptoe toward her. The others copied him. If not for the situation, seeing three grown men sneak so dramatically would have been amusing. They were almost beyond the current range of the Aberrant's strings.

The humming was growing louder, and Siobhan found her mind clear, if not calm, and her body surprisingly relaxed and ready for action, rather than paralyzed by deep-seated terror.

The three Morrows were huddled together. Sniffles, who'd been crying earlier, was now only pale-faced and tight-lipped as his eyes swept their path for strings. Chief led the way, and Bulldog pressed up behind both of them, looking over his shoulder every other second.

Which meant he didn't see the rounded leg of a broken table the others were stepping over, and when his foot landed on it, it rolled forward, sending him pitching backward. He let out a shout of surprise and reached out to grab onto Sniffles.

But Sniffles leaned away from him, and when Bulldog hit the ground, the fancy light crystal lamp he'd been carrying fell out of his hand. The glass body shattered against the floor. He cursed, trying to quickly regain his feet, but the strings had already been drawn by his noise, and he wasn't quick or nimble enough to get out of their way in time.

Chief turned to help, trying to haul him up, but the strings were too fast, touching Bulldog's arm as he tried to heave himself off the ground.

Expression twisted with terror, Bulldog grabbed onto Chief, holding him tightly and screaming, "Help me! Help me, don't leave me!"

Sniffles bolted for Siobhan, but she didn't let him into the room, holding a hand up to his face to stop him at the door. To her satisfaction, he didn't try to physically push past her, despite his fear.

Chief tore one arm back from Bulldog, grabbing his wand and shooting a stunning spell directly into the terrified man's face.

Bulldog slumped backward, the strings that were assimilating him slowing their advance through his flesh.

But the screaming had agitated the Aberrant's tendrils, and before Chief could free his other arm, one touched his wrist.

A boil began to bud on his right hand.

Siobhan was impressed with his composure as he pointed the wand at his own forearm, just above where the string was attached, and fiddled with the settings on his wand. A slicing spell shot out, cutting through the flesh and bone, almost all the way through the limb.

He gritted his teeth, holding back a scream of pain with a trembling, pale-faced exhale. He shot a second slicing spell at the same spot, severing the rest of the way through his right forearm.

Putting the wand in his mouth, he squeezed the flesh above the blood-squirting stump with his free hand, stumbling toward the storage closet with ragged gasps and a face so pale it looked green, likely more from shock than blood loss, though the latter would quickly become a problem.

"Your wands," Siobhan mouthed slowly, holding a hand out expectantly.

Sniffles gave her his immediately. Chief hesitated, but soon opened his mouth to let her take his, as well.

She examined his bleeding stump. It wasn't sprouting any flesh-strings, and she could see no boils. Behind him, his hand lay on the floor, only half-subsumed into string, and *not* transforming any further. Whatever the strings were attracted to, the severed hand no longer contained it.

She tucked both wands into one of her bigger vest pockets and stepped aside to let Chief and Sniffles enter the room, eyes sweeping over the entire shop once again.

The second infected Morrow was still being subsumed, but much slower now that he, too, was unconscious. The strings were unfurling his lower back, but his torso and head were still intact.

Bulldog had been forced into unconsciousness almost immediately, and the strings were only halfway up his arm. His expression was peaceful.

Siobhan turned around and they all retreated to the far side of the storage closet.

Tanya was glassy-eyed and had beads of sweat over her forehead despite the chill, but she looked to Siobhan with a calm, expectant readiness, as if prepared to leap to her bidding. "Should I search them?" she whispered, the words more breath than sound.

"Yes," Siobhan said, then turned to the Morrows. "Do either of you have any concussive blast spells left?" It was dangerous to cast them in a small, enclosed space, but it might be enough to break down the wall of the storage closet and let them escape directly into the side street.

Both of them shook their heads, which was a shame.

"How many stunning spells remaining?"

The leader shook his head again, but Sniffles said, "Four. Three in mine, one in his." He seemed sure, which was rather impressive, with all the chaos and mayhem they had just gone through.

Four stunning spells was enough to buy them a couple of minutes. Her attention turned to the Morrow leader. The slicing spell had done a relatively clean job on his forearm. There weren't any bone fragments, at least. She had plenty of healing supplies in her bag, courtesy of the secret meeting, but that bag was lying on the ground within the Aberrant's main string-sphere, dropped when the Morrows realized who she was.

If they didn't do something quickly, he would pass out and then die from blood loss. His grip on his severed forearm wasn't enough to stop the bleeding, and she doubted he'd be able to keep it up for much longer, judging from his pale skin and the faint trembling in his knees. She considered simply tying off the stump with a makeshift tourniquet and leaving Chief to his fate, but he might be useful, and even if he wasn't—even though he was a criminal that had threatened her—the thought of huddling in fear next to a slowly dying man while she had the means to help him made her queasy. *'It's not about him. It's about me and who I want to be.'*

She still had a handful of supplies in the pockets scattered throughout her clothes, and they already knew her as the Raven Queen, a wanted criminal known for doing blood magic. "I can patch up your arm," she offered, her breathy whisper almost lost amid the growing hum filling the building.

He stared at her a moment, then nodded jerkily.

"Kneel," she said, taking the little silver alchemy athame from her pocket and unsheathing it. It was meant for cutting ingredients and occasionally waving around a cauldron while chanting, not cutting a human, but she liked to have a backup.

His eyes widened, but she only used the athame to cut away his blood-soaked sleeve, which she wrung until the blood dripped out into the growing puddle on the floor, and then tied tightly just below his elbow as a makeshift tourniquet.

This would require much more power than shifting some teeth back into their proper place or knitting together a shallow cut. There was no way she could regrow his hand, but she needed to at least stop the bleeding and close the wound.

She dipped her finger in the pooling blood, using it to draw the flesh-mirroring spell array.

Tanya looked between the array, Siobhan, and the man, but didn't say anything. Instead, she offered Siobhan one of the beast cores, which the Morrows hadn't had time to find and take from her.

Siobhan accepted it with interest, imagining she could feel the faint sense of bottled power within the bright yellow crystal. She guided Chief to place one arm in each of the two inner Circles. She placed the beast core in the component Circle, warned him, "Do not move," then began to cast, using the Conduit still tucked uncomfortably inside the lip of her boot.

Despite her warning, Chief gasped and jerked as the meat of his stump moved under her control. Luckily, he didn't leave the Circle, but she sent him a harsh glare that made his Adam's apple bob with an audible swallow.

Without Siobhan needing to ask, Tanya moved to kneel beside him, holding one of his arms and gesturing for Sniffles to do the same on the other side.

The door to the upper floor, across the main room from the storage closet, flew open, distracting Siobhan.

An old man stood in the doorway above the small set of stairs, holding a spear and what looked like an antique wooden shield with metal banding around the sides, painted with a coat of arms. "Get out of my shop, hooligans!" he yelled, brandishing the spear from behind the protection of the shield. It was a rather belated response to all the ruckus they'd been making. Perhaps the old man had been waiting until it sounded like they were gone to come out in a show of bluster.

When no one responded, he took a better look at the ruined shop. His eyes widened, swept over the room, and without another word, he turned around and ran back up the stairs. "We have to get out! We have to get out *now!* There's some rogue magic *thing* growing down there..." His gasping voice came through the stairway door until he got too far away to be heard past the hum of the Aberrant.

The strings grew toward the open door, drawn by his voice, and up toward the ceiling, which was thumping with footsteps and letting through more muffled voices.

Siobhan resumed her magical adjustments. She couldn't actually mirror the regrown arm. However, she could mimic the way blood vessels shrunk as they grew into his remaining hand, forcing the ones in his stump to narrow artificially, and grow new paths between the veins and arteries. That would send the blood that would otherwise continue pumping out of him back into circulation.

"Is that blood magic?" Sniffles asked.

Tanya scoffed. "You're in the presence of the Raven Queen, and she's healing a man without any components. What do you think?"

"Is that...safe?" Sniffles seemed torn between leaning closer in fascination and shuffling backward to put space between himself and the blood magic, but any movement was restricted by his need to keep a firm grip on Chief's arm.

Tanya actually rolled her eyes, one side of her mouth twitching up in a smirk despite the stress-induced sweat still wetting her temples. "She's a free-caster. She's more than skilled enough for something like this."

"But...where is her Conduit?"

Tanya seemed stumped by this at first, too, but finally just said, "She's the Raven Queen," as if that were an acceptable explanation. "If I were you, and you make it through the night, I'd leave the Morrows. You do not want to be on her bad side."

Sniffles shuddered with his whole body.

Siobhan was curious about the reputation the Raven Queen had somehow earned behind her back, but couldn't split her concentration from molding Chief's stump. She didn't care to do a perfect job, and didn't have the power or skill to do so even if she had. She worked quickly, then started tugging at the skin, growing it a little but mostly just forcing it to stretch around the severed flesh. In only a couple of minutes, he was left with a raw, shiny forearm stump that looked suspiciously like a fingertip. It was sloppy, but definitely satisfactory for the work of a few minutes.

Siobhan released the spell. "You still need to see a healer. I did not clean the wound."

He gave her several quick bows, staring in wonder at his wrist, which probably still hurt quite a bit but wouldn't be fatal within the next few hours at least. "Thank you, thank you, er, Lady Raven Queen. Am I...do I owe you my life, now? Or...the life of my first-born child?"

Siobhan was picking up the beast core, but almost dropped it in stupefaction at his second question. *'Is he joking?'*

His earnest, frightened expression belied that.

She almost shook her head, but hesitated. Why would she turn down repayment for her help when it was offered? "I do not take payment in lives," she whispered instead, tucking the beast core into her jacket pocket. There was no way she was returning it to Tanya.

Her answer did not seem to reassure Chief in the least, but before he could continue to question her, Tanya butted in. "Mistress, is there any way to help Newton?"

There was no way to reverse an Aberrant transformation. Siobhan said so, and Tanya nodded reluctantly, her expression drawn tight with fear and dread.

'She's more naive than I thought, if she didn't know that. Or maybe just desperate for hope.'

"Well, do you have some way to get us out of here? Some way to break down the wall without the Aberrant being able to sense it?" Tanya tried.

Siobhan considered. She might be able to use the trick from Professor Lacer's class to turn small sections of the mortar between the bricks into sand, and thus open a hole for them, but there would probably be at least two layers of brick, and some sort of insulation in between them. Even if she got Tanya to help with that, it would take too long. "Silently, but not quickly," she whispered. "The strings would reach us."

"Well, is there maybe a way to travel with us through the shadows? Your shadow-creature seems big enough to carry us all."

Siobhan stared at Tanya, wondering if unrealistic, fantastical thoughts were a sign of shock, since the other woman seemed to be losing her grip on reality. The question was too inane to bother with a response. Besides, Siobhan's attention was drawn to a bright light that swept through the cleared front windows and the part of collapsed wall behind Newton.

She turned with excitement, a finger on her lip reminding the others to be quiet. The kind of lensed lantern that focused the beam in a single direction wasn't common among civilians, and someone was shining one such beam through the fog. The people up above could have somehow summoned the coppers, or, more likely, it had been the flare followed by all the previous noise and spellcasting. With the humming of the strings drowning out other sounds, she couldn't listen for the metallic clack of their footsteps that would signify the eponymous copper hobnails in the soles of their boots.

She had the sudden urge to call out for help, but the slowly searching strings were already almost a meter away from the doorway, crawling along the floor and hanging in vine-like patterns in the air. If she called for help, by the time the coppers got to them, they would be dead.

'We could write a note explaining the situation, wrap it around something, and throw it out one of the windows. They could open the storage room wall from the other side.' It could work, maybe, if the coppers had enough stunning spell charges on them and were willing to listen.

A copper stepped closer to the collapsed section of wall where Newton and the front door had once stood, shining his light through the string-filled opening. He called, "Is anyone in there? By order of the High Crown, reveal yourself!" The wand in his other hand sent out an almost-transparent pulse, likely the same revealing spell the copper team had used on Siobhan when they caught her and Oliver in that rundown building. That seemed like a lifetime ago.

The copper seemed to realize suddenly what he was seeing, and screamed over the humming, "Aberrant! Call the Red—" His words cut out in favor of a glass-sharp shriek, and his lantern fell to the ground as his arm exploded into thread.

The Aberrant's power was growing. That had been a lot faster than either of the other two.

Another copper—his partner—shouted in alarm, and through the fog and the strings Siobhan caught what she thought was the shimmer of a barrier spell springing into existence as he scrambled to back away. His footsteps rang loud as he retreated up the fog-filled street.

The first copper tried to run, too, but the strings got to his head too quickly. He slumped to the cobblestone street as the grey strings of his brain matter fluttered outward, illuminated by the bright beam of his lensed lantern.

49

THE CONSOLATIONS OF PHILOSOPHY

SIOBHAN
Month 1, Day 20, Wednesday 11:30 p.m.

FROM OUT OF Siobhan's line of sight, the remaining copper shot a couple of red stunning spells at the Aberrant's prime mass—their wands' default spell—though either because of his distance from their target or the Aberrant's gradual increase in power, the threads didn't still for as long as they had before.

The people above called out to the coppers for rescue, enticing the strings further up toward the ceiling.

One of the people that might have been able to save them had just died. Now the coppers would be more wary, more cautious. Maybe they would move too slowly out of care for their own well-being to save Siobhan and the others before it was too late.

Siobhan was terrified. She knew she was, but her body didn't agree. It was surreal to experience such a disconnect of emotion from physiological response. She felt detached from herself. She had grown used to feeling a little uncomfortable, a little displaced in her own skin, after using the artifact. This was different. She had never felt that her existence was a consciousness so distinct and separate from the meat suit she wore as a body.

It made her wonder again if there was any evidence of consciousness beyond the electrical and chemical signals processed by the brain. She didn't believe it—her sense of detachment was unreliable and there was no measurable evidence of such a phenomenon, but the curiosity it sparked made her feel more settled, more like herself.

She was a creature of curiosity, after all. *'If I cannot rely on others, I will rely on myself. I will find a way out of this.'*

Neither of the Morrows seemed as frightened as they had been before.

Tanya was still looking to Siobhan for salvation with out-of-character faith, but none of the clawing desperation that had been there after Newton first lost control.

All of the people who had been infected were now fully string, too, but Sticky Fingers was still breathing shallowly, resting in a coagulating pool of his own blood as the strings crawled over and past him, uncaring.

"An Aberrant's powers are always unique, like snowflakes, but they are often based on the circumstances in which they lost control," Siobhan muttered aloud, running her fingers over her cold-chapped lips.

Tanya nodded, a faint frown of confusion creasing her brow.

"Newton was casting a self-calming spell. The strings are imitating the hum of it. Transferring the calm to us. Can you feel it?" Siobhan asked.

"I feel it," Chief said, his voice a little too loud.

"The strings are drawn to movement. Especially to screaming. But they're ignoring him"—Siobhan pointed to Sticky Fingers—"because he's unconscious. I think they can tell the difference between a living, agitated body and someone in a state of complete calm. They ignored your hand once you cut it off, too," she murmured to Chief.

"So if it keeps giving off that sound, maybe we'll be calm enough to be safe?" Tanya asked.

Siobhan gave her a bitter smile. "If you would like to use one of the few remaining stunning spells to knock yourself unconscious and wait for rescue, you can. But I have a different idea."

Tanya hesitated before shaking her head. "No. The coppers will be calling in the Red Guard right now. Who knows what they'll do? Maybe they'll quarantine the whole building and kill everything inside. Newton—this Aberrant, I mean—it's a Blight-type. It spreads. I heard there's a town near Vale that had a bad Blight-type twenty years ago. The whole town is still trapped inside a sundered zone."

The words produced a small flutter of actual, physical anxiety in Siobhan's chest, and she closed her eyes for a moment to force it back.

"I'll follow you," Tanya added. "What do you need me to do?"

"Us as well," Chief concurred immediately.

Sniffles nodded rapidly.

"Do you know the spell Newton was using?" Siobhan asked.

Tanya deflated with disappointment. "No. It was a family spell, and I only know he used it when he became too stressed, or when he needed to relax to sleep. I could try to recreate it...?"

"No need." Siobhan handed Tanya both confiscated stunning wands, confident in Tanya's temporary trustworthiness as well as her composure. "When I give the signal, stun the closest strings, then switch immediately to the slicing spell." She sat down and began to unlace her left boot. She'd read that the human body didn't actually need its pinky toes for balance. In the worst case scenario, if this didn't work, her hands would be more useful than her feet, and the feet were farther away from her vital organs.

She could have taught Tanya the self-calming spell and tried to use her as the experimental subject instead, but doubted the woman would be willing to put her own life on the line.

And even if Tanya was willing, she didn't have the experience with the spell that Siobhan did. If she failed, creating another node of strings closer to the storage closet, that would make things worse for Siobhan, while still not absolutely proving that the idea couldn't work.

Siobhan couldn't trust anyone but herself with this task.

She stood, one foot bare against the floor. "Stay close. If this doesn't work, cut off the infected section immediately. I expect the strings will move quickly. Don't try to save too much of my leg. Aim for the mid-calf or the knee."

Tanya's lips firmed, and she nodded, her knuckles white around the wand's handle.

Siobhan reached out and touched Tanya's hand. "Steady, okay?"

"Okay," Tanya breathed.

Turning back to the main floor of the shop—now a wreckage of broken furniture and organic webs of the Aberrant's string—Siobhan took a deep breath, bringing her hands to her chest and creating a Circle with her thumbs touching her middle fingers. She exhaled on a deep hum, the spell coming easier to her than it ever had before. Her voice mixed with the humming of the strings filling the room. She matched their sound as closely as possible, a low droning, and kept going with every deep breath until her heartbeat was calm and the last remnants of acrid adrenaline had dissipated.

She had never been so placid. Even her thoughts felt slow.

Tanya stepped forward, and with a motion from Siobhan, used the last stunning spell from one of the wands on the closest string from only a few inches away. It and those nearby stilled completely, confirming Siobhan's suspicion that the efficacy of the spell decreased with distance, as was the case with many long-distance spells.

Still humming, she reached forward with her foot. She could feel her heartbeat attempt to spike with apprehension, and she paused to make sure she was as calm as could be again.

Then, she moved her foot forward the last couple of inches, touching her pinky toe to the string.

Nothing happened.

She drew her foot back, peering at it in what little light remained from the street and the tipped-over lamps inside the room. No buds forming.

'But maybe that's just because she stunned them. We've only got three stunning spell charges left. That's not enough to get all the way out of the room. It needs to work on the active strings too.' So, Siobhan waited until they began to grow forward again and let the string touch her once more.

It curled almost curiously around her toe and over her foot, but still didn't stop and pierce her, and no buds of infection grew in her flesh.

She pulled her foot back, then pressed it against the string a little harder, to make sure movement wouldn't trigger their attack suddenly.

The string grew upward and turned back on itself under the pressure of her flesh, heading slowly back through the air the way it had come, like a tree that was bound with straps would grow into the shape it was forced to conform to.

Still humming, she pulled her foot back, stepping away from the growing strings. They didn't follow her with any particular interest, as if deaf to the noise she was making because it matched their own.

Beside and slightly behind her, Tanya's mouth had dropped open.

"Come," Siobhan mouthed, making sure all three of her short-term allies could see and read the word on her lips.

Sniffles and Chief hurried out of the storage closet with soft steps, keeping Siobhan between themselves and the strings.

She jerked her head toward the door to the stairway on the other side of the room, then started to move, a little uneven since Sniffles was still carrying her other boot. She didn't want to waste time putting it back on while the Aberrant was still growing stronger.

Very carefully, Siobhan led the three of them through the room, physically blocking or turning the strings back on themselves where necessary.

She considered trying to save Sticky Fingers, maybe pulling him into a safer location at the least. *'He's a panicker, though, and hostile to the Raven Queen. He could get us all killed.'* They kept their distance from him and walked past. Neither of the Morrows protested.

Halfway to the stairway, the rogue magic sirens went off, their high-pitched ringing making the other three jump in surprise and agitating the Aberrant.

Her companions calmed almost immediately, probably due in large part to the effects of the Aberrant's humming, and Siobhan felt only the barest thump of alarm.

She knew, intellectually, that she was in danger of dying a horrible, gruesome death, the kind that would give someone nightmares. Her mind kept thinking of it, imagining it and yearning for all the things she had yet to accomplish with her life. But her body was too calm to feel it. Her heartbeat was placid, her muscles relaxed, and her veins free of the burn of stress-response chemicals.

The strings were a little more aggressive after the sirens started, but she reassured herself that even if her state of forced calm was no longer adequate to move through them, she would survive as long as they cut off the infected appendage quickly enough.

As they got to the stairway, Siobhan first turned back the strings curling around the door and along the walls, guiding them until they exited back into the main room against their instincts, then blocked the way so the others could pass ahead of her.

She looked up to the shadowed ceiling where the strings were matted and curled up, a feather of foreboding brushing against the back of her mind.

She turned and walked up the stairs, relaxed down to her faintly-vibrating bones and too lethargic to hurry.

The third floor was an apartment, and apparently housed the shop owner and a couple generations of his family.

Tanya, Sniffles, and Chief had stopped a little way into the living area.

Over Tanya's head, Siobhan saw a burst mass of strings writhing around the middle of the room. A middle-aged man was being turned, from the legs upward.

The strings had burrowed their way directly through the floor from the lower level in several spots, and one must have caught him. They were moving slower than they should have, and Tanya's outstretched wand was enough for Siobhan to guess they'd been stunned.

'Only a couple of charges left,' Siobhan thought.

Huddled against the far wall were two women and three young children. They were shivering in horror, one young boy's face pressed to his mother's neck to keep him from seeing the man's fate, but none were screaming, at least.

The grandpa had attempted to attack the strings, apparently, as his spear was caught up in the mass, but he was huddled against the wall to the side, warding off more pieces of the Aberrant with his paltry wooden shield.

Siobhan's eyes met those of the man dying slowly in the middle of the room. It was too late to cut off his legs, as his lower stomach was unraveling already. Even Myrddin might not have been able to save someone missing half their organs.

He was struggling against the forced tranquility. "Have mercy, save them," he gasped out, just before his lungs became visible from the inside of his chest cavity.

As she stepped around him toward the women and children, they huddled back away from her, and she realized it probably seemed quite sinister for her to have her hands in a Circle in front of her chest and be humming the same deep note as the strings. She couldn't stop to explain, but hoped they understood her intentions from the way she pushed the strings back from them and gestured with her head for them to move through the path she'd created.

It was too late to save the grandfather. The strings had bored through and around the edge of his shield, and as soon as they touched him it was over. He fairly exploded into flesh-strings, splashing against the wall and into his own shield.

A couple of the children screamed, and Siobhan had to move quickly to block the strings drawn by the noise. The one positive of the rogue magic sirens was that the strings were less aware of individual small noises, less likely to hone in on the subtle sounds of movement.

There were windows on this floor, barely large enough for the adults to crawl out of, but no way to get safely down to the ground. A jump from this high would break bones, at the least, and the bricks of the outer wall wouldn't provide nearly enough purchase to climb down.

Siobhan led them all to a bedroom at the far end of the upper floor where none of the strings had broken through yet, finally dropping the calming spell so she could speak. There was a window, and if they could get someone to bring a ladder, or create some sort of cushion against the ground, they could escape through it. And if not, they could take their chances with broken bones.

Chief began to explain the situation to the family members in hushed tones just loud enough to be heard over the combined sirens and Aberrant humming.

Looking through the window, Siobhan could see a line of bright lights being set up about a block away, facing the building but barely able to illuminate it through the thick, obscuring fog. "They're setting up a quarantine cordon," she murmured. "They want to be able to see anything that tries to escape."

Tanya moved to stand beside her, looking out with a hint of alarm. "Reinforcement coppers, probably. The Red Guard should be here soon, and they'll...handle things."

One of the women was crying silently, her hand held over her son's mouth to muffle his sobs, too.

Sniffles handed her the red Morrow handkerchief he'd had tied around his arm, but she threw it back in his face, which shocked him and brought a few more tears to his own eyes.

Siobhan drew Sniffles to the window, opening it as far as it would go and making him hold out the lamp he'd brought from downstairs. "Keep waving it. Someone should notice it, and they might be able to help you get down."

"You're not coming with us?" Tanya asked, then answered her own question. "Of course not. They would try to arrest you on sight."

Siobhan nodded silently. She had hoped to escape from the upper floor, but there was another problem she had to deal with. '*I left evidence downstairs. My bag, which is full of supplies, including a spare set of male clothing and the bracelets I gave Newton. The ones he never broke to ask for help. Even if I could afford to replace everything, who knows what the Red Guard could do with all that? They have magic the common person couldn't even imagine.*'

She wasn't sure if it was out of compassion, or her completely missing sense of urgency, but she took a couple of minutes to teach Tanya the esoteric calming spell, in case the other woman needed to block strings trying to enter the room. It took time and practice to get really good at a spell like that, but hopefully it would make some small difference.

Tanya seemed almost afraid to cast it, but picked up the mechanics quickly. She was a fourth-term University student, after all.

Satisfied that she'd done all she could, Siobhan took back the wand that still had two charges of the stunning spell and turned to leave the room.

Tanya reached out, grabbing hold of Siobhan's elbow to stop her. "I never meant..." She swallowed. "I never meant to make an enemy of you. Any offense I caused you by working with the Morrows, or the University, I apologize."

Siobhan's thoughts were too sluggish to work out the best way to respond to that. In the end, she only nodded silently, then left the room, turning back toward the stairway.

Strings were crawling along the walls and through the air from the lower floor. She tucked the wand between her teeth. With a deep breath, she brought her hands back to her chest, began to hum, and faced the stairway.

She tried to move, but her feet refused.

Not because she was incapacitated, but because she desperately, *wretchedly* wanted to do anything else but face the Aberrant head on. If it were possible, she would go to truly extraordinary lengths to avoid the thing.

But that could mean being forced to leave the University or being caught by the coppers. Neither of those were acceptable alternatives.

With only one road before her, she started to force her way down through the drifting strings, back toward the vibrating shadows and the origin of it all.

50

DECOHERENCE

Siobhan
Month 1, Day 20, Wednesday 11:45 p.m.

As Siobhan descended the stairs, she thought back to her first Defensive Magic lesson with Elwood Fekten. They'd talked about banshees and ways to defend against them. She'd looked over a couple of temporary deafening hexes after that, and knew one that she could have cast on herself, if she had the components and the wherewithal to *focus*, as it was rather complex.

The Aberrant's hum wasn't just in her ears, but in her bones. Still, she thought the deafening hex might do something. *Any* improvement would be useful, because she could recognize that she was slipping inexorably past extreme calm into both mental and physical slackness.

She couldn't feel her own face. That was more than the self-calming spell could have possibly done. At this point, she could barely even muster the care to worry about what would happen as the Aberrant continued to grow stronger.

The spot where the warding medallion had grown cold against her chest throbbed with a cold-burn. Siobhan slid her cupped hands up from her diaphragm to rub against the damaged skin, welcoming the temporary surge of wakefulness that accompanied the pain.

In the room below, the illumination of an overturned light crystal lamp showed the hive-like web of strings that had grown through the room—

through the air, across the floor, walls, and ceiling, and spilling out into the street.

The flesh-colored strings pressed sharply against her skin as she maneuvered through them, and she learned to avoid them more carefully the first time a vibration cut through her jacket and threatened to draw blood from her arm. It would be just what she needed to give the coppers a second blood sample to scry for her with.

As she made it farther to the front of the building, where Newton had triggered, the strings grew denser and began to respond aggressively when she was forced to push them out of the way. She had to freeze in place several times while they searched out the living creature moving among them.

When she finally reached the barrier sphere of strings around the huddled, amorphous mass that had been Newton, she spotted her bag on the floor inside, but just blinked at it lethargically for a while until she remembered that she was supposed to be retrieving it and escaping as quickly as possible.

Moving slowly, clumsily, she brought the Circle of her hands up to her mouth, pointing the wand with her teeth around the thick handle. She awkwardly leaned forward until the tip of the wand was almost touching the strings before triggering the stunning spell.

As soon as the strings stopped vibrating, she dropped the calming spell, switched the wand's settings to the cutting spell, and used the last three charges to cut the three lines of a triangle.

The closest strings seemed alerted to her presence without her actively humming, and, as quickly as she could while feeling like the whole world had been muffled in a bottle of molasses, she switched back to the stunning spell setting—of which only one remained—stuck the wand back in her mouth, and recast the calming spell on herself. She used what felt like the last bit of urgency in her soul to climb through the triangle-shaped opening she'd created in the barrier sphere.

With such a large hole, the strings didn't seem able to simply heal the wound, but they were already beginning to regrow new tendrils from the sliced edges.

She triggered her amulet, and immediately lost a couple of seconds to a disoriented blink as her body shifted. She almost lost concentration on the spell, too, and realized afterward that it had been dangerous to transform *while* casting. Anything could have happened, but mostly horrible things.

Casting took an effort of Will, and she was losing the ability to *care* enough to make the world bend under her heel. She looked down at the fetal mass of thrumming strings that still faintly resembled a human body.

'*Wouldn't it be ironic if I lost control casting the same exact spell as Newton, in the same spot? This was a mistake.*' It was the last coherent thought she had as she let the spell slip to keep the magic from turning on her.

Her mind lay fallow.

She didn't know how much time she lost, but a flash of fire and blood behind her eyelids sent a burst of fear through her.

She woke from her waking daze with a gasp, eyes wide, heart slamming against her chest with a sudden surge of energy. She'd been training herself for years to wake from her nightmares as quickly as possible, and apparently not even the absolute tranquility of an Aberrant's anomalous effect could overpower them. She never thought she'd be grateful for what was otherwise the bane of her existence.

She was still standing. Apparently, there were no searching strings within the sphere. If there had been, one would likely have found and subsumed her while she was catatonic with serenity.

Knowing her lucidity wouldn't last long, she shuffled closer to the origin point, the thing that had once been Newton.

She stunned it, point-blank against the part that should have been a head, and felt a wave of relief as every string in the building fell still and silent.

She could suddenly hear the sirens again, though she wasn't sure when they'd been drowned out by the humming, and shouts from outside filtered in through the muffling fog, some fearful, some authoritative.

'*This probably won't last long.*' Hurrying as fast as her still-clumsily relaxed muscles would allow her, she stripped out of her clothes, replaced them with the slightly worn set of men's clothing from the bottom of her bag, not bothering with the many buttons, and stuffed the female clothing as tightly inside as she could. She would have preferred to burn them, just in case, but the coppers might see something suspicious if she did that, and if the response was extra slow, she might end up burning down the whole building with Tanya and the others trapped above.

Sebastien retrieved her stunning wand from the hidden pouch at the bottom of the bag, then shoved her head ornaments into that same narrow, hidden space without regard for the feathers or the once-gentle curve of the wire filigree. With the evidence hidden as well as she could manage, she pulled the strap over her shoulders, the weight of her magical supplies a comfort she hadn't even realized she needed. She turned back to the fetal form that had been Newton.

Its strings were already starting to hum again, and the vibrations were spreading outward from there.

With a sharp grin that actually made her feel a pang of sorrow, she pressed her stunning wand again to the Aberrant's "head" and shot two consecutive stunning spells. '*There. Hopefully that'll keep it down long enough for me to get out of here.*' If not, she only had one charge left.

She knelt, the illumination of the lights from the cordon just enough for her to see Newton's two alarm ward bracelets, tangled through with strings.

She broke them without hesitation, pulling the pieces out of the string and shoving them into her pocket, then doing the same with the bracelet whose pewter bead around her wrist suddenly grew cold.

His clothes were torn to shreds, but some of the things in his pockets had fallen to the floor. Sebastien scooped up a handful of gold crowns and his Conduit, not sure if she should feel guilty for doing so. He'd had a wand, too, but she didn't see it. Maybe one of the Morrows had taken it off him.

The hole in the side of the string barrier was half-regrown already.

Pulling out her paper slicing spell array, she held it up near the opening by its edges, with the beast core Tanya had given her in the component Circle where she would normally have placed her little lantern.

The practice with Professor Lacer's air-sphere spell seemed to have helped her improve her grasp on the way the slicing spell molded air into a super-condensed arc. It was still much weaker than the slicing spells that had been in the battle wands—it was only meant for cutting fabric, after all—but it was enough to cut through the strings, and she managed to enlarge the opening again with a little effort.

She climbed back through the lopsided triangle, then made her way over fallen furniture and between the frozen strings to the farthest of the windows. The boards had been knocked free by the Morrow's initial concussive blast spells.

Moving slowly in the hopes that the fog would be enough to block her from the sight of the distant coppers along the cordon, she climbed out of the window and into the street. Just being outside of the building, finally, sent a wave of relief through her.

'Is there any way I can give the coppers a tip about how to deal with the Aberrant, and let them know to send a ladder around to the back of the building so the others can get out safely?' She tried to imagine a scenario in which she got the information to them without compromising her own safety. 'Maybe Oliver could do something. I should go to his house, since he's probably worried about me after I triggered the bracelet ward.' Damien, too, would have been alerted when she broke Newton's bracelets. 'Hopefully he doesn't panic and do anything stupid.'

Her relief had been preemptive. She'd only made it a couple of meters away from the window when a bright light burst into existence a short distance in front of her, making her squint and freeze instinctively.

"Halt!" a man's rough voice yelled. "Hands up, fingers splayed!"

She complied slowly, her eyes adjusting to see the red shields and magical tactical gear of the Red Guard.

A whole squad of them were standing a few meters in front of her, a couple with battle artifacts trained on her while the others kept watch to the sides and behind so nothing could sneak up on them.

"Oh, hells," she murmured aloud.

A Red Guard squad member shot a strange spell at Sebastien that she didn't dare to try and dodge. It prickled against her skin, tickling her insides until it reached her spine, and then bounced back.

The Red Guard woman who'd shot her checked the readings off a crystal tablet, then gave a quick handsign. "No anomalies. Human."

They relaxed a bit, and Sebastien was just about to slump with profound relief when she noticed a man to the left of the group peering closely at her, adjusting a complex metallic monocle attached by a clamp to the side of his head.

Sebastien felt the monocled man's attention activating the divination-diverting ward placed under the skin of her back, and knew it was over for her.

"Possible Nightmare-type," he snapped immediately.

She raised her hands even higher, fingers splayed wide. "Wait, wait! I'm human! I'm a University student, and I'm Thaddeus La—"

Before she could drop her professor's name in the hope of making them pause, a dark purple spell shot out of the center of the front man's shield. It hit her faster than she could blink.

51

THE IMPLIED INVISIBLE

SEBASTIEN
Month 1, Day 21, Thursday 12:05 a.m.

SEBASTIEN WOKE UP GASPING, a minty shock yanking her to consciousness hard enough it felt like her nose might start bleeding. She sat upright so fast she made herself dizzy, realizing with disorientation that she was lying on a portable cot in a square field tent.

A woman wearing the red shield symbol of the Red Guard, but without the tactical gear of the squad who'd found and shot her, said in a calming tone, "Easy. You might feel lightheaded or confused. You should lie back down."

Sebastien looked at the woman, who was standing across the tent, and slowly complied.

The woman's hard, wary expression didn't match her tone at all. There was a barrier spell up between them, wrapping around Sebastien. That, more than anything, helped Sebastien remember the situation she was in.

"The Aberrant is attracted to sound," she said immediately, hoping that being cooperative would lend her some goodwill. "I didn't have a chance to tell them before they shot me. It's drawn to sound, and it will infect anyone who's even slightly agitated with those strings. There's a spell that can protect against the strings, and stunning spells disable them for a short time. And there's—there might be some people upstairs who need help."

The woman didn't relax at all, though she motioned to someone at the open front side of the tent. They would presumably relay the information to the people that needed it. The woman scribbled in a small notebook. "What is your name?"

Sebastien almost gave the wrong name, and might have, if she hadn't taken to thinking of herself as Sebastien when in her male body. There were wards against untruth. Strong ones. "Sebastien Siverling. I'm a University student. Um, Thaddeus Lacer's apprentice." She tried not to sound awkward when she added the last bit. She realized belatedly that her shirt and vest were still both unbuttoned, and with a flush began to rectify her state of dress.

The woman's eyebrow rose, but she scribbled again in her notebook.

Sebastien's bag was on the table behind the woman, its contents laid out for display. Thankfully, the black and red feathered hair ornaments were not there. Either they hadn't found them, or the ornaments had been taken away for examination elsewhere, submitted into evidence against her.

When Sebastien stopped to listen, she realized she couldn't hear the humming any more, and the sirens had stopped, too. She didn't know if that was because they had moved her somewhere, or if they'd already dealt with the Aberrant while she was unconscious.

The fog outside the tent entrance and the brick building she could see across the street—a different one than they'd been trapped inside—suggested that she hadn't been moved too far. "How long have I been out?" she asked.

"Not long," the woman replied vaguely. "Did you have contact with the Aberrant?"

Sebastien hesitated. "Well—"

Before she could continue, a familiar voice snapped, "I am more than capable of dealing with whatever anomalous effect you think you have detected from my apprentice. Let me pass!"

Someone else said, "It's alright. Professor Lacer is with me."

Sebastien expected them to enter the tent, and turned toward the open side with a combination of dread and relief, but instead there was more distant, muffled arguing from other voices that she vaguely recognized. She frowned, rifling through her memory for a match. She wasn't the best with audible memories, and so she had just realized that it was Lynwood, the leader of the Nightmare Pack, and his adopted prognos sister Gera when the two of them walked in with Professor Lacer and another man who looked like an older, more severe version of Damien. Behind them trailed a man with an irritating cough and a sheaf of papers.

Gera's single scarred eye was staring milkily at nothing, but Sebastien could feel the extra pressure of her constantly running divination spell as soon as the other woman drew close. 'Did Oliver send her to help me?' Gera raised her hand to push back a lock of hair from her face, and Siobhan noted the wood bracelet held together with a bead of pewter around the woman's wrist. It was the same one Siobhan had thrown away.

Gera had divined her location, which was almost irrefutable evidence that Oliver had sent her.

Lynwood took a long look at Sebastien, examining her from head to toe, then turned to Gera.

She nodded.

Lynwood said, "I find myself needed elsewhere," already spinning on his heel. He bumped into the coughing man, barely stopping to mutter, "Excuse me, Investigator."

Professor Lacer, too, looked over Sebastien from head to toe, then gave the Red Guard woman who'd been questioning her a scathing glare that made the woman shift uncomfortably.

She straightened self-consciously. "Grandmaster Lacer," she said. "Welcome. Melinda Vernor." She bowed, receiving a slight nod of the head in return. "I'm surprised to see you here. Are you planning to help with the investigation?"

Professor Lacer somehow managed to give the impression of scoffing rudely without making a sound. "I am here on the invitation of Lord Titus Westbay, to provide my expertise and to make sure my apprentice is not mistreated."

"Er." Vernor looked rapidly back and forth from Professor Lacer to Sebastien. "I assure you, the spells used on him were not harmful. He is in adequate physical health, except for some...anomalous readings that were in effect before we encountered him. As I'm sure you know, it is our duty to ensure that no harm comes to the citizens of this country, despite the costs."

Gera hesitated, then offered the tent in general a moderately deep bow, the pressure of her attention withdrawing from Sebastien, easing the strain on her divination-diverting ward. "I am here to offer my assistance, as I have some skill in divination, and as I understand this person"—she gestured toward Sebastien—"is of significant interest to the disturbance going on in my...neighborhood."

The man who had to be Damien's older brother, Titus Westbay, gave Gera an ironic look. Apparently, it was a bit of an open secret that this part of the city was now territory of the Nightmare Pack. But he said, "Welcome. I am Titus Westbay, and this investigation is under my supervision. We would be appreciative of your insight."

Gera nodded regally, staring vaguely into mid-air. "As for the boy, he bears the blessing of the Raven Queen. This may be the anomalous effect you discovered."

Sebastien did her best to avoid seeming surprised. '*It's a good cover. There's no way for me to hide the fact that both the Raven Queen and I are resistant to divination magic. This way, it's not something that's unique to either of us, and it won't be a clue that someone could use to deduce we are the same person.*' She was impressed with

Gera's quick thinking. Perhaps Oliver had told her to say that. It gave her hope that there might still be a way out of all this.

Titus Westbay's eyebrows rose, and he shared a look with Professor Lacer. "The Raven Queen? How did you deduce this?"

"I am...acquainted with her, shall we say," Gera said, her head turning slightly toward Sebastien as if to check for a response. "She saw fit to grant me a boon. I have seen the effect before. She can grant it at will."

The investigator crossed one arm across his chest, thoughtfully resting his chin on the other hand. "It does make some sense."

Westbay gave him an inquisitive look. "Expound, please, Investigator Kuchen."

The man tucked away his handkerchief and looked through his papers nervously. "Well, we know the Raven Queen was here this evening. Two local gang members survived the Aberrant's break event and the subsequent incident, along with the surviving members of the family who lived above ground zero. They have told quite an interesting story."

Sebastien straightened her back, trying to control her apprehension. The wards against untruth made it more difficult, but they worked best on non-thaumaturges, the unaware, and the inebriated, since they only created a compulsion toward honesty. Truly debilitating wards against untruth were illegal, and while she suspected that wouldn't stop those in power from using them when they felt like it was worth it, here they were still manageable. She could lie if she wanted, with a quick mind and a strong Will. She would just need to lie like her words were a spell, and she was forcing them to become the truth with her unbreakable Will. "I didn't know it was the Raven Queen," she said, thinking quickly. "There was a woman inside the building. She was casting Newton's family spell, the one he uses to calm himself, and using it to protect against the strings. She saw me, and she winked at me, and I felt *something*, but I thought it was just a psychological reaction. Like a shiver, or something." She considered making the obvious suggestion that the Raven Queen had been involved in Newton's misfortune, but didn't want to get her real identity in even more trouble with the law if it was possible to avoid it.

Professor Lacer raised a hand to stop her. "Go back to the beginning. How did you find yourself in the city, so far from the University, *after* curfew?" he asked pointedly.

Investigator Kuchen interjected, bowing slightly to Professor Lacer. "Newton Moore, the Aberrant's previous name, was a student—young Mr. Siverling's student liaison, I am told. Tanya Canelo, the other student liaison, was also there for the entire incident, but has seemingly been rendered mute. She hasn't said a word since she was extracted from the house, despite no anomalous readings from her. We suspect she is simply refusing to speak."

'That probably serves Tanya well, since she can hardly tell the truth while explaining

why she was out tonight.' Sebastien was hoping to let the conversation go on as long as possible without her input so she could learn more about what they already knew, but all eyes turned toward her expectantly.

She swallowed. "Newton asked me to. He said he was going to do something dangerous, and he wanted backup. He gave me a warded, linked artifact, and I was supposed to be close enough to come find him quickly if he triggered it. I didn't expect *this*, though."

"What was he doing that was so dangerous?" Lord Westbay asked, at the same time Professor Lacer said, "And you *agreed* to this?"

Sebastien grimaced. "Well. Newton said it probably wouldn't be dangerous. He wanted someone available and able to find him just in case. He asked me to keep it a secret. And I...I had some other things to do in the city anyway."

"What things?" Vernor asked.

Sebastien cleared her throat awkwardly. "I was visiting a friend...at the Silk Door."

Vernor grimaced in distaste then muttered, clearly audible, "I suppose that explains your state of undress. Had to rush out in a hurry, did you?" She looked back at the dress on the table, obviously coming to some strange conclusion about its origin. "I hope you didn't forget to pay."

Sebastien didn't have to fake her blush. It was why the Silk Door was such a good alibi. It made sense that she would want to keep it a secret, and thinking that they had uncovered the scandalous truth, people would stop searching deeper. Sebastien had hoped she'd never have to actually use that alibi, but here she was, revealing herself as a regular visitor of the brothel only a couple of months after the waypoint between Sebastien and Siobhan had first been set up.

At least it was a high-class brothel. All the workers were treated well and compensated fairly, and none were there against their will, or under coercion, at least as far as she knew. The same couldn't be said of many other establishments.

"Yes, yes, *sex*," Professor Lacer said impatiently, waving his hand. "Hurry up and get to the relevant parts."

"Well. The artifact was triggered. I rushed out and did the compass divination Newton taught me to find him. It took me a few tries to get close—I think he was moving—and then suddenly...something happened. I felt really strange"—she shuddered at the memory—"and the divination didn't work anymore. I think that's when Newton lost control and the artifact broke. Right after that, there was a lot of screaming and the sounds of battle spells. I was able to find the building by following the sound."

She raised her hands to rub her face, but noticed some of Chief's dried blood under her nails, so hid her hands at her side instead. "It seemed really stupid to just rush into that, so I tried to be cautious, but by the time I got there the fighting had stopped. There were these vibrating strings everywhere, and there was a huge hole in the side of the building and furniture burning in the street. I was worried to get closer, so I was watching from around the corner to try and spot Newton. Then the coppers got there, and the strings started...eating? Or infecting? They were assimilating a copper. That's when I knew things were really bad." She pulled her knees to her chest.

"What an astute deduction," Professor Lacer muttered acerbically, but his eyes were searching, maybe even worried.

Sebastien resisted the urge to send him a peeved look. Her fake explanation was only slightly stupider than the real one, after all. She continued, her breath coming faster as she recalled the events of earlier that evening, without the artificial calming effects of the Aberrant to filter the experience. "The coppers used some spells, and I noticed the stunning spells seemed to actually work, but they didn't keep attacking. They backed away pretty far from the building, and I guess they were calling the Red Guard, but there were people still inside."

The weight of the undivided attention of Gera, Professor Lacer, and Titus Westbay was powerful. She could feel it pressing on her skin, and looked to the side, her hands clenched into fists. "They came out of a room to the side, and the one in front, a woman, was using Newton's calming spell to counteract those strings. She was leading three others toward the door, the one that goes upstairs, and I was watching through the edge of one of the windows. She saw me, though. She...she made a shushing motion, and then she winked, and I felt like something cold ran over my body." She looked up to Gera, not needing to affect an uncertain expression.

Gera nodded. "That was almost certainly when she bestowed her blessing upon you."

Vernor was scribbling rapidly, frowning at her paper, while Investigator Kuchen was pale, breathing shallowly, as if too afraid to cough out loud and disrupt Sebastien's retelling.

Professor Lacer leaned forward. "That was all? A shushing motion, and a wink? She did not communicate with you in any way?"

Sebastien shook her head. "No. She was too busy humming to talk. To be truthful, I didn't even know who she was. She had feathers growing out of her head. The wanted posters don't mention that. And it was dark."

"Humming?" Vernor and Investigator Kuchen asked at the same time.

"Newton's calming spell is esoteric. You have to take deep breaths and do a low hum through every exhale. I can show you, if you want."

"No," Vernor said quickly. "It could be unsafe."

"Newton taught you this spell?" Lord Westbay asked.

"Did he learn it from the Raven Queen?" Professor Lacer added.

Sebastien's mind kept flashing back to the moment before Newton's Will broke. He'd been frightened, terrified. She could see his face in her mind's eye. And what had happened afterward? She'd *felt* it, when it happened. Tanya had too. "He taught it to me so I could calm myself down when the other students became too irritating. He said it was a family spell, from his grandmother. So I guess you could ask her if that's true? I've used it a fair number of times, and it seems harmless."

"Deep breaths, Mr. Siverling," Professor Lacer said, stepping past the barrier and ignoring Melinda Vernor's aborted move to stop him. He crouched in front of the cot, placing a hand on Sebastien's knee.

Only then did Sebastien realize she'd begun to hyperventilate. She felt like she couldn't get enough air, like she was trapped.

"Exhale slowly." Professor Lacer's words were a command, and she thought she could feel his Will in the air behind them, reinforcing them. "The slower, the better. You must control your body. It does not control you. Exhale all the way."

Sebastien complied, and he guided her breathing for a few more repetitions.

He turned to Vernor with a scowl. "My apprentice has experienced a horrific ordeal, and then was attacked by the very people meant to keep him safe. I think it is best if I took him back to the safety and familiarity of the University."

"I have to get a statement from him," Vernor protested. "And we need some more tests, as well. He gave anomalous readings. You should know the implications, and the dangers, Grandmaster Lacer."

"You were seen coming out of the building through one of the windows," Investigator Kuchen said. "Please explain how this came to be."

Sebastien nodded. "Well, the four of them walked up the stairs, under the Raven Queen's protection, but I was pretty sure Newton was still inside. There was a body on the floor that seemed to be unconscious, but hadn't been infected by the strings. It was too dark to tell if it was Newton, so I just imitated what I'd seen the woman doing, and used Newton's calming spell to protect myself from the Aberrant while I crawled in the window."

"No one saw you do this?" Kuchen asked, his eyes narrowed.

Sebastien shrugged. "I don't know? The coppers were pretty far back, to get away from the strings, and the sirens went off around that time so I imagine they were distracted calling for backup. It was dark, and with all the fog, I guess they just didn't notice me. In any case, once I was inside, I was feeling really, strangely calm, and the unconscious person on the floor wasn't Newton, so I searched around looking for him. I had—a hunch, maybe— when I saw that huge ball of strings, that maybe he was inside, and I thought he might still be safe because he knows—knew—the calming spell. I'm not really sure what I was thinking. I feel like my judgment might have been impaired."

"Consistent with the reported anomalous effect," Lord Westbay murmured, to which Investigator Kuchen nodded rapidly, making his own notes.

"I picked up a battle wand that must have been dropped on the floor during all the earlier fighting, and I used it to cut through the sphere of strings and crawl through it. I had to put the wand in my mouth because my hands were occupied. There was a string...body inside. Not like the other people that were turned. It still looked mostly like a human form. It had the other half of the artifact Newton g-gave me, broken. That's when I realized it was him, and that he was...he was an Ab-Aberrant." She clenched her chattering teeth, then continued.

"I shot him in the head with the stunning wand a couple of times, and that cleared my mind enough to let me escape." Sebastien began to tremble.

"The boy speaks truth," Gera said.

Professor Lacer frowned down at Sebastien's clothing, then took off his own coat—the one that reached his knees and always fluttered behind him so dramatically—and flung it around Sebastien's shoulders. "That is the most asinine thing I have ever heard," Professor Lacer said, deadpan. "You deserve to be dead." He pulled out a beast core and, with a wave of his hand, the air around Sebastien fluttered with sudden heat.

She shuddered, both from the relief of the cold and his words. "I know," she agreed, refusing to duck her head. "I agree. I should have told someone from the beginning about what Newton was planning. But I didn't think it would come to this. As for climbing inside that building, I can only argue temporary insanity."

Professor Lacer's eyes narrowed at that. "Indeed."

"I'll need to see that artifact," Vernor said.

Sebastien pulled both of Newton's bracelets and her own that had been paired with his out of the pocket where she'd stashed them. She tossed them to the edge of the shield boundary, where Vernor used a pair of tongs to reach through and pick them up.

Once broken, the sympathetic connection between the bracelets ceased to exist. Neither could be used to scry for the other, but she wished she'd thought to cast the shedding-destroyer spell on her bracelet. Most thaumaturges would find it impossible to cast with skin cells too small to even see, and even the coppers' scrying spell probably wouldn't lock onto such a tiny sample, but she felt uncomfortable leaving it in the hands of the Red Guard.

"Did you retrieve anything else from Mr. Moore?" the woman asked.

"Um. I picked up his Conduit."

"We'll need to examine that too."

"Why?" Sebastien was pretty sure that the creation of an Aberrant had no effect on their Conduit, specifically.

Vernor motioned impatiently.

"I want to give his things back to his family," Sebastien said stubbornly.

"You will be able to. Ms. Vernor will return Mr. Moore's belongings to you once she has examined them to ensure they are safe and hold no important information about tonight's incident," Professor Lacer said, giving Vernor a hard look.

She pursed her lips sourly, but nodded.

Sebastien hugged herself, leaning forward to rest her forehead on her knees as she tried to think of anything else besides the events that filled the last hour of her memory. She wished they would become surreal, a poorly defined fog of impressions, but she knew that would never happen. Siobhan Naught's mind didn't forget, it only buried.

5 2

HIRAETH

Sebastien
Month 1, Day 21, Thursday 12:20 a.m.

"What do you think?" Lord Westbay asked Professor Lacer.

"I need more information. The Canelo girl's testimony is vital. Why was the Raven Queen here tonight? Why give my apprentice a blessing?" He said the last a little quieter, looking over Sebastien contemplatively. "How did she escape from the building?"

Despite the wondrous warmth he had created, Sebastien's shivers were not subsiding. With an effort of will, she lifted her head from her knees. She just had to keep going a little longer.

"Also, did she somehow trigger the boy's loss of control?" Kuchen muttered.

Thaddeus turned to Gera. "Tell me everything you know about the Raven Queen. At this point, being the only one in this room to have interacted with her directly, you seem to be our foremost expert on the woman."

Everyone else seemed equally enraptured by the promise of details on the elusive Raven Queen.

Gera shook her head. "The things I say must remain confidential. She has warned us against spreading rumors attached to her name. My brother ordered that we not speak her name to outsiders. They say she can hear when you pray to her, and she may be able to listen in when she is spoken of."

Professor Lacer scoffed. "That is nothing more than horror stories created to frighten children and adults so ignorant of the mechanics of magic they might as well be children. It is implausible in the extreme, and though I hesitate to use the word impossible, this approaches that hyperbole."

Gera shook her head. "You have not met her. But in any case, I doubt she is a woman in the sense you mean. She may take the form of one, but that means little. She presents herself as a human female, but when I met her there were anomalies, if you knew enough to notice them, and I do not dare to guess at her true form."

"Anomalies?" Professor Lacer asked impatiently.

"I believe she is a creature of night. Of dreams and shadows. My people have tales of them, passed down from many generations before. Her gaze is black and empty, a pupil without iris, and imparts an instinctive wariness when you meet it. She smelled of darkness, old blood, and the charge of a thunderstorm. Feathers grew from her scalp and wove through her hair, which shimmered with the iridescence of a raven's feather. And despite all this, everything about her screamed that she was utterly inconsequential, nothing more than a shadow in the corner of your eye, best ignored."

Sebastien was impressed with the hushed, theatrical tone of Gera's voice and the inventiveness of the description. She was more confident than ever that Oliver had sent the woman, because surely Gera had guessed who she was, even in this form, and was doing her best to differentiate Sebastien, and even Siobhan, from the identity of the Raven Queen. With Gera's help, the rumors would grow into such fantastical relief that an unassuming young sorcerer would be almost impossible to associate with the Raven Queen. *'The ward against untruth is almost certainly accompanied by a divination to suss out lies. She doesn't have my divination-diverting ward, but obviously she's got some other way to bypass both.'*

"She wields great power over the domain of dreams. I witnessed her grant a different blessing with this power, accomplishing what not even the greatest thaumaturges who I called upon for help before her could." She raised her hand to stop Professor Lacer before his mouth could even fully open to question her. "I will give no details of this boon. You may believe me or not, but I will not speak more of it." When he didn't argue, only scowling, Gera continued. "Stories say her kind may travel on the night wind or through the shadows themselves, and I witnessed this myself."

'Yes, definitely lying to keep me out of trouble.' Sebastien almost wanted to laugh aloud at the absurdity of it, and the shivers were subsiding as the amusement distracted her. The whole thing was ridiculous, totally unbelievable. Being in a tent with a group of powerful, influential people who were taking this seriously was almost surreal. But as long as they believed it, working from such a fallacious base premise would always lead them to the incorrect conclusion.

"She was there one moment and gone the next," Gera continued. "We searched everywhere for her, but there was not even a hint of her passing. Some of the stories say her kind can disappear as soon as there is no mortal eye looking upon them. She likely disappeared in the same way tonight. As for her purpose here, who can say for sure? The Raven Queen is mischievous, vengeful to those who anger her, and benevolent to those who please her. The Morrows disrespected her and gained her ire. The boy..." She turned her head back to Sebastien, and for a moment the pressure on the anti-divination ward increased, though Gera had been avoiding placing too much scrutiny on her for most of the conversation. "Perhaps he amused her with his curiosity and bravery, to get so close to a deadly Aberrant. Or perhaps she was sending a message. Her blessing is great. So can her wrath be. I say with complete honesty that it is my great desire to never gain her ire."

Sebastien gave the shallowest nod of thanks, which went unnoticed as everyone else was staring at Gera, who let out a breath in what was a convincing show of settling anxiety. "Shall we go to see the building? Perhaps I can provide insight into the events that transpired within, or I can help question some of the other witnesses. The Morrows, perhaps, if this Canelo is refusing to speak."

Lord Westbay and Inspector Kuchen left with Gera to look over the other survivors and the crime scene.

Professor Lacer hesitated, obviously interested in going with them, but remained with Sebastien while Vernor insisted on going through her own list of questions from the top. He refused to leave Sebastien alone with her, using a free-cast spell to create himself an invisible chair in the air, upon which he lounged with ominous relaxation.

Vernor asked for details as if trying to catch Sebastien in a lie, but seemed self-conscious around Professor Lacer, whose thundercloud scowl grew darker with every question and passing minute.

To Sebastien's relief, Vernor seemed to find nothing unusual about the bracelets or Newton's Conduit, and after recording all the data she could, including capturing their likeness from every conceivable angle with an artifact, she returned everything to Sebastien, except her battle wand, for which Sebastien did not have a license and couldn't argue to keep. She doubted she would have ever been allowed even those concessions without Professor Lacer, and it was probably against their protocol. His influence was surprising, and lent more credence to the rumors that he had once been part of the Red Guard.

When the woman turned back to her notes, Sebastien tucked everything back into her pocket. *'I'll burn the bracelets. Just in case.'* She wished she was powerful enough to free-cast the spell that would destroy any bodily shedding or remains, as that would have solved the issue from the beginning.

Halfway through, Titus Westbay returned to the tent, informing Professor Lacer that they were taking the Morrows to Harrow Hill Penitentiary for further questioning, but that Tanya was being remanded to the University infirmary at the insistence of one of the healers.

'Munchworth probably doesn't want her being forced to talk.' She wondered briefly if Tanya was safe. *'Would they orchestrate some "accident" to keep her quiet?'* But there was nothing Sebastien could do about that. Tanya had chosen her own fate, so she put it out of her mind.

When they reached the end of the questions, Sebastien's eyes burned with fatigue and her thoughts felt foggy.

Vernor began to ask the same questions again in different ways, and Sebastien resisted the urge to sag with defeat. "Newton was my friend," she whispered, pressing hard on her burning eyes to keep tears from welling in them.

Professor Lacer stood abruptly. "That is enough, I think. *Well past* enough. My apprentice has answered all your questions, and is in need of rest. He will be returning to the care of the University healers immediately. If he remembers any other relevant information, I will contact you."

Vernor tried to protest, but Lacer ignored her, effortlessly undoing the ward around Sebastien's bed.

"Wait!" Vernor yelled. "The confidentiality vow!"

Lacer sighed, running a hand over his face. "Quickly." His short beard and the hair of his eyebrows were both tousled, lifted from his skin as if they were afraid of his ire and trying to escape his face. Or perhaps it was static electricity. But it made him look wild, and even more dangerous.

Vernor hurried out, returning a minute later with a glyph-carved human skull, which she thrust toward Sebastien. "Place your hand on this and repeat after me," she said.

Sebastien leaned back from the skull, eyeing it suspiciously. "I will not do any sort of blood vow."

"No blood is necessary. With this artifact, your word is your bond," Vernor said impatiently, pushing the skull toward Sebastien.

"How does it work, then?"

"Rare components, advanced artificery," Professor Lacer said. "It will place a strong compulsion on you to adhere to what you promise."

Sebastien wanted to question them further, but it was obvious she wouldn't be leaving this tent without making the "confidentiality vow," and she was too exhausted to continue putting up a fight. She placed her hand on the skull.

It was warm under her frozen fingers, and she felt a tingle in her chest next to her heart.

"Be sure to state your full name. The one you were given at birth," Vernor said. She had obviously memorized the vow, and recited it quickly, pausing after every sentence for Sebastien to echo her. It was surprisingly simple and straightforward.

"I, Sebastien Siverling, will not divulge any details regarding the events of this night to those who do not have prior knowledge of them. This includes any information relating to the individuals involved, the events that took place, or the operations of the Red Guard. This restriction does not apply to members of law enforcement, including any members of the Red Guard."

'Will the vow truly restrict me, since Sebastien Siverling isn't the name my parents gave me? Even now I only use it some of the time.'

With that, Professor Lacer allowed her to pack up her belongings in her bag and led her out of the tent. He kept a hand around her shoulders, as if to support her.

It was well past midnight by then, and after such a long, difficult day Sebastien was embarrassed to admit that, without him to lean on, she might have stumbled under the weight of her exhaustion.

Despite the late hour, the street was bustling with coppers and more than a few members of the Red Guard. She couldn't see the building that had been the setting for Newton's last moments, but could tell where it was from the bright light diffusing through the fog and up into the sky about a block away.

Professor Lacer led them past the edge of the cordon, flashing his University token at the nervous copper guarding it.

Apparently, he'd paid his carriage to wait for him all that time. He helped her inside, sat across from her, and they were off immediately, bouncing briskly along the cobbled street.

Her eyes wanted to drift closed, but his steady gaze on her kept her from relaxing.

Suddenly Sebastien felt the searching tendrils of a divination sliding off her ward.

There was no overt indication of the spell Professor Lacer had just cast, except for his piercing gaze. "When was our first meeting?" he asked suddenly.

She wanted to ask, "What?" but she knew from experience in his classroom that he hated "inane" responses that vaguely requested a repetition of the initial question without imparting any information about the source of confusion, and which were most often used to stall for time. Instead, she was silent for a few seconds, then said, "We met on the last day to apply for the entrance examination. I don't know if you remember. We didn't speak. I had been arguing with Damien. Our first official meeting was during the oral portion of my entrance exam."

"What theoretical research am I helping you with?"

She was quicker this time. "Decreasing or even eliminating the need to sleep."

"What caused you to experience Will-strain earlier this year?"

She opened her mouth, then closed it and narrowed her eyes. "Why the questions?"

He gave her a small smile. "Good. I needed to be sure it was you. They say the Raven Queen is a shapeshifter, after all. I will admit I am slightly disappointed. Since you are indeed Sebastien, that means my apprentice is an incurable reckless idiot, and I am not about to have the opportunity to speak discreetly with the Raven Queen."

Sebastien's eyes widened. "You..." She trailed off, so many questions in her mind that she didn't know which one to choose. Perversely, she was reassured that he did indeed have a way to free-cast a divination that would suss out deception. It didn't seem to work on her, but she would know when he was trying to cast it.

"Do you have any messages for me, now that we are alone? I assure you, it is safe to communicate freely."

She shook her head silently, still in shock.

He pursed his lips in disappointment. "Any urges that seem illogical or out of character?"

"No."

"Think carefully."

'He took Gera's testimony much too seriously.' She was quite sure that the Raven Queen hadn't placed any strange geas or compulsions on her, since she *was* the Raven Queen. "I'm sure."

He settled back, one finger tapping against his large Conduit absentmindedly. "Do you have any idea why she gave you her blessing tonight? Specifically, a protection against divination?"

Sebastien suppressed a shiver of unease. "The prognos woman suggested that the Raven Queen was just being impulsive, or sending a message about her power? The coppers haven't been able to find her all this time. It could be a jab at them," she deflected.

"She most likely *was* sending a message," he agreed, "but not to the coppers, I think. What were Mr. Moore and Ms. Canelo really doing tonight?"

"You'll have to ask Tanya." Sebastien hesitated, wondering if Professor Lacer knew about Tanya's connection to the University faculty.

He noticed the moment of indecision. "You know something. Speak."

There was no magic spell behind the word to compel her, but the force of his command needed none. "She was sending paper bird messages to someone, after the gang battle. That spell is limited in range and needs a beacon of some sort to find its target, which I gather is usually the University token. So it seems likely that whoever she was communicating with was on campus."

Professor Lacer didn't react to the revelation, so she couldn't tell if he was surprised or if he already knew about whatever Professor Munchworth was involved in. It was even possible that Professor Lacer was involved with that same faction, but she had no way to know. "Did anyone else know about what was going to happen tonight?"

She shook her head. "The decision to leave seemed very last-minute. I didn't tell anyone, but I'm not sure if Newton or Tanya might have."

Professor Lacer seemed to lose interest in interrogating her. She wriggled her toes, which were again growing numb with cold and the restrictive press of her secret Conduit digging into her calf. In a small voice, she asked, "What are they going to do with Newton—the Aberrant, I mean? And the building? The other people? How are they going to handle something like this?"

"Everyone involved will be questioned, arrested for any illegal activities, and made to take a similar vow as yourself, though likely rather more restrictive. If it is deemed that there are no ongoing harmful or infectious side effects from exposure to the Aberrant, they will be allowed to resume their lives. The Aberrant will be dealt with by the Red Guard. If they deem the cleared building to be safe to occupy, it will be allowed to remain, and the family within it. With an Aberrant created from such a mediocre, low-level University student, I doubt there will be any issue with ongoing contamination. However, if I am wrong, the site will either be razed to cleanse the contamination or placed under a permanent quarantine barrier."

"And if there *are* ongoing side effects? In the people, specifically? What happens to them? To me?" She wrapped her arms around herself, feeling that if she didn't, she might crack apart, and her insides would spill out. Or burst into string.

She shuddered violently.

"The effects will be studied and neutralized if possible. The Red Guard has no lack of resources, Mr. Siverling, and I have no intention of allowing something like this to deprive me of my apprentice. You are only just becoming truly interesting." He gave her another small smile, but she couldn't tell if he was joking.

To her horror and shame, rather than shooting back a witty quip or even a more boring, ordinary response, her burning eyes filled with tears. They spilled almost instantly down her cheeks. She blinked, scrubbing frantically at her face. "I'm sorry. Everything that happened tonight...it just feels so *wrong*."

Newton wouldn't be there in the morning, wouldn't be there ever again, and yet somehow it seemed like she would be continuing with her ruse, unsuspected.

Lacer's smile slipped away. "You are overtired, and likely approaching Will-strain. I am taking you to the infirmary."

'*No, I need to talk to Damien as soon as he arrives, to keep him from doing or saying anything foolish.'* She tried to protest, but instead of calming, her tears came only faster, and began to draw out great, heaving sobs. She pulled her knees to her chest again, trying to pull her emotions back together in the same way.

She longed for her home. A home that maybe had never existed, though she once thought it had.

Professor Lacer gave her a solemn, inscrutable look, then gestured toward her with his Conduit. There was a brief moment of utter silence, and then the fatigue rolled over her, too heavy to resist.

'I don't want to sleep,' was her last thought, but it was too late.

Thank you for reading.

The story continues in *A Practical Guide to Sorcery Book III: A Sacrifice of Light*
Buy it now: https://books2read.com/SacrificeOfLight

If you would like access to:

- Illustrated excerpts from Siobhan's grimoire and portraits of the characters
- Exclusive short stories/bonus chapters/deleted scenes not available elsewhere
- The chance to read the latest pre-release chapters of the upcoming book as I finish them
- And other story-related goodies and opportunities...

Consider supporting me on Patreon:
https://www.patreon.com/AzaleaEllis

GLOSSARY OF MAGICAL TERMS

ABERRANT

Thaumaturges who have lost control of the magic they channel, but instead of dying, have been changed. They are usually much more magically powerful than they were in life, and almost always have physical mutations. Some Aberrants merely mutate into a dangerous beast-like being, rabid for death and destruction. Some mutate into grotesque or phantasmagorical forms, and have esoteric magical effects. Some mutations remain minor, while the mind and powers are twisted insidiously.

Uniformly, an Aberrant is no longer human, having lost their previous thoughts and desires. Almost all Aberrants are malicious, even those with seemingly benign effects. It is believed one is more likely to break and become an Aberrant with a corrupted Will from casting immoral magics.

ADDER STONE

A stone with a hole worn through the middle by natural means, it is said that adder stones impart clarity of mind and vision, and one can look through the hole to reveal illusions. Useful on their own, or as a component in spells.

ADHEL JUICE

Mixed with honey, it creates a strong sticky substance. It can be cleared through applying oil.

ALCHEMY

A ritual form of spellcasting that uses organic and inorganic components to create magical concoctions. The most common method of performing alchemy is through the use of a cauldron to create potions, philtres, draughts, and tinctures. It is the least expensive way to save a particular magic for instant use at a later time, but not the most efficient way. As with all ritual spells, the magic woven into alchemical concoctions is semi-permanent.

ALL-PURPOSE ANTIDOTE POTION

A mild antidote to common poisons and venoms, the all-purpose antidote is best used on mild irritants, or to buy time for a more thorough solution to serious toxins. It can be used in lieu of a sobering potion to diminish the effects of alcohol.

ANIMATION SPELL

Animation spells give temporary and false life to an inanimate object, such as in the case of the Glasshopper's eponymous confections.

ANTI-ANXIETY POTION

Also known as a calming potion, this is a weaker and less addictive version of the elixir of peace. The University infirmary keeps a large amount on hand for students struggling with stress.

ANTI-COUGHING PHILTRE

Suppresses the urge to cough. As coughing is often useful to clear liquid from the lungs, this philtre is used when there are extenuating circumstances, like broken ribs, that may cause more damage.

ARCANUM

A magical institution, teaching "secrets" of magic and the arcane.

ARTIFICERY

A craft of magic that embeds a pre-cast spell in an object for later release, or enchantment—changing the object's state. Battle wands, light crystals, and self-cleaning chamberpots are examples of artifacts. Enchantments and Wards are a sub-set of Artificery.

AUGER

A drilling artifact created in Osham. Though meant for mining and construction, it can also be utilized to brute-force wardbreak.

AVERY PARK

An area of greenery around southwest Gilbratha.

BALL OF LIGHT SPELL

Causes a spherical section of the air to glow with the illusion of a ball of light. Brightness, color, size, and location can be controlled.

BANSHEE

A humanoid magical creature that is dangerous to humans, and attacks with their voice through incapacitating screams and songs with a soporific effect.

BARK SKIN POTION

Grows a protective layer of bark over the skin of the drinker, while still allowing them most of their range of motion. While not as strong as plate mail armor, it is much lighter, and more effective than chainmail against atmospheric attacks. When damaged, chunks of bark will fall off, which can be useful against spreading attacks like rotting curses or acid.

BATTLE WAND

A wand-shaped artifact charged with offensive spells. For law enforcement, this is most commonly a stunning spell.

BEAST CORE

Beast cores, which resemble raw gems, are harvested from dead magical beasts, and can be used to power spells in place of other sources of energy. They come in many different colors, though the color itself is not as important as the brightness and clarity, with brighter and clearer cores being easier to drawn energy from.

Beast cores contain a total energy value of thousands of thaums, up to millions of thaums, and are generally rated either by their total energy value, or their per-second capacity if they were drained completely over the course of an hour.

When drained, beast cores will shatter and crumble, and cannot be recharged. Due to this, they are a rather expensive source of power, and are most commonly used for emergencies, for high-power spells that make it inconvenient to use lesser sources of power, or by those who have the coin to spend in exchange for convenience.

Beast cores become exponentially more expensive as their quality increases, similar to celerium.

BEAST KING

A figure shrouded in mystery and fear, the beast king is sleeping in Silva Erde, deep below the ground. While details about him are vague, diviners consistently find that if he wakes from his long sleep, calamity will follow.

BEWITCHMENT HEX

Draws the attention and interest of the victim.

BLACK STAR SAPPHIRE

A gem that can be used (as can many gems) as a Conduit. It is not as robust as celerium. As components, star sapphires can be used in space-bending spells, and it is said that a black star sapphire was used in a spell to travel within and through shadows faster than any mortal could otherwise move.

BLIGHT-TYPE ABERRANT

These Aberrants spread their anomalous effect, physically or otherwise, expanding their area of influence. If allowed to get out of control, they can cause true devastation. The first priority for this type of Aberrant is containment.

BLOOD CLOTTING POTION

Poured on a wound, clots blood and can stop excessive blood loss. It can allow someone to wait till medical attention arrives when otherwise they might bleed out. Not typically considered a battle potion, because it dos not have offensive effects.

BLOOD EMPEROR

The Blood Emperor was the leader of the Third Empire, also known as the Blood Empire. His invading forces, from an unknown land beyond the northern ice oceans, conquered the continent about three hundred years ago. His empire was eventually overthrown, but his policies shaped much of modern society even after the Third Empire's downfall. However, atrocities committed in the name of learning and power caused a severe backlash against all forms of blood magic and its practitioners.

BLOOD PRINT VOW

A spell that binds two or more parties to an agreement spoken while casting, bound by a thumbprint of blood. If at least one of the vowers cannot cast magic, a third party binder must be present to do so.

BLOOD-REGENERATION POTION

Boosts blood regeneration, but takes time and places strain on the body.

BRILLIG

A powerful race with strong affinity to magic, now extinct, or close to it.

CAIDAN'S THEOREM

If distance is measured in meters, a divination spell with the base cost B will require B x distance/100 ^ (B/100) thaums to cast.

CALMING SPELL

Forces calm and docility on the target.

CAT'S COUGH

An herb. Commonly smoked, it is addictive and gives a raspy, deep voice over time.

CATACLYSM

An apocalyptic event that destroyed civilization over ten thousand years ago, and which is still shrouded in mystery.

CHAMELEON SPELL

Allows a non-living object to partially blend in with its surroundings.

CHARYBDIS GULF

The sea inlet that bisects the main area of Gilbratha from the Lilies—the rich area where many of the nobles and socialites live—to the east. The Charybdis Gulf is dangerous, containing magical water beasts that will drown a swimmer and even capsize small fishing boats, yet despite this remains a large source of income and food, especially for the poorer citizens.

CINDER STAG

A powerful Aberrant that is contained within a sundered zone, the Cinder Stag still manages to affect the world outside the sundered zone with karmic flames of retribution that can follow a chain of cause-and-effect back to its source.

CIRCLE

Facilitates the three main elements of magic. It places a physical boundary around a spherical domain controlled by the thaumaturge, signifying that the things within are theirs to trade away and change as they wish.

COCKATRICE

Two-legged dragon-like creature with a rooster's head. (And more or less the shape of a chicken.) Weasels are their natural enemy. Can be the familiar of a witch.

COLD BOX ARTIFACT

Sometimes referred to as an ice box, this is an artifact which keeps the contents placed within it chilled or frozen by siphoning out their heat.

COMPASS DIVINATION SPELL

Uses a two halves of a spelled, linked bone disk as a sympathetic beacon and a stick with one burnt end. Using one half of the bone, the burnt end of the stick will point toward the other half, like a compass.

COMPREHENSIVE COMPENDIUM OF COMPONENTS

A restricted book that contains its namesake, including components that are illegal and unethical.

CONCUSSION-MODIFIED FIREBALL SPELL

Adds a force effect to the fireball spell, similar to an explosion.

CONCUSSIVE BLAST SPELL

Shoots ball of force which expands and weakens with distance, but can cause severe damage to a human (particularly their internal organs) or even break through walls at close range. It is often visible as a waver or fogginess in the air, but much less conspicuous than a fireball or stunning spell.

CONDUIT

Channels the thaumaturgic energy being converted as a spell is cast. For most sorcerers, this is a celerium crystal, which is resistant to the destructive effects of channeling magic. Witches may use their familiars as Conduits, and those sorcerers who cannot afford celerium may use lesser gems, such as diamonds or sapphires.

CONTACT STUNNING SPELL

Set into a ring artifact, releases the spell on firm, sudden contact, like a punch.

CONTINUE-MOTION SPELL

A complex, finicky spell that allows the caster to demonstrate an action as one of the inputs of the spell. The spell will continue this action, *exactly*, for as long as it is empowered. It is good for things like stirring a pot continuously, spinning thread, or weaving cloth, which require relatively simple, repetitive movements.

COPPERS

Law enforcement, named for the copper nails in the soles of their boots, the distinctive sound of which announces their approach wherever they go.

CRAFT

Specific path of magic: Sorcerer, Artificer, Witch, Magician, Shaman, Animist, Gestura, etc.

DEAFENING HEX

Causes deafness, usually temporary, though some variations will persist for a period of time after the caster stops focusing on the hex. Some variations can be used to some effect against a banshee in place of a vibration-canceler.

DEVIL

They possess living beings.

DINGLEBERRY BUSHES

Dingleberry bushes are named for their small, hard brown fruits that smell like feces and rot even before they fall to the ground.

DISSOLVING TINCTURE

A concentrated alchemical concoction that will dissolve other substances it comes into contact with, the dissolving tincture has many variants that can be adapted to the type of material the alchemist wishes to dissolve. Similar to a strong acid, but more versatile.

DIVINER'S SIGHT

Special magical sight of the divination realm, which reveals that which might not be seen with the normal eye. It is a catch-all term that includes any ocular enhancements, such as the ability to see in the dark.

DOORJAMB ALARM WARD

A small ward spell, carved into the underside of a door, will alert the caster when the door is opened.

DORIENNE INVISIBILITY SPELL

A spell that uses the self-camouflaging dorienne fish to create true invisibility through which light can pass. The dorienne fish itself sees through its skin and adjusts its pigment on one side of its body to what it sees on the other to appear invisible.

DRAGON SCALES

A magical component.

DRAKE

A miniature dragon creature. Not as intelligent or powerful. Can be the familiar of a witch.

DRAUGHT OF BORROWED GILLS

This concoction allows someone to breath underwater by dropping a small, living fish into a mucousy concoction and then gulping the whole thing down whole. The fish is kept alive within a bubble of potion within the stomach for a few minutes, during which time the fish's ability to filter oxygen from water is transferred to the drinker's lungs.

When the fish dies and the draught's effect wears off, the drinker must expel the water from their lungs quickly to avoid drowning. Often, use of this potion in dirty water can lead to complications and long-term side effects, so it should not be used recreationally.

DREAM-WALKING

Often practiced by shamans, it is a form of divination that sends their consciousness into the dream of another, most often for exploration or healing purposes.

DREAMLESS SLEEP SPELL

Keeps one from dreaming, using crystal and eagle feathers as components, and cast on the pillow Siobhan uses, or anywhere under her head. Uses alcohol and herb tincture as the Circle, which evaporates quickly and isn't uncomfortable to sleep on.

DRYAD

A creature of living wood, shaped like a humanoid woman. They come in different sub-species of trees, and can be very small when young. Sometimes they disguise themselves as trees before the unwary or unobservant, and short bursts of activity are often followed by long periods of "sleep."

DUELING BOARD

A game where the pieces shoot fake spells at each other and dodge attacks under the control of the players.

DYSENTERY SUSTAINING POTION

Diluted in large amounts of water, will keep a patient with diarrhea or dysentery hydrated with a small amount of calories and the immediately necessary electrolytes and minerals, and slightly slows the rate of expulsion, allowing absorption.

EARTH DISINTEGRATION AND STONE CREATION SPELL

One of Professor Lacer's practice exercises. Dirt or stone can be turned to sand and back again to stone using either transmutation, which creates the effect through natural processes, or through duplicative transmogrification, which copies the properties of existing material.

EARTH-ASPECTED WETA

Magical beast with a very tough hide.

ELCAN IRISES

A deadly, flesh-eating plant with purple-streaked flowers whose long, tapered petals open and turn to follow prey as it passes, releasing sweet-smelling pollen into the air. They lure their prey with their beauty and the soporific properties of their pollen.

ELEMENTAL PLANES

The five known Elemental Planes are accessible through planar portal spells from the mundane plane, where humans and other mundane races live. Each Elemental Plane corresponds to an element: Radiance, Fire, Air, Water, and Earth. Creatures, plants, and even the water and soil from the Elemental Planes will be imbued with the energy of their plane, and are powerful spell-casting components. Each Elemental Plane has sapient creatures, some of which are humanoid and can even cross breed with humans.

ELEMENTALS

Beings from the Elemental Planes. On the mundane plane (Earth), they are most often encountered as the familiars of witches, who use them as a Conduit to channel magic. When sapient and humanoid, they have specific labels.
Radiance—Angels
Fire—Demons
Air—Sylphides
Water—Undine
Earth—Erdgeist
Elixir of Euphoria
An alchemical concoction which, in low doses, combats depression, but is more often sold recreationally for the eponymous euphoria.

ELIXIR OF PEACE

Imparts a sense of well-being, and can be used in small doses to combat depression and anxiety, or for its recreational effects in larger doses. It is used in war to give soldiers who are dying some peace in their last moments.

ENERGY-REFLECTING SPELL

A general-purpose ward. A more expensive and inefficient defense than setting wards against more specific spells or incidents.

ERYTHREAN HORSE

Horse with partial magical lineage. They are extremely expensive, but don't look much different from a normal horse.

ETHERWOOD LEAVES

A luxury leaf for smoking. They are dark blue. The smoke is smooth and calming, great for blowing smoke rings, but nonaddictive.

EVER-INKING PEN ARTIFACT

Comes as a set with an inkwell. Spelled to automatically refill the ink cartridge of the pen with ink from the inkwell whenever not in use. More expensive ones refill based on the rate of expenditure, and some very expensive ones maintain a folded space within the pen's ink cartridge, so the user never needs worry about their inkwell running dry.

FABRIC CUTTING SPELL

This spell creates a short-range slicing blade of air that extends outward in an arc, the shape of which can be controlled to some degree by the caster's Will. Unlike many similar spells, it doesn't require the target to be within the Circle, as it uses compressed air as the cutting edge. At longer distances the cutting edge, visible as a faintly glowing shimmer in the air, degrades severely.

With practice and enough power, it can be used to overcome the inherent magical barrier that living creatures possess, and injure a human or animal.

FEVER REDUCING POTION/BALM

Cools the head, with some cooling to the body as well, along with pain relief. Encourages comfort, allows sleep, and should be given in conjunction with a sustaining draught.

FEY

A powerful race with strong affinity to magic, now close to extinct. They were supposedly so agile they could dance between raindrops without ever being hit.

FINGER BONE DIVINATION

Human finger bones can be used in (illegal) divination, after being processed and etched with symbols and glyphs. The diviner will shake them while casting the divination, throw them, and then read the spell's output in the way they have fallen, with certain glyphs in certain positions or crossing others. Depending on the amount of bones and what output options have been etched into them, this type of divination can have nuance and impart a greater amount of information than similar methods like dice-throwing or card reading.

FIREBALL SPELL

Shoots a ball of fire at about 12 meters per second.

FLEETFOOT POTION

Fractionally increases movement speed, but not reaction speed.

FLESH-FUSING POTION

A more powerful version of the skin-knitting salve, this potion is meant to seal larger wounds, ideally after the use of the blood-clotting potion.

FLICKER-FEATHER BIRD

Small birds that blink in and out of visibility with every flap of their wings.

FORTNER'S

A high class, bespoke clothing shop.

FREE-CASTING

Casting magic at will, without the stabilizing external Word of a physical spell array, a ritual, or special movements. The Word, and sometimes the Circle as well, is instead held solely in the mind. This feat is extremely difficult, and only a few are proficient in it.

GARDEN OF WONDERS

An element of a children's tale, which the University Menagerie seems to exemplify.

GASPING-TENTACLES SPELL

A spell which creates temporary tentacles growing from a solid, nonliving surface. Used to bind or obstruct movement from a distance, and often employed as a nonlethal method of detainment. Gone wrong, can strangle a victim to death.

GOLD DUPLICATION SPELL

A duplicative transmogrification spell that copies a source of matter. As with most attempts to create matter through magic, only the most skilled thaumaturges can create a truly perfect copy that will have the same magical properties as the original, and thus duplicated gold or other substances are often worth less than the authentic originals.

GOLDEN APPLE

Fruit from a magical tree that closely resembles a gold-skinned apple, and are said to improve organ function and thus increase a person's lifespan.

GREGORIAN SNAIL

Magical animal. Mucus can be used as a thickening agent in most salves and lotions, especially those meant for the face.

GREMLIN

Small humanoid creatures with spiky backs, large strange eyes, and small razor-sharp claws. They seem to have a great desire to fly, and collect feathers, steal eggs, and other futile attempts to reach the skies. They are sentient and somewhat trainable, but not considered sapient.

GROUP PROPRIOCEPTION POTION

Lets everyone who drank from the same batch instinctively know where the others were for a period of time. Its main component is a magical sea lichen that connects and disconnects any singular part of itself at will, still somehow communicating with the greater whole to capture prey and then confine it until it starved to death.

GRUBB'S BARRIER SPELL

A weak barrier spell that only protects against physical projectiles, with a minimum requirement of under 200 thaums to cast.

GRYPHON

Creature with the head and wings of an eagle, with the body, legs, and tail of a lion. Can be domesticated and flown.

GULD FISH

Minnow-sized fish that glint as if they are made of precious metals polished to a high sheen.

GUST SPELL

Creates a simple gust of wind, with the size and speed depending on the size of the Circle and the amount of power fed to it.

HAG

A magical humanoid. They have a natural predilection to the dark, and good night vision. They have some facility with hexagon/hexagram spells, dealing with balance. Hags who integrate with society may sell good luck talismans (or cursed objects.)

HANGOVER-RELIEF DRAUGHT

Taken in doses of a liter or more, this draught rehydrates, replenishes electrolytes, and mitigates the pain of a hangover. The University infirmary stocks many doses.

HARROW HILL PENITENTIARY

Gilbratha's jail, a stout stone building in the shape of a cross, within a circular wall that encloses the grounds.

HEADACHE-RELIEVING SALVE

Minty. An alchemical concoction that relieves headache pain and helps to rejuvenate the senses.

HEALING POTION

Generalized healing potions, of which there are many different variations of different strengths and capabilities, are an extremely effective method to preserve an injured or ill patient's life. They can be used for most types of wounds or illnesses, and are both convenient and practical. However, due to the price of components—many of which are from the Plane of Light—and the abundance of magical energy packed into these potions, they are expensive.

HELLFIRE

Is sometimes bright neon green.

HEMORRHAGING CURSE

This curse causes the target's blood vessels to rupture and encourages excessive, forceful blood loss. It can sometimes be recognized by the shape of its glowing force as it travels.

HENRIK-THOMPSON

A measure of scale for maximum Will capacity. It is measured by a crystal ball in an array that filters incoming energy and outputs a portion of it as light through the glowing crystal. It's the most widely-used metric, likely due to the fact that Will-capacity is the easiest to test, and often shows correlation to the overall caliber of a thaumaturge's Will. The brighter the light, the more power (thaums) is being channeled per second.

HOMUNCULUS

Very small people, who outwardly seem indistinguishable from humans, but are argued to be a different species due to their facility with certain magics.

HUMAN FINGERNAILS

A component in some spells, human fingernails are illegal due to the restrictions against blood magic.

HUMPHRIES' ADAPTING SOLUTION

An alchemical concoction that can be spelled directly into the veins to take the place of blood in a blood-loss emergency. Expensive, and the shelf-life isn't super long, so it may not always be on hand. Can also be used to keep creatures from the Plane of Water alive on the mundane plane, which was its original purpose.

HYDRA

Multi-headed snake. The number of heads ranges from two to nine, with more heads generally indicating a more powerful, intelligent creature, as information processing and bodily processes are divided among the heads based on their individual priorities and specialties.

ICE LION

A predatory, large, shaggy cat that lives near the northern ice oceans.

IGNORE PAIN SPELL

Muffles pain slightly, allows mind to detach from the focus pain draws, effects wear off quickly once spell is released, but it can allow someone to prepare to heal themselves. Recommended strongly against using this to do things like set bones or put sockets back into place, in case the sudden shock of pain causes the caster to lose control of the spell. Muffles pain by about 15%, so of moderate usefulness. May be good for exercise pain. Esoteric magic.

IMPOTENCE CURSE

A curse that removes the victim's ability to successfully complete intercourse, either through removing their libido, or suppressing their physical ability to copulate.

IMPROVED HEARING SPELL

An esoteric spell that uses hands cupped behind the ears to gather and direct amplified sound, and thus improve selective hearing.

INJURY-PROTECTION WARD

Makes physical damage less likely over a set diameter. Very expensive, but nebulous and thus not very powerful. Still can make a difference, either over time, or in dangerous circumstances.

JENTIL

Giants, who are known for building megalithic monuments.

KITSUNE

A sometimes fox, sometimes woman. In human form, the kitsune will still have her tails, more depending on how old and powerful she is, up to nine. They often use their tails to cover their bodies, wrapping around it in place of clothing, and are considered seductively attractive, though they do not appear often in Siobhan's part of the world.

KREIDAE SPIDER

A magical creature known for stealth and ambushes. Its silk is highly coveted for its transparency and use in camouflage or invisibility cloaks.

KUTHIAN FROG

Has sedative saliva, which is dried, powdered, and used as a component in stunning spells. Upon release from the spell, the treated saliva quickly degrades and becomes inert.

LANDRUM'S NOURISHING DRAUGHT

As with many spells, there are multiple variations of the nourishing draught.

Should be diluted in large amounts of water, which will thicken with the concoction. It contains vitamins, minerals, and electrolytes, as well as some complex sugars/starches. When given frequently, will keep the patient hydrated and with the resources their body needs to continue fighting. The nourishing draught should be created over low heat, to avoid killing the vitamins. Sometimes, it is then dehydrated for long-term storage.

Some versions also induce repeated swallowing, for patients who are insensate and cannot wake to drink. For those with extended nausea, some versions can also help them keep something down, though not stop diarrhea.

LIGHT CRYSTAL

A non-celerium crystal made into an artifact spelled to release light on command. The rich use them in place of candles or lamps, as they are much brighter and require less maintenance. But, though they also last longer than a candle or lamp, they are expensive enough that the common person cannot afford to buy one, even if it would save them money in the long run.

LIGHT SACRIFICE

Light can be used as a source of magical power just like heat, matter, and kinetic force. Converting light within an area to magical power will create an area of darkness, as the light is absorbed before it can pass through or be reflected.

LINO-WHARTON MESSENGER SPELL

A power spell with several pre-requisites. It binds a raven to a controller, allowing the controller to speak through the raven at a distance to transmit messages, or to complete simple tasks.

LIQUID FIRE POTION

When exposed to air, this potion catches fire.

LIQUID STONE POTION

Expands like an aerosol foam and hardens quickly upon contact with air. Can be used as a barrier or a splint for broken bones, among other things. Not permeable to air, or malleable once hardened, so it can suffocate if it lands on the face. Liquid stone's expansion is purposefully inhibited when in contact with living flesh so that those who carry it do not accidentally entomb themselves if a vial breaks accidentally.

It is softer than normal stone, similar with a similar durability as sandstone.

LOOMIS ANTI-AWARENESS FIELD

A spell, in artifact form on Siobhan's heirloom Conduit ring, that dissuades people from noticing or remembering a small object.

LORE-MASTER

A scholar who focuses on the stories of old, on the little-known or forgotten facets of magic and the creatures who use it.

LUGUBRIOUS

A powerful Aberrant.

LUNG-SEALING PHILTRE

When breathed in, this philtre creates a sealed bubble inside the lung, which can apply internal pressure to a puncture wound and keep someone from drowning in their own blood.

LYCANTHROPE

A type of skin-walker, lycanthropes take on and off the skin of a wolf, transforming into the animal at will. Divested of their wolf skins, they lose the ability to transform. A Lycanthrope's animal skin can be used to give a thaumaturge a lesser version of the animal-transformation skill practiced by the skinwalkers themselves, or as a component in taming and binding spells.

MAGICIAN

A person who uses magical artifacts rather than cast spells themselves. Often derided as scammers, charlatans, and unworthy by "true" thaumaturges. An artificer who uses their own artifacts is not considered a magician.

MALEDICTION

A curse spoken with a wronged person's dying breath with brings long-term misfortune to the cursed party. These are considered baseless superstitions by most.

MANDRAKE ROOT

A root plant whose tuber takes the shape of a humanoid being, and which can incapacitate and even kill with their cry if pulled from the muffling earth. They grow more expensive with age, and can be difficult to keep alive. They enjoy being sung to, and may die if not given enough personal attention even if conditions are otherwise optimal. The mandrake root's similarities to the human form make it valuable for spells that would otherwise need a human, such as simulacrum or surrogate spells, and they are most well known for their ability to receive, as a surrogate, a curse transferred from a human victim. They are also used in hallucinogenic spells and concoctions.

MAP-BASED LOCATION DIVINING SPELL

A divination spell that guides a drop of spelled mercury over a place-anchored map to find a location based on a sympathetic connection.

MENDING SPELL

Repairs mundane objects, but requires all the pieces as well as components that would otherwise be required to mend the objects by hand. The mending spell is able to achieve somewhat finer control and dexterity than one might with their hands and fingers.

MERMAID

Mermaids are a magical cephalopod. They lure prey by sticking tentacles above water and making them look like a human woman, who asks for help. When the victim gets too close, the "mermaid" suddenly comes apart into a mass of tentacles that grab them and drag them into the water to be eaten.

METANITE

A powerful Aberrant that the Red Guard has been unable to destroy or contain. It is a void-black form, which destroys everything it touches, but moves very slowly. The Red Guard uses space magic to adjust its path and evacuation to keep people safe from it.

MIMEO-MOTION SPELL

A more complex version of the continue-motion spell, the mimeo-motion spell allows duplication of the copied motion in multiple places. It is used most commonly for mass-producing books.

MIND-MUDDLING JINX

Causes the victim trouble reading, comprehending, and focusing. As with all harmful spells classified as jinxes, it is not permanent, and cast lightly, the victim may not realize they have been affected.

MIRRORED HEALING SPELL/FLESH-MIRRORING SPELL

Using blood of the injured person as a Sacrifice, this spell can mold flesh and bone to match the mirrored side of the body, and thus heal injuries without the need for rare and expensive components.
Uses glyphs "blood," "mirror," and then the physical part in need of mirrored healing, like "tooth." One large Circle around the whole area, and then two inner Circles, meeting in the middle, one which has the good side and one the injured side. Uses a pentagram inside a pentagon, for the combination of transmutation and transmogrification this spell requires. Relies more on the Will and Sacrifice than the clarity or complexity of the written Word. Requires a detailed, focused image of what the caster wants to happen. Using the the wounded person's own blood is especially efficient.

MNEMONIC-LINK TRACKING SPELL

Creates a sympathetic link between an object and the target, but depends on the caster's extreme familiarity with the target, and best augmented by an item that has a direct connection to the target.

MOONBEAMS & FAIRY WINGS

Moonbeams and fairy wings, harvested (from the Menagerie) at night, have mind-altering (recreational drug) effects.

MOONSEEDS

Commonly used in their dried form, similar to pepper, moonseeds are berries from a twining vine. The moonseed vine is nocturnal, growing off-white berries that resemble the pitted moon once dehydrated.

MYRDDIN

An extraordinarily powerful sorcerer who lived over a thousand years before. He has many incredible feats to his name, some based in reality and others in fiction, and has become enough of a household name that he's occasionally used in curses, E.G. "Myrddin's crusty black butthole."

NIGHTMARE-TYPE ABERRANT

This type of Aberrant is the most difficult to deal with, as they use stealth, memetic control, or subversion.

OKORA'S INSTANT COTTAGE

A spell that raises material from the ground to create a small cottage in the shape of a small model cottage used as a component. Size is dependent on power input and spell array parameters. It is easiest to cast with loose material that can be compacted together, such as snow or mud.

ORBS AND AMULETS

The Conduit shop at the north end of Waterside market

OSHER TREE

Young sapling that can uproot itself and move short distances. Sometimes confused for a dryad, but an osher has no humanoid form and is not considered to be intelligent.

PAIRED MOVEMENT WARD

When the ring holding a banner to the base of the spell is ripped away, the sympathetically linked counterpart held elsewhere also detaches. Spell must be cast ahead of time, with both halves of the pair together.

PAPER BIRD SPELL

Used to send letters or messages. The paper birds are spelled to take flight and deliver themselves to set destination or recipients. Unsuitable to fly in heavy winds or rain. They are created from special ingredients that make Siobhan feel they are not as practical as she suspected.

The special paper used to make them requires flicker-feathers from the sparrow-like bird of the same name, which the University cultivates in the Menagerie.

PASSWORD PUZZLE ARTIFACT

In the Night Market, inside a component shop, a stone puzzle disk that must be solved with magic to make the center rise up, allowing access to the warehouse in back and the half-troll, Harvester.

PENDRAGON PALACE

The home of the High Crown, the head of the Thirteen Crown Families and leader of the country of Lenore. It is built atop the white cliffs, to the northeast of Gilbratha.

PERIMETER ALARM WARD

Alerts the caster within when a perimeter has been breached.

PHILTRE OF DARKNESS

After brewing, when this concoction is suddenly exposed to air (e.g. when the bottle is smashed) the roiling liquid within bursts into clouds of magical darkness, which not even powerful night-vision can penetrate.

PHOENIX ASHES

An incredibly rare spell component, the ashes of a phoenix that has reached the end of one of its many life cycles are used to incubate the phoenix's egg as it rebirths itself. They are used in powerful healing and fire spells, and even supposedly spells that can effect one's destiny. Most famously, they were said to have been used by Myrddin to resurrect his recently-deceased lover. They sell for about a hundred gold crowns per gram.

PIERCING SPELL

A shaped spell that, unlike the area-effect concussive blast spell, is focused on penetrative power, and can gouge out a few inches of stone in a narrow diameter.

PIXIE

Humanoid creature with very delicate, multi-petaled flesh wings that constantly regenerate, dropping dandruff and little peels of dry skin. This "pixie dust" is an expensive magical component, and many humans keep them to harvest it. They are intelligent and mischievous, even sometimes malicious, prone to irritation and insults.

PLANAR DIVINATION-DIVERTING WARD

Protects against divination. The recipient will feel pressure under any type of divination/scrying attempt, and can add their Will to the artifact's inherent shielding capabilities to divert stronger and more determined attempts. The ward does not directly oppose a scrying spell, but turns aside, deflects, and hides instead, using its connection to the five Elemental Planes. The effects may also spill into the physical world, making it harder for people to notice and focus on the user.

When actively diverting, the disks may be painful as they consume the user's blood for power.

PLANAR PORTAL

A portal to one of the other Planes.

PLANE OF RADIANCE

One of the five known Elemental Planes, the Plane of Radiance hosts the element of Light in its many forms *and connotations*. Creatures and plants of the radiant element are very valuable spell components, and the most powerful, sentient Elementals from the Plane of Radiance are often called angels. The Plane of Radiance has sympathetic connections to the ideas of light, cleanliness, knowledge, strict justice, and healing.

PLANES-DAMNED

A curse word, referring to the Elemental Planes.

PORTABLE OFFICE

A wooden block that unfolds into a chair and desk made out of hundreds of smaller segments, created by Liza. She sells them for ninety gold.

POTION OF FEATHER-FALL

It uses a (preferably white) feather as a main component, and seems to reduce the effects of gravity on the imbiber, allowing them to jump from a high place without injury.

POTION OF MOONLIGHT SIZZLE

A potion that lets off a soft blue, bright glow that mimics the light of a full moon from its sizzling bubbles when the bottle is shaken. It's powerful enough to illuminate a small room on its own, and when sold at a reasonable price, much more affordable than light crystals or candles.

POTION OF NIGHT VISION

Allows one to see more clearly in the dark, in monochrome.

PROGNOS

Skilled in divination, have a single large eye in the middle of their head. It's said the best prognos diviners can see into the past to discover the identity of a criminal, but that's a myth. They are simply perceptive. They mature slowly and have longer lives than most humans.

PURPLE LOBSTER

A luxury food.

PUZZLE BAND RINGS

A wedding ring, historically used to keep women from cheating on their husbands, with the thought that they would be unable take the ring off for their infidelities and then fit the ring back together in time to keep their misdeeds secret.

QUINTESSENCE OF QUICKSILVER

The powder of a potion boiled down into a solid and then crushed. It temporarily frenzies the mind, making you smarter and granting a liquid creativity. Gives the illusion of power and lowers inhibitions. The effects of a single dose last about six hours on those who haven't built up a tolerance, and the come-down crash lasts a day or two. Long-term users lose their ability to focus and display various memory problems, becoming dependent on quintessence of quicksilver to function normally.

RADIANT MAIDEN

The progenitor of the Order of the Radiant Maiden. She is a powerful Elemental from the Plane of Radiance. These humanoid, often-winged beings have been referred to as angels.

RED SAGE

A powerful Aberrant that is contained within a sundered zone, but still manages to meet people. It has three eyes, each of which are said to see the future. All prophecies that it gives come true, but it seems that the Red Sage can either choose who it meets through a sort of subtle summoning (and thus control the prophecies it gives) or it chooses what to prophecy—it can be bribed to give a better fortune. However, in coming true *all* prophecies cause great suffering and destruction, if not to the recipient then to the people and world around the recipient. Two of its prophecies—and eyes—are in constant use, and ensure its continued existence and ability to affect the world. The Red Guard facilitates the prophecies from its third eye coming true to try and mitigate the damage, and attempts to control who can meet the Red Sage.

REGENERATION-BOOSTING POTION

This potion boosts the body's natural immune response, lending some of its power to boost the healing effect and taking the rest from the stored energy and nutrients of the injured person's body. It will struggle to fix anything larger than a small dagger wound, a bone fracture, or a hand-size burn. It takes time to work and is uncomfortable, and cannot be used in quick succession, but is much cheaper than a real healing potion.

REVEALING SPELL

Uncovers non-physical illusions and can see through non-magical darkness. Usually cast via a wand, issued to some coppers. A revealing spell shoots vibrational and magic waves, which penetrate and bounce back to the wand.

REVERSE-SCRYING SPELL

A divination spell with the base of a map-based sympathetic divination, but which targets instead the other sympathetic end of the connection which is being used to scry. Used to find the finder, historically most often in warfare.

REVIVIFYING POTION

Boosts organ function and energy levels. Can be used for many different illnesses, but is expensive due to its high magical load.

RUNE-INSCRIBED BASIN

A basin for far-viewing, a type of divination that uses water to see distant places, generally from the point of view of another surface of water. The basin can be used to contact other powerful diviners if they cast at the same time, with the same intent. Far-viewing in this manner does not transmit sound.

SACRIFICE

What you give up for the effect of a spell. It can be an object, like a blob of mud used to create a brick, or energy, like the heat from a flame. Components can have either a natural or a sympathetic link to the effects of the spell.

SELBY-FORMAN BINDING

A variation on conjuration/elemental binding used in the Second Empire.

SELF-CHARGING ARTIFACTS

Artifacts that contain the parameters to not only cast a spell, but to gather and transform the energy for that spell as part of their activation and release process. Creating a self-powered, or self-charging, artifact is a Grandmaster-level feat said to be pioneered by Myrddin, who supposedly came up with several methods, some of which have now been lost.
Self-powered artifacts cannot cast truly endless spells, as eventually the spell array breaks down— and more quickly with heavy use, but they are still widely coveted.

SELF-CLEANING CHAMBER POT ARTIFACT

Cleans and dries the nether regions, then processes the waste, removing the liquid from fecal matter and dehydrating urine into a thick paste, which it stores in a sealed container for later removal. An auxiliary spell keeps the smell from filtering out away from the chamber pot.

SEMPERVIVUM APRICUS

A low-growing succulent plant from the Plane of Radiance. Its juicy leaves grow in complex rosettes, glimmering with tiny motes of light that travel beneath the semi-transparent skin along with the water and nutrients. It is technically a "low-light" plant in the Plane of Radiance, and thus is able to survive on the mundane plane in areas with bright sunlight and long days, or with the help of artificial sunlight sources. They propagate by sending out root offshoots that grow into new baby plants.

SHADE (DUST)

Shades are predatory creatures that take humanoid forms and live in barren, arid areas such as deserts, where they will prey on the sleeping or stalk the lost traveler until they collapse from exhaustion. They are made of a fine powder which can be gathered and used as an expensive magical component.

SHADOW-FAMILIAR

An esoteric ritual spell that gives the user control of their own shadow, allowing it to move, stretch, and take unnatural shapes. "Life's breath, shadow mine. In darkness we were born. In darkness do we feast. Devour, and arise."

SHAMAN

A thaumaturge who specializes in contacting the spirit realm for the purpose of divination, as well as certain types of mental healing and wards. They often use mind-altering or hallucinogenic substances to facilitate contact.

SHIPP EVIDENCE BOX

Metal cube meant to put evidence in stasis. Has a transparent setting to allow examination of the contents within.

SIMPLE LOCKING SPELL

Learned from one of the warding books Katerin bought Siobhan, this spell locks a container that can be opened and closed, without need of a key or even a physical locking apparatus. Does not stop one from breaking in physically or magically, but will require some extra effort.

SIMPLE UNLOCKING SPELL

Used to bypass either mundane locks, or negate the simple locking spell. Cannot unlock a locking spell cast with greater power.

SINUS-CLEARING SPELL

A variation on the water falling spell, used to draw off liquid and thus clear the airways. Esoteric magic taught to Siobhan by a hedge-witch.

SIREN

Sometimes confused for mermaids, sirens are not in fact associated with aquatic animals, but with avians. Sirens have brightly colored feathers that sprout from the scalp and sides of their face where ears and hair would be on a human. They are best known for their mesmerizing voices, which are said to cause sailors to steer their ships into submerged rocks or even directly into cliff-sides in an attempt to get closer to the enchanting sound of the siren song.

Largely carnivorous, sirens are intelligent beings and those who are willing to integrate into human society are rare and coveted for their abilities.

SKIN-KNITTING SALVE

An alchemical concoction that mends small cuts over the course of about an hour. It can heal a deep scratch, cut, or a second-degree burn, but not a serious wound, and most (less expensive) versions will leave minor scarring.

SKINJACKER

A creature used in cautionary tales to children, which can take over a person's form and replace them.

SLINGSHOT SPELL

Created by Siobhan based on a Practical Casting exercise, it uses the glyphs "line," "movement," and "circle" to send a projectile revolving around a central axis. When it is released, the projectile shoots out, similar to a stone out of a shepherd's slingshot.

SMOKE CLOUD PHILTRE

A battle philtre that creates a sudden and thick smoke cloud when released from its container. Considered a battle potion.

SOBERING POTION

This potion speeds up the process of filtering alcohol from the body, but can cause an overwhelming need to urinate and, if overused, lead to dehydration.

SOUND MUFFLING SPELL

Creates a bubble of stilled air that suppressed the ability of vibrations to travel through it, and thus muffles sound.

SPACE-BENDING SPELLS

This type of magic can bend, and even fold space. They are extremely difficult and expensive. If a smaller area is filled with more space than it could normally hold, that space must come from somewhere, which will in turn be smaller than it normally is. There are usually visually-disorienting signs of the spell when you try to gain perspective or mentally measure the space.

SPARK-SHOOTING WAND

Artifacts charged with firework-like sparks of light. Can start a fire, with the right tinder, be used as a distraction, a signal, or a threat, though the spark-shooting spell is a non-combat spell.

SPEER'S PHILTRE OF STENCH

A powerful, physically painful stench that causes tears, mucus buildup, and vomiting, like a combination of a stink bomb and pepper spray. Used as crowd control to non-lethally incapacitate a large number of people. It has magical as well as physical properties.

SPIRIT

Ephemeral, small and often harmless beings, it is argued whether spirits are technically "alive" or merely accumulations of a concentrated type of magical energy over time, or perhaps imprinted residue from once-living beings. They may be summoned and contracted, but often have little ability to exert influence on the mundane world. Shamans often communicate with spirits to gain information through their particular brand of divination.

SPIRIT-TRAPPING SPELL

Useful for trapping spirits for communication or contracting. There are many variations on this type of Circle.

SPRITES

Tiny, insect-winged humanoids. They have some measure of intelligence, but are not considered sapient "people," rather more akin to interesting bugs.

STAR-MAPLE WOOD

A wood with properties from the Plane of Radiance, it can be used in regenerative and healing spells, as well as other spells using the Radiant attribute, or for its beauty. As it can be molded into an accessory while still living, it is rather valuable. As an accessory, sometimes is used to enhance beauty through improving health.

STUNNING SPELL

Red projectile spell. When high-powered, can leave scorch marks and a little steam or smoke at the point of impact. Uses a combination of low-current electricity and sedative material (the powdered saliva from a Kuthian frog), contained within a field of force, to incapacitate the target.

SUMMONING RITUAL

Summoning is said to slightly skew fate to cause a being that meets your requirements to come into contact with you. It has inconsistent results, and clarity of wording and intention is very important. One can summon spirits, animals, or even another person who has the capability to help you with a certain problem. Once summoned, you may come into contact with a being that meets your requirements as if through coincidence after some time has passed, or more directly and immediately. Some question the efficacy, hypothesizing that the vagueness of most types of summoning rituals leads to false interpretations of fulfillment.

SUNDERED ZONE

The strongest barrier spell known to man. From the outside, it looks like a perfect white dome, with all light reflected. They are used to quarantine Aberrants that cannot be killed. The sundered zones cannot be exited by the thing they were created to contain or anything tainted by them, but can technically be entered by sapient creatures who are able to give their informed consent.

SYLPHIDE

Powerful, humanoid elementals from the Plane of Air, given to song, laughter, and knowledge carried on the wind.

TATAROC DESERT

Known for its dryness, a line of standing stones through this desert signifies Lenore's border to the east.

THE BITTER PHOENIX

A tavern with a private back area where people partake of the illegal quintessence of quicksilver, and a powerful diviner will sell you information or make connections for the right price.

THE BLACK WASTES

An area where dangerous magic has infected the land itself. The environment shifts rapidly, with deadly and mutated land, flora, fauna. Time spent in the Black Wastes causes paranoia, hallucinations, and makes it difficult to find your way.

THE CHARMED HIGHLANDS

An area where celerium is mined.

THE CITADEL

The main University building, where the classes are held, and which also contains the supervised casting rooms. It looks like a coliseum made of white stone, with shimmering spelled windows and tall columns. It is huge and towering, and laid out in rings, like a cross-cut of a tree stump.

THE DAWN TROUPE

A powerful Aberrant which is not contained within a sundered zone. It manifests as a group of wealthy, attractive horse-riders with weapons and musical instruments. This Aberrant appreciates intelligence and talent, and will give boons to those who meet it and impress it. The Dawn

Troupe can be bargained with, and never breaks its promises. The Red Guard has agreed not to attempt to contain it, and as long as it receives a certain amount of people interacting with it—usually to attempt to gain one of its boons—it does not leave a certain area to go on a hunt. The Red Guard allows people to know about the boons so they will risk their lives to try for one.

THE ELEMENTARY

A shop in the Night Market which secretly sells, in the back room, items from the Elemental Planes. Their supplier, Harvester, is a half-troll.

THE GERVIN FAMILY

The Fourth Crown Family. They control much of the textile industry, as well as the high-end fashion industry.

THE MIRES

Gilbratha's slums, which get worse further toward the south of the city. The Mires are named for the sticky, stinking waste that lines the streets and wafts from the canals. They spread beyond the bounds of the white cliffs, which have been sunk, broken, or taken apart for use as building materials on that side of the city.

THE NIGHTMARE PACK

A gang consisting mostly of non-humans, which holds territory that houses a large percentage of non-humans. They are led by Lord Lynwood, a lycanthrope, and his adopted prognos sister, Gera.

THE RED GUARD

A special, semi-autonomous branch of law enforcement which handles rogue magic beyond the abilities of the normal coppers. Their operations are confidential.

THE SURIOR MOUNTAINS

An area where celerium is mined.

THE THAUMATURGIC UNIVERSITY OF LENORE

The most prominent and prestigious arcanum in the country, and the only one that can give a Mastery certification. It is matched in status only by Pendragon Palace, and looks down upon the city from atop the northern side of the white cliffs. Its grounds are extensive, and its structures include areas dug into the white cliffs themselves.

Every year, thousands of students, both new to magic and who have come from other arcanums to achieve their Mastery certification, take the entrance exam.

THE WESTBAY FAMILY

The Second Crown Family. They control the Gilbrathan coppers, and often have influence in the army as high-ranking commanders.

TIMED ALARM SPELL

Cast on a time-keeper such as a pocket watch, goes off at a set time to alert anyone nearby to the conditions of the spell being reached.

TITAN

A gargantuan, powerful, humanoid being prevalent in the early days of recorded human history, who survived the Cataclysm. A Titan might simply walk by and decide to crush half a human city like child kicking an anthill. They had enormous appetites and were entirely omnivorous, in the true meaning of the word. Extremely magically powerful. Now extinct.

TOME

A large, expensive book created with high-quality material meant for channeling magic. It has very thick pages, with a spell array drawn on each page. This allows the holder to carry portable spell arrays, open to any particular page, and cast the spell as quickly as they can place any necessary components and/or Sacrifices. Each tome usually carries between 12-20 spell pages.

TURTLE CREATION SPELL

Uses a turtle egg and duplicative transmogrification to create an anatomically-correct, edible, dead turtle.

UNDER-BED DUST BUNNIES

A magical creature that is spontaneously generated from the fluffy dust under a bed in a magical environment. Supposedly.

UNICORN/PEGASUS

A magical, horse-like beast with a valuable horn on its head. The pegasus is the progressed form of a unicorn, the wings growing after an intense accumulation of magic.

UTILITY WAND

A wand artifact with multi-purpose spells meant to be widely useful for a variety of emergency situations, not simply battle.

VAMPIRE

A sentient, magical, humanoid being, who often prey on humans for their blood. They often have blood-red hair, pale skin, and a mouth full of canine teeth. They are weak to things from the Plane of Radiance, and a common weapon against them is water imbued with energy from the Plane of Radiance. They have a natural predilection to the dark, and good night vision.

VIBRATIONAL SELF-CALMING SPELL

Esoteric, rather than using a written spell array, it uses the hands over the chest to form the Circle, and the vibration of the voice as a sympathetic component for forcibly calming the body. The longer you draw out the hum, the further it "stretches" your body into a calm state. Repeat ad nauseam.

WAKEFULNESS BREW

A pseudo-alchemical concoction, but more commonly classified as "kitchen magic," this spell marginally boosts the rejuvenating effects of caffeinated beverages. Better quality base materials take the wakefulness magic more smoothly, just as in standard alchemy.

WARD AGAINST UNTRUTH

The strongest legal wards against lies create a moderate vague compulsion, and are thus utterly useless against a strong thaumaturge who can imbue their lies with their Will. Illegal wards create stronger compulsions, but are considered blood magic as they take away the free will of a human.

WARDBREAKER

A specialist in diverting, subverting, and breaking wards.

WATERSIDE MARKET

A sprawling market within Gilbratha proper that has a lot of shops in the streets around. People of all ages and races can be seen, as well as thaumaturges who practice many different crafts, a testament to Gilbratha's diversity. Sells everything from food to magical animals. There are stalls as well as shops, with stalls being cheaper, but shops having a better selection.

WHISKERTON'S WHISKEY OF WELL-BEING

An expensive magical whiskey guaranteed to impart an additional sense of warmth and wellbeing by the shot, in addition to the standard effects of liquor.

WHITE CLIFFS

Gilbratha is built within a gargantuan circle of white stone cliffs that have been drawn up from the ground in what is undoubtedly a legendary feat of magic. These cliffs are intact to the north, but have sunk, crumbled, and been demolished for other purposes toward the poorer south.

The Thaumaturgic University of Lenore as well as many Crown Family houses have been built into and atop the cliffs, and nearer the bottom are many buildings placed on the staggered plateaus. Tubes run down from the University to transport people and goods, powered by magic.

WILL

The Will makes magic possible. The stronger a thaumaturge's Will, the more power they can channel, the less defined the Word needs to be, and the less power will be lost in conversion from input to effect. There are different facets to a strong Will.

WILL-STRAIN

Caused by over-exertion when casting magic. It starts with headaches, dizziness, and inability to concentrate. With more moderate strain, judgment is impaired. Sometimes thaumaturges display difficulty modulating emotions, with rapid swings from one to the other. Then hallucinations, with the more severe ones resulting in paranoia and even accidental harm to oneself or others. Beyond this, Will-strain damage is irreversible, and results in complete insanity and at times, the loss of higher brain functions. In extreme circumstances, loss of control while casting will lead directly to a "break" and the creation of an Aberrant.

WIT-SHARPENING POTION

While it doesn't actually increase intelligence, it will temporarily make the drinker more aware and improve performance in situations that require multitasking. In too high a dose, it can cause overstimulation through increased sensory input. It is somewhat addictive.

WITCH

A thaumaturge who uses a summoned contracted creature, often from one of the Elemental Planes, to cast spells, rather than using an inanimate Conduit like sorcerer.

WORD

The Word guides the transformation of energy or matter, steering the effects of a spell. It can be any type of instruction, though with sorcery it is most often written into the Circle as an array of glyphs and numerically-significant symbols. These are often supplemented with speech or written instructions, especially for complex effects.

WORTCUNNING

Magical herbalism, the study of plants and herbs, specifically for their healing and magical properties.

WOUND CLEANSING POTION

There are many different versions of this potion, and they come in different strengths and act in different ways. Uniformly, however, they work to clear the wound of dirt and debris, as well as kill any infectious agents such as viruses or bacteria. Formerly, this was understood to be overwhelming the "bad humors," and so, wound-cleansing potions often have strong scents due to components like distilled alcohol and herbal oil extracts.

YAK URINE

Used to help dyes stay color-fast.

ALSO BY AZALEA ELLIS

Seeds of Chaos Series (Complete)

Book I: Gods of Blood and Bone

Book II: Gods of Rust and Ruin

Book III: Gods of Myth and Midnight

Book IV: Gods of Ash and Amber

Gods of Smoke and Stars: A Seeds of Chaos Adventure—Available free to newsletter subscribers

A Practical Guide to Sorcery Series

Book I: A Conjuring of Ravens

Book II: A Binding of Blood

Book III: A Sacrifice of Light

Book IV: A Foreboding of Woe — Coming Soon

The Catastrophe Collector: A Practical Guide to Sorcery Series

Book I: Larva — Coming Soon

More books may have been published since you purchased this copy.

Here's a Quick Link to All my Books.

ABOUT THE AUTHOR

I'm the type of person that often has a wacky, shocking, or silly–but totally *true*–story to tell about my life.

(Like the time my brother and I were chased through a secluded strip of woods in the middle of the city, for over a mile, by a naked man with an erection.)

(Or the time a trucker threw an open bottle of pee out his passenger side window without looking right as I was walking by. You can guess what I got splashed with.)

I've got an active imagination that tends toward the outrageous and the macabre, which led to me being voted "most likely to borrow someone else's car to transport a dead body."

I write books about things that interest and excite me. I'm always in the middle of teaching myself something new, and if I'm not overwhelmingly busy I tend to get antsy. I believe that the impossible is only so if we believe it to be so. Therefore, nothing is impossible.

If you'd like to get updates from me, both about my books and about what I'm up to from time to time, the newsletter is the place to be, as I tend to be very scarce on other social media.

https://www.azaleaellis.com/newsletter

For more information:
www.azaleaellis.com
author@azaleaellis.com

f

Printed in the USA
CPSIA information can be obtained
at www.ICGtesting.com
LVHW091109131223
766336LV00013B/58

9 780999 675052